THE WIVES
of
FRANKIE FERRARO

CAMILLE

MARCHETTA

THE WIVES

of

FRANKIE FERRARO

St. Martin's Press
New York

DESIGN BY JUDITH STAGNITTO ABBATE

Library of Congress Cataloging-in-Publication Data

Marchetta, Camille.
    The wives of Frankie Ferraro / by Camille Marchetta.—1st ed.
      p.   cm.
    ISBN 0-312-18226-0
    I. Title.
    PS3563.A6346W58   1998
    813'.54—dc21   98-5325
                                                      CIP

First Edition: June 1998

10 9 8 7 6 5 4 3 2 1

for Terence

Part One

MIRANDA

1960—1961

Chapter 1

This is how Frankie Ferraro met his first wife:

It was June of 1960 and Frankie had just been discharged from the army. Not having anywhere else to go, he went home, back to the split-level house in Midford, Long Island, where his family had moved in 1952 when he was thirteen. His family then had consisted of his parents, his maternal grandmother, his older sister, Angela, and himself. Since then, his grandmother had died and Angela had married her high school sweetheart. Only Frankie's parents remained at home.

The night of his return, they ate as usual at the table in the kitchen, shiny with new appliances, Formica countertops, linoleum that closely mimicked marble. For dinner, his mother had made rigatoni with meat sauce, lemon chicken, banana cream pie, his favorite foods. "More?" she asked as he polished off his second helping of dessert.

"I'm stuffed." He patted his flat stomach. "That was great."

Dolly Ferraro smiled, her dark eyes alight with the pleasure of having made her only son happy, a prime concern of hers since his birth. Despite the strands silvering her black hair, the fine wrinkles creasing her skin, Dolly seemed young, her eyes brilliant with innocence and good humor, her body slender and supple. She could fall without effort into a perfect split, the envy of her small nieces who studied ballet, and dance without stop at family weddings—the peabody, the tango, the lindy, the fox-trot. Frankie was proud of her, his mother, lithe as a girl, who stopped polishing and cooking, washing and ironing, fussing and worrying, long enough only to watch *As the World Turns* for an hour each weekday afternoon, whose own world revolved unthinkingly about her husband, her children, and, since their arrival on the scene, her two precious grandsons.

Despite the clash of wills that went back as far as he could remember, Frankie was proud too of his father. Sal Ferraro was five feet ten and stocky, with light brown hair and broad, uneven features that individually were a mess, but together added up to a rugged handsomeness. He had sex appeal, that was for sure; and, until Frankie reached his teens and acquired the knack himself, he had been embarrassed by (and envious of) his father's ability to turn the heads of waitresses in restaurants, attract the attention of saleswomen in stores, elicit sideways glances and longing sighs from the women who worked for him. Accompanied only by an older brother, Sal had arrived in the United States from Sicily, at age fourteen, with nothing. Now he owned a business, a contract sewing factory, that supported his family in comfort, some would even say in style. A new Chrysler sedan was parked next to the black Dodge in the two-car garage.

"The family's coming Sunday. For dinner. Everybody wants to see you," said Dolly. She meant Angela, with Denny and the kids, his five aunts, four uncles, their spouses, and however many of his cousins were available.

"Good. That's great. I want to see them, too," he said politely. He doubted that any of the cousins his age would show up. Some had married and moved out of the area; some had jobs—as cops, as firemen—that kept them busy even on Sunday afternoons. Vic, his childhood playmate, had decided to be an actor and wasn't on speaking terms with his father. Of those who would come, three of his girl cousins, teenagers, had crushes on Frankie, which was embarrassing. But the rest were little and cute, and a lot of the boys were at least old enough to shoot baskets with. It wouldn't be such a bad day. Anyway, he couldn't get out of it, he knew, without really upsetting his mother.

"Angela's making the lasagna," she said, sounding surprised that her daughter was capable of taking on such an awesome responsibility. "She wanted to come over tonight to see you, but she had a class."

At the mention of his daughter, Sal smiled. "She went back to school," he said.

Frankie nodded, and said, "She wrote me."

"Angela always got good grades," said Dolly.

Not like me, thought Frankie.

"She shouldn't've gotten married so young," said Sal. "With a husband, a couple of kids . . ." Sal shook his head. "I told her to get that damn teaching credential first."

Frankie pushed his chair back from the table. He had heard this before. " 'Scuse me," he said.

"Wait," said Sal. "Where you rushing off to? I want to talk."

"We've been talking," said Frankie, who nevertheless sat back down.

"Sal," said Dolly, "he just got home."

Sal ignored her, his eyes fastened firmly on his son's face. "You know what you want to do? You made any plans?"

"He hasn't had time, Sal." Her voice held a plea for peace.

Which Sal ignored. "You turned twenty-one in May, Frankie, time you knew what you wanted to do with yourself."

"Maybe go back to school. Maybe get a job. I'm not sure yet. I thought I'd give myself the summer to think it over."

"You just gonna bum around, the whole summer?"

"I got some money saved."

"That don't mean you got to waste it."

Dolly looked anxiously between her husband and son. She didn't want this night to deteriorate into a fight. She never wanted any night to do that. "Sal," she said, "everything don't have to be decided tonight." Both men ignored her.

"I thought maybe I'd do some traveling," said Frankie.

"You been traveling," replied his father.

"Between army bases. I haven't exactly seen the world."

"You should've had the army send you someplace. Italy, maybe. You could've gone to Rome. We got NATO bases all over, right? You could've had the army pay."

"It's not like a vacation. You don't get to choose where you go." He could have ended up in Korea. There were still units patroling the DMZ. Or Vietnam. He didn't know much about the place, except there were troops on the ground, advisers they said, who sometimes came home dead. It was probably just as well, Frankie figured, that he'd never been stationed outside the USA. There was plenty of time now for him to see the world, going where he wanted, when he wanted, without putting his life on the line.

"Thank God you never got sent anywheres dangerous," said Dolly, "where there was fighting. I don't know what I would've done."

"There's no fighting now," said Sal, convinced as always that he was right.

The state of the world wasn't something he wanted to argue with his father. He didn't want to argue anything. Like Dolly, all Frankie wanted was peace. "Anyway, I figure I could do with a little R and R," he said, hoping the discussion was over. It wasn't.

"A week or two, maybe. Then you'll come work with me." The sentence see-sawed between a plea and an order.

"No, Pop."

"I'll start you at a good salary. How does eighty-five a week sound?" It was a good, though not overly generous, offer. Frankie shook his head. Sal ignored him. "Then, if you decide you wanna go to college, you'll have more money saved to help with the tuition."

"Uncle Sam will help with tuition, if I decide that," said Frankie.

"And you'll learn the business. I gotta leave it to somebody when I die."

"Yeah, well, I don't think you have to worry 'bout that for a while."

"What d'you say?"

"He don't have to make up his mind tonight, Sal," said Dolly.

"I told you, Pop. No."

"It's a good business."

"I know it's a good business. I just don't want any part of it, all right?" He was yelling, which was how conversations with his father usually ended.

"Don't take that attitude. It paid for this house. It paid for the food on this table. You didn't take that attitude when you wanted a car for your eighteenth birthday."

Frankie could hear the hurt right underneath the anger in his father's voice. He took a deep breath. "Look, Pop, I'm grateful. I really am. But it's my life."

"If there was something else you wanted to do, for chrissake—like be a doctor."

"Sal . . ."

"When I know, I'll tell you, okay? Now, get off my back." Frankie pushed the chair back from the table and, this time, didn't sit back down when his father told him to.

"Where the hell you think you're going? I haven't finished talking to you."

"Don't wait up, Ma. I don't know what time I'll be back." He picked up the keys of the Dodge from the table in the hall, and went down the short flight of steps leading to the garage. " 'Night," he called, and went out, closing the door quietly behind him.

*F*rankie had nowhere to go, no one he particularly wanted to see. With the happy sound of "Alley-Oop" blasting out at him from the car radio, he drove aimlessly down the pretty suburban street, past the pretty frame houses, four different types (split-levels like his parents', conventional two-storeys, ranches, Capes) alternating to provide a fiction of individuality. Even the landscaping of the houses was more or less the same: hemlock and juniper, boxwood and azalea arranged in neat patterns. There were no fences, giving the neighborhood kids free range over the yards. They were out now, in defiance of the heat and humidity, whooping and hollering, playing hide-and-seek or ring-a-levio, cops and robbers or war, shooting baskets, shooting marbles, just the way he used to when he was their age. It was all familiar, comforting. Boring. He felt anxious, restless. What the fuck *was* he going to do with his life?

His best friend, Jimmy, was at ROTC camp for the month. Barbara, Frankie's titular girlfriend, was at her uncle's wake. They had a date for Saturday night. For reasons he did not entirely understand, Frankie wasn't that anxious to see her. Or anyone else. He considered going to a movie (*Room at the Top,* which was playing at the one theater that sometimes showed foreign films, was supposed to be pretty good), or maybe to his sister's, play with the kids, have a beer with his brother-in-law, and wait for Angela to get home from school. Instead, he spotted a parking space in front of the Tic Toc Tavern, pulled into it, and went inside. He had been drinking at the tavern, with forged ID, since he was sixteen years old.

"Hiya," said the owner, a big man with thinning hair, sallow skin, and a belly that swelled out over his belt. He looked as if he hadn't seen daylight in years. "How ya doin'? How ya like this weather we're havin'?"

Frankie told him it beat Georgia's weather by a mile, ordered a beer, and went over to a booth and sat down. The place hadn't changed. The same worn red plastic banquettes ran along the wall, the same rickety tables and chairs stood in the middle, the same worn linoleum rippled on the floor, photos of the same celebrities hung askew on the wall—Frank Sinatra, Vic Damone, Mario Lanza, Joe DiMaggio—all autographed. "To Bill, a great guy, a pal, a champ, the best."

It was still early and the place was almost empty. Looking around, Frankie saw a waitress watching him. There was something hopeful in her look, something hungry. He wasn't surprised. Women always looked at him like that. Some men too. He looked like a movie star, like Rudolph Valentino, like Tyrone Power, with perfect features and smoldering dark eyes. This had caused him a lot of trouble over the years, despite his height and muscular build. For as long as he could remember, he had had to fight to prove that he was no sissy, no fag. And looking like a matinee idol seemed to raise expectations in women there wasn't a hope in hell he could fulfill. "Hello," he said, smiling politely.

"You want something to eat?"

Frankie shook his head. "Thanks. Not yet. I just finished dinner."

She returned his smile, and said, "You don't remember me."

He took a minute, shuffling through the deck of pictures in his mind. "Sure. Sure, I do," he said finally. "You're Cathy Clark, right? A year ahead of me in high school?"

"Right," she said, her smile blossoming with pleasure.

"Come on, sit down a minute. Bill won't mind. It's like a cemetery in here."

She looked around at the almost empty bar. "Yeah. Why not?"

What Frankie had been up to since graduation was no great mystery to Cathy (he was a frequent subject of gossip among the girls in the neighborhood), so most of what he had to say she already knew—first basic training, then MP school, then stints at Fort Ord in Monterey and Fort Gordon in Georgia. Fort Ord had been his favorite. Being in Monterey, he said, smiling at the memory, was like dying and going to heaven.

She hadn't done much since high school, Cathy told him, when he asked. She had worked in a supermarket before the Tic Toc. Here, at least, she had the tips. Sure, she dated, mostly local boys. "Nothing's worked out," she said, shrugging, meaning she was still not married or even seriously attached. Like most of the girls he'd grown up with, Cathy was biding her time, waiting for someone to offer her a home and family.

It wouldn't be him, thought Frankie. She wasn't as pretty as he remembered. Her blond hair looked brassy. She wore too much eye makeup, too much lipstick. There was a wary, knowing look in her eyes, a hard set to her mouth. Or maybe she only seemed that way to him because the women he had recently left behind in the South had seemed so soft, so innocent, so willing—even when they weren't. Still, when a customer called to ask Cathy for the check, Frankie asked her for a date. "Sure," she said, looking surprised, and pleased. "Why not?" She had off, she told him, the following night.

God, I need to get laid, he thought.

*T*here was nothing he wanted to do. That was the trouble, thought Frankie, as he lay in the too-short single bed, in the bedroom that had been his since he was thirteen years old, puffing on a Marlboro (a forbidden act, smoking in bed in his parents' house), mellow with the beers he'd had at the Tic Toc with the guys he knew from the neighborhood. After his years as an MP, he knew he couldn't be a cop like his brother-in-law, Denny, who believed that life offered no greater reward than being an agent in the FBI, an "Untouchable" like Elliott Ness. That's what came of watching too much television. It made you believe that tough shit jobs like police work were glamorous.

It might be interesting to be a newspaper reporter, but, since he had never managed more than a C in any of his English classes, that didn't seem a realistic choice. He wasn't particularly good at math either, but so what? He didn't want to be an engineer, or a scientist, or a schoolteacher like Angela. For that matter, he didn't want to be a doctor, or a lawyer, or a dentist. As for a movie star, that had been his cousin Vic's dream. And look at him— usually unemployed and always broke.

To be a senator, like Jack Kennedy, thought Frankie, now that would really be something. And how about making a run for the presidency? But that prospect was beyond the wildest of his dreams. You had to be a lawyer first, or a war hero, or something special, didn't you? And you needed connections. You had to know the right people. He tried to imagine himself making speeches and still heard in his voice the traces of Brooklyn and Long Island which the years away had softened but not yet completely obliterated. "Grow up, Frankie," he muttered to himself, and lit another Marlboro.

There was always business, but what kind? He thought about his father's factory, the large bright room with windows set high in the wall, smelling of sweat and scent and machine oil. From seven until four, six days a week, rows of women wrapped in aprons sat at the machines sewing while his father or Luigi, his second-in-command, stood at the wide table just outside the small office at the back, cutting fabric from patterns supplied by a design company. The garments (dresses, skirts, blouses, nightgowns) put together there ended up on racks in Macy's, Gimbel's, Abraham & Strauss, a dozen other stores.

When he had started working for his father, the summer he was thirteen, most of the women had been immigrant Italian. Now they were mostly Puerto Rican. Frankie liked working among them. He liked being teased and petted, flattered and flirted with. When he was fifteen, he had fallen in love with one of the girls, Concetta, a sultry beauty of seventeen. She had just arrived from Naples to join her sister, who had come the year before with her husband. During the day he couldn't take his eyes off her; at night she haunted his sleep. His father accused him of daydreaming, and docked his pay. They fought a lot that summer, his father and he.

Sometimes Frankie thought that Concetta wanted him to ask her out, but he didn't dare. His few words of Sicilian weren't up to a date. Anyway, neither his father nor Concetta's sister would have approved. Now he wouldn't be so inhibited. But now not even a harem, let alone the guarantee of money and comfort, could tempt him to spend his life overseeing the cutting and sewing of cheap fabric into sleazy, ready-made clothes.

What the hell do you want? he asked. Nobody answered. He put out his cigarette, turned off the light, closed his eyes, and tried to sleep.

*T*he next night he picked up Cathy, took her to dinner at a little Italian restaurant where the spaghetti and meatballs were nowhere near as good as his mother's, and then (though she had expressed a preference for the Doris Day movie playing at a nearby RKO) to see *Room at the Top*. Afterward they sat in his mother's car and made out. But the film had left Frankie feeling even more unsure and discontented, and the sight of Cathy's house, a few doors down, with its green aluminum siding, open front porch, and postage-stamp lawn looking parched in the light from the streetlamp, depressed him. I can't take much more of this, he thought, forgetting it was only his second night home. And when his hand under Cathy's skirt reached the smooth, damp skin above her stocking top, he still didn't have an erection. Disconcerted, worried, he let her small cry of protest stop him. He removed his hand and pulled away from her.

"I'm sorry," she said.

"It's all right."

She reached for the zipper of his pants. Frankie put his hand over hers, stopping her. "I want to," she said. "Don't you want me to?" He felt it wasn't right. He felt she was trying to live up to some code he shouldn't approve of, trying to repay him for something he hadn't lost. But he moved his hand to let her continue. More than fair, he needed to be sure that his dick wasn't dead.

She reached into his shorts, and took it out. "It's so soft," she said. "Smooth. Like silk." He felt her tongue circling its rim, felt it growing into her mouth.

Thank God, he thought. Thank God.

𝒯he next morning Frankie called Dan Colvington and accepted his invitation to the Cape. Then he drove over to Loughlin Motors, where his friend Jimmy's father gave him a deal on a 1956 beige-and-turquoise Chevrolet. During dinner with Angela and Denny that night, he told them he was leaving first thing Monday morning for Truro.

"Pop's not going to like it," said Angela.

"It's my life," repeated Frankie.

Angela looked like their father. She was small and compact, with fair hair, a pretty face, a great body, and enormous vitality. Denny Walsh, her husband, was a giant of a man, with bright red hair, freckles, and an unexpectedly easy-going manner. Their older son, Dennis, had the same red hair and freckles, while Sean, the two-year-old, was a throwback to his grandmother, Dolly. "Sean looks just like you," said Angela as Frankie swung the boy squealing up over his head and balanced him on one hand while Dennis clung to his leg. "Pop's going to offer you a job at the factory," she said.

"He did. Eighty-five a week. I turned him down."

"You're nuts," said Denny.

"Maybe."

"You're going to have to settle down one of these days," said Angela.

"One of these days," said Frankie, "I will."

𝒫inned to him since senior year in high school, Barbara expected that when Frankie did settle down it would be with her. Snuggling into his arms as they danced, she whispered how much she had missed him, how glad she was that he was home. Thinking it wasn't a good time to tell her that he was leaving Monday for Cape Cod, he pulled her tighter to him and murmured something wordless, which Barbara took for assent.

It was Saturday night and they were at the Carousel. Like most of the hangouts in the neighborhood, this one hadn't changed. It probably looked the same as it had when it opened, in 1947, right after the war, with wooden booths painted white and gold, brass divider rods reaching to the ceiling, and a miniature carousel on a shelf behind the bar. A jukebox alternated with a band to keep the music constant and loud.

When they had started going out together, Frankie was the high school's top jock, Barbara that year's homecoming queen. Everyone thought they made a terrific couple, even Frankie. Barbara was a knockout: white skin and long dark hair teased into a Sheba Queen of the Jungle mane, crimson lips and long red fingernails, a bosom that was easily a thirty-six. She was the height of neighborhood fashion. And a nice girl. Frankie had never even got his hand inside her blouse, though he never stopped trying.

If anything, Barbara was better looking now, slimmer, the baby fat all gone, her wild looks tamed by the requirements of her job as a receptionist in a local doctor's office. Frankie moved his hand down a few inches, and felt the tight curve of her ass under the confining girdle she wore. She looked up at him with startled eyes and he watched the battle in her face as she decided whether or not to tell him to cut out the crap and behave himself. Finally, she smiled, and snuggled her head back into his shoulder. And Frankie understood that her smile constituted a commitment that expected one in return. Barbara wanted wedding bells and rice, a gold ring and a champagne reception, and she wanted them from Frankie. She always had. She had written to him while he was away, and he had replied, often with more passion than he had felt, not out of a conscious desire to deceive, but a need to maintain another connection with home. Without actually saying so, without ever mentioning the word, he had led her to believe that once he was out of the army, they would marry. Now, of course, he was sorry. He didn't love her. He wanted nothing she wanted. He knew he had led her on, selfishly, for years. Now, selfishly, he didn't want to anymore. Her desire, instead of feeding his vanity, or his passion, made him feel stifled, claustrophobic. He moved his hand back up to her waist. Not even for a feel of her ample breasts was he willing any longer to hint that he could deliver himself to the altar; and, when he took her home, he kissed her only briefly, to be polite, before telling her that he was going away for a while. Her face clouded with disappointment; her eyes filled with tears. "But you just got back," she said.

"It won't be for long," he told her. He made the trip sound necessary, hinting that it was somewhere between an unbreakable obligation of friendship and an important business opportunity. He promised to send postcards while he was gone.

The next morning, when he called Cathy, he promised her the same thing. He said he would phone her when he got back, which seemed the right thing to do. Later, when the family arrived, he teased his aunts, told jokes with his uncles, shot baskets with the boys, flirted with the girls, and surprised himself by having a good time. Then, after everyone had gone, he broke the news to his parents. His father stormed, his mother cried, and Frankie remained unmoved. The next day he was up at five, showered, dressed, and packed by six. He had breakfast, kissed Dolly, shook hands with Sal, tossed his suitcase into the Chevy, and took off toward the rest of his life.

Exhausted from forty minutes of hard swimming, Frankie bobbed on the waves out beyond the breakers, treading water, taking it all in. An old man with silver hair was doing a languorous, graceful crawl toward the horizon. Two teenage girls, clutching at the tops of their suits, were riding the waves. On shore, the row of houses shimmered in the sunlight until they disappeared into a bright haze at the edge of his vision. Children were filling buckets with water and mixing it with sand to make play soup. A mother was helping her two little girls build a castle. A group of boys played volleyball. Gulls cried, wheeled, and dove. Dan was a golden dot on a fuchsia blanket in the sand, just in front of the weathered deck of the Colvington house. In Truro, on the ocean, it had been owned by the family since eighteen-something. A pretty, rambling, two-storey structure, its front covered with white-flowering wisteria, it was faded by sun and salt, inside and out. The windows stuck. The rooms needed painting. The furniture was comfortable, but old and worn. His mother would be horrified by the way everything looked, Frankie knew. Yet somehow, to him, the shabbiness of the house and its contents conveyed wealth more forcefully, more vividly, than his parents' eight-year-old split-level and its ever-changing array of carpets and curtains, coffee tables and couches.

Dan's parents, his brother, and two sisters, weren't expected until the middle of July, so the house was his for the next few weeks to do with as he wanted, and what he wanted was Frankie to pal around with. They had been assigned to MP school together. At first, both boys were wary of one another, the scion of Boston Brahmins not knowing quite what to make of the son of an immigrant, and vice versa. They were prepared to let unfamiliarity spill over into dislike. That had changed when they transferred to Fort Ord, where, on patrol, they had ended up more than once saving each other's asses. Discovering that they shared a respect for authority with an inability to conform, a sense of responsibility with an anarchic streak, a lethal punch with a sense of humor, they became friends. On leave, they were foils for one another, Dan blond and Frankie dark, Dan polished and Frankie rough, both charming, both sexy. The girls wouldn't leave them alone.

Kicked out of a number of prep schools before managing to graduate from one in Colorado that specialized in problem kids, instead of going to university Dan had traveled around the States, taking odd jobs to earn money until the draft had caught up with him. Now, with the wildness worked out of his system, he was at last ready, or so his parents hoped, to assume his rightful place in the world, first at Yale, alma mater to generations of Colvingtons, then as an executive in one of the family businesses. Dan seemed prepared to oblige them, at least as far as Yale was concerned. His acceptance undoubtedly guaranteed by major Colvington donations, he nevertheless had passed the SATs with scores that astounded all who had seen his high school reports. He would start classes in the fall.

*F*eeling more contented than he had since his discharge from the army, Frankie resumed his easy crawl and headed back to shore. "Better put some of this on," said Dan, tossing a bottle of suntan oil to him as he approached, dripping salt water. Dan was already deeply tanned, his blond hair transmuted to corn silk.

Frankie dropped down onto a towel in the sand, and said, "I'll be okay."

"You'll peel," said Dan burying his nose again in the book. It was something by Salinger. Frankie put his hands under his head, closed his eyes, and pulled the peace that had come upon him while swimming over him like a blanket. "Hand me a beer," said Dan a while later. Without opening his eyes, Frankie reached into the cooler, grabbed a bottle, and handed it to him. "Thanks, he said. "What do you want to do tonight?"

"Nothing," said Frankie. "I want to stay right where I am forever."

But the sun set and the insects swarmed, driving them inside. Frankie showered, dressed, and sat in a faded chintz armchair, waiting for Dan, reading by the light of an old wrought-iron bridge lamp a battered copy of *Magister Ludi* that he had found in the bookcase near the window. When Dan finally appeared, Frankie whistled appreciatively. "Well, you were worth the wait," he said, camping. "You're gorgeous."

"It takes time to be a lady-killer. And practice. Come on, let's go."

"Sure," said Frankie, returning his attention to the book. "Just let me finish the chapter."

. . .

hey had dinner in a restaurant where the view out over the ocean—the lighthouse lantern, the crescent moon, the stars dusted across the night sky—far surpassed the mediocre meal. They talked about Kennedy and how, if he got the nomination, Dan's family would not vote for him because he was Catholic, the very reason that Frankie's would be certain to, even though he was Irish. They talked about the future, Dan about his growing desire to join his father in the family publishing company after Yale, Frankie neglecting to mention the offer his father had made him: it didn't seem to add up to all that much. They talked about girls, about why it was they never wanted the ones who were available, and how eminently desirable the unavailable ones always happened to be.

Afterward they flowed into the throng sauntering through the streets, wandering in and out of the open shops, checking out what was happening and where, casting admiring glances at passing girls and curious ones at the large number of openly homosexual couples. When they reached the Provincetown theater, Frankie stopped to look at the poster for *The Three Sisters*. "Would you look at that," he said. "My cousin Vic's in the play. This must be the first time he's worked all year." They bought a couple of tickets for a night later in the week, and left a note for Vic at the stage door, telling him to look for them at Teeny's, where everybody ended up sooner or later. They walked there, and through the bar to the back, grabbed a table, and ordered a couple of beers.

A band was playing. "They're not bad," said Dan, who had heard them before. They had a good beat, the lead guitarist could sing, and the girl on the violin was terrific. "I asked her out," said Dan, "but she's dating the drummer."

A handful of couples on the dance floor were doing the lindy. At the next table was a large, noisy gathering. The central figure was a large man sporting a beard and waxed mustache. He looked like Ernest Hemingway. "The mayor's giving a party," he said. His voice had a heavy accent, Spanish, Frankie thought, Cuban maybe, though that idea may have come from the Hemingway connection. "We're all invited."

"Do you want to go?" asked Dan. "I know him."

"That guy?"

"The mayor."

"Sure," said Frankie.

"Dan? Is that you?" The voice came from behind them, and both men turned.

"Miranda!" said Dan, rising to his feet.

"I didn't know you'd come home," she said as he hugged her.

If Frankie had ever seen a Botticelli, he would have thought Miranda reminded him of one. As it was, she reminded him of nothing so much as the princess in Walt Disney's *Cinderella*. She could have stepped out of Frankie's dreams. Her hair was yellow, soft curls escaping from the tortoiseshell clip fastened to the crown of her head. Her eyes were a brilliant blue fringed by long lashes darkened with mascara. It was the only makeup she wore. Her nose was short and straight, her mouth full. Lovely bare shoulders swelled out of the ruffles of a white dress that fell in soft flounces to her calves. The long, delicate fingers of her small hands were tipped with pale pink polish, as were the toes exposed in white sandals. Her ears were the most beautiful ears Frankie had ever seen, set close to her head, small, perfect, like seashells, he thought.

"Looks like you're not the only one with a cousin in Provincetown," said Dan to Frankie. "A cousin by divorce and remarriage, anyway. Miranda Payson, Frankie Ferraro."

"Hello," said Miranda, extending a hand.

"I love you," said Frankie as he shook it. She laughed, a little embarrassed, a little pleased by his open admiration. "Marry me," he said.

Chapter 2

Standing behind Miranda was a pretty, dark-haired girl whom she introduced as Beth Monroe. "We've been friends forever, since nursery school," said Beth, assessing Frankie with cool, appraising eyes.

"Come on, sit down. Join us," said Dan. He pulled out a chair and Beth sat. Feeling as if he had wandered into a slow-motion movie, Frankie did the same for Miranda, managing to nod as she smiled and murmured her thanks.

"When did you get here?" asked Dan.

"We came yesterday," said Miranda. "But Mother's been here for ages. She'd love to see you, Dan. You'll have to come for dinner." She turned to Frankie. "You, too, of course."

The band began to play "Paper Roses." "Would you like to dance?" asked Frankie.

Miranda nodded, and said, "Order me a glass of white wine, Dan, would you?"

"You're not old enough to drink." The legal age in Massachusetts was twenty-one, not eighteen as it was in New York.

"We've got ID," Beth said as she watched Frankie with mingled distaste and fascination. "Who's your gorgeous friend?" he heard her ask as he led Miranda to the floor.

"Don't get your hopes up, honey," Dan replied. "I think he's taken."

He was. Completely. Nothing like this had ever happened to him before, he thought as he pulled Miranda into his arms. He felt as if he'd been struck by lightning, bowled over by a fast-moving object, escaped death to find life blissfully transformed.

Miranda shifted uneasily, trying to establish some neutral territory between them. "I can hardly breathe," she said.

"I'm having trouble myself," he admitted.

"That's not what I meant."

There was more teasing than complaint in her voice, but Frankie relaxed his grip anyway. "Leave room for the Holy Ghost," he said.

"What?"

"Once I dated a girl who went to a Catholic high school. At the dances, the nuns used to walk around the floor and tap you on the shoulder if you were dancing too close. 'Leave room for the Holy Ghost,' they'd say."

Miranda laughed. And Frankie pulled her close again, dipped his head, and rested his cheek against hers. A moment later, he gave in to temptation and nuzzled her ear. Startled, Miranda jerked her body away from his. "Sorry," said Frankie. "I couldn't help myself. You have the most beautiful ears I've ever seen."

"You can't go around licking people's ears, just because you happen to think they're beautiful."

"I don't. Usually. This is the first time."

"That you've licked a woman's ear?"

He smiled. She was teasing him. Good. Very good. "So soon," he said. "I usually wait till I know her better."

The band segued into "Alley-Oop." They danced that dance, and another, dancing until they were out of breath and their bodies glistened with sweat. "I've got to stop," said Miranda finally, turning from him, making her way through the crowd, not looking to see if Frankie was following, knowing he would be. The table when they got there was deserted. Miranda picked up her wine and drank, as Frankie signaled the waiter and ordered another beer. "Where are they?" she asked.

"There," said Frankie pointing to where Beth and Dan were dancing. "How are you and Dan related?"

"My mother is married to his uncle."

"The one in banking?"

"No, the one with the retail stores. Craig Colvington." Frankie looked at her with interest, waiting for her to continue. "You've heard of Colvington's?" He shook his head. "Next to Neiman Marcus they're the most special specialty store in the country."

"Oh?" said Frankie.

"You've never heard of Neiman Marcus." This time it was a statement, not a question, and her voice was tinged with amazement. "Where did you grow up? On a remote island in the Pacific?"

"On *Long* Island," he said. "New York. We shop at Macy's and Gimbel's, mostly. At A&S."

"Well, so do I, sometimes," she said defensively, and Frankie found her unwillingness to be thought a snob endearing. "I got this dress in Filene's basement." Again, he looked at her blankly. She laughed. "Oh, never mind. Who cares? What does your father do?" she asked, to change the subject.

Frankie thought about how best to phrase it. "He owns a business," he said. "A dress-making business."

"He's a designer."

"No. He does contract work for some of the Seventh Avenue labels."

"That's interesting," she said.

"No, it's not."

"Yes," she insisted. "It is. I mean, not fascinating, or anything. But I never actually thought before about how clothes get made. What the process is. Do you know a lot about the business?"

"Enough to know that dress you're wearing is shit." Miranda looked at him as if she couldn't quite believe what she'd heard. "You look beautiful in it. I don't mean that. But you'd look beautiful in anything. Look," he said, touching the side seam just a few inches above her waist. "The seam's coming apart. It wasn't stitched right." His index finger pushed through the fabric and rested on her skin. If he moved his thumb, a fraction of an inch, he could touch her breast. He removed his hand.

Her eyes dropped from his and she blushed. "You'd be a great guy to go shopping with, I guess."

"I hate shopping," he said.

*B*eth and Dan returned from the dance floor, and Frankie ordered another round of drinks. "I'm getting high," said Miranda.

"Here's to summer," said Beth, draining her glass. "This semester was awful. I think I failed French."

"Where do you go?" asked Frankie.

"Radcliffe," said Beth.

"Bennington," said Miranda.

"I've heard of them," he said. He had, not that he knew where they were. Miranda laughed. She knew he was teasing. "Here comes my cousin," he added as he saw Vic strolling in, a girl in tow. Three years older than Frankie, a childhood brush with polio had left him with a rolling gait, like a cowboy's. It had also left him ineligible for the draft. He had moved into Manhattan, enrolled in classes at The Actors Studio, and earned money bartending in Greenwich Village hangouts. Vic had the Ferraro looks: stocky, with fair hair and hazel eyes. He also had the Ferraro charm. And he had talent. Frankie had seen him in a play, in a small theater in the Village, above some church. The play had been lousy, but Vic had been good. Everyone said so, even the critics. Not that it mattered to his father, who hadn't spoken to him in two years. Of course Vic's mother called him regularly and passed on news in a roundabout way, allowing her husband to maintain the fiction that he didn't give a damn what became of his only son.

Standing, Frankie waved to catch Vic's attention. The cousins shook hands, hugged, then Frankie introduced Vic to the others, and Vic, in turn, introduced his date, whose name no one quite caught Small, with sharp features and wide brown eyes, she was appearing in the play with him; and when Frankie mentioned that she looked familiar, she suggested that he might have seen her in an episode of *Maverick* the week before. "That's it," said Frankie. "You played the schoolteacher."

"So what's everybody up to?" said Vic.

"The mayor's having a party," said Dan.

"Everybody's going to be there," said Beth.

"Who's everybody?" asked Frankie.

"Frankenthaler and Motherwell, probably." The names meant nothing to Frankie. "Everybody."

"They were at the house for dinner last night," said Miranda.

"Come on, let's go," said Beth. "There's nothing else to do. It might be fun."

"Can we get in?" asked Vic.

Frankie smiled and pointed to Dan. "The mayor's his best friend."

"We can get in," said Dan.

Frankie settled the bill and followed the others outside, where a logistical discussion about cars was in progress. He went up to Miranda, took her hand, and whispered, "Let's not go."

"We can't just—"

"You have a car?" he asked, cutting her off.

"Yes, but—"

He tossed his keys to Dan. "Take my car. Miranda's going to give me a lift home. See you tomorrow, Vic," he said; and, before anyone could argue, he led Miranda away.

"Well . . ." said Beth.

"Come on," said Dan. "Let's party."

The dim silver light from the moon danced on the water and bounced off the metal of forgotten toy shovels in the sand. Here and there a fire glowed, revealing indistinct shapes busy cooking lobsters, roasting marshmallows, playing guitars, singing folk songs, the plaintive strains of "Day-O" and "Scarlet Ribbons" blending with the hum of insects in the night air. Beyond the fires lay couples necking. Occasionally, one of the pair would leap up and walk into the shadows, to be followed moments later by the other.

This isn't really happening, thought Frankie as Miranda's car stopped in front of the Colvington house. Sitting in his mother's Dodge with Cathy in front of her ugly green house had been real, not this. "Do you want to go for a walk on the beach?" he asked as he got out of the car. In the pale light, the white MG looked as insubstantial as a dream.

"It's too cold," she said. The wind had come up, snapping the damp ocean air like a whip.

Frankie walked around to the driver's door and opened it. "All right. Let's go inside. There's some wine."

"I really should be getting home."

"I didn't get us out of going to that party to let you go home," he said. "Come inside." Still, she hesitated. "Just for a little while."

Finally, Miranda smiled at him and nodded her head so slightly the movement was barely perceptible. Frankie helped her out of the car; then, his arm around her waist, walked her to the front door. Inside, she let him take her sweater and settle her on the shabby sofa. "White wine okay?" he asked. "Or would you like a beer?"

"Wine, please." Frankie disappeared into the kitchen, and Miranda sat surveying the room. "Everything's so neat," she said when he returned.

"Our years in the army," said Frankie, setting a tray with pretzels and wine left over from earlier in the day on the table in front of her. "Always ready for inspection." He sat down, poured the wine, and handed her a glass. Miranda took a sip, then put the glass down and reached for a pretzel. His eyes followed the trajectory of her hand from the bowl to her mouth. It seemed to Frankie the most graceful gesture he had ever seen. He couldn't take his eyes from her mouth. Her lips were full, their outline clearly defined. Behind them, her teeth were white and straight. As she bit into the pretzel, he could see the pink tip of her tongue. How long did he have to wait, he wondered, before he could kiss her?

"I've always loved this house," she said.

"What's yours like?"

"Big. Not in the least cozy like this one. It's my mother's, really. The rest of us are just visitors. Even Craig. She comes here to get away from business, she says, but really it's to do more. The Cape is full of artists, in summer especially. She runs a gallery in New York. An art gallery," she added, to be on the safe side.

"Yeah. I figured," said Frankie.

Miranda seemed a little embarrassed. "Well, I wasn't sure. . . ."

"Keeps her pretty busy, huh?"

Miranda nodded. "She has a place in Boston, too. Tiny, really. She keeps it so she has someplace to go to make calls, write letters, meet with important collectors. Art's the most important thing in my mother's life."

"Do you have any brothers or sisters?" he asked, avoiding the obvious question. He didn't want to feel sorry for her, just now. He didn't want pity to temper his lust.

"Both. Do you?"

"A sister, Angela. She's married. She has two kids."

Her mother, explained Miranda, had been married four times: first, to Philip Nolan, a banker, father of Philip Nolan II, Miranda's brother. After three years of marriage, feeling artistically and emotionally deprived, Eva had left him for Zig Heller, a leading abstract expressionist (whatever that is, thought Frankie). Thanks to a combination of Heller's womanizing and constant belittling of Eva's talent as a painter, that marriage lasted only long enough to produce a girl, Joan. After the divorce, Eva installed herself and her children in a loft in downtown Manhattan (paid for by Mr. Nolan, who could afford it) and painted, eventually coming to the attention of E. DeWitt Payson, Ned, a noted gallery owner, who arranged Eva's first show and subsequently married her. He was Miranda's father. "He died," said Miranda, "when I was two."

"Of what?" asked Frankie.

"In a car crash. My parents were at a party. He'd been drinking. He was a big drinker. My mother refused to get into the car with him, so he took off without her. She followed in another car with some friends. They didn't see the accident, but they heard it. His car skidded off the road, hit a tree, and flipped over."

"That must have been terrible."

Miranda shrugged. "I didn't know him. I don't remember anything about him now. When I was five, my mother married Craig. He's been great. He's been a terrific father. Why don't you open another bottle of wine?" she said.

When he returned, he found her kneeling on the floor, leaning over a piece of tinfoil spread open on a plastic bag on the coffee table, meticulously rolling something that looked like tobacco into a cigarette paper.

"You roll your own cigarettes?" he said, not quite believing that his suspicion could be true.

"Doesn't everyone?" She stuck the rolled paper into her mouth and Frankie leaned forward to light it. He reached for one of his own cigarettes, but she stopped him. "Have some of mine," she said.

Frankie took a long drag and felt the sweet, satisfying marijuana smoke fill his mouth and lungs. He had had it only once before, in a nightclub in San Francisco, when he and Dan had somehow found themselves in the middle of a pretty wild party. He coughed. "Where did you get this stuff?"

"A friend." She rose from her knees and settled back onto the couch, smiling at him. "It's the greatest," she said. "Who's reading *Magister Ludi*?"

"I am," said Frankie. He had left the book lying on the coffee table when he and Dan had left the cottage to go to dinner, a lifetime ago it seemed.

"I read *Damien* last year. I loved it."

"This one's terrific," said Frankie, making a mental note to read *Damien* next. There was so much he didn't know, so much he wanted to find out about. He had read *Ethan Frome* in high school, and *A Tale of Two Cities*, but he'd hated them. He had thought Sydney Carton a fool and Lucy Manette just the kind of woman he'd like to slap around a little, if his father hadn't taught him that slapping women around was wrong. Except for Mickey Spillane, he'd never read anything he liked until he borrowed Dan's copy of *The Great Gatsby*.

He didn't tell Miranda that. He didn't want her to think he was ignorant. Instead they talked about Herman Hesse and what a fine writer he was, about *Room at the Top* and how awful the English class system must be. Eventually, they stopped talking altogether. They just sat in happy, companionable silence, enjoying the effects of the joint, sipping their wine, until Miranda reached for her stash again. Then Frankie reached for Miranda. "I've had enough," he said, "of that."

"Just a little bit more."

"Sssh. I'm busy." He ran his lips up her white throat to her ear, then traced its delicate whorls with his tongue. "I've fallen in love with your ears," he said. Then he kissed her. Frankie had never felt like this before, in the grip of such an overwhelming lust, yet relaxed and happy, determined and supremely confident. He felt he could make love forever, slowly, easily, climbing to heights of passion he had never even imagined. "Oh, God," he groaned as he felt himself rising and expanding. A part of him expected her to protest. After all, he had just met her. Anyway, he had never met a girl who didn't protest, at least a little, at least at first. But not Miranda, not even when he had slipped the white ruffle of her dress far enough off her shoulders to bare her breasts.

It was Frankie who stopped. He heard the sound of his car pulling up in front of the cottage, its motor die. "Dan's home," he said, moving away from her, settling a pillow in his lap, watching as Miranda adjusted her dress and hair. She really was so incredibly beautiful. He smiled at her. "You look fine," he said.

Miranda nodded, quickly folded the tinfoil, put it back into its plastic bag, and into her purse. "Don't tell Dan," she said.

"No. Don't worry." He felt a little hurt that she'd thought it necessary to ask.

"About the marijuana."

"About anything." He picked up his wineglass and took a sip.

"I knew you'd still be here," said Beth, preceding Dan into the room. Her cheeks were flushed, her eyes bright. She looked like someone who had had a good time.

"How was the party?" asked Frankie.

"All right," said Dan noncommittally.

"Fabulous," said Beth. "I met this sculptor—"

"She flirted with him all night."

"Only because you ignored me to talk to that redhead."

Frankie felt as if he were journeying back to Earth from a very long distance, from Jupiter maybe. "Anyone want some wine? I'll open another bottle."

"Not for me," said Beth. "I have to stay sober enough to drive home."

"I'm fine," said Miranda. "Perfectly fine," she insisted in response to Beth's dubious look.

Frankie opened another bottle of wine. Dan poured Beth a Coke. Half an hour passed in talk about the party, Miranda asking endless questions about who was there, what was said, by whom, to whom.

"You really should have come," said Beth.

"You know I don't like crowds," said Miranda. She smiled at Frankie.

Oh, God, I love her, he thought. I love her.

Then Beth stood. "Come on, Miranda. I'm dead."

Miranda got up, gathered her sweater and purse. As she started to follow Beth and Dan to the door, Frankie took her arm and whispered, "When will I see you?"

"Tomorrow? Dan knows where I am if you want to call."

"If?"

"Miranda, give me the keys," Beth called, her voice carried on a gust of chill air.

"I'll call you tomorrow," said Frankie, following Miranda outside.

"Not too early." She tossed Beth the car keys, kissed Dan lightly on the cheek, and got into the MG.

" 'Night," called Beth as she backed and turned the car.

They watched until the car disappeared into the night, then Frankie turned and went back inside, Dan close on his heels. "Well?" said Dan.

"Mind your own business."

"You were looking pretty peculiar when Beth and I got here. What happened?"

"Nothing. Nothing at all," said Frankie, lying. Something cataclysmic had happened, he knew it, something that would change his life forever. "Tell me about that redhead."

Chapter 3

*I*gnoring the marijuana-induced fog lingering in his head, Frankie rose early the next morning, showered, dressed, and, leaving Dan still asleep, drove into Provincetown, where he parked the car in one of the many spaces still available on Commercial Street. Overhead the sky was heavy with dark clouds threatening rain. In the dull light, the street looked worn and shabby. The shops hadn't yet begun to open and the few tourists out walking were in search of breakfast, not saltwater taffy and home-made fudge, hand-crafted jewelry and gaily colored clothes. For a moment, Frankie worried that perhaps he was too early, but when he reached the white frame building with its sloped mansard roof, he found the library open. He strode in as if he owned the place, then stopped, overcome by a wave of rare timidity. Libraries weren't familiar turf to him. Looking uncertainly around, he spotted a row of small wooden drawers with brass handles. Memories of high school and term papers came flooding back. Card catalogues. They would provide the information he needed. Then he saw the librarian, a large handsome woman with silver-streaked dark hair pulled up into a high crown, standing at a trolley sorting books, and instead Frankie went to her. Sensing his presence, she looked up before he spoke, staring at him for a moment as if he were some sort of apparition. He smiled and her eyes lighted with pleasure. "Yes?" The tag on her dark dress said "Mrs. DeSouza."

"I'm looking for a book on Motherwell."

"Robert?"

He hesitated a moment, then said, "Yes, Robert. And somebody else named Frankenthaler."

"Robert Motherwell and Helen Frankenthaler," she said, emphasizing the "Helen" to be sure he got it, but only slightly, trying to be helpful, not patronizing. With Frankie trailing her closely, she went to the card catalogue, looked through it, jotted a few notes on a pad, then smiled at him and, saying "Follow me," led him through the stacks to the art section, where she pointed out the shelves that held the volumes he might find helpful. Pulling one of the books down, she leafed through the index, nodded, and said, "This might be a good place to start."

He took the book, and, as his fingers brushed hers, he could feel her start, as if he had delivered a jolt of electricity. "Thanks," he said.

She took a second, then nodded, briskly. "If you need anything more, I'll be at the desk."

"Yeah, thanks," Frankie said again, "I'll be okay. You been a big help already." Watching her walk away, he thought what a great-looking woman she was, dignified, sort of majestic, yet sexy with her big breasts and that mass of hair piled on top of her head. She stopped at one of the tables, leaning forward slightly to talk to an old man reading a newspaper, and he admired the ample curve of her hip. He wondered how old she was. Forty, he guessed, maybe forty-five. (It never occurred to him that his mother was just forty-three. She had been eighteen when Angela was born.) Turning back to the shelves, he checked the index of several other books, took the ones with the information he wanted to a long oak table nearby, sat, and began to read.

Frankie thought he was smart. Everyone had always told him so, his parents, his teachers, if only as a prelude to complaining about his refusal to use what they called his "God-given intelligence." He'd believed them. And by now he'd matched wits against enough others to know that his weren't wanting. If anything, he felt usually that he had the edge. Uneducated was what he was, not stupid. He thought that if he'd ever bothered to study in high school, instead of expending all his energy playing football, drinking beer, and dating girls, he might have been a straight-A student like his sister. But books hadn't interested him then. Now they did. Now they fascinated him. They held all the secrets he was eager to learn.

But this modern art, whatever it was about, he knew he wasn't getting. Though he read the texts carefully, Frankie still couldn't make sense of the reproductions in the books he was studying. They looked like the kinds of things his nephews did in nursery school. He had received them regularly, once every couple of weeks while he was in the army: "To Uncle Frankie, Love" and the kid's name in the corner. It all seemed a crock to him, but if somebody like Dan, somebody Frankie knew to be intelligent, took it seriously, then the subject was worth further investigation. Anyway, he had no intention of making a fool of himself when he met Miranda's mother.

Feeling a presence behind him, Frankie turned as Mrs. DeSouza came up to the table. "We keep copies of art magazines on file," she said. "If you check *The Readers Guide to Periodical Literature,* you might find some articles that would be helpful."

"Good idea," said Frankie. "Thanks. Uh, where do you keep this guide?"

"Over there," she said, pointing. "Are you working on a paper for school?"

"Sort of," said Frankie. He stood, and began gathering up the books.

"Are you checking those out?"

"No. I finished. I was just going to put them back."

"Leave them. I'll put them away."

He grinned at her, feeling grateful as always for the infinite willingness of women to be of service. "Thanks, he said. "Thanks a lot."

*A*t noon, Frankie left the library and walked to Teeny's to have lunch with Vic. They sat in the dim bar at one of the small wooden tables, eating sandwiches and drinking beer. Nearby, two girls, hair teased to the limit, faces caked with makeup, eyes ringed with huge dark swirls of black, talked in low, confidential murmurs spiced with giggles, casting occasional surreptitious glances toward them. At another table, reading, sat a man, somewhere in his late twenties, in sandals, khaki shorts, and shoulder-length hair. Tending bar was Mac, the owner, who looked like a college professor on holiday, with curly gray hair and a long narrow face punctuated by steel-rimmed glasses. The filtered light from the windows revealed dust motes dancing a contented jig. The air smelled of stale cigarettes. Frankie lit a Marlboro. "Dan and me . . . Dan and I, we're coming to see the play tomorrow night," he said.

"You'll like it, I think. Chekhov's plays have this surface simplicity, a naturalness about them, but what they say about human nature . . ." Vic shook his head. "This is a pretty good production. We got great reviews, by and large." His voice was rich and deep, all trace of Brooklyn wiped out by years of training.

Frankie envied that voice, and the enthusiasm in it. He's always like this when he's working, he thought, even doing a crummy play in a dinky church hall. "You really like what you're doing, don't you? Acting, I mean."

"I love it. It's all I've ever wanted to do, my whole life."

"I remember," said Frankie, "when we used to come over your house, when we were kids, you always made Angela and me act out stories from movies with you. There was one where you played Chopin." Vic nodded. "And Angela was George somebody."

"Sand."

"And I was . . . I forget who I was, probably your servant, or something. What was the name of that movie?"

"*A Song to Remember.*"

"That's right. *A Song to Remember.* And you got in trouble with your father for banging on the piano."

"Not the first time I was in trouble," said Vic, the laughter fading from his face. "And not the last. Have you seen him lately?"

"Last Sunday. The whole family was at my house."

"Hail the conquering hero."

"Yeah. Sort of." Frankie felt sorry for Vic. As much as he sometimes longed to escape his family, he knew he wouldn't like it if he couldn't go home, not for a Sunday dinner, not even for a holiday. Not that Vic would be turned away if he did show up. His mother would throw a fit if anybody tried that. But when his father wasn't ostentatiously refusing to speak to him, he was trying to provoke a fight. It wasn't worth the aggravation. "He'll come around, Vic."

"I'm not planning on holding my breath. Ah, who gives a shit? Want another beer?"

When Mac brought the required brews to the table, Frankie took a swallow, then said to his cousin, "You're lucky. You know what you want out of life."

"You don't?"

"I want to be successful. Rich. I know that much."

"I wouldn't mind."

"But I don't know how I want to get that way."

"Start at the top, if you can."

"Of what?"

"Your father's company?"

"I think about it and I feel trapped. I feel like there's this weight on my chest and I can't breathe."

"You got any talent?"

"Not that I know of."

"Any outstanding qualities?"

"My looks?"

"You want to be a gigolo?"

"You want a rap in the mouth?"

"Well, there must be something you like to do more than anything." Frankie grinned. "Something else," said Vic, "since being a hustler doesn't appeal to you."

"Read," said Frankie. "I like to read."

"Well, you'll never get rich doing that," said Vic, laughing.

. . .

*W*hen Frankie got back to the cottage, Dan was sitting at the table drinking black coffee, reading the *Boston Herald,* the front page of which featured a large photograph of John Fitzgerald Kennedy. "You were up early," he said.

"I went to the library." Frankie poured himself a cup of coffee, lit a cigarette, and sprawled on the couch. "What do you think of this guy Motherwell?" he asked.

"As a person?"

"As a painter, bonehead."

"He's good. Very good. My father has a couple of his paintings. I like them a lot."

"Yeah?" said Frankie, impressed, though he hoped it didn't show. "Around how much would one of them cost?" he asked, and immediately regretted the question. Dan never asked what anything cost. He would walk into a store, pull a jacket off the rack, try it on, and say he would take it without ever looking at the tag. In a restaurant, Dan would sign the bill without looking at the total, let alone checking it. Frankie still wasn't sure whether he thought that stupid, or cool.

"I don't know," said Dan. "They're big paintings, so I assume they weren't cheap."

"Name me a painter you think is great," said Frankie, changing the subject.

"Living or dead?"

"Doesn't matter."

"Michelangelo. Da Vinci. Matisse. There are dozens of them. Why this sudden interest in art, Frankie? Wait, don't tell me. It's not an interest in art. It's an interest in Miranda, right?"

"You think all I care about is tail? that nothing serious ever crosses my mind?" Frankie was smiling, but there was an edge to his voice. He hated it when people seemed to question his intelligence.

"Tail *is* serious," said Dan. "To me, anyway. But I don't think I'd put Miranda in that category."

Frankie relaxed. He smiled. This he understood and accepted. He'd felt the same way, a little protective, when guys were dating Angela, though of course he'd been too young to warn them off the way Dan was doing now. "Don't worry," he said. "I can be as much a gentleman as you."

Dan laughed. "That's what I'm afraid of."

Frankie took another swallow of coffee. "You have her number?"

"She beat you to it," said Dan, looking up again from the paper, enjoying the look of momentary confusion on Frankie's face. "She called while you were out."

"What did she say?" asked Frankie, hoping he sounded calmer than he felt.

"We're invited for dinner tonight."

He glared at Dan. "Why didn't you tell me when I came in?"

"I wanted to see if you would ask me for her number."

"What do you think I am? Dead? She's the most beautiful girl I ever saw." Again, Dan laughed. "You're not interested in her, are you?" asked Frankie, suddenly nervous. He wasn't sure how he would handle a conflict of interest in this case.

"She's my cousin," said Dan.

"Not exactly."

"And she's not my type."

"I never noticed you had one."

"No? How do you think we've been dividing the girls all these years? You took the blondes. I took the others. You never noticed?"

"You're nuts. I just like women, all women." Frankie stood, picked up his cup, headed for the kitchen, and said, "I'm going to change and go for a swim. What time's dinner?" he added, with as much indifference as he could manage.

"Eight."

He looked at his watch. It was only ten past three. He had four hours and fifty minutes to kill.

Surveying himself in the mirror, Frankie smoothed back his hair, checked his face to make sure he had rid himself of every trace of stubble, adjusted the open collar of his sports shirt, tugged at the hem of his jacket. No, it didn't look cheap, he assured himself. What was he worried about? He'd paid a fortune for it.

"Are you ready?" called Dan.

"In a minute," said Frankie, continuing to study himself. Something was off, he knew it. But what? Then, almost of their own volition, his hands reached to the back of his neck and undid the clasp of the gold chain his parents had given him for his nineteenth birthday. That was better, he thought. Much, much better.

Outside, the air smelled of sea and salt and hot dogs cooking on charcoal fires. Children played in scattered groups, their cries punctuated by the voices of mothers calling them home. Chasing a stick thrown by a boy in sandy red trunks, an Irish setter yelped with delight while a collie played tag with terns on the sand. Far down the beach sat a lone guitarist, cradling his instrument, not playing, watching the light die.

They got into Dan's Austin Healey, and Frankie settled back into the comfortable leather seat, trying to relax. He didn't want to sweat. He hoped he had put enough deodorant on. "You like this aftershave?" he asked.

Dan sniffed. "Uh-huh. Nice and light. What is it?"

"Royall Lyme."

"I hate the ones that smell of musk. Or flowers."

"Like the inside of a whorehouse."

Dan laughed. "Remember that place in Oakland?" Frankie nodded, grinning. " 'What's that smell?' you asked."

" 'Cats,' said the madam. 'You mean this is a real cathouse?' you said. 'What's the matter?' said the madam. . . ."

" 'You don't like cats?' " joined in Frankie, and both laughed, the way people do when they were once happy somewhere together. "You ever miss the army?"

"No," said Dan. "Never. You?"

Frankie shrugged. "At least I knew what I was doing then." He looked out at the expanse of high, rolling dunes, gray in the dim light, at the hummocks of scrub pine hugging the edge of the road. "How many people will be there tonight, do you think?"

"Not many. Miranda said it was a small dinner party. That means not more than eight or ten. It should be interesting, though. Eva's evenings are always interesting."

They drove into the north Truro hills, turned into a gravel drive marked by two wooden posts, and continued for two or three miles through a gently rolling landscape marked by flowering fruit trees and purple lilac until they reached a large, white, gabled two-storey frame house with black shutters and a drape of climbing roses. "My uncle gave Eva this house as a wedding present," said Dan.

Frankie whistled. "Nice," he said.

"When someone marries you for your money, you have to be prepared to be generous." Surprised, Frankie looked at Dan. It wasn't like him to sound so cynical. Dan smiled. "Not that Eva isn't worth every penny," he added.

The door was opened by a stout, middle-aged, gray-haired woman wearing a print dress with an apron over it. This can't be Eva, thought Frankie, off balance for a second. "Hello, Mrs. Lyle," said Dan, kissing her cheek.

"I'm Mrs. Colvington's housekeeper," she said, having sensed rather than seen Frankie's confusion. "I'm so glad you're home," she continued, to Dan, "safe and sound. It's always a worry with a boy in the army. Go on into the living room," she ran on, without a pause for transition. "Everybody's there. Your uncle arrived this afternoon."

Inside, the house wasn't what Frankie had expected. He had thought it would look rich in an obvious, opulent way. But there was nothing opulent about it. It was big, huge really, and bare, with little furniture, though even Frankie could tell that what there was had cost plenty. Everything seemed to be cream colored. Only a spray of flowers in a vase, or an occasional painting, usually a large splash of garish color, relieved the bland monochrome of the decor. As Miranda had said, the house wasn't cozy. It was cold, uninviting. He looked at Dan to see if he noticed anything wrong, but Dan was smiling, perfectly at ease, comfortable, at home, the way he was anywhere. He led the way into a large room at the rear of the house with French doors opening onto a porch with steps sloping gently down the hill to the saltwater pond below. There was a small sailboat moored at the dock, and a rowboat, a black dot out in the middle of the dark gray water.

Two couples stood in the open doorway, talking. As Frankie and Dan entered, a small woman detached herself from the group and came toward them. She was dressed in a sleeveless hip-length tunic over tight toreador pants, both black, with heavy silver jewelry around her neck, on her arms, in her ears, her blond hair cropped short, like a boy's. This was Eva Colvington, a pint-sized older version of Miranda.

"Dan, how lovely to see you, darling," she said, with what to Frankie was one of the hallmarks of an aristocrat, that ability to say the word "darling" without sounding affected. "I was so delighted when Miranda told me you were here. Your mother never mentioned a word, and I did speak to her last week. I called to wish her a happy birthday." She smiled at Frankie. "Dan's family doesn't approve of me at all," she said.

"Nonsense," said Craig Colvington, her husband, as he joined them. He was a tall man, deeply tanned, with thick silver hair and the air of someone totally at ease with himself and everyone else. Someday, Dan might look just like him.

"Mother adores you," said Dan with great charm and a complete lack of truth.

"Flatterer," said Eva.

Frankie acknowledged the introductions with as much ease as he could muster, which wasn't much. He felt self-conscious, worried again about his jacket, concerned about what the wind had done to his hair. As he smoothed it down, he wondered where Miranda was. After a long day of waiting, even a few more minutes seemed intolerable.

The remaining couple drifted toward them. Colette Drake, a publicist with one of the big New York companies, said Craig, introducing them, and Nelson Clewes, the fashion designer. "Oh, sweet Jesus," said Nelson, looking from Frankie to Dan. "They're gorgeous." He was in his early fifties, extremely thin, with dyed yellow hair and startling blue eyes. There was nothing nelly about him but his voice.

"Now, don't be such a pederast, darling," said Eva. "These boys are family."

"It's not something one can help."

"Don't mind him," said Craig. "He's harmless."

"A lot you know," said Nelson.

"Are you two lovers?" asked Colette, turning a warm smile from one to the other.

Frankie could feel himself blush. He felt shocked, insulted; but Dan returned her smile, and said, "Just friends."

"My God, don't tell me you're actually straight? And just when I'd about given up hope." She was a homely woman, tall, with dark hair, a large nose, and wide mouth. But her oval eyes were lovely, and her body was perfect: high, round breasts, a small waist, slender hips, and long, elegant legs. She dressed with flair, in bright colors, in fabrics that clung gracefully to her in all the right places and stopped just below the knee. "He's blushing," she said, looking at Frankie. "How sweet."

Eva linked her arm through Frankie's. "I'd apologize for my friends," she said, "but they'd only say something awful again as soon as I'd finished. What would you like to drink, my dear?" She led him across to a trolley where the bottles were set out.

Frankie considered the array and asked for a scotch, though he would have preferred beer. Dan settled on a martini. "That's my department," said Craig, crossing to join Eva.

He had been to a lot of strange places, thought Frankie, seen a lot of strange things, but somehow this seemed the strangest. Anything less like an evening with *his* parents and their friends, he couldn't imagine. He took his drink, and settled himself in a corner of the couch. A moment later Colette dropped down next to him. "Tell me all about yourself," she said.

"Nothing much to tell," said Frankie. He gave her his best smile. Where the hell was Miranda? he thought.

Across the room, he could hear Craig telling Dan about the exclusive deal he had made with Nelson for specialty boutiques in the Colvington stores to carry his label.

"You could start with what you're doing here," said Colette.

Maybe he looked as out of place as he felt, thought Frankie. "I'd much rather talk about you," he said.

Laughing, Colette said that was a first: no man had ever suggested such a thing to her before. And then Miranda came in. That is, Miranda and Beth came in, but for a moment Frankie only saw Miranda, standing in the patio doorway, her shoes in her hand, her hair windblown, her color high, her breasts under a peach-colored summer dress rising and falling quickly, as if she'd been running. "There you are," said Eva. "I was just about to send out a search party." Eva's voice reached his ears like a radio message from another world.

"Sorry," said Miranda. "It was just so beautiful, we took the boat out for a row."

"We didn't realize the time," said Beth.

Frankie rose to his feet. He hadn't imagined her. She was real. And as beautiful as he remembered.

While Eva introduced Beth, Miranda kissed Nelson's cheek, then Dan's, and came to the couch to greet Colette. She extended her hand to Frankie, and he took it, resisting the urge to bend his head and kiss it, the way he had seen Stewart Granger do once in a movie. Then he had thought only a real jerk would do something like that. Now he wanted to kiss not only Miranda's hand but the inside of her elbow, and the soft skin just below her right ear. "Hello," he said.

"I'm glad you could come." There was just a hint of coyness in her smile. "I was afraid you and Dan would have other plans."

"Nothing important," he said.

She eased her hand out of his, crossed to a chair, sat, and strapped on her sandals. Her toenails, painted an opalescent pink, looked like jewels, like crescents made of mother-of-pearl set into the gold of her sun-tanned skin.

"Hi," said Beth. Her cheeks were flushed, her hair away. She had on a turquoise dress, cinched by a wide black belt.

"You look great," he said.

"You look just like your father," said Colette. At the mention of her father, Beth's face dimmed, as if someone had turned down her rheostat a notch. "Such an attractive man," she added, smiling sweetly before excusing herself to go join Nelson and Eva.

What the hell was she getting at? wondered Frankie.

"Bitch," muttered Beth.

"Oh, don't mind her," said Miranda. "Insinuation is just part of her job."

*M*rs. Lyle announced dinner, and everyone followed Eva's lead into the dining room and her directions as she placed them. Beth was seated between Dan and Nelson, Frankie between Colette and Miranda. Eva and Craig were at either end. At first, Frankie spoke little, watching the others, mimicking their table manners carefully. The main course was salmon, and the knives everyone used were the strangest he had ever seen, with oddly shaped etched blades and bone handles. The conversation was even stranger. A lot of the time, Frankie felt as if he were translating it from a foreign language whose subtleties and innuendoes were lost on him. A lot of the time, he didn't have a clue what anyone was talking about. They didn't even discuss politics in any way he was used to, in terms of the economy, the Cold War, or—these days most of all—religion.

"Of course, Kennedy will get the nomination," said Nelson. "He's the best-looking man the Democrats have. Which is also why he'll also be elected president. Nixon doesn't stand a chance."

"Oh, Nelson," said Eva. "Not everything has to do with sex."

"Oh, yes it does," said Nelson.

"If the public only knew what we know," muttered Craig.

"Ah, but they don't," said Colette. "And nobody's going to tell them." Her hand slipped onto Frankie's thigh and squeezed. He looked at her and smiled, an instinctive response. All his life, women had been good to him, and he was grateful.

The subject of art inevitably came up, a discussion—sometimes heated—of the current Provincetown Art Association show: Colette and Nelson condemning, Craig, Miranda, and Beth defending, Eva praising the exhibit which she had helped to organize, Dan admitting that he hadn't yet been to see it.

"You've been here for over a week," said Miranda accusingly.

"Well," said Dan, "truthfully, art is not my number-one priority."

"Burn the heretic, burn the heretic," said Nelson, an amused grin on his face.

"And you?" said Eva, looking at Frankie. "Are you interested in art?"

"Yes," said Frankie, careful not to look at Dan. "I am. Not that I know all that much about it. But I only just got here. I haven't had a chance to see the show yet."

"You really shouldn't miss it."

"Oh, I won't," said Frankie. He shifted his position slightly so that his knee touched Miranda's. She didn't look at him, but neither did she move away.

They discussed theater in New York, the current crop of best-sellers, Beth's impending trip to Sardinia with her family. Dan told army stories and Frankie, finally, relaxed enough to join in. They made an amusing double act, it turned out, and by the time dinner was finished Frankie was flushed with success. He hadn't made one grammatical slip. And they liked him. He was sure of it.

. . .

*L*et's go for a walk," whispered Frankie, pulling Miranda aside as the others, in a low murmur of conversation, wandered back into the sitting room after dinner.

"I can't," said Miranda. "Not now. It would be rude."

"I want to see you," persisted Frankie. "Alone."

She hesitated a moment. "When everyone goes," she conceded, finally, "meet me at the bottom of the porch steps." Turning, she followed the others, and, having no option but to wait, Frankie trailed after her and sat, forcing himself to listen to Nelson tell bad jokes for about ten minutes before signaling to Dan, who (good friend that he was) got to his feet to begin the ritual good-byes.

"Time I was off, too," said Nelson. "If I don't get enough sleep, my baby blues fade to gray. Give you a lift, Colette?"

Frankie thanked Eva and Craig, saying politely he hoped to see them again. And he meant it. They came in the package with Miranda.

"We're going to see *The Three Sisters* tomorrow night," said Dan as Beth and Miranda walked with them toward the door. "Would you like to come?"

Beth exchanged a brief look with Miranda, then said, "We'd love to."

"Your cousin's in it, isn't he?" asked Miranda.

"Yes," said Frankie; then, when the others had moved out of earshot, he whispered, "I'll drop Dan off and be right back. Wait for me." She nodded.

"See you," said Dan, waving a general good night.

"I'm at the Harbor Inn," said Colette, to Nelson, loud enough for anyone who was interested to hear.

"Is she ever hungry," said Frankie, getting into the car.

"Might be interesting," said Dan.

"She's all yours," said Frankie. "I've got other things on my mind right now."

*W*hen he returned, Frankie found Miranda, as promised, at the bottom of the porch steps. She wore a windbreaker over pants and a heavy sweater, thick socks, and sneakers. She was smoking a joint.

"I'm sorry I took so long. Are you freezing? You want to go inside?"

"No, I'm fine. Let's go for a walk." She stood up, and he slipped his arm around her waist as they set off past the dock, through the long grass bordering the pond. "Want some?" She offered him the joint. Frankie took a drag, and handed it back to her. "More," she said. "You have to catch up."

The night was brilliant with stars, and the reflection of the moon rippled on the water. There wasn't another house in sight. "Nice," murmured Frankie.

"I love it here," said Miranda. "By the water. It makes me feel so calm."

"With this stuff, you should feel calm just about anywhere."

"I don't smoke all that much," she said. "It's not that easy to get hold of," and, when Frankie looked at her questioningly, she added, "I know this guy in Boston, a musician. He deals a little on the side to make some money."

"You shouldn't be mixed up with people like that."

"I'm not mixed up with him. I hardly know him. It's just sometimes I get a little tense."

"What about?"

Miranda shrugged. "This and that," she said. "But I have to be careful around Eva and Craig. My mother probably wouldn't mind all that much. She shouldn't, the way she drinks. The way they all drink. But Craig is a real puritan."

"So's my father," said Frankie. "I guess I would be, too, if I had a kid."

"I can't imagine having children," said Miranda. "Can you?"

"Yeah," said Frankie. "I think it would be nice."

They came to a level area framed by dogwood and flowering cherry where the grass thinned and the sandy soil rose to the surface. They sat and Miranda again handed the joint to him. He took a drag, then leaned forward and put his lips against hers. She opened her mouth, and slowly he blew little rings of smoke into it. Murmuring contentedly, she closed her eyes and lay back. He stretched out next to her and pulled her into his arms.

"You should have changed," she said. "You'll ruin your lovely jacket."

"Do you like it?"

"Hmm," she murmured.

Frankie felt a quick rush of pleasure, unsure whether it was for her approval or her nearness. Snipping off the burning end of the joint with his fingers, he slipped it into his pocket. "I'm cold," he said, pulling her over until she lay half on top of him. "Keep me warm." He kissed her, her closed eyes, her open mouth. He traced the whorls of her ear with his tongue and felt her shiver. "Oh, baby," he whispered. "Oh, sweetheart. I wanted to do that all night."

He rolled her over onto the sparse grass, reaching under her jacket, inside her sweater, pushing aside her bra so he could feel her breast, small and firm under his hand, smooth and resilient to his touch. He ran his hand down her leg to her knee, back up the inside of her thigh and stroked her through her pants. She neither aided him, nor resisted. She seemed content to let him go as far as he wanted. Undoing the waistband of her jeans, he reached inside her panties and caressed the taut, silky skin of her belly. He heard her sigh and felt himself expanding, filling the night, filling the world.

When his fingers moved lower, she stopped him: a murmured protest, her hand over his. Pulling back from her, he collapsed, breathless, onto the sand, covering his closed eyes with his arm. Mingled with the disappointment, the pain, undermining the lust, he realized, was relief. He hadn't wanted to have sex with her, not like this, not quick and easy, on a beach in the middle of the night. He didn't want it to be casual and unimportant, dismissable by either of them. What he felt for her required solemnity, rite.

Frankie took his arm away from his eyes and opened them. Miranda had finished adjusting her clothes and was looking down at him, smiling, a vague, shy smile. "I love you," he said.

"I don't know why," she said. "I must be crazy, but I believe you."

"I'll love you forever," he said. "I swear it. For as long as I live, I'll love you. And after."

Chapter 4

The ringing phone distracted Frankie. "Ignore it, darling," murmured Eva Colvington, her body writhing under his, her long snake's tongue flicking at his ear. He tried to do as she asked, but then he noticed the company sergeant from Fort Gordon watching him, his face, his stance, everything about him radiating contempt. "What are you, asshole, some kind of pansy?" he said. It put Frankie off his rhythm. He stopped humping and tried to pull out, but Eva wrapped her legs around him, holding him in place.

"It's Miranda," called Dan from somewhere far away. "You awake yet?"

Frankie bolted out of sleep and sat up, the strange, erotic dream dissolving into a vague feeling of dread. "Yes," he said, sounding dazed. "What?"

Dan stuck his head in the door. "She wants to have a picnic today."

Frankie shook his head, where large banks of fog seemed to be obscuring anything resembling thought. "Fine with me," he said, sinking back into the pillow, closing his eyes, trying, and failing, to recapture the wisp of dream that lingered disturbingly at the edge of his mind. It must be the pot, decided Frankie. Powerful stuff.

They picked Miranda and Beth up at the house, drove to the beach at Race Point, and sat on blankets in the sand, eating fried chicken prepared by Mrs. Lyle, potato chips, peaches, plums from an endless supply in the wicker basket, drinking bottled beer from the cooler. After lunch, they built a sand castle, an elaborate structure of deep moats, crenellated walls, and tall, round keeps. They swam; they played in the surf; they lay in the sun and drifted off into an easy, contented sleep. Late in the day, they returned to the Colvington house where the four took turns in the big guest bathroom, with its old-fashioned brass-footed tub and hand-held shower. It occurred to Frankie that his mother, if this were her house, would have had it out of there in no time, replaced with a shiny new tub in colored porcelain, the best that money could buy.

"Anyone in there?" called Miranda, from the hallway.

"Me," said Frankie. He finished belting his pants, opened the door, and pulled her inside. He kissed her mouth and, pushing aside her terry-cloth robe, the tops of her breasts.

"Frankie, really," she protested.

"I know," he said. "I shouldn't. But I want to."

"You must have been spoiled rotten as a child."

"So my sister always says." He kissed her again, opened the door, and left.

*A*fter fortifying themselves with sandwiches, eaten in the large white kitchen under Mrs. Lyle's approving eye, the four drove off, in Frankie's car, to Provincetown to see Vic play Solyony in *The Three Sisters*. If Vic hadn't been in it, nothing would have prompted Frankie to go. Though he liked musicals all right, the few he had seen at any rate, like *Bye, Bye Birdie* or *The Music Man,* plays left him cold. The artifical sets, the made-up actors, the long speeches—he found it hard to get involved, to suspend disbelief, the key, his cousin had once told him, to enjoying the experience. But this night was different. It might have been the company, being with confirmed theater-goers who were obviously engrossed in the performance. Or the production, which, as Vic had said, was pretty good. Or maybe the play itself. Something in the sisters' longing to be somewhere else, leading a different life, struck a chord in Frankie. He found himself caught up in what was happening on stage, found himself moved by it.

"What did you *really* think?" Vic asked later, when he joined them at Teeny's. Miranda, Beth, Dan, they all raved, about him, about the production. Frankie, not able to formulate exactly what he had felt, murmured only a few words of faint praise. "Come on," said Vic. "The truth."

"I thought it was great," said Frankie. Vic laughed. "No, I really did."

"You don't have to sound so surprised," he said. His date was a dark-haired girl with large brown eyes, a sweet smile, and an air of total innocence. She worked as a receptionist in the hotel where Vic was staying and, as he pulled a chair out from the table for her, he said, "We can't stay long," adding as he dropped into the next seat, "I only came to collect my praise. If I don't get Maria home before midnight, her father'll have my head. And any other significant piece of anatomy he can get his hands on."

"I'm usually not allowed out at all during the week," she said, laughing. "Tonight was an exception. Thanks to Chekhov. My father's a great believer in education." He was a fisherman, she told them, a descendant of one of the Portuguese who had come to Provincetown in the middle of the nineteenth century to work on the whaling ships.

"I'm surprised you're allowed to go out with Vic at all," said Frankie.

"He knows I'm an honorable man," said Vic.

"Does it run in the family?" asked Miranda with a smile.

The image of her in the bathroom a few hours before, her breasts exposed, her face flushed, her hair awry, flashed into Frankie's mind, vivid as a color slide. "Knights in shining armor," said Frankie. "That's us."

They ordered something to eat, and when Vic left with Maria, the others remained to dance, fast dances and slow, drinking between sets, until Beth said, "I've got a headache. I can't breathe. Let's get out of here."

"Let's go to the beach," said Frankie as they came out into damp night air. Music floated on the breeze from the ocean. Somewhere in the distance a motorcycle roared.

"I want to go home," said Beth. "I'm exhausted."

"It's late," agreed Miranda.

They got into Frankie's car, Beth and Dan in the back, Miranda beside Frankie in front. She fiddled with the knobs on the radio.

"No music, please. My head," whimpered Beth.

Instead, Miranda rolled a joint. "It's going to rain tomorrow," she said, then lit it, took a drag, offered it to Frankie, who shook his head no, and to Dan, who also refused.

They sat in silence as Frankie, peering through a light alcoholic mist, drove cautiously along the dark stretch of lonely road, back to the house that seemed to him a castle and Miranda its princess, fragile and beautiful, remote even when seeming most accessible. He glanced at her. She sat with head back against the seat, her eyes closed, taking long, slow drags on the joint. Her face was perfect, he thought, and felt a wave of intense desire surge through him. In the rearview mirror, he could see Dan with his arms around Beth, holding her, as she rested her aching head against his shoulder.

When they reached the Colvington house, they walked in pairs to the door, Beth and Dan first, followed by Miranda and Frankie. She stumbled, and he put an arm around her. "Let's go for a walk," said Frankie.

"I can't. I'm not sure I can walk, I'm so tired. Anyway, I should look after Beth."

"She'll go right to sleep." He pulled her closer, murmuring "Please" as he kissed her ear.

Miranda shook her head. "I really can't. I'll talk to you in the morning," she said.

"I'll call you," said Frankie, conceding defeat, "as soon as I wake up."

She leaned forward and kissed him lightly on the mouth. Then she kissed Dan's cheek, and followed Beth inside.

"You interested in Beth?" said Frankie, getting back into the car.

He shrugged, and said, "She's leaving for Sardinia next week."

"Miranda's not going anywhere, is she?"

"Not that I've heard." They were silent all the way to the cottage, mellow from drinking, ready to sleep. "It was a nice day," said Dan.

"Yeah," agreed Frankie. "It was great." Maybe the best day of his life, he thought.

$\mathcal{F}$rankie and Miranda began dating, seriously dating. At least it was serious to him. He wasn't sure how Miranda felt. At times he thought that if she never saw him again, it would make no real difference to her. At others, he was convinced that she genuinely cared for him. But he never surprised on her face that look of rapt admiration he was used to getting from women. He never saw longing in her eyes. Sometime he wondered why. Mostly he tried not to think too much. Mostly he tried to enjoy the summer without calculating how soon it would end.

When Beth left, Dan began taking out a girl he had met at Teeny's, Caitlin, a skinny redhead, smart and full of energy. The four of them sometimes double-dated, sometimes triple-dated with Vic and Maria. But when Frankie could manage it, he got Miranda alone. On dull, rainy days, they visited the Commercial Street art galleries and the Association art show, and Frankie would listen as Miranda talked about brushstrokes and color, technique and form, light and space, trying in vain to understand what it was that she could see in paintings that to him looked mostly like drop sheets, the mishaps of amazingly careless workers. Afterward, they would go to Teeny's, and while she drank coffee or wine, and (now that he wasn't getting much exercise) he kept his beer intake to a minimum, Frankie would try to ferret out the secrets of Miranda's past. Yes, she'd had lots of boyfriends, she told him. And she'd been in love a few times, twice in high school, once the summer before her freshman year at Bennington with a guy from Amherst, a brilliant young man, a top athlete, a Rhodes Scholar.

"A what?" asked Frankie.

"It's a scholarship to Oxford, in England," explained Miranda. "Some wealthy South African politician established it ages ago. Anyway, we've sort of lost touch since he's been there."

"What's his name?"

"Stanfield Morrow." Frankie laughed. "What's funny?" said Miranda.

"He sounds like a company, a firm of lawyers, maybe. Anybody ever call him Stan?"

"No," said Miranda, beginning to smile.

"I didn't think so." His making her laugh was good, but didn't quite eliminate the knot of jealousy that had formed in his stomach. What must it be like, he wondered, to be Stanfield Morrow, assured of your place in the present, confident of your role in the future? "And since good old Stanfield?"

"Oh," said Miranda, vaguely, "you know . . ."

That was just it, he didn't. Frankie called to Mac for the bill. "How's it going?" he asked when Mac dropped the tab onto the oak table. Anything to change the subject.

"Working my ass off," said Mac. "One of the bums who worked for me quit."

"Hope you find someone soon," said Frankie as he ushered Miranda to the door.

*W*hen the sun shone, they went to the beach and lay side by side reading, or took the Colvington rowboat out into the lake and let it drift idly as they discussed what they liked or disliked about books, or films, eating their way through pounds of deliciously ripe summer peaches, exchanging brief, passionate kisses that promised more, later. When the wind was right, Miranda taught him how to sail the Sunfish. Sometimes, Frankie stayed with the Colvingtons for dinner. Craig was always gracious and Eva frequently flirtatious, yet both seemed to Frankie to be wary, watching him with appraising eyes, assessing his value as they might that of a toy Miranda had acquired, interesting but rather cheap, one that she would tire of even before it broke. They made Frankie uncomfortable, and he preferred the nights when Miranda and he would drive into Provincetown to have dinner, then go dancing or catch the acts at the clubs—folk groups, jazz musicians, transvestite comics who left Frankie feeling both disgusted and provincial. Afterward, they would sit in Frankie's car and neck. The nights would always end the same, with Miranda stopping him before he went too far, Frankie torn between frustration and acceptance, rage and relief.

. . .

$\mathscr{T}$he rhythm of the days, of the nights, had an eternal quality, like the ebb and flow of the sea, making it easy for Frankie to pretend that this time would last forever. But the middle of July inevitably drew near and, at breakfast one morning, Dan reminded Frankie that his family would be arriving the following weekend. Two weeks later, he and his father would leave for Switzerland and a walking tour of the Alps. Frankie took a swallow of coffee, and said, "I better clear out of here."

"Why?" said Dan. "There's plenty of room. My parents won't mind. People are always staying, all summer long."

"I'd feel funny," said Frankie.

"I'd like you to stay," said Dan, "at least until I go."

Frankie shook his head. "I appreciate that. But no. Really."

Dan shrugged. "If that's how you feel. What will you do? Go home?"

"I can't," said Frankie.

"Miranda," said Dan. Frankie nodded. "It's that serious?"

"For me."

"Are you sleeping with her?" Before Frankie could answer, Dan said, "I shouldn't have asked. It's none of my business. Sorry."

"I'm not sleeping with her," said Frankie. "Not because I don't want to, God knows . . ."

"Nice girls," said Dan.

"Yeah," said Frankie.

"And nice guys."

Frankie smiled. "Thanks," he said. He handed Dan the sports page. "What do you think about that?" he said, pointing to a picture of Rafer Johnson, who had won the decathlon trials in Oregon,

"Holy shit," said Dan. "Looks good for the Olympics, doesn't it?"

$\mathscr{F}$rankie called his parents and told them he would be staying on the Cape longer than he had planned.

"When are we going to meet this Dan?" asked his mother.

"In the fall, maybe. He won't be around the rest of the summer. He's going to Europe. He's a nice guy. You'll like him."

"I miss you, Frankie. I wish you'd come home."

He told her Vic was in Provincetown, and that he'd been spending some time with him, and that cheered her up: any link with family, however tenuous, was reassuring.

Then his father got on the phone. "You told your mother you seen Vic?"

"Yeah. He's in a play up here. I seen him. *Saw* him, I mean. He's good."

"Don't you be getting no bright ideas. Bad enough my brother's gonna have a heart attack over his son."

"Don't worry. I don't wanna be an actor."

"Just a bum, right? Hangin' around? Doin' nothin'?"

"I'll call again next week, Pop."

"It's a girl." Frankie could hear his mother whispering in the background. "That's why Frankie's staying."

"Jesus Christ, I got a psychic in the family," muttered Sal.

"Give my love to Angela and Denny, okay? And the kids," said Frankie. " 'Bye, Pop."

"Call," said his father. "Sonovabitch," he muttered about no one in particular, putting down the phone.

That done, Frankie went to Teeny's to ask Mac for a job. The grateful Mac hired him on the spot, and Frankie agreed to start the following afternoon. Mac also rented him the cabin the ex-bartender had vacated. "You can look around for better," he said, "but there won't be a lot left that's reasonable this time of year."

"It's fine," said Frankie. The cabin was one room with indoor plumbing, set in a small yard that was mostly sand and wildflowers. Inside it was clean and neat, though sparsely furnished. It had a double bed with a crucifix above it, a pine table and chairs, a sofa covered in a faded green, three tarnished brass standing lamps, an empty bookcase.

"If you want to hang pictures," said Mac, "feel free."

That night, when Frankie told Miranda about the job, she got angry. They had been to a party with Dan and Caitlin, on the beach, where someone who was really pretty good played the guitar and everyone drank beer and sang folk songs. When the crowd began breaking up into couples and drifting off into the dunes, they left. After dropping Dan and Caitlin off at the cottage, Frankie drove Miranda home.

"Everything was perfect," she said.

"I gotta work. I don't want to use up all my savings." He stopped the car in the drive, in front of the house, and tried to pull her closer to him along the car seat. She resisted.

"Beth's gone. Dan's leaving. What am I supposed to do while you're busy?"

"What did you do other summers?"

"Dated boys who had time for me."

"We'll still have plenty of time together. I'm only working a few hours a day." He reached out to stroke her neck, but she shrugged his hand away.

"If I'd known you were going to do something like this, I would have made other plans. I didn't even intend to stay this long. I only did because you're here."

She had changed her plans for him! The elation he felt at the thought lasted only a moment. He shifted in his seat, leaning away from her, and said angrily, "Jesus, Miranda, stop sounding like such a spoiled brat."

"Everything was perfect, and you've ruined it."

"We're spending too much time together anyway."

"I thought you were supposed to be in love with me." All Frankie could hear was the sarcasm, not the note of anxiety under it. From her pocket, she took a joint she had rolled at the beach, lit it, and took a drag.

"I am. That's the problem. You're driving me nuts."

She turned and looked at him accusingly. "Oh, so that's it. That's why you're doing this. Because I won't let you make love to me?"

"No! Damnit, why won't you listen? I can't hang around all summer doing nothing," he said, unconsciously echoing his father. "I gotta do something, earn some money."

"Do you want to stop seeing me? Is that what you're saying?"

"No. Don't be crazy."

"If that's what you mean, just tell me. You don't have to pretend."

"Miranda, I love you. You know that. I think I'd die if I couldn't see you."

She moved toward him, sliding across the seat, until she had him pinned against the car door. She put her arms around him. "Then tell Mac you've changed your mind."

Frankie was tempted. He had enough money to last the summer, beyond the summer, if he was careful, and in September, when Miranda went back to school, he could get a job then. He kissed her and felt her yielding in his arms.

"You'll tell Mac," she said.

But his instincts rebelled. Though he tried to convince himself that if he did what Miranda wanted, he would be reasonable, understanding, an adult, willing to compromise, deep down he felt he would be none of those things. What she wanted wasn't reasonable: she wanted only to have her own way. If he gave in, he would forever consider himself spineless, weak, pussy-whipped. "I can't do that," he said.

"I don't understand you." She pulled out of his arms.

"What you don't understand is some people have to work for a living."

She moved away from him, back toward the passenger door, opening it. "I'm going into Boston tomorrow."

"Why?"

"My sister, Joan, is arriving. Mother and I want to be there to meet her."

"When were you gonna tell me?"

"Tonight. Now. It's no big deal."

"When will you be back?"

"I'm not sure." She got out of the car.

"Miranda, don't be like this."

"I'm not being any way."

"Call me from Boston."

"If I can," she said. "Good night."

"Miranda—" The car door slammed shut. Frankie leaned out the window. "Call me," he said to her retreating back. Without answering, Miranda let herself into the house and, not even turning to wave, closed the door.

Chapter 5

Wearing one of Dan's shirts, Caitlin was at the stove, making breakfast. Dan sat at the table in the alcove, reading the *Herald*.

"Very pretty," said Frankie, his eyes at half mast, groggy from lack of sleep. "The old folks at home." He poured himself a cup of coffee, scraped back a chair and joined Dan at the table.

Caitlin blushed. "Eggs?" she asked. "Pancakes?"

"Pancakes, please," said Frankie. "This is what we've been missing," he added in the direction of Dan's bowed head. "Someone to take care of us."

"You look like shit," said Dan, looking up.

"I feel like shit," agreed Frankie. Grabbing the sports section of the paper, he checked the scores, then read the account of the Yankee game. He'd always been a Yankee fan. Joe DiMaggio was still one of his heroes: Italian boy made good, made better than good, made a star, married (no matter how briefly or disastrously) to an even bigger star, the brightest star in the world. The Bronx Bomber made Frankie feel that his own dreams of glory, no matter how amorphous, could one day come true.

The Yankees had won, but even that failed to cheer Frankie up. Nothing would cheer him up but a phone call from Miranda.

Caitlin brought the pancakes to the table, poured coffee all around, and sat. Yesterday, at the beach, she'd been reading *The Idiot*. Frankie had never read Tolstoy, had never heard of him, in fact. When he asked if it was any good, trying to sound nonchalant, as he always did when there was something he wanted desperately to know, Caitlin had said, "It's the the most beautiful book I've ever read." A secretary at an insurance company in Hartford, she was in Provincetown on vacation with a girlfriend. Well-read, smart, a wild dancer, someone who liked partying as much as books, Caitlin wanted to go to college, but her parents had said no, they couldn't afford the tuition, anyway it was useless for a girl to get a degree. Dan had suggested she apply for a scholarship or financial aid. Hard as it was to believe, the idea had never occurred to her, but she said she was going to look into it as soon as she got home.

"This is great, isn't it?" she said, picking up the discarded first section of the paper and looking at yet another picture on the front page of John Fitzgerald Kennedy smiling, this one with hand raised to acknowledge the cheers as he accepted his party's nomination for president.

"You don't suppose you think that because you're Irish?" said Dan, teasing.

"Now, why would you be thinking that?" she said, putting on a brogue. When Dan and Frankie laughed, she continued, "You don't have to be Irish to admire him. Did you read his book?" she asked. They admitted they hadn't. "Well, you should. He's a very intelligent man. A very brave man."

"And handsome," said Frankie, remembering Nelson's view on sex in politics.

"Looks don't matter a bean, and you know it."

"Only someone as beautiful as you could believe that," said Dan, with the practiced charm Frankie so much admired.

Again, the blood rushed up and filled in the spaces between Caitlin's freckles. She is beautiful, thought Frankie, who'd been so preoccupied with Miranda he'd failed to notice. Her hair was deep auburn, her cheekbones high, her mouth full. Pale lashes framed big green eyes. "Nice of you to say so," she said, and stood, beginning to clear the table. "I'll take a shower first, if you don't mind. Then I'll do these dishes."

"I'll do the dishes," said Dan. He reached and grabbed her hand, and pulled her to him for a kiss as she passed. "I'm not completely helpless."

"I've noticed," she said with a smile, then carried the pile of dirty dishes into the kitchen, leaving them with a clatter in the sink before going off to take her shower.

"I might as well move to Mac's place today," said Frankie when she'd gone. "Give you and Caitlin some time alone."

"It's not necessary," said Dan. "She'll be going back to Hartford on Sunday."

"The cabin's standing there empty."

"I'm not sure I want her staying here. You know what women are like," he said. "Ready to read commitment into anything you do."

"She's too smart. She won't misunderstand."

"Just do me a favor and stay until Sunday."

"Sure," said Frankie. "It's not what you'd call a hardship."

*T*wo days passed and Miranda didn't call. By Saturday night, Frankie was both anxious and angry. He phoned the house, but Mrs. Lyle said the whole family was still away and she didn't know when they'd be back. When he insisted, she gave him their Boston number, but whoever answered the phone there said they had gone to Europe. Frankie left his name and a message for Miranda to call as soon as she returned.

Dan insisted that their absence didn't imply anything sinister. It was summer, after all. People did travel. Sooner or later they came home.

On Sunday afternoon, Nelson Clewes and Colette Drake stopped into Teeny's for a drink. With them was another couple, the woman slender and dark haired with lively and intelligent eyes, the man distinguished looking with longish hair, Helen Frankenthaler and Robert Motherwell. Frankie recognized them from photographs in the art magazines he was now regularly reading. To his surprise, both Nelson and Colette remembered him from that long-ago dinner at the Colvingtons'. Yes, he told them, he was enjoying his stay on the Cape. Yes, he had seen the Colvingtons, often, but now they were away.

"In Paris," said Colette. "Craig always goes to see the collections, and Eva decided to tag along."

The collections, thought Frankie, what are they? "And Miranda?" he asked, not able to help himself.

Colette nodded. "Joan, too. I've never met a girl yet who could resist a trip to Paris." Even Colette's most innocent smile had an arch, insinuating quality, and Frankie wondered if she suspected how much he wanted to ask when the Colvingtons would be back, which he couldn't bring himself to do. For a moment, he thought she was going to tell him anyway, but instead she linked her arm through Nelson's, and, with a nod of farewell, turned away to join the others who had already seated themselves at a table.

"See you," said Frankie.

"I live in hope," said Nelson.

Frankie sent Mac to wait on them. He was, he admitted to himself, too embarrassed to do it. Dan would have carried it off, but he couldn't. He felt somehow demeaned. Which made him angry. Why the hell should he feel embarrassed about having to work for a living?

Early the next night, Colette returned to Teeny's alone, and when Frankie brought her wine to the table, she asked him to join her. Looking around, he checked to see if anyone required his attention, then pulled out a chair and sat. "I was surprised to see you yesterday," she said. "I thought you were here on vacation, with Dan Colvington."

He could hear the dollar signs in her voice when she spoke the name "Colvington," and the slight edge of surprise that any friend of that family might have to work to earn money. He shrugged. "I'm just helping out Mac for a few days. What about you? I haven't seen you around."

One dark eyebrow rose a fraction of an inch. "Were you looking?"

This he knew how to handle. "For a good-looking woman? Always."

Colette smiled. Frankie excused himself to wait on a customer. Sometime later, she beckoned and he brought her another glass of wine. When a group of privates from the nearby army base came in and started drinking, he forgot about her, and instead watched them warily. Before long, the soldiers started getting rowdy, and Frankie (his training as an MP combining with a naturally short fuse) decided to restore order. Before he knew it, he was down on the floor, ramming some kid's head into the sawdust-covered boards. Mac pulled him off.

"You okay?" asked Mac as the kid's buddies, anxious to avoid more trouble, got him to his feet and hustled him out the door.

"Sorry," said Frankie.

"No harm done," said Mac. "This time." The words held a warning.

"That's quite a temper you've got," said Colette, still there when the shift ended.

"Yeah," said Frankie, who'd heard it before.

"Where are you off to now?" she asked.

"Nowhere in particular."

"No one's waiting for you?"

"No one," he said.

"Well, then we have something in common. No one's waiting for me, either."

Never slow to take a hint, Frankie asked her if she wanted to grab a bite to eat, and she said it was a lovely idea, that she'd be delighted: she hated eating alone.

They walked around the corner to a restaurant in Commercial Street. Frankie had eaten there often enough with both Miranda and Dan for the pretty hostess to greet him with a smile and offer him a table by the window, overlooking the wharf.

Colette eyed the girl appraisingly as she walked away, and said, "She likes you."

"I like her," replied Frankie.

"Have you been out with her?" How strange he found the question registered on his face. Colette smiled ruefully. "I'm terribly nosy. My friends get used to it."

"You don't think you'd find out more if you beat around the bush a little?"

"No. People can never resist answering a direct question, even an outrageous one. *Have* you gone out with her?"

"No," said Frankie, laughing. "I've been too busy."

Colette changed her order three times before settling on Frankie's choice of steak and *pommes frites*. He asked for the wine list and studied it to see if he could remember the one Dan always ordered. "I bet you've been drinking wine since you stopped teething," said Colette, approving his choice.

"Since I was five," said Frankie who told her about the crates of grapes delivered every year to his grandfather's house, and about the giant press in the cellar where he had played as a child. "The wine always tasted like vinegar."

Firing nonstop questions as they ate, Colette managed to find out a lot, except the thing that seemed to interest her most, whether or not there was a woman in Frankie's life. When she approached that subject, he retreated. And because it was impossible to sit talking over a meal without discovering something about your companion, however little genuine interest you had, Frankie learned quite a bit about her, too: that she loved her job, that she handled publicity for all sorts of important accounts, from individual designers like Nelson Clewes to major department stores like B. Altman and Saks, from Broadway producers and big banks to stand-up comics and trendy nightclubs. If it wasn't for her, she told him, no one would know the Village Vanguard existed.

"That's great," he said, as if he knew what she was talking about.

She told him that she had been divorced for ten years and had no children. Her former husband, who had remarried and now had two daughters, was really a pretty nice guy. He was an internist, in Philadelphia. Sometimes she thought she was crazy for having given him up for . . . She laughed, and waved her hands. "For money. For success. For adventure. But *c'est la guerre,*" she said.

"Yeah," replied Frankie.

When they finished eating, Colette suggested that they catch the new act at the Harbor House, a comedian she'd seen at Upstairs at the Downstairs in New York. She had heard that he was trying out new material. Colette linked her arm through his and, though Frankie had every intention of refusing, he found himself accompanying her first to hear the comic, then afterward back to the pretty Victorian inn at Land's End where she was staying. "A nightcap?" she asked.

His head was already light from the wine at dinner and the drinks at the Harbor House. "Sure," he said, following her inside.

"I've got a bottle in my room." She took his hand, and led him through the dark lobby to the stairs.

He followed her, not certain yet what he intended to do, entertaining the possibility that, even if he did let this, whatever it was, maybe even go a little too far, he could still extricate himself with some grace, should he want to. But why the hell *should* he want to? he asked himself. The image of Miranda, breasts bare, eyes smiling, came into his head. And he pushed it away. It hurt to think of her. Miranda was gone, he decided brutally, and Colette definitely was not. He slipped an arm around her waist, and she smiled at him encouragingly. "Here," she said, handing him the key to the door.

The room was spacious, elegant, with large windows, a view out over the bay, and a double bed. The furniture was wicker, the wallpaper striped and hung with drawings of roses. It was a feminine room, too girlish for Colette.

"Scotch all right?" she asked.

"Fine," said Frankie.

"Water?" And when he shook his head, she said, "There's no ice."

"It doesn't matter." He sat in one of the wicker chairs.

Colette handed him the scotch, and stretched out on the bed, propping her head against pillows. "So," she said. "What happens now?"

He got up, put his drink on the dresser, and sat beside her. "This?" he said, and kissed her.

"How old are you anyway?" she asked, when she came up for air.

"Twenty-one."

Colette laughed. "Oh, my God, it's worse than I thought." She took his face in her hands, studied it a moment, then pulled it toward hers. "You're so beautiful," she said.

*H*ow old are you?" Frankie asked. Room service had brought breakfast, and he was lying, fully clothed, on the bed, eating, watching Colette as she dressed.

"This morning light is hell, isn't it?"

"Tell me."

"What difference does it make?"

"I'm curious."

She stepped into her dress, then came to the bed for Frankie to zip it. "Am I the oldest woman you've ever been to bed with?"

He grinned. "How do I know, if you won't tell me your age?" he said, pulling the zipper closed.

She swiveled around to face him. "I should have let you leave in the middle of the night and spared myself the inquisition."

"I'm glad you didn't," he said, kissing her. Every time he'd tried to leave, she'd made love to him again, until, finally, he'd fallen into an exhausted sleep. Now he felt lazy, grateful, not embarrassed, not guilty. He fingered the fabric of her dress. "This feels nice," he said. His father had never worked with cloth so fine, so luxurious.

"It should. It cost enough. It's silk," she added, as if it had suddenly occurred to her that he might not know. She pulled out of his arms. "Time to go."

Frankie had offered to drive her to the airport, but she'd refused. "If you really want to do me a favor," she'd said, "you'll let me leave you lying naked in bed. Icing on the fantasy cake, so to speak." But when she saw the look of outrage on his face, she smiled, ruefully. "Sorry, baby. I mustn't be greedy."

Completely unperturbed by Frankie's presence at her side, Colette settled her bill, then followed him out to the waiting taxi where Frankie handed her two small cases to the driver to put into the trunk. "When will you be back?" he asked, not quite knowing why he did, not at all certain he really cared. Perhaps it was just that the conventions of the situation seemed to require the question, and Frankie had been raised to be polite.

Colette laughed. "You are possibly the nicest boy I've ever met," she said, kissing his cheek. Then settling herself into the taxi, she added, "I have no idea."

Frankie closed the door, then leaned in through the open window. "I'm not a boy."

The driver started the motor, then turned to look at Colette for permission to go. She was staring at Frankie. "I'm forty-four," she said. Then she smiled at the driver. "Let's go. I don't want to miss my plane." The taxi pulled away, and Colette's arm extended out and waved. "It's been fun," she said.

*C*aitlin returned to Hartford, Frankie moved into Mac's cabin, and Dan's family arrived. Days he wasn't working, Frankie hung around with Vic, or spent with the Colvingtons on the beach, reading the copy of *The Idiot* that Caitlin had left behind, playing touch football with Dan and his siblings, sometimes joining Dan and his father for a game of golf. When the shows changed at the art galleries, he went to see them. Some mornings he spent at the library, letting the helpful Mrs. DeSouza steer him toward the things he needed: books on art, on theater, on wine; magazines about fashion, with sumptuous descriptions of elegant clothes, about people, full of gossip about who they were and why everyone was talking about them. Frankie felt as if he were cramming for an exam, one that he had to pass because he wouldn't be allowed to repeat the course.

On one of his nights off, a Sunday, about ten days after Miranda had left, Frankie was with Vic and Dan in Teeny's. The place was jammed. The bearded artist, the Hemingway look-alike, was there with an extended entourage. A transvestite entertainer, who was playing at a nearby club, came in dressed, unrecognizably, in a white suit, accompanied by a lesbian fan club that laughed at his every remark. Nelson Clewes arrived drunk and, to the delight of the group with him, grabbed the microphone from the band's lead singer and belted out the lyrics of "Itsy Bitsy, Teeny Weeny, Yellow Polka Dot Bikini," somehow still managing to appear dapper, even elegant. When Frankie asked him about Colette, all he said was, "I haven't seen her lately."

Maria had been grounded by her father for staying out too late, so Vic, Dan, and Frankie all took potluck dancing with the girls who had come without an escort, the ones up from some city for the weekend, or there for the summer working. It was an easy crowd, intent on fun.

It was close to ten when Frankie, on his way back from the john, saw that two women had joined Vic and Dan at the table. One was slender and brown haired, with straight brows over lustrous dark eyes, a beaked nose, and wide mouth. She was attractive, though not pretty, dressed in slacks and a shirt that managed, despite their simplicity, to look expensive. Joan, he assumed, since the other was Miranda. He had just enough time, crossing the floor, to get his flyaway feelings under control. Thank God I spotted her, he thought as he composed his face into what he hoped was an easy smile. "Hello, Miranda," he said when he reached the table. "So you're back."

He had come up behind her, startling her, and she jumped slightly, then swiveled around to face him. "This afternoon," she said. "I, uh, I went to Paris. To see the collections." He knew what she meant, because he had been reading about them in the fashion magazines. "Craig always goes. And mother."

She sounded nervous, which pleased him. "I heard. Colette told me." Miranda was thinner than when she'd left, and her face had a pale, drawn quality. She looked unhappy. Probably jet lag, thought Frankie, as he turned away from her to smile at her companion. "You must be Joan," he said. "Nice to meet you." When the band returned, he asked Miranda to dance. They were playing the Hank Locklin hit, "Please Help Me, I'm Falling." "You enjoy yourself in Paris?" he asked, taking her in his arms..

"It was hot," she said. "Crowded. Interesting, though."

After that they were silent. Never before had they been so uneasy, so awkward, with one another, not even on the night they met.

Returning Miranda to the table, Frankie asked Joan to dance, surprising everyone, including himself. For a while, the group alternated partners, Vic and Dan sometimes asking other girls to dance, but Frankie dividing himself scrupulously between the two sisters. Sitting one set out, at Joan's request, Frankie asked her what she did in San Francisco.

"I work at a museum. An art museum. I have a very unimportant job, but I'm learning a lot." She was a serious young woman, intense, without any of Eva's gaiety and charm, without Miranda's fragile beauty and tender appeal.

"You like it?"

"I love it," she said.

"When I was stationed at Fort Ord, I used to go to San Francisco all the time. Too bad I didn't know you then."

"Dan used to come in and take me out to dinner sometimes."

"Oh, you're *that* cousin. That sonovagun. He never told me you were pretty."

She laughed. "Miranda's right," she said. "You are a smooth talker."

"No," said Frankie, smiling. "She's wrong. Dead wrong. I always mean what I say. She oughtta know that better than anybody." He saw Miranda and Vic walking toward them from the dance floor, Miranda frowning for some reason. "Would you like to dance?" he asked. He took Joan's hand, pulled her to her feet. "Come on," he said. For the next few sets, he danced only with her, and when finally she said no more, she was exhausted, he stayed by her side and went on flirting. Not that Joan reciprocated. She smiled. She was polite. But he was making her uncomfortable. He knew it, but he couldn't help himself. He couldn't stop.

As the night wore on, the smile on Miranda's face became more and more strained. She went outside often, and Frankie knew it was to smoke a joint. He resisted the impulse to follow her, to grab her, shake the hell out of her, tell her how much he loved her. Let the little bitch suffer, he thought, the way he had suffered while she was gone. Once Dan went with her, and when they came back, Miranda's eyes were red.

"I'd like to go now," said Joan.

The evening came to an end, Joan driving Miranda back to the Colvingtons', Dan returning home, Vic to his hotel, and Frankie back to the cabin, where he lay awake until dawn, telling himself that even had Miranda loved him there was no way he could marry her, support her, give her the life she deserved, the life she had always had.

When he finally fell asleep, he dreamed that he was about six or seven months old, sitting in the middle of the floor of the family den, in the house to which he hadn't moved until he was thirteen, playing with a bright red truck that his sister Angela suddenly snatched away from him. He screamed, but no one came. And Angela, ignoring his cries, sat down and, humming softly to herself, played with the toy just beyond his reach.

Mixed with his screams, Frankie heard the sound of knocking and gratefully let it wake him. He opened his eyes. The dream fled, but not the frustration, or the rage.

Not bothering to put on a robe, he crossed to the door in his shorts, opened it, and found Miranda on the threshold. "Dan gave me the address," she said. She was wearing yellow pants and a white blouse printed with daisies. Her long blond hair hung loose, curling in soft wisps at the ends.

"Come in," he said. "Would you mind putting some water on for coffee? I'll be right back." He went into the bathroom, peed, washed his face, brushed his teeth, combed his hair. It was already hot, and he didn't bother to put on a shirt.

"I found some instant coffee. Is that all you have?" Frankie nodded, and she returned her attention to the kettle, waiting for it to boil.

"What are you doing here?"

"I missed you," she said.

"Yeah, I'm sure. Paris is such a boring city."

"I was angry when I left. I was sorry right away. I wanted to tell you, but . . ."

"They don't have phones in Paris?"

The kettle boiled. She turned off the gas, and poured water into his mug. "I didn't know what to say. I thought I could explain better when I got back. But you were so awful last night." Her eyes filled with tears. "Why did you flirt with Joan like that?"

"I wasn't flirting," he said, sipping tentatively at the coffee, trying not to scald his mouth. "I was just being nice to her. I was trying to get to know her."

"You embarrassed her. She's my *sister,* Frankie. She knows how I feel about you."

He put the mug down on the table. "How *do* you feel about me?"

Miranda walked around the table and stood in front of him. "I need you, Frankie. I need you to love me. Especially now."

Her answer left him feeling uneasy. "Why?" he asked. "Why now?"

She shrugged, then said, "Because when you love me, you make me feel safe, I guess. Nobody's ever made me feel as loved as you do."

"Do you love *me?*"

Miranda hesitated, as if searching her heart, as if trying to decide how far to go. Finally she nodded. He pulled her down into his lap, wrapped his arms around her, buried his face in her neck. "Say it," he said.

"I love you."

Those were the words Frankie had been waiting his whole life to hear, just from her. They were the only things she had to give that he really needed.

Miranda brushed his lips with her own, once, twice, then kissed his closed eyes. "Don't ever flirt with anyone but me, ever again."

"I won't," he said. "As long as you're with me. As long as you love me.
I hated being away from you. I've been going crazy without you."

He set her on her feet, then stood, and with his lips still on hers, their
tongues playing, he unbuttoned her blouse, undid her bra, and took them
off. He bent his head to kiss her breast, and heard her sigh. He opened the
buttons of her yellow pants, and slid them down. She stepped out of them,
then stayed in Frankie's embrace as he walked her backward to the bed. As
she lay down, he pulled off his shorts, then joined her, his mouth again on
hers, his hand stroking her breasts. Finally, he slid his hand down her thigh,
then, more slowly, up again, and into her panties. This time, she didn't stop
him. This time, he didn't want her to. He needed to make her his, forever,
and this was the only way he knew to do it.

"I love you," he said. "God, how I love you. Marry me. Please, marry
me."

Though later he wasn't sure, then, Frankie thought he heard her whisper,
"Yes."

Chapter 6

Though the thought of marriage was never far from Frankie's mind, he
hesitated to mention it again. Miranda was nineteen years old, he just twenty-
one. She was a college student, with her future already planned: she would
get her degree, then work in her mother's New York gallery until a man
suitable to marry came along. Frankie knew he wasn't that man. He wasn't
only unemployed, but unskilled, with ambition, but no direction. The Colvingtons would never approve of his marrying their daughter. Nor would
the Ferraros like the idea—they clearly thought Frankie too young and too
unsettled to take on the responsibility of a family. Then, there was the difference in their backgrounds. Acutely aware of it himself, he knew he
wouldn't escape both sets of parents' asking how, with nothing in common,
Miranda and he could expect to be happy together. They would laugh at
the idea of love conquering all. When want comes in the door (he could
hear Dolly saying it, quoting *her* mother), love goes out the window.

The idea of taking on his own family didn't worry Frankie. But the Colvingtons? The idea was daunting. And if he did, he would be on his own.
The kinds of battles his sister fought, and frequently won, when she wanted
something, were not for Miranda. Even knowing her for so short a time, he
knew that. Covert rebellion was more her style, taking advantage of the
relative freedom that Eva's busy work life and active social schedule allowed,

capitulating quickly when caught. And, though he urged her to stand up to her mother, as he heard more about her childhood, Frankie began to understand why she couldn't. Early on she had learned to be quiet when her mother had work to do, playful when her mother needed amusement, invisible when her mother claimed the center of attention. Rebellion had led to banishment. Submission got her the person Miranda often, and incredibly, described as "the best, most interesting, most beautiful mother in the world." Standing up to her was pointless, Miranda said. It always made matters worse.

Totally self-absorbed, having always depended on nannies to look after them when they were young, Eva rarely remembered to pay attention to what her children were doing, and was placated with any reasonable excuse when she did. Craig spent most of the week in Boston minding the stores. So, when Joan left to return to her job in San Francisco, with nothing but free time to fill, Miranda came to the cottage in the mornings, in the afternoons, whenever Frankie wasn't working. She returned with him there after dates, before he took her home. They made love every day, two and three times a day, sometimes more, as often as they could. "You do love me, don't you?" she said one afternoon about three weeks after the start of their affair. She lay naked in Frankie's arms, her skin the color of cream where her bathing suit had hidden it from the sun, of honey where it hadn't.

"Bet your ass," Frankie said, stroking her bottom "And such a nice ass, too."

She rolled away from him, sat up, and reached for the joint she had left lying in an ashtray on the bedside table. "What will happen," she said when she'd lit it, "when the summer's over?" He could hear the sudden note of anxiety in her voice.

It wasn't something he liked to think about. "You smoke too much of that stuff," he said.

"You drink too much beer. Here, have some." Frankie took the joint from her and took a drag. "I love the feeling," she said. "Like I'm floating, way out of reach of all my problems."

"You have problems?" He was always completely unable to imagine the nature of the pea capable of disturbing the rest of his princess.

"I don't want this to end," she said. "Do you?"

Frankie took the joint from her, and pinched it out. He pulled her into his arms. "No," he said, kissing her. "No, I don't want this to end. I never want this to end."

*F*or Frankie, Miranda was what he had always craved and never thought he could have: the distant stars of his favorite films, the enticing beauties of the magazine ads, the women, insubstantial as a dream, he had seen drift past him in limousines. He was obsessed with her. When apart from her, in the middle of some ordinary activity—browsing in a bookstore, mixing a drink at Teeny's, buying a new pair of jeans—the memory of their last encounter, of Miranda's naked body, of the feel of her lips or tongue or hands, would inflame him with a lust that seemed both unbearable and sweet, charging the hours between their sessions in bed with all the glorious excitement of anticipation, making him ready to go off like Apollo ascending as soon as he felt her under him. (He thanked God for the woman in Oakland who had taught him better.) Sex had never been this way for him before, so focused and sustained, so tender and generous. He believed it was the same for Miranda, but he wasn't sure. When he asked her, she said it was; but no matter how he stroked and handled her, covered her with kisses, held her whimpering with passion in his arms, still he felt there was a part of her he hadn't yet touched.

That Miranda wanted him, that she wanted their relationship to continue, brought Frankie to the border of ecstasy. What kept him from crossing over was doubt, the suspicion that, no matter what she said now, when the summer was over, when she returned to her real world, there would be no room in it for him. After all, she was so beautiful, she could have any man she wanted. Why would she choose him? The thought of her other lovers haunted him, their existence a shock and an outrage to his ego. This is 1960, he told himself, not the Middle Ages. So what if she'd lost her virginity before they met? But however hard Frankie tried to convince himself it was unimportant, the idea of that broken membrane tormented him. He wanted to have been the first for her. He had expected he would be for the woman he loved enough to want to marry.

"They said they loved me, but they didn't mean it," Miranda told him. "I didn't mean it either. I left them or they left me. What does it matter?"

But the look of anguish on her face made it clear that it did matter. It made Frankie suspect a wound still raw, still inflamed. It made him crazy. "Who left you?"

She laughed. "My father, for a start." Frankie didn't care about her father's dying, about how that first and primal loss might have affected her. It was the men who came after who worried him. But, when he persisted in questioning her, she pulled back inside herself where he couldn't reach her. "I don't want to know about the women in your life," she said.

"They didn't matter. You're the first," he told her, meaning it.

"You're the first," she repeated, and he wondered why he couldn't believe her.

. . .

*S*ometimes, when Eva required Miranda's presence for shopping expeditions or ladies' lunches, Frankie spent his time off with Vic. They went to the beach, or fished from the pier. Occasionally they drove in Frankie's Chevy through little Cape towns, stopping to see old mills, lighthouses, scenic coves, historical museums, the Marconi Wireless station, eating in quaint restaurants where the fried chicken was served in wicker baskets by pretty waitresses in black dresses and frilly white aprons. In one of those restaurants, their waitress had even more freckles than Caitlin, and Frankie smiled at her warmly, as if she were an old friend, causing the girl's eyes to light with the anticipation of romance.

"You're just like your old man," said Vic, when she had walked away.

Frankie stopped eating, the chicken leg midway to his mouth. He wasn't sure he liked the idea. "Yeah, like you never seen your father come on to a waitress, right?"

"I don't mean just about women. Remember when we were kids, when we used to go away on vacation together?"

Frankie bit into the leg. "Yeah," he said, his mouth full of food.

"How your dad used to want to stop and sight-see, and mine always gave him a hard time about it? I'll never forget the fight they had over that fort . . . what was it . . . Ticonderoga? We never did get to see it," he said wistfully.

"Old just don't knock your father out, that's all."

Vic shook his head, swallowed his mouthful of hamburger, and said, "When you leave a place, if you haven't tried to see what it's really like, soon it's as if you've never been there at all. It just blends into every town you've ever passed through."

It was true, thought Frankie. His father was curious about things; and adventurous, in his way. He had started his own business, for example, while Uncle Victor had always been content to work for other people. It was as if the trip to America from the old country had used up all his available courage. He was a good man, though, hardworking and responsible. Too bad he couldn't see those same qualities in his son.

When they left the restaurant, it was Vic who gave his name to the waitress, brandishing his Ferraro smile, suggesting she drive up to Provincetown sometime to catch him in the play. By then, it was late afternoon and there was heavy traffic on Route 6.

"Worse comes to worse," said Frankie, "Mac can handle the early crowd."

"Yeah, well, I have a performance to make."

"You'll make it," said Frankie, speeding up, cutting off a car to make a lane change.

"Alive, please."

Frankie took a pack of cigarettes from his shirt pocket, offered one to Vic, lit up, and exhaled a satisfying cloud of smoke. "You stopped seeing Maria? Or just playing the field?"

Vic shrugged. "You can't go on seeing a nice girl for too long. There's only so much rejection a guy can take."

"Some guys hang in till they marry the girl."

"Maria's sweet," said Vic, "but not for me." His face wore the same look as Sal's when he'd made a decision that was difficult but necessary, pained but self-congratulatory. Vic settled back in the seat, extended an arm out the window and flicked the ash from the end of his cigarette. "Is that what you're doing, hanging in?" he asked.

Frankie hesitated, not sure how to answer. If he said to Vic, "I'm fucking her," would that, he wondered, make his relationship with Miranda seem less significant? Would that open a door, give him a way out? Did he want a way out? Sometimes his feelings scared the shit out of him. "I'm in love with her," he said finally.

"That much I figured out for myself," said Vic. "I'll say this once, and I won't say it again. She's trouble."

"Trouble?"

"There's that mother of hers, to start with. Miranda's sweet, Frankie, and God knows she's gorgeous. But she's got no center. She's a marshmallow."

"You don't know what the fuck you're talking about."

"I just felt I had to say it."

"Next time, keep your mouth shut."

"Next time, I will."

There was a strained silence. Frankie again stepped on the gas and maneuvered the car into the next lane, this time without causing Vic heart failure. "You know what you're doing yet, after the summer?"

Vic laughed. "Looking for another job. That's how I spend most of my time."

"At least you got some direction in your life," said Frankie. "That's something."

On Labor Day, the Colvingtons threw a party, not a bash, just for twenty-five or thirty people. Frankie was ambivalent about going, seesawing between curiosity and dread, liking the idea of himself mixing with the Colvingtons and their friends, terrified he would somehow make a fool of himself if he did. He missed his friend's reassuring presence, the feeling he always had that Dan would cover his worst mistakes, his rough manners, his grammatical lapses: that Dan, as always, would somehow save his ass. But Miranda insisted, and Frankie swapped nights with one of the other bartenders.

Mrs. Lyle opened the door and ushered Frankie in. Newly installed in the hall was an abstract sculpture that looked like a car wreck, around which a group of people milled admiringly. Into their midst moved a maid, in uniform, carrying a tray of hors d'oeuvres. Carried on a murmur of voices came a laugh Frankie recognized as Eva's. "You know the way," said Mrs. Lyle. He thanked her and loped off down the hall, past tight clusters of guests deep in conversation. Turning into the sitting room, he took a glass of champagne (which he hated) from the tray of a passing waiter, and stood, too nervous to assess with any accuracy whether the glances thrown his way were hostile or admiring, looking for Miranda. He was starting to sweat, and prayed that the stains wouldn't make it through his jacket.

Eva, dressed as always entirely in black, was standing by the French doors talking to Walter Chrysler, one of Provincetown's preeminent citizens, famous for having converted an old church into an art museum. Craig Colvington was with Helen Frankenthaler and the mayor. Robert Motherwell stood engrossed in conversation with a burly, handsome man, Norman Mailer, realized Frankie. Joan, who had come in from San Francisco for the weekend, was with Todd Manheim, small and ferretlike, wearing a pale green printed shirt and white khaki trousers. Her head was bent close to his, as if fearful she might miss some pearl of wisdom falling from his lips. There was a show of Manheim's on at one of the galleries. To Frankie, his paintings looked like puke.

An arm threaded through his, and, with a rush of relief, Frankie turned his head, expecting to see Miranda. Instead, he found Colette Drake, her body wrapped in something turquoise that clung just enough to be sexy without looking cheap.

"You look great," he said.

"So, you stayed the summer."

"Yeah, I did."

"Have a good time?"

"Not bad."

"You fell in love." It was a statement. Before Frankie could decide how to respond, she said, "Don't even bother to answer. It's written all over your face."

"You never came back." His smile was tender, his eyes full of memories.

"Oh, I like it when you flirt with me." Colette smiled up at him, then released his arm. "I suppose I ought to turn you loose before she makes an appearance. She is here, isn't she? You did bring her?"

"She's here, somewhere."

"You wouldn't like to go out into the garden and neck with me while you're waiting?" Frankie laughed uneasily. He knew he was blushing. "No," continued Colette, "forget I said that. I don't know what gets into me sometimes. Whoever the lucky girl is, I want you to be faithful to her, forever. I love a good love story, don't you?"

Before Frankie could think of an appropriate answer, he saw Miranda entering through the doorway from the hall. She wore a simple white cotton dress that looked like a nightgown, and blossoms of dried flowers woven into her hair. Except for mascara, she wore no makeup. Frankie thought she was, hands down, the most beautiful woman in the room, maybe the most beautiful woman in the world. Then Miranda saw him and smiled.

"Oh, my God," said Colette, "Romeo and Juliet."

Frankie turned back to her, irritation now as plain on his face as adoration had been a moment before. "What?"

"You and Miranda . . ." said Colette.

"So?"

"So, I was surprised," she said placatingly, "that's all."

"I thought you'd guessed," said Frankie, remembering the night at Teeny's when Colette had seemed to sense his interest in Miranda's whereabouts.

"Oh, I knew you were interested. I knew you had a crush on her. But, quite frankly, I didn't think you were Miranda's type. No swipe at you, darling. I just figured she liked older. Well, well, well. I guess it's time to get my crystal ball polished. Hello, Miranda," she segued effortlessly as Miranda joined them. "You look lovely. Those flowers. A perfect touch. Just like a Botticelli." She dropped a peck on Miranda's cheek, grabbed a glass of champagne from a passing waiter, and said: "I think I'll break in on Joan and Todd Manheim. He's always good for a laugh, and I need one."

Botticelli. He remembered a reproduction he had seen in one of the books in the library. Yes, Miranda looked just like that Venus, thought Frankie as he slipped a proprietary arm around her waist.

"You two looked very serious," she said. "What were you talking about?"

"You," said Frankie, admiring the exquisite face, the delicate mouth, the straight nose, the azure eyes. They looked a little glazed, he noticed. "Have you been smoking?"

"I hate big parties. . . . I've decided I don't like Colette. Do you?"

Frankie hesitated, weighing his reply, considering the advantages of lying. There were none, as far as he could see. "Yeah. I do."

"She's a snake," said Miranda emphatically. "She'd sell her own mother if she could make a nickel doing it. Do you think she's attractive?"

"Sure. In a way."

"I always think she looks cheap." Miranda pulled away from him to take a piece of shrimp from one of the circulating trays, murmuring her thanks to the waitress.

"I don't know," said Frankie. "She's always got on real expensive clothes."

"Oh," said Miranda. "I forgot. You're the expert on clothes."

Never before had Frankie heard that tone from Miranda. When she had accused him of flirting with Joan, she'd sounded hurt, but not bitter, not bitchy. It surprised him. What had she seen looking at him and Colette that had set her off? Frankie began to feel a small, tentative flurry of guilt. "What's the matter?"

"I just don't see why you're so interested in her."

"I don't give a fuck about her," said Frankie, his guilt alchemized instantly to anger. Miranda looked at him, shocked. She'd never heard him swear before. Then, embarrassed, she looked around to see if anyone else had heard. "I'm sorry," he said. Watch your mouth, his father would have snapped if he'd been present. Swearing was for men, with men, never in front of women.

Miranda smiled tentatively, looking perplexed, anxious. "Our first quarrel," she said. His anger had completely defused hers.

"Our second," he corrected.

"Sometimes I get paranoid," she said. "I was jealous."

It was inconceivable to him that this girl, this ideal of loveliness, this embodiment of all he yearned for, this epitome of all his desires, could imagine for one moment that he might prefer someone to her. From the first, his feelings for her had gone far beyond sex, beyond even love, into worship. How could she not know that? "You've got nothing to be jealous about," he said. "I love you."

"I guess I'm scared someday you'll see who I really am, and change your mind."

"What are you talking about? You think I don't know who you are? You're the most beautiful girl in the world. And I've got you."

*M*iranda introduced him to her brother, Philip, a tall slender man with thinning hair, and his wife, a wraithlike figure with a slight stutter; then to Helen Frankenthaler. He stood silent and a little embarrassed, not knowing how to join the conversation as she and Miranda talked about Bennington, where Frankenthaler too had gone to school. When he met Robert Moth-erwell, Frankie did better. There were one or two paintings of Motherwell's that he actually liked, the ones in the *Je t'aime* series, which, if they didn't exactly correspond to his idea of art, were at least nice to look at. He managed to muster a compliment, and got an absent smile and murmured thank-you in response. Frankie didn't bother to compliment Todd Manheim when they were introduced, but that probably went unnoticed as Manheim never stopped talking about himself long enough for anyone else to get in a word, even a kind one.

"What do you see in that guy?" Frankie asked Joan as she stood with him and Miranda on the buffet line. There was lobster and crab and shrimp, most of it floating in what looked like green Jell-O, several kinds of salad, a large ham, string beans with almonds, mountains of bread, fruit, and cheeses with French names. At home, Frankie thought, there would have been at least one pasta, lasagna probably for this big a crowd, and sausage with peppers, meatballs, chicken cacciatore. He found, suddenly, he was craving his mother's cooking as avidly as he had at the army mess in Fort Gordon.

Joan helped herself sparingly to the goodies before her, some shrimp, a little rice, a heap of green salad. "Do you mean Todd Manheim?" she said. Frankie nodded. "I don't see anything at all in him, if you mean personally. But he's a very talented painter."

"He's not anywhere near as good as Frankenthaler," said Frankie, trying out an assurance he didn't feel. Her paintings looked to him like careless splashes of color—but at least the colors were usually pretty.

" 'Oh, no, he's not. Of course, he's not," agreed Joan as though shocked at the suggestion. Frankie grinned a small, self-congratulatory grin. "But his use of green is really very interesting."

"In his shirts, maybe," said Frankie. Joan laughed, and so did Miranda.

"Having fun, children?" said Eva, flitting past.

Did he imagine it, or did both Miranda's and Joan's smiles fade just a fraction? "Yeah," said Frankie. "Great party."

A few minutes later, while the three of them stood on the patio eating, Eva came by again and whisked Miranda away to meet someone. "I'll send her right back," she said, not meaning it. And though she towered over Eva, following in her mother's wake, Miranda seemed like a small craft in danger of being swamped. They came to a stop in front of two men, one in his fifties, the other somewhere in his late twenties, both blond, tanned, craggily handsome, sporting white trousers and shirts, lacking only the backdrop of the yacht they undoubtedly owned to make the picture perfect.

"Who are they?" Frankie asked.

"Tyler Banning, three and four," said Joan. "Bankers. Craig's involved with them in some business deal."

"Why did Eva want Miranda to meet them?" asked Frankie, although certain he knew the answer.

"I have no idea," said Joan coolly. Then, when she saw the look of anguish he couldn't quite control flicker across Frankie's face, she added, "Just being polite, I suppose. I've met them before. Miranda hasn't."

"We're thinking about getting married, Miranda and me," said Frankie, on impulse, not certain why, maybe just to test the water.

"Oh?" Joan's voice suggested shock carefully muted to polite interest.

"Miranda didn't tell you?"

"No," said Joan. "But then, we don't usually confide in one another."

Frankie thought about his mother and his aunts, about his cousins, and how they confided endlessly in each other, from the events they considered cosmic to the minutiae of daily life. Why, even he and Angela told each other everything. Almost everything. Of course they never talked about sex. "You're really a strange family," he said.

"It doesn't mean we don't care about each other," said Joan defensively. "By the time Miranda could talk, I was away at boarding school. We just never got in the habit. It's the same with Philip." She looked to where Eva was energetically fostering a conversation between Miranda and the Bannings, then turned back to Frankie. "You're both very young," she said.

"You ever been in love?"

Joan laughed. "I still am. I just haven't got around yet to telling Mother."

*E*very time Frankie made a move to reclaim Miranda, someone intervened. Once it was a woman who was positive she'd seen him somewhere, and he found himself unable to confess that it had probably been behind the bar at Teeny's. Another time it was Nelson Clewes. "Have you ever thought about modeling?" he asked Frankie. "You'd look stunning dressed properly."

"What's the matter with the way I dress?" said Frankie.

"Nothing," said Nelson, soothingly. "Nothing at all. Your clothes are perfectly acceptable. You even have taste, unrefined of course. But not flair, my dear. You don't know how to take dressing beyond necessity into the realm of art. Now, look at Craig. He's a man with style, with elegance. And the Bannings, those people Miranda is talking to, their clothes are stunningly simple, but perfect, don't you agree? They know how to dress, in the sense I mean. But you have something they don't, you know." Frankie waited, unable to conceive of any way in which he might outshine the blond gods across the room. "More than good looks, you have what Brando has: power, sensuality, sex appeal, not to mention a subtle hint of violence, always delicious." No one, not even his mother, had ever been so frankly admiring of

Frankie. "Oh, my dear," said Nelson. "I've made you blush. Hasn't anyone ever told you you're beautiful?"

"Yeah," said Frankie, embarrassment roughening the edges of his voice. "Some guy in a bar in San Francisco. I knocked out two of his teeth."

Nelson laughed. "Well, spare mine, please. I do get the message even when more subtly conveyed. But do think about modeling, and call me if you decide yes. No strings attached. There are some suits in my winter line that would look divine on you."

"Thanks, but I don't think modeling's for me," said Frankie politely. He thought all models (and dancers and hairdressers) were fags.

Nelson peered into Frankie's face, then sighed. "Perhaps you're right," he said. "You have the tiniest crow's feet around your eyes. I didn't notice them at first." Then someone else claimed his attention, and with a cheery, " 'Bye, dear boy," he sauntered off.

The champagne kept flowing, no glass remained empty, people began lurching from one group to another, and still the party showed no signs of abating. Miranda threaded her way back through the crowd to Frankie, and whispered in his ear, "Come upstairs with me. I need a smoke."

"No," said Frankie, who didn't want to be caught in anything resembling a compromising position. He didn't want to give Eva anything to use against him.

Before Miranda could argue, Craig joined them. " 'Ving a good time?" he asked.

"Swell," said Frankie.

"I'll be right back," said Miranda as she turned and headed for the door.

" 'V'you met everyone?" asked Craig, his speech slurred. His color was high and his blue eyes seemed to have trouble focusing.

"Just about."

"Do this every year," said Craig. "Good way to end the summer."

"Yeah, it's great."

"All good things come to an end," he said, his tone oracular, making Frankie suspect hidden meanings. He grunted something that sounded like agreement, and waited. " 'V'you made any decisions yet?"

"About what?" asked Frankie nervously, wondering if Craig could possibly have overheard his conversation with Joan.

" 'Bout what you're going to do. Go to school? Get a job? Get on with life?"

Someone suggested going for a swim, and a group headed down to the pond for a skinny dip. Nelson called for music, Joan turned on the stereo while Colette browsed through the stack of records and Eva got two of the waiters to push back the furniture and roll up the rug. Soon, the sound of Chubby Checkers filled the room.

"Get a job, I suppose," said Frankie.

"Know lots of people in New York," said Craig. "Call me when you get there, f'you need help." He's just being nice, thought Frankie, he's not really offering me a bribe. "Got a lot of potential, bright boy like you. Can see it. Just've to be sure you use it the right way." He clapped Frankie on the back and walked away.

"Dance with me, sweetie," said Colette, grabbing Frankie's hand.

All I need now, thought Frankie, is for Miranda to come back and see me. But she didn't. And when the dance was over, Colette awarded him a smile, then turned to Nelson who was clamoring for her attention, leaving Frankie standing next to Eva. Not knowing what else to say, he asked her to dance. A slow dance started and Eva stepped into his arms, tilting her head to look up at him. "You're even taller than Craig."

"Not by much," said Frankie. "An inch maybe."

"I've always liked tall men," she said, and a fragment of a dream he had once had hovered for a moment terrifyingly near before retreating again, out of reach.

Eva must have been a knockout, he thought, when she was young. Her face must have been every bit as beautiful as Miranda's. Even now, somewhere in her fifties, she was lovely and far more commanding a presence than either of her daughters, making up for her lack of size with an energy, a vitality, a tenacity that was formidable.

When the dance ended, instead of letting him go, she led Frankie out on to the patio. Though not so drunk as Craig, she was bright-eyed and unsteady on her feet. It's the champagne, thought Frankie, it's making everyone want to have a heart-to-heart. Keep your mouth shut, he instructed himself. Just keep your mouth shut. That's all you have to do. He didn't want to say anything he would regret later.

"You and Miranda have been seeing a lot of each other this summer." More than you know, thought Frankie smugly, nodding in reply. "I suppose you think you're in love." This time Frankie withheld the nod. "You're wrong, you know," continued Eva. "I've seen this happen so many times before, these summer romances that never last beyond October. You'll go to see Miranda at school, or she'll come visit you in New York, and you'll wonder what you ever saw in one another." If that's true, thought Frankie, why bother to tell me? Why don't you just let us get to October and find out for ourselves? "Why, only last summer, Miranda thought she was madly in love with the brother of a school friend. She was heartbroken in September when he left for England. He's a Rhodes Scholar," she added as if hoping he knew what that was so he could be impressed. "By Christmas, she had forgotten all about him."

"Miranda told me."

"Craig and I would have been happy to see that relationship go further, but they were both so young." Eva put a hand on his arm and smiled sweetly up at him. "I'm not telling you this to be unkind. You're such a dear, Frankie, I just don't want to see you hurt. I've grown quite fond of you."

"Thank you," he said.

"Miranda's just a child really," continued Eva. "She doesn't always understand that someone might be misled by what she says, or does." An image of Miranda naked, her hand on his cock, flashed into Frankie's head. "I couldn't bear to see you hurt," continued Eva, her voice full of sympathy and affection. "You're such a sweet person, a dear, kind, considerate person."

A movement behind Frankie caught Eva's attention. She smiled broadly. Frankie turned and saw Miranda. "There you are, darling. Come dance with Frankie. He must be bored with your old mother by now." And she walked away, leaving them alone.

"What was she saying?" asked Miranda.

"She was telling me about . . . what's his name? The Rhodes scholar?"

"Stanfield Morrow." Miranda frowned.

"Joan," Eva called in the distance, "darling, would you take some towels down to the pond? Those fools will be freezing when they come out of the water."

"Don't believe her," said Miranda, her voice pleading. "Don't believe anything she says."

*F*rankie lay awake all night, thinking, like a record player in repeat mode, playing over and over again in his mind all the conversations of the evening. By the time Miranda arrived the next morning, looking as if she too had spent a sleepless night, he had made a decision. "Do you love me?" he said.

She hesitated a moment, then said, "Yes. Of course I do."

"Your mother, last night; Craig, too; they both told me . . . no, they didn't actually *say* anything, they just made it clear they wanted me to leave you alone."

Miranda's face grew even paler. "You said you loved me. You said we'd be together. . . ." She looked as if she was about to cry.

Frankie put his arms around her and nuzzled her ear. "I'll never give you up," he said. "Never. You mean everything to me. I wouldn't want to live without you." He kissed her eyes, her mouth. "Do you believe me?"

Again she hesitated, but finally she said, "Yes, I do. I never really believed anyone before. Not really. But I believe you."

"We're going to get married," he said, "right away. As soon as we can."

"But . . ." Miranda paused, trying to formulate exactly the right protest.

"Until we get married, they won't leave us alone, they won't stop hassling us," said Frankie. "And the more serious they think we are, the worse it'll get," he continued, trying desperately to find a way through the dead weight of her resistance. "And what's going to happen when you go back to school? I have to get a job, Miranda. How often do you think I'll be able to come up to see you? And when I do, how will you be able to sign out weekends to stay with me?" He could see the uncertainty in her face, the fear. He felt like a rat for pressuring her, but he was afraid, if he stopped, somehow she would get away from him. He took a deep breath. "Look, we either get married," said Frankie, bluffing, "or we stop seeing each other."

"No—"

"You said you loved me."

"I do."

"Then marry me."

Finally, she said, "Yes. All right. I'll marry you."

Miranda couldn't stand up to him any better than she could to Eva. Relieved, Frankie smiled. "You won't regret it," he said. "I swear."

*J*oan returned to San Francisco; and, while Eva and Craig devoted themselves to enjoying the last few days of summer, Miranda and Frankie got blood tests and a license, went shopping for wedding rings and wedding clothes, buying matching suits of cream-colored Italian silk. She packed a bag of things she would need for Frankie to take with him when he left. He felt happy, adventurous, and fearful, as if at any moment Eva would discover what they were up to and find a way to stop them.

On Thursday, the Colvingtons returned to Boston with Miranda. Frankie worked until eleven at Teeny's, said good-bye to Mac, packed quickly, and spent the rest of the night hitting the clubs with Vic, who insisted on picking up the tab. He had said his piece, and now felt there was nothing he could do, except throw Frankie the only bachelor party he was likely to have, just the two of them, holding their fears at bay with a quantity of beer. After four hours of sleep, Frankie said good-bye to Provincetown, and headed for Boston. At eleven-thirty, he arrived, as planned, at City Hall. He felt nervous, not premarital jitters, but fear that Miranda wouldn't show up, that she would leave him standing there, waiting, a fool for having believed anyone so beautiful, so perfect, could ever be his. Stop torturing yourself, he commanded. She'll be here. But he couldn't stop. Eva might have found out, or Craig. They might have locked her in her room, shipped her off to Paris, done God knows what with her. Worse, she might have changed her mind. He kept thinking of all the reasons why she would do a thing like that, and suddenly they all seemed like good ones. After all, he had nothing really to offer her, nothing but his love.

"You look so sad," said Miranda, coming up beside him. She was wearing the Italian silk suit that matched his, and a small flowered hat.

"I was afraid you wouldn't come," he said. "God, you look beautiful."

"Come on," she said, "let's get married." And, taking his hand, she led him up the steps and inside.

Chapter 7

The excitement, the *elation,* that Frankie and Miranda felt for having kept their secret, deceived their parents, outwitted their enemies, lasted until Hartford where they stopped at a Howard Johnson's for something to eat. When the waitress walked away with their order, they became aware of a creeping anxiety. By the time she brought the check, Miranda couldn't stand it anymore. "Mother's probably frantic by now, wondering where I am," she said.

"Better call her," said Frankie, who had hoped to make it to New York and the safety of Vic's borrowed apartment before breaking the news to their parents.

When Eva finally picked up the phone, she sounded not worried but irritated. "Miranda, what on earth is so important you have to interrupt me while I'm working? You know how overwhelmed I am the first few days back."

In a nervous mumble, Miranda pushed out the words, "Frankie and I were married today. . . . We were married," she repeated. "Mother, did you hear me?"

Seeing the look on Miranda's face, Frankie opened the door of the phone booth and squeezed in behind her, putting his arms around her waist, resting his chin on her shoulder so he could hear Eva's end of the conversation.

"Yes, I heard you." Her voice now was slow, deliberate. "Where are you?"

"On our way to New York."

"Darling, I really think you should come back to discuss this with Craig and me."

"There's nothing to discuss."

"How can you say that? My God, you're not even twenty yet."

"We'll be back sometime soon." She and Frankie had discussed all the way from Boston how much of a cooling-off period to give Eva and Craig. Ten days had seemed reasonable. "I have to pick up some clothes."

"Miranda, darling, listen to me," said Eva, her voice coaxing. "Please come home. We have to talk."

"Mother, you mustn't be so upset," said Miranda.

Frankie could feel her wavering and tightened his hold. She turned her head so that she could see his face, and he smiled reassuringly. "Tell her you'll call her in a few days," whispered Frankie, "and hang up."

"Is that Frankie?" said Eva. "Is he there with you? Let me speak to him."

Frankie shook his head and Miranda said, "Don't worry, Mother. "I'll be fine. I'll call you in a few days. 'Bye."

"Miranda!" wailed Eva, for once sounding uncertain, out of control.

Frankie took the receiver from Miranda's hand and replaced it in the cradle. "You did great. I'm proud of you."

"And next comes your parents," she said, grimacing.

"Compared to yours," said Frankie, "they'll be a piece of cake."

*V*ic's apartment was a ground-floor room on West Thirteenth Street with a toilet a little bigger than a closet and an old-fashioned footed bathtub in the kitchen next to the sink. It was dark, hot, and airless, with an exhaust fan in one of the two dirty windows. The bed was a mattress on the floor, the scarred and frayed furniture someone else's cast-offs, the kitchenware scrounged from his mother. Thumbtacked to the walls were tattered theater posters, dating from the '30s and '40s, *The Philadelphia Story, Idiot's Delight, The Man with the Golden Arm,* and a framed photograph of a brooding, handsome man with the name Artaud scrawled under it. Frankie had visited the apartment a few times during his army leaves, but either he had forgotten how seedy it was or it had grown considerably worse in the meantime. Certainly it hadn't been cleaned since Vic's departure for Provincetown. "This was a lousy idea," said Frankie, when his gaze returned from its survey of the room to rest on Miranda's face. "The place is a mess."

"It's terrible," said Miranda, sounding as if she had never seen anything so awful, as if she could not have imagined people living like this.

"We'll move into a hotel tomorrow," he said. "I'm too tired to begin looking for one tonight." A number for the local grocery was tacked to the wall beside the phone, and Frankie called and ordered what he thought they would need through morning. He turned on the fan, found clean sheets, changed the bed with Miranda's help, then wiped the surface dirt off everything with a rag he found under the sink. When the food was delivered, he put it away, ignoring the condition of the refrigerator and the roaches in the cupboards. Then he scrubbed the bathtub and started the water running. "Come on," he said, when it was filled, "bath time."

"I'm too tired to move." Miranda was lying on the bed, eyes closed.

"It'll feel good," said Frankie. He began to undress her, slowly, enjoying himself, unbuttoning her blouse, letting her skirt drop to the floor, unhooking her stockings from the lacy white garter belt, rolling them down her long, honey-colored legs. Her underwear, like her skin, was soft and luxurious to the touch.

When she was naked, Frankie carried her to the tub. "Mmm," she sighed, sliding into the hot water, pinning her hair on top of her head. "Nice."

Quickly, Frankie took off his clothes. "Move over." She looked at him, startled, then smiled, and shifted her weight. He got in, reached up to the shelf above the tub for a new bar of soap, and began washing her feet.

Miranda, wide-eyed, watched the progress of his hands, trembling at the slide of his fingers along her body. "Where do you get these ideas?" she said.

From some guy at Fort Ord, reminiscing about a visit to his girlfriend, Frankie could have told her, but didn't. "They just come to me. Now you," he said, handing her the bar of soap. He should have asked for more details, he realized a few minutes later as he alternately collided with the faucet or came close to drowning his bride. Finally, he figured it out. He shifted under her, letting her straddle him, bracing his long legs against the edge of the tub. As she leaned forward to kiss him, her hair came loose and he twisted his hands in it. "Love me. That's right, oh, baby, love me," he whispered. "This is our wedding night," he said, his voice full of wonder.

*I*n the morning, they walked to Sixth Avenue and had breakfast, sitting over coffee and bagels, discussing finances and making plans. Miranda had a small allowance deposited into a checking account each month by the accountants handling her father's estate. September's was there, less what she had spent on wedding clothes, but Miranda wasn't sure whether or not Eva could intervene to cancel October's. He didn't give a damn, Frankie told her. They didn't need her allowance. He still had money left in his savings account, more than enough to manage on until he found a job. But when Miranda suggested going to work herself, Frankie (triumph mixed with guilt at having successfully wrested his prize from the lap of luxury) insisted that she continue with school. In his family, he said, men supported women, not the other way around.

"But I hate school," she said. "I only married you to get out of going."

Frankie looked so startled by that idea, Miranda burst out laughing. She was kidding. He grinned. "Tough," he said. "You're going." He had already learned that a firm tone was what she liked. *Needed*. It was what she was used to. "Tomorrow, I'll buy *The Times* and begin job hunting," he continued. "Today, we have to find a hotel."

To Frankie's surprise, Miranda said, "Oh, let's not bother. We can clean up Vic's. It won't be so bad. Anyway, it won't be for long. While you're job hunting, I'll look for an apartment."

"You sure you don't mind?" said Frankie, his desire to save money vying with his wish to give Miranda anything she needed to make her happy.

"I don't," she said. "Really." Then she laughed again. "Wouldn't Mother just die if she could see the place?"

"Maybe we should ask her and Craig to dinner before we move out," said Frankie, playing with the idea.

"They'd probably drop a net over my head and take me home."

"Home," said Frankie, "is wherever we're together."

They spent the rest of the morning cleaning Vic's apartment, scrubbing the floors, the walls, inside the cupboards, the refrigerator. They sprinkled roach powder everywhere. They took the sheets and towels to the laundromat to wash. They vacuumed the carpets and furniture with an old Eureka borrowed from the landlord.

"You're pretty good at this," said Frankie admiringly.

"I learn fast," said Miranda. By the time they finished, they were both hot and sweaty and covered in grime. "Bath time," she said, turning on the tap.

"Oh, you liked that?" He pulled her into his arms, nuzzled her neck, ran his tongue around her ear. Even it tasted gritty. "I'll have to see what other games I can dream up you might enjoy."

After a dinner of hamburgers and fries, Frankie left Miranda watching television and drove to Long Island to see his parents. Since it was a Saturday, he had called first to be sure they were home, so of course his mother had a meal waiting for him when he arrived. "I ate, Ma," he said, hugging her. "Sorry. I should've told you when I phoned." She looked beautiful, he thought, her face glowing with the pleasure of seeing him.

"You sure you can't eat something? A mouthful?"

"I'm stuffed."

"Something to drink?"

"A beer, maybe. I'll get it."

"That's all right. You go say hello to your father."

Frankie walked down the stairs to the den, surveying the house from an altered point of view. How new everything looked to him, how precise and predictable. Real wealth had a sheen to it, he had learned this summer, but it was subdued, not the brightness of a newly minted coin, but the soft patina of old money. A thought both startling and satisfying occurred to Frankie: this was no longer his home. He was a married man now. As he had said to Miranda earlier, home was where he lived with her, where he lived with his *wife*. "Hi, Pop," he said, entering the den, a dark room full of reproduction early-American furniture.

Sal stood, and the two men embraced. "So, you finally decided to come back."

"The summer's over," said Frankie.

Sal walked over to the television and turned down the sound, leaving Perry Mason to mime his way to the solution of the crime. "You look good," he said.

"You should bring your things in from the car," said Dolly as she entered, carrying a tray with beers in tall glasses for Frankie and Sal, and an ice tea for herself.

Frankie took a sip of beer, then said, "I'm staying at Vic's. He's taking a trip with some friends before he comes back to New York."

"And then what?" said Sal, his voice wary.

"By then, I'll have a place of my own."

"Frankie, honey, that's silly," said Dolly. "We got this big house here. . . ."

"Leave him alone, Dolly. He's a grown man. You can't keep him tied to your apron strings forever."

"I don't want him tied to my apron strings," said Dolly indignantly. "But what's so wrong about wanting to spend a little time with my son before he goes off and gets married?"

Sal laughed. "You always hafta worry ahead, don't you?"

"Listen, Ma, Pop," said Frankie, interrupting. They turned back to him, looking surprised to find him there, so used were they to arguing about him in his absence. "I met a girl this summer."

"You see!" said Dolly to Sal. "What'd I tell you?"

"It's serious?" asked Sal.

"Yeah," said Frankie.

"What's her name?" asked Dolly.

"Miranda. She's related to Dan. Sort of. Through marriage."

"When are we going to meet her?"

"Soon. Tomorrow. Unless you have plans?"

"What plans?" said Dolly. "I mean, Angela and Denny will be here with the children. But they'll want to meet her, too."

"She's here in New York with you?" asked Sal, his voice edged with suspicion.

"Yeah," said Frankie.

"Where's she staying?"

Above all, Frankie felt grateful that his father was so smart, that his questions were leading exactly to where Frankie wanted to go. "At Vic's," he said. "With me."

"Oh, Frankie," wailed Dolly. "She can't stay there. With you. It's not right."

Frankie cleared his throat. "We . . ." He hesitated. He knew they weren't going to like this. Then he took a deep breath and plunged in. "We got married yesterday."

Dolly sank back in her chair. She looked as if Frankie had just socked her.

Sal shook his head, trying to clear it. "You were married? Yesterday?" he repeated. Frankie nodded. "What was the hurry?"

"Not what you think."

"How'd you know what I think?" snapped Sal angrily. He always got angry when Dolly was upset.

"We're in love. We wanted to get married. It seemed easier doing it this way."

"It isn't what we planned for you, Frankie."

"At least tell me you got married in church," said Dolly, "by a priest."

"We got married at City Hall, in Boston."

Dolly started to cry. Frankie moved across to the couch, sat, and put his arms around her. "City Hall," she murmured, in the same voice she might have said "cancer."

"You'll like her, Ma."

"Is she Catholic?"

"No. Protestant."

"Oh, God," she wailed, though in other circumstances she wouldn't have minded so much. Then, returning to what really mattered to her, she said, "Even Protestants have church weddings. I don't understand what was the big hurry."

"I didn't want to come back to New York without her."

"I guess her parents are grateful," said Sal, with an attempt at humor. "You saved them a bundle."

"Not that grateful," said Frankie, smiling, knowing the argument had turned the corner. His sister would have had weeks, maybe even months, of emotional punishment if she'd eloped. But not him. Sin might apply equally to both sexes, but shame didn't. A fall from grace was, for a boy, if not inevitable, at least expected. It didn't make him an outcast; it didn't cause his parents to lose face in the eyes of the world—which is why a church wedding had no real importance. The virtue it implied, in the case of a son, was without social significance.

So when she couldn't get Frankie to agree to having a religious ceremony in a few weeks, Dolly moved on to what *was* essential, a reception to introduce Miranda to the family. Seeing no way out of that, Frankie agreed. Sal listened impatiently as they negotiated the details, then interrupted as soon as he could with more pragmatic concerns. How, he wanted to know, did Frankie intend to support his wife?

"I'll get a job."

"What kind of job?"

"Whatever I can."

Sal again offered him a place at the factory, and Frankie again refused. And again his refusal made no sense to Sal. Nor did it to Frankie now, when his circumstances were so different. Sal wasn't cheap, especially not when he was getting his own way. He would see to it that his son could support his wife. "If you could at least tell me what it is you want to do," he said, disgusted with what he considered Frankie's immaturity, his indecisiveness, his complete disregard for practical realities. "You're spoiled rotten," he said. "That's your problem."

Because he did understand that taking the job his father offered was, at the moment, the most practical thing to do, Frankie once or twice did try to say yes. But he couldn't. His throat squeezed shut, making it impossible for the word to escape. Marrying Miranda had opened up new worlds, worlds of expanding possibilities. He couldn't make himself walk back into the cage of his father's factory and let the door slam shut behind him.

"I'm not gonna beg you."

"I don't want you to beg me."

"I think you're nuts."

"So do I," said Frankie.

"At least we agree about somethin'," said Sal.

*O*n his way back to the apartment, Frankie stopped and picked up an early edition of Sunday's *New York Times*. He meant to start going through the want ads as soon as he got home, but didn't. Miranda had fallen asleep with the television on, images of Nixon and Kennedy flickering on the late news, exchanging shots in the war for the presidency. Frankie stripped off his clothes and got into bed beside her, watching to the end of the broadcast, letting himself be distracted by the soft slope of Miranda's bottom. She was wearing a cotton T-shirt and pink bikini underpants that left most of her bottom bare. He turned off the television set and leaned over her, sliding his hand up her leg and underneath the brief strip of fabric.

Her eyes opened. Dazed with sleep, she smiled at him. "How was it?" she said.

"A cinch. Miss me?"

"Uh-huh."

He kissed her. "We're going to see them tomorrow," he said. He felt power flooding him. "Don't worry. Everything's going to be fine. Everything's going to be just great."

Chapter 8

On Sunday morning, Frankie washed the Chevy (which he moved diligently once a day in accordance with the city's alternate-side-of-the-street parking regulations), buffed it to a high shine, and vacuumed the interior. That done, he showered and shaved, clipped and cleaned his fingernails, put on a new pair of slacks, a sports shirt, and a tweed jacket he had bought at Barney's on Seventh Avenue, then sat reading *War and Peace,* waiting for his wife. "What should I wear?" she asked, coming out of the bathroom in her bra and panties, her hair wrapped in a towel.

She sounded nervous, and Frankie found it touching that she should worry about meeting *his* parents. "Nothing fancy," he said. "It's only family." Half an hour later she emerged from the bedroom in a tan skirt, an ivory silk blouse draped with a strand of pearls, and small pearl studs in her ears. Her hair fell in a mass of shimmering blond to her shoulders. Except for a trace of mascara on her lashes and pale pink lipstick, she wore no makeup. "You look like a million dollars," he told her.

That pleased her, without reassuring her at all. The traffic to Long Island midday on a Sunday was heavy, as usual, extending what should be a forty-minute trip to well over an hour, and Miranda spent the entire time staring apprehensively into space or fiddling nervously with the radio dials. Relieved that he had convinced her to leave her stash of pot behind or for sure she would have arrived at his parents wrapped in a happy, impenetrable fog, Frankie kept up a steady stream of talk, dredging up from his memory sweet things, endearing things, about Angela and her family, about Sal and Dolly. "They'll love you," he told her. "Don't worry. They have to love you. I do."

His father of course was a pushover. "You've got the face of an angel," Sal said when he saw her. He sounded surprised, as if he'd expected the painted hussy of his wife's imagination to come walking through the door.

He kissed Miranda's cheek, then shook Frankie's hand, saying, "You did all right for yourself."

Dolly was a different story. She hugged Miranda to her birdlike body. She welcomed her into the family, but Frankie noticed an unexpected touch of reserve in her manner as she ushered everyone down to the den for a glass of wine and the antipasti she had prepared to tide them over until dinner was ready. Miranda seemed a little intimidated by her. Perhaps all mothers intimidated her, thought Frankie, but once his had left to return to her kitchen, Miranda, in the warmth of Sal's obvious approval, began to thaw. Denny soon found her sweet face and shy smile completely captivating. His sons, startled at first by her offer to play, watched with wonder as she nimbly wielded scissors, making hats and planes and rows of linked stars out of colored construction paper, and soon announced that Uncle Frankie's new girlfriend was a whole lot nicer than his last one. There was a rush of embarrassed laughter and Miranda said, smiling, "I guess that's why he married me." She was at her best right at that moment, confident, happy, completely unselfconscious. And Angela, who had begun to melt when Miranda joined the boys on the floor, was completely won over.

"Well?" said Frankie, cornering his sister as she left the den to go help Dolly.

"She's not what I expected."

"Which was?"

"Someone more . . ." She stopped, then said, "I like her. You can tell she comes from money, but she's not at all stuck up. She's sweet. You be good to her, okay?"

"That's the plan," he said.

Angela hesitated, as if debating whether to let it go at that, but she'd never been one to keep her thoughts to herself. "You've got a good heart, Frankie, I know that. But you're spoiled. Ma, Pop, me, every girl you've ever known, we all spoil you."

"You're the one who could always twist Pop around your little finger." He was starting to get annoyed. He had wanted approval, not a lecture.

"My one accomplishment. But with you, it's everybody. Even Miranda."

"Oh, please—"

"Whose idea was it to elope?" she asked, interrupting him. "Not hers. I'd put money on that. Every girl her age wants a big wedding."

"It was the only way."

"*Your* way. You never could stand to wait for something you wanted. Life's been easy on you so far, Frankie. But marriage isn't like that. It's hard. You have to learn to be patient, understanding; you have to be willing to compromise." Suddenly Angela stopped talking. Leaning forward, she kissed his cheek. "That's enough of that," she said. "I hope you'll both be very happy."

"Well, thanks," said Frankie, his voice heavy with sarcasm, watching as she went up the stairs to the kitchen, feeling as if he had been sideswiped by a six-axle truck. Five down, he thought. One to go.

His mother remained distant through drinks and pasta. She was worried, Frankie knew, and a little afraid, for him mostly, afraid that this beautiful stranger, who admitted she couldn't cook or clean or sew, would be unable to take care of him, afraid that she would break his heart. But during the lemon chicken, when Miranda helped Sean to cut his serving into bite-size pieces, Dolly began to weaken, and by dessert, when Miranda praised her banana cream pie, then asked for all of Frankie's favorite recipes, saying, "I know I can learn to cook, if I try," Dolly capitulated.

"Anyone can," she said. Her eyes had lost that wary look. She was smiling. "I'll teach you like I taught Angela."

"I told you, a piece of cake," said Frankie later, as they walked arm-in-arm down the front walk toward the car. "They loved you."

"I don't know about your mother," said Miranda.

They both turned to wave to the crowd on the Ferraro doorstep. "Come again soon," called Dolly.

"Her too," he said. "It was a stroke of genius, asking for those recipes."

While Frankie looked for work, Miranda started the process of transferring her credits from Bennington to Barnard. Once that was under way, she began apartment hunting, an exhausting and discouraging endeavor. What they could afford all looked worse than Vic's place, she insisted. There wasn't one she could live in. They were all just too depressing.

Though certain Miranda was exaggerating, Frankie didn't have time to go looking with her. Lacking all the right qualifications, finding a job was turning out to be more difficult than he'd expected. He registered with several personnel agencies, but most of the interviews they sent him on seemed to him to lead to the same dead end as working for his father, without the advantage of being well paid. The few jobs with a future were entry-level positions at various companies—in mail rooms, as a gofer, as a page at NBC, but the starting salaries were so low that he might have been able (just) to support himself on them, but certainly not a wife. Day after day, Frankie studied *The New York Times* and followed up leads, but slowly his energy flagged, his optimism waned. The jobs he found interesting he couldn't get, and the others he didn't want.

Carrying his new leather briefcase (which held *The Times,* a lined yellow pad, a pen, and his copy of *Anna Karenina*), wearing a white shirt, a striped tie, a well-cut navy suit from the place on the Bowery where the men in his family had shopped since 1934, Frankie was pretty sure personnel clerks wouldn't figure him for the odd guy out. Until they checked the application form. What he needed to do, it occurred to him one rainy Friday afternoon, after his third dead-end interview of the day, was go back to school, get a degree, enter the job market on a more or less equal footing with the other applicants he met at the agencies. That, however, was out of the question. Even with the government footing part of the bill, there was no way Frankie could pay tuition and support Miranda. And he absolutely did not want her to work. His ego wouldn't hear of it.

When he arrived home, Miranda, in jeans and a T-shirt, was sitting cross-legged on the bed, reading *The New Yorker,* munching on a brownie, a glass of milk nearby on the bedside table. She looked as if she didn't have a care in the world. In the background, ignored, the television flickered. Frankie put down his briefcase, and kissed her hello. "We should ask the landlord to call the exterminator," she said.

"Okay. But it won't do much good."

"You look so tired. Bad day?"

"Not great." He took off his suit and hung it carefully in the closet.

"Have a brownie," she said. "You'll feel better. I baked them this afternoon."

He changed into a pair of shorts, then poured himself a glass of milk, took a brownie from the plate on the table, and joined Miranda on the bed.

"You see anything today?"

She nodded. "A place on East Fourth. One room. It was awful."

"That's all?"

"I just got too depressed to look anymore. I walked home through the park."

He thought of the hours he had spent waiting in offices; the blank, discouraging faces of the men and women who had interviewed him; the frustration, the *anger*, he had felt seeing the secure, smug looks of the employed as he left the office towers still without a job. "Christ, Miranda, we can't stay here forever. Vic will be back anytime now."

"Tomorrow, I'll look all day."

"*We'll* look all day," said Frankie.

"That'll be fun," she said, leaning over to kiss him. "I'm sorry you're having such a rough time."

"I just want us to be settled." He felt he was failing: himself, Miranda, his father, everyone. He felt he would never make anything of his life.

"I feel settled," she said. "I feel like an old, settled, married lady."

Miranda returned to her magazine, and Frankie stretched out on the bed to watch the highlights of the Rome Olympics on television. That's it, Frankie thought after a while, that's what he'd like to be—an athlete, in top physical form, his body lithe, agile, perfect, an Olympic champion. Not that he was in bad shape. He sucked in his gut. In fact, he looked pretty good. Next week, he would join the Y, he decided, work out a couple of hours a day. It would help relieve the tension.

Gary Tobian did a perfect half-gainer. Frankie had seen the footage before, knew it moment by slow-motion moment. He could feel his own body, in perfect empathy with Tobian's, arc through the resistant air, turn, straighten, and slice into the cool blue water. He could smell the chlorine, feel the sting of it in his eyes as he surfaced, feel the hot sun on his face. His worries, heavy as wet snow, melted, dissolved, leaving him free to breathe again, making it seem possible that new ideas, new possibilities, could take root in his life and grow. A sense of well-being pervaded him, a sense of complete peace, of contentment. He reached out and touched Miranda's thigh, feeling the tight knot of muscle under the warm, smooth fabric of the jeans.

She turned and smiled at him, her face mirroring the peace and contentment of his own. "Aren't these brownies great?" She giggled for no apparent reason. "I ran into an old friend today, someone I know who used to play drums at a club in Boston," she said, "and he had such beautiful stuff."

The positive marijuana-induced impulses that entered Frankie's mind that Friday remained through the weekend, aided no doubt by repeated doses of brownie over the next two days. His ambition returned, and with it his optimism, his certainty that everything would work out just the way he wanted. When Miranda and he went apartment hunting, instead of despair, they were reduced to helpless laughter by the squalor of what they saw. The falling plaster, peeling walls, exposed pipes, the roaches, the rats in one case, caused hilarity, not disgust. They laughed as if they had never in their lives seen anything funnier than silverfish crawling up from a drain. Finally, late Sunday afternoon, their induced and buoyant optimism led them to a brownstone on East Tenth, just off University Place. The address was good, the building in great shape. The ground-floor apartment had two rooms, newly painted, with polished wood floors, a bathroom complete with toilet and tub, and access to a small garden. The bedroom was in the front and dark, but light from the garden filtered in through the French doors to the living room. The rent was more than they could afford, one-hundred thirty-five dollars a month, but, when Frankie agreed to do the maintenance in the building, the widowed owner, Mrs. Coro, reduced it to an even hundred.

"It'll be like having my kids home again," she said, smiling happily, seduced by their looks, by their charm, by their willingness to help, and, most of all, by how much in love they seemed.

"What a doll she is, that Mrs. Coro," said Frankie, as they walked away from their new home. "She reminds me of my grandma. I better pick up some kind of do-it-yourself book tomorrow."

"You don't know anything about plumbing, do you? Or anything else?"

Frankie grinned. "I can hammer a nail into a board. I can slap paint on a wall." Seeing the worried look on Miranda's face, Frankie put an arm around her waist and said, "I'll learn. It can't be too hard. My uncle Leo's a plumber, and he's no Einstein." Miranda started to laugh again, and Frankie joined in. "Come on," he said, "let's go celebrate." They went to the Lion's Head on Christopher, ordered steaks, drank beer, had chocolate cake for dessert. Then they went home and made love.

The buoyant feeling lasted through Monday morning, when Frankie was turned down for two more management-trainee jobs, one at an insurance company, another at a department store. In the afternoon, perhaps trying to regain the sense of well-being he had had while watching the Olympics, he applied for a job it would never have occurred to him to go after the preceding week. The ad in *The Times* read, "Staff wanted for exclusive health club. Good physical condition and athletic background required."

The club was located on Forty-third Street, just west of Ninth Avenue, in a sleek glass-fronted building some developer had rescued from the dilapidation of its neighbors. Pat Walewski, a thickly muscled man somewhere in his late fifties ran the place, one in a chain franchised by Mike Macklin, 1952 Olympic decathlon champion. His expression glum, Pat looked over Frankie's application. "You ain't got no experience," he said.

"Not in a health club—"

"Except for all that shit they teach you in the army," continued Pat, as if Frankie hadn't spoken. "Those motherfuckers can really make you sweat. How many sit-ups you do?"

"Five hundred. Six, maybe."

"Push-ups?"

"A hundred."

"Show me," said Pat, chomping down on the unlit cigar he seemed to like to keep permanently in his mouth.

Frankie took off his jacket, and dropped to the floor. At eighty push-ups, he collapsed. "I'm out of shape," he said. "I took it kind of easy this summer."

"Yeah," said Pat. He was about five feet seven, with a shaved head, and muscles bulging out of his short-sleeved shirt and straining the fabric of his khaki pants.

Mr. Clean, thought Frankie, that's who he looks like, the cartoon character in the television commercial. "It wouldn't take me long to get back."

Pat studied him with ice blue eyes, as coldly calculating as if Frankie were an item for sale in a store with questionable retail practices. "You know who Mike Macklin is?"

"Sure," said Frankie, and told him.

"Then you know we got a reputation to protect." Frankie nodded. With his teeth, Pat tore the end off the cigar, then stuck it back in his mouth. "I'm trying to give these motherfuckers up. You know what a franchise is?" he asked. Again Frankie nodded. "At least you ain't just pretty. There's more fucking meatheads around here than dustballs. Come on, let me show you the place." The reception room ran the length of the front and contained a desk behind which sat a blond boy in his late teens whom Pat introduced as Tom. There was a couch, a table with magazines, potted plants. Beyond a wide double door was a lounge with an assortment of vending machines. Behind that were the lockers and steam room. Upstairs was a studio for calisthenics, one filled with exercise equipment, another with weights, and a massage room. The offices were on the top floor. "Wha'dya think?" said Pat.

"Looks great," said Frankie.

"The pay's ninety-five a week."

"The ad said one fifteen."

"Yeah," agreed Pat. "But you ain't got no experience."

It was more than his father had offered. "Okay," agreed Frankie. "That's fair."

"You train two days for free. And you start right away. Tomorrow."

"Not tomorrow," said Frankie. "I got things to do this week. How's Monday?"

Pat smiled. "Never did like a pushover. It's a deal," he said, sticking out his hand.

Frankie took it and the two men shook. "A deal," said Frankie.

*W*alking downtown along Sixth, shirtsleeves rolled up, jacket off and looped over the arm carrying his briefcase, Frankie was oblivious to the seedy displays in the store windows, to the weary commuters surging toward bus stops and subways, to the blind beggar on the corner of Fourteenth Street, to Nixon's strained face on the front pages of the newspapers. In his head an argument raged about the pros and cons of the job at Macklin's. It didn't offer what he had considered a primary requirement—a future. Why then had he said yes to Pat Walewski? Because with the Olympics ending and the World Series about to begin his head was full of sports? Because there was an atmosphere in the club that he found more familiar and comfortable than the uneasy, alien world of corporate America he'd been exploring? Because the pay equaled that offered by the jobs he get. Because he wanted to phone his father with good news? All of the above, he decided. A wave of anger, compounded of disappointment and guilt, surged through him. Maybe he should have had the courage to hold out until something better came along. But how long would that have taken? Until he was broke? He had responsibilities. He had a wife to support.

The anger left him. A wife. Suddenly, the idea filled him with elation. He had somehow won the prize, hit the jackpot. Only twenty-one, he had already succeeded beyond the most fantastic of his dreams. He had hacked his way through the impenetrable forest, scaled the tower, and carried off the princess. Now (and this thought did make him anxious), he had to find a way to keep her, and keep her in style. Working at Macklin's, Frankie consoled himself, was only a temporary measure, a way to buy time until he got the chance he was looking for, a chance he was sure he would recognize once it came his way. And ninety-five a week wasn't bad, not bad at all.

On Wednesday, Macy's delivered a mattress, a lamp, and a television to the new apartment. Frankie and Miranda packed their bags, left Vic's, and moved in. By Thursday night, they'd stocked the place with essentials. Now armed with a home and a job, Frankie felt as ready as he ever would be to face the Colvingtons, and suggested driving up to Boston the next day to see Miranda's parents. At first, she refused. Though she'd avoided meeting Eva on her weekly business trips to New York, Miranda had spoken to her mother on the phone, and to Craig, and Joan. She'd even called her brother, Philip. She'd told them all that she was happy, that she and Frankie were managing fine, that there was no need for anyone to worry. But Eva and Craig continued to worry, continued to disapprove. They would always disapprove, Miranda told Frankie, of anything they hadn't themselves decided and arranged for her in advance. Seeing them wouldn't change that.

Frankie insisted. Visiting her parents was an obligation, one that could be postponed, but not shirked. The prospect of it was hanging over his head like a threat. He wanted it over, out of the way. He tried to allay Miranda's fears. Now that the initial shock was past, now that Eva had had time to get used to the idea of the marriage, she would have to accept it. What choice did she have, after all? What could she do? "What are you afraid of?" he asked.

"I'm not afraid," protested Miranda. "It's just so awful arguing with her. I always give in, just to make her keep quiet. We all do. Even Craig."

"You think she can make you leave me?"

"No," said Miranda, trying to sound emphatic, but failing.

"You bet she can't," said Frankie, pulling her into his arms, cradling her as if she were one of Angela's boys needing comfort. "There's nothing to worry about. We don't want anything. We don't need anything, from her, or from Craig. Not even approval."

*W*hen they got to Boston, they checked into a hotel, then phoned Eva at her office to announce their arrival. This time, she didn't complain about the interruption. "Miranda, darling, is everything all right?" she asked, as if all her daughter's past assurances of well-being were fictions whose time had come to be blown.

"Everything's fine," said Miranda. "Mother, we're in Boston."

"Boston?" repeated Eva, not quite believing she was finally about to get what she had been demanding for close to a month—the longest time, Frankie guessed, she had ever had to go without something she wanted.

"At the Ritz Carlton."

"You and Frankie?" said Eva.

Miranda looked at Frankie who was lying with his head in her lap, listening to the faint hum of Eva's voice coming through the receiver. "Yes," she said.

There was a pause while Eva ran through possible responses. Finally, she said, "We'll have dinner tonight. At the house."

"Yes," said Miranda again.

"Come at seven-thirty. And don't be late."

There was a click at the other end of the phone. Miranda stared a moment at the receiver, then replaced it in its cradle.

"That wasn't so bad," said Frankie, sitting up.

"That was the easy part."

He grabbed her, pushed her down onto the bed, and lay over her. "I've never stayed in a hotel this fancy before. But I bet you've stayed in plenty."

"Lots," she agreed.

"Ever made love in one?"

"No," she said, her eyes not quite meeting his.

"Me neither," he said, wanting to believe her. This is my hold on her, he thought, this is what she likes, what they can't give her. They'll never get her away from me.

*W*ith hours to kill before dinner, Miranda took Frankie to see the Isabella Stewart Gardner Museum. "This way you won't be too impressed by what Craig laughingly calls his humble abode," she said.

Eager to follow her lead (in cultural matters at least), wanting to learn from her, Frankie agreed, expecting to be impressed maybe, but certainly not to feel such a rush of pleasure entering the grand old house. He liked the proportion of the rooms, the light filtering through the leaded windows, the intricacy of the stonework, the patterns of the tiles, the grace of the arches. He liked its reverberations of wealth, of luxury. "God, what I wouldn't give to live like this," he said, standing in the middle of the courtyard, revolving slowly around, luxuriating in the sumptuous elegance of the stuccoed pink walls.

Miranda led him through the mock palazzo, pointing out its wonders, talking of Bellini and Raphael, of line and perspective. She showed him the Botticelli, but what he saw was only the resemblance between Miranda and the angel. "Now this . . ." she said, stopping in front of a painting in the Dutch room. "This I would love to have. I'd like to look at it every day of my life. It's by Vermeer," she added. Her voice had a note of awe in it, as if she was talking about something sacred.

Frankie studied the painting, trying to see what in the simple arrangement of figures (a young woman at a harpsichord, another singing, a man with his back turned, playing something that looked like a mandolin) could call forth so much emotion. Finally, he began to think that perhaps he had found its secret, in the fall of light, in the feeling of harmony it created, the feeling of serenity, of peace. He felt himself responding. The painting had somehow reached out and touched his heart. "Yeah," he said. "It's great. Someday maybe I'll buy it for you."

Miranda laughed. "Frankie," she said. "There are only something like thirty Vermeers in the world. You have to be rich as the Queen of England to own one now."

"Who knows?" he said, the laughter rankling. "Maybe someday I will be."

. . .

*M*iranda was right. In comparison to the Gardner Museum, the Colvingtons' house seemed almost modest. On Mount Vernon Street, in Beacon Hill, it was a red brick mansion, three storeys high, with long windows and black shutters, and urns filled with impatiens flanking the steps. Set back behind a low wall, topped by a wrought-iron fence, it had a small green lawn and manicured shrubs. As he parked in front of it, Frankie thought his Chevy looked like a battered mistake.

Mrs. Lyle answered the door. She started to smile, then changed her mind, said hello politely, and told them they would find Mr. and Mrs. Colvington in the drawing room. Expecting to be led up the stairs to some sort of artist's studio tucked at the back of the house, Frankie was surprised instead to be taken into a huge parlor on the ground floor. "Why do they call it a drawing room?" he whispered.

"Pretension," said Miranda.

A large, formal room, it matched Frankie expectations of how the rich ought to live, with oriental carpets covering polished wood floors, heavy silk paper on the walls, the window drapes coordinating with upholstered chairs finished in fringe, side tables buffed to a soft sheen. The paintings were landscapes in heavy gilt frames. Frankie assumed they were good, and he was right. They included two Cezannes, a Pissaro, and a Sisley. None of it was in what Frankie considered Eva's style.

As he and Miranda entered, Eva and Craig stopped talking, put their drinks down on the coffee table, and rose from the sofa to greet them. Eva was in a black dress, with a huge diamond pin at her throat. Diamonds glittered in her ears. "Oh, darling," she said to Miranda, "it is good to see you. I've been so worried."

Miranda bent her head to kiss her mother's cheek. "I told you I've been fine."

"I'm sorry we couldn't come sooner," said Frankie, "but it took a while getting settled." He extended a hand. For a moment, he saw anger in Eva's eyes, and resentment; but then she blinked, and managed a cool smile as she took it.

Craig looked pale under his tan and drawn, as if something, maybe Eva, had been giving him a hard time. He hugged Miranda to him, kissed her cheek. "You gave us quite a shock, young lady," he said. He shook Frankie's hand. "You could at least have let us know where you were."

"I called," said Miranda, sitting close to Frankie on the couch. Her voice sounded defensive, childish. He knew she was looking to him for protection. How had she managed, he wondered, before he had come into her life? He reached for his cigarettes, lit one, then saw Eva frown and offered one to her. She shook her head, murmured her thanks. For a moment, he considered stubbing his out, then defiantly took a drag.

Craig offered them drinks and, while he was making them, encouraged small talk—the drive from New York, the traffic in Boston because of "those damn Kennedy rallies," what Frankie thought of the Ritz Carlton Hotel.

"Not bad," said Frankie.

"It can't compare to the Carlyle," said Craig, "or the George Cinque."

The Zhorge Sank? thought Frankie. "I guess not," he said.

"You've been to Paris?" said Eva, who clearly didn't believe he had.

"No," said Frankie, shifting in his seat. "Not yet. I thought maybe Miranda and me might go next summer."

Startled, Miranda looked at him. Then, she smiled. "For a second honeymoon."

"We never really had a first."

"You never really had a wedding," said Eva, letting her exasperation show. "Would you tell me, please, why you couldn't wait to do things properly?"

Frankie took a sip of the scotch Craig had handed to him, then said, "To tell you the truth, Mrs. Colvington, we didn't think you'd agree."

"I most certainly would have asked you to take the time to think things over. I don't think that would have been unreasonable, do you?"

"We didn't want to wait," said Frankie.

"Miranda's a child. She's had so little experience. Did you ever stop to think perhaps you might be taking advantage of her?"

Again Frankie shifted uneasily in his seat. He had rushed Miranda into marriage because he was afraid he might lose her. Was that wrong? Should he have given her more time? Time to decide she didn't love him after all?

But she did love him. The image of her that afternoon in their hotel room, under him, naked, her angelic face contorted by passion, reassured him. He was right to have married her, whatever anybody else might think. Miranda had no regrets. And she never would have. He would make her happy. He loved her. Nothing was more important than that. Nothing. "Miranda knew what she was doing."

"I'm not a child," she said. She looked pale and nervous. Her fingers twitched at the fabric of her skirt. Frankie was almost sorry he had stopped her from smoking before they left the hotel, but he had wanted her there for the evening, not off in some distant world, unreachable if he should need her support. "I'm not. You just treat me like one. Frankie doesn't. Frankie treats me like a woman."

Eva sucked in her breath, then let it out in a hiss. "Sex," she said. "Of course at nineteen it seems like the most important thing in the world. Let me tell you, it's not."

Frankie felt the rush of blood into his face, felt the heat. Here he was, a married man, an experienced man, and he was blushing. "We love each other."

"I'm sure you think you do," said Craig, in a voice Frankie could imagine mediating a quarrel at some corporate meeting.

"We do," insisted Miranda.

"Because you like sleeping with one another?" said Eva, her voice edged with sarcasm. "Why shouldn't you like that? You're both young, healthy, attractive. But that, my dears, has almost nothing to do with love."

"Seems to me like a good place to start," said Frankie.

"Don't get fresh with me, young man."

"Sorry. I didn't mean to. I just don't see the point of all this. We're married. If you're right, and we've made a mistake, there's nothing we can do about it anyway. We'll just have to live with it."

"Miranda could go back to school. You could see each other weekends."

"No!" said Miranda.

"Give yourself time to think things over," said Craig. "Separately. So you can think clearly."

"We don't need time," said Frankie.

"If you decide you've made a mistake, there are solutions. And if not, well, Eva and I will learn to live with the situation."

"You don't have to live with it," said Frankie. "We're the ones who have to do that."

"Exactly," said Eva. "And how can you possibly expect to be happy together when you know almost nothing about each other, when you have so little in common?"

"You mean, because I have no money."

"That's only half of it," snapped Eva. "You've got no prospect of making any, either. What sort of life can you offer my daughter?"

"I don't care about money," said Miranda.

"Because you've always had it. Believe me, it's another story when you don't."

"I'm not like you," said Miranda.

"And what do you mean by that?"

"Nothing," said Miranda, her voice quavering. Frankie extended an arm and draped it around her shoulders to remind her that he was there, that she had nothing to fear as long as he was. "I only meant that I don't really care how I live, as long as it's with Frankie."

"It's not just a question of money," said Craig, in his mediating voice, assuming the role of peacemaker.

Frankie looked at him, waiting for Craig to list all the ways in which he and Eva found him to be an unsuitable husband, wondering how he could ever have hoped that these people would do more than just put up with him, as they had with Miranda's childhood illnesses, as if he were a case of the chicken pox, knowing however bad the attack she would soon recover? How could he have hoped that they would *like* him? Well, they'd expected her to be cured by autumn, but he'd shown them he wasn't so easy to get rid of.

It occurred to Frankie that he hated these people, the tall, blond Craig, the petite, blond Eva. The thought surprised him. He really had thought he admired them both. But no, he did indeed hate them, for their assurance that the world was theirs to dispose of as they liked, for their innate and unquestioning sense of superiority, for their instinctive and dismissive contempt for him.

"You're quite right, money isn't everything," continued Craig. "There are other matters to consider. Shared friends, shared interests, for example. You two come from such different worlds. How can you hope to understand one another?"

"So far," muttered Frankie, "we haven't had much of a problem."

"What religion are you, Frankie?" said Craig, ignoring the interruption.

"Catholic."

"Miranda was raised Episcopalian."

"It's not like I'm religious or anything."

"It's a cultural matter," said Craig. "A matter of values. Not better or worse. I'm not saying that. Just different. Are you a Republican or a Democrat?"

"I don't care about politics," said Miranda. "Just because you hate Kennedy—"

"We do not *hate* the man," corrected Eva. "We simply do not approve of him. For president."

"My point," continued Craig, in his quiet voice, "is that all these differences create a gulf. And one needs to find a bridge across it. You two never gave yourself a chance to do that. Why, you hardly know one another."

"We're married," said Frankie, repeating the one incontrovertible fact, the one they could do nothing about. "If we can't find bridges, we'll build them."

"Don't be a fool," said Eva. "Surely you can see how much better it would be to end this . . . marriage now, before there are more complications."

"We really do want what's best for you both," said Craig. "We really do want you to be happy."

"We are happy," said Frankie stubbornly.

Craig had run out of patience. The gentle, reasonable tone of his voice gave way to one of irritation. "And how long will that last?"

"If you think I'll let your allowance continue . . ." added Eva.

Frankie stood and said, "We didn't come here to ask you for anything. We just came because it was the right thing to do, you being Miranda's parents." He turned to Miranda, bent to take her hand, and pulled her to her feet. "There's not much point us staying for dinner, seeing how you feel."

"No," said Craig.

"Miranda," said Eva, taking her daughter's other hand. "Don't go."

Miranda stared at Eva. She said nothing for what seemed to Frankie like an eternity. He felt panic rising in him. She's not going with me, he thought. She's going to stay. I've lost her. Finally, she extricated her hand from Eva's. "Would you have Mrs. Lyle pack my clothes and send them over to the hotel?" she said.

Frankie put his arm around her waist, and began to move toward the door. Eva and Craig fell back, to make a path for them.

"You've had your chance," said Craig.

"We'll leave our address and phone number," said Frankie. "If you change your mind, call us."

"That bastard," muttered Craig as Miranda and Frankie passed into the hall.

"Well, that's over," whispered Frankie. "All over. And we're still alive."

Chapter 9

Five, sometimes six days a week Frankie worked at Macklin's Health Club, alternating shifts with Pat Walewski, Tom Murray, and seven or eight other trainers. When he worked days, Frankie left Miranda asleep. When he returned from the evening shift, he found her in bed, reading, usually novels, potboilers or classics, sometimes magazines. Together, they watched the news, then *The Tonight Show* with its temperamental host, Jack Paar. Sometimes a young comedian named Woody Allen would be a guest, and they would lie propped against the brass headboard of their new bed, sharing a joint, laughing until their stomachs hurt. They liked Jimmy Durante, too. But when Jonathan Winters came on, or Henny Youngman, they turned off the set and made love.

Unable to complete all the paperwork in time to start school that semester, Miranda had long hours to fill while Frankie was at work. "I read," she said one night when he asked what she did while he was gone. "I go for walks. Sometimes I have coffee with Mrs. Coro." Sitting on the floor, her foot on a flower-patterned plastic place mat, a present from Dolly, she was polishing her toenails a soft opalescent pink.

"Don't you get bored?"

"No, I'm enjoying myself. For the first time in my life, there's nobody telling me what to do." She dipped the brush back in the bottle, lifted it, then let it fall again, and looked up, frowning. "Why?" Her voice had changed key from contented to worried. She felt him judging her.

"You could clean up around here sometimes."

Puzzled, she looked around. "It is clean."

There were dishes in the sink in the kitchen, crumbs on the floor, a sifting of gray dust on the furniture. Frankie laughed. "Clean?" It was a hoot of derision. "My mother would throw a fit if she saw this place."

Miranda seemed to grow smaller, to shrink into herself. A tear slid from the corner of her eye. To conceal it, she dropped her head forward over her knee, her hair a shower of gold along her leg. Pretending total absorption, she resumed polishing her nails, and said, "I'm sorry. I just don't think about things like that."

What the hell do you expect, thought Frankie, if you marry someone who's been waited on hand and foot her whole life? He dropped down to the floor beside her, reached under the fall of hair, and lifted her chin. "Why don't you just tell me to shut up?"

"But you're right," she said, screwing the top back on the bottle of polish.

"I'm a pain in the ass."

"I don't know how to do anything."

"You do," he said. He rolled onto his back and pulled her down on top of him. "You do some things better than anybody I ever met."

"My nails," she said, protesting, but not seriously.

"Fuck your nails." Miranda's eyes widened in surprise at his language, and that excited him even more. "Fuck me," he whispered, another of his father's lessons forgotten. His desire for her was more avid than ever. He felt as if he were at a buffet dinner, the kind his mother and aunts prepared for family celebrations, where the food was so plentiful, so tempting, so good he had to keep going back to the table again and again. No matter how full he got, he never felt satisfied. He would never get enough of her.

If only he could be sure that Miranda felt the same. As eager as she seemed to please him, as willing to do whatever he asked, as often as she said she was happy when he asked her, still he sensed her withholding something from him. Just what, eluded him, but the sensation kept him feeling uneasy, anxious, insecure.

. . .

*O*n his days off, Frankie and Miranda shopped for their new home, fantasizing which of the tempting display rooms at Bloomingdale's would be theirs when they had the money, meanwhile buying a pine dining table and chairs from a warehouse store on East Seventeenth Street, and from Gimbel's a many-pillowed sofa and plaid armchairs, along with assorted side tables and lamps. At Fortunoff on Long Island they found dishes and cutlery, sets of pots and pans. From Azuma on lower Fifth Avenue they came away with bags of pretty and inexpensive Japanese imports—stoneware casseroles, pottery mugs, lacquer coasters and trays. What they couldn't pay for, they charged, but stayed within the budget Frankie had set. And when they disagreed, he gave way to Miranda, prompted by the notion that her taste was better, more refined, than his own.

When they got bored with shopping, they visited the museums, Frankie drinking in eagerly what Miranda had to say about the Monets at the Met, the Picassos at the Modern, trying to learn from her, trying to understand what it was about the Bellini painting of Saint Francis at the Frick, for example, that made her stand looking at it so quietly for so long. It felt as if she had moved a million miles away from him.

One day, after leaving the Frick, they walked to the brownstone on East Seventy-second Street that was the home of the DeWitt Payson Gallery. The staff greeted Miranda like visiting royalty, and Russell Schneider, Eva's assistant, a cherubic man in his early thirties, insisted on escorting them through the current exhibition, which consisted entirely of large canvases covered with pieces of jagged colored glass. You couldn't pay him enough, decided Frankie, to hang one of them on his walls.

They went to the Empire State Building, and the Statue of Liberty. They took the ferry to Staten Island. They lit candles in St. Patrick's Cathedral. They browsed in Scribners on Fifth Avenue, with its paneled walls and oak bookshelves, looking like the studies Frankie imagined while reading nineteenth-century novels. They spent over fifty dollars, a fortune, on *The Leopard* which was on *The New York Times* best-seller list, *The Complete Works of Shakespeare*, and several paperbacks including *Damien* and *Death in Venice*. "You know," said Miranda as they waited for the bus downtown, "you get the same look on your face when you buy a book as a collector does buying a painting."

"Yeah?" said Frankie. "Maybe because I never had none when I was little." His brow furrowed as he reconsidered the sentence. Any, he reminded himself. *Any.*

Miranda looked shocked. "You must have had books," she said, in much the same tone she would have used to insist that the Ferraros must have had food on their table every night even if Frankie couldn't remember eating it.

"Maybe nursery rhymes and fairy tales when I was a baby," he said, "but that's it."

"*The Secret Garden* was my favorite. When I was a child, I mean. I wanted to find a secret place that was all mine, where I could go and hide whenever I wanted to."

"Hide from what?"

"There was always something."

"Even now?" asked Frankie.

"Oh, now," said Miranda, smiling, her eyes not quite meeting his. "I never imagined life could be so wonderful."

I wish I had your guts," Vic told Frankie when he returned to New York. What he meant was he wished he had his cousin's ability to take what he wanted and not worry too much about the consequences. He still thought about Maria a lot, he said, though God knows he tried hard not to. He dreamed about her. When he couldn't help himself, he called her. Always her father answered and was very polite, but he and his wife remained in the kitchen, near the one phone. While Maria and he spoke, Vic could hear the low murmur of their voices in the background. At first it made him furious, but then he realized that it was just as well. She wasn't the kind of girl you could seduce and leave; and he was in no position to offer her anything more permanent, not now, not for a long time to come. His life was too uncertain. Maybe it always would be.

"She wouldn't mind," said Frankie. "Not if she loves you."

"Maybe she wouldn't," said Vic, "but I do."

Out of work again, Vic spent a lot of time with Frankie and Miranda. Sometimes the three of them went out to dinner, to the Lion's Head, to Julius's, to the Blue Grotto in Little Italy. Occasionally Vic would bring a date along, some pale, skinny girl, dressed from head to toe in black, an aspiring actress or dancer working at odd jobs while waiting for a break. If Frankie didn't have to be at Macklin's early in the morning, they would hit the clubs, staying until two or three, doing the lindy, the cha-cha, the twist. Other times, they would stay home, watching television, *Hawaiian Eye* or *The Untouchables,* the baseball play-offs and the Nixon-Kennedy debates, downing beers, eating hot dogs, pretzels, potato chips.

"He's got ideals," said Frankie as they watched a newsclip of Kennedy.

"He's full of shit," said Vic. "All politicians are full of shit."

The polls had Kennedy trailing. The fall session in the Senate so far had been a disaster for him. He couldn't get one of his bills passed.

A friend of Vic's who worked at a ticket agency sometimes got them passes for Broadway shows. At first Frankie went only because he thought Miranda would enjoy it, but soon he found he liked the experience—the dressing up, the mingling with the crowd, the eavesdropping on the conversations. He found that in the moment between the lights dimming and the curtain rising, he felt a sense of excitement that turned to irritation if he didn't like what he saw, but became a sort of wonder if he did. It was no different, he realized, from the way he felt at a Yankee game, watching Mantle rounding the bases after hitting a home run.

Frankie liked living in Manhattan. It was difficult and varied and interesting in ways he had only glimpsed on infrequent trips to the city as a child, visits to the Museum of Natural History organized by his school, the Christmas and Easter treat to the Radio City Music Hall with his parents. The movies, the theaters, the restaurants and dance halls, the elegant hotels and seedy bars, the museums and pawn shops, the Madison Avenue executives and Bowery winos, the rich patrons of the Plaza and the prostitutes on Broadway, the whole amazing range of life, all had been within his reach for years, and he hadn't realized it. Growing up less than an hour from Manhattan, he might as well have been in another state, another country. This is living, he thought. This is *really* living.

"Look," said Miranda one night, late, as the bus they were taking home after seeing *Becket* approached the Flatiron Building.

Frankie, distracted, in an exalted state from having actually seen Sir Laurence Olivier live, onstage, said, "What?"

It was a trick of light, of the density of air, of the texture and color of that night's sky. "It looks just the way it does in the Georgia O'Keefe painting."

"Yeah," said Frankie. "Get a load o' that!" O'Keefe, he thought. Georgia. On the way home from Macklin's the next night, he stopped at a library, looked up O'Keefe in the card index, pulled an oversized book from the shelf, and browsed through it until he found a reproduction of the painting. Sonovabitch, he thought. From the library, he walked to Twenty-third Street, and stood, watching. As the sky darkened around it, the building began to look more and more like the painted one and yet very different. Frankie thought about the science fiction story he had read when he was a kid, about a gangster whose efforts to reform his life, after receiving the eyes of an eight-year-old choir boy in a transplant operation, result in sudden and grotesque death. Now, looking at the building, Frankie felt as if he were seeing not through his own eyes but through someone else's, through Georgia O'Keefe's. It was a peculiar sensation. He wondered if that, maybe, was what art was all about, proposing new ways to see, other ways to understand.

. . .

One afternoon, while Miranda was at Gristede's grocery shopping, Frankie finally worked up the courage to call his old girlfriend, Barbara. He felt he owed her an explanation. Of course, she had already heard the news about his marriage, and the silence that greeted the sound of his voice was followed instantly by tears and recriminations. "You should've told me," Barbara kept saying. "You let me think . . ."

An image of what married life with Barbara would have been like flashed into Frankie's mind: the split-level house near his parents, the kids riding tricycles in the driveway, the Sunday afternoons drinking beer, watching baseball with his father and Denny. He felt as if someone were strangling him. "I'm sorry, Barbara," he said. "Really sorry you're upset. But I didn't exactly do it to hurt you."

"You bastard," she said.

With relief, he heard the sound of Miranda's key in the lock. "You're a great girl, Barbara. You'll find somebody who's right for you," he said. Replacing the receiver, he hurtled across the room to help Miranda with the groceries. Why is this different, he wondered as he took the bags from her? Why do I feel like this isn't real life, like it's a fairy tale and I'm the prince?

Next, Frankie called Jimmy Loughlin. From freshman year in high school, he and Jimmy had been inseparable. They'd been on the basketball and football teams together; they'd double-dated, got drunk, and gone joyriding. They were together, and drunk, when Frankie ran Sal's car into a lamppost. He'd had to work all summer for nothing to pay for the damage, but Frankie hadn't minded. The punishment helped ease his guilty conscience. It left him broke, though, and when Dolly didn't slip Frankie the money he needed, Jimmy would pick up the tab. They'd had that kind of friendship.

Jimmy, too, had heard about the marriage. "Your mom called mine," he said. "I figured you'd be in touch when the time was right." If he was annoyed not to have learned of it firsthand, he concealed it, offered his congratulations, and suggested they "get together and celebrate."

The apartment was by now in pretty good shape, so Frankie invited Jimmy and his girlfriend to dinner. Since neither Miranda nor he could manage anything more difficult than grilled steak, he called his mother for recipes, which she gave happily, and at length, though not without wondering aloud why her daughter-in-law had not yet taken up her offer of cooking lessons. "You know how it is, Ma. Getting settled hasn't left us a whole lot of extra time. But soon," lied Frankie, who doubted Miranda had any desire to transform herself into Dolly Ferraro's ideal of the perfect wife. Which didn't mean that she was unwilling to pitch in and help. They splurged and shopped at

Balducci's. They bought four bottles of Chianti Classico Riserva. Together, they made baked ziti, roast veal, fried cauliflower, stuffed mushrooms, a big salad, and zabaglione for dessert.

Jimmy and Donna arrived with flowers and wine. They admired the apartment, briefly, then described at length the four-bedroom ranch in Deer Park that they were in the process of buying, thanks to the down payment their parents had given them as a wedding present. The date had been set, the arrangements made, and Frankie (since he could hardly expect the return of a favor he hadn't extended) would not be best man. As the realization of that dawned on him, mingled with relief, Frankie also felt regret. It was another bridge burned. And though he doubted he'd ever want to return to Jimmy's side of the river, it would have been reassuring to know that he could get back, if he had to.

"Great food," said Jimmy. "This ziti's almost as good as Mrs. Ferraro's. You're a great cook, Miranda." He was tall, just short of Frankie's height, with sandy hair, brown eyes, and the beginnings of a paunch.

"Frankie made it," said Miranda, with a rueful smile.

"You're shitting me," said Jimmy. "Frankie cooks?"

"Jimmy," whispered Donna, her face flooding with color, "your language. Please." A pretty girl with teased dark hair, good bones, large eyes, and clear olive skin under heavy makeup, she shot Miranda a look of embarrassment combined with awe, the sort of look she might have bestowed on a fashion model or movie star, someone who inhabited a totally different, and superior, realm of beauty. Smiling apologetically, she said, "I told him, if he don't stop talking dirty, I'm gonna call off the wedding."

"Fat chance," said Jimmy.

"I've heard worse," said Miranda, smiling in return, looking like a princess granting a royal pardon.

"Bet your ass," said Jimmy. "Frankie don't exactly get no gold medals for a clean mouth."

"Not when I'm out with the guys," said Frankie, unable to help himself. If he chose to talk that way in front of his wife, that was one thing, but he didn't want anybody else using language in front of Miranda.

Jimmy caught the rebuke. "So, you watch your mouth now, and you cook. Next thing, you'll be telling me you clean house, too, like a regular little faggot." It was a word from their school days, one that could be spoken with affection or contempt, provoking friendly wrestling matches between friends or, between enemies, bloody fistfights. Now Jimmy's voice had an edge, though his mouth curved in a convincing smile.

"I clean house, too," said Frankie, matching the smile.

Jimmy's eyes narrowed, then he laughed. "Marriage," he said. "Is this what it does to a guy?"

"Just you wait," said Donna, smiling nervously.

"If Frankie's a reformed character," said Miranda, "don't blame me. I had nothing to do with it. He was like this when I met him. Wonderful."

Frankie reached over and took her hand. He had an impulse to kiss it, which he resisted. Jimmy would really think he'd gone soft. (What was it about Miranda that made him want to behave like a hero in a costume film?) He contented himself with a brief squeeze. "You see," he said, smiling at Jimmy, "like they say, love *is* blind."

"You got a job yet?" asked Jimmy when Miranda got up to clear the table.

"Let me help," said Donna, picking up the vegetable dishes and following Miranda into the tiny kitchen.

"I'm working at a gym," said Frankie.

Again, Jimmy looked surprised. "How come?" he said.

Frankie shrugged. "I like it. Keeps me in shape." He flexed a muscle for Jimmy's approval.

"Muscles don't buy houses," said Jimmy, unimpressed. "Look, Frankie, if this don't work out, you come see me, okay?" Right after high school, Jimmy had started working as a salesman at his father's car dealership. He was making good money. He was not at all worried about his future. "We always got room for another salesman. 'Specially someone like you, smart, a good talker."

"Thanks, Jimmy," said Frankie. Shove it up your ass, he thought.

"You can't beat the pay."

"If things don't work out, I'll give you a call."

I don't like this guy, thought Frankie. Not anymore, I don't. He didn't like that idea either, and tried to push it away, but it wouldn't go. Even last year, he remembered, during one of his leaves, before the camaraderie of booze had taken hold, he'd sensed a difference in their relationship. After the news bulletins about each other's lives had ended, after the sportscast was over, there was nothing left for them to talk about. When Frankie, in response to some question, had said that books were his chief escape from the alternating stress and boredom of army life, Jimmy had seemed not only surprised but disapproving. The only thing he ever read was *Playboy,* and he usually skipped the articles. He greeted accounts of where Frankie had been, what he had seen, and done, sometimes with skepticism, as if he suspected his friend of embroidering the truth, sometimes with hostility, as if anything alien to his own experience was suspect, a cover for something dangerous, like homosexuality or Communism. As for himself, Jimmy had been nowhere except to the Poconos for summer vacations, and ROTC camp in Connecticut. He'd done nothing special, which seemed to please him. He liked his life. He thought it was terrific. His smugness infuriated Frankie, while the ordinariness of the future stretching in front of his once best friend terrified him. He felt it reaching for him, trying to suck him back in.

"I don't know how you stand it, living in this city," said Jimmy. By the time Miranda served the dessert, the Chianti had washed away any reserve he might have felt about letting Frankie know exactly what was on his mind. "It's a hellhole. Shit everywhere. Mulinyans. Winos. It stinks of piss and garbage. Why don't you make him get you somewhere decent to live?" he said to Miranda. "There are plenty of great places in the neighborhood, right near the Ferraros. Cost you less here."

"I like living in the city," said Miranda.

"You do?" said Donna, sounding as if she found that hard to believe.

"It's exciting."

"Yeah. Like you might get shot any minute by some crazed drug addict."

"This is a pretty safe neighborhood," said Frankie. "Anyway, suburban living," he added, "it's not for me."

"You got something against grass?"

"Yeah. Mowing it." Miranda giggled, and Frankie looked at her and smiled.

"You know," said Jimmy. "You got a fucking screw loose. Ooops, 'scuse me." He leered at Miranda. "Gotta watch my mouth."

"We oughtta get going," said Donna. "It's gettin' kinda late."

"He can't drive like that," said Frankie.

"I'm fine," said Jimmy.

Frankie turned to Miranda, and said, "Make some more coffee." She nodded and started for the kitchen. "Please," he added.

"Fucking pansy," muttered Jimmy.

Frankie pretended not to hear. "Maybe you should let Donna drive."

"I'm fine," said Jimmy. "I seen you drive in worse shape."

"That don't make it a good idea," said Donna.

"Shut up," said Jimmy. Then he smiled. "Please," he added with exaggerated courtesy. But when he sobered up, he kissed Miranda good-bye, told her she was a great-looking broad, and didn't argue when Frankie insisted on walking him and Donna to their car. Before he got in, he threw his arms around Frankie. "It's been great to see you, pal. I missed you. We gotta do this again, soon."

"Yeah," said Frankie. He extricated himself from Jimmy's grasp, then went to Donna and kissed her cheek. "Good luck," he said.

She hugged him, and said, "You done okay for yourself."

"So's Jimmy," Frankie said. He had always liked Donna. He waved as the car pulled away from the curb, then went back into the apartment. Miranda had begun to clear up. "Well," he said. "What do you think?"

.

She didn't look at him, just kept scraping dishes and stacking them in the sink. "They seem like nice people," she said.

"They are nice people," he said. "But we don't ever have to see them again."

*D*an's visit the following weekend came as a relief. If being with Jimmy made Frankie feel as if he were confined to a holding pen, waiting for death, with Dan he felt as if he had traveled to a new world, one of rare beauty and infinite possibility.

Down from Yale for a long weekend, Dan brought them, as a wedding present, a first edition of *The Sun Also Rises*. He treated them to a night on the town—cocktails at the Carlyle, dinner at 21, drinks at the Blue Angel. By the time they got back to the apartment, Miranda was reeling. She staggered into the bathroom, not bothering to close the door. They could hear the sound of her peeing. Frankie walked over to the door and closed it, then opened the linen cupboard and pulled out sheets and blankets for Dan. "The couch opens. If you want a beer," he said, "there's some in the refrigerator."

"I've had enough," said Dan.

"We've all had enough," said Frankie.

Miranda lurched out of the bathroom. "I'm drunk," she said. Frankie put an arm around her and led her into the bedroom. "I'll be right back," he said to Dan.

"I'm drunk," repeated Miranda.

"I noticed," said Frankie. He helped her out of her clothes and tucked her into bed.

Miranda wrapped her arms around his neck. "C'mere."

He kissed her mouth, then unclasped her hands. "I'll be back. Don't go anywhere." She nodded drowsily. Her eyes closed, and she was asleep. Frankie returned to the living room, grabbed a corner of the blanket Dan was wrestling with, and helped him finish making up the bed. "She doesn't usually drink so much," he said.

"I wish I didn't.'

Frankie eyed the couch. "I hope it's comfortable."

"It beats an army cot."

Frankie sat in one of the armchairs, watching as Dan stripped down to his shorts. "Want some pajamas?"

Dan grinned. "You wear pajamas?"

"No. They were a Christmas present from my mom."

"Thanks. I'm fine."

Frankie lit a cigarette. "Must've shocked the hell out of you, Miranda and me."

Dan stretched out on the couch, propped a pillow behind his head. "I knew you were crazy about each other."

"But you didn't think she'd marry me."

"Not if Eva had anything to say about it."

"I thought, you know, once it was done, she'd accept it. But it's a couple of months now and she's still pissed."

"You care?"

"About the money and all that shit? About how cozy it would be to have rich in-laws just crazy about you? buying you things?"

"That isn't what I meant."

Frankie shrugged. "You know, I don't think Miranda gives a fuck. I don't think she cares if she never sees Eva or any of them again. But me? I like happy families. It's the way I was raised."

"Nobody's happy around Eva, except Craig maybe. She's like one of those women you read about in history, like Catherine the Great, dazzling when she's getting her own way, a monster when she's crossed. Craig gives in to her all the time, to keep the peace. He's afraid of her, I guess, but he loves her, too."

"To tell you the truth, she scares the shit out of me sometimes. And she's just this little bitty thing."

"She's got Philip right under her thumb. You know she kept him from marrying the girl he loved? Bullied him until he gave her up and married someone she approved of. And Joan? Well, she survives by staying out of the way, living three thousand miles away and keeping whatever she's up to secret. At least Miranda proved she had some guts."

"Yeah," said Frankie. There was a silence, then he said, "You want anything?"

"No, I'm fine."

"Think I'll hit the sack." He got up, and headed for the bedroom.

"Frankie," called Dan. Frankie turned. "I'm really happy about you and Miranda."

Frankie smiled. "Thanks. So am I."

$\mathcal{T}$he next weekend, on the last Sunday in October, Dolly and Sal held a reception for their son and new daughter-in-law in a purpose-built catering hall five miles north of Midford. It tried to live up to its name—The Versailles—with too many mirrors, too many crystal chandeliers, and succeeded only in looking gaudy. Not that anybody minded, except perhaps the groom. The entire family was invited, including (at Frankie's insistence) his cousin Vic, who shook hands with his father, then avoided him the rest of the day, spending his time laughing with his mother and aunts, joking with the boys, dancing with the girls, all to Uncle Victor's intense irritation. If there was one thing a Ferraro hated, it was seeing someone he disapproved of having a good time.

It was a raucous day, with Frankie fielding rough jokes from his uncles, and Miranda relentless questions from his aunts, all comfortable and familiar and irritating to him, but overwhelming for her. After about an hour, she disappeared into the ladies' room, reappearing sometime later with faraway eyes and an angelic smile on her face. She'd had the forethought to carry a brownie in her handbag.

"They're all so sweet," said Miranda as one after another of the uncles pressed envelopes full of money into her hands and kisses onto her cheeks.

"She's some looker," admired the uncles. "She's got real class."

"Not stuck-up at all," judged the aunts.

Uncle Charlie dragged Dolly to the microphone, whispered in the bandleader's ear, and the strains of a familiar folk song filled the room. *"C'e la luna, mezzo mare,"* sang Dolly in her high, sweet soprano. Her sister Santa joined in, swaying in time to the music. Soon, everyone was singing.

Frankie whispered a rough translation of the song's double entendres to Miranda, who began to giggle. "Do those nice women actually know what they're saying?"

"Sure," said Vic.

"Somehow in Italian it doesn't seem bad to them. Just sort of naughty."

Miranda laughed so hard tears streamed down her cheeks. "That's the silliest thing I've ever heard."

"That's because you're stoned," whispered Vic.

"Charlie could have been a concert pianist," said Dolly to Miranda when her performance was over. Charlie was her brother.

"Really?"

"He used to play piano in the silent movie houses," added Santa.

That set Miranda giggling again, causing Santa's eyebrows to lift.

"It's the wine," Frankie said to his mother. "She's not used to it."

"It's good wine," said Sal. "It goes right to the head." He turned to Vic. "Frankie tells me you're quite an actor."

"You should come and see me some time, Uncle Sal," said Vic. "Judge for yourself."

Sal hesitated a minute. "Maybe," he said.

Satisfied, Vic smiled. He'd made a dent in the family's defenses.

Frankie danced with his mother, with Angela, with his Aunt Santa, with his cousin Lucy who had a crush on him, with all the women. Miranda danced with all the men.

"Are your family parties always like this?" she asked Sal.

Sal nodded. "Aren't yours?"

"No," said Miranda, confirming all Sal's prejudices about people who cooked things in aspic and considered celery a food.

"Your family's great," said Miranda, as they drove home along the crowded expressway in Frankie's Chevy. "I love them." Her head rested against Frankie's shoulder. Her eyes were closed.

"They've got their good points," said Vic, sitting next to her in the front seat.

"They're so . . . colorful," she murmured. "So warm. My family's so up-tight and dull."

The grass is always greener, thought Frankie. Not that he would have traded them for anyone, not for the Kennedys, or the Rockefellers, and certainly not for the Colvingtons. He loved them, all of them. But . . . What?

But he didn't want to be like them. He had other aspirations, other goals. Sometimes he felt they were clinging to him, holding him back; and he wished that they'd been cruel to him, mistreated him as a child, denied him what he wanted, what he needed, so he could abandon them now without guilt.

They'd been good to him, though, his parents, his sister, his aunts and uncles. They'd been kind. They'd squandered money on him, lavished affection. They'd loved him. And for that, they'd exacted a terrible price—his gratitude, his love, and his loyalty. There was no way he could escape them. Ever. Not completely.

He reached over and took Miranda's hand. Her eyes opened and she smiled at him sleepily. "I love you," she said. The tightness in his chest eased. Now, at least, he had ties to another world.

*L*et's go to Tiffany's," said Miranda on his next day off. She had seen an ad in *The New Yorker* for a bracelet she liked. "I don't really want to buy anything, but it's a great place to browse."

If he were alone, Frankie realized as they approached Tiffany's elegant entrance, he would never dare to go in. He would be too intimidated, dreading that the sales clerks, suspecting he didn't belong, would either ignore him, or notice him and treat him like dirt. Entering, he found that the place bore only the most minimal resemblance to what he considered a store, to

Sears or Macy's, and his apprehension increased. He was dazzled by the sense of space and light. Everything glittered, sparkled, shone—the chandeliers, the marble floors, the jewels in their glass cases.

"May I help you?" said a young woman in a tan suit.

"Bracelets," said Frankie, his voice a whisper, as if he were in church.

Miranda's hair was windblown. As always, she wore little makeup. She had on an old tan cashmere coat and silk scarf over a sweater and tweed skirt. On her feet were plain brown shoes with low square heels. Frankie had been shocked when he'd seen what she was wearing, and had suggested that perhaps she ought to dress . . . well, *better* since they were going to Tiffany's. But now he could see it hadn't been necessary. Wearing rags, Miranda would still look rich.

The saleswoman smiled and nodded in a way that was almost a curtsy and led them to the correct counter. Miranda pointed to the bracelet she wanted, then asked to see several more. As she tried them on, Frankie studied her as he had once studied Dan. He adjusted the look on his face, the line of his body to reflect what he saw in hers—comfort, ease, assurance, interest, but not too much.

I'm at home here, Miranda's body language said, I belong. I may or may not buy this bracelet. If I don't, it's not because I can't afford it. I have more money than God.

Gradually, Frankie became aware that, as he watched Miranda, the saleswoman watched him. She would tear her eyes away for a moment to offer another bracelet, to point out a detail, to help with a clasp, but soon they would drift back, irresistibly, to Frankie's face. What's she looking at? he thought, feeling insecure and defensive.

But all at once he knew. He recognized the look. He had seen it all his life.

The woman was older than Frankie, about thirty-five he guessed, not unattractive, though prim in her suit and cream-colored blouse. She wore a wedding ring, a narrow platinum band, and an engagement ring with a respectable but far from large diamond.

I bet her husband's lousy in bed, thought Frankie. I bet she's not bad. He smiled, and she blushed.

"It's very pretty," said Miranda.

"What?" said Frankie. Noting Miranda's surprise at not having his full attention, he collected his thoughts and continued, "Oh, the bracelet."

"It's very pretty but perhaps not quite what I had in mind." It was a thin gold band set with a small aquamarine. Miranda took it off her wrist and handed it to the saleswoman. "Thank you."

"We'll take it," said Frankie.

Miranda's eyes widened with surprise. "But, Frankie . . ."

"We'll take it," he repeated.

"Will that be cash or charge?"

Holy Christ, thought Frankie, I didn't even ask the price.

"Charge," he said. He fumbled for his credit card, and handed it to her.

"We've been spending so much money," said Miranda when the woman had walked away.

"Don't worry about it." He put his arms around her, and asked, "Do you like it?" Miranda nodded, and Frankie kissed her lightly on the lips. Over the top of Miranda's head, he could see the woman filling in the charge slip. She looked up and their eyes met. This time she smiled.

Frankie felt a surge of power rushing through him. Suddenly, he felt giddy, lightheaded with happiness. It's a piece of cake, he thought. A piece of cake.

Chapter 10

The cream-colored envelope addressed formally to Mr. and Mrs. Francis Xavier Ferraro was buried in a pile of unopened mail, mostly bills, on the table next to the front door. As soon as he saw it, Frankie knew what it was. "Oh, shit," he muttered, dropping the rest of the pile back on the table.

"What?" said Miranda, who was, as usual, lying on the couch, reading a magazine, a glass of Pepsi within reach on the coffee table.

"An invitation to Jimmy and Donna's wedding." Frowning, Frankie tore open the envelope and scanned its contents, transferring the frown to Miranda when she giggled. "What's so funny?" he said.

"Nothing." She looked up from the copy of *Cosmopolitan* that she seemed to find so hilarious and gave him a cautious smile.

"What do you want to do about this invitation?"

Her smile faded. "Whatever you like."

"I know it doesn't matter to you. If we go, you'd show up stoned anyway. A wedding, a funeral, a meeting of aliens from Mars, you wouldn't notice the difference."

"I don't like crowds," she said, and returned her attention to the magazine in her lap. A moment later, she was smiling again.

Good manners vying with self-interest, it took Frankie days to decide whether or not to go to the wedding, a difficult decision complicated by the fact that his parents planned to attend, as well as Angela and Denny. The

Loughlins and Ferraros had been friends almost as long as their sons. Finally, self-interest triumphed. Frankie returned the cream-colored card with a refusal.

Three days later, Dolly phoned. "I just heard from Mrs. Loughlin," she said. "You're not going to Jimmy's wedding." Disapproval sounded the loudest note in her voice, with incomprehension and anxiety forming the chord.

"Miranda and me'll be in Boston that Saturday," he lied.

"Mrs. Loughlin's upset. So's Jimmy, she says. They think maybe you're mad Jimmy didn't ask you to be an usher." That was a reason Dolly would have understood: the men in her life—husband, son, father, brothers—were quick to take offense at any insult, real or supposed.

"I'm not mad." Frankie motioned to Miranda to hand him his cigarettes. She brought him the pack, and he put an arm around her, pulling her close.

"You didn't ask *him*."

"I know." He slid his hand from Miranda's waist down along the curve of her bottom. Miranda smiled, kissed his cheek, and wriggled out of his grasp.

"I explained you didn't have a church wedding." Dolly took a deep breath, then plunged on. "You're in a state of mortal sin, Frankie. Jimmy couldn't ask you to be in his wedding party. Father McMann wouldn't've let him."

"Ma, believe me, I'm not mad at Jimmy. I understand. In fact, I'm relieved. I couldn't be in his wedding party anyway." He lit a cigarette and took a drag. An idea, a revolutionary one, had just occurred to him. "I told you, Miranda and me have to go to Boston. For Thanksgiving."

"You mean, you're not going to be *home* for Thanksgiving?"

Never before had he voluntarily considered missing a holiday with his family. Frankie hesitated a moment, reconsidering, then said, "Ma, I'm married now. I've got responsibilities to my wife. I can't spend every holiday with you."

"You didn't last year either, or the year before."

"I was in the army. I didn't have a lot of choice."

"What about Christmas?" She sounded as if she was about to cry.

Frankie took another drag of his cigarette. Christmas? What did he feel about Christmas? He wasn't sure. "I don't know," he said.

"Frankie!" Dolly's voice had reached a wail.

"All right, Ma. I promise we'll be there for Christmas." He had made holes in the net, but hadn't yet slipped free.

"I'll try to smooth things over with the Loughlins," said Dolly, sounding calmer now that she had wrung a concession from him. "But you should go see Father McMann, Frankie. Talk things over with him. Mortal sin's no laughing matter."

"One of these days," he conceded, to end the conversation. Miranda had started the water running in the tub and was standing in the bathroom doorway, directly in Frankie's line of vision, taking off her clothes. He felt a sudden, imperative need to join her. "Say hi to Pop. I'll see you both soon," he said, hanging up, unbuttoning his shirt, quickly closing the distance between himself and his wife. If this was mortal sin, it had a lot to recommend it.

A truce having been declared with his father, it was Vic who spent Thanksgiving Day with the Ferraro family while Frankie and Miranda remained holed up in their apartment, alone, preparing and eating a traditional holiday dinner: turkey with wild rice stuffing, sweet potatoes, corn bread, cranberry sauce, green beans with slivered almonds, pumpkin pie for dessert. No lasagna—for Frankie a truly revolutionary act. Without stopping to analyze the reason why, he was dimly aware that the pleasure he was taking in the day transcended his being young and in love and content, at least for the moment, with only his new wife for company. His enjoyment had an edge of excitement, the thrill of guilt that came from having done the forbidden. As with his wedding, he'd broken the familiar code of behavior. He'd acted without reference to anyone's feelings but his own, and maybe Miranda's. The feeling of power, of freedom, that gave him was heady, though he suspected he'd soon be caught up again and knit back into the social fabric.

*O*n Friday, because of the holiday weekend, few of the club members showed up at Macklin's. Frankie had an easy afternoon, spending most of it clowning around with Tom Murray, one of the trainers, and working out himself. Though the club was officially open until eleven that night, at about eight Pat came into the weight room and told Frankie to go home. "The joint's dead. Tom and me can handle anything that comes up." Frankie looked at Tom to see if he minded, and Pat caught the look. "You got a wife," he said.

"So do you," said Frankie, willing to stay if Pat changed his mind. He liked Pat. He was a good guy to work for, fair, with a sense of humor.

"Yeah, but mine don't look like yours. Leastways, not anymore." Miranda had stopped in a couple of times to meet Frankie, and Pat had been loud in his appreciation of her. Now he put an arm around Frankie's shoulders. "Enjoy it while you can, sonny. It don't last long," he said.

Frankie took the subway to Fourteenth Street, then walked the rest of the way to East Tenth. It was raining; the night was damp and cold; the streets were full of exhausted shoppers wielding umbrellas, trying to keep dry department store bags full of sale items and Christmas gifts. One of them, the handsome middle-aged woman who occupied the top-floor apartment, stood on the front stoop, juggling a plastic umbrella and booty from B. Altman, trying to find her keys in an oversized handbag. Frankie unlocked the front door, stepped aside to let her enter, offered to help with her packages, and was relieved when she said she could manage. Bawling Miranda's name, he let himself into the apartment, and, for the first time since they were married, got no response. He opened the bedroom door and peered inside, hoping to find her asleep. The bed was empty. The apartment was empty. He felt a faint tickle of worry, which he tried to ignore. This wasn't like Miranda. She was always home when he got there.

He searched for a note and found none. He tried to remember how Miranda had said she would be spending the day, but nothing specific came to mind. Vaguely, he recalled something about a book she wanted to buy, but it was after nine. No bookstore he could think of was open. Maybe she had just run out to Gristede's for something? He checked the refrigerator, but—milk, coffee, orange juice, butter, bagels—all the necessities were in place. There was no sign of dinner, but that wasn't unusual. When Frankie got home late from work, if he wanted something to eat, he sent out for a pizza. Leaving the apartment door ajar, he ran up the stairs to Mrs. Coro's apartment. She didn't answer the bell, and panic set in. Banging on the door, he called the landlady's name.

"Who is it?" Her voice sounded tired, wary.

"Frankie Ferraro, Mrs. Coro. Sorry to bother you."

The door opened, and she peered out at him, her thin, usually neat gray hair now awry, her eyes glazed with sleep. She was wearing a bathrobe and slippers. In the background, Frankie could hear the sound of Fred Flintstone's voice coming from the television. "I fell asleep on the couch."

"I'm sorry," Frankie said again, "I thought maybe Miranda was up here."

"She's not home? Well, she's probably just gone around the corner to Gristede's," said Mrs. Coro reassuringly.

"Yeah," said Frankie, trying to smile. "That was my second guess." He backed away from the door.

"Call me when she gets back." Her voice had taken on an anxious note, as if, like Frankie, she'd started to picture Miranda lying raped and battered, dead in the street.

Nodding, he apologized again for disturbing her, and raced back down the stairs, hoping (though he knew he would have heard her) that Miranda had returned in his absence. The apartment was still empty. He closed the door, lit a cigarette, and tried to think what to do. He didn't even know how long she'd been gone. He couldn't call the police. Yet. Turning on the television, he sat on the couch and stared blankly at the screen. Most of the people Miranda knew in Manhattan she avoided because of their connection to Eva. There were only a few she might actually be with, a Bennington graduate now working at *Mademoiselle,* a couple of musicians from Boston in town looking for work, a high school friend studying at Juilliard. He looked up their numbers in her address book, and phoned. The two who were home hadn't spoken to Miranda all week. Frankie sat for a moment, thinking, then picked up Miranda's address book again, and went through it from cover to cover, looking for a name he might have forgotten, for some clue to where she might be. There were none.

Maybe it was the subway, a breakdown somewhere. Frankie got up, went into the kitchen, and turned on the radio, but the only bulletins that night were about the birth of the newly elected president's son. He turned the radio off, lit another cigarette, and dialed Vic's number. There wasn't much likelihood of Miranda's being with him, still it was worth a call to make sure. He let the phone ring ten times, then replaced the receiver, got up, and poured himself a drink.

You're as bad as your mother, he told himself, remembering the times Dolly had greeted him with hysterics when he was a half hour late home from a party. It's only ten o'clock, for chrissake, not three in the morning. The image of Miranda, a crumpled heap in an alley, came into his mind. "Oh, shit," he muttered, pushing the picture away, downing the scotch with a grimace of distaste, then pouring himself another. "Please, God, let her be okay," he murmured, sitting, burying his face in his hands, repeating the phrase over and over, the incantation a reflex action, the closest he had come to a prayer since the Christmas he was ten when all the candles lit to the Sacred Heart, the Blessed Mother, and a good number of saints had failed to deliver the ten-speed bike he'd wanted.

He heard the key in the lock, looked up, and saw Miranda standing there, surprise blended with apprehension on her face. "You're home," she said.

Relief instantly gave way to rage, and he said, "Where the fuck have you been?"

"I didn't expect you until after eleven." Closing the door behind her, Miranda came slowly into the room, wary of the storm of anger about to break over her head.

"I was worried sick. Where were you?"

"I had dinner out," she said.

Something, a slight hesitation, the way her eyes didn't quite meet his, told

Frankie there was more to the story. For the first time that night, for the first time ever, it occurred to him that Miranda might have been out with a man; worse, maybe not for the first time. Maybe she spent all the days and nights he was at work with another man. It was possible, as possible as Miranda's assertion that she spent most of her life on the couch, reading and watching television. But Miranda unfaithful was a shocking idea, an intolerable idea. How could he have thought it? Frankie felt himself begin to shake. Inside his head, disbelief battled with fear, common sense with rage. He wanted to hit her for frightening him. "Alone?" he said. Not meaning to, he moved toward her.

Seeing the menace in his face, she backed away until stopped by the front door. "No," she said.

He grabbed her by the shoulders and shook her. "Who were you with? Who?"

Afraid, she struggled against his hands. "Frankie, stop it! Let me go!"

"Who?" He was shouting. "Tell me who you were with!" Dimly, in the background, above the pounding in his head, he heard the phone begin to ring. He loosened his grip.

Miranda pulled away. Tears streaming down her face, she ran to the phone and answered it, as if about to cry for help. "Hello? . . . Oh, hello, Mrs. Coro. . . ."

The landlady's name was like a slap in Frankie's face. The wave of anger receded. His trembling stopped; his breathing slowed. He knew he had been about to do something irrevocable, something unforgivable, and he felt ashamed.

"I just got in . . ." Miranda's voice was shaky, but the strange note in it could have been mistaken for fatigue rather than fear. "I stopped to eat. I didn't realize how late it was. . . . Sorry. Frankie shouldn't have worried you. . . . Yes, really, I'm fine. . . . I'll come up to see you in the morning. 'Night." She replaced the receiver in its cradle and looked across the room at Frankie. With her right hand, she wiped away the tears.

He thought, even crying she's beautiful. "I thought maybe you were with her," he said. Miranda said nothing. She took off her coat, threw it over an armchair, and sat on the couch. She was wearing her best black wool crepe dress, with her pearl necklace and earrings. "Who did you have dinner with?" The rage had gone out of Frankie's voice. Only the fear was still there.

"My mother and Craig. They're here for the weekend."

"Oh, God," he muttered. He walked to the couch, shook a Marlboro out of the pack on the coffee table, lit one, and sat, leaving a distance, a neutral zone between them. "Why didn't you let me know?" he said.

"I was afraid."

"Afraid?" repeated Frankie, puzzled. Until a few minutes ago, he had never, as far as he knew, given Miranda any reason at all to be afraid of him.

"I wasn't sure you'd want me to see them—"

"They're your *family*, Miranda."

"And I didn't want to have to choose between you."

"I thought you did that when you married me."

Again Miranda's eyes filled with tears. "Oh, I did, Frankie. I did."

He closed the distance between them, and Miranda turned immediately into him, resting her head against his chest. "What did they say?"

"They wanted me to go back to Boston with them." Her voice was very soft.

He pulled back from her so he could see her face. "Boston! What the fuck for?" He hadn't meant to shout. Staring at him, her face pale, Miranda said nothing. "What good do they think you're going back to Boston would do?" he asked, this time in a more reasonable tone. "We're married." Miranda shrugged. He thought of how close he had come to hitting her. "I'm sorry," he said, "about before. It won't happen again. I swear it." He pulled her close to him again, and kissed her. "I was just so afraid," he said.

*Ɛ*va called the next morning. Wrapped in a towel, standing in front of the bathroom mirror, shaving, Frankie heard the phone ring. His face lathered with cream, he went into the bedroom to answer the extension. "Oh, Frankie," she said, "it's you," as if she would have preferred speaking to just about anyone else in the world.

"I live here."

"I haven't forgotten," she said. "I thought perhaps you'd be at that fascinating job of yours. What is it you do all day? Lift weights?"

He felt the anger rising, the hurt, and embarrassment. Bitch! Why should she make him feel ashamed of earning an honest living when all she had done to get money was marry it? Whore, he thought. "Sometimes," he said, adding quickly, "If you want to talk to Miranda, she's not here." She was upstairs having coffee with Mrs. Coro. "I'll ask her to call you when she gets home."

"No need. I just phoned to invite the two of you to dinner tonight."

"I'm working," said Frankie, without any pretense of regret.

Eva was silent for so long, Frankie thought perhaps she'd hung up. Finally, she said, "What time do you start?" He told her. "Then you'll have time to meet me for lunch." It was a demand, not an invitation.

"I'm not sure what time Miranda will be back," said Frankie, stalling, trying to decide whether or not lunch with Eva was a good idea.

"I was thinking more in terms of a tête à tête," said Eva, "just you and me, alone, getting to know one another." It was the last suggestion Frankie had expected. He kept quiet as he thought it over. "Frankie?" said Eva, "I really do think you and I must come to some sort of understanding, don't you?"

"I suppose."

"We're at the Carlyle. Be here at noon. Craig's got a lunch meeting. It will be just the two of us. I'm looking forward to it. And Frankie, I wouldn't," she added, her voice soft, confiding, "mention this to Miranda. She won't like it." And the line went dead.

Frankie returned to the bathroom to finish shaving. What the fuck is this all about, he wondered? He nicked his chin with the razor. "Goddamn it," he muttered. "Just what I need. To show up looking like a stuck pig." He rinsed his face, patted it dry, applied antiseptic powder to the cut, and went into the bedroom to plan his wardrobe—something expensive but casual, something to make him look as if he didn't give a damn. He pulled a pair of brown tweed trousers and a cream-colored shirt from the closet, rejected his leather jacket for a tan blazer, decided against a tie, and opened a new package of jockey briefs. Dropping the towel, he began to dress, hurriedly, wanting to make his escape before Miranda returned.

But as he was writing her a note, the front door opened, and Miranda entered. "You're going out?" she said, "I thought you didn't have to be at work until three?"

He waved the piece of paper. "I was leaving you a note."

"You're all dressed up." She went into the bedroom, pulled open a drawer, took out one of Frankie's sweaters and pulled it on over the one she was wearing. "It's freezing in that hallway. I'm chilled to the bone."

He crumpled the note and said, "Your mother called."

Miranda came back into the living room and looked at Frankie warily. "What did she want?"

"For me to have lunch with her."

"Just you?" She was more surprised than angry. Frankie nodded. Miranda sat on the couch and stared at him. "Why?"

He shrugged. "To get to know me better, she said."

"Don't go, Frankie. Call her back and tell her you've changed your mind."

"She's right." He went to the couch, sat beside Miranda, and took one of her clenched hands into his. "She and I really have to get this settled between us," he said, trying to pry open her fingers. "I have to prove I'm the right kind of husband for you."

She pulled her hand away. "It's none of her business. I'm the one you have to prove that to."

Startled, he sat back and studied her face. Why was she so angry? After all, he was only trying to do what was best for her, make peace with her mother. "What's that supposed to mean?" he said. "You don't think I'm a good husband?"

"That's not the point."

"It is to me."

As always, now that he was on the offensive, Miranda began to retreat. "Of course I think you're a good husband."

"I do my goddamn best."

"I know."

"And all you do all day is sit around here on your ass."

"That's not fair, Frankie. I wanted to get a job. You're the one who insisted I go to school. And I can't do that until January."

"Fuck the job. You don't need a job. But it wouldn't kill you to clean up around here every once in a while." For the second time in as many days, Miranda started to cry, and the sound pricked the balloon of his anger, deflating it instantly, leaving him feeling flat and ashamed. Frankie looked at her, abashed at what he had yet again done. "Oh, Christ," he muttered. "I didn't mean it. I'm sorry." She continued to sob, and Frankie gathered her into his arms. "Why don't you just shout back at me? I'm such a sonova-bitch."

"It wouldn't do any good," she said. "You wouldn't hear. You'd just get madder and madder. You'd end up hitting me."

"No," he said, horrified at the thought. "Never. I'd never hit a woman." The memory of how close he'd come the night before added to his shame. "Never," he insisted. "I'd never hit you. Forgive me?" said Frankie.

Miranda took a hanky from the pocket of her slacks, wiped her eyes, blew her nose, and nodded. "Instead of always wanting to be forgiven afterwards," she said, leaning her head back against the couch, closing her eyes, "why can't people just not do the things they do?"

"I don't know," he said. "I wish I could. But I've always had a rotten temper."

"I meant me, too."

Frankie leaned toward her and kissed her closed eyes. "I love you."

"I guess my mother loves me, too, in her way."

That reminded him. He looked at his watch. "I better go. It's getting late."

"I wish you wouldn't," she said, but there was no hope in her voice.

He kissed her mouth. "You tried to explain. Now it's my turn." He got up, walked to the hallway, took his coat from the closet and put it on, turning to look at Miranda as he buttoned it. "Look, I'm not mad at her. I understand. She wanted something better for her daughter. I'll probably feel the same way myself someday."

"That's not the point," said Miranda again, softly, as Frankie walked out the door.

*E*va was wearing black slacks and a sweater Frankie assumed was cashmere, a rope of heavy silver links around her neck and large silver hoops in her ears. "Come in," she said, stepping back to let him pass. "I thought perhaps you'd changed your mind."

It was twelve-fifteen. "Sorry," said Frankie. He wasn't about to explain that he was late because of a fight with her daughter.

"The room service menu is on the desk. We should order right away. I don't want you to have to rush your lunch."

"I'm not really hungry," he said, taking off his overcoat, draping it over the desk chair, and picking up the menu. "A roast beef sandwich, rare," he continued after a minute "on a roll with Russian dressing. French fries. And a piece of apple pie. Please," he added as an afterthought.

Eva laughed. "Boys," she said, "do have such healthy appetites. And to drink?"

"Just coffee," he said. He needed to keep his head clear.

Eva picked up the phone to dial room service, and Frankie went to the couch and sat. The Colvingtons had taken a suite, all done in reproduction French antique furniture, striped paper on the walls, gilt everywhere. His mother would love it, thought Frankie.

"Why don't you take off your jacket?" said Eva, when she'd finished ordering. "These hotel rooms are always so hot."

"I'm fine," he said, though he was beginning to sweat. Keep calm, he told himself. She's a woman, a pint-sized woman, not the Dragon Lady. You can handle her.

She came to the couch and sat at the opposite end. "That shouldn't take long to get here. The service is really quite good."

"Yeah." He shifted uncomfortably, studying Eva's face, waiting. Whatever it was, he wanted it to begin; he wanted it to be over.

"Do you think Miranda looks like me?"

"Yes. In a way." The features were the same, yet the overall effect was different, as if one face were chiseled in stone, the other carved in wax.

"Everyone says so. I can't see it myself."

"Joan doesn't."

"No, she looks like her father." She didn't sound pleased. "My son, though, with him I can see the resemblance. You've met Philip." Frankie nodded. "He's a very successful banker. Like *his* father. And quite an avid art collector."

"Yes." Frankie took his cigarettes from his pocket. "Mind if I smoke?"

Eva frowned. She didn't like it, he remembered, but this time she nodded, said, "Not at all," and continued, as if he hadn't interrupted, "Joan, too, is doing very well. There was a time when we despaired of her, one of those impossible adolescent stages. She wanted to be an artist. Her father is, you know?" Again, Frankie nodded. "He, of course, is a genius. Joan's talent, on the other hand, is quite small. She would have had her heart broken, if she'd continued. If we'd *let* her continue being deluded. But she will be a first-class art historian. Absolutely first class." She leaned toward him and added, confidentially, "I used to want to be a painter. Did you know that?"

"No," said Frankie.

"I had a great deal of talent, so everyone said. But I was a young widow, with three children to raise. I started running the gallery, to support us all, and somehow I never got back to painting." Her eyes shifted to a point above Frankie's head, as if the movie of her past were playing there. She sighed. "There's not a day that goes by that I don't regret it. Regrets are a terrible thing," she added.

"Yes."

"I would be very sorry if Miranda were to have any."

"So would I."

"From the time she was a very little girl, she has wanted to run the gallery. Her father left it to her, you know, not me. He didn't leave me a thing." She couldn't quite hide the anger that still caused her.

"No, I didn't know."

"Oh?" said Eva. "Miranda never mentioned that to you? How odd. I've merely been running it for her until she feels able to take over."

He wasn't absolutely certain why, but Frankie found all this upsetting. She should've told me, he thought. Why didn't she tell me?

"Of course," continued Eva, "it's a tough business. It requires not only knowledge but taste, and guts. One has to be able to inspire confidence. Quite honestly, I've always thought that perhaps Miranda isn't . . . well, *strong* enough to succeed. But then, it's what her father wanted, what *she* has always wanted. It would be a great pity if she never got the chance to try."

"I don't see the problem."

Again, Eva frowned, but before she could reply there was a knock at the door. "Lunch," she said. Rising, she went to the door, opened it, and instructed the bellhop to leave the tray on the coffee table. She signed the tab, adding a sizable tip, smiled him on his way, and resumed her seat next to Frankie. Leaning forward, she lifted the silver covers from both dishes. "Go on," she said, turning her smile on Frankie. "Mmm. Looks good. I haven't had a roast beef sandwich in ages. Coffee?" He nodded, and Eva lilted the silver pot, and poured them each a cup.

It was a bad choice, thought Frankie, biting into his sandwich. He felt awkward and uncomfortable with his mouth full of food, the Russian dressing oozing out from under the bread onto his hands.

"It's not just a question of college," said Eva, nibbling delicately at her salade Niçoise, picking up the thread of the conversation.

Frankie nodded, as if he understood what she meant. "I haven't wanted Miranda to get a job," he said. "We don't really need the money. But if it'd help her, later on, then I think maybe she should go work in the gallery. Until she starts school. Maybe even afterwards, if she's got time. You know, to learn the ropes." Eva smiled again, this time an impatient smile without warmth or humor, although tinged with admiration. I'm going to make her like me, thought Frankie. Sooner or later, women always do. "Well, it only stands to reason," he said. "You need experience to run a business."

"Yes, you do. But Miranda not only needs to get her degree, and take some business courses perhaps. I never had any, but I'm sure it would help. More important than that, she needs to travel, to meet people, the right sorts of people, not only artists, but curators, and collectors, *important* collectors."

"I won't get in her way."

"You're already there, Frankie. And that's the truth of the matter. Think about what Miranda is doing now. Living in a tiny apartment in Greenwich Village, wasting her life, going nowhere, meeting no one. It's not what I had in mind for my daughter."

"We're just getting on our feet."

"You're getting nowhere. And that's fine for you, if that's what you want. But it's not fine for Miranda. She deserves more."

"I know that."

Eva put her salad, almost untouched, back onto the tray. "Well, what do you intend to do about it?"

Frankie dropped the sandwich back onto its dish, wiped the dressing from his hands, and stood. He was furious, but less with Eva than with himself. He should be able to give Miranda more, but how? "If I had money, you would've wanted Miranda to marry me," he said. "You wouldn't've worried then about who was going to run the gallery."

"Perhaps I would have been *less* concerned," she conceded, "if Miranda had married someone who could provide for her adequately."

"One of these days," said Frankie, his voice angry, defiant, full of hatred, "I'm gonna have money. Plenty of money." But even as he said the words, he felt like a fool, like a kid bragging in a schoolyard.

"Oh, I don't doubt you're ambitious," said Eva, coolly.

A wave of fatigue hit Frankie. What was the use of arguing? Eva had made up her mind, and nothing he could say or do would change it. "I love Miranda," he said, his final, really his only defense.

Eva rose and went to him. She lifted her hand and put it on his shoulder. "You're so young, Frankie. When you're young, it's easy to mistake . . . other feelings for love." Her hand slid from his shoulder to his biceps, lingered there caressingly. "I don't wonder girls are mad about you," she said. There was nothing motherly in Eva's look, or in her touch. Oh, God, thought Frankie, as he felt his cock give a sudden lurch in his new Jockey shorts. Her hand traveled back up his arm to his shoulder, stroked the back of his neck. Then, as if in slow motion, Frankie saw her other hand rise, felt it slide up his arm and around his neck to where it joined the first. "Do I seem very old to you?" said Eva. Her eyes, usually ice cold, the steel color of the Atlantic in February, now seemed a warm, Caribbean blue.

"No," said Frankie, forcing the word out past the fear in his throat. He couldn't believe this was happening to him. He stared at her face, at her lips, slightly parted, the tip of her tongue peeking through. A reflex action, his head started to bend toward her mouth. Since puberty, he'd never said no to a woman who offered. If I do this, he thought, I'll have a hold on her forever. I'll be able to make her do anything I want. I'll be able to make her leave Miranda and me alone. But even as the thoughts coalesced in his mind, Frankie knew he was wrong. Eva would never relinquish control. She would use this against him. She would tell Miranda, if she had to. I'm sick, he thought. Sick. I must be out of my mind. He jerked his head back, but otherwise didn't move, uncertain how not to make an issue of Eva's actions, how to pretend this wasn't happening.

Eva rocked forward onto her toes, lifted her chin, and put her mouth softly against his. Frankie stood like a statue, frozen by fear, not even breathing. His cock, the only part of his body still capable of movement, throbbed in his pants. A few seconds, an eternity, and she rolled down on her heels, and stepped back. "You're a sweet boy," she said, her face impassive, her voice expressionless. She returned to the couch, sat, and regarded him steadily. "I really don't want to see you hurt."

Then leave me alone, he thought. Leave *us* alone. "I should go," he said.

"Miranda isn't in love with you, you know. Oh, I'm sure she's *fond* of you. I mean, why wouldn't she be? You're an attractive young man, and you're clearly mad about her. But the truth is, Miranda's in love with someone else. She has been for some time. Unfortunately, he happens to be mar-

ried. And I doubt very much he has any intention of leaving his wife. Not
for Miranda, at any rate." Once again, Frankie had that feeling, that he was
listening to someone speak a foreign language, one he knew only vaguely, a
word, an occasional phrase intelligible, but not enough for him to be sure
he understood correctly what was being said. "I've tried to break it up, God
knows. I've been throwing eligible young men at her nonstop. That's why
I didn't interfere this summer when she seemed so interested in you." A wry
smile flitted across Eva's face, then disappeared. "Of course, I never meant
her interest to go quite so far."

"What are you talking about?" said Frankie.

"Miranda married you on the rebound. To prove a point."

"You're crazy."

"When we went back to Boston last summer, to meet Joan," continued
Eva, as if Frankie hadn't spoken, "unfortunately we ran into Greg in a restaurant—Greg is his name, Greg Dyer. We've known him for years. He's
quite an important collector. He wasn't with his wife, but with another
young girl. Apparently, the next day Miranda went to his office and made
quite a scene. He told her that he no longer loved her, that their relationship
was over."

It was impossible to believe her. "How do you know all this?"

Eva shrugged. "Greg called me, to ask my help. He wanted me to talk to
Miranda, to convince her their affair was over. He was afraid Miranda would
go to his wife. His wife, by the way, is a friend of mine."

"The sonovabitch," said Frankie.

"Exactly," said Eva, dryly. "So I insisted Miranda come to Paris. I didn't
want to leave her alone to get into more trouble. I was hoping, given time,
she'd get over him."

"Maybe she did."

Eva again smiled her pitying smile. "The next thing I knew, Miranda and
you were married."

The blood was pounding in his head. He wanted to kill someone, but
who? Eva, Greg Dyer, Miranda, himself? I've gotta get out of here, he
thought. He grabbed his overcoat from the chair and headed for the door.

"Frankie!" Eva's voice stopped him as cold as a bullet in the heart. Frankie
turned, and looked at her. She seemed very far away, and obscured by mist.
"I'm sorry," she said. "but it's always best, I've found, to know the truth,
however much it hurts."

*I*t had started to rain again. Raising his collar to keep the icy drizzle from
running down his neck, Frankie crossed Fifth Avenue and entered the park.

He wasn't heading anywhere. He was just walking, aimlessly, trying to make sense of what he'd just heard. But it made no sense. She's lying, he thought, trying to convince himself. She's bound to be lying. But he knew she wasn't. No wonder Miranda hadn't wanted him to see Eva alone. The bitch, he thought, not sure to whom he was referring, his wife or her mother. Oh, God, Miranda. What he felt on his face were tears, he knew, not rain. In the distance, he could see a limousine decorated with flowers drive by along the transverse. He remembered today was Jimmy Loughlin's wedding day. Suddenly, he longed to be in his parents' house, dressing for his best friend's wedding, safe in a world where he knew all the rules, safe in the world where he belonged.

Chapter 11

*O*f all the tragedies in the *Collected Plays of Shakespeare* (which he was slowly reading his way through), *Othello* had given Frankie the most trouble. He couldn't believe that such a hot-shot warrior and brilliant statesman could be duped by even the craftiest Iago with evidence as flimsy as a lost handkerchief. "You have to think about Othello and Desdemona as people," Vic had said, when Frankie broached the subject to him one day in the steam room at Macklin's, "not as characters in a play, or actors acting a part. Even if you ignore the fact that he's black and she's white, he rose up through the ranks, and she's an aristocrat. There's a huge class difference between them. He probably never trusted her, maybe never thought he deserved her. Subconsciously, he's probably been expecting her to betray him. He's probably been waiting for it all along." Vic had played Cassio once in an off-Broadway production of the play.

As he left Central Park and began walking downtown toward Macklin's, Frankie didn't think about Othello, or Desdemona, or Iago. The words, "Put out the light, and then put out the light," kept reverberating in his head, but without his knowing why, without his being conscious of their origin, without his making any connection but that his life seemed suddenly dark, his future a black hole. What he wanted more than anything was to wring the truth out of Miranda, even better, to wring her neck. But later, while spotting some macho bullshit artist in the weight room, Frankie decided not to confront her with what Eva had told him, not to discuss it, not to make it an issue. Her relationship with Greg Dyer had ended before their marriage, he told himself. It had nothing to do with him.

That was true as far as it went, which was as far as Frankie was prepared to go. Beyond that lay dangerous territory, a place where he would have to admit, to himself, that if Miranda swore she no longer loved Dyer, he wouldn't believe her; if she confessed she did, there would be nothing he could do about it. Leaving her was unthinkable.

When Miranda called, wanting to know about his lunch with Eva, Frankie was evasive. "We understand each other better," he said, "that's for sure. I'll tell you all about it when I get home. I got a bunch of guys here shouting for help." In fact, the gym was almost deserted, but Frankie stayed late anyway, working out, trying to burn off the black mood enveloping him. Then, instead of going straight home when Macklin's closed, he walked to the Flatiron Building and stood looking at it. But this time it provided no insight, no exhilaration. It was only a peculiar gray structure in a bleak gray street.

"I cooked dinner," said Miranda when he walked in. "But I think it's ruined." It was the first meal she had ever, unassisted, prepared for him. He told her that it didn't matter, went into the bathroom to wash up, then returned to sit opposite her at the table. She looked the way he felt, close to tears. "Tell me what my mother said."

She made a pass at me, thought Frankie. She said you married me on the rebound, that you never loved me, that you're in love with somebody else.

The chicken was dry and tasted like cardboard, the rice like paste; only the broccoli, which Dolly always overcooked, seemed edible to Frankie. He pushed the food around on his plate, then looked at Miranda, and said, "The usual. She thinks you're wasting your life with me. She thinks you ought to be in school. She thinks I'm keeping you from meeting all the people you ought to know if you're going to run the gallery someday. You should've told me about that," he added.

"About what?" asked Miranda, seeming genuinely perplexed.

"About the gallery."

"Oh." She seemed embarrassed. "I never think of it as mine. I always think of it as Mother's." Frankie remained quiet a moment, as if weighing every word for truth. He had never before assessed her so coldly, and it flustered her. She began tearing a piece of bread to bits. "A gallery isn't like an ordinary business, Frankie, like a publishing company, or Craig's stores." She sounded as if she was repeating a lesson she had learned by rote at her mother's knee. "It may own a few paintings, but most of them belong to the artists, who can take them back anytime. The whole business is very insubstantial. It depends on knowledge and reputation, contacts and good-will. It could all fall to pieces tomorrow. What I inherited really is nothing but a building with a sign in front, which I suppose is why I don't spend a lot of time talking about it. Or thinking about it."

"The building must be worth a fortune," said Frankie, responding to the only piece of information he had really grasped.

Miranda dropped the last remnant of the bread on the table. She hesitated, as if trying to decide how much was safe to tell him. Finally, she said, "I suppose," and let it go at that. But later, in bed, when, instead of reaching for her, Frankie lay flat on his back, still as a corpse, Miranda said, "Is it just the gallery you're upset about?"

"I'm not upset."

"Whatever my mother told you, Frankie, it was a lie."

Probably, he thought. I wouldn't be surprised. I wouldn't put it past her. He opened his eyes and saw Miranda's mournful face hovering like a pale, sad moon above him. "She didn't say nothin'," he said. "I swear it. Now, can I please get some sleep?" He closed his eyes again, turned over, and pretended he didn't hear Miranda crying quietly into her pillow. It was the first time since their wedding that they didn't make love. The honeymoon was over.

As the days passed, Frankie worked hard to convince himself that Eva had lied; or, if not lied exactly, then exaggerated. Miranda had probably had a crush on Dyer, maybe even believed she was in love. After all, Frankie had once thought he was in love with Barbara; and, briefly, with a girl in Georgia. Only when he met Miranda had he known for certain what falling in love meant, what being in love was really like. It could have been the same for her, he figured. *Must* have been. Whatever she'd felt for Greg Dyer had begun to fade the moment she'd walked into Teeny's and seen Frankie there. Miranda had married him because she loved him. No other reason.

He kept that thought handy, like aspirin, for those moments of stabbing doubt when Eva's version of events rose up and clamored for acceptance.

Plagued by suspicion, before he left for work, Frankie asked Miranda what her plans were. He called home several times a day, just to say hi he told her, in case she was feeling lonely, but each of them knew it was to make sure that she kept to her announced schedule. If she was out, he would try her every fifteen minutes or so until her return. "I went to Gristede's for some milk," she would say, or the bookstore on Eighth Street, or the newsstand for a magazine. Sometimes he would ask Pat if he could leave work early, and would arrive home unannounced, to find her in the tub having a bath, on the couch reading, or sitting at the table, polishing her nails. Once he even found her scrubbing the kitchen floor. She smiled at the amazed look on his face. "It was filthy," she said.

What Frankie wanted was to keep Miranda locked up in the apartment while he was gone, with no access to anyone of whom he didn't approve. But after a week of torture, as he stood at the closet, carefully putting his clothes away, watching Miranda's expression reflected in the mirror on the door, he suggested instead that she go to work at the gallery, something he'd been thinking about since his meeting with Eva.

Miranda's face, emerging through the neck of her flannel nightshirt, looked wary. "I thought you didn't want me to work," she said.

"I didn't want you taking just any job. This is different. You won't be doing it for the money." And it would beat worrying where she was all the time. "You'd be doing it so's you could learn more about how the business works. You know, furthering your education. Christ, it's freezing in here," he said. He closed the closet door and, wearing nothing but his briefs, got into bed.

Miranda frowned. "Is this my mother's idea?"

Frankie pulled the covers up over his chest, took a cigarette from the pack on the bedside table, lit it, and said, "No, it's my idea. Don't you want to?"

Miranda hesitated a moment, as if weighing the consequences, then said, "Yes."

"You don't have to if you don't want to. I'm not trying to force you into . . ." He hesitated, looking for the correct word. *"Anything,"* he continued. "I mean. If you'd rather sit around here all day, reading . . ."

"No, I'd like to work. I'd really like to. I think it's a good idea."

Frankie nodded, and said, "You should call your mother and talk to her about it."

"I will. Tomorrow."

Miranda went into the bathroom, and Frankie began to read. He was up to Act Three of *Hamlet.* Shakespeare wasn't easy for him. A lot of it he missed. Sometimes he couldn't even understand the explanatory footnotes. But even when the meaning escaped him, Frankie responded to the language. He could hear its music. And when he finished a play, no matter what his level of comprehension, or of enjoyment, his sense of accomplishment was more than mere satisfaction. He felt virtuous. He felt full of grace.

That night, he had to struggle harder than usual to concentrate. Under the words of the play, distracting him, ran the sound of water, Miranda washing her face and brushing her teeth, the toilet flushing. When she returned, she opened the drawer in the bedside table, took out a half-smoked joint, rummaged for a match, lit it, and climbed into bed, careful to keep to her side. "I don't know why," said Frankie, stubbing out his cigarette, "he just doesn't kill him."

Miranda took a drag of the joint and offered it to Frankie. "Kill who?"

"Claudius."

Miranda thought a moment, then said, "He's not sure he's guilty."

"Of course he's sure." Frankie held the joint, considering whether or not to take any. Oh, what the hell, he thought, and took a drag. "His father told him."

"The *ghost* of his father," corrected Miranda.

"The same thing," said Frankie.

"Would you believe what a ghost told you, just like that, without proof?"

Frankie considered that, then said, "I don't believe in ghosts." Miranda started to giggle. "What?" said Frankie.

"Maybe Hamlet doesn't either."

Frankie laughed. "I never thought of that," he said. He continued reading, taking occasional puffs of the joint. When he got to the end of the act, he closed the book, put it back on the bedside table, and turned to Miranda. "That any good?" he asked, feeling relaxed, almost happy, with his cock pushing against his briefs, trying to make an escape.

"Yes." She was reading a collection of stories by Philip Roth. He buried his face in her neck, and she said, "I want to finish this."

His hand traced the line of her leg, found the hem of her nightgown and slid underneath. "Go on," he said. "Don't let me stop you." His hand traveled back up her leg. When it reached her waist, Miranda shifted slightly, freeing the fabric, giving him access to her breasts. Her breath caught as he touched her nipples, but her eyes never looked up from the book.

"Is it a long story?"

"Not very."

He took her perfect earlobe between his teeth, and bit gently. He ran his tongue into the caverns of her ear. Her breathing changed tempo, but still she kept reading, even as he slipped his hand under the elastic of her panties, across her belly, down between her legs. Finally, she closed the book and dropped it to the floor beside the bed. "You liked it?" he said, moving his finger inside her.

"Yes."

"Better than this?"

She put her arms around his neck and looked into his face. "I don't understand you, Frankie."

"I don't understand me neither," he said.

"Do you still love me?"

"Yes," he said. "Sure. You know I do." Christ, he thought, I love you so much it hurts. Miranda pulled up her nightgown and took it off over her head. She tugged at his briefs, following their path down his body with her mouth. Do you love *me*? he wanted to ask. But he didn't. Instead, he put his hand on the back of her head and, as her lips enclosed him, he pretended that she was giving him the only answer that mattered.

*M*iranda called her mother; Eva spoke to Russell Schneider; and Miranda went to work for the grand sum of seventy-five dollars a week, to be reduced to fifty in January, when she started school and cut back on hours. On her second day of work, she was late getting home.

Vic, who was playing Haemon in a production of *Antigone* that was set to open at the Fourth Street Theater the following month, had stopped by after rehearsals. As they sat drinking beer and watching *Manhunt,* Frankie kept checking his watch. Through the doors leading out to the garden, he could see the snow falling in lazy patterns, covering the dead grass and broken bits of slate with a thickening blanket of soft white flakes. It's the weather, he thought: that's what's delaying her. Finally, hoping to distract himself with someone else's problems, he said. "You hear anything from Maria?"

Vic looked away from the television screen, and said, "Yeah. She's dating someone, a local guy." He shrugged. "It's just as well," he said. "I couldn't see it working out between us." He took another swallow of beer and continued, "Anyway, I've got this thing going with Elaine Stiller. She's playing Antigone. She's the girl we saw in that *Twilight Zone* episode a couple of weeks ago."

"Christ," said Frankie. "She's a knockout."

"Yeah," agreed Vic. He didn't sound thrilled. "No talent, though. Can't act. You don't know how lucky you are, to be finished with all this dating shit."

Frankie wanted to tell him about his problems with Miranda. He wanted to ask Vic's advice, ask him what *he* would do; but he was afraid—afraid he would look like a fool; afraid he would seem weak, frightened; afraid he might cry. "Yeah," he said. "Real lucky." Sometimes Frankie had the feeling that he and his cousin were talking in code, each waiting for the other to understand the hidden message, the secret question, waiting for the other to deliver the answer.

The door opened and Miranda flew in, her hat caked with snow, drifts of it lying in the cuffs of her coat, flakes melting on her lashes. "It's lovely out," she announced, taking off her coat, and boots. She kissed Vic's cheek and Frankie's mouth.

"You're late," said Frankie, despite his resolution not to mention it.

"I couldn't get a taxi. I had to take a bus home."

"You planning to take taxis back and forth to work every day?" said Vic, laughing.

"I hate the subway," she said. "The bus isn't bad, if you're not in a hurry."

"You oughtta have a drink," said Frankie. "Warm you up."

"Ugh," she murmured, collapsing into a chair. "Well, maybe a little. I'm so cold. How are rehearsals going?" she asked Vic as Frankie got up to get her a scotch.

"Lousy. Which is about right for this point in the proceedings. And how's work?"

"Terrific," said Miranda. "Well, a lot of it is really boring, I suppose. I mean, I answer the phones, do some filing, fill out insurance forms. I'm supposed to help with all the paperwork. But today Todd Manheim came in. Do you remember him, Frankie?"

Handing her the drink, he said, "He's the guy who really knows how to use green. According to Joan, anyway." He turned to Vic. "He's a painter."

Miranda laughed, then took a small sip of scotch, grimaced at the taste, and said, "He stopped by today to talk to Russell about plans for his show. It's in April."

Frankie forced his face into an expression of amiable interest. He had pushed Miranda into a world he couldn't be part of, and he didn't like it. He didn't like it at all.

"The three of us went to the Plaza for a drink. That's why I'm late. Todd brought Polaroids of his paintings. We were trying to decide which to use on the announcements."

"You've worked there two days and they're asking your opinion already?" said Frankie, with more of an edge than he intended.

"I've known Todd for years," said Miranda. "And Russell. And I do know a little about the subject."

"Don't forget," said Vic, lightly, sensing the tension in the air and trying to relieve it, "she's the boss's daughter. That counts."

"No," said Frankie. "She *is* the boss."

Catching Vic's quick, questioning look to Frankie, Miranda said, "The gallery's mine. My father left it to me. That's my big, dark secret. And why my husband's mad at me. I forgot to mention it to him."

"I'm not mad," said Frankie, forcing a grin. He stood. "What are we going to do about food? Go out, or send out?"

"I'm not moving from this chair," said Miranda.

"Pizza," said Vic. "I'm dying for a pizza."

"Pizza it is," said Frankie, going to the phone, thinking about his mother, and how she always had dinner ready when his father got home from work:

spaghetti, rigatoni, ziti, veal cutlets, eggplant parmigiana, pot roast, chicken cacciatore. "What does everyone want on it?" he asked.

$\mathcal{T}$he following night, still working an early shift, Frankie again arrived home before Miranda. As he opened the apartment door, he heard the phone ringing. It was Eva. "She should be here any minute. I'll get her to call you," he said quickly, anxious to get off the phone. He'd come to the conclusion that there was no such thing as an innocent (or safe) conversation with his mother-in-law.

"I want you both to come for Christmas," she said with the presumption of someone used to getting her own way.

"Sorry," said Frankie. "We can't. We're spending Christmas with my family."

"Joan is coming home," continued Eva, as if Frankie hadn't spoken. "Philip and his wife will be joining us. I wanted us all to be together."

What you want is for me to be at the bottom of Boston Harbor, thought Frankie. He took the package of cigarettes out of his shirt pocket, shook one out into his mouth, and lit it. "I'm sorry about that. Sorry you'll be disappointed."

"Don't you think you should discuss this with Miranda?"

"We already discussed it."

"I know she'll want to see her brother and sister." Eva's voice was growing harder, colder, with every word.

"Yeah, well, I'm sure they can work that out," he said.

"Frankie, I must say I think you're being extremely unreasonable."

Unreasonable? he wanted to scream. Me! "I'm sorry you feel that way," he said.

"I hope you're not still upset about our little conversation. I hope you're not holding a grudge."

He took a deep drag on his cigarette. "We made these arrangements for Christmas weeks ago," he said, exhaling, watching the thread of smoke lift and curl and vanish. If only words would do that, he thought.

"I only told you because I felt it was in Miranda's best interests, and yours, as it happens."

"Do you want me to have Miranda phone you when she gets home?"

"You're impossible," snapped Eva. "Yes, have her call me," she added, and slammed down the receiver.

"Merry Christmas," said Frankie, pleased with himself, feeling powerful, if exhausted, as if he'd come off the victor in a duel.

The elation lasted until he told Miranda about the conversation. "I told her we couldn't go," he said. "She wants you to call her."

"I'm not going to call her," said Miranda, hanging her coat up in the hall closet.

"Just tell her what I did. That we're busy."

"I'm not going to call her," repeated Miranda, going into the kitchen. "What do you want for dinner?"

Frankie followed her. "It's no big deal," he said.

"Ha!" She opened the refrigerator, looked into the meat drawer, took out a package of chopped steak. "Hamburgers or meat loaf?" she asked.

"Meat loaf," said Frankie.

Miranda put the package on the counter, along with an egg, an onion, a jar of tomato sauce. She pushed a head of lettuce and some tomatoes toward him, then took a bowl from the cupboard and emptied the chopped meat into it. "Get the rice, would you? And hand me the oatmeal," she said. The recipe was on the box.

He got both boxes down from the shelf, put them on the counter in front of her, and said, "Do you *want* to go to Boston for Christmas?"

"No."

"Then, for chrissake, call your mother and tell her so." Miranda shook her head. "She'll blame me, if you don't call her."

"I'll write her a note."

"Why are you so scared of her?"

"I don't know," said Miranda. She began to slice the onion and tears filled her eyes. She brushed them away and looked at Frankie, "Until I married you, I either did what she said, or sneaked behind her back. I guess I just don't know how to fight her."

"It's not so hard," he said. He watched as she added the onion to the meat, the egg, the tomato sauce, the oatmeal, some salt and pepper. "What kind of stuff did you do behind her back?" he asked finally, hoping he sounded only casually interested, as if he were asking her nothing more important than where she'd spent her summers as a kid.

"Nothing much," said Miranda, looking at him, smiling a little. She turned the meat loaf into a Pyrex dish. "Drink, smoke a little dope. Nothing important."

"Did she know you were fucking your boyfriends?" He wished even as he said it that he'd cut out his tongue first.

She recoiled as if he had slapped her. "I didn't." She hesitated, and then continued, "There was one. That's all."

Were you in love with him? he wanted to ask. Do you still love him?

"Did your mother know about the girls *you* were fucking?" It was the first time he'd ever heard her use an obscene word.

Frankie moved behind her, slipped his arms around her waist, and kissed the back of her neck. "I'm sorry," he said. "I didn't mean that the way it sounded." She nodded, and slipped out of his grasp to wash her hands at the sink. "Miranda—"

"I don't want to fight with you, Frankie. All right? Not tonight. Not ever. Why don't you make the salad?" she said.

$$Chapter\ 12$$

$\mathcal{M}$iranda had classes Inauguration Day so Frankie sat alone in front of the television, eating a ham sandwich, drinking beer, watching John Fitzgerald Kennedy, without overcoat or hat, looking handsome, debonair, take the Oath of Office. Frankie liked the inaugural address. "Ask not what your country can do for you," said Kennedy, "but what you can do for your country." It reminded him of the St. Crispian's Day speech from *Henry V*, which he'd just finished reading. I'd like to do something, Frankie thought, something significant, something important. But what? As always, his mind drew a blank.

Now that she'd started at Barnard, Miranda worked at the gallery only on Tuesdays after class and all day Saturday. Though mutually agreed, the schedule left Frankie feeling irritable and restless, especially on his own days off. With Miranda busy, Vic doing matinee and evening performances of *Antigone,* and his own variable schedule at the club, Frankie had too much time alone in which to think, and none of what he thought made him happy. What he needed was a regular job, nine to five, so he could be at home when Miranda was. The want ads in *The Times,* however, presented no new solutions to the old problem. He still wasn't qualified for any job he wanted to do. Like hitting my head against a brick wall, he thought. But he didn't lose faith. One of these days he would get the chance he was looking for; and, when he did, he would take it. It was just that waiting sometimes depressed the hell out of him.

"You sure all this isn't too much for you?" he asked Miranda one Saturday morning before she left for the gallery. "I don't want you wearing yourself out."

"I'm not. I feel great." She got up from the table, leaving him to clear the breakfast dishes, and went to the hall closet. As she buttoned herself into her cashmere coat, she said suddenly, "You haven't changed your mind about my working, Frankie, have you?" She looked worried, and her voice had a puzzled, anxious note.

"No," he said guiltily. "Not as long as you feel you can handle it."

He didn't know what to do with himself, how to use up all his free time, all his excess energy. After reading for a while, he would start getting jumpy. When that happened, he would consider going to Macklin's to work out, and decide against it. He didn't want Pat, or anyone else, knowing he had no better way to spend his day off. Instead, he would take long walks along slush-filled streets, browse in bookstores, go to a movie. His cigarette consumption increased to two packs a day, and he developed a cold he couldn't shake. Then, in the same week, Mrs. Coro asked him to do some work on the newly vacant third-floor apartment, and Pat's doctor diagnosed angina and advised him to ease up on his schedule, leaving Frankie and the other trainers to fill in for him.

Frankie had done occasional plumbing and electrical jobs for Mrs. Coro, but nothing big. Unsure of himself, he worked slowly, in his much-reduced spare time. She didn't seem to mind. She trusted him and that mattered more to her than speed. He scraped the floors, then stained and polished them. He laid new linoleum in the kitchen. He replaced the plumbing fixtures in the bathroom and regrouted the tile. He patched the peeling plaster, scraped the windowsills, painted the ceilings and walls. It took him over a month, by the end of which time most of Eva's venom had worked itself out of his system. His cold went; and, instead of brief exchanges, soon he was having something like real conversations with his wife. He was feeling almost happy.

"How about it?" he said to Miranda, showing her around. "Not bad for someone without a clue what he's doing."

"It's great," she said.

"When we buy a house, I can do all the repairs myself."

"Maybe I should learn to sew," said Miranda, smiling. "I could make curtains."

"You could make clothes for all our kids," he said, getting into the fantasy.

"All?"

"How many do you want? Two, three, four?"

"Children," said Miranda. "You know, I can't really imagine having any at all."

"That's because," said Frankie, putting his arms around her, nuzzling his face into her neck, "you're still a kid yourself." She just turned twenty, he reminded himself, feeling years older, and far more mature. There was all of nineteen months between them.

Miranda returned his kiss, then eased herself out of his arms, walked across to the window, and looked out at Tenth Street for a minute before turning back to him. "They can be such little nuisances," she said, in a voice that suddenly resembled Eva's.

What must it have been like having Eva for a mother instead of Dolly, Frankie wondered, being treated all the time like a pest, instead of the most wonderful creature ever to have graced the earth? "I guess some people just can't stand kids," he said, deciding not to drag the witch of Boston into the conversation. "But you're great with them. Look at the way you love playing with Sean and little Dennis. You've got more patience with them than any-body."

"My mother always says it's much easier being nice to other people's."

"You're mother's full of shit," said Frankie, forgetting his good intention. Though he'd spent a lot of time recently questioning the assumptions he'd grown up with, never had he thought to ask himself what he really felt about having children. That he had taken for granted. Now, faced with Miranda's reluctance, he knew how important it was to him. He liked children; he wanted children; he wanted a son. His reaction wasn't rational, but instinc-tive. In his world, married couples who didn't have children, like his Uncle Charlie and Aunt Theresa, were to be pitied. And though the reason for their childlessness wasn't discussed, Frankie knew choice had had nothing to do with it. As Dolly would have said, it was God's will, not theirs. A wave of panic hit him. Miranda's world always seemed like a foreign country to him. He was never be sure of its customs. Could they be that different? "You do want kids?" he asked.

Miranda hesitated, then said, "Yes. Of course, I do. But I want to finish school first. Eventually . . ." She walked toward him across the newly pol-ished floor and stepped into his arms. "You don't want them right away, do you?"

"No," said Frankie, locking his arms around her, aware of their strength, knowing he could force her body to do anything his wanted, wishing he had that much power over her mind, and her heart, so that he could control her every whim, her every longing. "But someday."

*D*uring semester break at the end of February, Dan came to New York for a few days and stayed again with Frankie and Miranda. Before his arrival, Frankie worried that their relationship might have changed in the months since they'd last seen each other. With Dan at Yale, walking the path of privilege, and himself at Macklin's, heading nowhere in particular, with the army a fading memory, he was afraid that the bond between them would have weakened, that they would have as little to say to one another as he and Jimmy Loughlin now did. But within minutes of Dan's arrival, Frankie knew that everything was fine, that the friendship had held. It occurred to him how alone he would feel without Dan and Vic in his life. Having a wife was great, but a guy needed friends. He needed someone to talk to, discuss business with, politics, yack about sports. Though she tried, Miranda wasn't really all that interested in baseball.

They took Dan to *Antigone,* which they'd seen before on opening night, and afterward went with Vic to a Chinese restaurant, where they discussed the play, the production, Vic's performance, all of which Frankie had found interesting, if not the theatrical experience of a lifetime. The next night, Vic arranged house seats for them for *Camelot,* and afterward Dan bought him a bottle of Dom Perignon, in gratitude, he said, for Richard Burton. "Did you see him play Caliban on television a couple of years ago?" asked Vic.

No one had. A couple of years ago, admitted Frankie to himself, he would have run for cover if anyone had suggested he watch a play by William Shakespeare.

"He was great," said Vic, his voice tinged with envy. "Ugly as sin, full of self-pity and malevolence, sexy as hell, and very moving. It was some performance."

The three of them went to see *The Threepenny Opera,* the Matisse exhibit at the Met, the New York City Ballet do *Afternoon of a Faun,* his first and last ballet, Frankie insisted when it was over. For that, he knew, he would never acquire a taste.

On Dan's first visit to Macklin's for a workout, Pat Walewski looked him over and said, "You ain't in bad shape," he said. "Play any sports?" When Dan told him golf, Pat almost choked on his cigar butt. "You gotta be kiddin' me."

"What's wrong with golf?" said Dan, delivering the show of irritation he felt was expected.

"Don't get me wrong, kid," said Pat. "I know sports, and I know golf ain't easy. But it ain't baseball. For chrissake, it ain't football!"

Dan laughed, and neglected to mention that he was playing golf for Yale.

One night, leaving Miranda to write a paper on somebody called Rogier van der Weyden, Frankie and Dan went to Shea Stadium to watch the Jets pulverize the Raiders, stopping off afterward at the Hungry Lion for a drink. When he returned from phoning Miranda, Frankie noticed the three girls at a nearby table, swaying in time to "Angel Baby," all in clinging black outfits, heavy gold necklaces and earrings, penciled lines around their eyes like in pictures of the ancient Egyptians at the Met. One smiled encouragingly. "Just like old times," said Frankie.

"Not exactly," said Dan. "You call home these days."

"Don't let me cramp your style, man," said Frankie.

"Don't worry. You won't." Dan was no longer seeing Caitlin, who was engaged to be married, all plans for college now on permanent hold; but there was a girl in New Haven he dated, and another in Boston. He wasn't in love, and didn't want to be, yet.

Frankie picked up his stein, took a swallow of beer, and said, "Can you restrain yourself long enough to give me some advice?"

"I can try, but it won't be easy." Dan nodded in the direction of a woman sitting on her own, reading a copy of *Le Figaro*. Her face, free of makeup, was beautiful, with full lips, a strong nose, and dark eyes fringed by heavy lashes. Strands of blue-black hair fell carelessly from a knot held in a tortoise-shell clip. She wore a rust-colored sweater and tweed pants, a splash of color in the prevailing black. "What's up?" he said.

"Pat's talking about retiring."

"You're kidding. He looks like the type who'd rather die than stop working."

"He's got heart trouble. A couple of weeks ago, he had some kind of attack. Scared the shit out of him. He's decided to move to Florida."

"So," said Dan, forcing his mind away from the woman in the rust sweater and onto Frankie's problem, "you think you're going to lose your job?"

"Not exactly," said Frankie. "I mean, that could happen, yeah. But that's not what's worrying me. I'm thinking I should take over the franchise." When he'd first thought of it, the idea had seemed crazy to him. Running a health club wasn't what he'd pictured doing with his life. Working there had had been a stopgap measure, a way to earn money until he figured out how to qualify for the kind of job he wanted, the kind that combined high pay with lots of glamour and prestige, the kind that Stanfield Morrow might consider taking. But months had passed, and Frankie was no closer than before to having the necessary qualifications for those jobs. He hadn't found any shortcut to success—unless this was it. Buying Macklin's might not be the opportunity he wanted, but it was the one that was there, and Frankie had started to think he'd better take it.

Dan smiled ruefully. "I don't know what to tell you, Frankie. I don't know anything about that kind of business. About any kind of business."

"Neither do I. That's the trouble."

"How much would it cost?" Frankie told him. "You have that kind of money?"

Frankie shook his head. "I figured I could get a loan from a bank. I want an accountant to check things over. And my father. But it's a good business. It's making money. Pat let me take a look at the books."

"What does your father think?"

"I haven't said anything to him yet. You know my father. . . ."

"No," corrected Dan, "actually I haven't met him."

"Well, actually," mimicked Frankie, "next time you're in town I'll arrange it. But his reaction to anything I do is that I'm out of my mind. I just want to be sure of myself before I tackle him, sure this is really something I want."

"If it's a good business . . ." Dan shrugged, as much out of his depth as Frankie. He considered the issue a minute, then said, "Miranda's got the money her father left her. She could probably help you out with this."

"No," said Frankie, sharply. "I don't want money from Miranda."

"Most people I know aren't so fussy about where their stake comes from," said Dan, more amused than impressed by what his mother would call Frankie's "moral rectitude." "Well, what about a small investment from me?"

Frankie felt an unfamiliar surge of resentment. Dan's life was so easy, so secure, so *privileged*. Everything just fell into place for him. "That's not why I wanted to talk to you," said Frankie, sounding embarrassed, almost angry.

"You think I don't know that? But why not let me in, if you think it's such a good deal."

The wave of resentment receded, but still Frankie didn't reply. He just sat, shaking his head. Then he said, "I'm not sure why. I just don't feel comfortable about it." His refusal had been instinctive, competitive. He wanted to mark a separate territory, one where he had total control. "But thanks, Dan. I appreciate the offer. I really do."

They ordered another round of beers and a couple of cheeseburgers and sat not so much discussing the pros and cons of the plan as letting Frankie vent his dreams and anxieties: the golden opportunity he felt Pat's retirement presented to him versus the difficulty of raising money and the not-to-be-dismissed possibility of the business's failing.

"I feel I should grab it," said Frankie, finally. "I feel it in my gut."

"Then do it," said Dan. The flutter of a rust-clad arm distracted him. The woman was signaling for her bill. He turned his attention resolutely back to his friend. Smiling, he said, "What have you got to lose except your shirt?"

"Yeah," said Frankie, grinning, "What the hell?" He pulled a wad of bills from his pocket and peeled off enough to pay the tab. "You staying?"

"I'm not sure," said Dan, watching as the woman slipped into her coat and started across the restaurant. As she passed their table, he smiled. She nodded absently, not quite registering him, then continued on out the door. "I guess not," he said. "I guess I'm going home early like an old married man."

*D*an left to spend the weekend with his parents before returning to school. And on Saturday, with Miranda safely at work, Frankie drove to Midford. Embarrassingly, his mother treated him like visiting royalty, and his father as if he were a stranger. He felt like a stranger. It was hard for him to believe that he had ever lived in this house, with these people, that he had once been happy here.

"Why didn't Miranda come?" asked Dolly.

"She's working," said Frankie, earning a frown from both parents. He didn't react. Neither really disapproved, he knew; in fact they were probably grateful that Miranda wasn't at home and pregnant. And if they considered their son too young, and too broke, to bring children into the world, well, he felt pretty much the same way himself.

Lunch was sandwiches of leftover meatballs served on fresh Italian bread, followed by Entenmann's cheese cake from the A&P and strong Bokar coffee. The black Bokar tin had been a staple in the Ferraro refrigerator for as long as Frankie could remember. "If you'd've called earlier," said Dolly, "I would've made something special."

"It's fine, Ma. The meatballs were delicious." When they finished dessert, he turned to his father, and said, "Pop, can I talk to you alone for a minute?"

"Is everything all right?" said Dolly, always quick to worry.

"Fine, Ma. Everything's great. I've just got some business to talk over with Pop."

Relieved, Dolly smiled. "You two go ahead then. I'll clean up in here. Call me if you want anything," she added as the two men started out of the room.

Sal led the way down to the den, sat in the recliner, put his feet up, and looked at Frankie. "So?" he said. Frankie explained about Pat's retiring and about the franchise. He outlined for his father the cost, what the possible return would be on the investment, what the bank had said when he called about a loan. He presented everything in as positive a light as he could manage, holding his own fears firmly in check, painting Macklin's Health Club as the goose about to lay a golden egg for Frankie Ferraro. And still Sal sat there shaking his head.

"Why are you shaking your head?" said Frankie. He had known his father would react like this, but still it annoyed the hell out of him.

"Going into business is risky."

"You did it."

"Times was different."

"They were worse," said Frankie.

"Oh, I don't know about that. This economy don't look too good to me."

"It's an opportunity I don't want to pass up."

"You're so anxious to go into business, what about the offer I made you?" said Sal, taking what he suspected might be his last shot at bringing his son back under his control. "You come in with me, you got a guaranteed sure thing."

"I want to do something on my own, Pop."

Sal sat forward in his chair and glared at Frankie. "You're only twenty-one, for chrissake. You're a goddamn kid."

"It's important to me. Anyway, I'll be twenty-two in a couple of months."

"An old man," said Sal, leaning back and closing his eyes. Frankie waited. Finally, Sal opened his eyes. "Okay, you made up your mind. What d'ya want from me?"

Frankie felt the tension drain out of his body. "A couple of things," he said, trying to relax into the hard pillows of the Ethan Allen tweed couch. "I'm going to have an accountant check the books, but I want you to have a look at them, too, just to be sure I've got the story straight. And I need you to co-sign the loan."

"I'll give you the money," said Sal. "I got it."

"Thanks, Pop. But it'll be fine if you just co-sign the loan."

"You think I'd've turned down money from my father, if he'd've had it?" said Sal belligerently. "You kids don't know how damn lucky you are."

"I'm grateful, Pop. Really. I just want to do this on my own." He smiled. "At least, as much on my own as I can."

Sal took a moment to assess the situation, his annoyance with his son for always refusing well-intentioned offers receding before his pleasure that Frankie still welcomed his advice. "Okay," he said, "I'll check the books. I'll sign the loan."

*W*hen Frankie got home, Miranda was watching the news, a textbook open in her lap. Frankie dropped onto the couch next to her and kissed her neck. "Miss me?"

"Uh-huh," she said. "Where were you?"

A blur of bright color caught his eye, and he looked down at the textbook. "We saw that someplace. At the Frick." He looked up again at Miranda and she nodded. "It's by . . ." He searched his memory. "Holbein."

"Uh-huh," she said again, not nearly so impressed with his memory as he was. "Did you eat?"

"Lunch. With my parents. We had leftover meatballs," he said.

"You went to Midford?" He nodded. She looked annoyed. "I haven't seen your parents in weeks. Couldn't you have waited for me to go with you tomorrow?"

"I had a couple of things I wanted to talk over with my father."

"What things?"

It didn't occur to Frankie that Miranda was sounding very like a wife, which was too bad because he would have liked that. Instead, she reminded him of his mother and he got annoyed. "What are you getting upset about?"

"I'm not upset. I just think you could have waited for me."

"I'm sorry. I didn't know you'd mind."

"I like your parents. And they like me. Didn't they think it was peculiar I wasn't with you?"

"For chrissake, they don't think we're joined at the hip, Miranda."

She closed the textbook, dropped it on the table, and got up. She walked into the bathroom and closed the door. All the anger drained out of Frankie. He followed her, and when she didn't reply to his knock, he turned the knob and walked in. Miranda was at the sink, smearing her face and neck with cleansing lotion.

"I'm sorry," he said. Without replying, she reached for a tissue and wiped the cream from her face. Frankie closed the toilet seat and sat down. "I'm kind of jumpy right now."

"I've noticed," she said. She soaked a cotton ball in astringent and stroked it across her face.

"Pat's retiring."

Miranda turned from the mirror and looked at him. "It's not a problem," she said reassuringly, all the irritation gone from her voice. "We still have your savings. And there's my money. We'll be fine until you find something else."

"I'm thinking of buying the franchise."

"You're what?"

"It's a good business. It makes money. It's a way to get started."

"Oh," she said, turning away from him. She opened another bottle of lotion and smoothed some into her skin.

"What do you think?"

"Is that what you wanted to talk to your father about?" Frankie nodded. "Don't you think you should have discussed it with me first?"

"Maybe." Suddenly, he felt guilty, embarrassed. He'd been wrong and he knew it. "I didn't want to worry you, until I was sure what I wanted to do."

"I discuss everything with you."

"Do you?" he said. All the pain of weeks of worrying was back in his voice. Again, she turned away from him, picked up her brush, and began to run it through her hair. He stood and moved behind her, slipping his arms around her waist, burying his face in her hair. "I love you."

"Why don't you trust me?" she said.

"I guess I can't believe you love *me*."

She turned around in his arms and looked up at him. "I do," she said, "when you let me." She kissed him. "Buy the franchise, if that's what you want. If that will make you happy. Is that what your father said?"

"Eventually."

"I want you to be happy."

"Just love me," he said. "Just love me and I'll be happy."

Chapter 13

The gallery was crowded, noisy, and hot. The women were expensive, brightly colored, polished to a high sheen, their lacquered hair curling sleekly around their ears. They smelled of flowers. The men were rich, smooth, impressive in superbly tailored suits, their hair worn full and unbrilliantined in honor of the president's envied mop. Todd Manheim's opening was exactly the kind of party Frankie had once dreamed of attending. Now he grabbed another glass of the champagne he hated from the tray of a passing waiter and wished he were anywhere but here.

Things weren't going as he'd imagined. He wasn't the center of an admiring circle; he didn't have a large stock of intelligent and witty comments to dispense; in fact, he couldn't think of much to say when anybody bothered to address him. The adolescent awkwardness he had managed to avoid by virtue of his looks, his manners, his total acceptance in the homogeneous circle then surrounding him, Frankie now felt with a vengeance. It was obvious to him, and probably everyone else, that he wasn't in his proper element, wherever that was these days. He wondered how much longer he would have to stay.

Within minutes of their arrival, Miranda had abandoned him to a wax-model couple to make stilted conversation while she flitted like a parrot in a bright green suit from group to group—her job to charm the guests (many of whom she had known since childhood), answer questions, encourage sales, *not* to make sure that her husband enjoyed himself. Frankie understood that. So, as she swept past him an hour later, on her way to check the supply of canapés, he told her he was having a great time. "You don't look it," she said, sounding both concerned and harried.

He smiled at her reassuringly. "It's the paintings. Every time I look at them I feel sick to my stomach."

In her peripheral vision, Miranda caught Russell signaling to her. "I've got to go," she said. "Are you sure you're all right? I've got some stuff in my purse."

"I should've known, seeing what a good time you're having."

"Let me know if you want any," she said, moving away toward Russell.

Frankie stood by himself, trying not to feel like a wallflower, listening to the conversations around him, replaying the dialogue in his head, repeating the inflections of words and phrases he particularly liked, polishing his accent as he took stock of the room.

Across from him, Hugo Helm, someone Frankie recognized from the business pages of *The New York Times,* stood with Todd Manheim, studying one of the paintings, a studious frown furrowing the perfect Palm Beach tan of Helm's face. He gestured toward the canvas, seeming to point out to Manheim something that particularly intrigued him, and Frankie wondered if he was going to buy it. It was a large painting, of broad stripes in green and brown, and Frankie found it one of the more hideous in the show. According to the price list he had seen, that size canvas was selling for ten thousand dollars.

A few feet away from Helm and Manheim, Helen Frankenthaler was talking to Craig Colvington. Nelson Clewes, a pretty young boy in tow, was working his way around the room. Robert Moses, the city's esteemed master planner, was with someone Frankie didn't recognize, though he had seen Eva greet him with a kiss. But then, Eva had greeted everyone with a kiss, except Frankie. He had kept out of her way.

Eva was now deep in conversation with John Lindsay, listening as the handsome, blue-eyed mayor confided to her something that, judging from the rapt expression on her face, she must have found intensely interesting. The mayor obviously found *her* fascinating, watching her with frank appreciation as they talked. Frankie, on the other hand, eyed Eva with distaste. As usual, she looked rich, elegant, even beautiful, he conceded grudgingly, in a black evening suit with a brilliant diamond pin on its lapel. Several times since his arrival she'd attempted to speak to him, but each time he'd managed to evade her long enough for someone else to capture her attention. He didn't want to say more to her than good night if he could help it.

"Don't you know anyone here?" said a voice at his side.

Frankie turned and smiled at a rail-thin woman with light brown skin and sleek black hair, wearing a tentlike white dress trimmed in gold amulets. She was almost as tall as he, and strikingly beautiful. "My wife," he said, "but she's busy."

"So is my husband." She smiled at him, held out her hand, and said, "Kalima Burden." Her eyes reminded him of his mother's chocolate cream pie, a rich, luminous brown, set in clear white pupils, fringed by thick, dark lashes. Her nose was narrow and straight, her cheekbones prominent and high, her full mouth pouting over perfect teeth.

Frankie told her his name and shook her hand. "You look familiar," he said.

"Oh, I don't think we've met. I'm sure we'd both remember it." Her accent was strange, English, yet not quite.

"Are you a model?"

"No. Are you?"

"No," said Frankie quickly, uncomfortable with the idea.

"How wonderful. We have something in common."

Frankie laughed and looked around the room, wondering where her husband was.

"Am I making you nervous?"

"No," said Frankie, startled. "I was just wondering who you're married to."

Kalima pointed to a tall, fair-haired man with a slight stoop, wearing a pinstriped suit. "There," she said, "talking to Robert Moses. My husband, Nigel. Actually, *Sir* Nigel. And I, to be absolutely correct about it, am Lady Burden."

"Oh," said Frankie, impressed in spite of himself.

"It's not an hereditary title. My husband was knighted last year. He's in publishing, book publishing, which is how we know the Colvingtons. Craig's brother is a publisher. Do you know the Colvingtons?"

"Yes," said Frankie. "I know them. Some of them, anyway."

"Nigel is also a collector, which is why we're here. Are you a collector?"

"No," said Frankie. Then, feeling he owed something in payment for all of Kalima Burden's information, he said, "I'm married to Miranda Payson. Well, she's actually Miranda Ferraro now. We've been married six months."

"Newlyweds," said Kalima, her eyes scanning the room for Miranda, who'd joined Eva and the mayor. "She's very beautiful."

"So are you," said Frankie. "Where the hell are you from? I can't figure out your accent."

"Egypt," said Kalima. She smiled, and added, "My family likes to pretend that Cleopatra was an ancestor. It's always a good thing to be descended from royalty, if one's income is limited."

A waiter passed by and Frankie put his empty glass on the tray, took two more, and handed one to Kalima. He was beginning to feel lightheaded. " 'Other women cloy/The appetites they feed, but she makes hungry/Where most she satisfies,' " he said. The lines reminded him of Miranda, and so he'd remembered them. "Cleopatra," he added, "was supposed to be short and fat." He'd read that in some gloss of the play.

"No," said Kalima, surprise and profound disappointment combining in her voice.

"Yes. Short and fat, but charismatic."

"I detest that word." She took a canapé from an offered tray and bit into it. "These days, every television personality and hack politician is described as charismatic."

"How about intriguing? sexy?"

"Good," said Kalima. She smiled. "All good."

If my father could see me now . . . thought Frankie, deep in conversation with a dark, exotic beauty. He realized suddenly that he was enjoying himself.

Her father had been assigned for many years to the Egyptian embassy in England, Kalima told him, and she'd been educated there at a private girls' school, then at Oxford, graduating with a first in history.

"What's that?"

"Very good."

"Then you know all about Cleopatra." He was suddenly afraid that he'd made a fool of himself.

"Well, I do actually. Not that I believe she was at all fat," she said, smiling warmly, her tone soothing, depriving her words of sting. "I try not to let men know how smart I am. I'm afraid they won't like me. But then I can't help myself. I can't resist showing off a little. Sometimes I marvel that I ever found a man to marry me."

"You've got to be kidding," said Frankie. Kalima laughed. "You are kidding." Maybe she was deliberately trying to make him feel like an idiot.

The laughter faded from Kalima's face. She put her hand on Frankie's arm and looked into his eyes, her own seeming to melt into sweet dark pools. "Pay no attention to me," she said. "I'm a terrible tease. I didn't mean to hurt your feelings."

"You didn't," he said, feeling the blush travel up his neck, into his face. Needing to cut whatever bond linked them at that moment, he looked away, and found himself staring directly at Miranda. He smiled feebly. She frowned and returned her attention to the supply of champagne she was discussing with one of the waiters. "I never went to college," Frankie continued. It wasn't something he usually admitted, and he wondered why he did now.

"But you know your Shakespeare," she said kindly.

"I read."

"That's the most important thing, isn't it? To read widely, but with a purpose. Do you like the theater?"

Amazed, and relieved, that no one was attempting to claim her attention, Frankie directed Kalima through the crowd to a vacant bench. She'd been in New York for only a week with her husband, who had come on business, she told him, but in that time she'd seen five Broadway shows, the Italian drawings at the Met, the Max Ernst exhibit at the Modern, several gallery exhibitions, and had "practically bankrupted poor Nigel" at Bergdorf's. When their conversation got to Manheim, she said, "I do hope my husband doesn't buy a painting. I don't actually think I could live with any of these.

Well, if he does," she consoled herself, "he'll just have to keep it in storage with his other investments."

Frankie wanted to ask if you could make a lot of money by investing in art, but he didn't. He'd learned to let that kind of curiosity go unsatisfied.

"Trust you to be monopolizing the most beautiful woman in the room."

The familiar voice came from behind Frankie. Turning, he saw Colette Drake watching him, her eyes alight with speculation. He got to his feet and would have kissed her chastely on the cheek, except that she turned her face so quickly her lips met his. Putting an arm around her, he turned back to Kalima. "Colette Drake," he said, introducing the two women, "Kalima . . . I mean, *Lady* Burden."

Kalima rose and extended a delicate hand, its nails polished a deep mulberry to match the color on her lips. "How do you do?" she said.

"Colette," said Frankie, "is a publicist."

"I'm delighted to meet you," said Colette.

Kalima's eyes became flat, opaque, expressionless. "Oh, yes," she said, turning back to Frankie. "It's been a pleasure talking to you, but I notice my husband getting restless. It's half an hour past his usual dinnertime, and he's such a creature of habit." She reached into her small alligator bag and extracted a card. "I'm leaving tomorrow, but if you ever find yourself in London, do call." She smiled at him, nodded coolly to Colette, and moved off to claim her husband. Watching her go, Frankie felt regret, and a slight sense of loss, the way he did when he came to the end of a book he had enjoyed.

"Well," said Colette. "What were you two talking about?"

"Nothing much," said Frankie, circumspectly.

"You looked very cozy."

"Can it, will you, Colette?"

"My, my, my, temper," she said.

"You know I hate it when you start grilling me."

"A bad habit, my darling, but so hard to break. Especially since I usually learn such interesting things." Colette's smile made her look very like a cobra trying to appear friendly.

Frankie laughed. "You're too much," he said.

"I certainly hope so. Have you missed me? No, don't answer that. How could you with Miranda to keep you occupied? But you're looking marvelous, Frankie. Tell me what you've been doing with yourself."

He told her about Macklin's and his purchase of the franchise. "Another couple of weeks, and the paperwork will all be done. I'll own a business," he said, not even trying to keep the pride out of his voice.

"Congratulations," said Colette.

"It's just the beginning." Though his father saw the acquisition of Macklin's as the culmination of his son's ambition, as a business that would provide him, if he was lucky, with an income for life, Frankie knew otherwise. Though he had no idea yet what his ultimate destination would be, he was certain that Macklin's was just the starting point of his trip. "It's only the first step."

"That's the one that counts," said Colette. She put her hand on his sleeve, and feeling his biceps through the fabric, squeezed appreciatively. "Oh, Frankie," she said. "You really are a hunk." Uncomfortable, he shifted his position, moving away from her, waiting for her hand to drop. She removed it to reach for a canapé. "Sorry. I couldn't resist." She smiled at him. "I'm really very fond of you, you know."

"I like you, Colette. It's just sometimes . . ." He shook his head.

"Life must be hell for you. Women throwing themselves at you constantly."

"Would you cut it out?" Anywhere else, Frankie would have found a way to dump her, excuse himself politely, join another group, or just go, leaving Colette alone to cope as best she could with her hot pants. Those weren't, just then, reasonable options. He wouldn't go without Miranda; and he didn't want Colette to walk off, abandoning him again to the role of Invisible Man. He was stuck with her until another life rope got thrown his way. "Just cut the crap and tell me how you are."

"You know what your problem is? You don't know what a help I could be to you." Then she laughed. "As a *publicist*. Don't mind me, I'm exhausted," she said. "Endless parties. Endless meetings. Endless deadlines. I could use a week in Aruba. But I can't seem to talk my lover into taking me. His wife, silly cow, objects to his going without her."

Nelson Clewes, still trailing his pretty boy, came over to say hello. "Who was that absurdly beautiful woman you were talking to?" he said to Frankie.

"Don't tell me I've changed *that* much!"

Nelson kissed Colette's cheek, told her she looked fabulous, then turned back to Frankie for a reply. He shrugged. "I don't really know. She's married to somebody named Burden, Nigel Burden."

"Hmm," said Nelson. "The English publisher, right?"

"Right," said Colette.

As Colette eyed the handsome blond appraisingly, Nelson introduced him as the star model for his fall collection. Frankie didn't catch the name. His attention was again focused on Miranda, who was talking to a man in a navy suit. He was somewhere in his forties, ancient, only about an inch taller than she, stockily built, with a broad face, wide nose, full mouth, and brilliant blue eyes behind gold-rimmed glasses. His hair was thick, curly, and fair. Even at that distance, Frankie could see the arrogant, self-satisfied expression on his face. Miranda looked wary, unhappy.

"Who's the guy talking to Miranda?" he asked.

"Where?" said Nelson, turning.

"Greg Dyer," said Colette.

The temperature in the room seemed to plummet about twenty degrees. "Greg Dyer?" he repeated.

"A banker. From Boston. And a major collector."

"I know who he is," said Frankie. "Excuse me."

"Ugly cuss, that Dyer," said Nelson as Frankie moved away.

"But a real lady-killer," said Colette. "You know what they say, there's no aphrodisiac like intelligence."

"They're wrong," said Nelson. He smiled at his young escort. "There's no aphrodisiac like a big cock."

Colette's laugh drifted after Frankie and somehow seemed to mock him. He was headed straight for Miranda and Dyer, though he had no idea what he would say when he reached them, what he would do. Pretend not to know who Dyer was? Or punch him in the mouth and drag Miranda home by her hair?

"Frankie, you've been avoiding me."

Oh, shit, thought Frankie. He'd forgotten about Eva. "You were busy," he said brusquely, wanting to get past her to Miranda. "I didn't want to disturb you."

"Nonsense," said Eva. Turning to follow the direction of his gaze, she saw her daughter and Dyer. "Oh," she said, turning back. "I see. Well, I'm sure it's all perfectly innocent." She didn't sound sure at all.

"So am I," said Frankie, edging around her.

Eva put a restraining hand on his arm, and said, "Don't be an idiot."

"You want me to walk over you?" Frankie could feel the anger inside him bubbling hotter and hotter. Soon it would boil over.

"You really are a savage, aren't you?"

"If you was so worried about what I'd do, you should've kept your mouth shut."

"Please don't make a scene."

Eva was begging and somewhere under the rage, Frankie felt a small spark of pleasure. "Get out of my way." His voice was low, but the menace in it was unmistakable. Frightened suddenly, she stepped aside, and Frankie felt a thrill of triumph. "I won't make a scene," he promised. He didn't want to give her the satisfaction of proving himself the savage she thought him.

Miranda saw Frankie coming and composed her face into a study in tranquillity. By the time he reached her, she was smiling. "Frankie," she said, "I want you to meet a friend of mine, Gregory Dyer. Greg, my husband, Frankie Ferraro."

To Frankie, the word "husband" sounded full of satisfaction, with a hint of vindictiveness. "How do you do?" he said, trying to mimic Kalima greeting Colette. She'd done it so well, with just the right mix of manners and contempt. He was damned if he'd give this stuffed shirt the opportunity to brand him a hoodlum.

Frankie extended a hand and Dyer shook it. "Pleased to meet you," he said, not sounding at all happy about it. "Congratulations on your marriage. A little late, but nonetheless sincere."

"Thank you," said Frankie. He was taller than Dyer by at least six inches; he was younger, better looking. And, best of all, Frankie could sense his rival registering all that and not liking it.

"You took us all by surprise," he said.

"He took me by surprise," said Miranda, smiling up at Frankie as if besotted.

He put a possessive arm around her shoulders, letting his fingers stroke the green silk covering her arm. "It was love at first sight."

"For both of us," said Miranda. "It was overwhelming."

Is she telling the truth? wondered Frankie. "Is *your* wife here?" he asked, not so much curious as wanting to see what reaction he would get. He could feel Miranda flinch slightly, but the smile on her face never faltered.

Startled by the question, Dyer recovered quickly, and said, "No, she's in Boston. She doesn't like to leave the children. I'm only here through tomorrow in any case."

"Oh," said Frankie. "How old are they?"

"Quite old," said Dyer, with a laugh, uncertain where this conversation was leading. "Only two are still at home."

"Frankie's crazy about children," said Miranda. "He wants us to have lots," she added enthusiastically.

Who's the act for? he wondered.

"You're nothing but a child yourself," snapped Dyer. Then he smiled to cover the small crack in his veneer. "I've known her most of her life," he said to Frankie. "She always seemed more interested in paintings than children."

"Greg has quite a collection."

"You must have Miranda bring you by to see it next time you're in Boston," said Dyer, to Frankie, his eyes expressionless.

"Sure," said Frankie, "but we're not planning a trip anytime soon." What the fuck did she ever see in the guy? Frankie asked himself, secure for a moment in the knowledge of his own physical superiority. But maybe that wasn't what mattered to Miranda. She might need something else, something intangible, something he didn't understand, in order to love. Suddenly, Frankie felt as if all the air in the room were slowly being siphoned out. "What time do these things usually end?" he asked, turning to her.

"Soon, now. You don't have to wait for me, if you don't want to. I can take a taxi home."

"No," said Frankie. "I'll wait."

Then Craig Colvington appeared in their midst, probably sent by Eva. "Frankie," he said, "how good to see you. I must have missed you when you arrived." He barely waited to hear Frankie's mumbled hello before turning to Dyer. "Greg, can I tear you away from the newlyweds? Hugo Helm wants to meet you."

"Certainly," said Dyer, sounding relieved. He said good-bye to Frankie. "See you soon, my dear, I hope," he murmured as he kissed Miranda's cheek, sounding insincere, as if the minute he turned his back on them he would forget not only Frankie's but Miranda's existence. Frankie wasn't taken in. He knew he'd managed to get under Dyer's skin.

"He's an old friend of the family's," said Miranda, unnecessarily, as Dyer and Craig walked away.

"Yeah," said Frankie. "Eva told me."

Miranda studied his face a moment, then turned away and surveyed the room. "The crowd's thinning. Half an hour and it'll all be over."

"Okay," said Frankie.

"Well, there are a few people I should say good night to."

"Go on," said Frankie.

"You'll be all right?"

"I'm fine," said Frankie. And for the first time that night he really felt he was. He felt as if he'd scored some kind of triumph. He leaned forward and kissed Miranda lightly on the mouth. "Don't worry about me. I can take care of myself."

Chapter 14

Frankie's euphoria lasted until he got Miranda into a taxi to take her home. Then, when he slipped his arm around her to pull her close, she resisted briefly before settling into his shoulder without a word. Her body felt stiff, unyielding. She replied perfunctorily to all his attempts at conversation. She'd retreated to where he couldn't reach her, and the isolation he'd felt earlier came creeping back like flood water rising, cutting him off from what was familiar and safe.

In bed, Frankie smoked a cigarette and tried to read, finding it hard to concentrate, waiting impatiently for Miranda to emerge from the bathroom and come to bed. But when she did, Frankie could see the continuing resistance in her body, her shoulders hunched under the thin fabric of her nightgown, her head drooping on her slender neck. Slipping in beside him, almost weightless in her effort not to attract attention, she said good night, and closed her eyes. He almost lost courage. His success with women was not due to any great boldness on his part, to any overwhelming desire to meet challenges, leap hurdles, triumph in the face of adversity. The women had been willing and he had been eager. It had all been easy. Even Miranda, in retrospect, had been easy.

But tonight, no matter what the obstacles, Frankie needed to make love to his wife, not out of any great access of passion, but some half-realized need to reestablish possession, as if the act of sex alone could repel the assault Dyer's existence made on his claim to her. Putting the book down on the bedside table, he turned out the light, and slid close to the fortress of her body. He pulled her into his arms, traced her ear with his tongue. Opening her eyes again, she turned her head to him, and said, "I'm tired. It was an exhausting day." Still, his hand fondled her breast, moved down to her waist, then across the rise of her stomach. "Frankie, please. Not tonight." Desire drained from him, its place taken by fatigue as great as Miranda claimed to be feeling, and he let her go.

How could it be possible, he wondered, for her to prefer Greg Dyer to him? It made no sense. Dyer dressed well, and he must have a brain doing what he did; but he was built like a box; he had a face that looked like it had run into a wall once upon a time; and those glasses! Jesus Christ! What did she see in him? Lying there in the dark considering the question, Frankie didn't feel jealousy, didn't feel anger, didn't even feel pain. He'd spent so much time these past weeks convincing himself that Miranda really loved him that the resurgent possibility she might not left him only numb.

Feeling the bed begin to shake, he raised himself on his elbow and looked down at his wife, lying with her face turned into her pillow, crying. Her tears surprised him. Frankie hadn't considered the possibility that anyone but he had a reason to cry. "What's the matter?" he said.

"I'm sorry." Sniffling, she reached for a tissue.

"For what?" he asked, wanting to know the exact reason, out of so many possibilities, for her tears.

"Everybody's pulling at me all the time," said Miranda, ignoring the question. "Mother. Craig. You."

"Greg Dyer?" said Frankie. The words were out of his mouth without a conscious decision to speak them.

"Everybody," she repeated, too sunk in misery to notice the significance of Dyer's entry into the conversation.

Frankie sat up and turned on the light. "Are you in love with him?"

"What?" said Miranda, bolting upright, staring at Frankie with red-rimmed and frightened eyes.

Getting out of bed, he pulled on a robe, sat in the wicker chair facing her, and repeated, "Are you in love with Greg Dyer?" He spoke slowly, enunciating every word distinctly, trying to keep the flame low under the anger bubbling away inside him.

"Who told you about him?" she said.

"What difference does it make?"

"It was Mother. She told you."

"Answer me."

"How could she have done that?" Her voice lifted in a peal of outrage.

"Damnit, Miranda!" The anger boiled over, propelling Frankie out of the chair and across the bed. He grabbed her arms.

Frightened, she tried to pull away from him. "Leave me alone!"

Shaking her, he said, "Tell me. Goddamn it, tell me! Are you in love with him?"

"No! Now let me go!" Frankie released her, the anger receding, leaving hurt like a residue of sludge behind. He sat back on his haunches. Tears streamed down Miranda's face. Both of them were trembling. "I was," she said calmly, her voice now so soft it was difficult to hear without straining, "but that was before I met you." Hope again began to poke its way through Frankie's pain in tender, fragile shoots. He wanted so much to believe her. He wanted to believe her more than anything in the world. "How could she have told you?" repeated Miranda, stunned by the enormity of the betrayal.

"Easy. To make trouble," said Frankie.

"When did she tell you? Tonight?"

"Yeah," he said, finally, "tonight." How could he say he had known for weeks, sulked for weeks, been angry, withdrawn, and totally incapable of confronting her with his knowledge? In retrospect, it seemed childish, more childish than lying. He backed off the bed and settled himself again in the chair. "You want to tell me about it?" he asked.

"About Greg?"

"About Greg."

Reaching into the drawer of the bedside table, Miranda removed her stash, took a partially smoked joint from the plastic bag, and lit it. "There's not a lot to tell," she said. "Want some?" She extended her hand, offering him the roach. He refused. If he got to a mellow place tonight, he wanted to be sure it was the right place to be. Miranda took another hit, then started talking. Greg was a friend of her mother's and Craig's, someone she'd known as a child, she explained, and never thought of in any romantic way until one long holiday weekend soon after college. She'd run into him in a bookstore.

Greg had said hello, managed somehow to separate her from her friend, and invited her to dinner. It had sounded so innocent, a way to keep an old friend from being lonely while his wife was out of town, with Craig and Eva in Palm Beach, as it happened.

At dinner, Miranda saw a different Greg from the one she'd known most of her life. She had always, in a theoretical way, noticed his charm, but he was a being in another sphere, a friend of her parents', so it had never seemed relevant. That night, he turned its full force on her. He was amusing, witty, brilliant, seductive. He told her she was beautiful, intelligent, and extremely desirable. A few nights later, at Dyer's instigation, they again had dinner. Afterward, they stood on a street corner exchanging kisses in the rain. He tried to make love to her in his car, but Miranda became frightened and stopped him. He sent her gifts, silly trifles that made her laugh. He treated her like a doting father and besotted lover, a lethal combination. Finally, she agreed to go with him to a hotel.

The Ritz Carlton, thought Frankie. "That sonovabitch!" he said.

Miranda shrugged. "I was in love for the first time in my life. At least I thought I was," she corrected judiciously. A virgin when Dyer made love to her, Miranda was carried away in a frenzy of feeling. Sexually aroused, romantically involved, emotionally overwrought, she'd imagined the experience to be as meaningful to Dyer as to her. Though he never did more than hint, she never doubted that he was going to leave his wife and marry her when the last of his children went off to college. "I was a dope," said Miranda, with a smile that acknowledged the idiocy of having believed anything so trite.

As the months passed, Miranda began to pressure Dyer for a definite plan of action, and he became more and more evasive. They quarreled repeatedly. Finally Dyer told her he was committed to his marriage and had no intention of leaving his wife. He'd thought she understood that, and was sorry if he'd misled her. Under the circumstances, he said, he couldn't go on seeing her. The affair was over. That was in early June, just before Miranda had left for the Cape. Of course, she hadn't believed him. She thought he would miss her, change his mind, come after her. But he didn't. "At first I was terribly upset, wildly upset. But then I met you. And slowly, without even realizing it, I stopped caring about Greg. I mean, my ego was still bruised, but I knew I didn't love him anymore." When she returned to Boston, angry with Frankie for taking the job at Teeny's, Miranda had called Dyer, to test her reaction to him. He was polite, charming, and distant. She tried to match his attitude, to demonstrate that she, too, was an adult, sophisticated, able to handle the end of an affair with style. And she would have succeeded, too, if she hadn't run into him in a restaurant hand in hand with another young girl. "I snapped," she said. "I saw him with that girl, and I snapped. I mean,

I didn't really give a damn about him at that point, I'm sure I didn't, but the thought that he was starting all over again with someone new, that made me crazy. Eva and Craig were with me, and my sister, so I couldn't say anything then. But the next day I went to see him. I made an unbelievable scene in his office. A disgusting, awful scene. I was so ashamed of myself. . . . I guess I frightened him. He told Eva. And she dragged me off to Paris." Miranda sat silent for a moment, watching Frankie. Then she shrugged. "That's it," she said. Frankie said nothing. He just kept looking at her, assessing what she'd told him, weighing it for truth. "I need some ice cream." She dropped the roach into the ashtray, threw back the covers, and started to get up.

"I'll get it." He went into the kitchen, opened the freezer, scooped some chocolate ice cream into a bowl, and took it back into the bedroom.

"Don't you want any?"

"No," he said. He watched her sitting there, cross-legged, spooning the ice cream into her mouth, looking like a distraught little girl. God, how he wanted to believe her!

"Now, tell me about your first affair," she said, light-headed with pot, trying to reduce her revelations to insignificance.

"It wasn't the same thing," said Frankie.

"Why?"

"She was just some girl. I didn't love her, or anything." She'd been a year ahead of him in high school, Rita, a girl with a reputation for being wild, which meant that she bleached her hair, drank, smoked, and (it was widely believed) gave head. Frankie kept pushing to see how far he could get her to go, and that turned out to be all the way. Soon after, she dropped out of school and Frankie lost sight of her. But he wasn't about to tell Miranda any of that. It didn't seem to him the kind of thing a man told his wife.

He took off his robe and got back into bed. Miranda put her empty dish on the floor, turned off the light, and slithered back down under the covers. "I'm cold," she said, snuggling against Frankie, needing to appease him. He turned off his light and closed his eyes. "Mother shouldn't have told you," said Miranda. "It was cruel. To both of us."

"Let's just forget about it," said Frankie, hoping he could. "Go to sleep."

*O*f course he couldn't forget. Worry sat inside him like a giant rat gnawing at his brain, at his stomach, at his testicles. He couldn't concentrate at work, forgot to return phone calls to the bank, and to the lawyers handling the transfer of the Macklin franchise. Eating gave him a pain in his gut. Each night, when he took Miranda in his arms, he was terrified that his cock would fail to rise and do its duty. He didn't want her to know how disturbed he still was. He wanted to pretend that everything between them was fine, in the hope that pretending would make it so.

Miranda was apparently operating under the same impulse. When he returned home, she greeted him with cheery smiles, full of questions about Macklin's. She asked for help with school projects, coaxed him into spending hours with her on his days off planting spring flowers, planning garden parties for the summer. She responded to his lovemaking with a flattering intensity. She did what she could to convince them both that the path to their future wound through tranquil territory, not an obstacle in sight. Sometimes, however, she'd burst inexplicably into tears, and, when Frankie asked her what was wrong, she'd claim that she didn't know or explain her mood away as premenstrual blues.

$\mathscr{B}$y the beginning of May, the bank loan was formally approved and the paperwork completed. Frankie signed the necessary documents, handed over the cashier's check, and took possession of Macklin's. "Sonovabitch," said Pat Waleski, chomping on his cigar, pounding the new franchise holder on the back, "this calls for celebrating." Frankie phoned Miranda at the gallery and told her not to expect him home until late. But Pat got one of his spasms over dinner and, though he insisted he could manage fine on his own, Frankie accompanied him to Brooklyn Heights in a cab, handed him over to his wife (who didn't seem unduly worried), and took the subway back to the Village. When he got to the apartment, at about nine-forty, Miranda wasn't yet home. She's with Russell, he told himself, but he didn't believe it. What he believed was that his wife was somewhere with Greg Dyer. It was a crazy suspicion. Miranda hadn't known about his dinner with Pat long enough in advance to make any kind of a plan with Dyer, supposing that was something she might want to do. And how likely was it that Dyer would show up in New York the one night Frankie happened to be out of his way? He didn't know why he was so jealous. He didn't think he had any real grounds to be. In more logical moments, Frankie couldn't consider Dyer a serious rival. After all, the man was old; he was married; he was ugly. But however crazy, it was a suspicion Frankie couldn't get out of his mind. The jealousy raged through him, depriving him of logic. A senseless, bewildering, frightening emotion, it left Frankie feeling weak and vulnerable, hating himself and furious with Miranda.

Needing someone to talk to, he dialed Dan's number in New Haven. As he waited for him to come to the phone, Frankie poured himself a scotch. The high he'd been on with Pat hadn't survived the shock of the empty apartment.

"Frankie?" Dan's voice sounded distant, farther away than New Haven, maybe as far as Mars.

"Hi, buddy, how's it going?"

"I've got a chemistry test tomorrow," said Dan, sounding disgusted. "And I know sweet fuck all."

"Hey, I'm interrupting. Sorry. I'll call back another time," he said, suddenly as eager to get off the phone as he had been to call.

"It's okay," said Dan. "I'm grateful for the interruption. I've been studying all day. I didn't even stop for dinner."

"You should go get something to eat. You'll feel better."

Dan laughed. "You sound like my mother."

"Yeah," said Frankie, forcing a laugh. "Like mine, too. Everything going okay?"

"Except for chemistry, fine." He was pulling an A average, playing golf, dating—the usual. "What's up with you?"

Frankie knew the question was coming; still, when it did, it caught him by surprise and there was a silence while he tried to think how to answer.

"Frankie?" said Dan. "You still there?"

"Yeah," said Frankie. "Sorry. I had a mouthful of scotch. I just called to tell you the deal is closed. I've got Macklin's. As of today, it's mine."

"That's terrific. Congratulations. I'll come down to New York as soon as exams are over and we'll celebrate."

"Sure."

"You sonovabitch, you did it!"

"Yeah, I did. Listen, you go study. I just wanted you to know."

"Thanks for calling, Frankie. Give my love to Miranda."

And the line went dead. Frankie imagined Dan's lean body loping along the hall back to his room. He saw the neatly made bed, the orderly bookshelves, the desk lamp spilling a circle of light onto an opened textbook. It all seemed so safe, so well protected to Frankie, so distant from pain, so enviable. He poured himself another drink, turned on the television, returned to the couch and sat staring at the flickering black-and-white image of Alan Shepard being retrieved from the Atlantic after his fifteen-minute orbit of the earth. He couldn't pay attention. Only weeks before, he remembered, he had sat in exactly this position imagining Miranda dead. What he was imagining now, was it better or worse? He thought of a picture he'd seen in one of her books, *The Martyrdom of Saint Sebastian.* That's what he felt like, pierced by a hundred arrows, each small throbbing wound melding into an all-engulfing agony that stung and burned and tortured his body as well as his mind. If he drank enough, would it stop? Maybe if he smoked some dope. Getting up, he went into the bedroom, opened the drawer of Miranda's night table, took out the plastic bag, and rolled himself a joint. He lit it, took a drag, put the bag away and returned to the couch to wait for the drug to take effect. Whatever you do, he told himself, don't lose your temper. When she comes home, just keep calm. But instead of calming him, the marijuana made him jumpy, paranoid. He heard noises in the garden and imagined thieves. The flapping of the bedroom shade against the window sounded like a break-in, neighbors returning home like a police raid. He poured himself another drink to settle his nerves. Where the fuck is she? he thought.

At twenty past eleven, he heard Miranda's key turn in the lock. He sat still, his feet up on the coffee table, eyes closed. Just keep cool, he told himself. "Hi," he said, opening his eyes and turning to look at her as she entered.

Miranda paled, and said, "You're home."

"Pat got sick."

She forced herself to look away from him. Putting her books down on the foyer table, she took off her coat and hung it in the closet, saying over her shoulder, "Is he okay?"

"It was some kind of spasm. His wife didn't think it was anything serious."

"I guess it's a good thing he's retired."

"Yeah," said Frankie. He waited, wanting her to tell him where she'd been without his having to ask.

Instead of coming over to kiss him hello, she headed for the bathroom. Frankie heard the door close, the sound of bathwater running, the toilet flush. The door opened again, and Miranda came out and went into the bedroom. Getting up, Frankie followed her. He was driven by the need to smell her before she bathed. He needed to know if the odor of sex clung to her. Standing in the doorway, he watched Miranda undress. She took off her skirt and hung it up, folded her sweater and dropped it on a chair, unhooked her stockings and rolled them down her legs, leaving them in a heap on the floor. She took off the rest of her clothes, and, for once, Frankie studied her coldly. But he could see no marks, no telltale signs, only a fading bruise on her thigh for which he knew he was responsible. She put on her robe, gathered all the dirty lingerie up in her arms, and smiled. "Excuse me," she said, brushing past him. All he could smell was the faint scent of her perfume.

He followed her to the bathroom, watched as she dumped the dirty laundry into the basket, then turned off the tap. "Where were you?"

"Tonight?"

"Tonight," repeated Frankie.

She tested the bathwater, then looked at him. "At the gallery."

"The gallery closed hours ago."

"You said you wouldn't be home, so I went out to dinner."

"Who with?" When she didn't answer, Frankie repeated, "Who with?"

"I can't stand this, Frankie." Her voice was very soft. He couldn't tell whether she was angry, or frightened.

"Who with?"

"Why do I have to tell you everything I do, everywhere I go, everything I think?"

"You're my wife!"

"You're my husband, and you don't tell me!" She was angry.

"That's not true," said Frankie, outraged by the suggestion. "I tell you everything."

"When you were thinking about buying Macklin's, I was the last to know."

"That isn't the same thing," protested Frankie.

"It is to me."

"Don't try and change the subject," said Frankie. "Who'd you have dinner with?"

"Greg Dyer," she said defiantly.

He'd expected to hear just that. Why, then, did he feel so surprised? "Greg Dyer?" he repeated.

"Yes," she said.

This is what it's like, thought Frankie, when a volcano erupts. He could feel the rage flowing through him like red-hot lava looking for a way out, through his eyes, through his mouth, through his hands. With no clear intention of what he meant to do, he took a step toward Miranda. She stood her ground, as if no longer caring whether or not he struck her. The terror in her eyes stopped him. She was afraid of him. She was afraid of him and he loved her more than anything in the world. He turned and stormed out of the bathroom.

If she'd stayed where she was, Frankie might have poured himself another drink and tried to calm down. But she didn't. She followed him. "Frankie," she said.

The sound of her voice made him crazy. "Goddamn it!" Reaching out, his hand picked up the first object it found, a vase of dried flowers, and sent it crashing across the room. He knocked over the lacquer table it had sat on.

Miranda stood at the entrance to the living room, and watched him with growing horror. "What are you doing? Stop it!" He picked up a lamp, yanked the cord out of its socket, and sent it hurtling into the television set, where Jack Paar flickered and vanished. "We had dinner. That's all," she said, taking a few tentative steps toward him. "He was in New York and he stopped in to the gallery. It wasn't arranged. I hadn't planned to see him. It just happened." Never before had Frankie realized how satisfying the act of destruction could feel. He went through the room like a force of nature wreaking havoc, smashing everything in his path. "Frankie, please," Miranda pleaded. "You have to believe me. The whole thing was so innocent."

"Shut up," yelled Frankie.

"He asked me to dinner and I didn't see the harm. He only wanted to tell me how sorry he was, about everything."

"Just shut up!"

"Oh, God, I never thought you'd find out."

"Shut up, or I swear I'll hit you!" He moved toward her threateningly, fury and excitement making his heart race, his throat constrict. He was gasping for breath. Sobbing, Miranda collapsed into a small chair next to where the lacquer table had once stood. Frankie stopped moving and stared at her. "I'm the one with something to cry about," he said. He looked around the room at the upended furniture, the shattered glass, the sprays of dry flowers making odd patterns on the floor. Gradually, his breathing slowed until the only sound he could hear was Miranda crying. He turned and walked to the hall closet, took out his jacket, and put it on. Without saying a word, he left, closing the apartment door quietly behind him.

Chapter 15

The night was mild, with a fine mist falling like a curtain over the street. In the sky above the Hudson hung a pale sliver of moon. At the curb, one borzoi squatted while, nearby, another sniffed a lamppost. As Frankie came out of the house, their owner, a cartoonist named Mel, an interesting guy with a lot of radical political ideas (radical to Frankie at any rate), smiled and said hello. He lived across the street, and sometimes when they both had time to kill, they would stop and talk. Now, lifting his hand in a perfunctory wave, Frankie hurried by. He had no idea where he was going. He just knew that he had to get away before he did any more damage.

When he reached the park, he turned west and began tracing its perimeter. Usually he liked to look at the houses, trying to imagine the life that had once gone on inside, conjuring images of quiet wealth, of book-lined studies and hallways filled with ancestral paintings. This time Frankie ignored them. He could think of nothing but Miranda, her betrayal, his anger, how close he had come to hitting her, how for one moment he had felt that smashing his fist into her face would be the most sublimely fulfilling experience he had ever had.

His capacity for violence frightened him. For as long as he could remember, as soon as he struck a blow, he lost all control, all reason. It was as if, at the moment of contact, he was invaded by demons intent on killing. And afterward, staring down at someone lying in a pool of blood on the floor, or looking at his own bruised and bloodied face in a mirror, though still trembling with the aftermath of rage, he was filled with disgust. He remembered his father hitting him, bare-handed, on his back, his buttocks, his legs (how old had he been then? nine? ten? what had he done to deserve it?). Had Sal ever hit his mother? he wondered, or Angela? Frankie couldn't believe it possible.

The adrenaline drained slowly from his system, leaving him feeling depressed and weary. He was deep in the Village, wandering through its maze of streets, half the time not certain exactly where he was, oblivious to possible danger lurking in the shadows, to the late-night stragglers eyeing him warily as he passed. I should go home, he thought. But he didn't want to, though Miranda now would be safe from him. He didn't want to face her, didn't want to apologize, didn't want to talk about Greg Dyer. Circling back to Seventh Avenue, he turned into Thirteenth Street, and rang Vic's bell. On the second ring, Vic called out, "Who is it?" his voice a mix of irritation and wariness.

"Frankie."

Vic opened the door. His hair was rumpled, his eyes still filmed with sleep. He was wearing pajama bottoms and looked shorter and squarer than when fully clothed.

"You alone?"

"Yeah," said Vic. "I'm alone. You okay?"

"I had a fight with Miranda. Can I stay here tonight?"

"Sure. Come on in." Vic asked no questions. He pulled a sleeping bag out of a closet, offered it to Frankie, and collapsed back into his bed. "You know where everything is. I'm dead," he said, turned over, and went back to sleep.

*S*till awake at dawn, Frankie considered going home. At eight, he considered calling Miranda. He considered it again when he got to Macklin's. Instead, when Miranda phoned him, he told Tom to say he was busy. Then, for reasons not entirely clear to himself, he called Colette Drake and invited her to lunch.

Not wanting to go back to the apartment to change, Frankie borrowed a tie and jacket from Tom, and took a taxi uptown to meet Colette at L'Aiglon. As she walked toward him on her high heels, flamboyant in a bright orange suit, her sleek dark head thrust forward on her long neck, it occurred to him how much like a question mark she looked. The uneasy thought struck him that Colette was certain to be full of questions he was in no mood to answer. Getting to his feet, he leaned toward her and kissed her cheek. "You look great," he said, as the maître d' settled her into her chair.

Smiling, she said, "What a nice surprise this is," requested a martini, and then returned her attention to Frankie, and asked, "To what do I owe the honor?" Her dark eyes were alight with speculation.

Frankie had no idea how to explain his invitation. "It was a spur-of-the-moment thing," he said with a shrug. He needed a woman (not for sex, definitely not for that) but for comfort, admiration, affirmation: he needed a woman to want him. "I was thinking about you."

"Really? May I ask in what context?"

Before Frankie could reply, a waiter, like a good fairy, arrived with Colette's drink; then, whipping a notepad out of his breast pocket, he asked if they were ready to order.

"Do you know what you want?" asked Frankie.

Colette took a sip of her martini, and said, "Oh, yes, I always know exactly what I want. Unlike some people." Turning her gaze from Frankie to the menu in front of her, she ordered a shrimp cocktail, followed by grilled chicken. Frankie ordered Steak Diane. "It's wonderful here," said Colette. "It's my favorite thing, in fact. I'll have that, too. And forget the shrimp. I'll have the asparagus instead." She smiled placatingly at the waiter. He adjusted his notes, took Frankie's order for wine, bowed slightly, then turned and walked away.

Frankie laughed. "You always know what you want?"

"Well, almost always. You haven't answered my question."

"Christ, you're like a bloodhound." Colette opened her mouth to speak, and Frankie cut her short. "Can't we just relax and enjoy ourselves?"

"Sometimes you remind me very much of a spoiled brat."

"If you mean I always get my own way, you're wrong. I don't."

"No?" She studied his face for a moment; then, she groaned. "Would somebody please tell me what I'm doing here?"

He smiled. "You like me."

"Don't let it go to your head," said Colette.

"It's flattering."

"It should be. However, the question is—"

"More questions?"

"What exactly do you feel about *me*?"

"I think you're interesting. I think you're smart. I think you're sexy. Okay?"

It didn't seem to be okay. "A twenty-one-year-old married kid," said Colette gloomily. "And I'm having lunch with him. I must be out of my mind."

"Maybe we're friends," said Frankie. "Did you ever think of that?"

Suddenly Colette laughed. "Frankie," she said, "I could love you."

The laugh signaled the end of the discussion. Not that the questions stopped (with Colette they never would); they merely changed direction. Attacking her food with gusto, she asked how his acquisition of Macklin's was proceeding, congratulated him on closing the deal, and assured him that his gut instinct was correct—he was on the way, however faintly marked, to somewhere he wanted to be. They compared notes about plays they had seen, films, art exhibitions, sporting events, Frankie registering Colette's opinions for later review. (It was the way he sharpened and refined his own taste, honing it against that of people he respected.) Finally, almost regretfully, as if it was a duty she had to fulfill, Colette asked about Miranda. "She's fine," said Frankie, with what he hoped was sufficient aplomb. "Getting As or Bs in all her courses, working a couple of days a week at the gallery, enjoying herself."

"Not much time for play with that schedule, is there?"

"We manage," said Frankie curtly. I should've kept her locked up in that apartment, he thought. I should've never let her out of my sight. The despair he'd kept dammed up all morning flooded through him again. Christ, he thought, what am I going to do? "Anyway," he said," "we don't have to go out to have a good time." It sounded like bravado to him, and he was sure it sounded the same to Colette.

"No," she said. "I can see going out would not be necessary."

"How come we never talk about *your* love life?" he said, to get her off the subject.

"Maybe because while men may ask, they never really want to know."

"I do."

Colette took another sip of her wine, put the glass down on the table, and smiled. "So, you want to know about my lovers?"

"Yes."

"Who are they?" Frankie nodded. "Whether I loved them or not?" She leaned toward him and whispered, "What I do to them? What they do to me?"

Frankie felt a slight nudge against the V of his Jockey shorts. "Yes," he said.

"Oh, baby," said Colette, sounding disappointed. "You're not blushing."

"Maybe I am, where you can't see."

"Dessert?" said the waiter, offering a trolley full of sweets.

Startled, they looked away from each other to gaze vacantly at the trolley. Finally, Colette looked up at the waiter and smiled. "No, thank you."

Frankie shook his head. "Just the check, please."

When the waiter had moved out of earshot, Frankie leaned toward Colette. "Can we get a room here?" he said, nodding his head in the direction of the St. Regis lobby just beyond the restaurant. The question surprised him more than it did Colette. "Or we could go to your place." Maybe he needed more than comfort, after all. His cock, the final arbiter in these matters, seemed to think so.

Colette's stared at her hands, resting lightly on the soiled tablecloth, as if trying to read the answer concealed in their orange tips. "No," she said at last, shaking her head for emphasis. She looked up at him. "You're very tempting, but no."

"Why?" he said, not wanting to plead, but hoping to find a way around her reservations. Getting Colette to bed seemed suddenly important to him. Maybe, it occurred to him, that *had* been the point of asking her to lunch. "Why?" he repeated.

"Pride I suppose. I don't like pinch-hitting."

"It's not like that—"

"Frankie, let's cut the bull, okay? We both know why you called. And we both know why I came. But I've changed my mind. I've got nothing against a little fling now and then. God knows, I've got nothing against a little fling with a married man . . . or boy, as the case may be. . . ."

"Jesus Christ, Colette—"

"Shut up and let me finish. Because usually little flings don't hurt. Usually little flings are irrelevant. But not this little fling. This one, I think, is not about pleasuring ourselves and each other, it's about hurting Miranda. I don't like that."

"This has nothing to do with Miranda."

"Frankie, take a little advice from someone who knows. If you've got a problem with your wife, go home and work it out with her, not with me."

Seeing the waiter approach, they lapsed into a discreet silence. "Your bill, sir," he said politely, depositing the tray in front of Frankie.

He studied the tab, pretending to check it, though the numbers made as little sense to him as characters in Chinese. Finally, he reached into his wallet, counted out some bills, and dropped them on the tray. "Frankie," whispered Colette. When he looked at her, she raised her cupped hands to the air just above her head. "Tell me, is my halo on straight?" He laughed, and she reached across and took his right hand in both of hers and squeezed. "When you talk about this, and you will, be kind." He looked at her blankly and Colette's grin widened. "Private joke," she said.

Outside, he hailed her a cab. As it stopped, he kissed her good-bye, then watched as she got into the taxi in that single, fluid movement he associated with assured and successful women, like Colette, like Eva. "I'll call you," he said. "We'll have lunch. Maybe dinner."

"Lovely," she said, in a tone not designed to encourage him. As the taxi pulled away, she leaned forward and stuck her head out the window. "Go home," she called.

$\mathcal{H}$e didn't go home. There was no point, he told himself, since Miranda had classes all day. Instead, he returned to Macklin's and spent an hour or so checking the machines, ordering supplies, looking through paint and carpeting samples for the redecorating he planned to do. He worked out until Tom asked him if he was trying to kill himself; then he took a shower and went to a movie. By the time he returned to the apartment, it was after nine. For a moment, he stood at the door, straining to hear the sounds from inside: the bathwater running, the television on, the soundtrack of *Camelot*. There was only silence. Steeling himself, he put his key in the lock, turned the handle of the door, and entered.

Miranda had tried to clean up the mess. The furniture had been set aright and put back in place, the pictures straightened, the debris cleared. The one remaining table lamp was on. The books were back on the shelves. Though he knew it was no use, he called her name. It wasn't necessary to search the rooms to be sure she was gone. He could feel the emptiness. He looked anyway, in the kitchen, in the bathroom, in the bedroom where the door to the closet stood open. She had taken a lot of her clothes, her cosmetics, her address book, and the plastic bag full of pot from the drawer in the bedside table.

The scenes Frankie had been imagining all day included Miranda contrite and groveling, begging his forgiveness, promising never to see Dyer again; or Miranda stormily defiant, proclaiming her love, refusing to give him up. Miranda gone, fled out of his reach, beyond his ability to fight with her, reason with her, plead with her, even forgive her, that scenario had never entered his mind. Had she gone to Dyer? That's what Frankie wanted to know, and had no idea how to find out. Rage just then would have been a relief. He could have smashed something and had some small sense of satisfaction. But he felt no anger. Instead, he felt scared, sick to his stomach, icy cold.

Going to the phone, he looked to see if she had jotted down any notes on the pad beside it, but it was blank. Lightly, he colored the page with a pencil as he'd seen people do in detective films, and, as if by magic, a number appeared. He dialed it but it turned out to be only the number for the pizzeria from which they usually ordered. Again, he walked through the apartment, looking for clues. On the table in the foyer, lying beside the mail, he found the note she'd left him. Picking it up, he took the piece of ivory-colored bond out of its envelope, and saw that his hands were trembling. She had scribbled only a few lines: *Frankie, I don't want to fight anymore. I've gone away for a while, to stay with a friend. I think we both need time to calm down and think things through before we talk. I'll call you, but right now I don't know when.*

If she'd left him for Dyer, Frankie reasoned, wouldn't she have said so?

He sat on the living room couch, lit a cigarette, and made a list of Miranda's friends. When he'd written down as many as he could remember, he started to look up their numbers in the phone book, and then stopped himself. What was the use? How often could he phone around looking for his missing wife? What could he say? What would people think? And he couldn't call Eva, not yet, not until he was desperate; and not because she might worry, but because he wanted to put off as long as possible admitting to her that she had, after all, defeated him. Getting up, he began pacing, trying to decide what to do. He went back into the bedroom and stood looking at the robe Miranda had forgotten, hanging behind the door. Burying his face in it, he caught her scent. She'll come back, he told himself. He stretched out on the bed, in the dark, took a cigarette from the package in his shirt pocket and lit it. But what if she doesn't? he thought.

*D*ays passed and Miranda didn't return home, didn't call. Frankie felt as if he were trapped in a dark cave at the bottom of the sea. When he walked it was as if he were moving through water, pushing against the tide. Amazed that he could muster the energy, he forced himself to shower and shave every day, to dress and go to Macklin's. But once there he hid in his office, leaving whatever problems cropped up for Tom to handle. He didn't work out. There was no way he could lift weights, especially not the one sitting on his chest.

On Friday, his mother called to invite him and Miranda to Sunday dinner and Frankie said no. By now, Dolly was so used to her son's being too busy to visit that she sounded hurt, but not suspicious. Even Angela, when she called to yell at him for upsetting Dolly, seemed to notice nothing. "You only come around these days when you want something," she said. "That's not fair, Frankie. We're your family. You have a responsibility to us." He promised he would see them all soon, but that wasn't enough. "You've got people here who care about you. And you just don't give a damn!"

She sounded as if she was about to cry, but then so was he. "Get off my back, Angela, okay? I told you, I'll get there when I can." And he hung up on her.

When Vic, who was again out of work, called later that day to suggest a basketball game at the Garden, Frankie lied and said that he and Miranda were busy. "Is everything all right?" asked Vic. "You sound terrible." Frankie lied once more and said everything was fine. He couldn't go out. He was too afraid Miranda would phone while he was gone, and so he spent his evenings alone in the apartment, not watching the television that was left constantly on, not eating the food he occasionally ordered in. When finally he drifted off to sleep, he was awakened by the sound of the phone ringing, but always it was a dream.

On Monday, Frankie drove his car to Barnard and cruised the campus, hoping to spot Miranda on her way to or from class. The next morning, he parked near the subway and watched for her to come out. In the afternoon, he stood across from the gallery, waiting for her to arrive. Finally, from a phone booth on the corner, he called and asked to speak with her. Perplexed, because she thought she recognized his voice, the receptionist told him Miranda wouldn't be in for the rest of the week. "Do you know where I can reach her?"

"Have you tried her at home?"

"No. No, I haven't. I'll do that," said Frankie, hanging up quickly, feeling despair wash over him in a giant wave.

He thought he'd go out of his mind with worry. He drank to ease the tightness in his chest, collapsing into bed in a stupor each night. But still he washed the coffee mugs, the whiskey glasses, his soiled clothes; he showered and dressed and went to Macklin's. He took some encouragement from this: if he was really as near to going under as he felt, surely he would not be able to get out of bed?

The next Saturday morning, Dan called and, after a few minutes of casual chitchat, said, in a voice as devoid of curiosity as he could manage, "Oh, by the way, I ran into Miranda last night."

"What?"

"I was visiting some girl I know at Radcliffe. And I ran into Miranda. She was with Beth."

"Beth?" repeated Frankie. He felt as if his mind had gone to sleep.

"Beth Monroe. She was with Miranda on the Cape last summer."

"What did Miranda say?"

"Nothing. When I asked where you were, she said in New York. When I asked how you were, she said fine. She didn't exactly encourage questions. And Beth was glaring daggers at me the whole time. Of course," said Dan, sounding amused in a grim sort of way, "that might have had nothing to do with Miranda."

Needing to tell someone, Frankie said, "We had a fight. I lost my temper. You know how I get. I tore up the place a little. I guess I scared her. When I got home the next night, she was gone."

There was a pause. Then Dan said, "Well, you can't blame her. You're like a fucking maniac when you lose control."

"I didn't hit her," said Frankie. "I wouldn't."

"I didn't mean—"

"Oh, shit," said Frankie. "What the fuck am I going to do?"

"Apologize?"

"There's more, Dan. It's complicated. Real complicated. I don't think just an apology is gonna do it. Look, I've got to talk to her. Do you have Beth's number?"

"Yes. Just a minute." Frankie could hear the rustle of pages turning, then Dan's voice again giving him the number at the dorm.

"Thanks," said Frankie.

"You've got to keep your temper, Frankie, if you want to work this thing out."

"I know. I know."

"You say you wouldn't hit Miranda, but when you lose it, man, you go ape shit. There's no stopping you."

"I wouldn't hit her," said Frankie. "I love her."

"Just keep cool, okay?"

"If you think I'm such a sonovabitch," said Frankie, yelling into the phone, "why the fuck did you say you were happy we got married?"

"I thought you were good for her. I still think that."

"She doesn't love me," he said, all the pain in the world in his voice.

"You're out of your mind," said Dan.

"She doesn't love me," repeated Frankie. "She's in love with Greg Dyer."

"You're completely crazy, Frankie. Completely nuts, if you believe that. And if that's why you broke up the apartment, then no wonder Miranda split. She knew she was living with somebody who ought to be committed."

"Eva told me." He would not allow Dan to make him hope.

"That cunt," said Dan. "And you believed her? When you know she's been trying to break up your marriage from the beginning? When you know she'll do anything to get her own way?" Dan paused a minute, then continued in a quieter voice. "Frankie, talk to Miranda. You can work this out. You can, if you just stay calm." There was a silence, and finally Dan said, "Frankie, are you still there?"

"I'm here."

"Talk to Miranda."

"Yeah. I'll talk to her," he said. "Thanks, Dan."

Frankie replaced the receiver, poured himself a drink, lit a cigarette, and tried to decide what to do. Finally he picked up the phone again and dialed Beth's number.

Whoever answered left Frankie hanging for five minutes, then came back and announced that Beth wasn't in. Every couple of hours he tried again, and each time got a different girl and the same response. Afraid Beth wouldn't come to the phone if she knew who was calling, Frankie refused to give his name and, when he finally got her, late in the afternoon, she said, "Oh, I should have known it was you," sounding disappointed, as if she had hoped the mysterious caller would be someone else, Dan perhaps.

"Can you tell me how to reach Miranda?"

"She doesn't want to talk to you."

"Did she say that?"

"If she wanted to talk to you, she would have told you how to find her. Trust Dan not to keep his mouth shut."

"I just want to talk to her."

It took him five minutes to get her to agree to ask Miranda, to let her make her own decisions. "Hold on," Beth said, and he could hear her heels tapping along the corridor as she walked away from the phone. They must be going out, he thought.

An eternity later, he heard Miranda say, "Frankie, are you there?"

"I'm here."

"Oh." The sound was so soft, it was almost a sigh. Then there was silence.

"I've been worried sick about you," he said finally.

"I'm sorry."

"You should've left me a number."

"I didn't want to talk to you. I needed time to think."

He wanted to ask her if she had seen Dyer, but he didn't dare. If they started to quarrel, she'd hang up on him, and he couldn't let her hang up, not before she'd agreed to come home. "We have to talk," he said.

"I know."

"Come home, Miranda." He could hear her breathing at the other end of the line. He could imagine the look on her face, the small furrow between her brows as she decided what to say. "Please," he begged.

"I'm not sure that's a good idea."

"I won't lose my temper. I won't get mad."

"You always say that, Frankie."

"I swear it. I've learned my lesson. I'll never lose control like that again."

He waited until finally she said, "Maybe you should come here."

"So Beth can referee?"

"I'm not staying on campus," she said. She gave him the name and number of the hotel where she had taken a room. "What time will you be here?"

"I can be there tonight."

"No, not tonight. I've got plans tonight." She must have realized how that sounded because she added quickly, "A group of us are going out, old friends of Beth's and mine. I promised. Come about noon to-morrow."

"Okay," he said, disappointed, but not wanting to argue. "I love you," he said.

"I know." She sounded as if it was the saddest fact she had ever heard. "I'll see you tomorrow."

Frankie replaced the receiver and felt the adrenaline surge through his body. His heart raced, his breath labored, as if he'd been running a long distance. He felt wired. There was no way he could be alone. He would go out of his mind with anxiety. Vic answered his phone on the third ring. "You still looking for company?" said Frankie.

"What's up?"

"Miranda decided to visit a friend in Massachusetts."

"You two still fighting?"

"Yeah," said Frankie.

Vic was on his way to a party and Frankie agreed to tag along. It was at the apartment of some actor he knew, on Bank Street, and when they got there it was wall-to-wall people, loud music, pretzels and chips and dip, lots of booze. It was the kind of party where you had to hold your drink aloft over your head to avoid spilling it as you made your way through the tiny overcrowded rooms. Though Frankie was careful not to drink too much, he stayed on a high, moving from group to group as if he were the host, sociable and easy, keeping the conversation flowing, enjoying the admiring glances of the women, the camaraderie of the men. Never had he enjoyed a party so much.

That night he fell into a deep sleep, disturbed only by the dream of the ringing phone, and awoke at about six feeling refreshed and full of energy. In the shower, he again thought he heard the phone ring, but when he turned off the water, the apartment was quiet. By seven, he was on the road. The day was sunny, clear, a perfect day, and Frankie's spirits soared higher and higher. He turned on the radio and sang along with the Roommates, "That's the story of/That's the glory of love. . . ." Whatever he had to do to make things right with Miranda, he would do. Today he would solve the problems of his life.

He got to the hotel early and rang Miranda's room from the lobby. There was no answer. When the concierge checked, the key was in its box. Frankie sat in the lobby, waiting impatiently for her to return. She must have gone out for breakfast with Beth, he thought. By one, he was torn between anger and fear. From the public phone in the lobby he called Beth's dorm, hoping somebody there would know where to find them. The girl who answered the phone did. She told him there had been an accident and that Beth and Miranda were in a hospital, in Cambridge.

. . .

$\mathcal{N}$umb with shock, Frankie covered the miles to Cambridge in a daze, not thinking, not worrying, not noticing the route signs he followed instinctively, his mind in a state of suspended animation. Later, he wouldn't remember the policeman who had given him a ticket for speeding, the three people he stopped to ask directions to the hospital, or anything else about his trip. "I'm her husband," he said when the nurse on duty asked if he was a relative.

"Oh, Mr. Ferraro," she said. "We've been trying to reach you since early this morning."

Oh, God, he thought, I was out partying and Miranda was lying here, hurt. "Is she all right?"

"She's in intensive care," said the nurse.

As he walked the long corridors looking for the unit, Frankie saw Eva and Craig seated in a lounge with another couple and Beth. The air was thick with smoke, and no one was speaking, the only sound the occasional click of a cigarette lighter. He nodded curtly and continued on until he found Miranda's room. She was lying in a narrow white bed, with tubes in her nose and mouth, needles in her arm. Frankie stood looking down at her. He whispered her name, but she didn't move. "Miranda," he said again, loudly. There wasn't even a flutter of eyelids to indicate she might have heard. Please, God, let her be all right, he prayed.

After what seemed like hours, a nurse entered and asked him to leave, just for a few minutes, she insisted; and Frankie reluctantly returned to the lounge to talk to Beth. Seeing the look on his face, she got up and went to him. Her hair hung in lank strands. Her eyes were bloodshot, her face pale. She had a bruise on her forehead. She had suffered only a slight concussion, she said. Steven had swallowed so much water he was still under observation. Michael had escaped unscathed. (The names meant nothing to Frankie.) They'd known each other, they'd been friends, for years; and they were going all out trying to cheer Miranda up, she'd been so depressed since her arrival. The four of them had gone out to dinner, then on to a club to dance. They were drinking hard liquor, and Miranda was probably smoking a little; at least that's what Beth assumed she was doing on her frequent trips to the bathroom. By about two in the morning, they were seriously high, when someone, Michael, she thought, suggested they go rowing. Steven, who was on the Harvard rowing team, tried to veto the idea, but eventually he gave in to pressure. They broke in to a boathouse and made off with one of the sculls.

It all seemed like a terrific lark. There they were out on the river in the middle of the night, gliding through the dark, doing something whose only thrill was that it was forbidden. They were young, beautiful, rich, drunk as lords, and exceedingly pleased with themselves. Miranda dropped her oar, stood up, and began to sing. Steven, terrified they would be caught, grabbed for her. The scull turned over, hitting Beth in the head. She was stunned, but Miranda must have been knocked unconscious and trapped underneath. Steven kept diving, trying to find her, but it was pitch black and he couldn't see a thing. Eventually, Michael spotted her, floating facedown a few yards away.

"What was she doing here?" Eva demanded to know, looking accusingly at Frankie. "Why wasn't she in New York with you?"

I should've never let her out of the apartment, thought Frankie again. I should've locked her up and thrown away the key.

"Well?" said Eva. "Why was my daughter so depressed?" Her eyes were shadowed with fatigue and fear. Without makeup, she looked younger, more vulnerable, so much like Miranda it hurt Frankie to look at her.

He shrugged. "What difference does it make?" he said as he sat and lit another cigarette. Please, God, he prayed, I'll never ask for anything again, I swear. Just let her be all right.

"Greg," he heard Eva say, "how good of you to come."

Frankie looked up and saw Greg Dyer standing in the doorway. "I just heard," he said. "Mary Jo happened to call your house, and Mrs. Lyle told her. Is Miranda all right?"

He must be out of his fucking mind, thought Frankie. Before he knew what was happening, he was out of his seat and across the small room. He grabbed Dyer by the throat. "Are you crazy?" he heard himself say aloud. "Are you out of your fucking mind? Get out of here before I kill you."

"Frankie!" shouted Eva, "Stop it!"

"Let go of me!" demanded Dyer.

Frankie felt his hands tightening around Dyer's throat, felt Dyer struggling to get free. All he could hear was the sound of blood pounding in his head. As Beth's father came rushing to help, Eva and Craig pulled him away, thrusting him back across the room and into a chair. "Stop it, Frankie," said Craig. "This is no way to behave. Now, calm down."

"Get him out of here," said Frankie, his breath coming in painful gasps.

"He's a maniac. A maniac," murmured Eva.

Suddenly, they all became aware of the doctor standing in the doorway, a young man with thinning blond hair and a pale face. His look of dismay seemed to proclaim fights in the hospital lounge totally unacceptable. "Oh, Doctor," said Craig in his best chairman-of-the-board manner. "Sorry. The strain is getting to all of us, I'm afraid."

"I'm sorry," said the doctor. He didn't really have to say any more. They all knew immediately what he meant. "I'm sorry," he repeated. "But Miranda . . ."

"No," said Eva.

"She's dead?" said Craig, sounding incredulous.

The doctor nodded. "She never regained consciousness."

Frankie looked at Dyer. "Get the fuck out of here," he said.

Dyer turned and, without a word, left. Craig put his arms around Eva, while Mr. and Mrs. Monroe pulled Beth into a hug. Frankie could hear the soft sounds of weeping as he pushed passed the doctor. He raced along the corridor to Miranda's room, though he knew there was no longer any need to hurry. "Go away," he said to the hospital staff who were disconnecting tubes, removing needles. "Please." Silently, they exchanged looks, then turned and went out of the room, leaving Frankie alone with his wife.

Miranda didn't look dead. She looked as if she were sleeping. This is all a bad dream, thought Frankie. Any minute, now, I'll wake up. Any minute, the alarm will go off. Soon, I'll leave for Boston. He stretched out a hand and touched hers, lying motionless on top of the white blanket. It was still warm. "I'm sorry," he said. Then he began to cry.

Part Two

ANNABEL

1978

Chapter 16

He ought to go home, thought Frankie. As disagreeable as Annabel would be if he walked through the door of their apartment within the next half hour, later she'd be worse, much worse. Later, rather than the unhappy wife of an unsatisfactory spouse, she would have turned into Clytemnestra, Medea, a wronged woman in search of revenge. On the other hand, later, with any luck, the amount of alcohol he planned to consume in the meantime would serve as a pretty effective shield.

Annabel was Frankie's second wife.

"Another game?" he asked his cousin Vic. They were playing squash in one of the four courts now available in the renovated and expanded Macklin's Health Club.

"Can't," said Vic, wiping the sweat from his face with one of the thick white towels the club provided for a nominal sum. "Gotta get home." He looked questioningly at Frankie. "Don't you?"

If he left now, thought Frankie, he'd be able to see his kid before she went to sleep. His kid. Her name was Maud and she was five years old. Picturing the way her face would look as he walked through the door of her flounced and flowered bedroom to kiss her good night, he felt a quick rush of tenderness. She was the image of him, everybody said. She had silky olive skin that smelled of talcum powder, straight dark hair, and big doe eyes too often full of anxiety these days. If he went home now, he'd get there in time to read to her. He did that sometimes when Annabel was away on business. His daughter liked that. He liked that. But Annabel wasn't away. "There's no hurry," he said.

"Frankie, go home." Vic spoke with the ease and authority of a cousin, an older cousin, one who had alternately beaten Frankie up and saved his skin when they were kids.

Frankie grinned. "If I had Maria to go home to," he said as he led the way out of the court, "maybe I would."

Vic hesitated, then said only, "Yeah, I'm a lucky guy."

While Frankie made phone calls, Vic showered in the white-tiled, polished-chrome, blindingly clean bathroom adjoining his cousin's office. When he finished, he found Frankie still in workout clothes, seated in his big leather chair, feet up on the desk, hands behind his head, staring past the partially closed blinds into the lamplit space that was West Forty-third Street at night. The sound of something by the Bee Gees filtered in from one of the exercise classes in progress. They were in what had been the original club. Three years before, Frankie had bought the derelict property next door and expanded, renovating the old building and, in the new, adding a women's locker room, steam baths, saunas, squash courts, and a bar. That had followed the acquisition—in 1968, the year before he had met Annabel—of the entire chain from the conglomerate that had bought it from Mike Macklin. According to a recent estimate in *Forbes*, the company was valued at two hundred million dollars. In corporate headquarters on the Avenue of the Americas, Frankie now had a much larger and more luxurious office. He kept this one because it had been his first. His manager, Tom Murray, used another room, across the hall.

Hearing Vic, Frankie turned his head and said, "There's a hair dryer under the sink."

"This is okay," said Vic, smoothing his wet hair back from his forehead.

Frankie dropped his feet to the floor and stood. "Get pneumonia," he said. "I'm sure Maria won't mind as long as you're on time for dinner."

Vic let that go. He stuck out his hand. "See you Friday?" They played squash together regularly when they were both in town.

Frankie shook the offered hand, and said, "I'll be in Boston Friday. I'm not sure what time I'll be back. I'll give you a call."

"See you when I see you," said Vic, turning toward the door.

"Give Maria and the kids a hug for me."

Vic turned back. "You should bring Maud over sometime. The kids would love to see her. Come for dinner. Annabel, too," he added quickly.

"Sure," said Frankie, with the same lack of conviction. His family was sweet, but so boring, Annabel had told him on numerous occasions. And though Frankie didn't disagree with her (about some of them, anyway), still they were his family; he cared about them, and sometimes he felt it necessary to put in an appearance at a wedding, a funeral, a holiday dinner. But, when he insisted she go with him, Annabel behaved so badly, with such cool superiority, that he ended up wondering why he'd bothered, especially since, though *they* were careful not to let it show, nobody in the family liked her any better than she did them. They probably wouldn't even blame him for fooling around, he thought—if they ever found out he did. Though they might click their tongues in disapproval, his mother and his aunts would probably figure he deserved a little compensation for being married to such a woman. It was only their daughters engaging in extramarital sex that could cause their screams to shatter glass, their tears to flood the lower ground floors of their split-level houses, their threats to darken the sky over Long Island.

"An open invitation," said Vic.

Frankie smiled. "Soon," he said. "I want Maud to grow up knowing her cousins." That had been one of Angela's complaints too. Not only did she never get to see her brother, but her kids never got to see Maud.

"It's important."

"Yeah," agreed Frankie. "You take it easy."

When the door closed behind Vic, Frankie returned to his desk and sat, wondering why it was that his cousin managed to make all the right personal decisions and all the wrong professional ones, while he, Frankie, did just the opposite. Vic should, for example, have forgotten Maria. That would have been the sensible thing to do. And he did try. When he returned to New York from Provincetown, the autumn after he'd met her, he had dated steadily, diligently, hoping to find the one woman who would drive Maria from his mind. None did. The pittance he earned acting he spent on phone calls to her. The following summer, he turned down a guest part on *The Untouchables* (it was too small, not worth the trouble of flying to Los Angeles, he told his agent, who had worked for weeks to get him the job) because it interfered with his returning to the Cape in time to begin rehearsals for another season at the Playhouse. At the end of the summer, deeper in love with Maria than ever, he wrenched himself away again, returned to New York, got a small part in a Broadway play that turned out to be a hit, then toured with the company after the close of the run. He left the tour with money in the bank and the offer of another, bigger part in a new play. Convinced that finally he could afford a wife, he asked Maria to marry him. As crazy about Vic as he was about her, she said yes.

Fifteen years later, they had three children, a boy of twelve and two girls, aged eight and five. Vic's career was good, but not great. He was one of those solid, dependable, middle-rung actors who managed to work most of the time, in plays on and off Broadway, in guest roles on television, in featured parts in films. From time to time he was offered a continuing role in a series, but the ones he chose inevitably failed, while others he turned down ran for three, four, five years. Laughing, Vic said he often suspected that his bad choices were no accident. He wasn't happy living anywhere but Manhattan. Which was the only thing he and Maria ever fought about with any intensity. She hated living in the city, probably any city, but especially New York, where towering blocks of stone obscured the sky. She was used to light and space and air that smelled of the sea, not garbage. As a compromise, when one of the failed television series left Vic with surplus money, they bought a weekend place on Long Island, on the Sound, far enough from the fashionable Hamptons to be affordable. Then, when the building they were living in went co-op, they bought their three-bedroom apartment on Riverside Drive for a song.

No, thought Frankie, they weren't rich. Sometimes it was a strain for them to make ends meet; but they had each other and were happy. Whereas he had Annabel and wasn't.

When he had showered and dressed, Frankie considered calling his wife to tell her that he'd be late. But that would mean two arguments, one now, and one later when he got home. Which didn't seem to make a lot of sense. Instead he called Martha, his secretary, who never left work without a final, end-of-the-day wrap-up conversation with her boss. She gave him the list of phone messages, the details of his trip to Boston, and ran through his appointments for the next day, one of which was a lunch date with Colette Drake. Twelve years ago, she had started her own company, which now handled publicity for the Ferraro clubs.

"You better call and ask her where she wants to eat," said Frankie. "You know what a pain in the ass she is about that."

"I did. She suggested Cendrillon, if that's okay with you." It was Manhattan's newest "in" restaurant.

"Fine." Suddenly the air on the line went dead. "Are you there?" asked Frankie.

"Yes. Sorry. Patty just handed me a note saying your wife is on the other line."

"Tell her you don't know where I am."

"Mr. Ferraro . . ."

"I know. Lying wasn't part of the job description. Tell her the last you heard I was at the club, but I've probably left by now. For all you know, it may be true by the time you say it. I'm on my way out the door. Okay?"

Frankie heard Martha sigh. "Okay," she said. "But she's not going to be happy."

"If she starts yelling, hang up."

"An excellent suggestion. And when she asks you to fire me for being rude to her?"

"Don't worry so much about the details. I'll take care of you."

"Yes, Mr. Ferraro," she said, sounding not at all convinced.

"You're a good girl, Martha," he said reassuringly. She was that, as well as bright and efficient, attractive, too, though not in any showy kind of way. She was also reserved, unflappable, and polite (except when suffering from offended dignity), so he couldn't tell if she'd fallen in love with him, though he assumed that she had. Most women were a little in love with him. To start with, he thought sourly.

. . .

*F*or the first five years of his marriage, Frankie had been faithful to Annabel. If asked, he would have said that fidelity was irrelevant to the success of a marriage (the husband's fidelity that is), yet he was never seriously tempted to cheat on her. He was in love. And though his good looks and growing success continued to earn him tempting offers, though he never failed to be both grateful and curious, romantic that he was, his sexual interest remained focused exclusively on Annabel, his wife. He couldn't remember exactly when or why that had changed. Familiarity had played a part, but not a major one. More crucial (at some point after Maud was born, he thought), Annabel had stopped loving him—or pretending to. No longer did she make any effort to be agreeable, to be accommodating, to be civil, to be *nice*. Whereas once she had begged his advice about every last detail of their lives, now she planned vacations, business trips, decorating schemes, dinner parties, everything, without any regard for his preferences. Instead of bolstering his ego, she took pleasure in trying to deflate it. His business failures she attributed to lack of foresight, or worse, stupidity; his far more frequent successes she credited to luck. She was rude to his family and most of his friends. Whether the economy was up or down, the profits of Frankie's company rising or falling, she spent lavishly, and refused to listen if he asked her to economize a little. Worrying about money was just so middle class, she told him. And when he pointed out that he *was* middle class, *lower* middle class at that, barely a generation away from working class, Annabel smiled, and said, "But I'm not." Frankie thought he saw contempt in that smile.

Sometimes it seemed to him that Annabel, in producing a child, felt she had done as much as her marriage vows demanded, that Maud was as absolute a guarantee of her hold on him as she needed. Sure, not of him necessarily, but of her status as wife and mother, she no longer had to make an effort to hide her true self, the one he had failed to notice before he married her. But even when he finally acknowledged that she was a snob, that she was mercenary, selfish, demanding—even then, still dazzled by her, he continued to love her. It was a long time before he stopped, longer still until he noticed that he had. And when he did, after some agonizing over the question, he decided to remain married to her, for Maud's sake. However, he dropped the clause stipulating fidelity from the contract he renegotiated with himself.

Frankie's current girlfriend, Helen, sold advertising for NBC Television. Blond and pretty, she looked a little like Diane Keaton in her Annie Hall mode. She wore oversized clothes and floppy hats, which were attractive in an off-beat sort of way. Ambitious (though in Frankie's opinion not nearly as smart as she thought she was), Helen dreamed of climbing the corporate ladder to vice president in charge of something important, and had enrolled in the MBA program at Fordham. Tonight she had a class. So, with nothing in particular to do, nowhere in particular to go, Frankie headed for the club's bar, on the second floor of the new building. Designed by one of the most successful interior architects in the country, it had cost a small fortune to complete, and had been worth every penny. A large room, it had glass tables and upholstered chairs set in front of long windows overlooking Forty-third Street. There were leather couches, polished wood, loud music, and potted ficus trees. Trendier than the traditional bars in men's clubs, classier than the usual neighborhood hangout, it had an understated quality, a feeling of ease and comfort. But, even now, nearly empty, the cigarette smoke hung thick in the air. Frankie, who had given up cigarettes a couple of years before, would have liked nothing better than to ban smoking in the club, but the thought of plunging profits stopped him. If his customers wanted to die of lung cancer, he decided, that was their right.

Jake, the bartender, was on the phone. He didn't look happy, and, when he noticed Frankie coming toward him, he gestured with some relief to indicate that the call was for him. Frankie shook his head. Jake grimaced, then said, "Sorry, Mrs. Ferraro, I haven't seen him at all tonight. . . . Yeah. If he comes in, I'll tell him."

"Thanks," said Frankie, taking a seat at the bar.

"All in a day's work," said Jake, trying to keep any hint of how he felt (approving, disapproving, conspiratorial) from his face. "Want something to drink?" He was already reaching for the bottle of Glenmorangie that Frankie kept for his own use.

"Please," said Frankie. After years of pretending to like scotch, he had finally developed a taste for it. As he lifted the glass of fine malt whiskey, the phone rang again.

"It's Martha," said Jake, his hand over the mouthpiece. Again Frankie shook his head. "He's not here," Jake said into the phone. "She says to call your wife," he said, dropping the receiver back into its cradle.

Not even tempted, Frankie turned to say hello to Tom, the club's manager, who took the empty seat next to him. Tall, blond, a year or two older than he, Tom had worked as a trainer at Macklin's before Frankie bought the franchise, but had left to manage a gym on the Upper West Side. It had eventually gone bankrupt, and he'd hopped around the city from job to job until Frankie, after acquiring the company, had asked him to return to take over the day-to-day running of the original premises. Instead of responding with immediate and overwhelming gratitude, Tom had hesitated. "Before I say yes," he'd said finally, "I think I should tell you I'm homosexual." The news floored Frankie. He would never have guessed that the rugged-faced, deep-voiced, muscular athlete he'd known for years was a pansy. "Does that matter to you?"

Frankie felt self-conscious, uneasy, embarrassed. He wasn't sure why. It wasn't as if he expected Tom, after all this time, to make a pass at him. The idea was totally crazy. Yet . . . "I'm not sure," said Frankie.

"Think about it," said Tom.

Frankie did think. He thought about how long he'd known Tom, how much he liked him, how they'd always had a good working relationship. He thought about why he felt uncomfortable. No, *threatened.* He thought about Michelangelo and Leonardo da Vinci, about Alexander the Great and Gertrude Stein. He thought about his father, who was a world-class bigot, and his cousin Vic, who was not. He thought about who he was and who he wanted to be. He thought about it for three days, and then he called Tom. "I'm an asshole," he said. "If you still want the job, it's yours."

"I want it," said Tom.

They had been friends ever since.

*G*radually a group of club regulars began to collect in the bar, men Frankie and Tom had known for years, since they'd started working at Macklin's. Some were actors, usually out of work, one now a big success in a daytime soap, another with a burgeoning film career. Others had clawed their way up various ladders to positions of some responsibility, vice president at a television network, partner at a midtown law firm, a top-rank CPA, a stock broker. Sometimes Frankie threw a little business their way, sometimes they picked up a little more as a result of casual conversations with other members. But business wasn't the chief reason they continued to stop in at Macklin's before, during, or after a hard day's grind. What they liked was that the club had kept up with them. It had achieved success just as they had. Now it combined the virtues of familiarity, comfort, and—the most important one of all in a city like New York—trendiness. Thanks to the publicity Colette Drake never failed to provide, Macklin's was one of *the* places to go and be seen. And it didn't hurt that the club was co-ed. The bar was a great pickup place. It was where Frankie had met Helen, and a couple of the other women he'd been involved with in the past few years.

There were not a lot of women around that night, and, after about an hour of drinking at the bar, the lawyer suggested that they go get something to eat. Tom, as he usually did when the group was relentlessly heterosexual, claimed other plans. So did most of the others. But Frankie, now that several malt whiskies had banished his waiting wife completely from his mind, said food was just what he needed. Someone suggested heading downtown to Little Italy, but even with senses dulled by alcohol, he knew enough to veto that idea. Miranda's ghost still seemed to haunt the streets there, the restaurants. Anywhere south of Fourteenth Street depressed the hell out of him. Instead the three of them (the stockbroker, the lawyer, and Frankie), went uptown to Elaine's, where he was always assured of a table by the window, not so much because he had money, or was reasonably well known, but because he was handsome, and Elaine did have an eye for a handsome face.

At one of the tables sat Woody Allen and Diane Keaton; at another, there was a painter Frankie knew, a figurative artist (if you could call the bloated blimps he peopled his canvas with "figures") represented by the DeWitt Payson Gallery. He stopped to say hello, but refused the invitation to join him and his razor-thin, punk-haired girlfriend for dinner. Afterward, however, since nobody seemed overly concerned about showing up rested and alert at the office the next day, Frankie and his friends accompanied the couple to Regine for a couple of hours of mind-numbing music and dancing, then uptown to Eighty-second Street and Broadway, where someone had remembered a party was in progress. By the time they arrived, though the music was loud, the mood was mellow. The smell of pot hung in the air. Frankie saw joints being passed and pipes of hashish. Once, when he went to the john, he interrupted a blonde doing lines of coke. She took one look at Frankie's face and smiled. "Want some?"

"Not that," he said. He no longer did drugs.

"You don't know what you're missing."

She left the bathroom, but, when Frankie finished peeing, he found her waiting for him outside. He took a glass of something from a passing tray, and followed her into the apartment's study. Two men were at a table playing backgammon. A woman had headphones on and was watching Johnny Carson. Frankie sat on the sofa next to the blonde. "I'm Frankie," he said. What happened next remained a blur. The next day, all he could remember was that at some point his friends had retrieved him from a bedroom where he was in a state of advanced play with the Bathroom Blonde, as he came to call her. They took him downstairs, hailed a taxi, and dropped him off on Central Park West, in front of his apartment.

The doorman rushed out to meet him. "Good evening, Mr. Ferraro," he said, looking undecided about whether or not to offer help.

"I can walk," Frankie assured him. And he could, very well, considering. He started toward the entrance and then stopped. He remembered dimly that he didn't want to be here, that he had gone to great lengths to avoid being here. On the other hand, he couldn't at that moment think of anywhere else to go. He felt a sudden surge of anger. This was his place, after all. He'd bought it, paid for it, long before he'd met Annabel, long before he'd married her. Who did she think she was trying to keep him from it? He started walking again, through the door the cautious attendant held open for him, through the opulent art nouveau lobby, to the bank of elevators against the far wall. Fuck her, he thought. He was going home.

Chapter 17

All Frankie wanted was to make his way without incident to the guest bedroom, collapse onto the queen-sized bed, and sink into a deep and dreamless sleep from which he would awake, a considerable number of hours later, clearheaded and able to deal with the mounting problems of his domestic life. As he entered the apartment's large center hall, he began to hope that this might be possible. All was dark, quiet. His spirits lifted. Avoiding end tables topped by expensive unlit lamps, he made his way carefully along the hallway toward the promised sanctuary.

The apartment had large rooms and high ceilings. The sitting room, with its phenomenal view of Central Park, was used primarily for entertaining. For relaxing, or as much of it as was allowed, there was what his parents would have called the "den" but Annabel referred to as the "library." Paneled in alder and ash, it had deep shelves on three walls holding, in addition to the television set and stereo system, Frankie's books, which now ranged from paperback mysteries to valuable first editions. The dining room could seat sixteen comfortably. There were four bedrooms, the one Annabel now occupied, the guest room that Frankie had in the past several months made his own, Maud's nursery, and the housekeeper's suite, which was off the kitchen.

Over the objection of his parents, Frankie had bought the apartment in 1962, with money he had received in the settlement of Miranda's estate. After her death, when he couldn't stand to be alone in the apartment they'd shared, he had packed his clothes (along with the little Miranda had left behind), donated what remained to the St. Vincent de Paul Society, and had "gone home," as they put it, with Sal and Dolly. Numb with a grief that never seemed to lessen (though everyone had assured him it would), Frankie hadn't cared where he was; and, for a long while, the ties that bound him to his parents—the familiarity, the comfort, the love—held. Then he began to grow restless. Having lassoed him back into the family, wanting to tie him up and keep him there, his parents urged him to buy a place in the neighborhood. But whenever Dolly would find another house for sale nearby, whenever Sal would offer to lend him the money for a down payment,

Frankie would feel his throat tighten; he would feel a weight settle on his chest. Waves of panic would overwhelm him. He couldn't do it.

Colette mentioned the Central Park West apartment to him during one of their occasional nights of dinner and sex. A friend of hers (a former lover, suspected Frankie), a television producer, was moving, she said, to Los Angeles of all places, and selling the most wonderful apartment, one she would buy in a minute if she wasn't committed to living on the East Side. Curious, Frankie asked to see it. Immediately, without consulting anyone, he made an offer. Though the apartment had more rooms than he needed and the sixty-two-thousand-dollar price tag seemed high to him, he wanted the place. He liked the idea of himself living there, coming home to that impressive lobby, entering the period elevators, strolling through the high-ceilinged rooms, looking out at the same Central Park as New York's rich and famous. Dolly wept, Sal called him a fool, but Frankie, for the first time in over a year, had felt a sense of excitement, of hope.

He furnished the apartment slowly, gradually replacing items lent by his disappointed, disapproving, but always helpful parents with leather couches, chrome-and-glass tables, industrial carpeting, all of which Dolly refused to believe were the latest in Italian design ("Italian" to her meant not only spotlessly clean, but pretty imitation French) and Sal denounced as looking fit only for "a goddamn airline terminal. Like TWA." By the time Frankie met Annabel, the place was exactly the way he wanted it, masculine, comfortable, quietly expensive—and not at all to her taste. As soon as they were married, she started over. Now only his books remained. The apartment looked attractive, Frankie had to admit, with rose-patterned chintz upholstery and curtains, fringed lampshades, Chippendale tables, Meissen clocks, and oil landscapes by unknown but competent artists. It was still comfortable, but Frankie no longer felt at home. The place was Annabel's, not his, yet he remained fiercely possessive and proud of it, like an explorer who, though it had since been ruined by tourists, treasured the memory of the beautiful and unknown territory he had discovered long ago.

*J*ust beyond the door to Annabel's bedroom, a floorboard squeaked, and Frankie paused, wishing he'd thought of taking off his shoes at the front door. Then anger flared again. Fuck this, he thought. It's my goddamn apartment. And he proceeded at a normal pace toward the guest bedroom. Still, once he had entered and closed the door behind him, he felt a sense of relief. Safe, he thought. Smiling, he went through to the bathroom he now shared with his daughter. As he peed, he felt his head begin to clear as if the alcohol he had consumed was leaving his body in the steady stream of urine. He washed his hands and splashed his face with cold water. Despite a dull ache above his eyes, he felt sober enough. He didn't look too bad either, he thought, surveying his haggard face in the bathroom mirror. Then, beyond his reflection, he noticed the blue-and-yellow rubber boat sitting in the middle of the empty bathtub, a rubber Ernie resting on the ledge. Maud, he thought, feeling the familiar tug in his chest.

Leaving the bathroom through the opposite door, Frankie entered his daughter's room. In the dim glow thrown by the night light, he could see Maud's small body under the blankets, her dark head resting against the pillow, only her smooth cheek and tiny nose visible as she slept on her side, facing the wall. A stuffed animal and the worn blanket she couldn't seem to live without lay within easy reach. Leaning over, he inhaled her sweet smell, smoothed her hair back from her temple, and kissed her cheek. Disturbed, Maud flung her arm up as if to ward off an annoying insect, and Frankie felt a surge of pain as acute as if she had knowingly rejected him. When he returned from Boston, he promised himself, he would start spending more time with her.

Retracing his steps to the bedroom, Frankie felt an intense loneliness. Despite his wife and child asleep nearby, despite his mistress on East Seventy-seventh Street and his cousin on Riverside Drive, not to mention the rest of his enormous family scattered across Brooklyn, Queens, and Long Island, he felt alone in the world, with no one to whom he could go for comfort, or advice. Not switching on the light for fear it would make his headache worse, he held the thought as he started to undress, reveling in the comfort of self-pity. "Shit," he muttered finally. "I've got to stop drinking so much."

His impulse to reform was stopped dead in its tracks by the sudden spill of the overhead light and Annabel's irate voice saying, "And where, may I ask, have you been?"

The choked tones of her English accent, the thin, brittle quality of her voice, breaking in fury, grated on his ears. How could he ever have found it charming? wondered Frankie as he turned to face his wife. She was standing in the doorway, in one of her lady-of-the-manor ensembles, a heavy cream silk robe tied loosely over a matching gown. Her feet were bare. Tall and bulimically thin, she had long legs that gave her a loping boyish stride. Her face too was long, and narrow, startlingly asymmetrical, ending in a square stubborn chin. She looked like a Cubist portrait, Frankie had thought when he met her; and, dressed for public consumption, she did make a striking appearance, with her pale blond hair, her full mouth painted in vivid colors, her small gray eyes outlined heavily in black. When she was with people she wanted to impress, Annabel could be warm and amusing. At the moment, with hair hanging limp, without makeup, her face pale and angry, she re-

minded Frankie (as she did more and more lately) of the crabbed principal
of a girl's boarding school, or the menacing matron of a loony bin.

"Well?" Annabel dropped her hand from the light switch and clenched
it at her side.

His shoes off, his belt undone, Frankie continued unbuttoning his shirt,
but stopped there. Being naked in front of his wife these days left him feeling
too vulnerable. He said, his voice calm, reasonable, "I ran into a couple of
the guys. We had a few drinks."

"A few?"

"All right. More than a few." Impatience began to creep into his tone,
and a hint of guilt. "Look, Annabel, I'm tired. I'd like to go to bed. Do you
think we could save the argument for another time?"

"And having drinks with your *friends*," she continued, "was of course
more important than showing up for a dinner party—"

"Oh, shit!" Her goddamn dinner party had completely slipped his mind.

"—for which you were the host. I don't expect much of you, Francis—"

It sounded like "Frahnces," the way she said it. "Frankie," he corrected
automatically. From the start, she had refused to call him that. At first he had
been thrilled by the sound of his name delivered in her accent. Now it
irritated the hell out of him.

"But I don't think a little thing like common courtesy is too much to ask,
do you?" she continued, ignoring him.

She was right. As long as they were married, he should at least make an
effort not to embarrass her in public. "Annabel," he said, "I'm sorry.
Really—"

"You're sorry. And that's supposed to make everything all right?"

"What do you want me to say? What do you want me to do? I forgot.
And I apologize. Okay?" The truth was, he didn't feel all that bad about it.
Though once he'd stood in awe of Annabel's friends (how he hated to admit
that, even to himself), had thought them the quintessence of elegance and
wit, by now he couldn't stand most of them.

"Forgot? Of course. That's perfectly obvious," she went on, "but what I
do *not* understand is how you possibly could."

"For chrissake, let's not make a bigger deal out of this than necessary. It's
not like anybody was devastated by my absence."

"Not bloody likely. Insulted is more like it! I felt like a fool. Do you think
anybody believed that pathetic lie I told about an *emergency* at the office?
Emergency! 'What? Did the juicer break?' That's what Clive said. Everybody
laughed. *Everybody!*"

What little guilt Frankie had felt was wiped out completely by anger.
"Well, we know Clive wouldn't lower himself to do anything as amusing as
work for a living. So I'm glad he can get some enjoyment out of my job."

"Clive's no fool. Neither are the rest of my friends. They knew you weren't working. They knew you were out screwing some miserable little whore."

"If I was, I was at least having a better time than here with that bunch of parasites."

She moved away from the threshold, taking a step toward him. "Who the hell do you think you are that you can talk about my friends like that?"

Frankie held his ground. "Who do I think I am? I'll tell you who. I'm the poor slob who pays for your clothes, your hair, your nails, for your shopping sprees and exercise classes, for all the food you feed that supercilious bunch of jerks you call your friends. I'm your husband, that's who. And maybe you should keep that in mind. Maybe it'll inspire you to think of some way to keep me happy enough to go on footing the bill."

"Some husband!"

"And you're such a terrific wife. Right?"

"If you think I'd let you touch me, the way you come home, drunk, smelling of—"

"That's about the only I way could manage it. The only way I could stand to fuck you . . . if I was drunk!"

"You bastard!" She sprang at him, her hand raised. He grabbed her wrist, hard. "Let me go," she said. "You're hurting me!" That was the point. He wanted to hurt her. He could feel the rage inside him like a fire, burning, robbing him of air. Annabel swiveled her body, and, as Frankie eased his hold, she fell to her knees and buried her face in his groin. "Oh, darling. Oh, Frances," she murmured.

He released her and moved away. He'd never hit her, but he'd come close, closer than this. She had watched him in his rages, watched him punch walls, throw lamps, smash furniture. A lesser woman would have been cowed. Annabel was fearless. Frankie had to give her credit for that. Instead of terror, he'd seen admiration in her eyes, followed quickly by desire. In the early days of their relationship, arguments had always ended in sex, fierce, fast, and without a trace of tenderness. Frankie had liked that. It had added a new, unexpected, titillating dimension to their lovemaking. But what had felt permissible when he loved his wife (playful sex, experimental sex, even angry sex) did not when he stopped. Though he'd long ago dismissed as irrelevant the moral code taught in the weekly religion lessons of his childhood (the one that designated sex outside marriage—*any* sex not directed toward the begetting of a child—a mortal sin), somewhere along the way he had acquired a standard of his own, one more instinctive than reasoned. Sex as an expression of rage, of violence, was a sin, all right, one against humanity—not just the woman's (which in all honesty concerned him less) but his own. Not much of a code, maybe, but one he felt compelled to live by.

As Annabel rose slowly to her feet, Frankie buckled his belt, buttoned his shirt, stepped into his loafers. When he reached for the jacket he'd thrown over a chair, she said, "Where are you going?"

"Out."

"Oh, yes, go to your whore." She was standing in front of him, blocking his path to the door.

"Get out of my way."

"Maybe she knows some dirty little tricks to help you get it up. That's your problem, isn't it? You just can't get it up anymore."

Christ, how he wanted to hit her! "Annabel, don't make me do something I'll regret," he said. His face was white, his voice quiet.

"Hit me? You don't have the guts." She leaned toward him belligerently, offering her face. "Or do you? Go on! Hit me! Prove you're a man."

Hitting her wouldn't be enough. Maybe even killing her wouldn't be enough. He was afraid to put his hands on her even to move her out of his way. He was afraid that once he touched her, he'd be lost. "Get the fuck away from me!" he shouted.

She held her ground. Feeling desperate, Frankie pushed past her, and out of the room, all his willpower directed toward getting out of the apartment without striking her. "You bastard," he heard her shriek as he opened the front door. She was running in her bare feet along the hallway toward him. "Don't you dare leave!" Maud began to cry, and for a moment Frankie hesitated. But it was too dangerous to go back, much too dangerous. He slammed the door shut behind him. The elevator, thank God, was where he'd left it, and he stepped into it just as Annabel opened the apartment door. But fear of what the neighbors would think kept her quiet. She stood there white-faced, trembling with impotent rage, watching the elevator doors close, protecting each of them from the other's wrath.

*B*y the time Frankie cooled down enough to think calmly he was at Central Park South. It was four in the morning and, though spring with its budding trees and random flowering azaleas had definitely arrived in Manhattan, his wool jacket was no defense against the sharp wind coming off the park. Except for the headlight of an occasional passing car and a solitary beggar asleep on a bench, he was alone. Lines from the Wordsworth sonnet, "Westminster Bridge," came into his head and he laughed. No, the sight of *this* city asleep did not fill him with a sense of elation, though it was certainly beautiful, with its tall buildings looming like ghostly castles on his right, the park on his left fading into an enchanted forest, and overhead a midnight blue canopy studded with fairy lights. It scared the shit out of him. Now that he was aware once again of his surroundings, danger seemed to lurk in every shadow. Manhattan was no place for a lonely predawn stroll.

One of the passing headlights belonged to a taxi and Frankie stepped off the sidewalk to hail it. Without thinking, he gave Helen's address to the driver, then climbed in and settled back against the torn rear seat. "There's a bonus in it for you if you can get me there without hitting a pothole," he said.

The driver nodded. "I do it," he said. He was Lebanese. It seemed to Frankie that you didn't have to read a newspaper to find out where the world's trouble spots were. You just had to look at the licenses of New York cabbies.

As the taxi rattled along Central Park South toward the East Side, Frankie had second thoughts about his destination, none of which concerned Helen. It never crossed his mind that she might not be thrilled about a visit from him in the middle of the night. What did occur to him, however, was that, as a reward for being awakened from a sound sleep, she might expect an explanation, or worse, sex, neither of which Frankie was in any mood to provide. "I've changed my mind," he said. "Take me to the Carlyle instead." To be safe, he gave the driver its location. (It was never wise to assume these new immigrants actually knew where anything was.) "Nice job," said Frankie, when the cab pulled to a smooth stop in front of the hotel. The promised big tip earned him a smile, a rare sight in the city.

The sound of the taxi door brought the dozing doorman to life and he sprang to attention, wishing Frankie a good morning as he held the door wide. Inside, the lobby was deserted except for the wide-awake young woman at the desk. Hoping he didn't look as bad as he felt, he said, "I'd like a room for what's left of the night." He had no luggage; his clothes were rumpled, his face haggard. She should be forgiven, he decided, for eyeing him with such suspicion. Instead of affronted dignity, he tried a smile. It did the trick.

"Certainly," she said, taking his American Express card. She handed him a registration form, looked up questioningly when she saw his address, then away again when she realized it was none of her business if he didn't choose to go home.

The fact that she was pretty registered somewhere in Frankie's consciousness and he offered another appreciative smile before turning to follow the bellman who, despite the absence of luggage, was to lead him to his room. "Thank you," he said.

"Have a nice night."

Fat chance, thought Frankie. In the first place, he felt too rotten to enjoy the luxury of being alone. In the second, the Carlyle always reminded him of Eva. It was where she stayed when she came to New York, which, perversely, was why, on the occasions when he had need of a hotel in the city, he inevitably chose this one. He was still not beyond demonstrating, though he was usually the only one watching, that nothing good enough for Eva Colvington was too good for Frankie Ferraro. Refusing the tour of the room and its amenities, Frankie tipped the bellman to get rid of him, then stripped down to his shorts. He hung his clothes neatly in the closet, called room service to order breakfast (black coffee, a toothbrush, and razor), paid a brief visit to the bathroom, and got into bed. He wished he'd grabbed the copy of *The Ends of Power* from his bedside table, though Haldeman's account of the Watergate mess was hardly likely to lull him to sleep. Closing his eyes, he waited for the whiskey he'd drunk to do its job; but, instead, images of Annabel crowded into his aching head, contradictory and confusing images, Annabel as she had been when he met her, Annabel as she was now, hardly recognizable as the same person. Had she really changed so much? he wondered. Had he? It was at times like this that he grew desperate for a cigarette.

Frankie had met his present wife (a meeting he remembered only vaguely) at a party in London, in September of 1969. He'd stopped off there on his way home after spending a couple of weeks with Dan Colvington and his family in a villa they'd leased in the Veneto. After checking into the Savoy, Frankie had called Kalima Burden, and she'd asked him to a party for one of Sir Nigel's more important authors. Their house in Carlyle Square had been crowded, full of publishers, members of parliament, the cream of London's literary elite, and Sir Nigel's daughter Flora and her group of trendy friends, one of whom was Annabel. Flora had probably flirted with him. She usually did. But, by then, a combination of nonstop reading and increasing financial success had made Frankie less timid in social situations, and Flora was a lot less interesting to him than the writers present. Or Kalima. *She* had fascinated him from the beginning. And the more he saw of her (usually at parties hosted by Dan who had joined the Colvington Mead publishing company after graduating from Yale), the more Kalima made it clear that she returned his interest, encouraging him every way but sexually. At that, she drew the line. As she explained the one time Frankie had summoned the courage to broach the subject, she was a flirtatious but nonetheless faithful wife. And since her position meshed with Ferraro beliefs about the proper conduct of women, he took the rebuff with good grace. He and Kalima remained friends. However, when she was near, it was difficult for other women to engage his interest. They all paled beside her vibrant beauty.

But Flora was persistent, and Kalima was not at all dog-in-the-mangerish about her admirers. At her stepdaughter's request, a few nights after the party, she asked Frankie to dinner at the Burden home. Flattered, he went. Annabel was another of the guests. She and Flora owned a business together, an antiques store in Pimlico that they had started with items salvaged from the attics of their respective family homes, adding pieces on consignment from friends. They had built it slowly into a successful enterprise, a favorite with foreign tourists, especially American tourists, thrilled at the prospect of returning home from their vacations with a genuine piece of England's heritage. Unfortunately for Flora, and, as it turned out, for Frankie too, Annabel was the piece of England's heritage he took home with him, not that trip, but soon after.

In other circumstances Frankie would probably never have noticed Annabel. She wasn't pretty enough to attract his attention. But there she was, sitting next to him at Kalima's dinner table, being flatteringly attentive. Still, Frankie was used to that. In fact, Flora, seated to his left, was making her attraction to him equally clear. But poor Flora was neither as beautiful as Kalima nor as interesting as Annabel Lindsey. "Frankie," she'd said with a visible twitch of her narrow nose. "Is it short for Francis?"

"Yes. Francis Xavier."

"How lovely." She had called him Francis ("Frahnces") the rest of the evening.

What first appealed to him was Annabel's energy. She was full of life. She laughed a lot and had an opinion about everything. He admired that. He felt she was someone from whom he could learn a great deal. Somewhere between the duck and the profiteroles, he began to find her odd face attractive. And when Kalima rose to lead the ladies from the room, Annabel's long loping stride conjured for Frankie the aura of riding lessons and nannies, garden parties and race meets, the essence of Englishness. As he sat at the table with the men, wreathed in cigar smoke, lingering over port, discussing the implications of Neil Armstrong's walk on the moon, the riots in Londonderry, the war in Vietnam, and the death of Mary Jo Kopechne, the latter of riveting interest to the mostly rabid anti-Americans at the table, Frankie found himself anxious for the ritual to come to an end so that he could rejoin the women in the drawing room. And there, when he heard one of the footmen serving coffee address her as "Lady" Annabel, Frankie was caught. He was dazzled and intrigued. Humility and pride struggled. (She was too good for him. Like hell she was!) Pride won. He asked her if she'd like to go to the theater with him one night. Indeed yes, said Annabel. She would like nothing better.

"What love was ever as deep as a grave?" A line from a Swinburne poem, it was a question to which Frankie had thought he knew the answer. He was sure he'd buried his heart with Miranda. In the eight years since her death, though he'd had other lovers, he'd never experienced anything stronger for

them than affection, more potent than desire. He didn't expect to with Annabel either. She wasn't the sort of woman he believed he could love. For
one thing, she was as different from Miranda as it was possible to be.

Frankie had stayed in London longer than he planned. He went with
Annabel to the theater, to race meets, to private clubs to dance. There he
met celebrities who, he admitted (though only to himself), took his breath
away. "Oh, Francis, darling," Annabel would say, with a style not even Eva
Colvington could match, "I'd like you to meet Sir John Gielgud." Or Harold
Pinter. Or Ringo Starr. Or Twiggy. Or the duke of something-or-other.
Frankie was careful not to appear star-struck, but he was, not by the indi-
viduals themselves, but by the cumulative fact of them, and that he, Frankie
Ferraro, the boy from Brooklyn, had somehow gained access to their illus-
trious presence.

Mummy and Daddy had passed away, Annabel told him when she asked
him for a weekend to the family home in Kent, now occupied by her only
sibling, her brother Roland (the Earl of Melton!), his wife and two sons. The
home turned out to be a castle, with enormous state rooms hung with family
portraits by van Dyck and grounds landscaped by Capability Brown. The
place was going to ruin, she explained. The earl made a reasonable living as
a stockbroker, but had to scramble to make ends meet. He was exploring a
number of ways to boost estate revenues, and at the moment was planning
to follow the lead of many of his peers and open the castle to the public to
help pay for its maintenance, an idea Annabel hated. "All those grubby people
pricing the furniture. Ugh," she said with a delicate shiver of distaste.

He'd been invited to a house party, Frankie discovered to his dismay,
feeling like a Yankee outfielder among cricket captains, out of place among
the large group of guests, all of whom had known each other forever, or so
it seemed. Fascinated by their accents, their supreme self-assurance, their
impeccable manners, their extensive vocabularies and easy charm, he couldn't
seem to separate the genuinely interesting from the vain, the shallow, the
silly—or determine how they felt about him. They carried on in a code he
couldn't quite break. "Everyone's terribly jealous of you," Annabel had told
him one afternoon as they strolled around the lake that the great Brown had
created to provide an appropriate vista for the castle. "They are," she insisted
when Frankie declared that hard to believe. "It's not just that you're handsome or that you have money. Although we all care a great deal more about
money than we're willing to admit. But you know how to take charge of
your life. You make things happen. They just sit back and wait, expecting
that something will turn up. Nothing much ever does." Plenty was happening to him, Frankie thought. He felt as if he'd become a character in a
drawing room comedy, in a film by George Cukor, in a novel by Jane
Austen. Though not always comfortable, he liked the feeling very much.

After his return to New York, Frankie, who was in a lull between business ventures, began to find his life predictable and boring. The women he was dating seemed ordinary and dull. He called Annabel in London and asked her to come. She agreed and he sent a first-class ticket. Boredom vanished. For the next year, Annabel and he hopped back and forth across the Atlantic, for long weekends. They took trips together, somehow never to places that Frankie had expressed a desire to see, but wherever Annabel wanted to go. He didn't mind. It was all very romantic. His guard began to slip. Annabel was so confident, successful, strong, so completely the opposite of Miranda, surely she was safe to love?

In April of 1971, they were married. Flora was maid of honor, and Dan best man. The ceremony took place in the small stone church in the village neighboring Castle Melton, performed by the local vicar, to the clearly expressed dismay of Dolly and Sal. Except for his parents, Angela and Denny, Dan and his wife, all the guests at the wedding breakfast were relatives and friends of the bride.

"Very nice people," Dolly had said to her son with as much enthusiasm as she could muster. She would have felt more comfortable among Martians. "But what a shame the way they've let this place go to ruin!" The evidence of damp on the wallpaper, the threadbare upholstery on the furniture, all the signs of neglect, amazed her. "How can people live like this?" she whispered to her daughter. Angela had laughed, and repeated the comment to Frankie, who had not found it funny or endearing. It had reminded him of Annabel's remark about tourists pricing the furniture. It embarrassed him; and it confirmed the distance he had put between himself and his family, a distance he was willing to travel, because he loved them, to drop in on their world from time to time, but that was it. Staying was out of the question, no matter how comfortable a place it seemed.

He'd gone too far to be able to get back, that much was true. And he couldn't honestly say he regretted it, anymore than he regretted the loss of his Brooklyn accent to the more acceptable (to him, at any rate) mid-Atlantic one he now had, thanks in large part to the influence of his wife. But marrying Annabel had been a mistake. Frankie was clear about that much, though even now he didn't see how he could have known it at the time. To quote his father, what was he after all, a goddamn psychic?

A knock at the door interrupted that disturbing flow of thought. Frankie sat up and switched on the light. "Just a minute," he called. It was seven already, he hadn't slept, and he felt like shit. Going into the bathroom, he took the terry robe from its hook, put it on, and returned to the bedroom to remove the chain from the door. "By the window's okay," he said to the waiter, who was bearing aloft a silver tray containing the coffee and toiletry articles Frankie had ordered. He took the copy of *The Times* from the doorknob, dropped it on the desk where he'd left his wallet and keys the night before, and extracted a couple of dollars from the leather billfold.

"Shall I pour the coffee, sir?" the waiter asked.

"No, thanks. Just leave it." Frankie managed a smile, and offered the money. The waiter took it with a murmured thank-you. Frankie nodded, then turned away, picked up the newspaper, and carried it to the table by the window. As he sat in the brocaded chair, he heard the door shut. Wearily, he closed his eyes. He didn't know how he was going to get through the day.

Chapter 18

Determined to keep his promise to himself to see more of his daughter, after leaving the Carlyle, Frankie returned to Central Park West. Once there, however, instead of going up to the apartment and risking another scene with Annabel, he waited outside. Feeling embarrassed, uncomfortable, wary, like a burglar casing the planned site of a robbery, he leaned against a nearby lamppost and watched the entrance. His discomfort did not improve his mood. Neither did the questioning looks of the doorman. What the fuck was he doing, lurking outside his own home? Frankie asked himself, more than once. But before his anger could build to a great enough pitch for him to storm inside, the consequences be damned, he saw Maud, accompanied by the housekeeper, coming out of the building. She was wearing a denim jacket over a blue plaid pinafore, and denim Mary Janes with white-ruffled ankle socks. Her long dark hair was fastened over each ear with berets. Her face was pensive, somber, as if she expected to get little pleasure from the day. But she looked beautiful, he thought as he walked toward her, and said, "Hello, sweetheart."

"Daddy!" she said, her voice a blend of pleasure and anxiety, a hesitant smile forming on her face.

Frankie swept her up into his arms. "I hope you're as glad to see me as I am to see you. Good morning, Mrs. Ashby," he added, smiling at the housekeeper, a lean figure in a long gray coat and small gray hat.

"Good morning, Mr. Ferraro," she said politely. Tall, with silky white hair and pale skin the texture of dried rose petals, April Ashby was somewhere in her early sixties, though she seemed older, much older, like something carefully preserved from the last century. She and her late husband had worked for Annabel's parents. Her son worked for Roland, in his City office, not at the castle. Frankie couldn't rely on her for help.

"I'll take Maud to school today," he said cheerfully, as if what he was suggesting was a usual occurrence.

Mrs. Ashby's face folded into a frown. "I really don't——"

"You must have a lot of things to do," Frankie continued, interrupting her. He smiled. "And if you don't, well, you've earned an hour or so of free time. Go have a coffee, a Danish, read a magazine."

The frown did not diminish. "Lady Annabel——"

Frankie removed one arm from Maud's compact body and raised it to hail a taxi. "Tell her Maud's with me. Enjoy yourself," he called as he settled himself and his daughter inside and closed the door in April Ashby's disapproving face.

As the taxi pulled away from the curb, Maud craned her delicate neck to peer anxiously after the housekeeper's diminishing figure. To get her attention Frankie said, "I kissed you good night last night. You were sleeping."

Turning to look at him, she said, "You did?" She sounded surprised.

"That's right," he said. "I meant to come home in time to read you a story, but, well, something came up. . . ."

"You had to work late." Except for the sweet, high-pitched tone of her voice, she sounded very grown-up. Annabel disapproved of baby talk. So did he, for that matter.

"Not exactly," said Frankie, feeling guilty and reluctant to add to the guilt by lying to his daughter. "I ran into some friends. I'm sorry about that."

"Will you read me a story tonight?"

It's like going to confession, thought Frankie. Saying you're sorry isn't enough. You've got to promise not to commit the same sin again. No wonder he hadn't gone in years. "I have to go away today, for a few days, but when I get back, I will. I promise."

"Two stories?"

Frankie grinned. "Well, I'll read you one. And you can read one to me." Maud was just learning how, and loved to show off her accomplishment. "You're looking very pretty today," he said, changing the subject.

Finally his daughter smiled without reservation. "I have new shoes," she said, wiggling her feet for his approval. "They have straps." Her accent, despite Annabel and April Ashby, was completely American. It was all the television she watched, Frankie supposed, and her school. He doubted he spent enough time with her to be an influence.

As the taxi bumped and rolled through the Central Park transverse toward Maud's Park Avenue school, Frankie listened to his daughter chatter happily about her clothes, about her teacher, about her best friend, Georgia, whose "daddy takes her to the mu-zeen," she informed him, her eyes wide with sincerity. She doesn't even know the meaning of the word blackmail, thought Frankie, and she's great at it. "They have pictures there. Bigger than the pictures we draw at school." She sounded as if she could not quite imagine anything in the world quite so big. "Can I see them?" she asked, but without conviction.

Why would that be? wondered Frankie, who had always assumed that his daughter was spoiled, as most affluent kids were supposed to be. Who said no to her so often that she doubted even such a simple request would be granted? Whatever toys she wanted, she got. Birthday parties were huge celebrations. The apartment the day after Christmas looked as if FAO Schwarz had opened a branch store on the premises. Friends were imported on demand for play dates. Anywhere she wanted to go, if Annabel and Frankie weren't able to take her, which was usually the case, Mrs. Ashby always did. What had Maud ever been denied that now made her sound so tentative? The company of her parents, he realized with a fresh surge of guilt. He reached out a hand to touch the shining dark hair that hung straight to Maud's shoulders. Twisting a strand of it around his finger, he said, "When I come back from my trip, we'll go." There was no trace of smugness in her answering smile. It was simply, purely, radiant. Something inside Frankie did a somersault. He was enjoying himself, he realized. He liked spending time with his child.

Then why didn't he do it more often? he asked himself later, when he was back in a taxi on his way to work, after he had left Maud with her teacher, spent a few minutes exchanging pleasantries with the parents of her schoolmates, promised Georgia's very attractive mother that of course he'd ask Mrs. Ashby to phone to arrange a play date for the girls (he noticed that she did not suggest Annabel do it). Annabel would say it was because he was a selfish bastard, because he always put his own interests first, because he cared about no one's pleasure but his own. Frankie didn't believe, didn't *want* to believe, that was true. The way he saw it, he spent far too much of his life trying to keep other people happy—his wife, his parents, his employees. With most of them, he succeeded, or at least he did most of the time. Annabel was his only failure, Annabel whose complaints, whose demands, whose refusal to be satisfied drove him crazy, made him run for the hills, take cover, keep out of her way as much as possible. But keeping out of her way meant keeping out of his daughter's as well. He had to do something about that, about his wife, about his child, about his marriage. He couldn't let things go on as they were. None of them could stand it. But what was the best thing, the *right* thing to do? He wasn't sure, and the uncertainty left him feeling paralyzed.

*T*he corporate headquarters of Ferraro Clubs, Incorporated, or FCI for short, was in a suite of offices in a fifty-storey building on Avenue of the Americas at Fifty-fourth Street. There was a fountain in front and a small park behind, which Frankie's own office overlooked. Only about twenty people worked for the company, including two vice presidents, several executives, their assistants and secretaries, a receptionist, a mailroom clerk, and a trainee who ran errands and filled in where and when needed. It was a small group of comparatively well-paid people who managed to keep office politics to a minimum; and, despite Frankie's quick temper, calm usually prevailed. For the past few years, as business improved and his marriage deteriorated, this place, like the Forty-third Street club, had become a refuge from problems. However, one look at his secretary's face when he arrived warned him that there was no escaping them that day.

"Good morning, Mr. Ferraro," Martha said, her voice cool.

" 'Morning, Martha. What's up? There's a problem?" It could be more bad news from Boston, where the health club was being renovated, he thought hopefully; or another delay in the shipment of new equipment for White Plains despite promises given only yesterday; or . . .

"No problem," she said unconvincingly. She took a breath. "Your wife would like you to call her. As soon as you get in, she said."

"What time did she phone?" If enough time had passed, Annabel might have gone out, making it safe to return her call.

"Let me see," said Martha, referring to her notes. "Her first call was at five past nine." She ran her pencil down the list. "And her last was three minutes ago."

"It must be important," said Frankie with a try at a smile.

"Apparently."

Under the coolness in her voice, Frankie could hear the suppressed rage. "Look, Martha, I'm sorry if, uh, if Annabel gave you a hard time." Tall and slender, with thick brown shoulder-length hair, she had an oval face with regular features, a strong chin, and nice hazel eyes, not a beauty, but not bad, either. She dressed well, simply, without flash, in classic styles that suited her. And, more important than any of that, she was a good secretary, intelligent, trustworthy, reliable, someone he could depend on. He didn't want to lose her.

"*Lady* Annabel, I believe she likes to be called."

It must have been some fucking conversation, thought Frankie. "Yeah, well, I think she'll settle for Mrs. Ferraro." At least for the time being. "Okay. If you get her on the line for me, I'll talk to her." Taking another look at Martha's face, he went on, "Never mind. I'll do it myself. I'll just get a cup of coffee first."

"I'll get it," she said quickly.

Frankie's spirits lifted a quarter of an inch. He laughed. He couldn't help it. Martha blushed. Getting coffee was one of the duties she felt was beneath her. She must be desperate for him to call Annabel, before Annabel called again, which she would. When she was in this kind of mood, she never gave up. "Thank you," said Frankie. Then, his face sobering, he turned and went into his office, sat at his desk, and picked up the phone.

The housekeeper answered. "Mrs. Ashby," said Frankie, "would you tell my wife I'm on the phone." He didn't bother to say please. And when a few minutes later he heard Annabel hiss his name, he cut her short with, "What the hell did you say to Martha?" It was always best to take the offensive.

"Oh, yes," said Annabel bitterly. "Of course. Poor Martha. Did I hurt her feelings? How dreadful of me."

"If you're mad at me, then take it out on me—"

"Is she one of your little tarts? Are you fucking her too? Did you spend last night with her? Is that why you're so angry?"

"If you said anything like that to Martha, if you even hinted, if you insulted her, I swear to God I'll strangle you the next time I see you."

"You are, aren't you?"

"I am not! Jesus Christ, are you crazy? She's my secretary!" As if that would have stopped him if he'd found Martha attractive, which he didn't. "I like her. I rely on her. And if she quits because of you—"

Martha chose that moment to enter. She blushed again, but otherwise showed no sign of having overheard the conversation. Without looking at Frankie, she put the mug of coffee down on his desk, then turned and hurried from the room.

"This is pointless," said Frankie, his voice calmer. "You didn't call just to hurl dumb accusations at me, did you? You wanted something?"

"What I want . . ." said Annabel. Her voice, like Frankie's, had grown quieter, but heavy with sarcasm. "What I *need*, I'm beginning to doubt you could ever give me." The feeling's mutual, he thought, but he kept his mouth shut. He'd run out of steam. Gone was the anger, the desire to fight. All he wanted was peace. "However, I would appreciate," she continued, "your not interfering with the way I raise Maud."

They went on bickering for a few minutes about whether or not Frankie should have told Annabel what he intended, about whether or not Mrs. Ashby had been mortally wounded by the slight to her authority, about whether or not Frankie would promise not to repeat the offense. "She's my daughter. If I want to take her to school, I will," he said finally. He took a sip of the coffee, then added, "I don't know why you're making such a big deal out of this."

"I am not, as you put it, making a big deal," said Annabel. "I am simply asking you not to interfere with my arrangements for Maud without checking with me first."

"Fine," said Frankie, though he wasn't sure he meant it.

"I hope you mean that, Francis."

"Whatever you want."

"Oh, yes," she said. He said nothing and after a moment she asked, "Will you be home this evening?"

"I have to go to Boston."

"I see."

"I did tell you." He was sure he had. "I'm meeting with the architect and the contractor about those renovations."

"Well, I'll see you sometime, I suppose."

"Late Friday."

"I'm leaving for London Friday morning. I'm spending the weekend with Roland and Elizabeth, then Flora and I are going scouting." Annabel and Flora still owned the shop in Pimlico, plus another on Columbus Avenue, which they had opened two years before. Both were doing well in a small way, selling the furniture that Annabel had begun recently to design plus antiques that she and Flora somehow still managed to acquire at reasonable prices. Three or four times a year they went off together to hunt for more.

Annabel would be gone at least a week, maybe longer. The relief accompanying that thought felt almost like happiness. "Have a good time," he said.

"Why not? I have no doubt you will." And she hung up.

Frankie replaced the receiver, took another swallow of coffee, then pressed the intercom. "Come in, would you?" he said, when Martha answered. A moment later, the door opened and she entered. She looked calm, collected. "Look, if my wife said anything to . . . well . . ." Embarrassment stopped him. "Anyway," he said finally, "she asked me to apologize for her."

"Sure," said Martha, as if she believed him. "It's okay. It's forgotten."

"Thanks."

"Sure," repeated Martha. "Is that all?"

"Yes," said Frankie. "That's all. No, wait a minute. Call the store and see what time Annabel is expected there today." He wanted, if possible, to go home and pack for his trip to Boston without running into her. "It would be great if her assistant didn't know it was you asking."

If she wasn't the sort of person who liked to maintain a dignified demeanor in front of her employer, Martha might have rolled her eyes. Instead, she said, "I'll hold my nose." Whether to disguise her voice or in protest wasn't clear.

Frankie laughed. "If it'll help," he said.

. . .

*A*fter changing into a clean shirt from a supply he kept on hand, Frankie spent the remainder of the morning working. He reviewed the figures for the purchase of a piece of property in Miami with Louie Sutter, the company's financial officer, then called the real estate broker to say no. During the period of inflation and high interest rates that had followed the 1973 OPEC oil embargo, Frankie had stopped expanding, concentrating instead on selling off the less successful facilities and improving the others. Basically he had laid low. Now he was feeling anxious to make a move. However, with many of the existing clubs still needing renovation and interest rates remaining high, he was reluctant to take on debt he wasn't sure he could handle—the sort of decision that would please his conservative father, but one Frankie regretted having to make. Miami had possibilities. He returned phone calls, answered letters, read an article that Martha had called to his attention about the results of some recent studies on health and diet, and made a note to review the menus of the clubs' snack bars and restaurants. At ten to one he put on his jacket and left the office to keep his lunch date with Colette.

Miss Drake had not yet arrived, the maître d' informed Frankie when he entered the restaurant, but their table was ready, if Mr. Ferraro would care to be seated. Cendrillon was French, fashionable, modeled after La Coupole, though on a much smaller scale, given the price of New York real estate. The thing to do was to sit in the front, near the door, but when Frankie saw that "Madame's favorite table" would result in a nonstop stream of greeters, he asked for another, a booth in a corner, against the wall, which caused a moment of shocked surprise followed by a quick yes, as the maître d' tried to conceal his pleasure at having so desirable a property suddenly free to be auctioned to the highest bidder.

"I can't believe where they sat us," said Colette when she arrived to the sound of Jacques Brel singing softly in the background. Frankie stood to greet her, and she absently returned his kiss, then added, "I saw an empty table near the door." She turned to call the retreating maître d', but Frankie took her arm.

"I like this table," he said as he eased her into her seat.

Colette hesitated, then decided she had bigger fish to fry, and smiled. "Why you insist on hiding your light under a bushel . . ." she said, sitting.

She was wearing an orange wool jersey two-piece dress, with a sashed waist and a loose flowing skirt, a heavy gold necklace and earrings, and a ring that might have come from a cereal box except that it, too, was made of gold. Thanks to genes rather than plastic surgery, her face was virtually unlined. To conceal the gray, she had dyed the hair she now wore in a flattering bob a lighter shade of its original brown. She ate sparingly, went to health spas at least twice a year, and worked out regularly—with a private trainer, rather than at one of the clubs, despite the deal Frankie had offered her. As a result of all this hard work, Colette looked years younger than the sixty-one she'd die rather than admit to, still quite a woman, still sexy, something Frankie remained aware of, though they'd stopped sleeping together sometime in the late '60s when she'd married a widower eleven years her senior, a retired lawyer, who worshiped the ground she walked on.

Over a glass of white wine, they discussed the pending media campaign. Once again Frankie refused to appear in the print ads. He didn't like calling attention to himself. He found it embarrassing. Which, in Colette's opinion, was ridiculous. Men would flock to the clubs, she argued, in the hope that somehow they might end up looking like an Italian stud. Women, too, just to catch a glimpse of him. "You'll find another way to make them flock," he said. "So far you've been doing a great job."

Pleased with the compliment, Colette smiled; and, as she worked her way through her seafood salad, she went on talking about plans for the summer promotion. Frankie tried to keep his mind on what she was saying, but an image of Maud's unhappy little face kept getting in the way. Finally, she dropped her fork, leaned toward him and said, "You're facing a wall, so I can't suspect you of being distracted by another woman. Unless there's one on your mind. Is there?"

"What makes you think it's a woman?" said Frankie. "Why not business?" Colette still asked too many questions.

"Because I know how well your business is doing."

And how awful my marriage is, thought Frankie. "It's my daughter," he said. He wasn't in the habit of confiding in Colette. He didn't really confide in anyone, at least not about the things that really bothered him, but this seemed different. And Colette was a friend. "I don't spend enough time with her."

"Most men don't spend enough time with their kids," she said, not sounding in the least judgmental. She probably wouldn't spend much time with her children either—if she had any. "Did your father spend a lot of time with you?"

"Not a lot, I guess." He thought about it for a while. "I mean, he was home for dinner every night—that's the way I remember it, anyhow. And around every weekend. Summers we went away two weeks, maybe three, with my uncle and his family." He took another bite of grilled chicken, and said, "More time than I spend with Maud, anyway."

"So he was a pretty good dad?"

"Well, he never showed up for events at school, plays and stuff like that, the way I do for Maud. I didn't mind, though. I would have been embarrassed if he'd seen me prancing around on stage wearing pirate drag. But it was different when I started playing football. He always used to come to the games."

Colette smiled. "Did he help you with your homework, teach you to shoot baskets, tell you about the birds and the bees?"

Frankie laughed. "Pop? No way. I learned all that stuff on my own." He looked at Colette and grinned. "You think I would have turned out better if he had?"

"I don't remember having any complaints."

He reached across the table and took her hand. "Don't tell me your memory needs refreshing?"

"Hmm," she said, as she disengaged her hand. "What a nice thought." She returned his smile. "Oh, Frankie. You are so incredibly good for my ego. I think that's why I keep you around."

"I thought I was the one keeping *you* around."

"As if your ego needed boosting!"

"I don't know," he said, pushing the plate with its half-finished *pommes frites* away from him. "It feels pretty low at the moment." He put his elbow on the table and rested his chin in his hand. "How do you rate me, Colette?" Having started to talk, it was not so hard, he found, to keep going.

Her eyebrows lifted a good half inch over her startled brown eyes. "Rate you? How? As a person? a man? a lover?"

"In general," said Frankie.

"Well," she said, then kept quiet as she thought about whether or not she wanted to play this game with him. "Do you mind if I smoke?" she asked.

"It's going to kill you."

"We all have to die someday." Reaching into her purse, she extracted a silver case and a lighter, which Frankie took from her. She leaned toward him to take the offered light, inhaled deeply, then released the smoke. "Let's see," she said. "You're smart, though probably not as smart as you think. You're stubborn. You've obviously got a good head for business. You're ambitious, but not greedy or dishonest, which is nice."

"Thank you." He handed her back the lighter.

Taking it, she tucked it into her purse, then said, with a smirk, "Of course you think all you have to do is whistle, and any woman in the world will come running."

"I don't," he said.

"Maybe not at this particular moment, but usually. It's because your mother and sister and all those aunts of yours spoiled you rotten, I suppose. Or because you're so good looking. You really are, you know." She held up her hand as Frankie again started to interrupt and, when he sat back in his seat, she continued. "But you don't treat women badly, not even the ones who make complete fools of themselves. You don't insist on getting more than you're offered. Or offer more than you're prepared to deliver. I always liked that. You're considerate, as a lover as well as a person. You've got the world's worst temper. It's frightening, really. But you usually get it under control before you do any serious damage."

"Not always."

A busboy cleared the table; a waiter took their order for coffee, and Colette said, "Have you ever hit a woman?"

"God, no!" He was about to add that he'd come close a few times, but he didn't. It wasn't anything he was proud of. "Except maybe Angela. My sister. She used to annoy the shit out of me when she was little."

"I believe you. Some wouldn't, if they'd seen you in action, but I do. So, all in all, I'd say you're a pretty nice guy. As guys go.

He laughed. "According to what I read in the newspapers, that's not much of a compliment. You know what some doctor I met at a party the other night told me? He said that, since the start of the women's movement, impotence in this city has gone up at least forty percent."

Colette's eyebrows lifted slightly, then she shrugged. "Even that's not enough to keep husbands faithful, though, is it?"

Frankie's smile faded. "How the hell did you find out?"

"I didn't find out. I guessed." Her eyes widened with curiosity. "Who is she? Or is it *they*?"

"None of your business." He was too irritated with himself for having given the game away to be polite.

The waiter arrived with their coffee. Colette took a sip, then asked, "Does Annabel know?"

Frankie shrugged. "She's not stupid."

"No, she's not," That was at least one fault no one could lay at Annabel's feet. "So, life at home is hell." Again, Frankie shrugged. "Which is why you keep away. And don't get to see a lot of your daughter."

"You got it," he said.

"Poor baby."

"I don't seem to have much of a talent for marriage."

"If it's any consolation, not many people do. You know your problem, Frankie?"

"Probably not, but you're going to tell me, right?"

She hesitated a moment, but then couldn't resist. "You don't really see women as people. . . ."

Frankie snorted in disgust. "Now you're going to start quoting me some shit from the women's magazines about equality, about marriage being a partnership. . . ."

"I wasn't. Now that you mention it, though, what's wrong with that idea? You treat me like an equal, don't you? Why not a wife?"

"Where I come from, men wear the pants—"

"And you think Annabel's fighting you for them."

"My pants, my shirt, my cock!"

"And you had no idea before you married her that she was like this?"

"She was a different person. Completely different."

"She wasn't! That's my point. When you fall in love, Frankie, you don't just fall, you get struck by lightning. It blinds you. And you end up marrying a fantasy, not a woman. Miranda, the beautiful, the sweet WASP angel, who turned out to be—"

"I don't want to talk about Miranda."

Colette didn't argue. She let Miranda rest in peace. "And Annabel, *Lady* Annabel, the English aristocrat, cultured, sophisticated, amusing. A ball breaker, from start to finish. But you never noticed, did you? Of course not!"

"I knew she was smart. Strong. Capable. That's what I liked about her. And about *you*. You've got quite a reputation as a ball breaker yourself."

Colette took a final drag of her cigarette, carefully put it out in the ceramic ashtray, and said, "Okay. Sorry. I knew I shouldn't have opened my mouth."

Frankie was silent for a moment. Then he said grudgingly, "I asked for it."

"Yes, you did."

He signaled for the bill, checked it briefly, then paid it with a credit card.

"Are you planning to stay mad at me for long?" asked Colette as she walked with him to the door.

"I'll let you know," he told her. He tipped the girl at the counter, and helped Colette wrap herself in a gray wool coat.

"Go fuck yourself," she whispered, stepping past him through the door he held open for her.

"Good advice," he called after her, watching her petite figure stride angrily away from him. "At least I'd stay out of trouble that way."

Chapter 19

*T*he prospect of spending time with Dan and his family cheered Frankie up, and during the drive from the club in Boston to the Colvingtons' house in West Newton, he was able to push thoughts of Annabel to the back of his mind and consider instead the way in which his friend, Daniel Jessup

Colvington III, after screwing up most of his early life, had finally pulled it together. A successful publisher, married happily (to a poet, no less), he and Amy had four children, three boys and a girl. The kids were, well, kids. And Amy was great. They lived as modestly as it was possible for the rich to live, largely ignoring Dan's trust fund, rarely spending more than his (ample) salary allowed, enjoying an ordinary, affluent, upper-middle-class life. Their rambling Victorian house with its three gables and front porch in a pleasant Boston suburb was a long way in cost and pretension from the mansions inhabited by Craig and Eva Colvington and others in the family. Instead of an army of servants, a young Danish au pair helped with the housework and the children when she wasn't attending classes at a community college; the boys had chores befitting their ages; Dan did what he called "his fair share"— a claim greeted by hoots of derision from his wife, who did what the rest left undone, most of the work as it usually turned out. They had two televisions, one for Benja, the au pair; and two cars, Amy's station wagon and Dan's Porsche (an extravagance, along with his twenty-seven-foot sailboat). The Colvington cottage on the Cape they shared with Dan's parents and siblings. For two or three weeks each summer, they rented a house somewhere in Europe so that the children wouldn't grow up ignorant of other cultures, and sometimes, during school holidays (for the same reason) they traveled in the United States. Dan had it all, and Frankie envied him, though that was nothing new. From the moment they'd met, he'd envied him. Not in any mean sense. He didn't want Dan to lose his looks, his charm, his education, his wealth, his patrician self-assurance, his happiness. Frankie only wished, somehow, to acquire their equivalent for himself.

Turning into the Colvingtons' gravel drive, Frankie could see in the spill of the outdoor lights that the exterior of the house was newly painted, gray with white trim. Soon the garden would be a riot of color, but now only a few of the azaleas were showing pink and white blooms. Dan and Amy spent what free time they had gardening. It wasn't much. Though both had left behind the radicalism of their pro–civil-rights marches and anti–Vietnam War protests, Amy was a member of PEN's Freedom to Write Committee, as well as a volunteer at a local organization for battered women, while Dan kept active in civil rights groups. Their garden was a haven, a respite, a reminder, they said, that life could triumph and beauty survive no matter how hard people tried to destroy them.

As Frankie opened the trunk of the rented car to get his bags, the front door opened. "Hello," called Amy. "You've made good time." She stood on the threshold, in jeans and a sweater, holding the baby, three-year-old Luisa, known as Lulu.

"The house looks great," he said as he climbed the steps and entered into the center hall. Furnished in a combination of family pieces, acquired antiques, and contemporary furniture, there was nothing shabby about the place, yet it lacked the sheen of homes decorated by professionals, the coherence and high finish of his apartment, for example. The house was idiosyncratic, but attractive and comfortable, warm and welcoming—a home. "Mmm, you both smell delicious," he added as he kissed Amy's cheek.

"That's the pot roast," she said, laughing. She was a small, fragile, darkhaired woman with large oval eyes and a long narrow nose. Frankie had seen faces like hers in paintings of Renaissance Madonnas. The Colvington clan had not been happy when Dan married her, though most had come around by now. "Hungry?" she asked, shutting the front door with a hip.

"Starving." He put his bags down and held out his arms to the baby. "Come to Uncle Frankie, sweetheart?" Delighted to be the center of attention, Lulu beamed and allowed herself to be appropriated. "So you remember me?" he said, nuzzling her neck.

Lulu nodded. "You give me a book." She meant last time. She hadn't quite got the hang of verb tenses yet.

As Amy rolled her eyes, Frankie laughed. "I brought you another. It's in my bag."

"How are Annabel and Maud?" asked Amy. When he assured her that they were fine, she inquired after the rest of his family, then said, "Dan should be home any minute. Though you can expect an evening punctuated by phone calls. One of his prize authors is threatening to leave."

"As long as I have you to keep me company, I'll survive."

"Me and the boys," she said, then laughed at Frankie's groan of mock dismay. Where discipline was concerned, Dan and Amy tended to err on the side of leniency, unlike Annabel and Mrs. Ashby who pounced on poor Maud for every small offense. His daughter had wonderful manners, thought Frankie, but she didn't smile easily. She didn't smile like Lulu. "They're on notice to behave," continued Amy. "And Lulu's been fed, so you won't have her to contend with." She held out her arms for the baby. "Let me have her. Why don't you take your bags upstairs and settle in? Your usual room. I'll make the drinks."

"My book . . ." said Lulu as Frankie picked up his things and started for the stairs.

"I'll bring it when I come back down," called Frankie.

"Greedy little beggar," muttered Amy, heading for the den.

At the top landing, he was intercepted. "Uncle Frankie!" said Danny, the oldest boy, hurtling out of his room into the hallway, his brothers hot on his heels.

All except the eight-year-old Ben were blond and blue-eyed and looked like Dan. Ben was dark, like his mother. "Did you fly up or drive?" he asked.

"Daddy has a new car," volunteered Aaron. He was five and dressed for some reason as Robin Hood. "It's black."

"A new Porsche," said Danny.

Knowing that Amy wouldn't mind his bags being dragged along the hall carpet and occasionally banged into the woodwork, Frankie let the boys take them and followed in their wake up another flight of stairs and into the guest room, a large light space with a pitched ceiling, oak furniture, and a private bath. While he unpacked, the boys leaned against the walls, sprawled in the armchair, practiced karate, keeping up a constant stream of talk, perhaps waiting for the usual gifts, perhaps just glad to see him, perhaps both. They were brats, but nice brats, and Frankie loved them, he supposed, as much as if they were his by blood. "These are for you," he said, tossing them the presents he'd brought, nothing much, palm-sized games for the car, some books, the new Macklin T-shirts. They were noisily grateful and followed him back down the stairs to the den to show their mother.

"My book," said Lulu when she saw the boys holding their loot. And when Frankie handed her the brightly illustrated story he remembered as a favorite of Maud's at that age, she smiled happily and, prompted by her mother, thanked him.

"Now, go away, all of you," said Amy. "I want to talk to Uncle Frankie. Danny, would you look after the baby for me?" The younger boys raced away without a backward glance while eleven-year-old Danny picked up the baby. "Thanks, sweetie. I'll be up in a few minutes." Turning to Frankie, she offered him his drink—scotch, water, no ice.

"Thank you," he said as he sprawled into a broad armchair. "It's good to be here."

"How did your meeting go?"

"No major problems," he said. From the airport, he'd gone directly to the club to meet with his contractor before driving to West Newton. "Just a lot of irritating small ones. I've got another meeting in the morning." He asked her what she was working on, and, while he listened to her talk about the book of poems she was getting ready for publication, about the difficulty she had making time to write, about the center and its endless stream of pathetic women, what he was thinking was how much he admired her, how much he liked her, and how big a fool he'd been not to have understood her attraction from the beginning. For Dan, who could have had anyone, to have chosen her, well, at the time, it had boggled Frankie's mind. It wasn't just that she came from outside Dan's social circle (both her parents were immigrants, her father a Russian Jew who owned a bakery, her mother an Italian, who helped in the store), since he was always attracted to women like that, but Amy had not seemed interesting or exciting, glamorous or good-looking, only ordinary and dull. It had taken Frankie years to appreciate her; and, now that he did, he'd revised, among other things, his earlier opinion of her looks. Now he found her beautiful.

"What?" said Amy, when she noticed his expression.

"I don't know how you do it," he said, "going to that center week after week, never losing hope, never giving up." He couldn't tell her what else he'd been thinking. It would sound too much like flirting, and his mood wasn't sufficiently lighthearted to make that seem harmless. Which it would be, he assured himself.

"Oh, I lose hope often enough," she said, smiling grimly. "But sooner or later it turns up again." A cry came from somewhere in the house and Amy got to her feet. "Lulu," she said. "I better see what's going on. It's time for her bath anyway. Will you be all right on your own for a few minutes?"

"Take your time," he said. Watching her as she left the room, Frankie allowed himself the brief luxury of imagining that she was his wife, that this was his house, that the children he could hear in the distance were his children, that he was contented, happy. A moment of satisfaction, followed immediately by an ache of acute loneliness. He took another swallow of scotch, then, to take his mind off his own problems, picked up the copy of *Newsweek* from the coffee table.

Barely two paragraphs into a story on Nicaragua, the world's latest hot spot, he heard the sound of the front door opening and closing. Then, jacket off, tie loosened, shirtsleeves rolled, Dan stood in the doorway. "What? No children? No noise? A man sitting quietly alone reading a magazine? Am I in the right house?"

Frankie stood. "The boys are somewhere, doing God knows what. Amy's with Lulu. And presumably Benja is putting the finishing touches on your wife's famous pot roast. How are you?"

"Great." Shaking the hand Frankie offered, Dan studied him for a moment, and then said, "And you?"

"Not too bad." Sitting again, Frankie checked his friend's face for signs of change, and didn't find many. Dan had a paid membership at Macklin's (business was business, friendship was friendship, the two shouldn't be confused, he believed). He worked out regularly, ate wisely, drank moderately. His figure was trim, and his blond hair was thick and free of silver. But the lines around his eyes, his mouth, scoring his cheeks, were deeper than Frankie's, which hardly seemed fair since, by all reckoning, Dan had a healthier, happier, more sober existence. But that, supposed Frankie, was the advantage of dark skin and a cuisine heavily dependent on olive oil.

Dan poured himself a light drink, sat, and the two men talked baseball until Amy returned. She'd changed into a dark skirt and pale pink sweater, combed her hair, fixed her makeup. She always did for dinner, at least when

Frankie was there, and he wondered if she bothered when alone with her husband. It was a lot of trouble to take for someone who would love you no matter what you looked like.

"Lulu asleep?" asked Dan as his wife stooped over his chair to kiss him hello.

Seeing the look she gave him, the way he touched her, Frankie felt another twinge of envy.

Amy shook her head. "Danny's reading to her. Frankie brought her a new book," she said with a smile in his direction. "So you still have a chance to say good night. And Ben wants to talk to you. He says it's important." Dan raised a questioning eyebrow and Amy elaborated, smiling. "He has a crush on a girl at school, and she won't talk to him."

"Already?" said Frankie.

"Already," said Dan. He got to his feet. "Excuse me for a few minutes."

"Sure," said Frankie. "But if it's advice about girls Ben wants, I'd be happy to have a talk with him."

"I think I can handle it," said Dan. "I haven't forgotten everything I used to know."

"He used to be some lady-killer," said Frankie when Dan had left the room.

"He still is," said Amy, sitting in the chair vacated by her husband. Frankie looked so surprised she laughed. "Oh, Frankie. What are you thinking? No, no, no. I only meant that women generally find him irresistible. And who can blame them? I do."

"And you've been married how long? Thirteen years?"

She nodded. "Not that I couldn't cheerfully strangle him at times."

"And here I thought he was perfect." On the one hand, Frankie was kidding. On the other, he couldn't see a lot of flaws in Dan, certainly nothing worth getting upset about.

"No, that he's not," said Amy decisively. "But he is honest, and honorable. I trust him," she added. To be faithful, she meant.

Frankie was silent a minute, and then said, "You sound so certain."

"I am." She laughed again. "Though I know it's crazy. In the light of history, I mean. Women have always been betrayed by the men they trusted most. Husbands, lovers, fathers." She shook her head. "You should hear the stories the women at the center tell!"

"And you think the same isn't true for men?"

The note of bitterness in his voice surprised her. "I wasn't making a case for the moral superiority of women," she said.

"That's all you read in the newspapers and magazines these days. What saints women are. Or would be, if men weren't such bastards."

"The rhetoric's running a little high," agreed Amy.

"A little!"

"But you can hardly blame women, you can hardly blame *us*," she corrected, wanting to make it clear whose side, if it came to out-and-out warfare, she'd be on, "when you think about the years, the *thousands* of years, that women have been denied their most basic human rights: to be educated, to own property, to participate in choosing the governments that shape their lives. They weren't even permitted to choose whom to love, to marry, whether or not to have children—"

"I'm not saying there haven't been injustices—"

"I should hope not," she snapped.

"Or even that they've ended. But I'll be damned if I'll take the blame for it!"

They argued, not quite angrily, but with a noticeable edge until Dan reentered the room.

"You know what they say," said Amy. "If you're not part of the solution, you're part of the problem."

"Let me guess," Dan said. "The women's movement. Right?" Amy looked at her husband blankly for a moment. Then, retreating from her high moral plane, she laughed. Grinning, Frankie nodded. Dan shook his head. "Conversations haven't been this heated since the bombing of Cambodia."

*D*inner was family style. The dark oak table was set with washable place mats and inexpensive pottery dishes. In addition to the pot roast, there were mashed potatoes, string beans, salad, and, for dessert, an apple pie from Amy's father's bakery. Frankie, who hadn't had a home-cooked meal in weeks, overate but refused a third glass of red wine. No one drank much, he noticed, except Danny, who downed four glasses of milk. Conversation was general to start with: Benja, who was little and blond, spoke in lightly accented English, played the violin, and hoped to be admitted to the New England Conservatory the following year, reviewed a recent concert she'd heard. Danny ventured the opinion that Benja was very talented; Ben seconded that, noting that she never made the violin squeak; and Aaron announced that he did, when Benja let him play hers. The boys talked about school, about Little League, karate lessons, about whether or not they liked the idea of going to Greece that summer. But eventually the conversation turned to politics, as it always did in that house, and an assessment of Jimmy Carter as president.

"He's a good man," said Amy.

"He'll never get reelected," said Frankie. "Not with inflation running so high."

"If he would get out there and *lead,*" said Dan.

*A*fter the boys were put to bed, while Amy and Frankie did the dishes, Dan made one last, unsuccessful, pitch to keep the departing novelist. "Fuck him," he said later when the three of them retired to the den to talk. "Let him go. The best of luck to him," he added.

At ten, Amy excused herself to go to her office, a small sleeping porch adjacent to their bedroom, to work. "You're a lucky guy," said Frankie when she was out of earshot.

Dan grinned smugly. "I like to think maybe I'm just smart."

Frankie's good humor vanished. Bleakness settled over him like a shroud. "Yeah," he said. "Could be."

"Hey, I was joking."

"I know," said Frankie.

"Want another drink?"

"No, I'm fine."

"Me, too," said Dan, kicking off his shoes, settling back in the armchair, feet up on the footrest.

Frankie leaned back against the sofa cushions, stretched his legs out in front of him. "I didn't know what you saw in her at first," he said. "Amy, I mean. She was so quiet. So shy. So *nice.*"

"Took me by surprise, too," admitted Dan.

"I think she's great."

"Yes."

Frankie waited for an elaboration to come, a qualification maybe. But Dan remained silent. He's waiting for me, thought Frankie. He knows something's bothering me, and he wants to know what. The temptation to open up was strong, but not strong enough to overcome Frankie's resistance to seeming weak and self-pitying in front of his best and most admired friend— the strong, happy, completely-in-control-of-himself-and-his-fate Dan Colvington. Frankie changed the subject to business, and the two of them sat up until long after midnight trading stories, problems, plans. "We'll have the house on the Cape for a couple of weeks in July, before we go to Greece," said Dan, leading the way up the stairs after declaring the evening officially over. "You should bring Annabel and Maud up for a few days."

"That'd be great," said Frankie. The light was still on in the master bedroom, he noticed as he left Dan at its door. Was Amy waiting up for him?

Would they talk before going to sleep? Would they make love? "See you in the morning," he said, continuing up the narrow staircase to his attic room. Why didn't Dan's life ever fall apart? he wondered, lying awake in the brass bed, hands behind his head, staring at the papered ceiling, trying to ignore his need for a cigarette. How come all the pieces in Dan's puzzle always fell into place? How come luck never gave him the finger? And it wasn't even possible to hate the sonovabitch. He was just too good a guy.

*S*ince Amy had a board meeting at the center, and the children had Benja, after work the next evening, Dan walked the short distance from his Berkeley Street office to Macklin's, which was at the unfashionable end of Newbury Street, not far from the Avenue Victor Hugo Bookshop, where Frankie had bought a number of his first editions. Despite the renovations currently going on, the club continued to operate and, at the end of the construction day, even managed to provide a more or less tranquil setting for its members. They played squash, showered, dressed, then walked back to Berkeley Street to have dinner at Grill 23. As Frankie was downing his last oyster, wondering whether he should call Helen and go directly to her place from La Guardia, he noticed that Dan's attention had strayed from his smoked salmon to a point somewhere in the distance. "Who is it?" asked Frankie, resisting the urge to look over his shoulder.

"Craig and Eva," said Dan, mustering a smile.

"Shit," muttered Frankie.

"They have someone with them," said Dan. That was good. It meant that any conversation would be short and polite. As they neared the table, Dan stood, and said, "Craig, Eva, how are you?" He shook his uncle's hand and kissed Eva's cheek.

Following Dan's example, Frankie got to his feet. "Hello," he said, forcing himself to extend a hand.

"Frankie, you're looking positively worn out. I do hope everything is going well for you." Eva had had a face lift and assorted other surgery. Her skin stretched tautly over her cheekbones, her figure was trim, and her small breasts high. She wore a close-fitting black knit dress and large silver earrings. She reminded Frankie of a corpse.

"Couldn't be better," he said.

Craig, too, had aged. His thinning hair had turned silver, and there was a slight stoop to his broad shoulders. He introduced their guest, whose name Frankie didn't catch, though he noticed that she was about his age and attractive.

"I was planning to call you next week when I'm in New York. There are a couple of matters we need to discuss." Eva didn't need to say what. Frankie knew. She wanted to sell another painting from the private collection and needed his permission.

"Anytime," said Frankie.

"Well, do give my best to your lovely wife," she said, smiling sweetly at Dan. The wattage of her smile decreased significantly as she turned to Frankie. "You, too, of course."

"Bitch," said Frankie as he sat and adjusted his napkin on his lap. When Dan said nothing, Frankie continued, "I know, I know, I should sell her the gallery, auction the paintings, get her and Craig out of my life."

"Yes," said Dan.

"I can't," said Frankie. Miranda's "fortune" had been worth more than he, in his wildest speculations, could have imagined. In addition to the trust fund, the gallery, and the the building that housed it, there was her father's collection of paintings (including works by most of the leading abstract expressionists), whose value fluctuated wildly with the economy and the art market. To avoid a court battle, Frankie had negotiated a settlement with the Colvingtons. He kept the trust fund and the title to the building, but allowed Eva to go on running the gallery at a handsome salary plus a piece of the commissions, all sales from the private collection subject to prior approval by him. That last, especially, drove her crazy.

"You mean, you can, but won't," said Dan.

"Right," agreed Frankie. For all the aggravation the continuing association with Eva cost him, it provided him with pleasure, too, exquisite pleasure, knowing that he had power over her, that he could deny her what she wanted, that he could make her foam with rage as desperate as his, but impotent.

"Making life difficult for Eva, not to mention yourself, won't bring Miranda back. What's the point?"

At the sound of Miranda's name, Frankie felt the familiar twist of pain in his gut. "Revenge?" he said.

"Exactly," said Dan. "I repeat. What's the point? Let it go, Frankie. Forget Eva. Forget Miranda, too, for that matter."

As if he could, thought Frankie. As if he didn't try. Forget Miranda. That would be the day. "If Eva had kept her mouth shut. If she hadn't tried to make trouble . . ." He stopped and shook his head. "I know. I'm as much to blame as she is."

In a smoothly choreographed operation, the busboy cleared their appetizer plates as the waiter slid their steaks onto the table in front of them. He topped their wineglasses. "Anything else?" he asked.

"Thank you," said Dan. "That's fine for now." He waited until the waiter was gone, then returned his attention to Frankie. "Miranda's problems started long before you made an appearance in her life."

"I know," he said.

"Then stopping blaming yourself. Her death was an accident. A tragic accident. They happen."

"If we hadn't fought. If she hadn't run away—"

"If," said Dan, interrupting. He shrugged. "You thought Miranda was perfect, a princess out of a fairy tale. She wasn't. She was a beautiful, lonely child, desperate for love, desperate for attention. She was too eager to please. Eva, you, everyone. She was too afraid of *failing* to please, and she used drugs to mask the fear, and the pain. A simple story. Classic. She had no center, Frankie. No sense of her own worth."

"I loved her."

"I know. And she did too. If that boat hadn't tipped over . . ." Dan stopped. "Listen to me. *If.* I'm as bad as you are." He took a swallow of wine and then continued. "I don't know. Maybe Miranda was so badly damaged that all the love in the world wouldn't have made it all right. Frankie, let it go. Let *her* go. Get on with your life. You've got Annabel to think about, and Maud."

Frankie's eyes slid away from Dan's. "Yeah," he said. He cut a piece of steak, put it in his mouth, chewed it, swallowed, then gave in to temptation, and said, "My marriage is shit. I'm miserable. And Annabel is . . . I don't know what. Disappointed, discontented, angry. We make life hell for each other. And for Maud. I don't know why I don't just get out. Get out," he repeated, "before I lose it completely. Sometimes I feel as if I really could kill her. That's how mad she makes me." He laughed grimly. "I work my temper off at the club. I screw around. . . ." Frankie stopped, then said, "Surprised?"

"No," said Dan. "You haven't seemed okay to me for a long time."

"We tried a marriage counselor last year."

"And?"

"Annabel's English. She doesn't get it. And me? I don't like her enough even to try to make the marriage work. I think she feels the same about me."

"I'm sorry."

"Yeah," he said; then he continued, "Amy told me she trusts you. I told her she was nuts. She knew I was joking."

Dan smiled bleakly. "Trust is a lot like faith, Frankie. You either have it or you don't."

From somewhere behind him, Frankie heard the sound of Eva Colvington's laugh. "And if you lose it, do not pass go, do not collect two hundred dollars, go directly to hell?"

"In a manner of speaking."

"I think I'm already there."

Chapter 20

When he arrived at La Guardia, Frankie made two phone calls. The first was to his apartment, where Mrs. Ashby confirmed that Lady Annabel had indeed left for London. The second was to Helen, just in case she was waiting for him to put in an appearance. She was, but Frankie felt only a fleeting pang of guilt at disappointing her. That's all he ever felt. Unlike marriages, illicit relationships have no set rules. Their terms are constantly up for re-negotiation, making it difficult to know just what to feel guilty about.

Helen had been involved with a married man once before. He'd been older, and richer. They'd been very much in love and would have married, her story went, but he had died, suddenly, before he could get a divorce. She'd been heartbroken, she said, devastated, suicidal. To Frankie, who had once been all of those things, Helen seemed none of them. When they met, three months after her lover's death, she appeared vibrant, eager, ambitious, too, which he admired. He liked Helen. She was good company: intelligent, fun loving, an inventive bed partner; but he wasn't in love with her. And as he listened to her grumble into the phone about his taking her for granted, his showing up without warning or, worse, his failing to show up when expected, Frankie realized that another renegotiation was pending. Helen was beginning to have expectations. "I haven't seen you all week," she said, her voice full of reproach.

"I'll call in the morning. We'll do something," he said, not knowing whether or not he meant it, just trying to comfort her and keep himself from feeling like a complete prick.

As he made his way through the terminal, Frankie imagined Helen in her neat, one-bedroom apartment, with its beige walls, beige furniture, and framed Lautrec prints, blowing out the candles she'd lighted in anticipation of his arrival, pouring herself a glass of wine from the open bottle, sitting on the sofa where they sometimes made love, listening to—what? Eric Clapton, or Billy Joel, playing on the top-of-the-line stereo system he'd given her for Christmas. She would be feeling disappointed, lonely, sorry for herself. But he had made no promises. And she had gone into the affair with her eyes open, avoiding the nice-boys-with-marriage-in-mind who wanted to date her in favor of someone like him (affluent and married) who provided an edge of excitement, of danger, a reprieve from the trying-to-make-ends-meet humdrum reality of her life, someone who wouldn't get in her way while she tried to build her career. He'd learned that much from the copies of *Cosmopolitan* he'd scanned while in her apartment.

Exiting the terminal into the rain-drenched April night, he saw the black town car from Superior Limo waiting at the curb, and Lionel, one of the regular drivers, leaning out of it, waving. "Over here, Mr. Ferraro," he called. He opened the rear door for Frankie, then took the carry-on and briefcase and disappeared behind the open trunk. When, a few minutes later, he slid into the front seat and closed the door with a soft, solid thud, he said, "There's an accident on the Triborough. Everything's backed up for miles. Friday nights!"

"Wouldn't you know," said Frankie. All he wanted was to get home and go to sleep. The conversation with Dan had depressed the hell out of him. "Well, do your best."

"You going home?"

"Yeah," said Frankie. "I'm going home." He liked Lionel, who was an interesting talker when conversation was wanted, but kept his mouth shut when it wasn't. He was discreet, too, a good thing since he sometimes drove Annabel. Sensing this was a night for buttoned lips, he concentrated on driving while Frankie sat slumped in the leather seat, staring out the window, occasionally closing his eyes when a headlight caught him at the wrong angle. The rain didn't help. The glare off the wet road was a killer.

It took some doing, but the driver found his way around the traffic, and, forty minutes after leaving La Guardia, the car slid to a smooth stop. Frankie said, "Great job, Lionel," and got out of the car, waiting in the lobby until the driver brought his bags. He handed him a twenty, saying, "For Ireland." Lionel and his wife were planning a trip there for their anniversary.

The driver smiled. "Thanks, Mr. Ferraro. See you next time."

"Good trip, Mr. Ferraro?" asked the doorman as he carried the bags to the elevator.

"I've had worse," said Frankie. Dan hadn't said anything new. He hadn't said anything that Frankie hadn't thought himself a million times. Then why had their conversation disturbed him so much? Not just because talking about Miranda, thinking about her, always upset him, he realized as the elevator made its way slowly to the seventh floor. His real problem was that he didn't know what to do about Annabel, about Maud, about his life. He felt confused, out of control. No wonder he was depressed. Opening the door into the darkened apartment (Mrs. Ashby in a gesture of what? frugality? contempt? had put out all the lights), Frankie wondered if the marriage counselor had been right. Maybe he did need continuing therapy and a prescription for something like lithium. But it wasn't only Annabel who had a cultural aversion to psychotherapy. His was, if anything, deeper. From his father, who had once exclaimed about the wife of a cousin whispered to be seeing a psychiatrist, "What's the matter with her? Is she nuts or something?" Frankie had learned to go to the family for help, or to no one.

Switching on all the lights, he walked quietly to the guest bedroom, dropped his bags inside, and continued down the corridor to his daughter's room. She was asleep, curled around a stuffed animal, a puppy, with one small hand clutching the worn security blanket. Frankie leaned over, inhaled the sweet scent of lotion and talc, brushed her hair back from her forehead. He owed her a better life, he thought. She shifted in her bed, disturbed by something. Were thoughts like radio waves? he wondered as her eyelids fluttered. She looked at him sleepily. "I'm home, honey," he said. "Go back to sleep. I'll see you in the morning." He leaned over and kissed her cheek. Her eyes closed. A much better life, he thought as he retraced his steps to his room.

*W*hen Frankie awoke, Maud was sitting in the armchair near his bed, motionless, silent, watching him. "Morning, honey," he said. She continued to stare at him, as if she couldn't quite believe he was real. Her eyes didn't seem to blink. Frankie found it disconcerting. He frowned. "Where's Mrs. Ashby?" he asked. Shouldn't someone be taking care of his daughter? Isn't that what he paid all that money for each month?

"Ashers said I shouldn't wake you up." Ashers was Annabel's nickname for the housekeeper. Maud's face crumpled with distress, and she said, "Did I wake you up?"

Frankie thought of the mornings that he and Angela had raced through the apartment in Brooklyn, or the house in Midford, not giving a damn about their parents' need for sleep, hurtling into Sal and Dolly's room, demanding attention. "No," he said, "I woke up by myself." He sat up. "It must be late." He looked at the clock on the bedside table. "It is. It's almost nine." He needed to brush his teeth and pee, but getting up seemed the wrong move just then. "Come here," he said, holding out his arms, "and give me a hug."

Maud got up from the chair and crossed the space to the bed. She was wearing pink denim pants and a long-sleeved white shirt printed with rosebuds. Her hair was braided with pink ribbon ending in a cluster of silk roses. "I have shoes on," she said, sounding worried as she allowed herself to be lifted into her father's lap.

"Not a problem," said Frankie. He pulled the sneakers from her feet and dropped them onto the floor. "That okay now?" Maud nodded, but the worry didn't leave her face. Maybe taking off her shoes was against one of Mrs. Ashby's rules? Poor little kid.

"I dreamed you came home," she said.

"It wasn't a dream. You woke up when when I kissed you goodnight."

"Oh," she said solemnly, as she made the necessary adjustments to her memory.

"Well," said Frankie with forced cheerfulness, "aren't you going to school today?"

"It's Saturday."

So it was. The day after Friday. "Well, what *are* you going to do?"

Again Maud shrugged. "I'm going to the park," she said finally.

"With . . ." Frankie searched his mind for the correct name. "Georgia?" he said.

Maud shook her head. "With Ashers."

That sounded like a load of laughs. Frankie lifted one of her braids. "What's that?"

"What?" she asked.

He walked his fingers lightly across her nape. "A spider," he said.

"No!" shrieked Maud, sounding for the first time like a child.

"Oh, yes," said Frankie, his face breaking into a wide, reassuring smile, so that she would know it was a joke. "A big, black spider." He walked his fingers along her neck, down her back. "I'll catch it," he said, tickling her. Before long, he had Maud helpless with laughter, one of the best sounds Frankie had ever heard, and a rare one, he realized, feeling more than ever like a prize shit.

A knock at the door silenced them. "Mr. Ferraro? Is that Maud with you?"

"Yes," called Frankie. "It's Maud." Who the fuck did she think it was? Some hooker he'd picked up on the way home from the airport?

"I told her not to bother you."

"She's not," said Frankie. "We're playing."

"I told her not to leave her room."

If the old lady thought for a minute that he was decent, in a pair of respectable pajamas, silk preferably, she'd come barging in and drag Maud off. But she couldn't be sure. "She's fine, Mrs. Ashby."

"Really, Mr. Ferraro—"

"We'll be out in a little while," Frankie interrupted, hoping she'd take the hint and go away. She did. "How about," he said, turning to his daughter whose face had resumed its worried expression, "you and me spending the day together?"

"Doing what?"

She wasn't a kid who surrendered easily. "We could start with the museum," said Frankie, remembering that he'd promised to take her. "That's something you'd like to do, right?" Maud nodded. He reached for her shoes and put them on her, double knotting the laces as Dolly used to when he was little. "After that we'll see." He lifted her up and set her on the floor and then got up himself. He wasn't wearing much, just a pair of boxer shorts. "You want to wait here while I get dressed or go back to your room?"

"Here."

Afraid of Mrs. Ashby or worried that he'd disappear? "Fine," he said. "I won't be long." He turned on the television and immediately a cartoon show appeared on the screen. It was definitely Saturday.

Her face wearing its familiar troubled expression, Maud stared at the screen as it faded in, and said, "I'm not allowed to watch television in the morning."

"Just this once," said Frankie. "It won't kill you."

When he had showered, shaved, and dressed, Frankie returned with Maud to her room, which was, as always, tidy—the bed made, toys put away, no dirty clothes in sight. In the closet, he found a canvas bag he remembered from when she was baby, and into it he threw, after consultation with his daughter, a coloring book and crayons, the stuffed animal she had been sleeping with the night before, the worn blanket she liked to keep handy, and a couple of A. A. Milne books from her shelf. "Anything else?" he asked.

Maud nodded, then went to the closet and removed her denim jacket. "In case I get cold." Everything she said sounded as if she'd learned her dialogue from a prepared script. It was the way all children learned, he supposed, mimicking adults, but in Maud's case the effect seemed more stilted than cute.

"Good thinking," he said, giving her a smile. "Okay, let's go." He set off down the corridor, Maud following closely behind. At his room, he stopped. "Just one more minute, honey, while I get some things I need." While she stood in the doorway watching anxiously, Frankie put on his jacket, checked for his wallet and his keys, then picked up the phone and dialed Helen. She answered so quickly he thought she must have been sitting by the phone waiting for his call. "Something's come up," he said. "I've got to spend the day with my daughter." He flashed a reassuring smile at Maud, in case she'd taken offense at his phrasing, but her expression didn't change. "She's right here, waiting," he interrupted, when Helen started to protest. "I can't talk. I'll phone you tomorrow, okay?" He heard her phone slam into its cradle, and the line go dead. Frankie hesitated. He should call her back, but, then, there wasn't a lot he could say to her with Maud listening. So he replaced the receiver, and said, "I'm ready. How about you?"

"Ready," said Maud, her face serious, determined.

Frankie took her hand and headed for the front door. There was one more hurdle to get over before they were free, and Maud was as aware of it as he. Saving Frankie the trouble of tracking her down, Mrs. Ashby intercepted them in the front hall. Dressed as usual in a tweed skirt and twin set, she stood there, like a sentry, between them and the front door. "You're going out?" she said. It sounded like an accusation.

"Yes," said Frankie.

She looked at the canvas bag in Frankie's hand. "May I ask when you'll be back?"

"I have no idea," said Frankie. For some reason, maybe because Maud was usually around, he never lost his temper with Mrs. Ashby, never raged, never shouted. He was always calm, reasonable, polite.

She wasn't fooled for a minute. Mrs. Ashby pushed, but never too far. She was afraid of him. "Really, Mr. Ferraro, I don't think Lady Annabel would approve—"

"Of my spending the day with my daughter?"

She bit her lip, a rare sign of nervousness. "What shall I tell her if she calls?"

"That Maud is with me." Holding firmly to his daughter's hand, he opened the front door and started out.

" 'Bye, Ashers," said Maud.

"Now, be a good girl, Maud," said Mrs. Ashby, frustration and worry sounding clear in her voice. "And do mind your manners."

"I'll call you later," said Frankie, "to let you know what our plans are. I don't want you worrying." He flashed her the winning Ferraro smile.

There was a noticeable softening in Mrs. Ashby's hard edge. "I'd appreciate that," she said.

"And don't stay in all day. Get out a little. Enjoy yourself."

A smile began to form, but she quickly suppressed it. "Thank you," she said politely.

Frankie pulled the door closed and looked down at Maud. He felt as if he had rescued his daughter from a tower, a prison, a gorgon. "We did it," he said. "We're free."

The Metropolitan Museum of Art seemed a strange place for a kid to want to go. Frankie knew he would have hated it at Maud's age. Not that anyone in his family would have thought of taking him, and the best the school could do was an occasional field trip to the Museum of Natural History. As they waited in the hazy sunshine for the cross-town bus, Frankie asked his daughter if she wouldn't like to see the dinosaurs instead; but though Maud said that would be fine, her face turned glum and Frankie realized she was trying to please him, not herself. That made him so sad he could have wept there on the street corner. What a peculiar little girl she was. "But you'd rather see the paintings, right?"

Frankie could see relief flood through Maud. Her face brightened and she nodded. "Georgia said they were big."

"Oh, they are," agreed Frankie. "Some of them, anyway."

The bus came and they rode through Central Park with Maud on Frankie's lap (which she seemed to prefer to a seat), looking out the window, absorbed in the display of Saturday activities, the joggers, walkers, bicyclists, the riders on horseback, the parents pushing kids in strollers, the woman walking six Dalmatians. Someone was flying a kite, a giant colorful pentangle with a streaming pennant, she pointed out to him excitedly. Something to remember for her birthday, he thought.

The Metropolitan had become one of Frankie's favorite places. Since Miranda had introduced him to it, he had spent hours there, at first trying to swallow the whole vast collection in one frantic gulp, then moderating himself to sips, covering the whole haphazardly, returning again and again to what he liked (a category that expanded slowly over the years), paying little attention to what he didn't. At one time or another, he had seen it all, which is not to say that he felt he knew enough to take on Eva Colvington, or Kalima Burden, but he looked carefully, read about what interested him, and often was deeply moved by what he saw. Still, he felt as if something essential in the nature of art eluded him, something mysterious, something profound, something he wasn't educated enough, or perhaps just smart enough, to comprehend. But where to start with his five-year-old daughter? that was the question. Already her eyes had grown wide at the sight of the vast lobby with its towering floral displays. Keep it light, Frankie told himself as he checked the canvas bag and their jackets, keep it simple. He flashed his membership card, fastened a completely unnecessary but (to her) very desirable entry button to her shirt, and walked up the central staircase, Maud holding tight to his hand. He guided her through the galleries, stopping to look only at paintings he thought might please her, ones she could relate to, Siennese Madonnas, Renaissance Nativities, Cassat portraits of mothers and children, anything with a dog or a cow, the Degas ballerinas, and Poussin's "Abduction of the Sabine Women," which he hoped would satisfy his daughter's craving for size and drama. It did. She stared at it, looking very pleased with herself, while Frankie gave her a censored account of what was going on in it. "I bet Georgia didn't see this one," she said when he'd finished. At least he hadn't bored her to death, Frankie thought as he stood outside the ladies' room, anxiously waiting for his daughter to reappear.

They ate lunch at a restaurant in mid-town where the booths were replicas of cars. Maud loved it, though the only thing on the menu she would eat

was a grilled cheese sandwich. When they finished, Frankie took her to FAO
Schwarz and bought her a doll, one with long, dark, combable hair, which
didn't seem very like bribery to him since he rarely indulged her with im-
promptu gifts. Following another impulse, he called Mrs. Ashby to tell her
that they wouldn't be home until after dinner, then took Maud in a taxi to
the garage where the Ferraros kept their car, the green Jaguar that Annabel
had insisted they buy over Frankie's objections, but which he had to admit
(at least to himself) that he loved. "Where are we going?" his daughter asked
as he buckled her into the seat.

"To see Grandma and Grandpa."

For a moment, Maud looked perplexed, as if she had no idea who they
could be, and again Frankie felt a familiar twinge of guilt. However much
he strained to escape it, one of the most important things in his life was his
sense of family, and that was yet another thing he was denying his daughter.
Then she smiled, and said, "Oh, good," and Frankie felt his spirits lift. "I
like the way Grandma makes 'paghetti," she added.

"Me, too," said Frankie. "It's the best."

When Dolly answered the door, she was wearing a pastel polyester pants
suit with a print blouse. She had on earrings and lipstick. "Oh, Frankie," she
said when she saw him. Instead of the expression of pure pleasure he'd imagined, what he saw on her face was joy tinged with dismay. "Why didn't you
let us know you were coming? And Maud! Oh, my, how you've grown."
There were tears in her eyes as she stooped to kiss her granddaughter, who
eyed her warily. Maud wasn't used to so much emotion.

"You're going out," said Frankie. It sounded like an accusation.

"No, no, that's all right. Come in. We're just going to your Uncle Victor's
for dinner. It's not important. Sal," she called, "look who's here."

"I should've phoned," said Frankie.

"Don't be silly," said his mother as she picked Maud up to give her
a hug.

"What the hell?" said Sal, coming up the stairs from the den. His hair was
thin and almost completely white. His stomach strained against his belt. He
looked happy, healthy, and years younger than his age. Someday he was
going to retire, he said, but not yet. "What're you doing here?" He clapped
Frankie on the back. "Good to see you, son," he said, and offered his hand
for a shake. "Or should I say stranger?"

"You're looking good, Pop," said Frankie.

"I'm feeling good," replied Sal, studying his son's face and clearly not
liking what he saw. "And who's this?" he continued, turning to Maud and
offering her his best smile. "Do I know you, little girl?"

"I'm Maud," she said, sounding surprised to have been forgotten.

"Maud? But you're too big for Maud. She's just a baby."

"I grew up," she said.

Dolly and Frankie laughed, but Sal kept a straight face, extended his arms, and said, "Well, if you really are Maud, then how about you give your Grandpa a kiss?"

Maud considered that for a moment, then leaned toward him to kiss his cheek, as Sal lifted her out of Dolly's arms and into his own. "Still lethal to women, eh, Pop?"

"You bet your life," said Sal. He looked at Dolly. "You better call Victor and Milly. Tell them something's come up." And before Frankie had time to decide whether he wanted to or not, he found himself and Maud, with his parents, in the Jag, on their way to his uncle's for dinner. Sitting beside Frankie in the front seat, Sal said, "Some car," worry about its cost mingling in his voice with satisfaction that his son could afford the price. "Expensive to run?"

"Nothing I can't handle."

Worry won out. "That's right, throw it away."

"It's a beautiful car," said Dolly, smoothing the waters. "And so comfortable."

"Mommy likes green," said Maud, sitting in the back next to her grandmother.

"All shades," said Frankie. "Especially the color of money."

*D*epending on your point of view, dinner at Uncle Victor and Aunt Milly's was just a quiet family affair or a raucous get-together. Having started with Sal and Dolly, Milly had thought it only right to ask Angela and Denny, whose boys were teenagers now and out with their friends on weekends. Then Vic had called, so Milly had extended an invitation to her son and his family. By the time Frankie and his carload got there, the others were also arriving. Kissing and back-slapping and shaking of hands started at the front steps and continued through the hallway into the den. There were some awkward explanations about Annabel's absence, which surprised no one and relieved them all, and a few barbs thrown by Angela who said she was surprised to learn that Frankie wasn't dead, as she'd feared from his long silence; but mostly everyone was just happy to have him there, to reclaim him and his daughter for the family.

Frankie held Maud in his arms until the hubbub subsided and her shyness gave way to a desire to join Vic's three kids playing. Then he let her go, leaving it to the women to settle the occasional disputes that came up and to make sure that she ate some of what Aunt Milly had so painstakingly prepared (baked ziti, veal cutlets, mashed potatoes, stuffed mushrooms, fried

cauliflower, a salad of iceberg lettuce with enough wine vinegar in the dressing to bring tears to the eyes, and, for dessert, a chocolate cream pie). He
was having a good time, he realized after several hours of frequently volatile,
but essentially good-natured conversation about houses and kids, sports and
travel plans, business opportunities lost and found. Much of the furniture was
covered with plastic, the pictures on the walls might have been bought at a
sidewalk art sale, the rococo lamps were more suited to a bordello than a
split-level on Long Island, but for once he failed to notice. He was happy;
and so was Maud when he checked to see how she was doing. That came
to an end at about ten when, tears flowing, she came running to him at the
dining room table where he was still seated. Close on her heels was Cara,
Vic's youngest, also crying. "What is it?" asked Frankie, lifting Maud onto
his lap. "What happened?"

"She hit me," said Maud.

There were accusations and rebuttals and counteraccusations, which none
of the women took seriously. "Poor babies," said Dolly. "They can't keep
their eyes open."

"Time to go," said Maria. It took half an hour before all the leftovers
were distributed, belongings gathered up, good-byes said. "When are you
going to bring Maud to see us?" she asked as she walked outside with Frankie.

"How about next Saturday?"

"Great," said Vic, bringing up the rear, Cara in his arms. "We'll be on
the Island. Come for the whole weekend."

"I'll give you a call," said Frankie. "To confirm. I don't think Annabel
will be back by then, but I'm not sure." His meaning was clear, all dates
were off if Annabel returned.

$\mathcal{T}$he week passed quickly for Frankie. He couldn't remember the last time
he'd felt so comfortable in his own life. If he had no early meetings, he would
take Maud to school. On Tuesday, he put in an appearance at a parents' day
gala, startling Maud's teacher, who was used to Mrs. Ashby filling in for both
Annabel and Frankie. She was full of praise for Maud, though she expressed
concern about her quietness, her shyness, about how well behaved she was.
Then she caught herself and laughed. "What a thing to be complaining
about!" she said. To hide his own concern, Frankie flashed her the Ferraro
smile, which made her a little more inclined to forgive him for what she had
previously thought of as unpardonable parental neglect.

By Wednesday, aided by a bracelet from Winston's, Frankie had persuaded
Helen to speak to him, but he arranged to meet her for dinner late in the
evening so that he could spend some time with his daughter before she went

to sleep. Other nights he didn't go out at all, but stayed in playing board games with Maud, erecting Lego villages, reading to her and, once she was asleep, sitting in the comfortable armchair in the library, his feet up, enjoying the unaccustomed solitude, the peace, catching up on his own reading, finishing the Haldeman book, starting Kundera's *The Farewell Party,* and working his way through the poems of Wallace Stevens. "That would be waving, and that would be crying," he read. He wasn't sure he could explain what it meant, but the poem touched him. "Just to be there, just to be beheld/ That would be bidding farewell. . . ."

When Annabel phoned, she spoke to Mrs. Ashby, and once to Maud, never to him, which suited Frankie fine. The only thing he wanted to know about his wife was when she would be back in New York. Not before the weekend, the housekeeper informed him when he asked, since there was a party at Castle Melton she planned to attend. Frankie's anxiety gave way immediately to relief. This period of contentment, of happiness, wasn't going to be snatched from him just yet. He called Vic to confirm plans for the weekend, then told Mrs. Ashby that he was taking his daughter away for a couple of days. Her lips tightened, but she said nothing, and dutifully packed Maud's bag. "Now, don't just hang around," Frankie said to her on Friday as they were leaving. "Call a friend. Get out a little." Did Mrs. Ashby have any friends? he wondered. She must. Everybody did. The housekeeper nodded, forced a grim smile, and said she would be sure to take his advice. He was getting the hang of this servant thing, thought Frankie, pleased with himself.

"She'll miss me," said Maud as they were getting into the elevator.

"She'll live," said Frankie.

$\mathcal{V}$ic and Maria's house was a ramshackle frame bungalow set on a bluff overlooking the Long Island Sound about ten minutes from Port Jefferson, an old fishing village that reminded Maria of home. The area was a blue-collar haven for refugees from urban blight, and was alternately tumble-down and newly built, houses dating from the Revolution scattered amid the development communities of three-bedroom ranches, Cape Cods, and mock colonials with mowed lawns and neat shrubs. Where the Ferraros lived had so far escaped the contractors' roving eye. It remained wooded and beautiful.

Except for a storm that blew in late Saturday night and out again early on Sunday, the weather was good enough for the children to play on the sandy beach below the house, and for Vic to take them all for a sail in the sixteen-footer he kept moored at a local club. It was a lazy weekend, its peacefulness disrupted only by the children's squabbles and an argument between Maria and Vic that blew in and out much like the storm. Watching them fight filled Frankie with a perverse envy for the sense of commitment running beneath their anger, the trust, and the lack of lingering resentment when it was over, all qualities missing from his relationship with Annabel, or Miranda for that matter, though he was far from understanding why.

As soon as he realized it was there, he pushed the thought of his wives from his mind. He didn't want to spoil his weekend. He was having too much fun watching Maud get dirty. Half an hour after he combed it, her hair was falling out of her pigtail. By the end of the day her designer clothes were covered with unidentifiable stains. She groused and played, cried and laughed, just like a normal kid. Seeing her like that gave Frankie so much pleasure that, with the additional incentive of missing the worst of the traffic on the Expressway, he left on Sunday later than he'd planned, bundling his daughter into the car in her dirty clothes because she'd spilled orange juice on her pajamas that morning. Mrs. Ashby's going to have a fit, he thought, buckling Maud into her seat. But two hours later, as Frankie juggled the weekend bag and the sleeping Maud in his arms, trying to open the apartment door without ringing the bell and disturbing the housekeeper whom he sincerely hoped had gone to bed, the door was flung open not by the disapproving Mrs. Ashby but by Annabel, looking jet-lagged and irritable.

"You're back," he said, sounding disappointed. He felt like a schoolboy caught in a prank. He felt like a fool.

"Obviously," she said.

Oh, shit, he thought. Already.

Chapter 21

"I'll just put Maud to bed," Frankie said softly to Annabel. "It won't take me long." He tried a smile. "I've got the hang of it now." Startled, Annabel looked ready to protest. Then, thinking better of it, she nodded. Letting him do it was easier than finding Mrs. Ashby or doing it herself, figured Frankie as he dropped the canvas bag on the floor of Maud's room, carried her into the bathroom and put her whimpering with fatigue on the toilet. Her teeth would survive one night without brushing, he decided. Returning to her bedroom, he stripped off her dirty clothes and tucked her, still in panties and undershirt (guaranteed to cause Mrs. Ashby heart failure) into bed, retrieved her blanket and stuffed toy from the canvas bag, and placed them near her. When he leaned over to kiss her good night, her eyes opened and her arms went around his neck. With a five-year-old's unerring instinct for melodrama, she said, "I love you, Daddy."

She was a knockout, this kid of his. "I love you too, honey," he said, kissing her sun-flushed cheek. Her arms dropped and she was sound asleep.

Turning, Frankie saw Annabel standing in the doorway, her expression unreadable. She crossed the room, and he stepped aside so that she could take his place by the bed. With the awkwardness that characterized all her movements, she leaned over and touched Maud's hand, kissed her, then straightened, and said softly to Frankie, "She's awfully sweet, isn't she?" Stooping, she picked up the clothes he had left in a heap on the floor, deposited them in the hamper, and said, "Would you like a nightcap?"

They went into the library where Frankie poured a straight vodka on ice for Annabel and a scotch and water for himself. "Well," he said, sitting in an armchair facing the sofa where she was seated, "how was your trip? Successful?"

Annabel shrugged. "Not very. It's getting harder and harder to find anything decent. We picked up quite a nice Louis Quinze armoire in Champagne-sur-Seine, but nothing else exciting. A pity. We're low on stock at the moment." Frankie asked her about the party at Castle Melton (such fun), about her brother and his family (quite well, really). Annabel asked him about his weekend. "You went to Long Island, I think Ashers said. To your cousins?"

Frankie nodded. "It was quiet. Relaxing."

"How lovely."

"Yes," agreed Frankie. Rummaging around in his mind for a topic of mutual interest, he came up with "How's Flora?"

Annabel put her feet up on the sofa and stretched out, letting the silk dressing gown she was wearing fall away to reveal her long, slender legs. "She's in love. Or thinks she is. He's a bit of a climber, but Nigel and Kalima are ecstatic. I think they despaired of ever getting her settled." Annabel smiled at him, a knowing rather than happy expression. "After failing to get you, she seemed to lose all interest in men."

Had Flora really had a crush on him? Frankie often found it hard to see beyond the good manners, beyond the careful social mask, to decipher what English people (his wife was no exception to this) were really thinking and feeling. But he liked Flora, and was glad to hear she was happy. "Can you blame her?" he asked, with a grin designed to counter the arrogance of his words. A protest would only have made Annabel sneer.

She ignored the question. "Kalima of course wanted every last bit of news about you," she said. "The woman's obsessed with you." Another of her dearly held beliefs was that Kalima had Frankie had been lovers. "You'd think Nigel would notice. Or perhaps he does, and doesn't care."

"He knows Kalima and I are just friends. He's not a fool."

"Meaning I am?"

Here it comes, thought Frankie. But, reluctant to let the mood of the weekend go, he ignored the surge of irritation, and said calmly, "You're the last person I'd call a fool."

"Well, thank you for that much, at least." She put her glass down on a coaster on the table beside her, and said, "Francis, we can't go on the way we've been."

"No," he agreed, surprised that she should be the first to raise the subject. "What do you suggest we do?"

"I'm not sure." Call it quits, he wanted to say. I'm sick of the fighting, fed up with the trouble. Let's get a divorce. But images of his daughter collected in the past two weeks, flashed through his mind like a photo montage, and he couldn't get the words out. He took a swallow of scotch, a long swallow, and said, "Try harder maybe? For Maud's sake?" He closed his eyes and added, "For ours?"

"Yes," she said. "If you want to."

Opening his eyes again, Frankie glanced across to his wife, lying on the sofa, looking tired, unhappy. "Don't you?"

"Of course." Annabel lay still for a moment, then, as if rallying weary troops for one last push, she stood up. "Well, I'm exhausted. I ought to get myself to bed while I still have the energy to move." Passing by his chair, she leaned over and kissed him, so casually that it might have been nothing out of the ordinary. "Good night." It had been months since they had exchanged anything other than cool greetings and heated insults. Surprised again, it took Frankie a few seconds to remember to return the pressure of her lips. Then (and it was as if some alien creature had taken possession of his body) his hand found the opening of her robe and slid up her warm bare thigh. "Mmm," murmured Annabel. She straightened and smiled down at him.

It was an invitation, no doubt about that. Was it one he wanted to accept? Did he have any choice? Frankie stood. He circled his arms around Annabel's waist, lowered his head, and kissed her. Her mouth opened; her tongue met his. "I thought you were tired," he said after a while.

She returned his smile. "I'll let you do all the work."

This ought to be easy, thought Frankie as he walked with Annabel, his arm around her shoulder, his fingers stroking her neck, down the hall to the room he now thought of as hers. His wife had no hips, no breasts worthy of the name, a face that was more interesting than pretty, yet there was something not just sexy, but erotic about her. She had turned him on from the beginning.

It wasn't easy. He got through the preliminaries all right: Annabel out of her robe and silk teddy and into bed, himself naked and on top of her. But the stirring of desire he had felt in the library, though it continued to flicker, failed to build. Sensing his desperation, Annabel too tried. Her mouth sought his nipples, her nails traced patterns on his back, on his buttocks, on his thighs. Now, he thought, now; but the blood pounding in his head, in his chest, seemed to be making a determined effort to avoid his penis. Annabel slid slowly down his body, her mouth aiming to take possession of it, but Frankie stopped her. What do I do now? he wondered. What the fuck do I say? "It's no use." He could hear the embarrassment in his voice. "I guess I'm kind of tired myself." Without a word, Annabel moved away from him. She settled her head on her pillow, her back a fortress erected against him. Frankie, touching her shoulder, leaned over her. He felt sorry for her, he realized; embarrassed for himself, but sorry for her. She was a proud woman and he'd humiliated her, without meaning to certainly, but he wouldn't put money on that making her feel any better. "Annabel, we need time, that's all. Time to make friends again."

"Go away," she said, her voice pinched and cold. "Just go away."

There didn't seem to be any point in arguing, so Frankie got out of bed, gathered his clothes, tried to think of something comforting to say, gave up, and retreated to the guest bedroom. He hung up his jacket and trousers, threw the rest of what he'd been wearing into the hamper, stared morosely for a moment at the neatly made bed, then put on the brocaded bathrobe Annabel referred to as a dressing gown. There was no way he could sleep. Returning to the library, he poured himself another drink and resumed the chair he had vacated such a short time ago. Now what? he thought.

$\mathscr{T}$he terms of the peace treaty had been vague, unspoken beyond an agreement to try harder; but an act of sex had clearly been needed to ratify it. Now Frankie wondered if his failure to rise to the occasion (that thought caused a grim smile) had canceled the truce. Apparently not, he discovered at breakfast the next morning. Already dressed, in slacks and a long-sleeved silk shirt, Annabel didn't look as if she'd slept any better than he, but instead of cold and withdrawn, instead of hostile, she was polite. A definite improvement. "Good morning, Francis," she said, with the hint of a smile as he entered the dining room where she was having her usual breakfast of tea and cold toast with marmalade.

No, he thought, revising his opinion, she was aiming for something warmer than polite: cordial perhaps. It was a word Annabel used often to describe someone she had found agreeable. Frankie made up his mind to go her one better. He would be friendly. Going to her, he put his hand on her shoulder, kissed her cheek. "Hi," he said. "Sleep okay?"

"Well enough." Her smile firmly in place, she turned her attention back to Maud, who was seated next to her, eating fingers of buttered toast, looking both surprised and pleased by her father's appearance.

What did she expect, wondered Frankie, that I'd run for the hills, disappear from her life, now that her mother's back?

"Daddy, look!" said Maud. She was wearing a new print pinafore. "Mommy bought it. At Liberty's," she announced triumphantly. She'd been taking trips with her mother to England since she was old enough to travel, although most of her memories seemed to revolve around the animals at Castle Melton.

"Nice," said Frankie. "You look very pretty this morning." He turned to Annabel. Well, it wouldn't kill him. "And so does Mommy."

Annabel's smile broadened a fraction, but she said nothing, and Frankie went to the sideboard where the boxes of dry cereal were lined up, poured some Cheerios into a waiting bowl, added milk, and took his seat at the table, listening while Maud continued to regale her mother with stories of her adventures with Frankie, the Fabulous Father. "How lovely," said Annabel from time to time. "That sounds wonderful. . . . Did he really? . . . How marvelous . . ." She managed to keep all trace of irony from her voice.

When it was time for Maud to leave for school, Frankie stood, and said, "Get your jacket, honey, and whatever else you need for today. I'll meet you at the front door."

"You're taking her to school?" said Annabel when Maud had left the room. She couldn't quite conceal her surprise.

"I have time this morning. I might as well."

Ordinarily she wouldn't have been able to resist needling him, but this time she contented herself with a slight, bemused shake of her head, and said, "Maud will get positively spoiled from all the attention."

"I don't think there's much chance of that." He started for the door, then turned back. "About last night," he said. Then he stopped. It needed to be discussed, but he was damned if he knew what to say.

Annabel came to the rescue. "I'd just as soon not talk about it, Francis, if you don't mind. As you said, we probably just need some time to make friends again."

Frankie nodded. "What if we start by going out to dinner tonight? Just us."

"That would be lovely."

"Good," he said. He returned to her side and again kissed her, this time on her mouth. "I'll be home about six-thirty."

"See you then," she said with a smile that was almost warm.

*C*onversation between Frankie and Annabel was usually a minefield, with one or the other of them inevitably stumbling into an unexploded shell and setting it off. But over dinner that night, in silent agreement, they skirted the hot topics, like money and family and which of them was less sensitive to the other's needs, less willing to compromise, more to blame for the god-awful state of their marriage, and stuck instead to more or less safe topics like what plays Annabel had seen in London, the progress of the renovations in Boston, and the latest political scandal in England.

"I don't get it," said Frankie. "I mean, what all the fuss is about. At least here when a politician resigns it's over something that matters, something to do with the law, or the Constitution, like Watergate. Not sex."

"Well, you know, we thought that whole Watergate mess was a bit of a tempest in a teapot, a lot of bother about nothing."

"That's the point I'm making, how different our priorities are."

"Oh, I don't think it's quite that," said Annabel.

"No?" said Frankie, willing to listen, hoping to learn, even from his difficult wife.

She shook her head. "No. I suspect it's that the English are politically sophisticated and sexually naive. While Americans are naive about both."

"You don't see us booting people out of office because of some sex scandal."

"Only because it's all kept so quiet. You don't have a press that revels in revealing the sordid details of a politician's life."

"What about Wilbur Mills and Fannie Flagg?"

"Well, reporters could hardly ignore a car plunging into the Potomac, could they? But they don't go digging for dirt, that's my point. At least not yet."

"Never happen," said Frankie adamantly.

"I do hope you're right," said Annabel, not sounding at all optimistic. "There's something so utterly distasteful about that kind of thing. Pornographic, really."

The dinner was a success. The food was excellent, the wine better, the service quietly efficient. The restaurant was empty of people they knew, which was rare but fortunate, since any encounter with either Frankie's friends or Annabel's usually provided a freighter full of ammunition for a quarrel. This time, they managed to get through the entire meal without so much as the exchange of warning shots. Afterward, they stopped into Studio 54, where the disco music made it difficult to talk, and impossible to argue. In the taxi on the way home, they necked as they hadn't in years. It was titillating, not like being with your wife at all, thought Frankie as he paid the driver and followed Annabel into their building, admiring her long lanky stride, the subtle roll of her almost nonexistent buttocks under the flowing silk jersey dress. It occurred to him that she wasn't wearing panties. She walked quickly, barely acknowledging the doorman, with whom Frankie exchanged a few brief remarks before hurrying after Annabel, who pushed the button to call the elevator, entered as soon as the door opened, and positioned herself in a modified spread-eagle against the far wall, her face saying Come and get it. As soon as the doors closed, Frankie did. He pressed his body against hers, explored her mouth with his tongue, sent his hands out to investigate the truth of his theory. Praying that all his neighbors were happy at home and not inclined to visit between floors, he raised her skirt higher and higher until he could feel the warm bare flesh of her thigh, of her hips, of her bottom. "Oh, nice," he murmured, as his fingers touched the wiry blonde curls between her legs. The elevator slowed to a stop, and reluctantly Frankie pulled away.

Annabel slid her skirt down into place as the doors opened. Then, before stepping out of the elevator, she extended a hand to touch the fly of Frankie's pants, smiling with satisfaction as she felt the swollen length of his cock pressing against the zipper. "Good boy," she said, giving it a quick pet, then striding off down the corridor to the front door.

"Don't ring," called Frankie. "I have my key." The last person he wanted to see just then was April Ashby.

*R*atified, the truce held. Frankie moved back into the master bedroom. He phoned Helen, invited her to lunch, and, over a somber meal at the romantic Café des Artistes, put a formal end to their relationship, which made them sad, as well as fearful, the way people often are before setting off alone on a journey whose hazards are certain while the destination is not. Recognizing the bar at the club as an occasion of sin (a phrase remembered from the religion lessons in grade school), Frankie avoided it and returned home from work in time to read Maud to sleep and keep any dates that Annabel had arranged. They entertained at home, each making an effort to be pleasant to people they normally would have taken delight in drawing and quartering; they went to parties, to the theater to see the stylish *Dracula* with Frank Langela, and *Othello* at the Roundabout, a play that always depressed the hell out of Frankie, though he never understood why he had such a strong reaction to it. Sometimes they even stayed home to read or watch television. It was as if they were newly married and still in love, though they were neither of those things. They were two old hands bailing frantically to keep their marriage from sinking.

About a month after their reconciliation, at the point where both Frankie and Annabel were becoming used to getting along, where each was convinced that the crisis in their relationship was past, when guards were dropped, and life began to seem more or less normal again, they attended a dinner party given by Angus Taylor, an interior decorator, only modestly successful, but of enormous use to Annabel. She claimed to be fond of him. She said she found his camp and bitchy manner "rather amusing." Frankie did not, and the apartment, a penthouse in the east eighties was so "done" it set his teeth on edge. But he liked Andy, Angus's current lover, a regular at Macklin's, a handsome blond actor, now appearing in *A Chorus Line*. The other guests included Lorena Davis, the Met's newest star, thanks to glowing reviews for a recent performance in *Don Giovanni*; Maddy Schiffer, a buyer for Bloomingdale's; Harry Mason, a stockbroker, and his wife, Tara, whose new apartment Angus was in the process of decorating. With the exception of Lorena Davis, Frankie had met them all before and, if they weren't exactly his favorite people, at least they were gainfully employed, not like the general run of upper-class deadbeats whom Annabel tended to invite to dinner parties because they happened to be old school "chums" of hers or her brothers, well-connected spongers most of them, despite their having, as Annabel put it, "pots of family money." Her guests tended to talk only about each other— with style and wit, Frankie had to admit—amusing if you were one of the group, boring if you weren't.

That had been one of the major disappointments of Frankie's marriage, the inadequacy of the dinner parties at his home. Even people he admired, like Dan and Amy Colvington, couldn't seem to make evenings take off, rise above the ordinary, leave him with that buzz he got from feeling he'd learned something new, experienced something different. Life isn't a great-books course, Dan had said to him once. But Frankie hadn't really believed him. Dinners with the Colvingtons were always enlightening as well as fun. So were parties at Vic and Maria's, where conversations with their friends— actors, directors, journalists, musicians—tended to wander over a wide range of subjects. And, at the Burdens', gossip was only spice added to a mix of history and literature, politics and art.

However, Angus's party was shaping up to be one of the best Frankie had been to in a long while. The evening's star, without question, was Lorena

Davis. In her early thirties, she was black and beautiful, with a rich voice and great comic flair. Somehow she managed to orchestrate the conversation so that everyone got a chance to speak, about everything from terrorists in Italy and riots in Tehran, to a heated discussion about cities and their art collections, which continued until Andy (a native) mounted a courageous defense of Los Angeles. Angus silenced him by shoving a piece of chocolate gateau into his mouth.

During dinner, Frankie had sat between Maddy Schiffer and Tara Mason. After, without giving it much thought, he followed Tara away from the table to a loveseat near the French doors that opened onto a small balcony overlooking Madison Avenue. He'd met her before, but they'd never exchanged more than a few words, none of them memorable. Over dinner she'd come to Andy's defense of Los Angeles, revealing a wry sense of humor Frankie hadn't suspected. A small woman, in her late thirties, she was fashionably thin, with dark hair and eyes, a slight bump in her nose, and wide full lips. Wearing a simple black suit, a long strand of pearls, with pearl-and-diamond studs in her ears, she looked expensive, elegant. Like Eva Colvington, thought Frankie, who was better looking, though nowhere near as warm or appealing.

"You own the DeWitt Payson Gallery, don't you?" asked Tara as she took the offered cup of coffee from the tray Andy was passing.

The question surprised him. He kept a low profile where the gallery was concerned, leaving Eva to handle the publicity as well as the business. "Yes," he said, "I do."

"I never see you at the openings."

"I don't often go."

"Harry and I have known the Colvingtons for years." Tara's smile faltered and Frankie knew she had just remembered about Miranda. She recovered quickly. "And we've bought quite a few things from Eva. Well," she added, "Harry has at any rate. Eva convinced him they were good investments."

"They probably are. She usually knows what she's talking about."

"I think it's smarter to buy only what you like. Then, when the art market crashes, at least you have the consolation of owning something you love."

Frankie smiled, and said, "It'd be hell for business if everyone felt the way you do."

"I suppose so." Tara's laugh was an infectious giggle, much younger than she was. "People are so rarely sure of what it is they love the market would be bound to crash." Frankie found himself joining in, and the sound of his laugh drew a surprised look from Annabel, followed immediately by a frown. "Sad really," said Tara, sobering quickly.

Taking advantage of a moment of quiet, Annabel tried to draw them into the main conversation, and intermittently Frankie and Tara obliged by casting their vote for best movie or most horrible restaurant experience, half-heartedly following the flow of talk while for the most part going with their own conversational drift. They found they were both Dylan fans, though they disagreed about Frank Sinatra (Frankie thought he was the kind of guy, slick and crude and obsessed by gangsters, who gave Italians a bad name); they admired F. Scott Fitzgerald and Gabriel Garcia Marquez; thought *The Virgin of the Rocks* one of the most beautiful paintings in the world; were unanimous in disliking Todd Manheim, but differed over Pablo Picasso.

"You would like Picasso," she said. "All that macho posturing."

"You should meet my friend Amy Colvington."

"Any relation to Eva?"

"A niece. By marriage. Amy's very gung-ho about the women's movement."

"You don't approve?"

"Me? Hey, I—" He was about to put on his party shoes and tap dance, but decided against it. "I'm not sure. I'm still thinking about it."

Tara laughed, then said dryly, "At least you're honest." She worked for a small private foundation, the kind that supported worthy painters and writers and scholars for a year or two while they completed their projects. She enjoyed what she did, felt it was worthwhile. "There are no more Medicis, no more Sun Kings. The rest of us have to do what we can to keep culture alive. If we don't want to sink into barbarism."

Frankie couldn't have agreed more. Not sinking into barbarism was one of the chief aims of his life.

A month or two before Frankie might have suggested to Tara that they have lunch. Her acceptance would have indicated a returned interest, although not, Frankie understood, necessarily a romantic one. Lunch itself would have determined whether they were headed for sex, or friendship, or nothing at all. He prided himself on being the kind of man who could be friends with a woman, something which, in a million years, his father couldn't pull off. Not that his interest in Tara was platonic. Far from it. He found intelligence to be a great aphrodisiac, even if it was never quite the thing that pushed him off the mountaintop and plunged him into love. But for reasons entirely to do with the desire to save his marriage, Frankie ignored the voice in his head suggesting he ask Tara out. Instead, at the end of the evening, he shook her hand and told her how much he'd enjoyed talking to her. From the way she smiled at her husband when he joined them, Frankie didn't think she was disappointed. "Maybe the four of us can have dinner one night," she said.

"Great idea." He turned to Annabel. "Do you have one of your cards with you?"

Frankie was sure she did, so her slight hesitation surprised him. "Of course," she said, opening her purse and extracting an engraved business card which she handed to Tara. "I'll so look forward to hearing from you." She didn't sound convincing.

"Call," ordered Frankie as he maneuvered Annabel out the door toward the elevators while Tara lingered to say a few final words to Angus and Andy.

"We will," said her husband, without conviction. Which again surprised Frankie. He would have thought that, if there was a possibility of picking up a client, Harry Mason would never say no to a meal.

*V*irtuous, that's what Frankie felt as he stepped into the spring drizzle to hail a cab. And puzzled. He had successfully resisted temptation and was proud of himself. He had handled Tara, Angus, the evening, everything very well. Yet Annabel, who was standing behind him, waiting under the awning, out of the rain, was radiating hostility with such force he could feel it even at that distance. A taxi stopped. Frankie opened the door and motioned to his wife. Without once looking at him directly, she ran to the cab and got in. He climbed in after her, closed the door again, gave the driver the address, and sat back. What the fuck do I do now? he wondered. What do I say? Was there any chance of avoiding a fight? Not much, he thought, though he was damned if he knew why. Despite the alcohol he'd consumed in the course of the evening, he felt cold inside and out.

Silence reigned for the entire ride back to Central Park West, up the elevator, and into the apartment. This was something Annabel was good at, though Frankie wasn't. He held out until after they'd said a polite goodnight to Mrs. Ashby (who had opened the door at Annabel's first imperious ring), until he and his obviously irate wife were alone in their bedroom. Then he said, "You want to tell me what's going on?"

Annabel was pulling off her earrings, her bracelets, her rings, dropping them into a tray on her dresser. Without turning, she said, "As if you didn't know."

"If I knew, I wouldn't ask."

Their eyes met in the mirror for a moment before she wheeled around and said, "You just can't resist trying to humiliate me, can you?"

"What the hell are you talking about?"

"You and that slut, Tara Mason."

"We were *talking,* for chrissake."

"Talking! You were so oblivious to the rest of us. . . ." Her voice was rapidly rising in pitch. "So oblivious to *me,* I'm surprised you didn't try to fuck her right there in the middle of Angus's sitting room."

"You've got to be kidding!"

"It was a disgusting display. Tasteless. I've never felt so humiliated in my life." She was crying.

"We were talking, that's all. I didn't know there was a law against it."

"You think I'm such a fool, don't you? You think you can tell me any old load of rubbish and I'll believe it. Well, I won't!"

"Why are you doing this? It was a nice evening. I enjoyed myself for a change. Can't you leave it at that?"

"When are you seeing her again?"

"You heard. When the four of us have dinner."

"As if I'd lower myself to associate with that whore."

"Oh, forgive me. I didn't realize she wasn't up to your social weight."

"Hardly. But she's right at your level, isn't she? Right in the gutter where you're comfortable. I must have been out of my mind to listen to Roland!"

"What has Roland got to do with it?" asked Frankie suspiciously. Maybe he *had* drunk too much. He was having trouble trying to follow the path Annabel's mind was taking.

"He gave me some brotherly advice. He said I should try to hold on to you, at least until something better came along."

"Someone richer, is that what he meant?"

"Someone of my own class," said Annabel viciously. "How I ever could have fallen in love with you!"

The first thing Frankie understood was that he had Roland to thank for the peace of the past four weeks. The second was that his wife loved him; the third, that she hated herself for it. And for that, the fourth and last, he hated *her*. "That's it. I've had it." He turned and headed for the door.

"Admit it, why don't you? You want that little tart."

Turning again to face her, he said, "Okay. I want her."

"You're going to see her again."

"Sure. Tomorrow. We've decided to skip the preliminaries and just meet at the Hilton for a quick fuck."

Annabel covered the distance between them so quickly Frankie didn't have time to raise his hands to ward her off before she struck him in the side of the head with her hairbrush. "You bastard!" she screamed.

He grabbed her by her wrists and squeezed until she dropped the brush. "What's wrong with you? Are you crazy?" He released her wrists and grabbed her by the shoulders, shaking her as if she were a rag doll. She tried to pull away, but he wouldn't let go, just went on shaking her, yelling at her. "I've had it. You hear me? I've had it."

"Let me go. You're hurting me." She was sobbing, frightened now.

"How much do you think I can take? Jesus Christ!"

"Oh, Francis, please . . ."

The sound of his name increased his fury. "Frankie," he said, shaking her harder. "Frankie. Frankie."

"Daddy . . ."

Later, Frankie was surprised that Maud's voice had been able to make itself heard over the pounding of blood in his ears, his shouts, Annabel's sobs. But the one word, a soft frightened cry, sounded as loud as an alarm bell. Immediately he released Annabel and went to the door. Maud was standing outside, her eyes wide with fear. "It's all right, honey," said Frankie, picking her up, thanking God that his daughter was such a good little girl that even when terrified she did as she was told. She was forbidden to open the door to her parents' room.

"I heard noise. I got scared."

"I heard it, too," he said. "It's nothing to worry about."

Frankie carried Maud into the bedroom where Annabel had managed to get herself under control. Her eyes were red, but she had wiped the tears away. She smiled, and said, "Were you frightened, love?" Maud nodded and Annabel held out her arms. "Daddy's right. It's nothing to worry about. It's all over now. Come, I'll put you to bed." She took Maud from Frankie's arms and, resting her cheek against her daughter's, carried her from the room, saying, "I'll be right back." It was at least ten minutes before she returned. "She's asleep," she said. Then she saw the suitcase on the bed. "What are you doing? Where are you going?" There was panic in her voice.

"It's like you said, Annabel. It's over. All over."

Chapter 22

After spending the night at the Carlyle, Frankie returned to Central Park West and again intercepted his daughter and Mrs. Ashby. This time the housekeeper seemed to be expecting him, and she turned the child over without a word of protest. But once in the taxi, Frankie began to wonder if taking Maud to school that day had been a good idea. His daughter was such a serious little thing that she seemed very grown-up; but she wasn't. She was five, so young, and as he did his best to explain why he would no longer be living with her and her mother, Maud's face crumpled with distress; her eyes filled with tears. All she really understood was that something bad was happening. Feeling like a rat for upsetting her, Frankie lifted her onto his lap. "I'll see you when I can," he said desperately. "We'll spend weekends together. We'll go away again. We'll still have lots of good times. I promise."

The taxi stopped. Frankie paid the driver, then took Maud by the hand and walked with her to the entrance of the school. "Don't be upset, baby. I love you. Remember that." Maud looked at him, then nodded. "Now, you be a good girl," he said, turning her over to her teacher.

"See you later," called Maud. Those were his usual parting words. Frankie didn't see any point in correcting her.

*T*o delay arriving for as long as possible, Frankie walked the couple of miles from Maud's school to his office, continuing the game he'd played during his long wakeful hours at the Carlyle, trying to predict how Annabel would react to what had happened. Would she think that this quarrel, like all the others, could be patched up and smoothed over? Or would she feel, as he did, that they'd done their marriage about as much damage as possible; that it was beyond repair; that it was time to toss it out, onto the garbage heap with their other failed hopes and dreams? When he arrived at the office, what would be waiting for him, a call from Annabel begging for a reconciliation or one from her lawyer asking for a meeting to discuss divorce terms? He guessed that Annabel would want to try again. And he hoped that he would have the guts to say no and stick to it. They both deserved better than the constant shit they served up to one another.

Entering his office suite, Frankie felt his body stiffen, as if bracing for a blow. But, instead of the expression of suppressed rage she usually wore after a series of phone calls from Annabel, Martha greeted him with a reassuring, a *comforting*, smile, as if she knew he'd had one hell of a night. "No messages?" he asked.

"They're on your desk. Coffee?"

"Coffee would be great," he said, heading for his office "And a bagel or something. I didn't have any breakfast."

"Off the trolley okay?" The food on the catering cart, while no match for that from the nearby deli, was edible, and convenient. "Or do you want me to send out?"

Martha wasn't usually so willing to please, at least not when performing tasks she considered menial, which led Frankie to believe he must look even worse than he felt. "I'm desperate," he said. "The trolley's okay." He continued into his office, and, leaning over his desk, picked up the stack of pink slips and leafed through them as he walked around to his chair. There were messages from real estate agents, from builders, from suppliers, from Tom, from his mother, but none from Annabel. Sitting, he checked the morning mail for hand-delivered letters. Nothing. What was she up to? he wondered. Her silence scared the bejezus out of him.

The first call Frankie returned was to Tom, who never called unless it was important. "Rico quit," he said when he came to the phone.

"Fuck," said Frankie. That was all he needed. Rico was the head chef of the Forty-third Street club's restaurant and largely responsible for its success.

"He's going to Michael's Pub."

"He want a raise?"

"It's not the money. It's the glamour."

Frankie thought a minute. "Screw him," he said finally. "We'll find somebody else." The question was where? "Better start asking around."

"What do you say, you pick up my expenses while I try out all the good restaurants in Manhattan?" said Tom.

Frankie laughed. The sound surprised him. He hadn't thought himself capable of a laugh that day. "Okay. But keep off the beluga," he said.

Martha entered as Frankie hung up the phone. She'd transferred the coffee from a paper cup to a mug and the bagel from a paper dish to a ceramic plate. As she put them on the desk in front of Frankie, she said, "Your mother phoned again."

Suddenly he was worried. It wasn't like Dolly to keep phoning. If she wanted to teach him a lesson about something, like not paying enough attention to her, she did it, not by pushing, but by backing off, until he pleaded for forgiveness. "Did she say what was wrong?"

"I asked her. She said nothing. But she didn't sound like herself."

Frankie picked up the phone and began to dial. "Rico's leaving the club," he said as Martha headed for the door. "Start calling around. See who's out there."

"Sure," said Martha.

"Doesn't your roommate . . . what's her name? Jill? work for the food editor at *McCall's*?" Looking surprised that he was familiar with any detail of her personal life, Martha nodded. But then, Frankie was sort of surprised himself. "She should know who the hot young chefs are."

"I'll ask."

Frankie said, "Hi, Ma," and Martha left, closing the office door behind her.

"What's up?" he continued. "You okay?"

"I'm fine," said Dolly.

"And Pop?"

"We're fine. We're all fine . . . Frankie, Annabel called me this morning."

"She *what*?" Annabel never called his mother unless he made her.

"She said you had a fight last night."

"So?"

"And that you walked out on her."

"Jesus Christ!"

"Frankie, don't swear. I don't like it."

Frankie took a deep breath, then, his voice lower by at least a decibel, he said, "Ma, this is none of your business."

"You know I don't like to interfere—"

What Frankie knew was that any argument to Dolly was a call to her to make peace.

"What happened is between Annabel and me. Stay out of it, Ma."

She said firmly, "She's your wife, Frankie."

"Exactly. That makes her *my* problem."

"No matter how much you love someone, you can't agree about everything all the time. So when a husband and wife argue, that's not what's important. What's important is they make up afterwards."

"I can't believe she dragged you into this."

"Who else was she going to talk to? It's not like the poor thing has a mother she can turn to."

"A mother! Jesus fucking Christ! Give me a break!"

"Frankie!"

He was yelling and he never yelled at his mother. At least he hadn't since he was fifteen and Sal had threatened to beat the crap out of him if he ever did it again. Frankie took another deep breath, and said, "Sorry."

"Don't talk to me like that ever again." She sounded close to tears.

"I said I'm sorry."

"I'm only trying to help."

"I know." I have to get off this phone, he thought, before I rip it out of the fucking wall.

"You got a wife. You got a child. Church wedding or no church wedding, marriage is forever. Forever! You understand me?"

"Ma, I don't want to fight with you. But keep out of this."

"That means," continued Dolly, ignoring him, determined to make her point, though years of experience should have taught her that she didn't have a prayer of persuading her son to do anything he didn't want to, "you are married until you die."

"Well, that's just too bad for me, isn't it? I can't expect to get lucky twice."

He heard her gasp. "Frankie! How could you say such a thing?"

Exactly what he was asking himself. He took a breath, and said, "Look, Ma, I started out upset this morning. And you're not making it any better. I'm saying a lot of things I'm going to regret when I calm down a little. So I think maybe we should hang up now. I'll talk to you later. At the end of the day."

"You'll call Annabel?"

"Ma, I'm going to hang up now. Don't worry. Everything will be okay."

"Frankie—"

" 'Bye, Ma. . . ." He replaced the receiver and picked up the mug of coffee. It tasted like acid. He put it down and stared at the bagel, which suddenly looked as appetizing as cold oatmeal. Oh, shit, he thought, pushing them both away. Now what?

$\mathcal{F}$rankie wouldn't have believed it possible, but he took care of business. He dealt with real estate agents, contractors, club managers, and even spoke for a quarter of an hour to Colette without her guessing that anything was wrong. For minutes at a time, while he talked on the phone, considered a problem, attended a staff meeting, he managed to forget that his life was falling apart. As busy as he was, he might even have managed to put it out of his mind entirely, except for the steady stream of phone calls from family and friends.

The one from his father came midmorning. After giving Frankie hell about the way he'd talked to his mother, Sal tried to find out what, if anything, his son had decided to do. "I don't have any plans," Frankie told him, and got off the phone as fast as he could, before he started yelling at Sal too.

With his sister, however, he made no effort to hold back. "What kind of shit are you trying to hand me?" he asked her. "You can't stand Annabel. Never could." That wasn't the point, Angela told him. In different circumstances, maybe a divorce wouldn't be so terrible. But there was Maud to think about. Or was he so selfish that he didn't give a damn about his daughter? Frankie yelled. Angela started crying and slammed down the phone. Great, thought Frankie. All that'll get me is a another phone call from Pop

But it was Vic who called next. "I'm supposed to invite you to dinner, if you'd like to come," he said, adding, "I wouldn't if I were you."

"Annabel talked to Maria."

"Yeah. And me, too."

"What are you supposed to do? Grill me a steak and talk me into going back to her? She's off her fucking rocker!"

"That's more or less what she said about you."

"She called my mother. Angela. I don't know what's going on in her head. Listen, tell Maria thanks, but I'm kind of busy. I'd like to bring Maud out to the Island again sometime soon, though, if that's okay?"

"Anytime," said Vic. "Anything I can do?"

"Game of squash tomorrow?"

"You got it."

When Dan called, he said that Annabel had kept him on the phone for over an hour. She'd sounded pitiful. "Pitiful?" said Frankie. "Don't make me laugh. This is a plot, a campaign. It's not me she wants, it's my money. It's security. It's . . . Oh, shit, I don't know what the fuck she wants."

"As long as you're sure what *you* want—"

What he wanted was peace. Not knowing how to get it, he went on winging it, letting his emotions carry him in whatever direction they happened to blow.

"I know how difficult Annabel can be," said Roland, when he called from London, "but you've taught her quite a lesson, Francis, if *that's* what you wanted."

"It's not," said Frankie.

"I've never seen her so upset. I think, you know, that she'd agree to just about anything, if you'd return home."

Frankie had never been comfortable around Roland, who reminded him of a character from an old black-and-white movie, the rich second banana who never gets the girl. He'd always suspected that Roland didn't think much of him either, a feeling confirmed by Annabel, usually in the middle of an argument, when she was pointing out the many ways in which her husband had fallen below her high expectations. His voice dripping with sarcasm, Frankie said, "I didn't know you cared so much, Roland."

"Of course I care," he said in his most lord-of-the-manor tone. "Annabel and I may not be close." They had hardly known each other growing up, each sent away to separate boarding schools at some ridiculous age like seven or eight, which sounded like child abuse to Frankie. "But she is after all my sister."

"Don't worry. It won't be a messy divorce, unless Annabel makes it one."

That's what Roland cared about, the notoriety. And of course not getting stuck with the care of his difficult sister. "Francis, you don't mean to go through with this madness," he said, a hint of panic replacing the note of sincere concern in his voice.

"There's a call on my other line I have to take. 'Bye, Roland. Give my best to Elizabeth," he said, and hung up, pleased with himself for having kept his temper. Roland was not a person Frankie wanted to let see him out of control.

*P*eople don't like to think of themselves as weak, as gutless, as moral cowards. Frankie was no exception, and usually he gave himself credit for being a pretty courageous kind of guy, willing to stand up for what he believed, to take on anybody in a fight, to give as good as he got, if not better. But he didn't consider himself a superman. He knew that under enough pressure, like most people, he would cave. So what surprised him, what filled him with brief, heady moments of satisfaction, of elation, was that all the phone calls, the entreaties, the arguments, instead of weakening his resolve, strengthened it. Sometimes he thought that was because, as his mother and sister never hesitated to point out, he was stubborn as a mule, resented being put in the wrong, and always refused to give in gracefully. But the self-doubt was fleeting. He knew that more than pigheadedness was driving him. When he tried to imagine spending the rest of his life with Annabel, he couldn't. Every scenario he wrote in his mind ended in a quarrel. All the things about her that he'd once found desirable, endearing, lovable, now filled him with loathing and rage. One night lying alone in his king-sized bed at the Carlyle, he woke from sleep, dripping with sweat, and half the bedclothes on the floor. Trembling with terror, he tried to reassemble the fragments of the dream that had awakened him. Finally, he remembered—he'd dreamed he was strangling Annabel. No way am I going back, he promised himself. He was afraid it would take very little, too little, to turn the dream into reality.

*T*he days settled into a pattern. After restless and frequently sleepless nights, Frankie would return to Central Park West in time to take Maud to school, coping as best he could with her questions about where he slept and when he would be returning home. He would arrive at his office feeling depressed, and spend hours every day responding to phone calls about his personal life. When he finished work, he would go to the Forty-third Street club to play squash, have a drink in the bar afterward, and join whoever was at equally loose ends for dinner. He avoided drinking too much, avoided restaurants where he might run into Annabel, avoided parties where he might find himself in situations he didn't feel equipped to handle just then. Sometimes he thought about calling Helen, but resisted the temptation. He didn't really want to see her. He had no interest in renewing their affair. All that was prompting him was the idea that he ought to have sex, even if he didn't particularly want it. Instead he went to the theater, or to the movies, often alone. Sometimes he returned early to the hotel to read. A book, Frankie had long ago discovered, was a pretty effective shield against despair.

As predictable, as soothing, as this pattern became, by the end of the second week, Frankie knew he had to call Annabel. He needed more clothes. He wanted to make arrangements to take Maud away for the weekend. He wanted the phone calls from friends and relatives to stop. Above all, he wanted matters between them settled. But, on Friday morning, Eva Colvington called to discuss the sale of a painting and he couldn't face another difficult conversation too soon after that one. He *would* phone Annabel, he promised himself, but later. First, he'd take Martha and her roommate, Jill, to a small Italian restaurant in SoHo to test the work of a young chef whom both Tom and Jill had separately voted terrific. Knowing he was on show, the chef took great pains with the lunch. The food was delicious, the girls pretty, the conversation entertaining, and, for as long as they were in the crowded, cheerful restaurant, Frankie was able to put Annabel out of his mind. But, in the taxi heading back uptown, he could feel the tension begin again to build.

"What do you think?" asked Martha when they'd dropped Jill off at her office.

"About what?" asked Frankie.

"The food," said Martha calmly. Knowing something was wrong, though not exactly what, she'd taken to treating him with exaggerated patience and courtesy.

"Funny name, Brendan. For an Italian chef, I mean."

"Maybe he isn't Italian."

"Maybe," said Frankie. "What did you think?"

"I liked the food. I thought it was delicious."

Frankie mustered a grin. "I guess that's it, then. No point looking further."

Martha blushed and smiled in return. "If he wants the job."

"If we want him," corrected Frankie, "we'll make it worth his while." His grin faded and he resumed staring out the taxi window. The promised rain had made its appearance, making Sixth Avenue look as dismal as he felt, snarling the traffic to a crawl. The air was hot and heavy. The constant blaring of horns made his head ache. He rubbed his eyes.

"You okay?"

"Just tired. I was up late reading." The taxi stopped at a light, and Frankie said, "Come on, let's walk the rest of the way. It can't be any slower than this"

*S*ettled behind his desk again, Frankie stared at the phone, willing himself to pick it up and dial. What's the worst that can happen? he asked himself. And immediately imagined Annabel hanging up on him, himself storming over to Central Park West in a rage and forcibly taking his clothes and his child, while Annabel screamed and Mrs. Ashby looked on in mute disapproval. Not the way he wanted the encounter to go. "Shit," he muttered; then "Go on, do it." His hand reached for the phone, but Louie Sutter, his CFO, opened the door, without knocking (there were times when Frankie thought he let the informality in his company get a little out of hand), and asked if they could talk about the employee benefits package just as Martha buzzed him to announce that Annabel was on the line. For a minute, Frankie was tempted to consider Louie's very real presence a reprieve. Then he thought better of it. "Give me half an hour," he said. He waited until the door closed, then depressed the flashing button on his telephone. "Annabel?"

"I was afraid you wouldn't speak to me." Her voice was soft and . . . well the word "chastened" came to mind.

"I was just about to phone you. We have to talk."

"Yes," said Annabel. "We do." They agreed to meet at seven-thirty that night at the apartment. "Shall I ask Mrs. Ashby to prepare something for us to eat?"

Frankie considered the suggestion. "Sure," he said finally. "That'd be nice."

The impending meeting with his wife weighed on Frankie like his mother's warnings that his father would deal with him when he got home, like the summonses to the principal's office that had shadowed his high school years. By four, he couldn't stand it anymore. Annabel had an appointment with a decorator late in the day, she'd told him, and wouldn't be home until close to seven. While she was out, he decided, he would pack up the remainder of his clothes, much easier than doing it while she watched. He buzzed Martha and asked her to get him a driver immediately, preferably Lionel. And when a few minutes later she told him that Lionel was available and would be waiting downstairs by four-thirty, he asked her if she could spare him a couple of hours.

"For what?" she asked.

Frankie explained the situation briefly and, when Martha looked both startled and hesitant, he said, "I know, I know. It's a lot to ask, but I could really use your help." Still she hesitated, obviously torn between her desire to keep herself out of his personal life and her instinct to help him if she could. "You have other plans?" he asked finally.

She shook her head and, as if agreeing to her own execution, said softly, "Okay."

When they got to the apartment, Frankie thought it best not to use his key and instead rang the bell. Mrs. Ashby opened the door. She didn't look merely surprised to see him, she looked shocked and confused. "You're very early," she said.

"Yes," agreed Frankie as he ushered Martha past her and into the hallway.

"Lady Annabel isn't at home."

"I know. You remember my assistant, Martha?" She'd been there for dinner a couple of times, and had worked out of the library once when Frankie had broken his leg skiing and couldn't get in to the office. Mrs. Ashby nodded, and mumbled something that might have been a greeting.

"We just need to get a few things," he said. "It won't take long." He started off down the hallway, Martha hurrying after him. "Where's Maud?"

Mrs. Ashby, after an almost imperceptible hesitation, said, "In her room."

But Maud, who had heard his voice, came racing along the hallway toward him crying, "Daddy, Daddy!" as excited as if she hadn't seen him in a year.

"Hiya, honey," he said, swinging her up into his arms and over his head while Maud shrieked with pleasure. Then he brought her to rest against his shoulder, and said, "Do you remember Martha?"

Maud nodded, and smiled shyly. Martha returned the smile and complimented the little girl on the outfit she was wearing, a pair of checked pants and a white T-shirt, both with pockets made of appliquéd St. Bernards. "Daddy bought them for me. To wear until I'm old enough to take care of a real dog." That was how she remembered the conversation, though Frankie was sure he had never promised her a dog.

"Maud, it's time for your dinner," said Mrs. Ashby. Shock had given way to disapproval. One thing was certain, whatever was happening, whatever Mr. Ferraro was up to, however innocent it might seem, Lady Annabel was not going to like it.

"I don't want dinner," said Maud, beginning to whimper. "I want to be with my Daddy."

"You can't right now," said Frankie. "I've got some work to do. When I'm finished, we'll play." He turned to Martha. "I won't be long." She nodded, but then stood in the hallway watching as Frankie carted the still-whimpering child off to the kitchen, Mrs. Ashby's grim form trailing after them. Returning a few minutes later, he found Martha waiting for him in the library, looking through one of his books. Frankie took it out of her hand, looked at it, and smiled. It was a first edition of *The Great Gatsby,* signed by Scott Fitzgerald. It was dated Paris, 1925. "Great book."

"Of all of his, it's my favorite."

"Mine, too," agreed Frankie. He looked around the room sadly, as if suddenly aware of everything he would be leaving behind when he left. Temporarily leaving behind, he assured himself. Still, it didn't seem fair. This was his home. These were his books. He could feel the anger flare, a small hot lick of flame in his gut. Watch it, he warned himself. Don't lose control. "Well, come on," he said. "I want you and my things out of here before Annabel gets home."

While Frankie gathered the papers he needed from drawers in the library desk, the stack of books as yet unread, the photographs of Maud and his family, Martha packed them carefully into shopping bags retrieved from a cupboard in the kitchen. She folded the clothes that he removed from drawers and closets and placed them carefully into the suitcases lying open on the bed in the master bedroom. When he'd taken everything he could think of that would make the next few months seem less bereft of comfort, Lionel came upstairs to help carry the bags down. He and Frankie were loading them into one of the elevators when the door to the other opened and Annabel got out. She looked at Lionel, at the bags, at Frankie. Her face paled. Without saying a word, she turned and moved quickly toward the open apartment door, her leggy awkward stride almost breaking into a lope. "Wait for Martha," said Frankie to Lionel as he started off in pursuit, hoping to head Annabel off before she slammed the door, and chained it, making it impossible for him to get inside. "Annabel!" he called.

His voice stopped Martha short on the threshold, preventing a collision with Annabel whose face convulsed with rage at the sight of her. "How dare you!" she said.

What? Be there? Help Frankie? Exist? What?

"Lady Annabel—"

Annabel shrieked at her, "Get out! Get out of my sight. How dare you come here! How dare you!" She was blocking the doorway and Martha couldn't get past her. Afraid to get too near, she backed up just as Annabel's hand lashed out. "Do you hear me? Get out!" Her fingers grazed Martha's cheek.

"Cut it out, Annabel," said Frankie, grabbing his irate wife by the wrist. "Go on down with Lionel," he said to Martha, pulling Annabel away from the door. "Drop the luggage at the hotel, then have him take you home." Martha nodded, then sidled out the door. She didn't even try to speak. She looked embarrassed, afraid, angry. "Martha, I'm sorry," said Frankie, then he kicked the door shut and focused his attention on his wife. "Are you out of your fucking head?"

"You bring your whore to my home and you accuse *me* of being out of my head?"

"She's my assistant. My *assistant*," repeated Frankie. "She works for me. I pay her salary. When I ask her to help me, she helps me. Even if it's something she doesn't particularly want to do, like helping me tonight. Why can't you get that through that thick skull of yours?"

"Don't lie to me!"

"Jesus Christ!" shouted Frankie. "I can't fucking take any more of this. I really can't." He was still holding her wrist, Frankie noticed, and he let it go. For a moment, Annabel stared at him, then she began to cry. Turning, she walked away from him into the library. He followed her, noticing, as he poured drinks for both of them, how unfamiliar the room seemed minus the few books and photographs he had taken. He handed her a glass, which she took without touching him, then sat in the armchair facing her. She'd removed the jacket of her beige linen suit, and he could see her lacy bra through the cream-colored silk of the blouse. "Do you have a lawyer?" he asked.

Delicately she blew her nose, and said, "I don't want a divorce."

"We'll both be better off, Annabel. We make each other crazy."

"I'll change."

"You won't. I won't. I don't even want to anymore. I just want out."

"No," she said.

"We'll let the lawyers work out the details. Whatever you want, within reason, you can have. What I want is joint custody of Maud."

"Maud," she repeated bitterly. "It's always Maud. She's the only reason you didn't leave me long ago."

"That's not true," said Frankie. I did love her once, he thought. I must have.

"You've never cared about me."

"I married you," said Frankie. Why would he have done that if he hadn't loved her?

"Oh, yes," she said. "And now you think it was the worst mistake of your life."

"This is pointless." He stood up. "Find yourself a lawyer, if you don't have one already." Reaching into his pocket, he fished out a card. "Tell him to call this number."

"You certainly came prepared." She took the card.

"That was why we agreed to see each other tonight, wasn't it? To get everything settled?" He started for the door. "I'm going to spend a little while with Maud. But I won't be staying for dinner. I'm not really hungry."

"No," agreed Annabel. "Neither am I."

"I want to take her to Long Island tomorrow, if that's all right with you." Annabel hesitated, then she nodded. "Thanks," he said.

Instead of replying, she looked down at the card in her hand, then took a sip of the vodka, refusing to watch him as he left the room.

Thinking about it in the taxi on the way to the Carlyle, Frankie decided that the evening hadn't turned out to be such a disaster. He had never really expected to get through it without a fight, and, as their fights went, this one with Annabel had been pretty mild. When he got back to the hotel, he found his luggage waiting in his room. And remembered Martha. He looked up her number in his address book, dialed it, and waited. It seemed to take her a long time to answer, and, when she did, she sounded curt, angry. "It was horrible," she said. "I've never felt so humiliated. Please don't ever put me in a situation like that again." Frankie promised he wouldn't. He said he was wrong to have dragged her into his personal life. He thanked her for her help. He apologized for Annabel. He begged her pardon. Reluctantly, Martha gave it.

. . .

*T*he following morning, Mrs. Ashby delivered Maud to him in the lobby of the apartment building. Her face was impassive. "What time will you be back tomorrow?" she asked.

"Eight," he said. "Maybe later. It depends on the traffic."

"Very good," she said.

On Sunday night, it was Mrs. Ashby who greeted him at the upstairs door. "I'll put her to bed," she said, taking the sleeping child from his arms. "Good night, sir."

"Good night," he said, feeling both relieved to have avoided seeing Annabel and worried. Everything seemed somehow to be going too smoothly, too quietly.

Monday morning, as usual, he picked Maud up and took her to school. But on Tuesday, at ten minutes past the usual time neither Mrs. Ashby nor his daughter had appeared. When he asked the doorman to phone upstairs, he looked startled, and said, "But they've gone, sir." Without waiting for an explanation, Frankie raced through the lobby to the elevators. He waited an eternity for one to reach him, another for it to climb to the seventh floor. Even from the hallway, he could feel the emptiness of the apartment inside. Using his key, he entered. Everything was neat, tidy, dishes put away, beds made. He checked closets and drawers. There were clothes remaining, but not many. In Mrs. Ashby's room, there was nothing left. From her phone, he called Annabel's store. No one there knew where she was. Or they said they didn't.

What Frankie felt first was panic. Maud was all right, he knew. She was safe. But where was she? Retracing his steps through the apartment, he tried to put himself in Annabel's shoes, tried to follow the path her mind would take, and just as he realized that of course he knew where she'd gone, he walked into the library. Instantly his fear was swamped by rage. His heart pounded in his chest; his breath came in short, labored gasps; he felt as if he'd run a marathon. His books, his precious first editions, had been pulled from the shelves, their jackets torn, their covers ripped from the bindings. They lay in confused piles on the floor where his wife had thrown them.

There was an address book in the top drawer of the desk. Frankie took it out, slammed the drawer shut, and looked up the number for Castle Melton. Without pausing to consider the time, he dialed. "Lady Annabel, please," he said to whichever servant answered the phone.

"I'm afraid Lady Annabel is sleeping," said the polite male voice at the other end.

"Then wake her up," said Frankie.

"I have instructions—"

"I said, wake her up."

But Annabel didn't come to the phone. Elizabeth did. "It was a long flight, and she's exhausted, Francis. In any case, I'm afraid she doesn't wish to speak with you."

"I have to talk to her."

"Perhaps later. When she's calmed down a bit."

"Elizabeth, please—"

"I'm sorry, Francis."

Elizabeth might look like a wimp, but she wasn't. There was no getting past her when she'd made up her mind to stand firm. "Do you know what her plans are?" he asked.

"Oh, yes," said Elizabeth brightly. "Annabel told us that she's brought Maud home, to stay."

Chapter 23

In Manhattan, in summer, the air wraps itself around you like a warm wet towel, settles over your face making it hard to breathe, dampens your clothes until they cling to you, heavy and oppressive. On the narrow cross-town streets, it lies as thick as a blanket, while on the avenues and near the parks, it shimmers in a dense golden haze, hitting the sidewalks with a bounce that carries aloft the smells of garbage, gas fumes, urine, body odor, horse manure, and occasionally a whiff of some precious perfume in the wake of a tanned woman in a sleeveless linen shift and large dark glasses. Waiting at the curb for a taxi or a bus is an ordeal. Walking to a subway, a grocery store, a meeting, requires careful planning of routes mapped through the lobbies of air-conditioned buildings, cool caverns offering a few moments of relief from the sweltering outdoors.

All day long, in the grip of a fierce nostalgia, a longing for the time when his worst problem had been how to evade his mother's watchful eye, Frankie had been thinking about the days before air-conditioning. He remembered the steamy nights lying awake in the Brooklyn apartment where he had lived as a child, the sweat-soaked sheets, the whine of a mosquito overhead, the smell of citronella in the air, the bursts of sound from neighbors sitting on their stoops until three or four in the morning, hoping to catch a breeze from the motionless air. He remembered the heaviness of his body in the morning, as he lay too exhausted to do anything but scratch the bites on his arms and legs. "Remember how hot it was?" he asked Vic that night as they sat drinking in the bar at Macklin's.

Vic nodded. "We used to sleep out on the fire escape sometimes, the whole family, trying to get a little more air. Not that it did any good."

"We got a window fan, when I was about ten, one of those big exhaust fans. It was supposed to cool the whole apartment."

"Yeah, I remember. We had one too."

Frankie laughed, a small involuntary sound, more like a grunt. "Sure you did. As soon as somebody in the family got something, everybody got it."

"Remember when Uncle Leo bought the television set?"

"Yeah. What year was that?"

"How old were we? Nine? Ten? Maybe 1948. I'll never forget that first night, all of us sitting around watching that one little screen."

"And Uncle Leo jumping up every five seconds to adjust the antenna on the top."

"Diagonal roll. Horizontal roll. Snow."

"Aunt Sara yelling at all of us to be quiet."

"And every once in a while a glimpse of Milton Berle."

Frankie laughed again, a bigger sound this time, and said, "When I got home from school the next afternoon, there was a set in our living room, right between the two front windows, opposite the door, so it was the first thing you saw when you walked in."

"I think we had ours by the weekend. And from that day to this, my mother says, she's never had to worry about what my father's up to. 'If he's not at work, or eating, you can bet your bottom dollar he's in front of a television set.' "

Vic did a good imitation of his mother and Frankie grinned to show his appreciation. "You think she ever really worried?"

"You got to be kidding. About that self-righteous sonovabitch?" There was more affection than anger in the description. "He's as straight arrow as they come."

"I can't make up my mind about Pop. Some of those ladies at the factory really had the hots for him. And a lot of them were pretty good to look at. It would take some kind of guy to turn down offers like that." Frankie signaled Jake, the bartender, for a refill. "But Ma, I don't think it ever crossed her mind that he might cheat on her. I mean, sometimes she'd pretend to be jealous, but she was just trying to make him feel good, like he was some kind of Casanova."

"Some women don't want to know," said Vic, putting his hand over his glass as he met Jake's eyes and gave a slight shake of his head.

The bartender passed Vic by, then topped up Frankie's glass with the

Glenmorangie, shorting him by a shot. Frankie didn't notice. He took a sip of his drink, then said, "Yeah. Some guys have all the luck." The past was forgotten. His wife and child were back in full possession of his mind. The lethargy that weighed on him like a bale of wet cotton had nothing to do with the summer heat wave paralyzing the city. It was depression. He was rid of Annabel all right, just as he'd wanted. The only problem was that he'd lost Maud at the same time, and that he hadn't expected.

Casting an occasional sympathetic glance at his cousin, Vic sat quietly for a while, nursing his drink. Finally, he asked, "You decided what you're going to do?"

"If Annabel won't talk to me?" Frankie had called the castle several times that day and each time she'd refused to speak to him. Even Roland wouldn't come to the phone. They let Elizabeth do their dirty work for them. "I have to see my lawyer." He took another long swallow of scotch. "Find out what my options are."

"Annabel's hurt and angry too, don't forget."

"Cunt," muttered Frankie.

"When she calms down a little, when you calm down a little, you'll come to some kind of arrangement."

"You don't know her like I do."

"No," agreed Vic.

"I know you never liked her. Nobody in the family did."

"We should've made more of an effort," said Vic, sounding more politic than convinced.

"She never gave you a chance," said Frankie, signaling for another refill.

Vic stood. "Why don't you come home with me? Have some dinner." When Frankie hesitated, he continued, "Come on. What's the point of sitting around alone, getting drunk?"

Frankie grinned. "I thought you were keeping me company?"

"You'll feel a whole lot better tomorrow if you stop drinking now and let Maria feed you."

Frankie looked around the bar and saw a number of people he knew. Some of them would be available to share a few drinks and later on a meal. It had been a while since he'd had a night like that. Maybe it would do me good, he thought, then quickly decided it wouldn't. Vic was right. The next day would be hard enough without having to get through it with a hangover. "Thanks," he said to his cousin, "I'd like that."

At two in the morning, wide-awake and sober, Frankie called England. At three, he tried again. Both times the butler answered the phone and told him that everyone was still asleep, though Frankie doubted that Roland was since, presumably, he had to show up at his office at something like a reasonable hour. Even if he didn't do much before he left for a long drunken lunch at some club or other, Frankie thought sourly. Between phone calls he made lists: lists of what to do, lists of demands to put to Annabel, lists of concessions he was willing to make. When he phoned again at four (nine Castle Melton time), Elizabeth came to the phone. Sounding polite, even friendly, she said, "Do give it a few days, Francis. Annabel's feeling awfully rough. And I promise I'll get her to ring you when her mood improves." Like when hell freezes over, thought Frankie, who didn't know whether or not to believe in Elizabeth's goodwill but thanked her anyway and asked to talk to Maud. Elizabeth hesitated, then said, "She's down at the stables, having a riding lesson. But even if she was here, Francis, quite honestly I couldn't let you speak to her."

"Annabel's orders?" Somehow Frankie managed not to yell.

"She'd be awfully upset," Elizabeth replied, not quite answering his question.

"Well, we wouldn't want that, would we?" He hung up and phoned Roland at his office. When his secretary said he was in conference, Frankie finally lost control and shouted into the phone, "You tell that cocksucker I want to talk to him." He heard a gasp at the other end of the line, followed by a loud slam. She'd hung up on him. Immediately, he felt ashamed. He redialed the number, got through to the secretary, asked her name, and, when she told him, said, "Well, look, Beryl, I shouldn't have lost my temper like that. Not at you, anyway. I shouldn't have said what I said. I'm sorry."

"I'll tell him you phoned," she said coolly, not acknowledging his apology.

He forced himself to go to bed and even managed to sleep for a few hours. At seven he showered and dressed. He had checked out of the Carlyle the day before and had brought his bags (the removal of which had assumed in his mind the mythic proportions of the firing on Fort Sumter) back to the apartment; but he'd forgotten to buy food, so he went to the coffee shop in the Mayflower Hotel, ordered a bagel and coffee, and, while the minutes crept past, sat reading *The New York Times*. No matter how bad the news (civil war in Nicaragua or soaring interest rates in the good old USA), for once Frankie didn't give a shit. Not even Bjorn Borg winning for the third time at Wimbledon cheered him up. All he wanted was to get his personal life straightened out. Finally, it was time. He folded the paper, paid the check, and, at eight-forty, left to keep the appointment with his lawyer.

· · ·

𝒩athan Felder, who had looked after Frankie's business affairs for years, had recommended Karen Coster, a partner in a high-profile Park Avenue firm, to handle the divorce. "I don't know," Frankie had said when Nathan mentioned her. "A woman." He didn't like the idea for a lot of reasons, but settled on one. "Won't she side with Annabel?"

"Karen's represented a lot of men, some of them clients of mine. I didn't hear any of them complain." That wasn't quite accurate. Litigants in divorce cases complain about their lawyers almost as much as about each other. What Nathan meant was that Karen Coster got her clients the best possible deals in the most difficult circumstances. He arranged a meeting, after which Frankie felt even more unsure. Though Karen reminded him a little of Colette, he didn't like her: probably because she didn't flirt, and he was never quite sure of how to relate to a woman who wouldn't flirt with him. (Except for Martha, of course, but then he rarely thought of Martha as a woman.) When he decided to hire Coster, it was not because of her personality, which he found unpleasant, or her success record, which was impressive, but because it had occurred to him that having a woman represent him might be useful. She might make him look more sympathetic in court; she might understand Annabel's stratagems and ploys much better than he or any man ever would; maybe she would even anticipate a few.

Karen Coster, however, had not anticipated Annabel's flight to London. Or rather, it had come sooner than she'd expected, before she had thought to warn her client of its possibility. Not that she apologized for that. "You should cancel your credit cards," she said when Frankie had filled her in on his abortive attempts to reach his wife.

"Why?"

"I think you'll find she's charged the airplane tickets to one of them."

"Probably." He still didn't get what she meant.

"Why do you think your wife left?" said the lawyer patiently.

He'd spent a lot of time thinking about that. "To improve her bargaining position, I suppose. She knows I'll do anything—almost anything—to get Maud back. And to even the score. To cause me as much pain and trouble as she can. The way she sees it, I'm the bad guy. I'm the one who wants this divorce."

"Exactly," agreed the lawyer. "And another way to hurt you is in the pocket, like run your credit card bills sky high." Frankie was about to protest when he realized that was exactly what Annabel would do. "Cancel your credit cards," Coster advised. "Close your joint bank accounts. Cut off any other access she might have to money or credit."

He wanted to do it. Oh, how he wanted to do it. And yet he hesitated. Deeply ingrained in Frankie was the idea that he should support his wife and child, that however much he wanted a divorce, taking care of them was still his responsibility.

"She won't starve, will she?" asked the lawyer, a hint of sarcasm in her voice.

"No. She's staying with her brother and his wife. They're not exactly rolling in it, but they have more than enough to take care of her. And she has the income from the business, too."

"What business? You never mentioned a business. Is it hers?" Frankie told her about the two antiques stores. "They're in her name?"

"She has a partner," said Frankie. Then he remembered another detail that might be important and said, "I put up the money for the Columbus Avenue store."

The lawyer's normally severe face grew gentle as she smiled with delight. "Really? Is there anything in writing?"

"Yeah. I didn't see the point at the time, but Nathan insisted."

"Very smart man, Nathan. You'll do what I said, cancel her credit?" Though still looking dubious, Frankie nodded. "Think about it this way: the more uncomfortable you make her, the faster she's likely to decide she's made a mistake and return to New York."

"That could still take a helluva long time," said Frankie. "And I want my daughter back. Can't we get a court order or something?"

She hesitated, and then said, "It's a difficult situation, Mr. Ferraro. Neither of you has filed for divorce. There's no interim agreement in effect. Your wife's not in violation of any custody arrangements."

"So there's not a goddamn thing I can do?"

"You could hire a solicitor in London. The English courts might at least grant you visitation rights," said Karen Coster calmly.

"In England?"

"In England."

At that moment, what he wanted more than anything, thought Frankie, was the satisfaction of wringing Annabel's neck.

On the way back to his office, Frankie stopped at the bank to get himself a supply of travelers' checks. While there, he considered taking his lawyer's advice to close the joint account, but he couldn't bring himself to do it. Neither did he cancel the credit cards. Leaving his wife and child without access to money, well, to him it didn't seem like something an honorable man should do. Instead, he told Martha to book him on a night flight to London, called a staff meeting and, over sandwiches ordered in from the deli, did a quick run-through of current business and anticipated problems. When the meeting ended, Frankie called Vic to let him know he was leaving, then his mother to tell her that Annabel and Maud were in England and that he was going after them. Convinced that she would never set eyes on her grand-daughter again, Dolly got hysterical. Frankie, who was afraid of much the same thing, did his best to calm her down and then gave up. "I'll call you from London, Ma," he said, and hung up. When his father called a few minutes later, Frankie asked Martha to say that he'd already left. For once, she didn't give him a hard time about lying. Then, as Frankie was on his way out, Colette called to ask what he thought about the ad for the launching of the renovated Boston club. It had been lying on his desk for three days without his having looked at it. "What did you think?" he asked Martha.

"It looks great."

"Fine. Tell her," he said, and continued out the door.

"Mr. Ferraro thinks it looks terrific," Frankie heard her say as he headed toward the elevators. "He's had to go out of town for a few days," she added after a pause. "He said he'd call you when he gets back." There was another pause. "England," she said finally, her stock of lies apparently used up.

*B*efore returning to the apartment to pack, Frankie had to keep an appointment at the DeWitt Payson Gallery where Eva Colvington was waiting for him. Usually, Frankie looked forward to his meetings with Eva. She never made much of an effort to be amiable, never tried to hide how much she resented his continuing control of the gallery, which only reinforced Frankie's sense of the power he had over her, a source of heady satisfaction that made all the aggravation of dealing with her worthwhile. This time, with so much else on his mind, it was unlikely he would get much pleasure from their encounter, yet he never considered canceling. He only did that to irritate Eva, not to suit himself.

The gallery hadn't changed much since Miranda had taken Frankie to see it shortly after their marriage. The brownstone itself had a new roof, and its exterior had been repaired and repointed, but the interior, despite constant redecorating, still had the same flow of space, the same neutral walls. The greatest changes were in the lighting (which altered every time someone came up with a new design for fixtures) and in the list of artists represented. To the roster of the established and successful, the names of "brilliant" new painters and sculptors were constantly added, and occasionally dropped. Six of them were currently having a group show. To Frankie, their work just looked like more of the same overpriced crap: blobs of multicolored paint applied sparingly to a white canvas; tufts of fabric glued to a black ground; a sanded plank angled against a wall, which, before he noticed the small card with the artist's name, Frankie thought had been left behind by a carpenter. The only piece he liked was one by a kid named Luke Fairoaks, a takeoff on the fashionable hyperrealist sculpture. Fairoaks had placed anthropomorphic cats, huge human-sized figures, dressed in thirties' fashions, in an art deco living-room set. The whole thing looked like some nutty illustration from a period mystery novel. At least it made Frankie smile, no small achievement that day. "That guy's got some talent," said Frankie to Eva as he followed her tiny, black-clad form through the gallery to the office in the back.

The look she gave him over her shoulder said, "A lot you know." But she forced a smile. "I'm so pleased you think so."

Decorated in shades of beige, the office had teak furniture, leather chairs, and a red color-field painting hanging on the wall opposite the entrance. Frankie found it stark but beautiful in its way. The whole made a perfect backdrop for Eva. She crossed to the desk, turned the only papers visible on its surface to face him, motioned him into a chair, and, sitting, handed him a pen. Frankie read the papers quickly, then looked at her, and said, "Could I see the painting?" It was one from the private collection.

"See it? Why?" She sounded as if he'd asked her to perform some unspeakable act.

"Because I can't remember which one it is," he said reasonably, "and I'd like to know before I agree to sell it."

"Must we keep acting out this same charade?"

"If it's one I like, I might want to keep it."

"Highly unlikely," she said, not quite able to control the sneer in her voice.

"Oh, it's a piece of shit, is it?"

Whatever reply she was tempted to make, she swallowed. "Frankie," she said sweetly, "this gallery sells only works by artists of great talent, even genius. I should have thought you'd know that by now."

"All I know is that as long as there are enough fools out there, you'll be sitting pretty."

"And you," she snapped.

"And me," he agreed easily, though financially the gallery for him was a wash. "Now could I please see the painting?"

Eva gave her blond head a short impatient shake, then shrugged, stood up, and headed for the stairs leading down to the storage area, which was cluttered with stacked canvases and small sculptures, most shielded by protective coverings. "Here it is," Eva said as Frankie followed her in. The painting she indicated was one of several that had recently been shown to a buyer and lay still exposed. It was a Barnett Newman, acquired by DeWitt

Payson years before the artist became successful. "Well?" said Eva. He studied the painting for a minute, for effect. "For goodness' sake, Frankie!"

"You can close the deal," he said, and turned, without waiting to see how Eva took the news. He went back upstairs, to her desk, picked up the pen, signed the papers.

"That's a relief," she admitted, following him into the room. Just once had Frankie refused to confirm a sale. The painting had been a Rothko, from the private collection, a painting that he had, for reasons he didn't fully understand, loved. Eva had thought he wanted only to annoy her. He'd certainly succeeded. "Thank you," she said graciously as she took the signed papers from him.

"Always happy to oblige."

Eva moved around the desk towards him. "Are you?"

"Within reason." What small degree of lust he had felt for her had long since been laid to rest. With Miranda, he thought, when he could allow himself to think about that. Now Eva only repelled him. He wanted to move away from her but held his ground.

She put her hand on his arm. "Frankie," she said softly, "we don't have to be enemies."

"Don't we?"

She shook her head, the waxwork perfection of her face acquiring a mournful cast. "You know how fond I am of you."

"Oh, for chrissake, Eva, give it a rest, will you?" He couldn't take any more and stepped away from her. It was not a good day for games.

"Fine," she snapped. "Have it your own way. Sell me the gallery. Sign over the paintings. I'm sure we can come to some equitable financial arrangement. That way you'll be rid of me forever."

"No," said Frankie.

"You're so goddamn impossible," said Eva, who rarely swore.

"Part of my charm," said Frankie.

"Go to hell," she shouted as he headed for the door.

"Not before you," he said, and left.

It was July and, thanks to the package tours, the London flight was crowded. Even first class was full. Too tired to read, feeling cramped, restless, Frankie tried to watch the movie, *Saturday Night Fever,* but something about John Travolta reminded him of himself at that age, which made him feel worse. Closing his eyes, he began counting his options. The next thing he knew they were circling over Heathrow. It was early morning and the sun was shining, giving off a thin yellow light, which Frankie took as a good omen. Pursuing Annabel through a rain-drenched English landscape would only have added to his depression. From the airport, he took a taxi to the Savoy, where Martha had booked him a room. From its windows he could see across the Thames to the Royal Festival Hall and the new National Theatre building, great hulking concrete structures, not beautiful certainly, but serious, impressive. It was a nice enough view during the day, but at night it would be spectacular, the river walks, the bridges, the Houses of Parliament and Big Ben to the west, to the east the dome of St. Paul's, and St. Bride's tower, all alight. But except for a dutiful glance out the window when the bellman had indicated he should look, Frankie was oblivious not only to the sights of the city, but the amenities of the room. He had only one thing on his mind. He took a shower, shaved, and changed his clothes, deciding against the multicolored woven linen jacket, which he thought might be a bit too flashy for the occasion, donning instead a St. Laurent black-and-white slub silk. Then, dressed for battle, he left the hotel for the agency where Martha had reserved a car. On the long flight to London, he had come to a decision. For now, perhaps forever, he would forget about solicitors, barristers, the complicated forms of the English court system. Instead, he would swoop down without warning on Annabel at the castle where she was holed up, and confront her face-to-face. If he could just see her, speak to her, he was sure they could come to some mutually acceptable arrangement. After all, as his father always said, money talks.

The car Frankie rented was a black Bentley, a comfortable sedan with leather seats and a burl walnut dashboard, a far cry from a mini, but not quite as ostentatious as a Rolls would have been, nothing for the Earl of Melton and his family to sneer at. Crossing the river at Waterloo Bridge, he followed the signs past Elephant and Castle and through the bleak south London suburbs. A Saturday, there was no rush-hour traffic to contend with, and it was still a little too early for the crush of weekend travelers. He adjusted quickly to driving on the left. Turns and roundabouts required some thought, but otherwise it was only necessary to follow the flow of traffic, keep up with the going rate of speed, and remember to pass on the right. Below Bromley the real countryside began, the gentle green landscape of the "garden of England." Frankie knew the way. He had traveled it often enough when courting Annabel, though rarely since their marriage. Now he followed not so much the route numbers as the signposts to the villages whose names had always amused him: Leaves Green, Biggin Hill, Tatsfield, Pilgrim's Way. He passed Chartwell, once the country home of Winston Churchill. Puffs of white cloud floated dreamily in the azure sky; window boxes bloomed with scarlet petunias; pink roses climbed cottage walls; and with every passing mile Frankie felt his spirits brighten. He was again a knight on his way to do battle. Justice was on his side. Right would prevail. Nothing could stop him.

Just south of Bough Beech, Frankie turned the Bentley into a narrow country lane and continued several more miles past oasthouses and hop fields, through the timber-framed black-and-white village of Melton, beyond the small Norman church, turned right, and drove through the open gates, across the moat, and along the drive cutting through the sweep of park up to the turreted stone magnificence of Annabel's birthplace, a sight that never failed to leave him feeling impressed, both with it and with himself for having gained entry into its hallowed halls. Stopping the car in the gravel drive in front of the broad steps, he got out. Looking around for signs of life, he could see only one of the gardeners trimming a hedge. From the stables, which were behind the house, he could hear the distant whinny of a horse. Otherwise, all was quiet. He climbed the steps to the massive oak door and rang the bell. A moment later, the butler appeared on the threshold. "Mr. Ferraro," he said, with a hint of disapproval.

"Hello, Rhodes. Is my wife at home?" said Frankie brightly, though he knew better than to expect an answer.

The butler blinked once, and said, "If you'll come this way, sir." He led Frankie along the stone paved hallway and opened the door into the ground-floor sitting room, one not used by the family but reserved for people who had had the presumption to show up without invitation to make demands of the occupying lords. "Would you care for some refreshment while you wait, sir?" asked Rhodes, the request a concession to Frankie's tentative status as a member of the family.

"Some coffee would be nice."

Rhodes nodded politely, then soundlessly moved toward the door while Frankie sat in one of the needlepoint armchairs and picked up a copy of *Tatler* from the table. He didn't bother to open it, but instead stared blankly at the landscape paintings on the paneled walls and considered what he would do if Annabel refused to see him. Well, he knew where her rooms were. He didn't think anyone would try to stop him, but, if they did . . . The sound of the door opening interrupted his war plans. He looked, hoping to see Annabel, but it was Elizabeth who entered. She was wearing a wool cardigan over a taupe-colored linen skirt and yellow blouse. It was never summer in the castle. "Francis," she said, "hello."

She extended her hand for him to shake but, when he took it, he leaned forward, kissed her cheek, and said, "Hello, Elizabeth. You smell wonderful." She was wearing a spicy scent, not too heavy. With silky blond hair, perfect skin, but otherwise unremarkable features, Elizabeth was far from the beauty everyone pretended her to be, though Frankie had always found her attractive in an understated way. He'd never, however, suspected the strength of character he'd witnessed over the past few days. Annabel and Roland clearly relied on her to defend the ramparts.

Elizabeth smiled at him, and asked, "When did you arrive in England?"

"This morning. Surprised to see me?"

"No," she said. "We rather expected you'd come. That is, Annabel was sure you would."

He began to feel that something wasn't quite right, that things weren't about to go the way he'd planned. "Well, I'm glad she knows me so well. Where is she?" Elizabeth hesitated and Frankie started to move past her, toward the door. "Is she in her room?"

"She's not here," said Elizabeth.

Frankie stopped. "Not here? You mean she's gone out for a while? Into the village?" But he would have seen her if she'd passed him on the way into Melton. "Riding?" he said, when Elizabeth shook her head.

"She and Maud left yesterday."

"Left?" He hadn't expected this. He felt as if all the air had been knocked out of him. He felt as if he might faint. "But where did they go?"

"I'm sorry, Francis." She sounded genuinely regretful. "Annabel didn't say."

Chapter 24

For a long time, in his brother-in-law's presence, Frankie had felt ill-at-ease, afraid that his accent, his manners, his style of dress were all wrong, that next to Roland he would seem flashy and pretentious, deserving of the contempt he saw frequently in Annabel's eyes. But he'd got over it. Coming straight from the stables where he'd been when Elizabeth had sent for him, still in jodhpurs, boots, and riding jacket, all worn from long use, Roland looked the complete country gentleman, aristocratic and self-assured, a man who could handle himself no matter what the situation. But Frankie knew he wouldn't last a minute in a street fight. Or in a boardroom brawl either.

Rocking back and forth on his heels, hands in his pockets, Roland also claimed not to know where Annabel had gone. Announcing she had no intention of "hanging about" waiting for Frankie to show up, she'd left, he said, with Maud, taking one of the cars. The Jaguar, he added, for the first time sounding irritated. By now she could be anywhere in the British Isles, or on the Continent for that matter.

Mrs. Ashby had been left behind, but Elizabeth refused to let Frankie speak to her. "I won't have you hounding the poor dear. She's frantic enough as it is. She has no idea where they've got to. And she's convinced that they'll never manage without her." Except for Elizabeth, the encounter between Frankie and Roland might have turned nasty, but she kept the two men from each other's throats and managed, somehow, to get Roland to second her invitation to join them for lunch. It was the height of civility. Too high for Frankie. He refused, but politely. "Do you want her back, Francis?" asked Elizabeth, as she walked with him down the stone steps to his car.

He considered lying on the chance that, if he said yes, she might admit to knowing where Annabel was. But Elizabeth didn't know, he was sure of that, and if she repeated the lie when Annabel phoned, well, his errant wife might return, but the complications in the long run wouldn't be worth it. Finally he said, "I want my daughter back."

"She's a lovely little girl."

"Yes," agreed Frankie.

"Divorce is so hard on children."

"Yes," said Frankie again.

"It's such a pity, really," said Elizabeth sadly, without explaining exactly what was, divorce in general, or Frankie and Annabel's in particular. She leaned toward him and kissed his cheek. "I'm sure when Annabel calms down, the two of you will be able to work something out. She's just so terribly hurt at the moment."

"We both are," said Frankie firmly.

"Of course," said Elizabeth. Then, her pale face still serious, she stepped back, watching as he got into the Bentley, lifting her hand in a cursory wave as he drove off, growing smaller and smaller in the rearview mirror, until, when he reached the first bend in the road, he saw her turn and start back up the stairs. It occurred to him that this might be the last time he ever saw Elizabeth, whom he realized he liked, even admired, the last time he ever saw Castle Melton. The thought filled him with sadness. He'd wanted to be a part of this world, but once in it he'd felt like an actor cast in a role for which he wasn't right, the person who ended up spoiling the whole production. Now all he wanted was for the curtain to come down. He knew there wouldn't be any applause.

*W*hen Frankie got back to London, he went directly to the store in Pimlico, where the pretty shop assistant claimed not even to have known Annabel was in England. Flora, herding him upstairs to the office to prevent his further terrorizing the assistants or customers, swore that Annabel hadn't confided in her. Frankie insisted she was lying.

"I'm not!" Flora offered him a glass of champagne, then remembered he hated it, took an open bottle of white wine out of a small refrigerator, and poured them each a glass. "I never lie." She smiled wryly. "Unless I absolutely have to, of course."

"You're Annabel's best friend."

Flora shrugged as if she wasn't quite sure she deserved the title, and said, "She was no doubt afraid that, even if I managed to resist you, I'd eventually give in and tell Kalima. Who of course has never been able to refuse you anything." She handed him a glass of fine crystal etched with a floral design, a remnant from an estate sale and not worth selling.

"You'd be surprised," said Frankie. He took a taste of the wine and put the glass down. Whatever it was, it was too dry for him.

Flora looked startled. Then she laughed. "Oh, no, don't tell me."

"What?"

"You actually propositioned my stepmother and she refused?"

"I didn't," he lied. "But if I had, you bet she'd have refused. She loves your father."

"Well, I'll be damned," she said, not quite believing him.

"What you ought to be is spanked for having such a dirty mind."

Depressed at the thought of spending a Saturday night alone in a foreign city, Frankie asked her to have dinner with him. But she was going to the theater with her fiancé, Flora told him, sounding so regretful that he suspected her crush on him might have survived the engagement. "You won't be too lonely?"

"I'll manage." He stood up, kissed her cheek, and said, "Enjoy the play."

" 'Bye, Frankie."

Her face looked so sad that Frankie kissed her again, this time on the lips, briefly. " 'Bye." Then, without looking at her again, he left.

*B*ack at the hotel, Frankie poured himself a scotch from the bottle he'd bought at the duty-free shop in New York, then sat in the ladder-back chair at the table by the window, opened his address book, and called Kalima to let her know that he was in London, in case she hadn't already heard. She too was busy that evening. "A dinner party, not at home, my darling, or of course you would come. Shall we lunch tomorrow? You'll tell me everything then." They agreed to meet at the hotel at one. "Nigel's playing golf. Isn't that thoughtful of him? I'll have you all to myself."

Replacing the receiver, Frankie turned the pages of his address book back to A and methodically began dialing the phone numbers of people who might know where Annabel was. Some weren't home; others hadn't heard from her in "simply ages;" still others made it clear that, even if they had, they wouldn't tell him. He reached the Ds before being overwhelmed by a sense of déjà-vu. Memories of himself alone in the Greenwich Village apartment, of Miranda late or missing, of his panic trying to find her, all came flooding back. He slammed down the phone and stared blankly out at the sight-seeing boats making their way up and down the river below him. He was wasting his time. Anyone who knew where Annabel was hiding could be trusted not to give her away. And wherever she was, she was perfectly safe, enjoying herself, enjoying the thought of the misery she was causing him. He'd hear from her only when she was good and ready.

He got up to freshen his drink. What should he do now? he wondered. The rest of the day, the night, stretched bleakly before him, a featureless landscape to be traveled slowly, hour after tedious hour. Finally, he called the concierge and asked him to arrange a theater ticket (just one: it sounded pathetic); and half an hour later he was walking across Waterloo Bridge on his way to the National to see a production of *The Cherry Orchard*, in the hope that Chekhov could rescue the day from being written off as a complete waste. But all the play did was compound his sense of loss. Arkadina's heedlessness mirrored his own; by being inattentive, frivolous, silly, she had lost something important, something irreplaceable, something precious. When the ax sounded in the last act, Frankie felt drained. Sunk in gloom, he followed the crowds back across the bridge. The play of lights on the water, on the Gothic spires of Westminster, on the dome of St. Paul's, gave the city a warm amber glow, and made the dark sky seem as rich and soft as velvet. Frankie observed the breathtaking view without much enthusiasm; and, reaching the Strand, he hesitated, not certain what to do. It was close to eleven. Between jet lag and the amount of driving he'd done that day, between anxiety and disappointment, he should have been exhausted, but he wasn't. The thought of returning to the lonely hotel room oppressed him. On the far side of the street were theaters and restaurants still alight. The broad avenue was alive with traffic, taxis and buses sweeping up from Waterloo Station and along from the Aldwych and Charing Cross, passenger cars on their way home or off to late-night rendezvous. The walk signal flashed and Frankie made a decision. Crossing the Strand, he plunged into the dark precincts of Covent Garden, and turned into a narrow road with no sidewalks and few lights. He continued on until he found what he was looking for, the brick facade of Joe Allen's lit by a single overhead light.

. . .

*R*oom service knocking on the door woke Frankie the next morning. Opening a wary eye, he checked the bed beside him, saw that he was alone, and felt a sense of relief as welcome as an aspirin. Then he remembered. A hamburger at Joe Allen's; too many drinks at the bar; a scuffle ended by the bartender; a pretty waitress, who (probably out of pity) had helped him the few blocks back to the Savoy. After coffee and sandwiches, suddenly sober and remorseful, Frankie had escorted her back downstairs and put her in a taxi, making one less problem to deal with this morning. "Come in," he called, though not too loudly. His mouth felt wadded with cotton wool and his body hurt from aching head to throbbing ankle. (He must have hurt it somewhere in his travels.) "Just leave the tray over there, by the window," he said as he groped for his money. Handing a pound to the waiter, a slender young man, with curly ginger hair and a small, delicate face, pale except for the flush of color across the cheeks, Frankie asked, "What time is it?"

"Nine, sir. It's the time you requested breakfast be sent up."

"Thank you."

"Thank *you*, sir," said the waiter, pocketing the tip.

Moving carefully, Frankie got up, and, naked, hobbled into the enormous marble bathroom to pee. He stared at the huge tub, as if trying to remember what it was for, then started the water running. A bath was just what his aching body needed. Returning to the bedroom, he picked up the breakfast tray, carried it into the bathroom, and got into the tub. He drank black coffee, ate some of the thin cold toast, soaked until the water cooled, then took a shower. When he had shaved and dressed, he studied himself in the mirror that backed the closet door. Except for his eyes, which had a slight pink cast, and a faint purple bruise high on his left cheek, he didn't look bad. One of these days, he thought, it's all going to catch up with me.

*K*alima was late. She was always late. It wasn't her fault, she claimed when she arrived at last. It was Flora's. "She phoned just as I was about to leave the house. She said you're frantic. Are you?"

"Yes," said Frankie. "Do you want to eat here or go somewhere else?"

"Here," said Kalima. "It's raining. And the River Restaurant is lovely." She removed her trench coat and handed it to Frankie to check. "My shoes are ruined," she said, regarding her black pumps dolefully.

"Why don't English women ever wear sensible shoes when it rains?"

"I'm not English," said Kalima. In a tomato red linen dress, sashed around her waist, heavy gold jewelry, and a diamond the size of a small egg on her right hand, she looked stunning. She always looked stunning, Frankie thought, and, no matter how chic and contemporary her clothes, like the queen of an ancient and mysterious country.

"Sorry. Women *in* England, then?"

Kalima laughed. "Because I suppose, if we did, we'd never get to wear anything *but* sensible shoes. It rains at least once a day, you know." She sighed. "At least, that's what it feels like to me."

They sat at a table overlooking the river, which had a silver sheen in the watery light. Over Bloody Marys, they talked about Nigel and the offer he'd received from an American company to buy his publishing house; about Flora and her wedding plans; about politics; about Kalima, who was deeply involved in groups concerned both with peace in the Middle East and the position of women there. "What do you think of Jimmy Carter?" she asked hopefully.

"He means well," said Frankie. He paused a moment, then continued, "To tell you the truth, I haven't been paying much attention to politics lately."

"Poor darling," she said, reaching out to lay her elegant dark hand on top of his. Unlike Amy Colvington, Kalima was able to separate the political from the personal. She never made you feel small for ignoring the world's problems in favor of your own. "You have no idea where Annabel is?" she asked.

"No one seems to," said Frankie. "But she'll turn up. Even if she's willing to give up me, my money, her business, she'd never give up her social life. There's nothing in the world that matters to her more than that." Kalima frowned. "What?" asked Frankie.

"I was just wondering why, when the last veil drops, the sight is so rarely pleasant?"

"What do you mean?"

"That quotation—from St. Paul, I think . . ." Kalima took a sip of her drink, then continued, "about seeing through a glass darkly?"

"Yes?"

"I think it's rather like that when we fall in love. Only we don't see our beloved through a glass, but through veils. Veils of illusion. Which he—or, in your case, *she*—lets drop one by one, sometimes deliberately, sometimes by accident—a kind of psychic striptease—until they're all gone, every last one of them, and we can see the object of our desire clearly. And discover someone we don't like, don't want, can't wait to get rid of."

Frankie laughed. "I never took you for a cynic."

"But I'm not," she said. The waiter arrived with their lunches, leg of lamb for Frankie, chicken for Kalima, who tasted it, sighed happily, then said, "I'm not a cynic. Really I'm not. I'm such a complete romantic that I believe if we could just see one another as we are to start with, we'd all live happily ever after."

"You think you see Nigel that way?"

Kalima sighed. "That's the problem with my theory. We all think we're so clear-sighted, levelheaded, without illusions. But few of us are. I hope I see the real Nigel. I'm not completely sure."

"But you love him?"

"Devotedly."

"I think I hate Annabel. It's a terrible thing to say, but it's how I feel. I think she only married me for what she could get."

"But isn't that why you married *her*? Why we all marry the people we choose?"

"I loved her," he said, and then added, for the sake of absolute honesty, "Well, at least I thought I did. I *believed* I did." He smiled ruefully. "I don't know what happened. I don't think I've changed that much. But her? When I compare her to the woman I fell in love with, they don't even seem like the same person."

"You see," said Kalima, "the veils have gone. And I expect," she continued, "that Annabel feels much the same about you."

But Frankie didn't see. Though there was no getting away from the fact that he'd been flattered that someone like Annabel would look twice at him, still, not only had he loved her, he'd admired her, for her self-assurance, her poise, her social graces, her business skills. And he hadn't concealed anything about himself. He hadn't hidden behind any veils. Annabel had met his family, his friends. She had seen his temper at first hand, known his interests, his ambitions. He'd kept nothing back from her, nothing except perhaps the feelings of insecurity that swamped him from time to time. He'd entered into his marriage in good faith, determined to make her a good husband.

Had Annabel married him with the same good intentions? He doubted it. She'd wanted his money, imagining him to be richer than he was, as obscenely rich as wealthy Americans were always reputed to be in the London tabloid press. She'd wanted him, too, that he was sure of, but in a Lady Chatterly sort of way, with a passion she hadn't been able to muster for the belted earls and Horse Guards officers she usually ran with (who, in any case, seemed to Frankie to prefer booze and horses to women). She'd loved him—for his looks, his ambition, his aggressiveness, the violence that lurked just beneath his surface—for all the wrong reasons. And, despising herself for it, she'd hated him too. Even as she introduced him into her world, she let him know (subtly to start with, more directly after they were married) that he had no real place in it, that he would never belong, never be welcomed, but only tolerated because of her. She'd made her contempt clear, for his manners, his way of dressing, the way he spoke, how he made his money, for everything he was and hoped to be.

"I loved her," repeated Frankie. "That's how big a fool I was."

"Are you staying over tonight?" Kalima asked kindly, to change the subject. "Come and have dinner with Nigel and me. Just us, and one of his authors. You'll adore her."

The author was a fierce, plump woman who wrote intricate and bloody mysteries. The evening was the kind that Frankie loved, with good food (prepared by Kalima), excellent wine, and interesting conversation. He admired Nigel, who was intelligent, well-read, knowledgeable about a wide range of subjects, and able to discuss them with a verbal flair that could have been daunting, except that, in addition to having a great deal of charm, he managed often to be funny and never pompous. It was a lot like watching a play, Frankie thought, as he listened to his hosts spar with the novelist, who talked in a rapid fluting voice, and had a wryly self-deprecating delivery. For large blocks of time, he managed to put his problems completely out of his mind. Only after he'd dropped the author at her house in Pimlico, refused her invitation to go in for a nightcap ("You'll be perfectly safe, darling," she'd said. "I'm a lesbian."), and was alone in the taxi did the depression drop on him like a net, wrapping him in folds from which he felt powerless to escape.

Nevertheless, he slept and awoke the next morning only when room service arrived with his breakfast. It was eight o'clock. He poured himself some coffee and phoned Elizabeth to see if she had heard from Annabel. She had not, Elizabeth assured him; and asked when he planned to leave for New York. "Why do you want to know?" asked Frankie suspiciously.

"So that I can reach you, if I need to."

"I'm booked on a flight this afternoon." There was a hint of apology in his tone. "But I can always change it, if you hear anything."

At nine, Frankie phoned the solicitor Kalima had suggested, explained to the polite assistant the reason he needed an immediate appointment, and, thanks to his dropping Lady Burden's name, was granted one for eleven-thirty. To kill time, he walked in the light rain from the hotel to St. Martin's Lane and browsed in the secondhand bookstores that lined the alleys across from the brooding gray hulk of the Coliseum where the English National Opera performed. The memory of his first editions, lying in devastated piles on the floor of his library, deprived him of the heart to buy anything, and soon he continued on to Trafalgar Square, went into the National Gallery, and, on the way to the Seurat, caught sight of a Sisley landscape, a winter scene, bare and white, with dark smudges of barren trees and a gray sky. He liked the painting. It looked the way he longed to feel: solitary, peaceful.

. . .

*H*enry Dowson, the solicitor, was a heavyset, elderly man with the smooth round face of an aging cherub. He confirmed what Karen Coster had told Frankie in New York. If Mr. Ferraro liked, he could start proceedings for joint custody. . . .

Mr. Ferraro did like, Frankie assured him.

And, in the meantime, petition the court to grant him rights of visitation. But since, at the moment, he had no idea where his wife and child were . . .

"Do it," said Frankie.

"Have you considered hiring a private investigator to find them?"

He's been watching too many American movies, thought Frankie. But then it occurred to him that a detective might not be such a bad idea after all, and he asked, "Do you know someone?"

"Yes," said the solicitor. "A company that's done some excellent work for me."

"If Annabel doesn't turn up in the next few days, I'll give it a try."

The meeting took less than an hour, at the end of which the two men shook hands, the solicitor promised to be in touch, and Frankie left the shabby office with its tufted leather sofas and paneled walls feeling, despite how little he'd accomplished, comforted, optimistic, as if he'd acquired a reliable ally, someone who would help him win his battle against the irrational and vindictive woman his wife had turned into. (Or had always been? Frankie wasn't sure.) But as he stood in the drizzle outside the ancient stone front of the law office in Gray's Inn Road, hand up to hail a taxi, Frankie's pleasant fantasies of a vanquished Annabel were interrupted by an image of Maud. Savoring his imaginary victory over his wife, he had forgotten his daughter; she had slipped completely out of his mind. Now she was back and with her the ache of her loss. If he wanted to keep Maud in his life, he realized, somehow he was going to have to make peace with her mother.

*B*ut all thoughts of an amicable settlement fled from Frankie's mind as soon as he returned and opened the bills he found waiting for him in New York. Annabel had run riot. The American Express card was at fifteen thousand dollars, the Visa at twelve. There was a bill from Harrod's for eight thousand pounds. She'd been buying clothes, jewels, furs. She'd spent eight hundred pounds on a single dinner at Le Gavroche and six hundred at Trumps, a disco, the night after she'd arrived in London. There was only one charge for gas, he noticed, and that was from a filling station on the outskirts of Melton. He felt abused, betrayed. Here he had tried to do the decent thing, had tried to provide for his wife and daughter, to make sure that they weren't desperate, stranded, and what had Annabel (that bitch, that cunt) done in return? Yet again she'd shown a complete disregard for him, for his feelings, for his possessions. She'd squandered his hard-earned money. She'd walked all over him. He'd make her pay, Frankie swore, if it was the last thing he did. . . .

His rage kept him awake and he spent most of the night in the sitting room in a chair near the window, drinking, calculating the numbers of crimes being committed below him in what, from his seventh-floor vantage point, seemed the most tranquil and idyllic of settings, Central Park, Frederick Law Olmstead's testament to grace and beauty. You can't judge a book by its cover, he told himself, appearances are deceiving. He thought about Salome and the Dance of the Seven Veils; about John the Baptist, and his head on a platter. He thought about Kalima and what she had said over lunch in the River Restaurant. He wondered how he could have been so taken in by Annabel, how he could ever have loved her. She isn't even pretty, he thought with disgust.

At four, he went to bed. At six he got up, showered, dressed, and went through the credit card statements again. The billing period for most of them had ended shortly after Annabel's arrival in England, he noticed, so thousands of dollars more than the amounts shown were probably owed by now. It occurred to him that if he could see those charges, he would know where she was. Or at least where she'd been. If they were all in the same location . . . He thought about the detective agency that had been recommended to him. He wondered if he could hire them to kidnap Maud and bring her home.

It was still only seven-thirty. Frankie left the apartment, took a taxi to the club, and worked out for an hour, hoping to rid himself of some of his anger, his anxiety. Tom saw him and waved and, when he was finished, Frankie stopped into his office to say hello. "You okay?" asked Tom.

"I'll live." They went down to the bar where, in the morning, coffee and bagels and assorted muffins were served. The new chef was working out great, Tom said. Restaurant receipts were holding. Word of mouth was good. "Glad to hear it," said Frankie.

From the club, he went to his bank and did what he now mentally kicked himself for not having done days before. He transferred the money out of his and Annabel's joint account and made sure she had no access to his line of credit. Back in his office, after assuring the receptionist, assorted colleagues, and Martha that he felt a lot better than he looked, Frankie spent an hour tediously canceling his credit cards and arranging for others to be issued in his name alone. When he asked for recent charges, he found Annabel's trail leading from the Connaught Hotel in London, south to Dover, across the Channel on the hovercraft, up to Paris. The last posting was from the Hotel Crillon. Annabel wasn't counting her pennies. Or his.

Frankie phoned Karen Coster and, when she advised him to publish an announcement disavowing any further expenses incurred by his "spouse," he ruthlessly trampled his instinctive repulsion at the idea, asked Martha to take down the lawyer's dictated statement, and to call *The Times* to get it into the next day's edition if possible. Once it was done, he started to like the thought, to be exhilarated by it. If only he could be rid of Annabel herself so easily, by announcing his wish in a newspaper, by walking three times around his house (or block) chanting "I divorce you." If only life were that simple.

The exhilaration soon passed. Were Annabel and Maud still in Paris, he wondered, or had they moved on again? He thought he would go out of his mind with longing for his daughter, with worry that he might lose her forever, with anger toward the woman who was causing him this misery. When he called his mother to report that no, he hadn't brought his daughter back, and that, in all honesty, he had no idea when, if ever, she'd come home, he didn't bother to sugarcoat his words, to offer any hope, provide any comfort. Lashing out at Dolly was a way of sharing his sorrow, and her wail of distress could just as easily have come from him.

Unable to wait patiently for Elizabeth to call, Frankie phoned her at least once a day. She always came to the phone and always told him the same thing, that she'd heard nothing as yet. Frankie was no longer sure whether or not to believe her. And, having canceled the credit cards, he had no way now of keeping track of Annabel's progress. He phoned the detective agency recommended by Henry Dowson and hired them to find his wife and child. It would take time, he was told, to pick up their trail. Frankie agreed to the suggested retainer and told them to get to work.

He felt like a character in a television soap opera. Things like this didn't happen to real people. They reached amicable agreements and got quietly divorced. But then Frankie would browse through *The Times* or see a headline in the *Post* and know that he was wrong. Real people did unimaginably terrible things to each other. From some points of view, he and Annabel could be seen to be acting well. At least they hadn't started waving knives and guns at one another. At least not yet.

*E*arly the following week, Frankie was just getting out of the shower when the phone rang. He wrapped the towel around his waist, trailed water into the bedroom, looked at the clock. It was only seven. Annabel, he thought as he picked up the receiver.

"Frankie . . ." It was Dan Colvington. "Frankie," he repeated.

"What?" Dan's voice sounded funny, and Frankie was scared. Something's happened to one of the kids, he thought. "Dan, what's the matter?"

"It's Amy," he said finally. His voice was soft, controlled, full of pain. "She had a cerebral hemorrhage last night." The kids had been asleep, and Dan in the den reading a manuscript. Amy had gone up to bed, not more than ten or fifteen minutes before he finished and went up to join her. He'd found her on the floor of the bathroom. "I didn't hear a thing," he said. "Not a thing." His voice broke.

"I'll get there as soon as I can," said Frankie. He got off the phone, threw on some clothes, made himself coffee, called the limo service, and packed. In less than an hour, he was on his way to La Guardia.

Boston was hotter, steamier than New York had been. After checking into the Copley Plaza, Frankie called Martha in New York to let her know where he was and why.

"Oh, God," she said. "I can't believe it."

Amy dead. Who could believe it? thought Frankie. He felt awash in tenderness for her. He remembered how he liked her, *loved* her, the times he'd wished she were his. Poor Amy. And the kids. And Dan. Poor sonovabitch. "You can leave messages for me here, at the hotel," he said to Martha. "I'll check in when I can."

"Tell Mr. Colvington how sorry I am."

"Yeah, I will. And, Martha, call my parents and my cousin Vic. Let them know."

"Yes," said Martha. "Flowers?"

"Let me see what Dan says first."

"Larry called a little while ago." Larry was the manager of the Boston club. "He's having a problem with the interior designer."

"You handle it," said Frankie. "Okay? Come here if you have to."

"I'll see what I can do," she said. And the line went dead.

*T*hough he dutifully checked his messages and called the office, Frankie for the next three days put all thoughts of business, all thoughts of Annabel and Maud out of his mind. He thought only about Amy and Dan and the kids. He made himself available, and useful, as Dan had been when Miranda died. He went with Dan to make the funeral arrangements. He made phone calls and took messages. He tried to keep the kids busy, the boys anyway, answering their questions when Dan wasn't around, taking them to and from the funeral chapel for one brief farewell visit on the last day of Amy's wake. Nights, after the others had gone to bed, he sat up late with Dan, monitoring the amount of alcohol consumed, listening while his friend talked, about Amy, about their life together, about the night she died, over and over again, about everything but what he intended to do now that she was gone. But then Dan couldn't quite believe yet that she *was* gone. "I still think it's a nightmare," he said. "And that I'll wake up soon."

"I know," said Frankie.

The funeral home was different, but the Episcopal church where the burial service was held was the same, as was the cemetery where Amy was buried. Frankie felt as if he'd entered a time warp and emerged on the day of Miranda's funeral. It was all familiar and terrible, even to the presence of Eva and Craig Colvington. Both in the church and at the cemetery they were in Frankie's line of vision, Eva pale and small in black, Craig tall and somber in a dark blue suit. They're remembering too, thought Frankie when, at the cemetery, his eyes met Eva's across Amy's flower-draped coffin. He saw the familiar flash of anger. She still blamed him. But that was no surprise. He still blamed himself.

Dan stood holding Lulu in his arms, his sons between him and Amy's weeping parents on one side and his own on the other. As the minister began the Lord's Prayer, Lulu began to cry, not because she understood what was happening, but because she didn't. Dan turned to find someone to hand her to and Frankie, who was standing behind him, took the child and walked away. Benja raced after him. "Let me," she whispered.

"That's all right," said Frankie. "I've got her now." He carried Lulu to one of the waiting limousines, removed his sweat-stained jacket, and sat with her in the back of the car, quieting her finally by telling her a story, freely adapted from one of Maud's books. By the time Dan and the boys returned, she was asleep in his arms. "Thanks," said Dan.

"Do you mind if I have one of the cars wait with me for a minute?"

"Take your time," Dan said, shifting the sleeping Lulu to his own lap. He didn't have to ask why. He knew.

Miranda's grave was only a few hundred feet away. Frankie had stopped visiting it years before when he realized that his being there did her no good and depressed the hell out of him. But now, well, he couldn't leave the cemetery without "paying his respects," as his father would have said. He spoke briefly to one of the limo drivers, then walked the short distance to where Miranda was buried. The tombstone was a simple granite slab. Inscribed on it were the words, "Miranda Payson Ferraro, beloved wife." What a fight he'd had with Eva over that! Frankie stood there for a moment, his mind blank. Then he thought, I don't even have a flower to leave. Finally, he whispered, "I wish I'd known how to make you happy. I wish . . ." His mind went blank again and, turning away, he walked back to the limo. Lunch was being served at the home of Dan's parents.

*I*t was after midnight when Frankie returned to the hotel. He'd had a lot to drink, too much, and had to walk carefully so as not to lose his balance, and to speak slowly, precisely, if he wanted to be understood. Dan had been in even worse shape when Frankie had left him to take a taxi back to the hotel.

There was one message for him, said the desk clerk as he handed Frankie his key and a slip of white paper. It was from Martha who, he remembered, had come to Boston to meet with the interior designer. Call her, that was all it said. Nothing about the message implied that it was urgent. If he'd had a little less to drink, Frankie probably would have waited until morning to talk to her. Or, if the thought of being alone hadn't filled him with such dread, he might have phoned her instead of deciding to knock on her door. But without consciously making a decision, and certainly (he told himself later) with no ulterior motive in mind, when he got off the elevator Frankie turned left toward Martha's room instead of right to his own.

"Who is it?" she said, her voice sounding sleepy and anxious.

"Me. Frankie."

"Just a minute."

Frankie waited what seemed a long time and was no more than a few seconds. When she opened the door Martha's brown hair was tousled, her face without makeup was pale. All she had taken time to do was throw on one of the hotel's terry robes. "Oh, God," she said when she saw him, "Are you okay?"

"Fine." He waved the slip of white paper at her. "You left a message."

"It's nothing important," she said. "I just wanted to remind you that I was in Boston. And to let you know that the furniture we chose is all in stock and there won't be any problem with delivery. At least, that's what they say."

"Oh," said Frankie. "That's good."

"Yeah. You sure you're okay?"

"Look, can I come in a minute?"

Martha hesitated. Finally, with a small sigh, she said, "Sure."

Frankie stepped past her and she closed the door. "Do you have anything here to drink?"

"You think that's a good idea?" And when Frankie nodded, knowing the uselessness of arguing with a drunk, she said, "In the minibar, I guess."

He looked, found a miniature bottle of scotch, and opened it. Martha handed him a glass. "I don't have any ice."

"That's okay." He emptied the bottle into the glass, then walked into the bathroom, turned on the tap and splashed some water into it. Martha's toothbrush and toothpaste were standing upright in a glass. Jars of cosmetics were neatly aligned on the counter. A zippered bag lay next to a hair dryer, its cord wrapped tightly around its handle. Even the used towels were folded and hanging on their racks. When he returned to the bedroom, he found Martha sitting in one of the armchairs, her feet up under her, her robe tucked tightly around her legs. "You're a very tidy person," he said.

"Yes." It sounded like an admission of guilt.

"So am I."

"I know."

"But not as neat as you," said Frankie, dropping into the second armchair, stretching his legs out in front of him.

Martha sat quietly for a moment, and then she said. "How's Mr. Colvington? And the children?"

Frankie shrugged. "He lost his wife. And he didn't even want to," he said. "She was beautiful, intelligent, talented. She had a great husband, one who loved her, and four terrific kids. She was the woman with everything. And now she's dead."

He saw Martha's eyes fill with tears and closed his own. He remained that way for what seemed a long time, not saying anything, taking an occasional comforting swallow of scotch. Finally he put his empty glass down, "I should be going," he said, his eyes opening. But instead of standing up, he buried his face in his hands. His shoulders began to shake. He was thinking of Miranda, Annabel, Maud, Amy, his sense of loss embracing them all.

"Mr. Ferraro," said Martha softly. Without thinking, she got up from her chair and knelt on the floor beside him. She touched his arm. "I'm so sorry, Mr. Ferraro. I know how much you cared about her."

"I love her," said Frankie, meaning Amy, meaning the others. His hands dropped from his face and reached for her. "Hold me," he said. "Please." He held on to her as if she were a life raft and he a drowning man.

She put her arms around him comfortingly, and said again, "I'm so sorry."

Frankie lifted her from the floor into his lap. "Hold me," he repeated. "Hold me, Martha. Please. Hold me."

Chapter 25

At four that morning, Frankie awoke as suddenly (and soberly) as if doused with a bucket of cold water. He knew exactly where he was; he knew who was in bed beside him. He stifled a groan. I must have been out of my fucking head, he thought; then, reassuringly, yes, he had been. Out of his head with grief. Martha would understand.

However, he didn't feel like hanging around to discuss the matter. They could talk later, he decided, slowly withdrawing his leg from between the legs of his sleeping secretary (no, personal assistant, he corrected himself, feeling his face contort in a fleeting, unworthy leer: she had assisted his person most ably, he remembered). Martha's breathing was deep, steady. Trying not to disturb her, he inched his way out of the bed, groped around the graying room, retrieved his discarded clothes, and (ignoring the headache, the flannel mouth, the desperate thirst, the need to pee) quickly donned his pants, shirt, and shoes. Gathering the rest into a bundle, hoping he'd got everything, without a backward glance at the bed, he slipped quietly into the corridor and hurried away.

Back in his own room, Frankie undressed again, took a couple of aspirins, and went to bed, sleeping until after eight, when he awoke, looked at the clock, and felt the relief of a condemned man temporarily reprieved. Martha, thank God, was on a plane to New York. He wouldn't have to deal with her until later, maybe not until tomorrow.

When he had showered and dressed, he called Dan, who was leaving for the Cape with his kids. "Come and see us, Frankie," he said.

"I'll call you in a day or so, see how you're getting on. We'll fix a date then." In the background, Frankie could hear the boys fighting, Lulu crying, Benja trying to quiet them. When Miranda had died, with nothing, no one, to pull him back, Frankie had slipped over the edge, falling into a shadowy world somewhere between living and dying. It had taken him a long time to get back. "Dan, take care of yourself, okay?" he said. "Think about the kids. How they need you."

"I know. That's what's kept me going these past few days." He laughed, a grim sound. "Though today I wouldn't mind trading them all in for a nice well-behaved dog."

Pity for Dan, something he'd never in his life expected to feel, overwhelmed Frankie. But, as he replaced the receiver, he realized that sympathy for his friend, worry about the kids, grief for Amy, all of that accounted for only part (though today perhaps the larger part) of the dense black cloud enveloping him. Self-pity made up the rest. He had to do something about that, but what? He'd tried to put his life in order, and look what had happened. Annabel, goddamn her, had hold of his balls and wasn't about to let go.

Keeping busy would help get him through. It always did. In New York there was a pile of work waiting on his desk, but that was about the last place Frankie wanted to be just then. So, he called Jack Haggerty at First Boston. Renovation costs were running higher than estimated, which was no surprise to anyone. Not wanting to be left short of cash, Frankie had scheduled an appointment for the following week to renegotiate the loan. Now he asked Haggerty if he had any free time that day. "All you need," he said, agreeing to meet Frankie at the club at eleven. Haggerty wanted a look at how everything was coming along before agreeing to advance any more money.

Leaving the hotel, Frankie stopped at the front desk where he handed the clerk his credit card and received in return a manila envelope, his name scrawled across the front in Martha's handwriting. Waves of embarrassment, guilt, and curiosity, washed over him, but he resisted the temptation to open it until he was in a taxi on his way to the club. It contained a pair of briefs and a tie. There was no note, but the open envelope seemed to release great gusts of hostility into the air. Terrific, thought Frankie resentfully, stuffing it and its contents into a pocket of his garment bag. Now she's pissed at me. Then, a few minutes later: I didn't rape her, for chrissake. All she had to do was say no.

At the club, Frankie left his bags in the office reserved for his use, then spent half an hour with Larry, the club's manager, who seemed to want to talk only about Martha, and how much she'd accomplished (and with such intelligence and tact) in Frankie's absence. When he got to the part about taking her out to dinner the night before, to thank her, Frankie stood, bringing the conversation to an end. "She's a great girl," he said. Then, prompted by the ghost of Amy Colvington, he quickly amended, "I mean *woman*. Excuse me, I gotta make some calls." Retreating to his office, he phoned the New York office, where Martha had not as yet arrived. After picking up his messages (none from Annabel, none from Elizabeth), he returned a call to the manager of the Newark club, who said, "You're making all these expansion plans, so I think you oughtta know the building next door is about to come on the market." Frankie could hear the longing in his voice. The poor guy had seen the renovations in New York and heard about what was going on in Boston. He was feeling like a neglected kid.

"It's an interesting idea. Let me think about it, and we'll talk," Frankie said, though he had no intention of spending a penny more than necessary before a divorce settlement was signed.

*S*uitably impressed with the renovations, Jack Haggerty agreed to lend the additional money on the understanding that this was the last Frankie was going to get, so he'd better watch his costs. Frankie took the warning with good grace, and bought Haggerty lunch. On the way back to the club, lost in thought, he headed instinctively for the Avenue Victor Hugo, where he had once spent hours browsing happily for books. But when he found himself in front of the familiar storefront, he couldn't bring himself to go in. His collector's instinct still seemed to be on hold. All he was desperate to get his hands on just then was his daughter. Quickening his pace, he returned to his office and phoned Elizabeth, who was out, and Roland, who was in a meeting, as was the solicitor and the private detective. He dialed his mother's number. Sometimes it was comforting to hear the voice of the one person in the world who loved him completely, unconditionally. "Poor Dan," she kept murmuring as Frankie told her about the funeral. "Oh, those poor children."

"They'll be okay, Ma," he said reassuringly, as much for his sake as for hers.

What was left of the afternoon, he spent reviewing contracts he had thrown into his briefcase before leaving for Boston. He found it difficult to concentrate, though there were few interruptions, and none of them calls from the New York office, where no doubt Martha was handling everything in her usual efficient way, he thought bitterly, though he knew he had no right to feel anything but grateful. Finally he gave up, worked out for a while, showered, dressed, and took the shuttle home.

The apartment was dark, silent, unwelcoming when he got there, though neat and very clean, he noticed, thanks to the daily woman whom Martha (yes, her again) had found. Turning on all the lights as he went along, he dropped his bags and jacket in the guest bedroom, where he was still sleeping, and continued along the hallway to Maud's room to switch on the lights there too. Its emptiness only made him feel worse. He retreated to the library where the bare shelves stared back at him, reproaching him for the mess he'd made of his life. Muttering curses as he went, Frankie returned to the bedroom, picked up his jacket and keys, and went out, leaving all the lights on. At the curb, he hailed a taxi.

"Where you go to?" asked the driver, another Lebanese.

Good question, thought Frankie. "Forty-third between Ninth and

Tenth," he said finally. There would be people at the club he knew. He could eat, drink, talk. It occurred to him that he couldn't have much of a life these days, or he'd be able to think of another place to go to have a good time.

The restaurant at Macklin's was crowded, a sight that managed to lift Frankie's spirits, though not by much. He sat at the bar while he had something to eat, talking to Jake, making conversation with whoever temporarily occupied the next stool. Though he went easy on the booze, by midnight he felt relaxed enough, tired enough, to tackle the empty apartment again. He said no to accompanying a couple of bond traders to Studio 54, returned home, fell asleep within seconds of his head touching the pillow, and awoke the next morning feeling pretty good. Until he remembered Martha.

Should he bring her flowers or not? wondered Frankie. Would a gift please or offend her? She'd have to explain to all the endlessly curious young women she worked with what had prompted it, and she'd be embarrassed, he decided. So he arrived at the office empty-handed, to find that Martha wasn't there. Which was strange since, give or take a few doctor's appointments, she always arrived before him. Her typewriter had its cover on; her calendar was open to the correct date; not a paper marred the surface of her desk. The blotter was new, he noticed, and felt another surge of annoyance. He'd spent the day worrying about her and she'd been changing blotters!

His private office was equally tidy. On his desk, side-by-side, lay a folder full of correspondence and a typed list of phone messages. Sitting, he buzzed the receptionist on the intercom and asked her to order him coffee and a bagel from the deli. He read through the messages to see if any were urgent, then picked up the phone to call Colette, whose name appeared a total of six times. Before he could dial, the door opened and Louie Sutter walked in, and said, "How'd the meeting with Haggerty go?"

"We got the money."

"Great."

Frankie smiled. "Wait till you see the club, Lou. It's gonna look terrific."

"So Martha said."

"This morning?"

Louie shook his head. "Yesterday. When she got back from Boston."

Where the hell is she? wondered Frankie.

In partial answer to the question came a knock on the open door. Standing on the threshold was a chubby dark-haired girl in a full flowered skirt and ruffled white blouse, the wrong clothes for her plump figure. Smiling hesitantly, she said, "Mr. Ferraro?"

"Yes," said Frankie.

"I just wanted to let you know I'm here."

"And you are?" he asked suspiciously.

"My name's Carol. I'm your temp."

"My temp? *Secretary?*" he said. The girl nodded. "Where's Martha?"

"Martha?" she repeated.

Frankie turned to Louie, and said, "Did Martha say anything to you about taking the day off?"

"No. Not a thing."

"Great," said Frankie. "Shit," he muttered.

"Do you want me to stay?" the girl asked timidly.

Distracted, Frankie said, "What?" He was trying to figure out what was going on. Then, "Yeah, sure," he continued. "Just answer the phones. Take messages. I'll let you know when I'm ready to talk."

"You sure she didn't mention it to you?" asked Louie, sounding worried.

Frankie shook his head. "But if it was something bad, like an accident or something, she wouldn't have had a chance to arrange for a temp."

"You're right," said Louie; then he grinned, adding, "though with Martha, you never know." He stood and headed for the door. "Give me a buzz when you find her."

"Sure," said Frankie, who was feeling more annoyed with every passing minute. Here he'd finally worked up the courage to . . . well, apologize, he supposed, and she was avoiding him. He called her at home, but there was no answer. He remembered the name of the magazine her roommate worked for and called there, but Jill was in a meeting, he was told. What is it with these women? he asked himself, as he hung up the phone. First Annabel, now Martha. Why couldn't they just stick around and settle an issue face to face, once and for all? A timid knock on the door interrupted him, and when he called, "Come in," the temp entered nervously, carrying a paper bag with his breakfast.

"This just came for you," she said.

Frankie opened the bag, took out the bagel and coffee. "There's a mug out there somewhere," he said. He thought a minute. "Carol, right?" She nodded. "See if you can find it." He hated coffee in a paper cup.

"Yes, certainly," said the temp eagerly, grateful to be performing some service, no matter how insignificant.

Waiting for Carol to return, Frankie opened the correspondence folder to look at his mail. There, on top, was an envelope addressed to him in Martha's handwriting.

"Is this the one?" said Carol, walking back across the office toward his desk, holding out a ceramic mug for his inspection.

Frankie barely looked at it. "That's fine. Just put it down. And close the door again when you leave," he said. Then, picking up the envelope, he ripped it open.

Dear Mr. Ferraro. Well, that seems kind of silly, doesn't it? wrote Martha, in her neat, careful hand.

> *Dear Frankie, I suppose I should say, I spent all day trying to decide how to handle what happened last night, wondering if we could just put it behind us and go on as if nothing had changed. That's what I would like to happen. Honestly, though, I don't think I could pull it off. I think from now on I'd always feel self-conscious with you, and a little embarrassed. Not that I think there's anything to be embarrassed about really. You were upset. I felt sorry for you. One thing led to another. It usually does in circumstances like that. I understand what happened was just, well, friendly, I suppose. Which isn't a bad thing. It just changes every-thing in a way that I'm not comfortable with. Nothing between us would be natural and easy anymore. And I wouldn't like that. So, I've decided to take the two-weeks vacation I'm due in lieu of notice. I've arranged for a temporary secretary to fill in until you find someone to replace me. You'll probably be upset when you read this and maybe even angry that I've left you in the lurch, but I think when you calm down a little you'll realize it's for the best. I've enjoyed working with you. Good luck with everything.*
>
> > *Fondly*
> > *Martha.*

When he finished reading the letter, Frankie read it again. He started it a third time. Shit, I know what it says, he thought, and put it down; then picked it up again, opened the top drawer of his desk, stuck it inside, and slid the drawer closed. He didn't know what to feel. Rather, he felt a whole lot of things all at once. Relieved that Martha had spared him an awkward scene. Frustrated because he was used to scenes (they were no big deal, and he felt the need to apologize). Guilty about (maybe) having taken advantage of someone who deserved to be treated with respect. Annoyed at having to go through the trouble of replacing his secretary. Worried that he might not find anyone nearly as smart, as hardworking, as trustworthy and reliable, as Martha. Hurt (and possibly angry) that she claimed to have slept with him only out of pity. A mercy fuck! The whole idea of it was insulting.

Again Frankie picked up the phone, dialed; again no one answered. She's probably gone away, he thought, trying to remember where her family lived. Upstate New York somewhere, he thought. He buzzed the personnel office and asked for her records. When he got them, he found an address and phone number for her parents, in Pawlings. He was about to call them when he realized that, if he did, and Martha wasn't there, he'd terrify them. Better to wait until Jill phoned him back. If she phoned him back. She didn't. On his way to a meeting later that day, he stopped at a florist and sent Martha an arrangement of flowers, expensive flowers, orchids that would survive for weeks, the florist assured him, as long as they were watered. He enclosed a note (finally, all he could think of to say was "I'm sorry"). All he had wanted to do was apologize, and, having done it, Frankie felt better. Soon he could hardly remember why he'd been so upset.

"What happened to Martha?" everyone asked.

"An emergency at home," he lied. "She may not be coming back."

Perhaps at another time Frankie might have made more of an effort to track Martha down, to settle things with her in person, to try to coax her into returning. He certainly thought about it from time to time. But Carol, despite her lousy clothes sense, was sweet and efficient and didn't have a problem running his errands or playing with the truth on his behalf, so he asked her to stay on permanently. The manager of the Newark club, realizing that Frankie wasn't seriously thinking about either renovating or expanding the premises, quit to go to a new gym that was in direct competition to Macklin's. And there was still no news about Annabel or Maud. A missing personal assistant was no competition for a missing wife and child.

A couple of weeks later, over lunch, Colette mentioned that her secretary had just quit. "If you'll settle for a PA, I may know of someone." Colette raised an eyebrow. "Remember Martha?" asked Frankie.

"Certainly I remember Martha. What happened? Did you fire her? In which case why would I want her? Or did she quit?"

"Neither. She had some personal trouble she had to deal with. But I think that's probably all taken care of by now."

Colette looked at him speculatively. "She's in love with you. That's why she left." She leaned toward him. "Did you fuck her?"

"Are you crazy? Look, do you want her phone number or not?"

Colette smiled. "Sure. I'll talk to her."

"She's worth her weight in gold," said Frankie. When he got back to the office, he told Carol to phone and give Martha's number to Colette. A few days later, he received a polite note from Martha thanking him for the recommendation. Colette had offered her a job and she'd taken it. The good deed was like penance, Martha's note like absolution. He put her out of his mind.

*F*rankie kept busy. He worked long hours, phoned Elizabeth every day, played squash with Vic, visited his parents, went up to the Cape to spend the weekend with Dan. They swam with the kids and built sand castles on the beach; they played softball and soccer. They went sailing. Amy's presence haunted them. She was there and not there, which was, at the same time, both distressing and comforting. Danny, the oldest boy, tended to be sullen and withdrawn. The other two were apt to burst into tears for no reason at all. Lulu wanted to be held. Her preference was for her father, but anyone would do.

"Thanks for coming," said Dan when it was time for Frankie to leave.

"I'll be back," promised Frankie.

Dan's parents were arriving the next day to stay with the children while he returned to Boston for a few days. Amy's new book of poems was on its way to being a bestseller (one of the rewards of dying young, he said bitterly), and Dan felt he had to do the interviews she could not. "We're going to Mykonos, the middle of August," he said. "Think about joining us." Dan looked pinched and sallow beneath his tan. His hair looked more gray than blond. He had aged years in just a few weeks.

"You're still going?"

Dan shrugged. "I think it's best for the kids. To tell you the truth, Frankie, I'm not sure I could handle my job day-in day-out the way I feel right now."

"You could if you had to."

Dan took a minute, then said, "You're right. People do what they have to. I'm lucky I can afford to goof off and grieve."

"I wouldn't call you lucky, Dan."

Dan's eyes filled with tears. "So much for the golden boy."

Frankie let that go, and said, "If I find Maud in time, maybe we'll both come."

"Good luck."

"You too," said Frankie. The two men shook hands. Then they hugged.

"Are you two crying?" said Ben. The image of his mother, he was standing on the porch of the house, in his bathing suit, his silky body the color of toast perfectly done. He looked wary; he looked as if he might like to cry himself.

The two men stepped apart. Frankie laughed. "What's it to you, big guy?"

"Men don't cry," said Ben.

"Sure they do," said Dan. "When there's something to cry about."

*T*ime dragged. Frankie felt as if he were floating through the days, living in a dream state, waiting for something to happen to wake him up. What did, the last week in August, was a call from the detective agency in London. They'd traced Annabel to Cap d'Antibes. She and Maud had been staying at a villa belonging to some Americans, Harry and Tara Mason. Angus Taylor's stockbroker, thought Frank, and his sexy wife. "Are the Masons there?"

"Only Mr. Mason. That is, he was there."

"He's left?"

"They all have. Mr. Mason, Mrs. Ferraro, the child. They've gone cruising, on the Masons' yacht."

Frankie didn't doubt for more than a minute that Annabel and Harry Mason were lovers. He had thought there must be someone. He just hadn't known who. He could feel the blood throbbing through the veins in his head, his heart pounding in his chest, his throat beginning to close. Rage was stopping his breath. He could barely speak. "Are they just friends, or what?" he asked to make absolutely sure.

"If you'll forgive my saying so, sir," said the detective politely. "I think there's a bit more to it than that."

"You have any proof?"

The detective cleared his throat, then said, "Well, sir, as to that . . . we . . . we do have some photographs."

The photographs would come by courier; and, until he got them, Frankie decided, he would do nothing. Then he changed his mind and called Tara Mason. "I got your number from Angus Taylor," he said.

"Oh?" She sounded surprised to hear from him. And wary.

"I thought we might get together finally, go out for a drink, dinner maybe."

"Harry's away," she said. She wasn't being coy. She was digging for information.

"So's my wife."

There was a long tense pause, after which Tara Mason said, "You know."

"Yes," said Frankie. He laughed. "Though I gotta tell you, I haven't known for long. The news came as kind of a shock. How long's it been going on?"

"About a year."

"You've known all that time?"

"No. Well, that is, I knew there was someone." She took a breath. "Harry told me it was Annabel before he went off to meet her in Cap d'Antibes." She laughed bitterly. "He was so pleased, he couldn't keep it to himself. *Lady* Annabel. God, is he impressed!"

They met for a drink at the Plaza. Though embarrassed by the circumstances, their need to know every last detail of their spouses' affair overcame any reluctance they felt about revealing their own hurt and humiliation. Sipping her way through several martinis, Tara told Frankie that Annabel was the latest in a long series of Harry's lovers; she told him that she had no idea why she stood for it, except that she loved her husband; she told him that she was one of the quaint, old-fashioned types who believed marriage was forever. Until Harry decided to leave, she was more or less happy to have him stay. So far, he had always come back to her. "Does Annabel have any money?" she asked.

"Not much.

"Then I expect he'll come back again. Harry's expensive. And I have all this family money; my husband's very attached to it." She had, through most of the conversation, avoided looking directly at him. Now she met his eyes. "What are you going to do?"

"I've wanted a divorce for a long time. For months anyway. I haven't changed my mind." He told Tara about the fight he'd had with Annabel the night of Angus Taylor's dinner party. "Now I really don't understand what it was about." he said.

"Guilt?"

Frankie shrugged, then said, "Or jealousy. Maybe it occurred to Annabel that in the long run Harry and I might both want you, not her."

"Do you?" She sounded surprised.

"Oh, yes," he said, mustering a genuine smile for the first time in weeks.

"Thank you," said Tara, returning the smile. "A pity the timing's so rotten."

The next day he sent her flowers, and a note assuring her that everything would work out for the best, which might not be true, but it was the thought that counted.

*S*hortly after Frankie arrived home the following night, the courier arrived, as promised, with the photographs. Seated at the desk in the library, a full glass of scotch on the table beside him, he picked up the ivory-handled letter opener that Annabel always used, and slid it under the sealed flap. The delicate knife broke, and, impatiently, Frankie flung it aside and ripped the envelope open, sliding the photographs out onto the desk. Most of them were innocent enough: Annabel and Maud, sometimes alone, sometimes with Harry, shopping in Nice, in Cannes, in Cap d'Antibes, playing in the sea, sitting by the villa's pool, going into or coming out of restaurants, on the deck of the Masons' yacht. However, there were others (and it was these that had made the detective stutter) of Annabel and Harry alone, in an open arcade overlooking the sea, in a small power boat a short distance from shore, on the deck of the yacht. There was no doubt about what they were up to. The arrangement of clothes, sometimes the lack of them, the positions of arms and legs. Oh, they're fucking, all right, thought Frankie, waiting for the anger to build and explode, expecting at any moment to leap out of his chair, to send the contents of the library flying, photographs, paperweights, lamps, tables, anything that came to hand.

But it didn't happen. Oh, he was angry, on principle, but he couldn't duplicate the rage he'd felt the preceding night. That must have been shock, he thought. He didn't care enough about Annabel to feel jealous, or betrayed. He was even willing to concede that his wife, after all, was doing no more than he himself had done. Remaining seated, calmly sipping his scotch, he rifled through the photographs again, and slowly an idea began to take form in his mind. A wave of excitement swamped the remaining anger. The depression that had dogged him for weeks began to lift. Without checking his watch, he picked up the phone and dialed Castle Melton. "It's close to midnight, sir," said the outraged butler when he answered.

"Sorry to wake you, Rhodes," said Frankie cheerfully. "Please ask the earl to come to the phone. Tell him it's an emergency."

"But sir—"

"If he's asleep, wake him up. It's urgent."

"Yes, sir," said the butler, sounding certain that whatever he did would be wrong.

Frankie waited with what seemed to him extraordinary and unusual patience the few minutes it took Roland to come to the phone. "Frances, what on earth . . ." he grumbled.

"I suppose you still don't know where Annabel is?"

"I was asleep," said Roland irritably.

Ignoring the complaint, Frankie continued, "Or *who* she's with."

"I don't know what you're talking about, Francis."

"Some photographs just arrived. Sent to me by a detective I hired."

"Look here, Frances, this sort of thing isn't—"

"You're wrong, it's done all the time," said Frankie, interrupting. "The photographs are of Annabel and a man named Harry Mason. Maybe you know him?"

"No," said Roland, paying attention now.

"They were taken with a telephoto lens, so the quality isn't always the best, but it's good enough to give a really clear idea, I'd say a *graphic* idea, of what's going on," said Frankie, describing the photographs in tedious detail until Roland stopped him.

"What do you want me to do?"

"Phone Annabel.

"I tell you I don't know where she is!"

"I do. Annabel's with Mason on his yacht, cruising the Mediterranean. His wife gave me the number."

"His wife?"

Frankie repeated the number. "This could get messy, Roland," he said, rubbing it in.

"I'll call her in the morning," said Roland wearily.

"Call her now. Tell her I wouldn't like to see these pictures in the *Daily Mail*."

"You wouldn't!"

Frankie had counted on that—Roland's panic, his fear of seeing his family name splashed across the front pages of the tabloids, fodder for the insatiable London gossip mills. It's why he hadn't called Annabel himself. His soon-to-be-ex-brother-in-law would take care of matters much more efficiently than he could do on his own. "Tell her she should call me. And the sooner the better."

"I'll tell her," he said. All the fight had gone out of him.

"I don't want to use these pictures, Roland. But I will."

"Don't do anything, Francis, I beg of you, without talking to me again."

"Tell her to call me," Frankie repeated and dropped the receiver into its cradle. He got up, feeling edgy, excited, the way he did when he was about to negotiate a big deal. Sitting down again in one of the armchairs, he picked up a copy of *Esquire,* leafed through it, put it down again. Too anxious to read, he sat staring at the wall, trying not to think, drinking his scotch, pouring another, waiting. When the phone rang, he leaped out of the chair to grab it. Less than an hour had passed since his conversation with Roland.

"Francis?" It was Annabel's voice. She sounded as if she'd been crying.

"Yes?" said Frankie, choosing not to argue about his name. He had bigger fish to fry.

"Promise me you won't use those photographs. You have to promise me!"

He recognized the same note of panic he'd heard in Roland's voice and felt a deep sense of satisfaction. "I hope I won't have to," he said.

"I'll do anything," said Annabel. She started to cry. "Anything you want."

"I'm glad to hear you're willing to be reasonable. Let me talk to Maud."

He heard Annabel catch her breath. "But she's asleep," she said.

"I want to talk to her," he insisted.

"I'll get her," said Annabel, sounding exhausted, and resigned.

Again Frankie waited. Finally, he heard Maud's sleepy voice saying, "Daddy?"

"Honey, hello. I'm sorry I had Mommy wake you, but I wanted to talk to you. Are you all right?"

"I miss you Daddy."

"I miss you, too, baby. But we'll see each other soon, okay? Very soon. Now put your Mommy back on."

"Yes, Francis?" said Annabel, getting back on the line.

"I want you and Maud back here by the end of the week."

"But—"

"By the end of the week, Annabel."

"All right. Whatever you say."

Frankie heard the line go dead. There was a smile on his face as he replaced the receiver. A wild sense of elation flooded through him. He felt in control again. He felt powerful. His life was back on track. It was finally going his way.

Part Three

THIRD
TIME
LUCKY?

1982

Chapter 26

*F*inancially, Frankie got out of his marriage to Annabel better than he expected, better than he deserved, something he was the first to admit. He did not (as Dan Colvington might have in his place) do the polite, the gentlemanly, the quick thing, and allow her to divorce him somewhere easy like Reno. Instead, in the autumn of 1978, within weeks of her return from Europe, he sued Annabel for divorce in New York, charging her with adultery, being careful not to give her the opportunity to gather evidence for a countersuit (he lived like a monk for months). Thanks to the photographs supplied by the detective agency, Annabel's "kidnapping" of Maud, and the fact (of particular outrage to the judge, a courtly man in his late sixties) that the child had been a witness to her mother's "adultery," Frankie might have walked away from the proceedings with sole custody of his daughter and without a penny to pay in settlements or alimony. He might even have walked away with Annabel's New York store. But with victory assured, Frankie decided to ignore his lawyer's advice and his own craving for vengeance and be generous, not to the wife he had come to resent, and despise, but to the mother of his child, an icon who figured loudly in both Dolly's lamentations about her son's divorce and Frankie's harsh assessment of his own behavior. When he thought of his daughter, he remembered his sins and suffered an embarrassment of self-loathing. The sight of Maud's sad face plunged him into an agony of remorse. Consequently, he agreed to alimony as well as child-support, and he gave in to Annabel's request for joint custody. Though he insisted on keeping the Central Park West apartment (minus all the furniture but Maud's), he bought his former wife another in the east seventies. Despite the recession, and the sky-high interest rates, he was doing all right; he could afford to indulge his guilt and be magnanimous.

After the divorce, her affair with Harry Mason finished, Annabel began to travel even more frequently, in pursuit of old treasures and new romances, which meant that Maud spent most of her time with Frankie. This pleased him, for his sake; but for Maud, he was troubled. To Frankie, it seemed that Annabel considered her daughter variously as a roadblock on the road to her next marriage, a prop to be used whenever presenting herself as a doting mother might be to her advantage, and, above all, a weapon to be deployed against him in a war that never seemed to end, though its objectives grew steadily more obscure. Then Annabel would surprise him with what appeared to be a burst of pure love for the child, and Frankie would think he'd got it all wrong, that it was only some sort of cultural quirk he'd failed to understand that made his former wife seem to him to be a cold and selfish, if exquisitely tasteful, money-grubbing bitch.

Having Maud with him so much complicated Frankie's life, but he found he didn't mind. He liked to be home to put her to bed, to be there when she got up. When traveling on business, if Annabel was away, he tried never to be gone overnight. If he was, he had not only his daughter's tears to contend with, but Mrs. Ashby's disapproving face. He had agreed to that too, finally, keeping Ashers, a high price to pay to ensure some stability for Maud, but when he saw how his daughter clung to the woman during the weeks leading up to and following the divorce, he didn't have the heart to say no.

Between Maud and Mrs. Ashby, it wasn't easy to have a sex life, but Frankie managed. Though age had coarsened his skin and lined his face, he was handsomer than ever, if less beautiful. Rigorous exercise kept his body in shape, while strands of silver at his temples added a certain distinction to his looks. Moreover, at the time of his divorce, as well as the easy charm, the winning smile, the arrogant acceptance of his own physical attractiveness, all so seductive, Frankie emitted an aura of power, of success. It was as if a neon sign hung around his neck flashing "rich and available." More than ever, women threw themselves at him, cornering him at parties, joining Macklin's in pursuit, calling his office and his home with offers of tickets to Yankee games, to plays, to concerts, issuing invitations to dinner parties, asking friends to fix them up.

At first, as always, Frankie had a hard time saying no. He enjoyed the attention; he expected it; he had, after all, been getting it since the day he was born. He liked being told how attractive he was, how desirable, what a good lover. Who wouldn't? And, if nothing else, it kept him from confronting the question that hung unformulated at the edge of his mind: why, if he was such a prize, had neither of his wives been able to love him, or, rather, to love him enough to ward off disaster, to keep them all safe?

Then one morning Frankie stared at the image in his bathroom mirror and heard himself saying, I'm too old for this. He had had four hours' sleep. His eyes were bloodshot, his complexion sallow. Neither toothpaste nor mouthwash had rid him of the foul taste in his mouth. All he wanted was to crawl back into bed for another few hours; but he had to catch a plane to Miami, meet with a real estate broker about a possible site for a new club, and get back to New York in time to take his daughter and her school friends out to dinner. It was Maud's seventh birthday and Annabel was in London.

The next day he lost—badly—to Vic at squash. Exhausted, Frankie stood for a minute, gasping for breath, then laughed, and said, "I've gotta get more sleep."

Vic nodded. "In case you haven't noticed," he said, forcing a smile, "you're not eighteen anymore."

"I've noticed," said Frankie.

Later in the week, Frankie was foolish enough to complain (or was it brag?) in a phone call to his sister about one particularly persistent and annoying woman who hadn't let herself be dropped politely but kept calling, asking for another chance. Instead of sympathetic, Angela was angry. Her voice spitting irritation, she said, "Frankie, just *when* are you going to grow up?"

"Last time I looked, I had." He was almost as annoyed with himself for mentioning the matter as he was with Angela for getting on his case.

"*Please*. You're like a little boy, a spoiled, *greedy* little boy."

"Greedy? Me? Why?" He was offended. "Because I work hard? Because I've built a successful business? Because I have money in the bank?"

"I'm not talking about money—"

"And spoiled?" he went on, not listening to her. "I'm up every fucking morning by six. Most days I take Maud to school. I'm at the office by eight-thirty. I work my ass off until I leave to go home to spend time with my daughter. I'm not a goddamned playboy, you know, just because I like to go out every once in a while and get laid."

"Your mouth, it gets worse every day. You have to talk to me like that?"

"You just piss me off sometimes."

"I'm worried about you, that's all."

"Okay, okay," said Frankie, in response to the conciliatory note in her voice. "I'm sorry."

But Angela's white flag was only an inch or two up the pole. "You can't go on like this, running around like a crazy person, out to all hours, a different woman every night—"

"Don't exaggerate," he said, irritation and complacency at war in his voice. The truth was, he could have a different woman every night if he wanted to, which he didn't.

She paid no attention to him. "Neglecting—"

"If you say my daughter," Frankie interrupted again, "I'm gonna hang up on you."

Angela paused a moment, then, "I was about to say your health," she went on. "You're a wonderful father." She doesn't know the half of it, thought Frankie. "But you've got to settle down. Forget Annabel, forget

Miranda. Oh, I know, we're not supposed to mention that name, but I'm mentioning it. That was a terrible, terrible tragedy. But it was a long time ago. Look, I loved her, you know I did—"

"Angela, for chrissake!"

"But she was a very mixed-up girl. What happened to her was not your fault. You know it wasn't. And Annabel. I never thought she was the right woman for you. If you want my opinion, you should thank your lucky stars you got rid of her."

"I *don't* want your opinion, Angela. That's the point I've been trying to make."

"Well, the point *I'm* trying to make is, you should stop acting like some kid who's been left alone in a candy store."

"You have a very active fantasy life. Does Denny know about this?"

"We're not discussing Denny. We're discussing you. Find yourself a nice woman, Frankie, a *sane* woman. And when you do, marry her."

"Never," said Frankie.

"You'll be better off in the long run."

"Never," he repeated.

Frankie might have ignored both Vic's veiled warning and Angela's outspoken attack if they hadn't coincided with his own growing sense of fatigue. As it was, he soon found himself following at least part of his sister's advice. He stopped running around so much. He gave up nooners and stayed home several nights a week. To his surprise, he liked his new way of life and rarely felt lonely, even when, with Maud gone, he rambled around the enormous Central Park West apartment on his own. Sometimes he watched television, but mostly he read, voraciously, the way he had when he'd first discovered books: *Remembrance of Things Past,* Tolstoy's short stories, Vasari's *Lives of the Artists,* anything he could find by Barbara Tuchman, all of Dashiell Hammett, whatever caught his eye as he browsed in bookstores. Friends complained he was turning into a hermit, but he got out a lot. He just did different things. He took Maud to visit Dan and his children, to spend weekends with Vic and Maria and their kids. He saw his parents more often, as well as his sister and her family. He planned events to keep his daughter entertained; he worked out at the gym; he dated enough to service his libido and keep up with the latest plays and films. But he was, no doubt about it, fucking less, drinking less, sleeping more. He looked good, felt great; business began to boom; all was reasonably right with his world. And then he met Kelly.

It was at an opening night party for a Mamet play in which Vic had one of the leads. Everyone was in the restaurant bar, milling around, swapping opinions over cocktails before dinner. Frankie's date was in the ladies' room. He was with his parents and Vic's (all of them dressed in their finest, the men in navy suits, the women in flowered dresses), trying to explain how a decent family man like Vic could appear in a play where he had to use "language like that," when he spotted Kelly in the group surrounding his cousin, who should by rights have been doing his own explaining. She was wearing a long green dress that hugged her body, making every man within reach long to do the same. Cut high in front, deep in back, it was slit to above the knee. About five feet eight, with legs that never stopped and a high firm bosom, she had a mop of frizzed auburn hair, skin like cream with a sprinkling of brown sugar freckles, high cheekbones, a short, straight nose, and eyes the color of peridot, pale, almost translucent, set a little too close together. Her tiny chin might have been considered a flaw had anyone noticed, but her mouth captured all the attention. It was wide, with well-defined lips resting in a permanent pout. The vibrancy of her colors caught men's eyes, but it was her mouth that held their attention. Frankie was no exception. Giving in to an impulse he hadn't felt in a long time, he excused himself to his family and started to make his way through the crowd toward her. So intent was he on reaching his goal that he failed to notice Colette who, refusing to be ignored, planted herself firmly in his path, forcing him to stop. Trapped, he complimented her on her dress, told her she looked beautiful, which was of course an exaggeration though in fact she did look pretty good for a woman on the dark side of sixty. Though he had long ago stopped thinking of her in erotic terms, Frankie still saw Colette as an attractive woman, still vital, still sexy, and their friendship had the sort of intimacy that only former lovers can achieve, if they have the sense to stay on good terms with one another. "The redhead talking to Vic, do you know who she is?" he asked.

Colette looked quickly, then said, "Kelly Helm. Hugo Helm's daughter."

Frankie recognized the name: Hugo Helm, of the Helm Theater Group, multimillionaire, and noted art collector, currently in discussions (so the gossip went) with Michael Graves about building a museum to house his booty in Oak Park, not far from the family home. Helm frequently bought paintings from the DeWitt Payson, and Frankie had run into him at the occasional gallery opening he attended. But he had never met Kelly. He would have remembered that.

Colette's husband joined them, greeting Frankie with a firm handshake and warm smile. A vigorous seventy-seven, with a thick head of silver hair and an athlete's trim body, Jake was somebody Frankie could never feel quite comfortable with, but he stayed politely for a few minutes of social chitchat before excusing himself to continue his progress across the room. He reached the group around Vic just as Kelly's escort put his arm around her to urge her back into the tidal flow of the party. Frankie's arrival stopped them, and

they waited politely while he told his cousin that he had given the performance of a lifetime. "And this time I mean it," he said. Vic laughed. "No
kidding," continued Frankie. "You were great."

"Do you usually lie?" asked Kelly.

Frankie turned to her, caught the look of admiration, of *interest,* in her
eyes, and said, "Only to avoid a bloody nose. Vic gets a little hostile when
you don't like his work."

Vic laughed again, then said, "Kelly Helm, my cousin Frankie Ferraro."

"Pleased to meet you," said Frankie, shaking the hand she offered. It was
slender and elegant and there wasn't a ring anywhere in sight. Vic introduced
Kelly's date, one of those preppie blonds Frankie instinctively resented.
Without registering his name, Frankie smiled politely and released Kelly's
hand to take his. "I've seen you at Macklin's," he said.

"Oh, you're that Frankie Ferraro," said Kelly.

Frankie shifted his attention back to her. "Is there more than one?"

"Two at least," said Vic good-naturedly. "We have a second cousin by
the same name. He's a cop in Hartford."

Everybody laughed and the four exchanged polite patter for a few more
minutes until Kelly's date managed to catch the eye of someone he knew in
another group and used that as an excuse to maneuver Kelly away.

"What do you think?" said Frankie when they were out of earshot.

"Nice. But not my type."

"Who's not?" said Maria. She kissed Frankie hello, said, "You're looking
very handsome tonight," then linked her arm through her husband's and
smiled up at him.

"Anybody but you," said Vic.

A shadow crossed Maria's face, and Frankie shifted uneasily. Vic had had
a brief affair the year before. He'd been guest starring in a movie, on location
in Memphis, away from home for a couple of months, missing Maria and
his kids. Feeling lonely, he'd given in to temptation in the shapely form of
the actress playing his girlfriend. When Maria found out, she'd packed up
the children and taken them home to her family in Provincetown. It had
taken Vic over a month to talk her into coming back.

"You should have denied everything," Frankie had advised, too late,
when his frantic cousin had told him what happened.

"I don't want to lie to her."

"Nobody *wants* to lie."

"I feel like a bastard when I do. I feel like some second-rate Casanova in
a cheap melodrama."

"So, you feel better now?"

"She says things will never be the same between us," Vic had said, sadly.

"Maybe they'll be better," Frankie had told him, though he didn't believe it. "Well, she's definitely *my* type," he said to Maria, to shift focus away from her domestic problems to his own romantic ones.

"She can't be more than eighteen."

"Oh," said Frankie, who hadn't given Kelly's age a thought until then.

"Twenty-one, at least," said Vic. "She mentioned a college graduation."

"Didn't you bring a date?"

Frankie could hear the disapproval in Maria's voice. "I did," he said easily, looking in the direction of the ladies' room. "And what do you know? Here she comes." He kissed Maria's cheek. "Not a good time to make a move, I guess."

Maria shook her head, but then she laughed. "We must be out of our minds," she said, adding, when Frankie and Vic looked at her blankly, "Women. Why we put up with you, I'll never understand."

*O*ne of the (few) advantages of age, decided Frankie, was that he no longer felt the need to grab every opportunity that came his way the moment he became aware of it. He had learned how to wait. If not for long. His first phone call the next morning was to Colette, the person most likely to know how he could get hold of Kelly Helm. "Well, did you do it?" she asked, saving him the trouble of finding a tactful way to broach the subject of another woman.

"What?"

"Ask her out. Kelly Helm. The woman you just about trampled me to get to."

"Don't exaggerate, Colette."

"Well, did you?"

"I was with someone," said Frankie righteously.

Colette laughed. "Always the gentleman," she said. "It's one of the things I've always admired about you. Well, you missed a great opportunity. Someday, when Hugo Helm sells those theaters of his, she's going to be worth a fortune." There was a Helm Theater in most major American cities, usually a lavish house where touring companies of hit Broadway shows played.

"She's an only child?"

"There was a brother, but he was killed a few years ago in a car crash."

"Jesus, how awful," said Frankie.

"He was drunk, or stoned, or something." There was no trace of sympathy in her voice. "The word is, Helm doesn't think Kelly has what it takes to run the company, but that doesn't mean she won't end up rich. Meanwhile, she's working for Abel Ellis, to keep her in stocking money." Ellis, who specialized in big, splashy musicals, was one of the more successful of New

York's theatrical managers. "You can find her there," she added, her voice sounding like a smirk.

"What makes you think I'm looking for her?"

"How long have we known each other, Frankie? Since 1960? What is that, twenty-two years?"

Frankie groaned. Then he said, "You think she's too young for me?"

Colette laughed. "Yes. But who am I to talk? Anyway, you never know, she may turn you down. Call me," she said. " 'Bye, sweetie." And she hung up.

$\mathcal{K}$elly didn't turn Frankie down. And the following night, as soon as Maud was asleep, he took a taxi across town to meet her at the Helm family's New York home, a penthouse apartment on Fifth Avenue with a view of the Metropolitan Museum of Art and, beyond it, Central Park. "Anytime you want," he told Kelly, "no trouble, you just walk across the street and into one of the world's great museums."

"I never go," she said, and Frankie thought he detected a faint note of pride in her voice. "Not anymore. My father used to drag me to museums all the time when I was young. And I hated it."

Was that how Maud was going to feel one day, wondered Frankie, as if he'd *dragged* her to museums? But no, he reassured himself, Maud *liked* to go with him; she loved it. He dismissed Kelly's attitude as (there was no other word for it) adolescent. She was in a transitional stage, separating from her parents' values in order to develop her own. She would come around. It never occurred to Frankie that she was a bit old for teenage rebellion: twenty-two, Kelly told him over dinner at the River Club, as old as his friendship with Colette, twenty-one years younger than he, who allowed himself to be comforted by the gap's not being quite as large as he'd feared. She didn't have a steady boyfriend; she hadn't since senior year in college. Her escort to the party where she and Frankie had met was "just a friend from work."

Mindful of the age gap, feeling unusually diffident, Frankie was prepared to be patient, to wait for sex until he was certain Kelly was as eager to consummate the relationship as he. He had to wait only until he took her home, when Kelly returned his good-night kiss with such enthusiasm, such hunger, that wonderful mouth providing so much pleasure, that soon they both lay naked on the sofa in the sitting room, spent, surprised by the ferocity of their coupling. They began to see each other two nights a week, then three. Soon they were seeing no one else. Since her parents were rarely in New York, usually they went to bed in Kelly's pink-and-white flowered bedroom. Frankie hated the room; it reminded him of a birthday cake; but

Kelly had been allowed to choose every last detail when she was sixteen and she loved it. She was like a little girl who never had to grow up, Frankie sometimes thought. He found that sweet, in a way. But whenever Maud was with her mother, Frankie insisted that Kelly spend the night at his apartment, which he'd had redecorated in neutral colors, lacquer finishes, all simple, comfortable, masculine. The Rothko painting, source of a major battle with Eva, had pride of place in the sitting room.

If sex was the bond between them, decorating and art were not the only areas where their tastes differed. Kelly read only when beside pools or on planes. Though she had accompanied her father to the theater from early childhood, usually it was only for the length of time it took him to check the receipts. Consequently, she had seen the high points of many productions, but rarely one straight through from beginning to end, unless it was a musical deemed suitable for the children. Her theatrical likes and dislikes, as well as her attention span, had been shaped accordingly. Shakespeare and Chekhov bored her. Straight plays were too dreary, she said. She liked comedies, as long as the laughs came along at a brisk pace. Musicals she adored. She had seen *Torch Song Trilogy* ten times.

Frankie remembered a time when he'd felt much the same, so he was determined to be patient. Besides which, unlike Annabel, Kelly wasn't a woman determined to have her own way just to prove a point. She would agree eagerly to accompany him anywhere he wanted to go, and do her best to appear interested when she got there. But sitting next to her as she tried, just to please him, to enjoy the Philharmonic playing Beethoven's Seventh was not only irritating, it spoiled his own pleasure. So, much as he did with Maud, Frankie accommodated his tastes to Kelly's. They went to movies, Hollywood blockbusters usually, to rock concerts and sports events, especially basketball and hockey, which Kelly liked because they were fast moving. Soon Frankie found himself missing exhibitions he wanted to see at the Met, the Morgan, the Whitney. Plays he intended to get to closed before he remembered to order the tickets. Unread books piled up on tables in his library. His record albums lay gathering dust.

On the other hand, he was having fun, he told himself; he was having a great time. He could still outdance most of the kids at the clubs. And since he wasn't drinking much or doing drugs, he could handle the pace. "I feel young again, like a twenty-year-old," he told everyone. "Kelly's the best thing that ever happened to me."

"Welcome to the land of the living," said his buddies. "She's quite a girl, all right," said Vic, leaving it at that. Frankie's sister Angela just rolled her eyes when Kelly's name came up. And Maria said nothing with such determination that Frankie knew she thought he was making a fool of himself. Again.

He didn't care. Nothing could detract from the pleasure he took in being seen with a very beautiful, very desirable, very *young* woman, who was obviously besotted with him sexually. And if that wasn't satisfying enough to his ego, Kelly's virtually unquestioning admiration, her assumption that his every judgment was just, his every opinion right, fed that insatiable animal until it was plump as a Strasbourg goose. After Annabel, for whom he could do nothing right, Kelly came as a welcome relief.

And Maud liked her. Kelly seemed able to sit happily for hours admiring Barbie dolls and discussing their wardrobes. She took Maud shopping, buying her glittery hair bands, plastic purses, black lace dresses that made Mrs. Ashby's face pale when she saw them. Now nine years old, still serious, but decisively feminine, fascinated by clothes and makeup, Maud was thrilled with her new companion. And since Frankie, old-fashioned about such things, avoided any hint of a sexual relationship with Kelly, his daughter never saw her as a rival, only as another playmate her father had thoughtfully supplied.

Still, several months into the affair, Frankie began to grow restless. That was his pattern. He started to tire of the pace of his life, to resent the restrictions, the responsibilities, the burdens, that having a single designated girlfriend put on him. He longed for the freedom, for the relative quiet, of his bachelor life. Once, he would have paid attention to the stray thoughts creeping into his mind at odd moments, thoughts about the differences in his and Kelly's ages, their interests, their stamina, and acted on them. Now he ignored them, dreading where his freedom would lead—to the bar-hopping, the brief encounters, the "relationships" that lurched from interesting to moribund in a month or two. The thought of his next affair (the preliminary moves, the sidelong glances, the come-on smiles, the flirtatious banter, the first date, the first sex), no longer filled Frankie with anticipation, with excitement. What he felt above all was dread.

To avoid all that, how far was he prepared to go? The question plagued him. The memory of his first two marriages didn't inspire confidence. He no longer trusted his judgment. He approached women, even the acquiescent Kelly, as a soldier does a minefield, or a cop the door of an armed and dangerous felon. He moved carefully, quickly. In the heat of passion, his guard as well as his cock stayed up, waiting for the hidden enemy to appear. He was alert to danger, prepared to fight or, better yet, to flee. He couldn't afford another big mistake.

As the first anniversary of their meeting drew near, his ambivalence grew. Though he had succeeded, so far, in putting her off with vague comments that sounded like promises but weren't, he knew he was fast approaching D-day. Kelly was waiting for him to declare his intentions. And even if she was prepared to go on being patient, her parents would not be so accommodating.

Her parents! Sometimes Frankie thought it was not so much Kelly herself he was reluctant to let go of, as Hugo and Rose Helm. A self-made man, Hugo unreservedly admired Frankie's success, while Rose was one of those women who blossomed in the presence of a handsome man. They welcomed Frankie into their life, into their family. He, and Maud too, were invited to their homes in Oak Park, Aspen, Palm Beach. There he met stage and film stars, dined with CEOs of multinational corporations, partied with Saudi princes, talked finance with leading economists. He skied and sailed, swam and played golf. Hugo asked advice about his new museum, and offered tips on the stock market. All of it was enjoyable, easy, casual, until he invited Frankie to partner him in a father-son golf tournament, an invitation both flattering and touching. A few weeks later, Rose invited his parents to dinner. Based on past experience, Frankie expected the evening to be a disaster. Instead, it was a success, a grand success. The parents got on like a house on fire, Sal said later. "Such nice people," Dolly assured her son. "And that apartment! Everything done just right, not a thing out of place, not a speck of dust anywhere."

"You went looking, Ma?" asked Frankie.

"You know what I mean," said Dolly.

Frankie knew exactly. His parents' former reservations about his relationship with a woman so much younger than himself were now consigned to the dusty old trunks in their minds, the ones holding the collection of doubts and fears that had caused them sleepless nights worrying over the progress of their children's lives, all saved to be pulled out later when disaster struck, so that they could blame themselves for not having intervened in time to ward it off.

That was the way it went, the tide turning slowly against Frankie, until even those who didn't necessarily approve of the relationship began to assume that it was permanent, that it was just a matter of time before he and Kelly would marry. This certainty had such force it almost convinced Frankie that he'd made his decision, when he had not, when in fact he hung suspended, paralyzed, between his desire to run from Kelly and his reluctance to give up her parents, to relinquish their houses, their country clubs, their friends, and, most of all, their approval and affection. Unlike the families of his wives, the Colvingtons and the Lindseys, the Helms adored Frankie, and the warmth of their acceptance was like sunshine after a long spell of cold gray days. He didn't want to come in out of it.

And he hated the idea of hurting them, for as much as Kelly might believe that she loved him desperately and that her life would be meaningless if they parted, she was young and would recover fast enough. It was the Helms, relying on him to replace their son, to take care of their little girl, who would be devastated. How could he do that to them? And yet, how could he marry

Kelly when he wasn't sure that she was the wife he needed, or that he needed any wife at all? How could he marry her when he couldn't be honest with her, couldn't bring himself to tell her, to tell her parents, to tell *his* parents, the one thing that would destroy their faith in him, the secret that he had kept hidden, for years, from them all?

Chapter 27

The name of his secret was Hannah, not a name Frankie would have chosen, but then he hadn't been consulted, about that or anything else leading up to or following her birth. Martha, her mother, had made it clear that she didn't hold Frankie responsible for the one night of accidental (that's how he thought of it, anyway) passion that had produced this unexpected result, this child, whom she knew he didn't want, but she did, very much. It was her choice to keep it, and that made it, in her mind, *her* child, no one else's. She not only accepted the responsibility, she gloried in it. She took charge. She made the decisions, all of them. That (she was firm on this point) was the way she preferred it.

Frankie got the message: Martha would rather choke than ask him for help. "Then why bother telling me? You should have saved your breath," he'd snapped one night, shortly after Hannah's birth, when Martha had again refused to take money from him.

"I was a fool. I was feeling guilty. I thought you ought to know. A man should know when he's having a child."

"What a man should do is pay," Frankie had said.

Martha laughed. "Well, you'll just have to find another way to work out your guilt. Money won't do it this time."

"I didn't mean 'pay' in that sense." He felt embarrassed, as if she'd caught a glimpse of his naked psyche and found it lacking. "I meant take care of."

"Look," she said, her tone friendly, reasonable, "I would take the money if I needed it. If the baby needed it But we don't. We'll manage. Don't worry so much."

Martha's attitude should have filled Frankie with relief. He didn't love her; he didn't want the child. When he'd learned Martha was pregnant, six months pregnant by then, mixed with the shock and anger he'd felt was regret that she hadn't, when it was still possible, had an abortion. Though without telling him, of course. The thought of abortion made him uneasy. He couldn't escape the idea that it might be a sin, a mortal sin; and though mortal sins (as far as he knew) were not graded in order of seriousness, to him it seemed that this might be a worse one than fornication or adultery, and would trouble his conscience as the others never had.

Martha refused to accept that anything should trouble Frankie's conscience. The way she carried on, Hannah's conception and birth might have been a result of spontaneous generation. She might have done it all herself, like one of those single-celled organisms that divided in order to procreate. So adamant was she about accepting sole responsibility that Frankie, at first grateful, eventually came to resent it. "She's my goddamn kid," he'd end up shouting whenever Martha made some decision without first consulting him.

"I knew I shouldn't have told you," Martha would reply quietly, as if surprised and troubled by her own lack of foresight. "I knew I should have kept my mouth shut." She was very good about keeping her mouth shut. Only her friend Jill had been with her when Hannah was born. Martha hadn't even called Frankie until three days later.

Frankie confided in Dan and discussed matters with Vic, both of whom agreed that he'd done (or offered to do) as much as duty required. "You think you should marry her? Would that make you feel better?" asked Vic; and, when Frankie replied with an emphatic no, he added, "Then be grateful. She's let you off the hook. Not every guy's so lucky."

The trouble was, Frankie didn't feel lucky. He felt insignificant. He felt marginalized. He felt out of control. He didn't like it.

Martha was a good mother, instinctively good, like some women are, loving, attentive, playful, only rarely impatient. She enjoyed her child. And except for Pina, a Salvadoran woman who looked after the baby when Martha had to go out, she took care of Hannah herself, without even doting grandparents to help, since Dolly and Sal were unaware of her existence, and Martha's parents, supportive once their initial outrage had passed, lived too far away to be of much practical use.

What she needed, Frankie often thought after one of his visits ("checkup visits," Martha called them) was a husband. Or, to be more accurate, what Frankie needed was for her to have one. If someone else were taking care of her, then maybe he could stop worrying about not doing it himself. As it was, though she never asked him for a thing, he couldn't quite escape the feeling that somehow he was failing her, failing the baby, failing to fulfill his role as a man.

The thought of handing off this burden was so appealing that one night he said to her, "You know, you really should think about getting married."

She knew he didn't mean to him. "Married!" she repeated, a hint of a sneer in her voice. "You think I couldn't, if I wanted to?"

"Of course, you could," he said placatingly, knowing that somehow, without meaning to, he had offended. He did a quick, surreptitious survey. Diet and exercise had rid her of all the excess weight of pregnancy. Her slender body was firm; her thick hair fell to her shoulders in a shimmering brown mass; her face, with its wide mouth and large hazel eyes, was undeniably pretty. "I mean you're attractive, intelligent. You're sensible. About most things anyway. You're a good manager. A great mother. A fantastic cook," he added, savoring the taste of the grilled steak she'd prepared. Even when he was dating heavily, Frankie usually managed to stay for dinner once a week or so.

"Anybody can get married if they want to. Beautiful, homely. Smart, stupid. Fat, skinny. Good cook, bad. Look around."

"You mean, you just have to find the right person."

"Seems to me, most people find the wrong one." She refrained from pointing an accusing finger, but Frankie got the message. "Don't you have to be somewhere soon?" she added, watching sourly as he cleaned his plate.

"Trying to get rid of me?"

"Now, why would you think that?" she said.

Only rarely did Martha ask Frankie for advice, and then, usually, it was about work. "I want the status, and God knows I want the money," she confided to him when Colette, who wanted to spend more time in Boca Raton with her retired husband, offered Martha a promotion from personal assistant to executive with accounts of her own. "Still, doing publicity seems so frivolous and unimportant somehow."

"Is there something you'd rather do?" he asked.

"I don't know. That's the problem."

"You must have some idea."

She looked at him. "You grew up wanting to own a health club, right?"

"I took an opportunity when it came along."

"There was nothing you wanted to be? Like a doctor? A lawyer? A cop?"

"President. I thought it would be great to be JFK. Turns out I was wrong." They were quiet for a moment, as a rerun of November 1963 flickered by in their memories. Then Frankie said, "It's great to save the world, but most of us don't get the chance. We just do the best we can; and with any luck we don't hurt anyone or anything in the process. Unless you've got a better idea, you should take the job."

"I can't work the long hours Colette does, not with the baby."

"Look," said Frankie, "if what this is about is staying home with the baby, I've told you, it would be much easier for you if you would let me help out."

"That's not what this is about," she said. "It's about what to do with my life."

Martha took the promotion, and Colette was delighted to have someone she could rely on. "I like the girl. She reminds me of me. Don't laugh. She's got my pride, my stubbornness, my need for independence. Though not my ruthlessness, I'm sorry to say," she told Frankie. To Martha, she said, "You only have to worry about the lunches and the meetings. For the rest, you can work as much as you want to at home. All you need is a couple of phone lines, a typewriter, and a messenger service."

That decision made, Frankie tried to convince Martha that she had another, possibly even more pressing, problem to solve. He hated her apartment, the same one she had once shared with Jill, who now lived with her new husband. It was in a large block in the east eighties. Part of a low-cost housing development, the building had no redeeming features—no architectural distinction, no personality, no charm. Neither did the apartment. It did, however, have two precious bedrooms. And it was affordable, which made it infinitely desirable to Martha, who told Frankie that he didn't have to visit if he found it such an insult to his aesthetic sense. "It's fine," he protested. "You've done some pretty interesting things with it," he added, referring to the odd bits of carved wood molding interspersed with framed reproductions of Impressionist paintings on the walls, the drape of fabric on the windows, the furniture salvaged from the Salvation Army, which Martha had painted and distressed, the secondhand sofa and armchairs she'd reupholstered herself in colorful fabrics that would take the hard use of a small child. Very handy was Martha, and she'd done what she could to transform the place into somewhere cozy, somewhere pleasant to be. Still, there was a coldness at its heart that no amount of redecorating could touch.

For over a year Martha resisted Frankie's attempts to get her to move, until one of her clients, a dancer with the New York City Ballet who was leaving to form a company in his native Chile, offered her his rent-stabilized two-bedroom apartment on West End Avenue. "If you'd told me sooner you were looking for a place," Frankie said when Martha told him that she'd signed the lease, "I might've been able to help."

"I wasn't looking. This just came up."

"Maybe I could've found you somewhere bigger, better." Even to himself, he sounded petulant.

"Bigger, better, I couldn't afford. This one's great. You'll like it."

"And if I don't?"

Martha took her time, running through a list of possible answers. It was one of the things about her that pissed the hell out of Frankie, the way she thought everything over so carefully. It made fighting with her difficult. Quarrels never escalated as satisfactorily as with everyone else. Finally, she said, "Frankie, if we're going to have any kind of relationship, if we're going to stay friends, then you have to understand that where I live, how I live, is *not* your responsibility. It's not even your business."

"It's not my business where my child lives?"

"*My* child." Martha's voice sounded weary, as if she'd had this conversation a few times too many and was bored by it.

"So you keep saying. What if we go to court and let a judge decide?"

He'd never threatened her before, and wasn't sure why he had this time. Except that he wanted to ruffle her calm, get underneath that self-control. He succeeded, though not in the way he'd expected. She laughed. "Go to court? Who are you kidding? Tell the world you have an illegitimate child? Please! You don't want your parents to know. You don't want anyone to know. Any more than I do."

"Don't count on that," he said. "I may change my mind, if you keep pushing."

"Me? Push?" She took a deep breath, then exhaled. "Oh, go away," she said. "Talking to you when you're in this kind of mood is a waste of time."

Frankie left, but the next day he took Colette to lunch, at what was (for that week at least) her favorite restaurant, an Italian place on Second Avenue in the east sixties. "I don't get it," he said, "why she won't take my help. Why she tries to squeeze me out."

"If you ask me, Martha's been very generous with you," said Colette. "Mmm, delicious," she added, savoring the taste of the *cozze napoletana,* a house specialty.

"Generous? Martha?" When he was the one doing all the offering of money, of help, of anything she wanted?

"She welcomes you into her home, lets you play with her child. She feeds you, for heaven's sake. You think many women would do that? In the circumstances?"

"*Our* child," corrected Frankie, ignoring the rest.

"Lucky for you she's decided to forgive you."

"For what? We're not talking rape here. I didn't demand sex at gunpoint. She could've said no."

"She felt sorry for you. And you took advantage of it."

"For chrissake!" But she was only repeating what he'd told her. "Let's change the subject, okay?"

Colette diverted her attention for a moment to the *risotto al limone* the waiter had just brought, then asked, "Do you think she's in love with you?"

It wasn't the most shocking suggestion Frankie had ever heard. Women always seemed to be falling in love with him, or at least that's what they claimed. But Martha? She'd never exhibited any of the usual signs: a desperate desire to please combined with a clamoring for attention and the need to manipulate. "No," he said, "I don't think so."

"I don't either," said Colette, which opinion sent an unexpected surge of disappointment through him. (It was, after all, always pleasant to be loved.) "And you don't love *her*." It wasn't a question.

"Of course not."

Colette sneered. "And you ask what she has to forgive you for?"

That was one thing he didn't have to feel guilty about. "Love's not the issue," he said. "Hannah is. And what Martha and I have to do is figure out what kind of relationship to have so that the baby doesn't suffer. That's what's important."

"She's a sweetheart." Colette adored Hannah and was terrific at playing granny, free with advice, generous with gifts and time, though she stopped short of offering to baby-sit. Changing diapers, she said, was one experience she planned to miss.

"A doll," agreed Frankie, surprised again by an unexpected surge of feeling, a rush of pure love for his daughter, a tenderness he had believed reserved only for Maud. He smiled. "She said my name the other day. Well, it sounded more like "Fan-key, but I got the general idea." Hannah was then thirteen months old, and Frankie pushed away the thought that what she ought to be calling him was "Daddy." Martha would never agree. And, if she did, what would happen if, when they were out together, they ran into someone he knew? What if Hannah called him Daddy then? How could he explain?

Not that he ever took her or Martha anywhere, not out for dinner, not to the park, not even for a walk around the block. That idea, once it entered Frankie's mind, refused to go away. It bothered him. It wasn't as if he was ashamed. In fact, he thought, allowing himself to get angry, the secrecy wasn't his idea. It was Martha's. She was the one who had put "father unknown" on the birth certificate, the one who had refused to name him to anyone, not to her parents, not to her friends, not to Colette even after she'd guessed, leaving her to pry confirmation out of Frankie. As far as he knew, Martha had only told him. That being the case, he saw no reason to spread the news around, though he wasn't *ashamed*. He wanted to make that point perfectly clear—to himself anyway. So, that August, while Maud was with Annabel at Castle Melton, Frankie invited Martha to spend a few days with him on the Cape with Dan and his kids. She refused. He pleaded. Dan knew. The kids wouldn't care. Then why deprive Hannah of a few days away from Manhattan's sweltering summer? A few days of sea and sand?

The appeal to parental guilt worked and Martha gave in. They drove up to the Cape together with Hannah asleep in the back of the car. And once there, Martha fitted effortlessly into the routine of the house. She helped the au pair clean up and cook meals; she ferried kids to visit friends; she swam and built sand castles, did jigsaws and played board games. Frankie had thought he would find it peculiar to have her there, in a place almost as familiar to him as his own home, but the truth was that most of the time he forgot she lay sleeping, Hannah in a crib beside her, in the small bedroom under the eaves. Martha might have been another of Dan's sisters, or one of his own cousins, so little did her presence disturb him. Only Hannah, with her dark hair and eyes, her olive skin and Ferraro smile, had the ability to ruffle his calm, to tug at his heart strings, to make him long for Maud, to make him wish that somehow the four of them could be transformed magically into a family.

"We're friends. That's all." Frankie had said to Dan after intercepting a speculative look. But he wasn't sure even that much was true. And when he returned Martha and the baby to West End Avenue, he felt an unaccountable sadness, a sense of loss, which he didn't understand, and tried to ignore.

Gradually, however, as he stopped dating so frenetically, Frankie found himself spending more and more time visiting Martha and Hannah at their new apartment. Though he'd been prepared, on principle, to dislike it, he didn't. Built in the late 1930s, the building had character. It felt solid and permanent, an indelible part of New York's historical landscape. It carried the conviction that, like the pyramids, it had occupied its place forever, which by the city's standards it had. The apartment itself, big and bright with large windows overlooking West End Avenue, had what Eva Colvington would have called "elegant proportions." Martha's possessions, the painstakingly acquired and repaired furniture, the fabric finds, the recovered cushions and chairs, the intricate arrangements of pictures and ornaments, all of which before had had a desperate quality, here seemed to form themselves into harmonious and comfortable patterns. They seemed at home. And that's how Frankie felt when he visited. On evenings when Maud was with Annabel and he didn't feel like being alone, he would call and accept Martha's invitation to visit, showing up in time to play with Hannah while Martha cooked. After the baby went to sleep, they would hang out, like roommates, like pals, the way he and Vic used to when they were kids, like Dan and he did that summer after Miranda died when going out to score had been the last thing on their minds. He would sit with Martha in the rescued armchairs to watch *M.A.S.H.* or *Barney Miller* or *Hill Street Blues*; sometimes they would play games—Scrabble, Monopoly, gin—those kinds of games a refreshing change, thought Frankie, from the emotional and sexual ones he usually engaged in with women. Sometimes they would sit and talk. Except for sex, no subject seemed to be off limits. They discussed the books they lent back and forth, the movies they saw with other people, the sporting events Frankie went to with other friends and Martha watched on TV. Sometimes Frankie even found himself confiding in her about business.

Eventually he realized how much he preferred Martha's and Hannah's company to his own, a thought which seemed at the same time both normal and peculiar. Of course he would prefer company to solitude, who wouldn't? But Martha's company? She was, after all, nothing to him. Except the mother of your child, some annoying inner voice would prompt, a voice that sounded very like his father's. When he caught himself indulging in that kind of gross sentimentality, Frankie laughed. When not irritated, he was amused by the romantic notions Sal Ferraro had managed to impart effortlessly, under cover of teaching his son the many ways "to be a man." It was hard not to laugh. Who could take such notions seriously? The landscape of Frankie's world was strewn with the wrecks of marriages, two of his own included. Families lay scattered like body parts after a bomb blast, a husband here, a wife there, children moving back and forth between them. The parts inevitably got stitched into new family units, which sometimes held, sometimes didn't. Those that didn't recombined yet again. And while it didn't make Frankie particularly happy to know that the family wasn't the holy, the sacrosanct, entity his parents believed, still he was grateful not to have had to live the rest of his life with Annabel.

But though difficult and unhappy, his relationship with Annabel, and with Miranda too, had had a certain clarity. They had been marriages, begun in passion, ended in despair, each with a beginning, a middle, an end, if not neat, at least definite. His relationship with Martha wasn't so clear-cut. Believing it to be one thing, it had turned out to be something entirely different, but exactly what he didn't know. It had no name, no shape. He and Martha were not spouses, not lovers; and Hannah's existence somehow made it impossible for him to consider her only a friend, as he did Colette, or Kalima. And while he'd known, or thought he'd known, how to behave with both of his wives, with all of his girlfriends, while he'd understood with them what role he had to act, with Martha he had no idea. He found that ambiguity disturbing, unsettling. He felt somehow in the wrong.

*K*elly, to start with, had not seemed like another complication, just a welcome distraction. With her, Frankie knew exactly who he was, and what he was doing. Her willingness to follow his lead, to trust in his judgment, made a welcome change from Annabel's constant sniping and Martha's irritating independence. Moreover, Kelly had a winning way of combining adoration with accommodation, slotting neatly into Frankie's life, adjusting to his schedule, rarely questioning his own assessment of how much of himself he could spare for her, a lesson learned from having a workaholic father. Her days were pretty full, too, what with work, exercise classes, hair and nail appointments, shopping. And though clearly self-centered, though a bad haircut or a spot on a favorite dress, in her mind, ranked equal on the scale of tragedy with a plane crash on the Potomac or war in the Middle East, Kelly was also extremely good-natured. And if Frankie's flights of temper, his preoccupation, his forgetfulness, sometimes reduced her to tears, those tears seemed to have less to do with genuinely hurt feelings than with a deep-seated belief that an occasional brief scene, ending in an abject apology and a small but expensive gift, was necessary to keep romance alive. That she had learned from her mother.

So the months passed with Frankie, rejuvenated by lust, soothed by ad-ulation, yet again not giving any serious thought to the consequences of his pleasure. And by the time he realized how deeply he was embroiled with Kelly, how inevitable marriage was beginning to seem, when he realized how necessary it had become to tell her about Hannah, he also realized that he'd left it too late. No matter how he broke the news now, he would still look like a sneak and a liar, if not to Kelly herself, then certainly to her family, who were, after all, the ones who mattered—and to his family, who perhaps mattered most of all.

Finally, the pressure built to such a point that Frankie felt he could no longer put off making a confession, and he stopped by Martha's, unannoun-ced, to discuss it with her. "What are you doing here?" she asked ungra-ciously as she let him into the apartment.

Frankie thought he saw a flash of pleasure in her eyes before her irritation masked it. He noted the black jersey dress skimming the curves of her body, the high heels, the strand of fake pearls, the careful makeup. "You look great," he said. He realized he'd never before seen her dressed in anything but work or casual clothes.

"Thanks," she murmured, stepping aside to let him in.

Through the open door into the kitchen, he could see Pina at the sink, washing dishes. "Going out?" he asked.

"Yes," said Martha, volunteering nothing else.

"Hannah asleep?" Martha nodded, and Frankie walked to bedroom and peered inside. Almost three, Hannah no longer slept in a crib, but in the four-poster single bed he'd bought her. She lay on her stomach, her face turned away from him toward the wall, only her dark curls visible above the quilt. Jemima Puddleduck, a gift from Colette, lay just beyond her out-stretched fist. Turning back, he saw Martha looking at him with obvious impatience. Which he ignored. "We have to talk," he said.

"Now?" There was dismay in her voice.

"It will only take a minute."

She sat on the plaid couch and Frankie noticed how its peach tones flat-tered her skin. She looked flushed and soft and . . . yes, sexy. "There's noth-ing wrong is there?" she asked, suddenly worried. "You're all right?"

"I'm fine. I just wanted to tell you that I'm getting married."

Some of the color left her face, which could be explained by the anger in her voice when she said, "That's what's so important you couldn't wait to tell me?"

"It's important to me," said Frankie.

"And that's all that matters?"

Since that wasn't the argument he wanted to have, Frankie decided to ignore the remark. "I'm sorry if this isn't a convenient time for you."

"Well, now you've told me, congratulations." She smiled. "I hope you'll be very happy. It's Kelly, I assume?" And when Frankie nodded, she said, "From all you've told me, she sounds like a very nice person." She stood.

Frankie remained seated. "Nothing's definite yet. I'm planning to ask her soon, but before I do, I think I should tell her about you. And Hannah."

"There's nothing to tell."

"Hannah's my daughter."

"Her birth certificate very clearly says 'father unknown.' "

"What's that got to do with anything? You know the truth. I know the truth. And I don't see how I can get married with that kind of secret on my conscience."

"It's not your secret. It's mine. And why your conscience has to be so sensitive about this one issue beats me. You must have other things you could confess instead, other sins to offer up to make you feel better."

"I want to tell Kelly the truth," said Frankie stubbornly.

"Are you sure you know what that is? Maybe I lied. Did you ever think of that?"

"Of course I thought of that," said Frankie. "Do you think I'm a complete idiot? But all you have to do is look at the kid. Anyway, you wouldn't lie."

"I would. I'd tell everyone you were crazy." There was a rising note of fury in her voice, fury and fear. "I'd say you were making the whole thing up."

"And I'd have you in court on a paternity suit!"

The intercom sounded. "This really isn't a good time," said Martha, more calmly.

"I don't want to fight with you," said Frankie. She walked to the door, spoke into the intercom, replied to the muffled voice at the other end, buzzed the visitor into the building. "But I want Hannah to be part of my family," he continued as she turned back to him. "I want her and Maud to grow up as sisters."

"No," said Martha. "No, absolutely not."

"You're being completely unreasonable."

"We've been over this a million times! Hannah's mine. You can't have her, Frankie. You can have anything else you want, maybe, but you can't have her." Again a buzzer sounded. Plastering a smile on her face, she opened the door. "Hi, Mark," she said.

He was short, just an inch or two taller than Martha, with broad shoulders and a youthful, slender body. He had shoulder-length blond hair, a beard, and horn-rimmed glasses. He looked like a guitar player in a rock band. Sensing the tension in the air, he hesitated on the threshold. "Have I got the wrong night?"

"No," said Martha, smiling pleasantly. She introduced the two men, and then said, "Frankie was just going." She turned to him, still smiling, and said, "Aren't you?"

Frankie felt a surge of the old familiar rage, the desire to do damage. Who the fuck did she think she was, brushing him off like this? But Martha held the door open for him, apparently oblivious to his anger.

"Nice to have met you," said Mark politely.

"Yeah," said Frankie, gaining control. "Great. Be seeing you," he said to Martha, hoping she noticed it was a threat.

"Next time, call first," she said, and closed the door.

Chapter 28

The February night was bitter, with a brisk wind pushing heavy dark clouds across a plum-colored sky. There was snow in the air. Leaving the warmth of the apartment building, Frankie felt the cold like a knife cut. He buttoned his cashmere coat up to the collar, wrapped his scarf tightly around his neck, pulled his hat firmly around his ears, and wished he had remembered to put a sweater on under his jacket. There were few pedestrians in sight, but the steady stream of empty taxis along West End Avenue was visible proof that the city was still in the grips of a recession. Doing his bit for the economy, Frankie raised a hand to signal one to stop. You had to be crazy to walk on a night like this—crazy or poor.

On Broadway there were more people, though not enough to qualify as a crowd, most scurrying quickly toward the warmth of the subway entrance or a nearby restaurant, but Amsterdam and Columbus seemed dark and empty. So did his apartment, with that exaggerated emptiness even a happily reclusive person feels when canceled plans force him unexpectedly to spend the evening at home, alone.

Frankie had intended to arrive in time to see Hannah before she went to bed, then to stay and have dinner with Martha, during which he planned to have a calm and reasonable discussion with her. But he'd been delayed at work. A conference call with club managers, originally scheduled for earlier in the day, had finally been put through at seven-fifteen. Hurrying to leave his office, he'd forgotten to call ahead as he usually did, to inquire (politely) if it was a convenient time for him to visit. But Martha was always home at night, with Hannah, at least he always assumed she was, so the oversight (which had occurred to him only in the taxi on the way to her place) hadn't seemed important. So much for assumptions! Who was that guy anyway? he wondered.

Leaving his coat and hat on a chair in the hallway, Frankie went into the library, poured himself a scotch, sat in his armchair, put his feet up on the hassock, and stared blankly at the array of photographs on the shelves where his first editions used to be. The cold had dampened his anger. Now what he felt was relief. He had been reprieved. Willing to do what was right, thanks to Martha's stubbornness (beyond his understanding or control), he couldn't follow his best instincts. Continuing the deceit was not his fault, not his responsibility. Without Martha's agreement, he couldn't confess. After all, the secret was not his, it was theirs. He was off the hook.

The scotch drove the damp from his bones. He poured himself another, then sat back and tried to see past the inertia and (to be honest) the fear of complications that had kept him quiet for so long, tried to consider the matter of his illegitimate child rationally, tried to weigh the ethics of the situation. If on the one hand it was wrong to confess without Martha's okay, wasn't it equally wrong to marry Kelly without telling her first about Hannah? More pragmatically, wasn't the truth a ticking time bomb set to blast any marriage sky high?

But if Martha *wouldn't* tell, if he *didn't* tell, it was unlikely that Kelly would ever find out. Unlikely, but possible. Some one of the three or four people who knew might spill the beans, even if inadvertently.

If he told Kelly now, the odds were she would be surprised, but not especially upset. He was certain she would respond to Hannah just as she had to Maud, as an incidental part of his past life making no real difference to her own. She was so young, so easygoing, so accepting. Sometimes he thought there was no offense, no crime, he could commit that she wouldn't excuse and forgive him. Her parents were a different story; but they too could be handled. And his? Dolly would weep and Sal would rage but finally they would, as always, resign themselves to the inevitable, to the fact that boys after all would be boys.

Oh, yes, the irony was that if he owned up now to the truth, everyone would be shocked; everyone would be disapproving, but ultimately forgiving. In a year or two or ten, however, it would be a different story. That Hannah's birth had preceded his marriage to Kelly would somehow get lost in the avalanche of emotion. He'd be painted a liar, a seducer, a betrayer of women—not only of his wife, but of Martha too. He'd be seen as no better than a bigamist. It would hardly be fair, but who would care about that? Who would defend him? And convicted of behaving like a scoundrel (a term taken from his former brother-in-law Roland's vocabulary) he would end up an object of contempt.

Frankie shuddered. Get a grip, stop exaggerating, he told himself. But he could see the future as well as any seer: another marriage ended in a barrage of accusation and misery. Somehow he had to prevent that happening. He couldn't let himself slide back into the body-wearing, soul-numbing exploits of his past. He was too old for one thing, forty-three. The body didn't bounce back as quickly anymore from the ravages of excess. Neither did the mind, he suspected. He poured himself his third scotch of the evening.

Quick and decisive action, that's what Frankie admired. He longed for the moral certainty of a film hero; he craved the satisfaction that must come with cornering and wasting the villain. But only when he lost his temper was he capable of acting without thought. Even in business, he temporized. Seize any opportunity offered but do nothing illegal, or worse, immoral; keep your word; pay your help a decent wage; remember employees aren't serfs. When he had to close a club (as he had a few months before when the escalating recession had made keeping it open a fool's game), it cost him sleepless nights. Finally, he salved his conscience by giving plenty of notice, by being generous with severance pay, by transferring some employees to other clubs, by assisting others to look for new jobs. It wouldn't, after all, have helped anyone if misguided benevolence had caused his entire company to go bust.

In his personal life, Frankie found even that level of conviction difficult to reach. It always seemed to be higher up the mountain, shrouded in fog, and he too weary and out of breath from climbing to get there.

"Fuck this," mumbled Frankie, getting to his feet. There were times when trying to think a problem through was no help. He carried his glass into the kitchen, scrambled himself an egg, made some toast and coffee, forced himself to eat, then left the mess he had made for the housekeeper to deal with when she arrived in the morning. Walking through the apartment, turning out lights he had earlier put on, he forgot briefly about the women in his life and reveled instead in pride of ownership. Since Annabel had left, taking with her the chintz curtains, the Chippendale furniture, the gilded paintings, the Crown Derby knickknacks, Frankie again felt comfortable in his home. There were now overstuffed chairs covered in heavy gray cotton, furniture in lacquered woods, chrome lamps, kilim carpets. There were few pictures: the Rothko in the sitting room, a Morris Louis in the hall, some Dine lithographs, and a few silk screens he'd picked up here and there over the years. All was exactly the way he wanted. All was his.

For now at least. The emptiness of his bedroom reminded him immediately of Kelly, who was in Philadelphia for an out-of-town preview of a new musical. What would happen when she got her hands on the place? The thought was not a comfortable one, and as he hung his Armani jacket in the closet, he pushed it out of his mind. Going into the bathroom, he saw his face in the mirror and frowned. Worry seemed to add ten years. And scotch didn't help. Praying he would sleep, he crawled into bed, wishing after all that Kelly were there.

From the thought of Kelly in his bed, his mind leaped suddenly to Martha in hers. Was she alone? Who was that guy? He tried to remember what making love to Martha had been like, and couldn't. He'd been very drunk that night. All he could recall was a feeling of comfort, of peace, but then that was the way he always felt when he was with her. No, not always, *usually* felt, he corrected himself, remembering how often he was furious with her for being so obstinate. An image of Martha making love to . . . what was his name? Mark? began to play in his mind. Hannah asleep in the next room. Frankie didn't like the picture. He turned over, adjusted his pillow. Enough, he thought. Turning on the radio, he settled back down, and, listening to Barry Grey's soothing voice, drifted off to sleep.

*T*he next morning, while Frankie waited in his shiny, stainless-steel kitchen for the Braun coffeemaker to produce the requisite four cups and the microwave to cook his oatmeal (like everybody else, he was watching his cholesterol count), the phone rang. It was Annabel. He stifled a groan. Since any conversation inevitably ended in a fight, when he could, he avoided talking to her, leaving it to Mrs. Ashby to arrange Maud's schedule. But Annabel wasn't content with that. To her, nothing in the world was worse than being ignored. Doing battle was so much more exciting than moldering away in obscurity, like some insignificant island nation no one had discovered any practical use for.

"Caught me," said Frankie.

"I thought this might be a good time," said Annabel.

"Not that good. I'm late for a meeting."

"Certainly you are," she said, not believing him for a minute. "You're such a busy little mogul, flitting from here to there, doing oh such important things."

"You want something, I suppose? You didn't just call to be pleasant?"

"I have to leave for London. Something came up rather unexpectedly."

"A last-minute invitation to a party?" Frankie always promised himself he wouldn't provoke her, but then, when he had her within range, he could never resist taking a jab at that determined chin, that aristocratic nose. Nothing gave him more pleasure than blackening her eyes, figuratively speaking of course. It had been a long time since he'd felt compelled to do physical violence to his former wife.

"No, actually," said Annabel, her tone turning nasty in reaction to his. "Business. Flora's onto this château in France that's going to be sold up," she explained, though she didn't have to. "It's owned by friends of the Burdens, so we have first dibs. I'm going with her to have a look."

Frankie knew Annabel so well, he got the picture immediately. The château and its contents were for sale, that much was true. But Flora could easily have gone alone, if it was just a question of doing a valuation. There had to be a party involved, one of those weekend house parties, with lots of money and lots of titles invited, a happy hunting ground for Annabel, who needed a constant supply of social contacts, likely clients, potential lovers, maybe even a prospective husband or two. "So while the other guests are enjoying themselves, you and Flora will be skulking around pricing the furniture," he said.

"Exactly," replied Annabel.

He was right, thought Frankie, without much satisfaction. "And to think the idea of people doing the same at Castle Melton used to make you cringe."

"It's not the same thing at all," said Annabel irritably, though of course it was. "In any case, I wanted to let you know that I'm sending Maud back to you this afternoon."

"Fine," said Frankie. "Just pack her up and ship her back."

"Frances, for heaven's sake, Ashers does all the real looking after. It won't be any bother for you. But if you don't want her, she can just stay here. She'll be perfectly fine. I wouldn't even have bothered to call, except you make such a fuss when I go away without letting you know."

"Of course I want her," said Frankie. "You know I don't mind having Maud here. I prefer it, in fact. What I mind is the way you treat her."

"Oh, don't start that again!"

"She's your daughter, Annabel—"

"And I adore her—"

"Not some kind of prop you rent and return when it suits you."

"A pity you didn't feel that way when we were married, instead of whoring around, never coming home, leaving me alone night after night with the baby—" She was angry now, with a faint hint of tears in her voice.

"Give me a break!"

"You were the one who wanted the divorce. You can't blame me now for trying to make some kind of life for myself!"

"I don't blame you—"

"You always were such a selfish bastard!"

"I'd love it if you married again. It would save me a fortune in alimony!"

"I'd have remarried ages ago except that I want you to pay and pay, and go on paying—until there's not a thing left for your little teeny bopper to enjoy."

She meant Kelly. Frankie smiled. "Jealous?" he said.

"Fuck you!"

"Why Lady Annabel! I'm shocked!"

"It's impossible to have a civilized conversation with you!"

"Francis the barbarian, that's me."

"Expect Maud directly after school. I'll be in touch when I return."

Frankie heard the slam of the receiver at the other end and set his handset back into its cradle. He felt much better, he noticed. Though he dreaded the thought of any conversation with Annabel, he always did feel better afterward. Maybe it was childish to keep sniping at one another. Maybe they ought to stop. But that wasn't likely. Frankie wasn't sure what her excuse was, but for himself he knew it was a continuing and active . . . not hatred exactly, not quite that strong, but something near it, a combination of resentment, hurt feelings, a need for vengeance. He might have been able to get past it if he could get her completely out of his life, but Maud made that impossible. So, forced to deal regularly with Annabel's unpleasant reality, Frankie found he could stand it, he could almost enjoy it, if he could make her suffer, even a little. And there was no real harm in it. Though they irritated the hell out of each other with no effort at all, they no longer did any real damage. Except perhaps to Maud, and that Frankie didn't like to think about.

The thought of Maud reminded him that he'd better start changing his plans for the next few days. He called Kelly in Philadelphia and told her he would not be joining her there for dinner that night, a change she didn't seem to mind since she was having fun playing with the cast and crew. Then he called Martha.

"Can we talk later?" she said, sounding pleasant, though harried. "I have an early meeting. And Hannah and I both slept late this morning. I'm not even showered yet."

"You had a nice time?"

"When? Oh, last night? Yes. Very nice," she said, without contributing any details. "Look, I'm sorry I got so angry. . . ."

"I seem to have that effect on people."

She laughed. "Well, you're not always easy to deal with."

"I know you think you're the height of reasonableness. But the truth is you're stubborn as hell."

He heard her sigh. "I really can't talk now, Frankie," she said. "What about later? Can you stop by?"

He felt a surge of regret. He wanted to see Maud, have dinner with Kelly, be with Martha and Hannah. Arab sheiks had the right idea, he thought. Just get everyone under one roof, all the wives, the girlfriends, the children. Ignore the women you'd grown tired of, the ones you'd grown to hate, fuck the others anytime you like, one big reasonably happy family, or at least no more unhappy than any other, and all the logistical problems solved. "Maud's coming back this afternoon."

"I thought she was with Annabel until the end of the month."

"It seems she's heard about a party this weekend. And she wants to go. The party's in France."

"Oh." Though she never said a word against her, Frankie knew how much Martha disliked Annabel, which wasn't surprising given the way his former wife had delighted in tormenting her.

"I'll stop by when I can."

"I know," she said, as if whether he did or not was a matter of small importance, which he knew it wasn't. He knew she wanted Hannah to have a daddy, even if it was one she called "Frankie." "Call first, okay?" added Martha lightly. "Just in case."

In case of what, exactly? he wondered, sampling his oatmeal. Cold. "Shit!" he muttered, tossing it into the bin. He left the bowl and cup in the sink with the frying pan and dishes from the night before. When he got to work, he would have a Danish, a muffin, anything. To hell with his cholesterol! He had more important things to worry about.

On Wednesday night, at about nine, Frankie picked Kelly up at her apartment, and they walked over to Madison Avenue, to Marechal, a little French place on the corner of Ninety-first Street. (Was it a coincidence or a pattern, Frankie sometimes wondered, that he'd chosen yet another woman who couldn't cook?) There were patches of snow left from the preceding night's storm, but the cold spell had broken, and it was clear and mild, a signal to optimistic New Yorkers that, though it might only be February, spring was on the way. There were people in the streets walking, strolling really, coats unbuttoned, scarves loose, heads bare. A feeling of good humor seemed to float on the breeze that carried the usual scraps of paper, empty polystyrene cups, discarded plastic bags. A couple in jeans and leather jackets, with long dirty hair, studied the display in the window of a jewelry store where Frankie had once bought Annabel a very expensive diamond bracelet. Casing the joint? he wondered. A pretty girl wearing an oversized Yankees' jacket and a cap smiled and nodded as she walked past with her two Airedales. "Someone you know?" asked Frankie. He walked with his arm draped around Kelly's shoulder, his face turned toward her so that strands of permed red hair, lifted on the wind, sometimes tickled his nose. He caught the scent of pineapple, her shampoo.

"No, I thought you did." She turned around to look after the girl. "I miss my dogs," she said sadly. The Helms had two at their home in Chicago, chocolate Labradors. "I should really get one. Not another Lab. A sheepdog maybe. They're so cute."

"In a New York apartment? Anyway, who'd look after it when you go away?"

Kelly looked at him as if he'd lost his mind. "The housekeeper," she said. She was in a state of high excitement. She'd bought a pair of shoes at Bergdorf's that were just perfect to wear with the cocktail dress she'd bought at Bendel's the week before. "And the sexiest bikini," she said. "It almost doesn't exist. Wait until you see it."

They were scheduled to spend the weekend with her parents at their house in Palm Beach. (Golf, a polo match, a cocktail party, a trip up the inland waterway on someone's yacht for lunch at a lakeside restaurant.) And this seemed the perfect opening for Frankie to tell her that the trip was off, until Annabel returned at least. He chose not to take it, asking instead about work, listening with interest to Kelly's tales of the out-of-town woes of the play Abel Ellis was currently trying to bring to New York. These involved a dipsomaniacal leading lady, an egomaniacal director, and a mechanical set that kept breaking down in the middle of the show. "What a business," said Kelly. "I'm learning so much from Abel. Working with him has been a wonderful opportunity." She said that as if Abel Ellis might actually have turned down Hugo Helm's request to hire his daughter.

"Do you think you'd like to produce some day?"

"God, no. It's hell!"

"How about taking over your father's company?"

She shook her head. "Daddy doesn't think I have the temperament for it. He knows I'm not all that interested in business. Anyway . . ." She hesitated. Glancing up at him, she smiled, then looked away, and, fastening her eyes on some spot in the distance, she said, "I suppose I'd like to do something, but I can't decide what. Maybe because so many things seem unsettled. . . ."

"That's life," he said. "Unsettled."

*I*t took the usual three tries before Kelly was satisfied with their table (the first rocked, the second was in a draft). As soon as he was sure she was comfortable, Frankie broke the news. Startled, she looked up from the salmon quenelles to meet his eyes, her own clouded with tears. "I know you're disappointed, but I don't see how I can leave Maud," he said. Though he would have enjoyed a weekend in Palm Beach, he only mildly regretted not going. There would, after all, be other times.

Kelly clearly felt otherwise. "I was really looking forward to it," she said.

"Go," said Frankie, feeling the first faint twinges of guilt. "You don't need me to have a great time."

"It won't be the same." She blinked her pale green eyes to keep the tears from falling. "I don't know what Mother and Daddy will say."

He reached across the linen-covered table, past the freesias in the ceramic vase, and took Kelly's hand. "I'm sorry," he said. He didn't like disappointing her. "I'll call your father in the morning and explain." Kelly sighed. "As soon as Annabel gets back, we'll go. I promise."

Kelly took her hand from his, reached into her purse, removed a handkerchief and dabbed at her nose. "She's so selfish. Doesn't she ever think of anyone but herself?"

"Rarely," said Frankie.

"Didn't it occur to her that you might have plans?"

"She thought if I did, I could just leave Maud alone with Mrs. Ashby."

Kelly looked at him hopefully. "Would that be so terrible?" She lowered her eyes to the tablecloth, and said, "My parents left me alone with my nanny all the time."

"I know I'm not reasonable on this subject. I know it wouldn't be the end of the world if I left Maud with Mrs. Ashby for the weekend. And if it were an emergency, maybe I would. But it's not. And I can't do it. Having Annabel and me for parents is no picnic. Maud's had a rough enough time in her life, even before the divorce, without being made to feel now that she's not wanted, that she's in the way."

She looked up again. "And the way I feel? Doesn't that matter?"

"Yes," said Frankie curtly. "But you're an adult." Well, almost, he added to himself. "You're not a bewildered little kid trying to make sense of the world."

"Maud knows you love her."

"Maud spends her life being batted back and forth from one parent to the other, like some fucking tennis ball."

"She doesn't feel that way. She doesn't! I'd know if she was unhappy."

How could she, when even he wasn't sure? "I'm sorry, Kelly," he said, "but there's no way I can leave her this weekend, not with the way Annabel just dumped her and took off. It would be like, well, a double rejection. I can't do it."

"All right," said Kelly, sounding exasperated. "Then let's just take her with us."

Frankie thought that over a minute, then said, "We could."

"And Mrs. Ashby, if you like" added Kelly, "though God knows there's enough staff there to look after her when we're busy."

"And Mrs. Ashby."

Smiling, Kelly reached for his hand, lifted it to her face, and rubbed her cheek against it. "You see how easy it is to make everybody happy." It was something her father always said.

And delighted that she would get to dance at Au Bar in her daring ink blue cocktail dress, cruise up Lake Worth in her sailor-boy shorts suit and matching cap, in gratitude, that night when they returned to her frilly adolescent bedroom in the Fifth Avenue apartment, Kelly spread herself like a banquet, offering herself like a sacrifice to a god, willing to do anything, anything at all, to please him. Not that that took such a great effort. Everything about her pleased him, her mouth, her tongue, her long carefully manicured nails, the fall of her hair as gentle as rain, her skin as soft as dew, her sex as wet and warm as a summer night. This is the answer, he thought, making love to her, though he couldn't remember the question. And later, when he tried to extricate himself from the damp tangle of limbs and sheets in order to go home to his daughter, she coaxed him into her again. "Oh, I love you, Frankie," she said.

"I love you," he repeated, an echo in the dark.

"I want your baby. I want your baby so much." Oh, Christ, he thought. And when he was getting dressed he asked her if she was still taking the pill.

"Sure," she said, as if surprised by the question.

"Good."

She frowned. "You do want children?"

"I have children." Tell her now, he thought. Go on, tell her. Get it over with. But he didn't. Instead, he said, "A child, I mean."

"I don't."

Frankie could hear the anxiety in her voice. "You're twenty-two years old," he said carefully. He zipped his pants, buckled his belt. "There's plenty of time."

"I don't mean right away. There's lots I want to do first. But someday."

"Someday," agreed Frankie, with a reassuring smile. He put on his jacket, leaned over and kissed her. "Sure, someday."

She put her arms around his neck and held him still for a moment. "You're such a good father." She kissed him again. "It's one of the things I really love about you. It's why I don't mind your leaving me like this, in the middle of the night. I know you have to be there for Maud."

For Maud, for Hannah, for the children Kelly wanted someday to have. Frankie wasn't sure just how he would manage that logistical feat.

. . .

*W*as he a good father? Looking at Maud's solemn little face the next morning it was hard to believe. He rarely lost his temper with her, never seriously, and always made it right as soon afterward as he could. But no matter how much effort he put into relieving the pain and minimizing the anxiety that were an inevitable part of her life, only rarely did she seem to him an ordinary, happy, carefree little girl.

"Kelly and I were thinking about going to Palm Beach this weekend. Do you think you'd like that?" They were standing in the lobby of the building the next morning, waiting for the doorman to hail a taxi to take them to Maud's school. Outside, it was drizzling slightly and she had on boots and a yellow slicker over her skirt and sweater. From under her blue cap, a stream of long dark hair cascaded down her back. "The weather should be nice, so you can swim. And maybe have a tennis lesson, if you want to."

Maud looked as if she were carefully weighing the question. "I like Kelly," she said finally. "Are you going to marry her?"

Frankie looked down at her. "Who said that?"

"Mommy said you were probably going to. She doesn't like Kelly."

"No," agreed Frankie, "but we do, so I think that's good enough, don't you?"

Maud nodded, then said, "Are you?"

"I'm thinking about it," said Frankie.

Maud nodded again. "And you'll have a baby."

Times like this made Frankie wonder about ESP, about thought waves propelled through the air from an unconscious transmitter to an unconscious receiver. "Maybe."

"Married people always have babies."

"Not always," he said. "But how would you feel about it if we did?"

Maud thought that over for a minute. "I'd like it," she said. "I think. It would be fun to have a baby brother—"

"Or a sister," said Frankie.

Maud nodded. "Except . . ."

Frankie waited. "Except what?" he asked finally.

"Would you love the baby more than me?"

"Oh, no," said Frankie. "Never."

"Mommy said—"

"Never mind what your mother said." The impulse to tell her about Hannah, just then, was almost overwhelming. He wanted to take Maud to West End Avenue, to introduce her to her little sister. He wanted to see them together. He got hold of himself. What would Martha say? What would Maud think? How could he explain? "Look at Grandma and Grandpa, don't you think they love Aunt Angela and me just the same?"

Maud considered that, then said, "I think they love you best."

Resisting the urge to smile, Frankie thought about Hannah, about the curve of her cheek, the length of her lashes, the sound of her laugh. "This is something I really know about, honey. Love isn't like a pie where the pieces get smaller and smaller the more people who have to eat it. There's always enough to go around. More than enough. Anyway, I could never love anybody better than you."

Maud smiled. "There's a taxi," she said, gesturing to one sliding to a stop at the curb where the doorman was standing, ready to open its door.

"What about Palm Beach?" he said, ushering her through the doors into the damp morning. "We'll take a boat trip on the lake. Last time I saw pelicans nesting there. Sitting in the trees. They looked like something out of a horror movie."

Maud laughed. "Cool," she said.

The worried look was gone from her face and Frankie sighed with relief. He helped her into the taxi, tipped the doorman, and when he'd given the driver the school's location, he said, "We'll have a good time. A great time." Still, he couldn't quite rid himself of the idea that he'd just missed the chance of a lifetime.

Chapter 29

Staying with Mr. and Mrs. Helm was almost as good as staying at a hotel, Maud told her father, showing him the neatly wrapped miniature soaps, the sewing kits, the packets of shampoo, the powders, the lotions, the shower caps in baskets on the shelves above the sink in the bathroom. He had exactly the same in his room, he assured her when she asked, and promised she could see later.

Maud was a good traveler, undemanding, patient, curious. She was no trouble at all to have around. Neither was Mrs. Ashby these days. Over the years, her allegiance had shifted subtly from Annabel to Maud; and, as long as Frankie did nothing to upset the child, she was prepared to overlook his many other failings, which included his having been born neither English nor a member of the upper classes. She treated him now with more respect than she had ever done during his marriage. As a result, they'd moved from a state of guerrilla war to one of respectful cooperation. They needed each other; Maud needed them both. For her sake, they were determined to get along.

"Did you leave word where we could reached, Mrs. Ashby?" Frankie asked when Maud had finished giving him the tour of their rooms. It was Friday evening, a few hours after their arrival in Palm Beach. "I meant to do it myself, but . . ." He shrugged.

"Oh, yes," she replied. "At Castle Melton."

"Thanks," said Frankie. They both knew that Maud's whereabouts would be of no interest to Annabel while the house party in France was in progress, but, since Frankie insisted on knowing where his daughter was every moment of the day and night, he felt he ought to stick to his own rules and keep Annabel informed. He smiled at her. "I know I can always count on you."

"I should hope so," she said, responding to the flattery with a smile of her own.

Just a hint of a kind word and the old dragon stops breathing fire, thought Frankie. If only he'd realized that years ago. If only he'd once considered her a person and not just Annabel's flunky. If only he hadn't allowed her snobbery to intimidate him. If only he could learn not to respond to intimidation with rage. If only . . . well, his life would have been a lot easier. "Are you comfortable?" he asked. "Do you have everything you need?"

Everything was perfectly satisfactory, she assured him. She and Maud had adjoining rooms at the top of the house in what had been servants' quarters when the staff ran to double digits. The rooms were light and airy, freshly painted and simply furnished, each with a television. They were, however, far from luxurious, and the bathroom was down the hall. "Not what we're used to, of course," she added, "but it will do." Compared to life at Castle Melton (a drafty old pile with inadequate plumbing, but much idealized in her memory), life everywhere else could only fall short.

"May I go swimming?" asked Maud, who was sitting on her bed fiddling with a remote control, changing channels on the television set.

"In the morning," said Frankie. "Dinner is in half an hour," he added, turning to go. "Don't be late."

The Helms' house was on the ocean side of the boulevard. Built in the late twenties, it was a pastiche southern colonial with a white stucco facade, a green hipped roof, and green shutters. Hugo and Rose had owned it for about ten years. It had (including those for staff) fifteen bedrooms, countless bathrooms, a huge sitting room, a dining room that could seat twenty with room to spare, and a library with paneling ripped from the walls of some French château. Since it was still too early for cocktails, Frankie headed there. The room had neither comfortable chairs nor reading lamps, but was well stocked with books, most dating from when the house was built, many of them first editions. (Now when he found one, instead of making an offer to Hugo as he once might have done, Frankie put it back in its place on the shelf). One of the most valuable was a copy of *The Great Gatsby,* and, as he stood leafing through it, reading sections at random, he thought about the way his initial admiration for the silk-clad gangster hero had turned, somewhere along the line, to repulsion; he realized that Nick Carroway, the book's narrator, had become muddled in his mind with Dan, who had lent him the book when they were stationed together at Ft. Ord, so many years, so many mistakes ago.

The door opened and he heard Kelly say, "I knew you'd be here." Slipping her arm around his waist, she asked, "Found anything good?" He told her the title, and she frowned. "Never read it." She craned her neck a little for a better view. "Who's it by?"

Shocked into silence, Frankie didn't reply immediately. "Fitzgerald," he said finally, "F. Scott." Then a horrible thought struck him. "You've heard of him?"

"Sure." Annoyed, Kelly removed her arm from his waist and moved away. "I'm not a complete ignoramus, you know."

"That's not what I meant," he said apologetically, denying even to himself that the thought had crossed his mind. "I thought maybe it was one of those generational things: somebody popular in mine, completely ignored in yours. Like, uh . . ." He searched for a name. "Erskine Caldwell," he said.

Kelly brightened. "No, him I don't know," she said. The sounds of people gathering in the garden filtered through to them. "Time for cocktails," she added.

Frankie slid the book back into its place on the shelf. "I better wash my hands again." He kissed her cheek. "You're so young. I keep forgetting that." He laughed. "At least I keep trying to forget."

"Not that young," said Kelly, rubbing against him.

She was wearing a striped silk dress with a wide pink belt pulled tight around her waist. Frankie ran his hand over her bottom, then dropped his head to kiss her neck. "Not *too* young, anyway," he said. He pushed her away. "Tell your mother I'll be right there."

$\mathcal{B}$y the time he joined the rest, Mrs. Ashby had brought Maud down and discreetly removed herself to wherever it was the help had dinner. Maud stood next to Hugo, who greeted Frankie heartily as if they'd not seen each other just an hour before. Rose, wearing a flowered silk chiffon dress, introduced him to the other guests as "Kelly's friend" and Maud as "his adorable little girl." A petite woman in her early sixties, Rose was trim and girlish, with prominent cheekbones, short hair dyed red, a couple of shades lighter than Kelly's, and skin (still without a trace of her daughter's freckles) that once must have been fine as porcelain, but now had begun to pleat across her cheeks and throat. Her husband, who was five years older, looked a good ten years younger. He was a big, broad, handsome man, blustery, with a barking laugh. No one who saw the way he fawned over his wife and daughter would believe that he had a girlfriend stashed in an apartment in Chicago. Frankie had met her. About Kelly's age, she worked as a secretary in the ad agency that handled the Helm account. The three of them, Frankie, Hugo, and the girl, whose name was Carline, had had dinner together one night in January, in New York, when Kelly and her mother were at a spa in Miami. That dinner had demonstrated to Frankie how deep in trouble he was. It was like a scene out of a movie: Joe Kennedy on the town with Jack. And though it wasn't as clear-cut as asking his intentions, Frankie got the message. Hugo Helm trusted him like a son. Now all he had to do was marry Kelly and legitimize the title.

The night was balmy, with a gentle wind coming off the ocean, and the guests stood around the floodlit mosaic fountain, nursing their drinks (a Shirley Temple for Maud), making desultory conversation, the men in linen jackets with narrow lapels and tan trousers, the women brightly colored in silk dresses, their hair sleek and straight, their lips carefully defined in garnet or ruby. When one of the servants announced dinner, Rose led them into the garden room, where most informal meals were served rather than in the larger, more impressive, dining room. It had one wall of long windows overlooking the ocean, and the remaining three hung with paintings from the Helms' collection, several of which (including a Manheim) had been bought from the DeWitt Payson Gallery. An arrangement of lilies in a silver epergne dominated the table, which was laid with Limoges china and Baccarat crystal, with candles in silver holders along its length. Orange trees in tubs scented the air.

Rose arranged her guests according to a plan settled earlier in her mind, seating Frankie between her daughter and his, commenting as she did so on what an attractive little group they made. Hugo too beamed at them fondly, and, as always, their obvious affection seduced Frankie. It was so different from anything the Colvingtons or Lindseys had offered.

They were eleven in all, the Helm family, Frankie and Maud, Hugo's banker and her lawyer husband from Chicago, a theatrical manager and his wife from London, and a couple who ran a literary agency in Stockholm.

All had been friends of the Helms' for years, so the conversation was easy, the laughter frequent. Everyone fussed over Maud. They talked to her in the same loud, bright interrogative snips of conversation she heard from Anna-bel's friends. Sometimes it seemed to Frankie that only his family had the knack of being natural with children, ignoring them unless urging them to eat or scolding them for getting into trouble. Even he didn't have it. He paid too much attention to Maud. He analyzed her every word and look. He probed to find out what was on her mind. He suspected he was obsessed with her, and was becoming the same about Hannah. The thought of whom led him to wonder what Martha was doing for the weekend. Why hadn't he asked what her plans were? Then he remembered he hadn't left a phone number where she could reach him in case of an emergency.

"Frankie?"

Someone was talking to him. Who? He looked quickly around the table, caught Rose Helm's inquisitive look and smiled. "Sorry. Part of my mind's still in New York."

Hugo's laugh boomed. "Takes at least three days to unwind," he said.

"Don't say that," said the banker from Chicago, with a groan. "I have a meeting at eight-thirty Monday morning."

"Hugo asked what your plans were for tomorrow," said Rose.

"Kelly and I are going to take Maud to the beach in the morning. That's about as far as we got in terms of planning."

"I thought we were playing golf," said Hugo.

Frankie looked at Maud's fearful face, then turned to Hugo, and shook his head. "Sorry. How about Sunday?"

"Sunday's good."

"Really, Hugo," said Rose. "Must you play both days?"

"Yes," he said, in a pleasant voice that nevertheless discouraged argument. "And tomorrow afternoon?" His glance swept the table. "What about a boat trip?"

"Can we see the pelicans?" asked Maud.

"Absolutely," said Hugo. "I ordered them to be there, specially for you. That suit everybody?" Maud smiled and nodded. "That's settled, then."

"Ferraro," said the English theatrical manager. "Your name sounds very familiar."

"Frankie owns a chain of health clubs," said Hugo. "Macklin's. Very popular on the east coast."

The theatrical manager shook his head and said, "You Americans. So health conscious." Like Hugo, he was a big man, portly, with smooth pink skin and thinning blond hair. "It's as if you expect to live forever."

"Don't pay any attention to him," said his wife, a pretty woman, slender, with straight brown hair, cinnamon-colored eyes, and a mouth that seemed always on the verge of a smile. "The only exercise he approves of is lifting a glass."

"Very good for you, drink. Thins the blood. Prevents heart attacks."

"Frankie owns the DeWitt Payson gallery, too," said Rose, wanting everyone to have the full list of her future son-in-law's credits.

"Where I've dropped quite a bundle, let me tell you," said Hugo

The banker's husband looked up from his plate in surprise. "I thought Eva Colvington owned it." He had a thick head of curly white hair and a feisty manner. He was the kind of guy who liked to think of himself as knowing everyone and everything. "Wasn't she married to Payson at one time?"

"Eva runs the gallery for me," said Frankie, hoping to short-circuit the conversation.

"She must be an enormous asset," said the banker. Curious, she looked at Frankie, willing him to explain the connection. She was in her early forties, a good twenty years younger than her husband. She had a mane of blond hair that spilled down her back, which was bare from the halter neckline of her tartan silk dress to her waist. Her cheekbones were pronounced, her nose perfectly sculpted, her body lean and muscular. She had the look of someone who spent a great deal of time trying to be beautiful.

She was beautiful, Frankie supposed, objectively speaking. But she was not attractive, not sexy. She had an artificial, antiseptic quality that killed desire, in him at least. Nevertheless, the smile he turned on her was as warm, as full of suggestion as a mixed dinner party with husbands present would allow, though all he said was, "There's no one who knows more about twentieth-century art than Eva." Then, before anyone could pose another question he didn't like, he turned to the Swedish couple, who looked like aged Viking twins, and asked them what they thought of Palm Beach.

Careful not to allow his attention to wander again, whenever the conversation seemed in danger of flagging, Frankie tossed in another bone for the others to chew on: what time of year was best to visit Venice; why soccer had never caught on in the United States; whether the oil embargo against Libya would help stem the tide of world terrorism; if *On Golden Pond* was a good movie or just another piece of sentimental Hollywood fluff. By the time Rose stood, signaling the end of dinner, Frankie was confident that he had successfully forestalled any further probing into the details of his private life.

His optimism proved unfounded. As he left the garden room, Maud's hand clasped firmly in his, the theatrical manager fell into step beside him. "It's come to me now. Why your name is so familiar. Annabel Lindsey married some chap named Ferraro. No relation, I suppose."

It wasn't that he was a particularly fascinating subject, Frankie understood.

It was just that, new to the group, he was the only one with secrets left to explore. "No relation," said Frankie, cheerfully. "Me."

"They're divorced," said Maud, in tones borrowed from her mother.

"I do beg your pardon," said the manager, embarrassed.

"No problem," said Frankie. He smiled. He had to, otherwise it was going to be a very long weekend. "Excuse me. It's time my daughter was in bed."

*F*rankie delivered Maud to Mrs. Ashby, then returned to his room (Kelly's was across the hall, a concession to her parents' sense of decorum) and called Martha. Her machine picked up and Frankie was annoyed. Where the hell *was* she? He left a message, giving the Palm Beach number, "in case of an emergency," he said. "Have a good weekend," he added, wondering how she spent her time when he wasn't around. She worked, of course, cleaned house, watched television. She read. She looked after Hannah, fed her, bathed her, took her for walks. Maybe she saw friends. But Frankie didn't know who they were, whether they were male or female. Except for Pina, Jill, and now Mark, he had never met any of the people in Martha's life. Which suddenly seemed strange to him. He knew whom Annabel saw, what she did; and he hardly ever spoke to her. To Martha he talked practically every day, and had since she started working for him. In . . . 1967, two years before he had even met Annabel.

How could he not have learned more about Martha in all that time? Because he had never been interested, Frankie reminded himself. And he wasn't really all that interested now. It was just that he felt, well . . . ashamed of having so little curiosity about someone whose life was so intimately linked to his. Why, that asshole of an Englishman had displayed more interest in him than he had about Martha in all the time he'd known her. I really am a self-involved sonovabitch, he thought, climbing the narrow staircase to the third floor, on his way back to Maud's room. No, he corrected himself as he hit the landing, I just like to keep my nose out of other people's business. That's a virtue, he added, piling on the reassurance, a definite virtue.

Maud was already in bed, waiting for him. Mrs. Ashby, who was standing at the dresser, tidying clothes, acknowledged his presence with a nod, then kissed Maud good night, and excused herself to go to her own room. When she'd gone, Maud inched further from the edge of the bed, making room for Frankie, who took the book from the bedside table, settled down beside her, and began reading Chapter Three of *Black Beauty*.

"I wish I had a horse," murmured Maud when Frankie reached the end of the chapter. She was exhausted, but not yet willing to give in to sleep.

"You have a pony," Frankie reminded her. It wasn't hers exactly, but there was a pony in the stables at Castle Melton that Maud rode when she was there.

"That's Oliver's," said Maud. Oliver was Roland's younger son. "I want one in New York."

"Maybe," said Frankie. He sat up and turned to look at her. "When you're older. If you save your money—"

"I'll never save enough. Horses are expensive."

"You bet they are. And not just to buy, but to keep. They eat a lot. And who'd take care of it?"

"A stable hand," she said, sounding surprised by his lack of knowledge.

The conversation seemed familiar to Frankie. Yes, he'd recently had a similar one with Kelly, he remembered, about a dog. "You can't have everything you want, Maud," he told his daughter. "And you can't expect to get what you want just by asking for it. That's not the way the world works. That's not the way I work."

"I don't want everything. I just want a horse."

"No. Or, at least, not right now."

"Please, Daddy?"

"I said no."

She frowned, considering her options. "I'll ask Mommy. She could buy it. She has lots of money," said Maud finally.

If he wasn't careful, thought Frankie, the irritation he had felt with the cross-examiners at dinner, with Martha for not being home when he called, was going to spill out and swamp his daughter. "Even people you think have lots of money, like Mommy and me," he said, hoping he didn't sound as annoyed as he felt, "still don't have enough to spend stupidly. We can't buy everything we want, everything *you* want, or we'd end up with none at all." He paused for a moment, then went on. "Remember the time you spent your whole allowance on that pink plastic purse?" Maud nodded. "And you had nothing left to buy Mrs. Ashby a birthday present?" Again Maud nodded. "What happened?"

"I cried," said Maud.

Frankie stifled a laugh. "And?"

"I asked you for more money. And you gave it to me," she added triumphantly, as if she'd just proved her point.

"Well, there's nobody to give me more money when *I* cry," said Frankie. "Which is why you can't have a horse. I don't want to talk about this anymore. Okay? I want you to go to sleep." She looked sulky but said nothing, and Frankie started to stand up. It looked as if she would let him go, but then she said, "One more chapter. Please?"

"Will you close your eyes and not talk anymore?" Maud nodded and Frankie settled back into the pillows beside her, and opened the book again.

She wasn't spoiled, he thought. She was sweet tempered, thoughtful, generous. Which was peculiar, since neither he nor Annabel possessed any of those virtues. It was just that at times Maud could not resist a power play. But then, who could?

*W*hen he returned to the sitting room, Frankie found the others drinking coffee from delicate demitasse cups and sipping brandy from crystal snifters. "Help yourself," called Hugo, motioning to the trolley where the coffee and drinks had been laid out. Frankie poured himself a brandy, then joined Kelly on the couch. The conversation was fragmented, gossip mixed with golf scores, shopping anecdotes with weather forecasts. "Let's get out of here," he whispered.

Kelly nodded. She placed her cup carefully on the glass-topped coffee table and stood. "We're going dancing," she said. "Anybody want to come?"

Only the Swedish couple did, and the four of them got into the Helms' Lincoln, Frankie driving, and headed for Au Bar, whose principle virtue, as far as he was concerned, was that the noise level precluded conversation. They stayed a couple of hours, mixing partners, until the Swedes pleaded exhaustion. When they returned to the house, they found that everyone but the maid who let them in had gone to bed. A chubby dark-haired girl, with skin so fair it seemed improbable in that climate, she agreed cheerfully to bringing the couple the hot water and lemon they wanted and to letting Kelly lock up when she and Frankie were ready to turn in.

When the Swedes had murmured polite good nights and headed up the broad staircase to their room, Frankie took Kelly's hand and led her through the darkened house toward the patio doors. Outside, the air was warm and wet, heavy with the scent of jasmine. The lights had been turned off earlier and only the quarter moon lit the way down the few steps to the pool. Set in a slate surround, it was bordered by a patch of grass, and, on three sides, by beds of flowering shrubs, separated at its far end from the sandy beach by a high stone wall with a heavy wooden gate in its center. The key to the lock was concealed under a stone frog. Frankie stooped to retrieve it, then opened the gate, took Kelly's hand and tugged. "No, wait," she said. She slipped off her shoes, then reached under her dress to pull down her pantyhose.

"Good idea. If I can be of any help . . ." said Frankie, as he kicked off his loafers and removed his socks.

"Done," she said, letting the wisp of silky fabric fall in a heap. She slipped her arm around his waist. "I'm glad Maud's here. She's such a great little kid."

"You have a lot in common."

Annoyed, Kelly pulled away from him. "I wish you'd stop doing that."

"What?"

"Insinuating that I'm a child. I'm not. I'm an adult. I'm a woman."

"And I don't treat you like one?"

"No, you don't."

He turned and wrapped his arms around her. He kissed her neck, her ear, then whispered, "Not even when I do this?" He slid his hands down her back and cupped her bottom, pulling her close to him. "Or this."

Kelly relaxed against him; she returned his kiss; but when he let her go, she said, "I'm old enough to know what I want, Frankie. I love you. I want to marry you. I want to have children with you. And your pretending that I'm too young to know my own mind won't change that." Though Frankie had been expecting this moment for weeks, he still felt as if it had crept up on him without warning and put a gun to his head. He put his hands in his pockets and started walking. She hurried after him. "What do *you* want?" she said, touching his arm.

He stopped, looked at her, considered a number of replies, and finally settled on the truth. "I don't know," he said. Moonlight reflected off the water illuminated her face. He watched her eyes cloud with hurt. He saw it tug at her mouth. He felt awful. Still, he told himself, it would be disastrous to let guilt and pity lead him where he didn't want to go. "You have to understand, Kelly. I've got two marriages behind me, neither one of them any good. You can't blame me for being cautious."

"Don't you love me?"

"I thought I loved *them*. Miranda, Annabel. And maybe I did. Maybe love just doesn't last. Maybe I do something to kill it. Or maybe what I felt was a whole lot of other things I mistook for love. I'm not sure. And this time I'd like to be. I don't want another failed marriage."

"You don't want to marry me," said Kelly sadly, moving away from him.

"I care about you. You know I do. I just don't want to make another mistake."

"I don't know how I'm going to explain to Daddy," she said.

Frankie took hold of her wrist, pulled her to him, and said, "There's nothing to explain."

"He was so sad after my brother died . . . we all were . . . but Daddy especially. Since he met you, though, he's been better, much better."

"I wouldn't hurt him for the world," said Frankie. "I'm crazy about him and your mother, too. All I'm asking for is a little more time."

"How much time?"

"Jesus, Kelly! How the fuck do I know? Until I'm sure!"

A slap of icy cold water hit their feet. Kelly screamed. Both of them leaped backward, out of the way of the rising tide. "It's freezing," she said, forgetting for the moment to mind that he'd shouted at her.

"Let's go swimming," he said.

"Are you crazy?"

"In the pool, then."

He took her hand and pulled her after him back along the beach and through the gate. He locked the door again, replaced the key, picked up their shoes, his socks, her stockings, then led her up to the pool house. "Turn around," he said, his hands on her shoulders, directing her into position, her back to him. The zipper glided down her back with almost no resistance. He slid her dress off her shoulders, and followed it down her body with his hands, taking the strip of thin silk panty with it. She wore no bra. He buried his face in her neck and reached in front to caress her breasts. "Mmm," he murmured, then abruptly released her. "Grab some towels," he said as he began to remove his clothes. Then, naked, they went back out into the warm night and slid into the pool's moonlit water. It was almost as hot as a bath.

"I've never done this before. Been swimming naked here, I mean," said Kelly. "There are always so many people around. Mother, Daddy."

"Ssh," said Frankie. He kissed her lightly on the mouth, then turned onto his back, pulling her on top of him. With his feet, he pushed off from the side and they floated together out into the pool, her face resting on his shoulder, her legs tangling with his. The water felt like a thousand fingertips gently caressing his body. His cock pressed against Kelly's thigh, searching for room to grow. He stroked her wet buttocks, then released her, twisting away, diving beneath her, teasing her with his mouth and hands. She caught the spirit of the game, diving and circling, sliding against his body and away again. They played until they were both crazy with desire and Frankie maneuvered Kelly to the shallow end of the pool, braced her against the tiles, and plunged into her. "Oh, I love you," she murmured, her legs straddling his hips, her arms circling his neck. "I love you."

"Ssh," whispered Frankie as she came, his mouth covering hers to prevent her cries from waking her sleeping parents. Then he buried his hands in her wet hair, pressed his face tight against her slender throat, and for a few short moments forgot everything.

*T*hey slept in Kelly's room. That is, Kelly slept. For most of the night, Frankie lay awake. Thoughts of Kelly and the Helms, Martha and Hannah, jarred him back to consciousness whenever he managed to doze off. Just before six, he crossed the tiled hallway to his own room, thinking that he might do better without Kelly's body beside his, a reminder of what he needed to forget if he hoped to get any sleep at all. Being alone didn't help. An hour later, feeling centuries older than the young buck who had sported so friskily in the pool the night before, Frankie dragged himself from the bed and into the bathroom. After showering and shaving, he felt better, but his nervous system was crying out for a caffeine fix. While trying to decide which would be the least offensive option at that hour of the morning, phoning the kitchen to have one of the staff bring him a cup of coffee or going down to forage for one on his own, he thought of Martha. Crossing to the writing desk, he picked up the phone. She would be awake; at least he assumed she would be; didn't all small children get their mothers up at dawn?

But when she answered, Martha didn't sound either awake or pleased to hear from him. "What time is it?" she asked querulously.

"Close to eight," said Frankie. "I thought you'd be up by now."

Frankie heard the clatter of items being picked up and dropped, and then Martha's voice, sounding outraged, saying, "It's seven-fifteen. Frankie, it's Saturday!"

"I thought Hannah woke up early."

"Sometimes she does. This morning, she didn't. What do you want?"

"Did you get my message?"

"Of course I got your message."

Ears straining, he listened for background noise, something to let him know if she was alone or if someone else was there. "I just wanted to be sure you're all right. You and Hannah. When nobody answered the phone last night, I was a little worried."

"I know it's hard for you to believe that anyone has a life apart from you, but we do. At least, I do. Keep that in mind, Frankie, will you?"

"I don't know what's wrong with you lately."

"Wrong with *me*?" There was a note of fury in her voice.

"You fly off the handle for no reason—"

"Frankie, I'm going back to sleep now—"

"Martha, don't hang up! Martha!" As Frankie shouted her name, he caught a movement in his peripheral vision. Turning, he saw Kelly standing in the doorway, wearing a short robe of turquoise silk, loosely tied, one perfect small breast beginning to slip through the wide V of the opening. Confusion, disbelief, hurt, anger made their way quickly across her face. He put down the phone and stood.

"Who's Martha?" Her voice sounded small and full of pain.

"No one." Just then, he couldn't come up with anything that sounded more reasonable.

"Is that why you don't want to marry me? Because there's someone else?"

"No. That's not why. I told you why." He went to her, and pulled her inside the room, closing the door again behind her. "There is no one else," he said, holding her in his arms, looking her straight in the eye.

Her pale eyes filled with tears. "Who is she?"

"She works for Colette," he said. "You know Colette."

"And you called her at seven on a Saturday morning?"

"I woke up thinking about something. You know how I am. I never thought of the day or the time." All of it was true, if not exactly truthful, and for a brief moment Frankie couldn't help feeling proud of himself for having so artfully avoided lying. But then his conscience surfaced. He could tell her now, he thought; he could tell her the whole truth, and nothing but; he would be understood and forgiven; all would be well. But, finally, he couldn't do it. He was ashamed of himself, but he couldn't. "I love you," he said. "You know I do. There's no one else. I swear it. I love you."

Pulling away, Kelly stared at him hard. And for the first time Frankie could see that she really was Hugo Helm's daughter. "Then marry me," she said.

$$\boxed{\textit{Chapter 30}}$$

Kelly wanted a June wedding. Frankie suggested waiting a year, until the following spring, but that provoked hurt looks and accusations about his trying to weasel out of marrying her, which he denied vehemently. He wasn't trying to weasel out of the wedding. He didn't have the courage for that. What he was hoping was that fate would intervene to save him—and for that he needed time. Then, over the champagne Hugo opened to celebrate the announcement, an unexpected ally won Frankie a reprieve. Insisting that four months were not nearly long enough to plan the kind of wedding Kelly wanted to have, Rose convinced her daughter to wait until December.

Not wanting weather to be an issue, Kelly vetoed both Chicago and New York as sites and, defeating the whole idea of a Christmas wedding, chose Palm Beach instead. The ceremony would take place in the Lutheran church on Royal Palm Way and the reception at The Breakers. Very sweetly, thought the bridegroom, Kelly asked Maud to be her maid of honor, and any reservations the little girl might have been tempted to muster against her father's getting married were completely overwhelmed by the excitement of helping to choose what kind of dress she would have, what flowers she would carry, how she would wear her hair. While Frankie golfed with Hugo and the men, Maud pored over bridal magazines with Kelly and Rose and which-ever of the women guests was not lying on a chaise in the sun. When she ventured an opinion, it was received as if offered by a French modiste. She was included in discussions of cars and attendants, of menus and table linens. It was heady stuff for a nine-year-old.

While Frankie pretended, Kelly glowed with happiness. Her red hair, her pale green eyes, her alabaster skin, all shone. She looked radiant. It was a sight her parents were used to, having successfully provoked it over the years with puppies, ponies, fur coats, sports cars. But nothing, they agreed, had ever succeeded as well as Frankie. For that, Hugo and Rose were grateful. They were delighted by the engagement, and with the prospect of having him for a son-in-law. They foresaw nothing but a rosy future ahead for the couple. "Third time lucky," said Hugo buoyantly when Frankie, finding himself briefly alone with the older man before the others gathered for cock-tails, cautiously mentioned his fears, trying to secure in advance forgiveness against the day when he would fail Kelly, fail all of them.

Since he usually enjoyed basking in Hugo's approval, such optimism should have delighted Frankie. Hugo's conviction that both Frankie's former wives must have had "something wrong upstairs" not to have found him an ideal husband should have brought him peace with its absolution. Instead he found himself more and more irritated by Hugo, and by Rose too. Blinded not only by affection, but by the arrogant assumption that anyone Hugo deemed worthy must, like a painting that struck his fancy, be the prime article, they refused to see Frankie's flaws. Hugo Helm did not make mistakes.

The reaction of his own parents irritated Frankie too, but, at least it al-lowed for the possibility of error, a relief in the circumstances. "For chrissake, don't fuck up this time," Sal said when Frankie phoned with the news, "or you'll break your mother's heart."

Dolly begged him, again, to get married in church, this time not just because it was the right, the Catholic, thing to do, but as a talisman against disaster. "You have to ask God's blessing, Frankie. How else can you expect to have a good marriage?" When Frankie told her he *was* getting married in church, a Lutheran church, to which congregation the Helms nominally belonged, Dolly protested feebly, but not for long: any church was better than none. "I'll pray for you," she said before hanging up, conjuring for Frankie the image of her kneeling before an altar, her head bowed, not following the mass, which had been changed to the vernacular for the benefit of people like her, but saying her rosary just as she had since she was a girl. The rosary, made of beads of pink glass, blessed by the Pope, was a gift from Frankie, bought on a trip Annabel and he had made to Rome. It had caused an argument, as everything had in those days, since Annabel's taste required bringing back some bruised and battered antique that Dolly would have been ashamed to display in her house, where everything had to be new and perfect. She had loved the rosary and, wielding it, had prayed for him more relentlessly than ever, which comforted him when he thought about it. Who knows how much more trouble he would have got into it if his mother had given up in despair?

*N*o one, it seemed, had any reservations about his forthcoming marriage, which Frankie ought to have found reassuring but didn't. Angela, whom he had counted on to give him hell, called him at his office when he got back from Palm Beach to assure him that Denny and she were overjoyed at the prospect of seeing him settled finally with a nice girl. So, she added, were Dolly and Sal—except for the matter of the church wedding.

Over drinks after their usual squash game, Frankie turned to Vic for reassurance. "You think I'm out of my mind?" he asked.

Vic shook his head. "Kelly's a good person," he said. "You'll be all right."

"I'm scared shitless."

Vic laughed. "With your track record, I'd be, too." Then his smile faded, and he said, "Frankie, all you need to make a marriage work is a lot of goodwill."

"I thought it was great sex."

Vic grinned. "It doesn't hurt. But I've always found that being on time for dinner is what really counts." He stood up. "Congratulations, Frankie. And I mean it."

The handshake turned into a hug and for a moment Frankie felt as if Vic were a life raft he was hanging on to. He let go and stepped back. They left the club together, and shared a taxi uptown. "Call me when you get back from Boston," said Vic as Frankie got out of the cab on Central Park West. "We'll have dinner, the four of us."

"Sure thing," said Frankie. He stopped to ask after the doorman's sprained ankle (an injury earned in the line of duty—hailing a cab on a wet night for a tenant) and then, looking forward to the evening ahead, went inside. Maud was waiting for him. His new fiancée, thank God, had tickets to a rock concert that he had used his daughter as an excuse not to attend. Kelly had pouted, but not for long. It occurred to her that a friend was someone she could talk to endlessly about the wedding. And so he'd arranged for them all to enjoy themselves, thought Frankie, not without a flicker of guilt.

. . .

*A*nnabel returned from Europe midweek; Maud left for her mother's apartment; and Frankie flew up to Boston for a meeting with Jack Haggerty, who was trying to convince him that interested buyers were begging to pay through the nose for his company. Though Frankie had found it necessary to put all expansion plans on hold and to close the Newark club, his efforts to keep the others solvent through strategic renovation, innovative programs, and clever publicity had resulted in substantially increased profits. FCI had weathered the recession well. Things were looking good, and soon, if luck and the economy held, he would be as rich as his former wife had always pretended he was. Too late for her to get her hands on a penny, Frankie thought with some satisfaction as he left the meeting. "I'm going to ask Kelly to sign a prenup," he said to Dan that night when dinner was over; the children variously studying, watching television, and in bed; the housekeeper tidying up the kitchen; and he and Dan settled in the study to talk.

"Kelly's a sweet girl, levelheaded. I don't suppose she'll refuse." Dan poured Frankie another whiskey and himself a glass of Perrier. For a long time after Amy's death, he'd drunk heavily. Then, just as friends began to stop being sympathetic and begin wondering whether he was an alcoholic and, if so, what they should do about it, Dan ran his car off the road and returned home with stitches in his head and his arm in a sling. The look of terror on his kids' faces had been enough to convince him that it was time to give up that particular crutch.

"Why should she refuse? Her old man's got plenty of money. One of these days it's all going to be hers. And I sure don't want any of it!" Dan laughed. "What?" said Frankie. "You think I'm marrying Kelly for her money?"

"No . . ."

The reply lacked the conviction necessary to smooth Frankie's ruffled pride. "Goddamnit," he snapped, "all you fucking Colvingtons are the same! All you fucking WASPS are the same. Not only do you marry each other all the time for name, for position, for money, but you suspect everyone else of doing it, too, and then have the nerve to look down your noses at them because of it—"

"Stop shouting, okay? Who the hell do you think you're talking to? Eva Colvington? One of your wives? I've got kids sleeping upstairs!"

Frankie and Dan rarely crossed swords. They may have started in different places, but years of borrowed books, long conversations, shared experiences, had brought them to essentially the same world view. And, when they did find themselves at odds, they had enough respect for each other to agree to disagree and let it go at that. This time was different. Frankie felt that his honor had been impugned. He took a sip of whiskey, and said quietly, "Level with me, Dan. What *do* you think?"

"Not that you're marrying Kelly for her money."

"Why do I keep hearing a 'but'?"

Dan got up, went to the bar. "Human motivation is complex," he said as he topped up Frankie's glass.

"Just cut to the chase, okay?"

"I'm trying." Sitting again, he looked at Frankie, and said, "All of us— even sociopaths, I suppose—live by some code of ethics, of honor, idiosyncratic, maybe not making a whole lot of sense to other people, maybe not even making sense to ourselves a lot of the time. Your code happens to be a very romantic one—"

"And yours isn't?"

"We're talking about you. Anyway, one of the rules in your very romantic code is that you shouldn't spend a nickel you haven't earned yourself."

"I bought my apartment with money from Miranda's estate."

"You wouldn't even have done that if Vic and I hadn't talked you into it. Now, here comes the 'but.' In spite of your reluctance to sponge, as you see it, the only women you ever fall in love with are women with money. Why?"

"How do I know? Why do the women you're attracted to, even the people you make friends with, always come, as your folks say, from the wrong side of the tracks?"

"My folks would never say anything that direct," said Dan, smiling.

Frankie sat for a moment, thinking. Then, finally, he said. "It's not the money I'm attracted to. It's the aura." He looked at Dan, who didn't seem inclined to say anything more. There was silence for a moment, and then Frankie asked, "How is Eva, by the way?" She'd had a stroke a few weeks before.

"Her speech is slurred. She can't use her right hand. Craig says she hates people seeing her the way she is now. She doesn't even want Joan or Philip to visit."

Frankie tried to find some reserve of sympathy under the mountain of rage he felt toward his former mother-in-law. But there was none there. "Even dying, she's a cold, vain bitch," he said.

*T*he Helms decided to stop over in New York on their way back from Palm Beach to Chicago. Rose and Dolly, after a good half hour weeping with joy into the telephone together, agreed on the necessity of a celebratory dinner. And Frankie, on his return from Boston, found himself immediately caught up in a whirlwind of prenuptial activity.

"Who's invited?" he asked Kelly.

"Just your parents and mine. Angela and Denny. Maud."

"So what's the big deal?"

"Daddy suggested Le Cirque," said Kelly, laughing, "but your father said he can't stand French food."

"Your mother wanted to invite your aunts and uncles," said Sal when Frankie called him. "But I told her she was nuts. I mean, how many times can we ask them to ante up 'cause you're gettin' married? You had any sense, you'd elope."

"If it was up to me—" said Frankie. But he couldn't tell his father that, if it were up to him, he wouldn't be getting married at all.

Finally, a date and a time were selected, and a restaurant, Italian to suit Sal's limited palate. "Twelve-ninety-five for a dish of macaroni," he muttered when he saw the menu. "Are they crazy?"

"Just enjoy it, Pop," said Frankie. "You're not paying."

"That's not the point," said Sal. "Did you get a load of these prices?" he called across the table to Hugo. "I'm glad it's you footin' the bill, not me."

"I'll get my revenge, don't you worry." A broad smile spread across Hugo's jovial features, and everybody laughed, including Maud.

She was wearing a new pink silk dress with a lace collar and matching pink ribbons woven into her long dark hair. On her feet were cream-colored shoes and lace-trimmed socks. Her normally somber face was alight with excitement. It was probably the only party she'd ever attended, thought Frankie, including those for her birthdays, that hadn't been spoiled for her in advance by her parents arguing: where to have them, whom to invite, what the entertainment should be—no matter how simple the plan it was never simple enough to prevent disagreement. They had a lot to answer for, Annabel and he.

"I like weddings," Maud confided to Frankie later when he went into her room to say good night. "Everybody's so happy."

"Most of the time, anyway."

"There's a boy at school who really likes me, Daddy," she continued, ignoring his caution. "His name's Christopher."

"And do you really like *him*?"

"Oh, yes. I want to marry him when I grow up."

Frankie smiled. "That's a few years off yet. By then, you may have found someone you like even better."

"I'll never like anybody better than Christopher," she said emphatically. "He's very handsome. And he's smart. He knows all about snakes. And stars. He got a telescope for Christmas last year. And when Mrs. Rabin calls on him he always knows the answers." She smiled shyly. "He says I'm pretty."

"You are. You're beautiful. And lots of boys are going to tell you that and say they love you. But what they say isn't important. What they do, that's what counts. Whether they're nice to you, or mean. Whether they listen to you or make fun of what you say. Whether they respect you—"

"What's 'respect'?"

He knew how his father would reply. "Respect," Sal Ferraro would have told his granddaughter, "means people should treat you like a lady, they shouldn't say bad words in front of you, they should open the door for you, walk on the curb side of the street, they should mind their manners."

Frankie, however, didn't want to lie to his daughter, bamboozle her, teach her the double standard he'd been raised to consider the way of the world, so he thought about it a minute and then said, "It means taking other people seriously. It means accepting that their needs, or desires, or opinions, may have as much value as your own."

"Do you respect me?" asked Maud.

"Yes," said Frankie, with no hesitation. "Very much."

"And Mommy?"

Frankie thought for a moment and then said, "Maybe the trouble between your mother and me is that we didn't respect each other enough."

"But you respect Kelly?"

"Yes," said Frankie quickly, giving the necessary answer without being sure it was an honest one.

"Do you respect her more than anyone in the world?"

For reasons beyond his understanding or control, Martha's face flashed into Frankie's mind. Irritated, he pushed it away and dealt with the issue at hand. "Not more than you," he said to Maud, who had clearly begun to think that respect was a synonym for love. He picked up the copy of *Black Beauty* that was lying on the bedside table, and opened the book to the page where the marker rested. "That's enough conversation for tonight," he said, and, as Maud snuggled contentedly against him, he began to read.

*S*everal times a day since his return from Palm Beach, it had occurred to Frankie that he ought to phone Martha, but, instead of doing it, for over a week he allowed himself to be distracted by whatever business or family matter happened to turn up. He wasn't avoiding her, he told himself, he was just busy. He wasn't reluctant to tell her the engagement was official, there were just other more pressing matters to deal with. It wasn't as if the news would come as a shock, after all, or that she would care—as long as he kept quiet about Hannah. Over the years, she'd made it abundantly clear that she felt they had no claims on one another. Still, he couldn't make himself phone her and was wondering if he would ever get around to doing it when Colette phoned him, a business call in which she tried, this time, to convince him to appear in a television commercial promoting the clubs. He refused, as he had formerly refused to appear in the print ads. Reluctantly, Colette conceded defeat, and then, because gossip was her métier, she asked about his trip to Palm Beach. She'd heard rumors as far away as Boca, she said; and, when Frankie confirmed the news of his engagement, after the smallest hesitation, she offered him her congratulations.

"Thanks," he replied. He waited for her to continue, for her to tell him what a terrific girl Kelly was, how she hoped they'd have a long and happy marriage, how she was sure he was not about to make another fucking mess of his life.

After another pause, all she said was, "Have you told Martha?"

"Not yet." There was a defensive note in his voice that he was unable to control. "It's been one thing after another since I got back."

"Yes, well . . ." There was an even longer pause. Finally, she spoke the words he'd been waiting for: "I hope you'll be happy, Frankie. You know that." The trouble was, she didn't sound as if she thought he had a prayer.

Annoyed, Frankie hung up. Now that someone finally seemed to share his own reservations, he found he preferred unadulterated enthusiasm. And what did she mean asking if he'd told Martha? Determined not to be railroaded by an old crone with more mouth than sense, he began going through the folders on his desk, the quarterly financial reports, the recommendations for expansion, the suggestions for cutbacks; but the idea of Martha kept pulling his mind from the pages in front of him. Finally, he depressed the button of his private line and dialed her at the office where, now that Hannah was old enough for nursery school, she spent her mornings. She wasn't in. She was out at meetings all day, the receptionist told him.

It took Frankie until four in the afternoon to reach her. "I just walked in the door," she said, sounding breathless and happy when she answered the phone, making Frankie think of hotel rooms and clandestine rendezvous rather than the dreary office settings in which he had, until then, been imagining her out of his reach.

"I know. I've been trying to find you since this morning," he said accusingly. "Your office told me you had back-to-back meetings all day."

He was fishing, but either Martha didn't notice or she didn't mind. "Not *all* day," she said. "Just this morning. I spent the rest of the time shopping. I decided I needed a new spring wardrobe." For whose benefit, Frankie wondered, Mark's? Martha laughed. "Luckily, I had to pick Hannah up at school or I would have bankrupted myself."

"Listen," he said, before he changed his mind, "could I stop by for a while tonight? I haven't seen you or Hannah for a while."

"Sure," said Martha. "Of course. What time should we expect you?"

. . .

*F*rankie rang the doorbell promptly at six-thirty. Pina let him in, mumbled something about Martha getting dressed, then ushered him in to Hannah's room where the little girl looked up, smiling at him with delight. In a few weeks, she would be three years old. She was wearing a tutu, ballet slippers, and a crown, which meant that at some point recently she'd been playing the heroine of one of the fairy tales she loved to have read to her, Cinderella or Sleeping Beauty. But just then she was on the floor, putting together the tracks of a wooden train set, bought after the trip from Grand Central to Pawlings to visit to her grandparents had led to a fascination with trains. She looked adorable, and, feeling the familiar tug at his heart, Frankie sank down beside her and offered his help, which Hannah took more for the pleasure of having a playmate than because she needed it. Her fingers worked with amazing dexterity, and, as she skillfully fitted the pieces of the track together, she talked constantly, parroting words and phrases and rhythms borrowed from her mother, from Pina, from anyone she heard speak. "This goes here. And this funny piece, it goes wite here. Oh, Madwe de Dios, I dwopped it."

As he sat playing with the child, Frankie felt more relaxed than he had in days. Hannah's laugh was better than a tranquilizer, he decided, regretting that he'd waited so long to visit. Finally he heard the murmur of Martha's voice, speaking softly in Spanish to Pina. "I have to talk to your mommy," he said, getting to his feet. "I'll be back in a few minutes." But Hannah stood up and followed him out of the room.

Martha looked up and smiled. "I was just coming in to say good night."

Her hair fell sleekly to her shoulders. The dress she wore looked expensive, a green printed silk with a wide belt cinched tightly around her small waist. A strand of pearls hung just to the deep U that exposed the curve of her breasts; pearl-and-jade earrings dangled from her ears. Frankie wondered if they'd been a gift. She looked very nice, he thought, very attractive. "You didn't say you were going out," he said, a note of accusation in his voice.

"I hadn't planned to. Something came up."

Then he noticed that her smile was forced, and her eyes bloodshot and swollen. "Something's wrong," he said, worried. "You've been crying." But if something was wrong, why was she dressed for a party?

Martha shook her head, and said firmly, "I got some mascara in my eye. Do I look terrible?"

He wondered if she was lying, but all he said was, "No, you look great. Very pretty."

"Thank you," she said, but the quality of her smile did not improve. "Well . . . I better get going. Kiss Mommy good night," she said to Hannah, extending her arms.

Hannah went to her and Martha lifted her up. A genuine, if brief, smile lighted her face as she and her daughter exchanged a kiss. "Hav'a nice time," said Hannah.

Martha laughed. "I will, sweetie," she said. "You be a good girl for Pina."

"And Frankie," said Hannah.

"Yes," agreed Martha, passing her daughter to Pina, who took her and headed back toward the bedroom.

"Can I talk to you a minute before you go out?"

"Sure." She reached into the hall closet to get her coat, then turned to face him. "What is it?" she said, a hint of impatience in her voice.

"It's official. Kelly and I are getting married. In December."

"You didn't tell her about Hannah?"

"No," said Frankie guiltily.

"Good," she said, as if she had expected as much. "Congratulations." She put on her coat, buttoned it. She kissed his cheek. "I hope you'll be happy, Frankie, you and Kelly. Stay as long as you like," she said. "Until Hannah goes to sleep," she added, and, opening the door, she left.

What had he expected, Frankie asked himself? That Martha would weep and wail and beg him not to do it? That she would be angry and hurl recriminations? When had she ever done that? And why did he always feel, despite his conviction that he had in no way wronged her, as if he deserved whatever blame she chose to heap on him. He should be grateful, he thought, staring at the closed door, that she always let him off so lightly. Instead of which he felt let down. Disappointment swept through him and a sense of loss so profound it made him want to weep. He didn't understand himself at all. Familiar strains from some work by Tchaikovsky, though what particular piece he had no idea, drifted toward him together with the sound of Hannah laughing. Turning away from the door, he went into her room. She was dancing for Pina, her plump legs under the ruffled tutu twirling in time to the music coming from the cassette player on her dresser. "Look, Frankie," she called when she saw him. She spun faster and faster, flapping her arms. "Look," she called again. The music ended and she fell to the floor, remained still for a moment, then looked up and smiled. "I'm a swan," she said. Her look was one of total joy, complete trust.

Picking her up, Frankie clutched her to him. He never wanted to let her go. "You're beautiful," he said. "The most beautiful swan I've ever seen."

Chapter 31

*E*va Colvington died at the beginning of May. A second stroke, massive and merciful, finished her off, no doubt to her relief, Dan said when he phoned to tell Frankie the news. She'd hated growing old, feeling her body slow, her intellect falter, seeing the light that had attracted so many willing victims fade to extinction. Above all, she'd hated losing her power to command. Sitting in her wheelchair, at a loss for words for the first time since she'd learned to speak, she'd watched with frustration and rage as the world proceeded around her, taking no note—except for the very basic necessities—of her needs and desires. When her son, Philip, on one of his duty visits to the hospital, had asked her how she felt, Eva, after struggling to find the word, had spat out, "Trapped."

Frankie neither sent flowers personally, nor attended the funeral, though he had to fight off a craven impulse to keep up appearances by doing both. He did authorize a huge floral tribute from the DeWitt Payson Gallery, but Eva had earned that. The gallery had been the one true love of her life and it had thrived under her devotion, as had the artists she'd nurtured over the years, transforming them from nonentities to art-world celebrities with the magic of her regard. In acknowledgment of that, Frankie closed the gallery for the day, sent Russell Schneider north for the funeral, and, when he could, dodged phone calls from distressed artists, important buyers, and assorted members of the press, all wondering if the gallery could survive Eva Colvington's demise.

Oh, yes, Eva had been set free, but so had Frankie. The gallery had provided him with only a modest income over the years, fluctuating art markets and expensive overheads (including Eva's cut) taking their toll on profits, but his determination to hold on to it had always had less to do with a desire to make money than a need to make Eva eat crow. But if the regret that others had prophesied he would someday feel, for nursing for so long as self-diminishing an emotion as anger, failed to materialize, nevertheless Frankie did catch a hint of relief in the rush of feeling following the news of her death. As the memories flooded in, as he tallied once again the ways Eva had caused him misery and heartbreak, it occurred to him that now he could close that particular ledger. Death had balanced the account.

. . .

*W*hat *are* you going to do about the gallery?" Martha asked a few days after the funeral.

"I'm not sure," said Frankie. The strain between them had gradually dissipated, vanishing completely on the fifteenth of April, Hannah's third birthday, when he, without having been invited, arrived at her party with a clown in tow. Tempted briefly to climb on her high horse and protest, Martha was undone by her daughter's delight. And, since then, motivated by a vague sense of alarm, a fear that, if he failed to play his cards right, he'd lose something valuable, Frankie had resumed stopping by to see them almost as frequently as in the days preceding the appearance of Kelly in his life. Martha didn't protest. And sometimes she even asked him to stay for dinner. "Do you want me to light the candles?" he asked.

"I don't think they're really necessary." There was a hint of alarm in her voice.

The table was set with Italian ceramic dishes, with matching candleholders on each side of a jug of pink tulips. Frankie took a book of matches from the wicker basket on the kitchen counter where Martha kept a collection and said, "I like candlelight."

She shrugged. "Suit yourself."

"There," he said as the candles caught the flame. The lights in the apartment were soft, and the candles added a glow that seemed to him not so much romantic as cozy. "Very nice." He poured the wine, an excellent Chianti that he had opened earlier, then sat, aware of a feeling of contentment he attributed to the prospect of a good home-cooked meal and the fact of Hannah asleep nearby.

Martha carried the casserole dish to the table, set it down, and began serving the chicken cacciatore. "Do you think Russell Schneider can run it?" she asked.

"Yes," said Frankie, who had been weighing his options, trying to make a decision. "But Eva was right about one thing, I *am* a philistine when it comes to contemporary art. I don't know much, or like much. She loved the stuff. She understood it. So does Russell. And he's managed to establish a reputation for himself, in spite of having to play second fiddle to her all these years. He's liked, he's respected. But he doesn't have her power, and power is where the money is. Anyway, it's time I got out. This is great," he added, after tasting the chicken.

Martha thanked him for the compliment, offered him a basket full of crusty Italian bread, and said, "What about Joan?" She meant Miranda's half sister.

"She's a big-shot curator at some museum in Los Angeles, making quite a name for herself. She's not going to want to give that up to run a gallery."

"But she's someone you could talk to about what to do."

"I thought I was talking to *you* about it," he said.

Martha smiled. "You might find it more helpful speaking with someone who knows a thing or two about the subject. And Joan's family, after all."

"Family," said Frankie. "I never thought of her that way myself." Joan. He tried to remember what she looked like and could only recall a small pale face and dark hair. "She probably hates me. I should call her," he added, thinking Martha's advice wasn't half bad. "I mean, what's the worst she can do? Hang up on me?"

Martha laughed. "You do have that effect on people. Want some more chicken?"

"Yes, please," he said, not because he was still hungry, but because the chicken tasted so good, the bread (from a nearby specialty store) like manna, the wine as rich and mellow as his mood. He had not felt so at ease in . . . he couldn't remember how long, and he wanted to extend the moment. For as long as he kept eating, he could. For that length of time, he didn't have to think about how to explain his evening to Kelly when he saw her later; or wonder if Martha's plans for that night included a visit from Mark. He could save all that for his walk home. "More wine?" he asked, reaching for the bottle. Then he said, "I'll call Joan in the morning. Dan will know where I can reach her."

*J*oan was still in Boston, Dan told Frankie, staying at the Colvington house helping Craig sort through Eva's things. "Hard as it was for the rest of us to understand," said Dan, "he loved her . . . He's in a pretty bad way."

"It takes time," said Frankie.

"Yes," said Dan. Memories of Miranda's death and Amy's, the months, the years of misery following on each, crowded the airwaves between them. There was a silence. Then Dan said, "Poor Eva. For all her scheming, I never thought she got much happiness out of life."

"She got exactly what she wanted." Money, status, success. She'd been delighted with her lot, almost to the end, and Frankie saw no reason to feel sorry for her now that she'd lost it all to death.

Dan laughed. "You're right," he said. "She did. And who am I to pity her just because the things she cared about don't matter a damn to me?"

Of course they didn't matter to him. Unlike Eva, who'd spent the first part of her life playing the humiliating role of poor relation, Dan had been born with all the money and status anyone could ever want. Success was a guarantee that had come with his birth certificate. But, even as he thought it, Frankie knew he was being unfair. Dan possessed an innate decency having nothing to do with wealth or family. He'd been born with character, that ineffable quality resulting from (who knew?) a random gene or a gift of divine providence, like the genius of Mozart, of Rembrandt. With or without the privileges of his birth, Dan would still have been a man of integrity, the sort of man Frankie aspired to and, in his own opinion, fell short of being.

So instead of calling Dan on his remark, Frankie let the old punishing anguish of Miranda's loss reach out and take hold of him, and said bleakly, "Her kids are the ones I feel sorry for." And for their sake, he added silently, I hope she rots forever in hell.

When he returned to his office from a staff meeting at the White Plains Macklin's, Frankie phoned the Colvington house and heard in the new housekeeper's voice the same note of disdain he used to hear long ago in Mrs. Lyle's, a note very like the one that Eva had used when speaking to him. But Frankie had had the pleasure of listening to Eva beg from time to time. The housekeeper, however, remained outside his circle of power, an irritant he couldn't rid himself of as long as his relationship with the family continued.

That relationship, however, was nearing its end. There were some decisions still to be made, some ties still to be cut, but soon it would be over. Then why, Frankie asked himself as he waited for Joan to come to the phone, had a weight of sadness replaced the relief of a few days before? The answer came back, as always, Miranda. He'd managed, despite everything, to hold on to a small part of her, which even now, after so long, he was reluctant to let go.

"Frankie?"

He heard surprise in Joan's voice and a note of caution. "Joan, hello. Listen, if this is a bad time . . ."

"No, no, it's not. Thank you for the flowers, Frankie. They were splendid, the most gorgeous arrangement of roses. Mother would have loved them. It was thoughtful of you to send them."

"Joan, about Eva—"

"She wanted to die," said Joan quickly, as if she knew he couldn't possibly say anything nice, not wanting to hear (at least not at that moment) anything critical. "There's no point being sorry. It's just a bit . . . well, bewildering. Mother was such a powerful personality. It's hard for me, for any of us, to imagine a world without her."

"Yes, I'm sure," said Frankie, careful to keep any hint of hostility out of his voice. Joan certainly didn't need him to complicate whatever process she was going through to come to terms with her mother's death. She stumbled on a few sentences, repeating more or less what Dan had said. Frankie kept his own comments short and neutral, realizing as Joan talked that it wasn't dislike he heard in her voice, but wariness, one stranger trying to size up another. That, he realized, is what they were, despite the years that had passed since their first meeting, strangers. "I'd like to see you, Joan," he said when she faltered to a stop. "Before you go back to Los Angeles."

There was a pause, and then she said, "Of course. You have to decide what to do about the gallery." Trust Eva's daughter to get the point immediately.

"I'd like your advice."

Again there was a slight hesitation, and Frankie wondered if she was looking for a polite way to refuse. Finally, she said, "I suppose I should come to New York."

"Yes. You ought to see everything. I can put you up at the Carlyle. Or you can stay at my place. There's plenty of room."

"Your place sounds good. When were you thinking of?"

"As soon as it's convenient. Whenever you're able to leave Craig. Just give me a couple of days' notice so I can make sure to keep my schedule clear for you."

A few hours later, Joan called Frankie back to let him know her travel plans. The following Wednesday, he sent a car and driver to meet her at La Guardia, and, when she arrived at his apartment, he was there, waiting for her.

Joan was older than Miranda, older than he, Frankie figured, by five years at least. Like him she had aged well. Although there were faint lines at the corners of her large dark eyes, the skin over her prominent cheekbones was taut and smooth; her brown hair, which she wore in a long bob, had no trace of gray. As slender, but much taller than Eva, she had her mother's sense of style, though she favored strong colors rather than black. She wore a fashionable plaid culotte skirt and blue jacket with bold brass buttons.

"You look great," said Frankie.

"So do you." Casting an admiring look at his perfectly creased trousers, his silk tweed jacket, and bow tie, she held out a hand, which Frankie dutifully took before leaning forward to kiss her cheek.

"How's Craig doing?" he asked. Joan shrugged and shook her head. Frankie said, "He'll feel better once he gets out, plays a little golf, starts trying to live a normal life." He picked up her bag. "Come on, let me show you to your room."

*T*wenty minutes later, they were in a taxi crossing Central Park. Outside, it was hot and humid, but from the air-conditioned comfort of the cab, the park looked a cool oasis of lush grass and flowering trees. Joan sighed, and said, "I forget how beautiful New York is."

"It has its moments," said Frankie.

At the gallery, they were greeted by Russell Schneider, alerted to their arrival by Frankie's assistant. As he ushered them through the space, he called their attention to the present show, paintings by a young "graffiti artist," a recent discovery of Eva's, and sculpture by one of the gallery's most respected elder statesman who specialized in nudes executed in some polymer, painted naturalistically. It was the last show Eva had installed before her stroke and it had been very successful, Russell assured them. What he didn't add was that her death had boosted sales. The sculptor had been mentioned kindly in a *Time* article about Eva, and the graffiti artist was reviewed well in *Newsweek* and *Art World*. His career was made. Even from the grave, Eva apparently wielded influence.

She had made preliminary plans for subsequent installations, Russell told them in response to Joan's question, nothing definite as she was never one to get too ahead of herself, preferring to be free to respond to the whims of the market. He had a few ideas of his own about how to implement or (if need be) change those plans, he said, which he'd like to discuss. Though doing his best to look assured and in control, his worry was obvious. When Eva had hired him, Russell was just out of Cambridge and the Fogg, ambitious, enthusiastic, naive. Now he was a distinguished man in his middle fifties, with receding gray hair and a wife and two children in a nearby Park Avenue apartment. In more caustic moments, Frankie tended to think of him as Eva's flunky. When feeling more generous, he could admit that much of the gallery's success was due to Russell, who had the taste, the expertise, and the tact to have functioned expertly in Eva's frequent absences, so much tact that he'd managed to keep her approval without making an enemy of Frankie. So it was not with any pleasure that he now acknowledged to himself that the man's future, which was in his hands, didn't look promising—something else to worry about. He smiled reassuringly. "We'll talk soon, Russell," he said.

"I hope you won't make any decisions without getting my input first. I worked with Eva a long time. I think I have something valuable to contribute to the discussion."

"I'm sure you do. Like I said, we'll talk."

For a moment, Russell looked ready to press the issue; but after a moment, he said only, "Fine. Whenever it's convenient. Now, let me show you the storeroom."

.   .   .

$\mathscr{F}$or the rest of the day, Frankie and Joan sorted through the stored paintings and sculptures and a stack of drawings they found, some placed neatly
in a large drawer, others framed and intermingled with the oils and water-
colors. When they got hungry, they sent out for tuna sandwiches and drank
black coffee made in the gallery's small kitchen. Joan worked quickly and
efficiently, jotting down notes in her neat decisive hand, patiently explaining
to Frankie what she took to be the merits—or frequently the demerits—of
a particular work. Once he heard her give a little gasp of surprise. "How
could I have forgotten this?" she said. She was referring to a painting of small
squiggles in a pink plane, which Frankie recognized as a Klee. "It used to
hang in our living room when Mother was married to Ned," she said. "Isn't
it beautiful?" she asked, her voice a sigh of ecstasy.

Not wanting to break the mood, Frankie grunted something that could
be taken for assent, then checked the inventory list and confirmed that the
painting had been bought by Payson and so belonged to Frankie, as Miranda's
heir. "How much is it worth?" he asked. When she told him, Frankie whistled. He'd always known that, sitting in the storeroom, gathering dust, was
a fortune; but he'd lost track of how much everything had increased in value
since the time when, numb with grief and anger, he had sat with Eva as she
tried to explain the worth of what he was determined to despise, if only
because she loved it.

$\mathscr{B}$y five-thirty, Joan had seen everything there was to see, and, though
she was still full of the energy of excitement, Frankie had had enough. He
told her she could return for another look the following day and for as many
days thereafter as she liked, but, for today, they were finished. Returning to
the Central Park West apartment, they found Maud there, with Mrs. Ashby,
settling in for another stay since Annabel was again on her way to Europe.
Frankie introduced Joan to Maud and the housekeeper and, though both
were perfectly polite, Frankie could sense that something was up. When his
guest went off to bathe, he walked down the hall to his daughter's room and
knocked. Her voice, calling "Come in," was faint and hurt, and when he
opened her door he saw her lying on her bed, crying. "Honey, what's the
matter?" he asked, crossing the room quickly and dropping to the bed beside her.

Sitting up, Maud fixed him with a stern, suspicious look. "Is Joan your
new girlfriend?"

That was the last thing Frankie had expected to hear. For a moment
surprise kept his mouth shut, then he said, "Joan? No. She's a friend, that's

all." He explained her presence in New York, though not the nature of their relationship. He wasn't up to that.

"You're still going to marry Kelly?"

"Yes."

"You're sure?" said Maud. Her light nine-year-old voice was as stern as a nun's, demanding that he tell the truth.

Frankie wanted to say yes again, unequivocally, but the word got stuck in his throat. He couldn't get it out. Finally, he said, "Things happen, Maud, that we don't always foresee, so I can't promise absolutely. But I can tell you that as of this moment I have every intention of marrying Kelly next December, as planned. Okay?"

Maud considered a moment, then nodded, and said, "I love Kelly."

"So do I," said Frankie, though all he felt then was the need to placate his child.

To put her mind at rest, Frankie phoned Kelly and asked her to join Joan and Maud and himself for dinner; and, since the women's movement had made little impression on Kelly and her girlfriends, who still thought it only natural to sacrifice each other to accommodate the whims of the men in their lives, she agreed immediately to canceling the date she'd made when Frankie had said he'd be busy. They dined at the small French restaurant on Madison Avenue where the waiters knew Kelly and serenely accommodated her search for the perfect table. Throughout the meal, she dominated the conversation with talk of the wedding, and Maud, secure in the glow of Kelly's unshakable self-confidence, added her own excited commentary, while Joan observed the group with interest, listened to the babble of conversation, and commented when required. A successful evening, thought Frankie as he paid the bill; and when Kelly, without a word of complaint, allowed herself to be dropped off at her apartment (she never expected to have Frankie for the night when he had Maud), he was again struck with his good fortune at having found a woman so self-assured (or was it self-involved?—he pushed the thought away) that it never occurred to her to be jealous.

At home, Frankie turned Maud over to Mrs. Ashby, stopped into his room to phone Martha for a report on the day's events, went to his daughter's room to read to her until she dropped off to sleep, and then joined Joan in the library. She had changed into a blue silk robe over matching pajamas. Without makeup, she looked younger, plainer, and a little sad. "A nightcap?" he asked.

"That would be nice. Thanks." Frankie poured them each a brandy, handed her a crystal snifter, then sat on the couch across from her. "What happened to all your books?" She nodded in the direction of the bare shelves.

"Annabel, my ex-wife, she went through here like Sherman through Georgia. I didn't have the heart to start over."

Joan shook her head. "Relationships," she said ruefully. She took a sip of brandy, then said, "I'm living with someone now, you know?" Frankie nodded. Someone had told him, Colette perhaps. "It's been five years," she continued. "We've had our ups and downs, but . . . I think we're going to make it." Then she said, "You do know, I'm a lesbian?"

Frankie shifted uncomfortably, and said, "I'd heard."

"Not from my mother," said Joan dryly. "You'd have thought—considering the life she led—she might have had a more liberal attitude about that, about a lot of things. But she didn't."

"Whatever the sex of your lover, your mother wouldn't have approved," said Frankie. Now that Joan had raised the subject, why hold back? "Nobody was good enough for her children."

"True. But the real issue for her wasn't money, you know, or status, for that matter. It was control."

"She did like that."

"And you weren't controllable. Anyone could see that. You were like Vesuvius, like Etna, ready to erupt ready to bury everything and everyone in your path. And as long as she loved you, Miranda wasn't controllable either."

Frankie heard only one thing. "You think Miranda loved me?"

Joan shot a surprised look at him. "Why else would she have married you?"

"To get away. Escape from Eva. Show Greg Dyer she didn't care anymore." That was what Eva had said, that Miranda had married him on the rebound, because her pride was hurt. Though Frankie had tried hard not to believe them, even now, over twenty years later, Eva's words still reaped their harvest of doubt and pain.

Joan shook her head sadly. "Miranda married you because she loved you."

"Then why—" He stopped. Still it was hard for him to speak about her.

"It was an accident, Frankie." He shook his head. He knew that, without quite being able to accept it. "Miranda was a druggie," continued Joan. "She was fatherless and, in every significant way, motherless. Drugs filled the gap. They comforted her. Maybe in time she could have given them up, as she grew older, more secure. But she never got the chance to try. That's all. And it's very sad. But it's not your fault. Or mine."

Hearing the pain in Joan's voice, Frankie realized for the first time that someone other than himself had struggled with an overwhelming sense of guilt for Miranda's death. Miranda, that beautiful girl, full of golden promise. Miranda, dead at twenty.

"For years," continued Joan, "when I wasn't blaming Mother, or you, I was blaming myself for not loving her more, for not taking better care of her when she was growing up. But now I can see that none of that mattered.

Miranda was enjoying herself that night. She was out with her friends, having a good time. A boat tipped over. What could we have done to prevent that? Nothing. Just as we could have done nothing if she'd been in a plane crash, or run over by a car."

"I know," said Frankie. "I tell myself that, but . . ."

"The guilt never quite goes away."

"No," said Frankie.

"If I had a daughter, I'd take better care of her."

"I try."

Joan smiled. "I can see you do. Maud's a lovely little girl."

"Yes," said Frankie as an image of Hannah's laughing face flashed into his mind.

"I'd like a child," said Joan, again with sadness in her voice. Frankie shot such a surprised look at her that Joan's face lightened and she laughed. "There are ways," and when Frankie shifted uneasily in his chair, she laughed again, and said, "Relax, I wasn't thinking of you. Between Kelly and Maud you have enough on your plate."

And you don't know the half of it, he thought. "You can run away from a lot of people, Joan. Your parents, your lovers, your brothers and sisters; but you can't run away from your child, not if you want to keep your self-respect, you can't. So think about it hard, about your life and how you want it to be, before you make any decisions. Okay?"

"Okay." Joan smiled, put her glass down, and stood, pulling the belt of her robe tighter, and said, "Well, I don't know about you, but I'm exhausted."

Frankie stood, went to her, and kissed her cheek. "Thanks," he said. "For helping me out like this. I appreciate it."

"It's been a pleasure." She crossed to the door, but turned again before opening it. "Miranda loved you, Frankie. I read her diary. I found it when I went to get the things she left in her hotel room. Remember, you asked me to do it? It was a young girl's love, an infatuation. Maybe, if she'd lived, she'd have gotten over it. Maybe it would have turned into something deeper. But she loved you enough to suffer every time she disappointed you, every time she made you unhappy. She loved you the same way you loved her."

"Her diary? Where is it?" Finally, he would be able to read Miranda's mind. Finally, all his questions would be answered. Excitement flooded through him, followed immediately by frustration at having to wait to get his hands on it, and anger that he had not been given it years ago.

"I burned it."

"Burned it?" There was rage in his voice. "Why the fuck did you do that? Who gave you the right?"

"It was her private diary, Frankie."

"*You* read it!"

"And I shouldn't have. There were things in it Miranda never meant anyone else to see. For a long time I was ashamed that I had."

"What else did she say?"

Joan stood by the door, looking like one of those movie heroines prepared to take cyanide rather than talk, looking suddenly very like her mother. "You don't need to know anything else," she said firmly.

"If you're lying to me—"

"I'm not. I swear."

"She loved me."

"Yes," said Joan. She opened the door and went out, leaving Frankie alone. He poured himself another drink. Miranda had loved him. Relaxing into his chair, Frankie sat sipping the brandy, letting his mind play with the idea. Soon he felt a sense of relief, of release. He felt the old wound finally beginning to heal.

$\mathcal{J}$oan spent the next few days at the gallery. On Sunday she had lunch with a friend from Sotheby's, to whom, with Frankie's permission, she showed the Payson collection on Monday. Over dinner that night, this time just the two of them at the Café des Artistes, she gave Frankie her expert opinion. A large number of the works in the storeroom, she told him, belonged to artists (those still living and the estates of the dead) the gallery currently represented. Many among the living were most likely looking for new dealers, and the most successful would be snapped up immediately, taking their work with them when they went. The others would, by necessity or choice, hang on for a while, in the hope that whoever took over the running of the DeWitt Payson would do better for them than Eva had. As for those whose estates the gallery handled, their works (in most cases, anyway) had jumped in value and a hefty commission could be expected from any sales. Eva had not, or at least Joan had found no record of it, bought anything herself, but in the collection (over a hundred works) left by DeWitt Payson to his daughter, there were, in addition to the Klee, a Rothko ("I assume that's the one in your living room," she said), two Klines, a Rhinehart, a Motherwell, three Frankenthalers, a Morris Louis, a de Kooning, and sculptures by Epstein and Nevelson, among others, bought when the artists were young, before they had made names for themselves. The only pieces of real interest to Frankie (aside from the Rothko, and the Morris Louis that was hanging in his hall) were a small oil sketch of a young girl by Picasso and a drawing of a woman in a hat by Matisse.

"You don't, I suppose, want to keep the gallery?" asked Joan.

"If you'll run it," said Frankie.

Pleased by the gesture of good faith, Joan smiled, then shook her head. "I love what I'm doing, Frankie. I really do. Curating suits my temperament. Running a gallery wouldn't. But thanks."

"I knew you'd say no."

"Armand Hammer paid a fortune for Knoedler's."

"I remember. What did your friend say about the private collection?" he asked.

"Sotheby's would be willing to handle a sale."

"There are a few things I want to keep."

"No problem. Just remove them before any formal appraisal is done." They both sat silent for a moment, eyes not meeting, staring into space, watching the end of an era come slowly into view. "You're sure about this?" said Joan finally.

For a moment, Frankie hesitated. Then, he said, "Absolutely. It's time."

*T*he next day, after Joan left for Los Angeles, Frankie stopped by the gallery to tell Russell what he planned adding (why kick a fella when he's down?) that the decision had nothing to do with a lack of confidence in his abilities, just a need Frankie had to put this part of his life behind him. This resolution was not unexpected, and Frankie could see that, though Russell grumbled, his agile mind had already begun to consider how to put the months it would take to tie up loose ends to good use. There were any number of possibilities, many of them, no doubt, far more appealing than staying on as second-in-command to an absentee gallery owner, of limited knowledge and taste.

When he left the gallery, Frankie took with him a small package that one of the staff had wrapped in brown paper. Back in his office, he phoned Hugo Helm, as a courtesy, to tell him his decision, and to offer him first refusal (at the reserve price) of any painting he wanted before it went to Sotheby's. "You can tell me what there is over dinner," said Hugo. He and Rose had again stopped over in New York for a few days on their way to London to see a play Hugo was checking out for a possible run in his theaters. "Nothing I like better than a bargain."

At the end of the day, before returning home, Frankie stopped in to see Martha and Hannah, spent an hour playing with his daughter, then, as he was leaving, handed Martha the small paper-wrapped package he'd brought with him. "For you," he said, and was surprised by her surprise, until he realized (with some embarrassment) that he hadn't given her a gift since she'd stopped working for him.

Curious, Martha tore open the paper, then gasped when she saw what it was. "It's not real!" she said. It was the Matisse drawing.

"Sure it's real," said Frankie. "What do you think, I'd give you a fake?"

"Not a fake, a reproduction. Frankie, I can't accept this."

"Yes, you can," he said stubbornly.

"It must be worth a fortune."

"I have no idea," said Frankie. "It doesn't matter. I want you to have it . . . If you like it, I mean."

"Of course I like it."

"Consider it a thank-you."

"I didn't *do* anything."

"It was your idea to call Joan," who, he told her, was not only handling the arrangements for the auction with Sotheby's, but had undertaken to try to find a buyer for the gallery. "So, you see, it's thanks to you I got this whole mess sorted out."

"Thanks to Joan, you mean."

"Don't worry about Joan," said Frankie, beginning to sound annoyed. "I know how to say thank you to her, too." He was planning to give her the Klee. "Now, will you just take the drawing, for chrissake, and stop making such a big deal out of it?"

She leaned forward awkwardly, kissed his cheek, and said, "Thank you, Frankie." Although she was smiling, there were tears in her eyes.

"I knew it was something you'd like."

"I love it," she said. "I'll treasure it. Always."

*A*fter putting Maud to bed, Frankie showered and changed into a suit for his dinner with Kelly and her parents. He was in the hall, waiting for the elevator when Mrs. Ashby opened the door and called to him, a note of urgency in her voice. "Your sister's on the phone. She said it's important."

He raced back inside, to the library, and picked up the receiver. "What is it?" he said, too frightened to be polite. As soon as Angela spoke his name, he knew whatever had happened was terrible. "Frankie, it's Pop." He could hear how hard she was trying not to cry. "He had a heart attack. Anyway, we think he did. Ma called the paramedics. He's at Saint Jo's. He's still alive, but, oh, Frankie, it doesn't look good."

"I'll get there as soon as I can," he said, and hung up without saying good-bye. As he headed for the door again, he saw Mrs. Ashby, and her anxious face recalled him to the world existing outside the cyclone of fear enclosing him. He remembered he'd made plans that now had to be broken. "Would you call Kelly for me?" he asked. "Tell her I can't make it tonight. Tell her it's my father. Tell her I'll call her as soon as I can."

"I hope everything will be all right," said Mrs. Ashby, with regained composure.

"I hope so. I don't know when I'll get back. Explain to Maud, would you? if she wakes up and I'm not here."

Mrs. Ashby assured him that she would take care of everything, and Frankie hurried away, not bothering with the elevator, taking the stairs. At the garage around the corner where he kept his car, he waited impatiently for the attendant to bring it to him, then drove like a taxi driver across town, ignoring yellow lights, jumping traffic lanes, fiddling with the dials of the radio past the sounds of Kim Carnes, Sheena Easton, the Moody Blues, searching for something soothing, something classical, stopping when he heard the sound of Schubert. Through the Midtown Tunnel, along the expressway to Long Island, the music changed from Schubert to Smetana to Brahms. In the hospital lobby, the desk attendant directed him to the room where his family was waiting, and he found them sitting side by side, Angela's arm around Dolly's shoulder, Dolly weeping copiously. Denny, sitting forlornly in a nearby chair, stood as Frankie entered, his face bleak with worry. "How is he?" asked Frankie, as he kissed his mother and sister.

"He's still in the emergency room," said Angela. "They're still working on him."

When he shook his hand, Denny said softly, "It's bad . . ."

Surrounded by doctors and hospital staff, Sal died at eleven-thirty that night while his family sat waiting in another room. They were allowed to say good-bye to him, what was left of him, with Dolly on the verge of collapse and Angela weeping. Frankie touched his father's hand, and, bending over, kissed his forehead. He was still warm. Frankie felt a surge of pure love, unlike anything he'd ever experienced for his father before, and his eyes filled with tears of sorrow, and of regret for all the good thoughts left unspoken, the good deeds left undone. Denny, his own eyes wet, finally ushered them all from the room. They took Dolly home, found some sleeping pills in a bottle in the medicine chest in the bathroom, gave her one, and put her to bed. Angela insisted on staying the night.

"We have to start calling people," she said. There were relatives to be notified, and a lifetime of friends.

"Tomorrow," said Denny. After picking up the few things he and Angela needed from their house, he was returning to spend the night with the women. "We'll take care of everything tomorrow."

"I'll be back first thing in the morning," said Frankie. Though he knew no purpose would be served by his staying and what little hope of sleep he had would completely vanish if he attempted to spend the night in his old room, in his narrow bed, he was reluctant to leave. Finally, he kissed Angela, hugged Denny, got into his car, and headed back to the city. As he neared his apartment, instead of turning into the street leading to his garage, he continued west, until he saw a parking space in front of Martha's apartment. Without thinking, he did a U-turn at the corner, pulled into the space, then got out, hurried up the steps, and rang Martha's bell once, twice. It seemed an eternity before he heard her sleepy voice asking who it was.

By the time he got upstairs, Martha had thrown a robe on over her night-gown, but her hair was uncombed, and a smudge of mascara that had escaped the makeup remover lay under her left eye. She seemed more worried than annoyed. "What's happened?" she asked as she stepped aside to let him in. He told her and she said, "Oh, Frankie, I'm sorry. I know how much you loved him." Instead of inquiring why he'd felt it necessary to tell *her* at this early hour of the morning, she said, "Can I get you something? Coffee? A drink? Have you had anything to eat?" She made him a turkey sandwich, which he washed down with a glass of scotch. He felt dazed. The world he'd inhabited his whole life had altered drastically, in a moment, in a failed heart-beat; and this new world seemed foreign, unreal. He asked for another scotch, then relaxed into the cushions of the couch, and closed his eyes. Tomorrow he would ask himself what instinct had led him to Martha, but for the mo-ment all he felt was the necessity of being there. As she stooped to take away the plates with the remnants of his hasty meal, he opened his eyes, took her hand, and pulled her down next to him. Without meaning to, he began to cry. She put her arms around him. "Oh, Frankie," she murmured as he clung to her. Caught in the emotion of the moment, he didn't think about Amy Colvington, or the night after her funeral when Hannah had been conceived. If he had, Frankie might have dried his tears, thanked Martha for the food, and gone. He thought of nothing but his father and felt, unquestioningly, that Martha was his only refuge from sorrow, his only comfort. So he held her, and, when she finally stirred, he said, "Don't send me home, please."

She was silent for a moment; then she said, "I won't. Go inside. Lie down. You need to sleep."

He followed her into the bedroom, stripped down to his shorts, and got into the bed. "Don't go," he begged as he saw her about to leave the room.

Martha hesitated, then she returned to the bed, and lay down beside him, on top of the covers. He turned toward her and pulled her into his arms. "Thank you," he murmured, and drifted off to sleep.

She lay still, hardly breathing, until she too fell asleep. To be awakened later, much later, by someone touching her breast, kissing her throat. Frankie was lying next to her on top of the covers, one leg thrown over hers. "Frankie," she said aloud, just before his mouth reached hers.

He had awakened and found her too far away. He needed her closer, as close as he could get. "Oh, Martha," he said, "please. I need you." Her arms went around him, her mouth opened for his tongue, her legs spread to welcome his hand. "Oh, Martha," he said again as he plunged into forgetfulness. "Oh, Sweetheart."

Chapter 32

"You're not about to sneak out, are you?" asked Martha.

It was about five in the morning and Frankie was standing in the dark, pulling on his pants, his emotions seesawing between grief and guilt. He felt like a complete shit. "No," he said, though, until she spoke, he hadn't decided whether to wake her to say good-bye or leave without facing the music. Romantic or martial, he didn't want to hear it. "No. I wouldn't do that. I was going to wake you."

"Good," she said, sitting up and turning on the light.

Her hair was a tangled mess. There were dark circles under her eyes. Along her right cheek ran a crease left by her pillow. She looked awful. Pushing aside the covers, she reached for her robe and slipped into it, giving Frankie a fleeting impression of a slender but rounded female body. It occurred to him that he'd never seen her naked.

"Would you like some coffee before you go?" she asked. "Some breakfast?"

"No, thanks. I want to get home before Maud gets up." Somehow he couldn't quite meet her eyes. She nodded and left the room. While Frankie finished dressing, he could hear, from the bathroom, the faint sounds of water running, a toilet flushing, the medicine chest opening and closing. He supposed he'd often heard those same sounds while visiting, but at this hour of the morning, in these circumstances, they had an intimacy he found disturbing. So did being in Martha's rumpled bedroom. He'd seen it only once before, shortly after she'd moved in, when she'd shown him proudly around the apartment. The pine bed, the night tables, the chests of drawers she had bought in Vermont one summer when on vacation with her parents. A quilt, acquired during a trip to Pennsylvania to visit a girlfriend, served as a spread. Home-made curtains in a heavy cream cotton hung on the windows. There was a pine trunk, a rocking chair, and on the walls framed posters of Matisse paintings (a view from a window of some French seacoast town, a recumbent Odalisque wrapped in transparent lace). There were books everywhere (novels, biographies, books about parenting, sewing, current events) and photographs on every surface, mostly of Hannah, one of Martha in ski gear, another of her parents. None were of him. It was an ordinary room, a comfortable room, and one Frankie felt he had absolutely no right to be in. Hurriedly, he found his jacket and put it on, then went into Hannah's bedroom for a quick look at his sleeping daughter. That too he found unsettling, and heartbreakingly sad that he should feel so ill at ease. He closed the door softly and turned, just as Martha emerged from the bathroom with a fresh-scrubbed face and hair neatly pulled back in a ponytail. She looked very young. "Hannah's still asleep," he said. Then, forcing a smile, he added, "You look just the way you did the day I hired you."

"I wish," she said, smiling in return. She walked with him to the front door and they stood together awkwardly for a moment, neither able to decide just how to say good-bye. "When's the funeral?" she asked, finally.

"I'm not sure. Thursday, I suppose. I'll let you know." She gave him an odd look, and Frankie realized that she'd asked only because she couldn't think of anything else to say, while he, for reasons he had no wish, or time, to explore, suddenly wanted her there, at the funeral. It would be a comfort, he thought. "You'll come, won't you?"

"I don't think that's such a good idea," she said, her voice wary.

"It'll be all right," he urged. Why shouldn't it be? The few people who knew she was anything more to him than a former secretary could be relied on to say nothing.

"When you know the day, we'll talk about it."

"There's nothing to talk about," he said stubbornly.

"You'd better get going," she said, forestalling an argument.

He nodded, but, instead of opening the door, he said, "Martha . . ." and then stopped, not knowing what to say next.

"I'm okay with this, Frankie," she said. "Really. You don't have to worry. We're friends, right?"

"Right," he said. He puts his arms around her and hugged. "Thanks."

For a brief moment, she returned the hug. "I am sorry about your father," she said; then she pulled away and opened the door. "Off you go."

He leaned forward and kissed her lightly on the cheek. "I'll call you."

Martha nodded. " 'Bye," she said, and closed the door.

With Dolly too dazed by grief in those first hours to make any coherent decisions, it was left to Frankie and Angela to arrange the details of the funeral. Together, they notified family and friends, chose the funeral home, the mahogany casket, the simple cross with lilies for the memorial card, the hymns for the mass. Occasionally, their mother would emerge from her cocoon to express a preference: Sal should wear his brand new pinstripe suit instead of last year's navy one and hold Dolly's old black rosary, the one that Frankie's gift had replaced. But, for the most part, she would just nod her agreement to anything they suggested.

Unlike the funerals of Frankie's youth that had gone on for close to a week, from midmorning to late night, in an orgy of grief, his father's wake would last just two days, with two hours for viewing in the afternoon, and the same in the evening. Mass cards and donations to charities were requested in place of flowers, though many, still convinced of the superiority of the old ways, sent large wreaths and floral displays, so that the air in the parlor remained heavy with the sweet scent of death. On a black-draped gurney with a prie-dieu running its length rested the half-open coffin, a blanket of roses covering its lower end. In it, Salvatore Ferraro lay painted and cold, his broad, capable hands crossed on his chest, a rosary twined through his thick fingers. A Madame Tussaud's version of his father, Frankie thought, kneeling to pray. As in a salon arranged for a musical evening, straight-backed chairs faced the coffin and proceeded in neat rows to the back of the room. Comfortable sofas and tables topped by porcelain lamps ran along walls hung with landscape oils of uncertain origin. In a velvet armchair in the front, flanked usually by Angela, sat Dolly, in black. Grief came in waves for her, too, so that fits of weeping alternated with faint smiles and thank-yous mustered for the friends and relatives who stood before her to offer condolences. Not since her wedding had she been so much the center of attention.

As Frankie paced, talked to Vic, to his uncles, to his cousins, to friends of his father's, to Dan (down from Boston for the funeral), he felt often like a host at a macabre party. He felt as if the whole idea of a wake was medieval, barbarous. But, then again, he felt he needed to see Sal's body lying so still, so alien from the father he'd respected, admired, been ashamed of, and ultimately, above all, loved; he needed it to help him grow accustomed to the loss, to the idea that he would never again see his father, talk to him, fight with him; he needed it, finally, to help him make the transition into a world where he, Frankie, was the man of the family.

On the first night of the wake, Kelly and her parents came for an hour, their long black limousine occasioning much comment as it pulled into the funeral home's parking lot. Frankie greeted them in the hall. Though he was pleased, *touched,* that they had come, for the first time since he'd met the Helms, Frankie didn't have to stifle a persistent and guilty wish that Hugo were his father. Just then, the only father Frankie wanted was lying dead in the other room.

The Helms sat with Dolly for a while, then mingled with the rest of the family, talking to everyone, alternating sympathy for Sal with praise for Frankie, whom, they said, they already considered a member of their family. Kelly remained in the hall, apologizing tearfully for not being able to go into the parlor. She would faint, she said, or throw up, or do something equally awful. The sympathetic looks being cast her way by Dennis, Angela's redheaded twenty-six-year old son, reminded Frankie that he couldn't just leave her there, as he'd been about to do. Sitting next to her on the sofa, he slipped a comforting arm around her shoulder and assured her that he understood, that her coming had been enough, that he himself often considered the whole practice of wakes primitive, all the while resenting being called upon to comfort her when he was, after all, the grieving party. Guiltily, he pushed the resentment away. He was upset, and overreacting. Kelly was young. She would change.

The next afternoon, watching how Maud behaved, Frankie wondered about that optimistic assessment. From the moment she'd learned of Sal's death, Maud had been disturbed and worried and full of questions. When she understood there was to be a wake, and what that was, she asked if she could go. Wanting to spare her what he had experienced as a child, at first he resisted the idea. When Maud persisted, he phoned Martha to get her opinion. "She wants to say good-bye to her grandfather, Frankie. I think you should let her," Martha had said, adding quickly, "if her mother agrees." But Annabel was somewhere in Europe, and he didn't consider it necessary to track her down to get an okay. Instead, he consulted Mrs. Ashby, who seemed to find it only proper that Maud "pay her last respects" to a member of her immediate family. So, on the last afternoon of the wake, he had a driver bring his daughter directly from school to the funeral home. Maria noticed the town car arriving and called Frankie away from a conversation with one of the FCI managers and Tom, who had recently been promoted to corporate vice president. Excusing himself, Frankie went to greet his daughter, who looked, he thought, more apprehensive than frightened, as if, unfamiliar with the protocol of wakes, she was worried she might do something embarrassingly wrong. He kissed her, and said, "We'll just go in and kneel down and say a prayer for Grandpa. He looks different," he warned.

"Like he's sleeping?" she asked.

Frankie shook his head. "No," he said. "Your grandpa is gone. What's left is more like a statue that looks like him." He took Maud's hand and led her inside and up to the coffin. They knelt and Maud studied her grandfather solemnly, then closed her eyes. Her lips moved as she said a prayer. When she opened her eyes again, Frankie took her hand and led her to Dolly, sending a prayer of his own heavenward that his mother would manage not to get hysterical at the sight of her granddaughter. (There was no telling what would set her off.) But, as always, what was of paramount importance to her was not upsetting the children, and she managed to greet Maud with a smile, then introduce her proudly to a second cousin who had come from Philadelphia for the wake. As quickly as he could, Frankie took Maud out to the hall, but instead of sending her back to the city with the driver as he'd planned, he left her to be entertained by her cousin Sean, Angela's younger son, on whom she'd had a crush for most of her nine years. And when the afternoon visiting hours came to end, and Frankie, with Dan seated beside him, drove the short distance to his parents' home, what he heard coming from the back of the car, rather than silences broken by sighs, was Maud babbling naturally about school, and Dolly responding as if genuinely interested. Moved by the power his daughter had to heal, Frankie was sorry that he'd not agreed to letting her see Dolly sooner.

Every day between the afternoon and evening sessions, his aunts conjured, as if by magic, meals of pasta, lemon chicken, veal cutlets, eggplant parmigiana, overcooked vegetables, green salads, for family members and friends who had driven long distances to attend the wake. Seated at the dining table, Maud listened wide-eyed to the boisterous conversation. Everyone had some reminiscence, some funny anecdote to tell about Sal; even Dolly laughed and contributed a story or two of her own. What did his daughter make of it all? wondered Frankie. Did this seem any different to her than the family parties she was used to, the gatherings for Christmas and Easter, the Sunday dinners? Did she even notice, as he did, as everyone else at the table did, that Sal was missing?

After dinner, Maud didn't want to leave with the driver and went home finally only because Frankie promised she could attend the funeral mass in the morning. But when he looked in on her later (after the evening viewing hours, the drive back to the city, the quick drink at the Stanhope where Dan had insisted on staying), Frankie found her still awake. Seeing him, she began to cry. "I miss Grandpa," she said.

"Yes, I know. We all do," he said, and stayed with her until she fell asleep.

As they were getting ready to leave for the funeral in the morning, the phone rang. It was Kelly. Her parents had left for London, and she wasn't feeling well, she said. She thought it was a virus. She hoped he didn't mind, but she really couldn't go with him. She was very, very sorry. Frankie assured her again that he understood. And then, he did. Not only was Kelly spoiled, with an undeveloped sense of responsibility, but she would never voluntarily do anything that caused her a moment of inconvenience, a millisecond of unpleasantness. The initial annoyance caused by this insight quickly gave way to relief. At least he wouldn't have to spend the day looking after her.

In the drive cross-town, through the heavy traffic, Maud sat quietly beside Frankie in the car, probably paying as little attention as he was to the first of the day's bad news on *Morning Edition*. As they traveled the expressway, from time to time she would sigh, and Frankie would ask if she was too hot or too cold; that settled, they would relapse into silence. Without argument, she agreed to wait in the hall of the funeral home with Maria and her children while Frankie joined the others for the final awful moments in the parlor, the last prayers, the final kiss, the closing of the coffin.

"Let perpetual light shine upon him," said the funeral director. "May he rest in peace."

Frankie helped his mother from her seat, and supported her as she walked to the coffin to say good-bye. For one awful moment, he thought she was going to throw herself across his father's dead body and wail. He'd seen that happen, when he was a child. But Dolly only stooped and kissed Sal's cheek. She touched his hand, and whispered, "I won't be long," which is what Sal used to say to her when she went up before him to bed. Then, as she tried to linger, Vic took her arm, and said, "Come on, Aunt Dolly. That's enough." Frankie kissed his father's cold forehead, and said, " 'Bye, Pop," then turned to take his mother's other arm, leaving Denny to cope with Angela, who had finally, after days of keeping hold of herself, begun weeping in soft violent sobs.

When they arrived at the church, Denny took the women inside, while Frankie, his nephews, Vic, and two cousins of Sal's took their places beside the coffin, lifted and carried it up the stairs, placed it on the black-draped gurney, and escorted it down the aisle. He thought he was oblivious to everything and everyone, but still he noticed Hannah, who smiled at him, while Martha, holding her, remained pale faced and somber, barely nodding in acknowledgment of his look. After a conversation that at any other time would have turned into a full-fledged argument, she'd agreed to come to the mass, but when he'd offered her a car and driver she'd refused, insisting she would make her own arrangements. What arrangements? he'd wondered, thinking that never in his entire life had he met such a stubborn woman. Next to her now stood Colette and her husband. They had all come together, Frankie realized. In the pew behind them stood Dan. He was glad that they were there, that they'd cared enough to make the effort. Their presence comforted him; their affection compensated, at least a little, for the wealth of love Sal had taken away with him at his death.

The mass now was in English, of which Frankie didn't entirely approve. Yet he liked hearing his nephews read the lessons; and, as he stood at the lectern delivering the eulogy, looking out over the crowded church, his eyes shifting from his mother to Maud, to his sister and Denny, to Martha and Hannah, over the entire congregation, he was glad to be able to express aloud his feelings for his father, something he regretted now never having been able to do to his face. "He was a good man," he said. "Opinionated, stubborn, but decent, hardworking, and reliable. More than anything in the world, he loved his family, and we returned that love." He told anecdotes that caused ripples of laughter to flow through the crowd. "I disagreed with him often," said Frankie in conclusion. "I fought with him, but I respected him always and I loved him. I'll miss him all the rest of my life." Later, he watched the others file up the aisle to take Communion and wanted to join them, but couldn't. He was in a state of mortal sin, a state he didn't entirely believe in, yet wasn't prepared to risk the wrath of God to try to disprove. His father would have been in the same state, thought Frankie with grim humor, except that the hospital chaplain had made it to his bedside before Sal had breathed his last. Would he have the same good fortune? Was there a hell and would he burn in it? he wondered, as he sat listening to the tenor sing "Panis Angelicus." If he were to die tomorrow, suddenly, like his father (men his own age did) . . . it was a terrifying thought, and not just because of the damnation that might await him. His life wasn't in order. In fact, it was a mess. Maud would be taken care of, but Hannah? Why hadn't he included Hannah in his will? Why hadn't he even *thought* of it? What kind of self-centered *prick* was he? Then the priest began the closing prayers, and Frankie pulled his mind back to the service and his father, a good father, he thought with another twinge of conscience, who never would have let a child of his go unprovided for.

After the pallbearers returned the coffin to the hearse, Frankie joined his mother and sister in the informal receiving line on the steps, a painful and, perhaps for Dolly, a comforting duty to accept the ritual sympathy of friends and family. Dan pulled him into a bear hug, then enfolded Dolly in his arms, murmuring words of sympathy as she wept for Sal's loss and Dan's kindness in being there. When Colette and her husband drew near, a reluctant Martha trailing in their wake, Hannah in her arms, Frankie greeted them, then turned to his mother, and said, "You remember Colette and Jake, don't you Ma? And Martha? She used to work for me."

"Yes," said his mother, "Yes, I do. Martha," she repeated. "Thank you for coming, dear. Is this your daughter?"

"Yes," said Martha.

"She's beautiful."

"I'm so sorry for your loss," said Martha, taking Dolly's hand briefly.

"Frankie," said the Hannah, "I got new shoes." She wriggled to show him.

"Very pretty," said Frankie, leaning forward to kiss the little girl's cheek. Then he smiled at Martha, and said, "Thank you."

She nodded, then hurried on, heading unintentionally toward Vic, standing with his arms around his father who seemed to be in a state of shock. Aware of movement in his peripheral vision, Vic looked up to find himself staring directly at Martha. Keeping his face carefully neutral, Vic nodded. Martha acknowledged him with a faint smile, which she then turned on Maria, who was standing next to her husband with her three children and Maud. Maria stared at the mother and child for a moment, then turned to Frankie, her look of suspicion followed quickly by one of outrage. Her eyes grew cold, and she turned away again. Nothing much ever got past Maria. Frankie shrugged, then an idea seized him. Without stopping to ponder its origin or consequences, he walked over to the group, took Maud's hand, and pulled her aside. "Would you like to ride back to the city with Colette?" he asked. "She can take you home."

"I want to stay with you," said Maud.

"I told you," said Frankie. "You can't come to the cemetery. So either it's go home or wait at Grandma's for hours with nothing to do." (That wasn't quite true. She would have Maria and Vic's girls to play with.) Maud hesitated, but finally she agreed to go. Frankie swung her up in his arms and hurried with her across the parking lot to where Jake was backing his Mercedes out of its space. He saw Frankie and stopped. Rolling down his window, he said, "What's up?"

"Will you give Maud a ride home?" he asked.

Colette's surprise turned instantly to pleasure. "We'll take her out to lunch first, if that's all right with you?" she said.

"Thanks," said Frankie, opening the rear door where Martha was sitting on the far side, Hannah beside her.

"This isn't fair, Frankie," said Martha.

"Take care of her for me, will you?" he said, ignoring her protest. He didn't quite understand what he was doing or why. He just knew it was important to him. "I'll see you at home, honey," he said to Maud, and kissed her. Then he leaned across her and kissed Hannah as well before closing the door. Waving, he watched the car pull out of the lot; then, walking back, he passed Dan, who was heading for his Porsche.

"Sometimes you should try thinking before you act," he said.

"Maria knows."

"Hannah looks just like you. Be grateful your mother and Angela were too out of it to notice."

Not knowing what to say to that, Frankie shrugged. "Thanks for coming."

He hugged Dan again, and then moved quickly to rejoin his family. His worst fear had come true. Someone had recognized Hannah as his own. And yet, instead of resentment or worry, instead of guilt or remorse, all Frankie felt at that moment was relief. Something was over. Something was beginning. He didn't know what. But he could figure that out later. Now what he had to do was bury his father.

Chapter 33

The sense of elation Frankie felt watching Maud drive away with Martha and Hannah soon gave way to a vague feeling of apprehension, not altogether explained by Maria's stony disapproval, following him all day like a guilty conscience. If that was the worst, well, he could live with it. Maria wouldn't say anything to anyone but Vic, or to himself, if she managed to get him alone, which she wouldn't (Frankie intended to stay well out of her way for a while). But what if someone else had spotted the resemblance?

Worn out, wrung out, needing to escape the barrage of emotions that had assaulted him all week, Frankie got into bed that night desperate for sleep, but the pillow-top mattress he lay on seemed only marginally more comfortable than a bed of nails. His body could find no comfortable position, and his mind was prey first to a jumble of disturbing thoughts, his fears about Martha and Hannah jostling with worry about his mother, and then, overwhelmingly, with grief. The pain that he'd felt while standing at his father's grave came rampaging back, like some mythological beast intent on devouring his guts. He didn't try to fight it. He gave in, letting it have its way with him, until, what seemed hours later, nothing was left but a void, into which he sank in a dreamless stupor.

Morning came quickly. Looking haggard, his skin bleached of color except for the purple shadows under his dark eyes, Frankie sat in his kitchen, eating the oatmeal prepared by an unusually solicitous Mrs. Ashby. For once, he was grateful that his solemn little daughter was not inclined to babble. In answer to his questions, Maud offered only grudging responses. Yes, they had all stopped for lunch on the way home; yes, she had eaten, a grilled-cheese sandwich; Colette had insisted on buying her a doll, though she was too old for that sort of thing. It was a pretty doll, she conceded, briefly looking pleased. She didn't mention Martha or Hannah and neither did Frankie. It wasn't until they were in the taxi on the way to her school that Maud got around to mentioning what was really on her mind: Was he going to die? Was Mommy? Yes, Frankie told her. Someday. But not for a long, long time.

When he got to the office, Frankie called Martha, to get her version of yesterday's ride. "Maud's a sweet little girl," she said. "Well mannered, and so pretty."

Instead of pleased with the compliment, Frankie felt disappointed, as if he'd hoped for something more, though he couldn't imagine what. He considered remarking on the resemblance between the two girls, or telling her about Maria, but then thought better of it. There was a silence, and Frankie knew that Martha was searching for a polite but firm way to demand that, in future, he respect her wishes to keep their personal lives separate, except, of course, for Hannah. Not in the mood for that discussion, he said, "It was a helluva day. And I hardly slept at all last night. I'm worn out."

He could almost hear her gears shift. Finally, her voice full of sympathy, she said, "You have to give yourself time, Frankie. But I guess I don't have to tell you that."

Except for being impossibly stubborn, she was a genuinely nice person, and, briefly, Frankie felt remorse for so blatantly trying to manipulate her. But it wasn't really a manipulation, he told himself. He wanted her sympathy; he needed it. There was nothing fake about his pain. "I didn't know I loved him that much," he said.

"Feelings are always a little confused, aren't they? Love, anger, resentment, everything all mixed up together."

"Like one minute you're crazy about someone and the next you'd like to murder them?"

"Yes," agreed Martha, laughing "You see it with children all the time. First they're all over you, wanting a hug. The next thing you know they're screaming, 'I hate you.' Sometimes I think it's only when someone dies, when they're gone forever—maybe because then they can't make any more demands on us—we let ourselves love them completely. And even then, there's usually a little guilt mixed in."

There was nothing confused about his feelings for his daughters; he knew that for certain. "You love Hannah completely," he said.

"Oh, I do. I'm head over heels in love with her. But there are moments, and pretty often too, when I'm angry, when I resent her for taking up so much space in my life, and that frightens me. I think I'm a terrible person, an awful mother."

He'd never seen that side of her; but he could imagine it was there; she was, after all, only human. "You're a wonderful mother."

"I try."

Face it, he thought, there are times you'd give anything to lose all the baggage (the wives, the kids, the business, the family), times when you'd like nothing better than to be an orphan, a beach bum, earning just enough to live, taking each day as it comes. Yes, there were those times. Like Martha said, often. But never for long. Deep down, he cherished his obligations, his responsibilities. How he met them was how he measured himself against his father and his uncles, how he defined himself as a man.

"And I think I succeed more often than I fail," continued Martha. "So do you, Frankie. You were a good son. You don't have to have any regrets about that."

Putting down the phone, Frankie sat at his desk, thinking about what Martha had said, thinking about his father. Sal hadn't always understood or approved of his son's actions, but then his viewpoint had been narrow, conservative, *bigoted,* not to beat around the bush. He'd had the limitations of a man of his age and class. And Frankie had never seen it as his duty to turn into a carbon copy of his father. He'd tried to be different, hoped to be better, and, if he hadn't succeeded, if he'd come up against his own limitations, at least he had made the effort, and had done it without being uncaring, or disrespectful. Sal had had his love and, ultimately, Frankie had earned Sal's respect. Yes, he'd been a good son.

And, over the next few months, Frankie went on being one to Dolly, spending almost as much time with her as Angela did. He helped her sort through Sal's clothes, dispose of his effects, implement his will, organize her finances. Dolly had never paid a bill in her life, and, after spending several frustrating hours trying to teach her how to do it, Frankie gave up and transferred her billing address to his accountant's office, leaving her with only a personal checkbook and small petty cash account. He was fairly certain that she could keep good enough records to avoid bouncing checks. After all, she'd managed a household for close to fifty years, hadn't she?

For the moment, agreed Angela and Frankie, they wouldn't try to talk Dolly into moving. Later, if and when the house got to be too much for her to deal with, then they would talk about selling it. Meanwhile, they insisted that she spend the weekends with one of them. Once, at the height of the summer, Frankie even took her to the Cape. She liked the attention, but hated the disruption. She was tired, she pleaded. She wanted to stay home. Neither of her children would listen to her.

Depending on his schedule, Frankie sometimes picked Dolly up, sometimes sent a driver for her. He would take her to movies (if he could find one with a G rating); to the theater to see *Crimes of the Heart* (which she thought depressing) and *Sister Mary Ignatius Explains It All for You* (which she found sacrilegious); to dinner at pretty restaurants (the Russian Tearoom, the Tavern on the Green) with Maud if she was staying with him, since she seemed to distract her grandmother more effectively than anything else. Twice he invited Kelly to join them, but, however hard she tried, and she did try, she couldn't hide her boredom. She strained to take part in the conversation, but could rarely think of anything to contribute, and who could blame her since most of it revolved around household problems she had no experience of, and family members she didn't know? She fidgeted. She fixed her makeup. Frankie found himself charged with keeping both his mother and Kelly entertained, two irreconcilable tasks.

"Your mother's such a darling woman. I just love her," Kelly said to him shortly after the second strained meal.

Perhaps she meant it, since boredom and affection aren't irreconcilable, at least not where family is concerned. "I'm glad," said Frankie, preferring polite indifference to Annabel's active disdain. He didn't, however, ask Kelly again to join them, nor did she press to be included in his plans. She understandably preferred time spent with her friends to dull evenings passed with his mother. When he could, ignoring the fatigue he suddenly felt trying to keep up with Kelly's boundless energy and active social agenda, Frankie joined her, accompanying her to Tramps and Trax, to Cachaca and Zinno, often enough for his neglect not to become a major issue, though she did complain about his refusal to go with her to East Hampton or Martha's Vineyard on the weekends. Soon, they were seeing each other less frequently than before their engagement, though both proceeded on the unconscious assumption that after their marriage, when they would of necessity be together every day (choice no longer having anything to do with the matter), a shared life would breed shared interests.

In addition to Dolly and Kelly, Frankie had to find time for Hannah (now included in the will his surprised lawyer had just redrawn) and Maud, except for the three weeks in August she spent with her mother at Castle Melton. Never had Frankie been busier than that summer after his father's death, juggling the demands of his personal life with his business responsibilities. Keeping the Ferraro Clubs operating in the black in the middle of a recession was no easy feat, and Frankie was, as well, negotiating with Russell Schneider, who had put together a financial package that would enable him to buy the gallery. There was also a problem concerning the authenticity of one of the paintings destined for the Sotheby's sale. With so much already on his plate, he knew he ought to get rid of the business from which Sal had never been able to retire (thereby, in all probability, shortening his life). But Frankie, even when chest pains forced an emergency visit to his internist (the diagnosis was indigestion), couldn't bring himself to sell it. Reacting to a chance comment from Martha about the booming market in exercise gear, he decided instead to use the factory to produce sportswear to sell in boutiques in his clubs, and expand from there into specialty and department stores if the line were successful. For that he needed to find clothes designers, fabric designers, and fabric manufacturers to supply him.

Frankie couldn't remember a time when he'd had less sleep (no more than four or five hours a night) or felt more stressed, not even during his divorce, which is why, when Annabel asked to see him soon after her return from England, he tried to avoid meeting her, insisting that they could discuss on the phone whatever it was she considered so important. "I want to *see* you, Francis," she insisted. "It won't take long, I promise. And I won't be difficult." Neither seemed a promise Annabel was likely to keep, but Frankie, knowing he would get no peace until he did, agreed to meet her that night in the Edwardian Room at the Plaza.

When Frankie arrived, exactly on time, Annabel was already waiting, seated at one of the window tables with a view of the lighted lamps and horse-drawn carriages that lined the perimeter of Central Park. She looked stunning, he conceded grudgingly, in a purple suede dress, a silver choker set with amethysts encircling her slender neck, her long blond hair arranged in an intricate upsweep that showed off the amethyst earrings he'd given her one anniversary. She must have had a face lift. He was sure she had fewer wrinkles on that fine English skin than the last time he'd seen her. As he sat, he noticed something else, a large diamond on the ring finger of her left hand. "You look great," he said as he took his seat opposite her, happily aware that he no longer found her at all sexually attractive. Whatever the spell she had cast on him, it was broken.

She smiled. "A compliment. Why, thank you. One good turn deserves another. So do you," she went on, after surveying and finding no fault with his new single-breasted pinstripe suit. Then her smile faded. "Francis, about your father, I'm sorry. Truly sorry. I was fond of him, you know." She had sent a huge floral arrangement to the funeral home and a polite little sympathy note to him at the apartment.

"You could have fooled me."

"No, I was," she said. "He disapproved of me so, it rather got my back up. But, well, he was quite a man."

Impervious to her charm, resistant to her bullying, unmoved by flattery or airs—quite a man, thought Frankie. "Yes, he was. But it wasn't my father you wanted to talk to me about."

"Let's order first," said Annabel. Through cocktails and appetizers, she kept up a steady stream of small talk, about Maud, about her summer in England, about a weekend at a house party with the Burdens. "Flora's getting divorced," she told him.

"I'm sorry to hear that," said Frankie. "I liked Jeremy." He was a literary agent, a working-class lad who'd made his way to the top of London's intellectual ladder, representing authors who regularly appeared on the short lists for the Booker and Whitbread awards and frequently walked away with one or the other.

Annabel shrugged. "She married him on the rebound," she said. "When she realized she couldn't have you." To stop the ritual denial Frankie was about to issue, Annabel held up her hand. "Now, don't play shy."

"She may have had a crush on me. Briefly," said Frankie.

"But more than just *you*," said Annabel. "Flora wanted a husband. And Jeremy wanted a wife with connections. They were happy enough for a while. And now . . ." She shrugged again. "They've realized they don't suit. They'll be much happier apart."

"Like so many."

"Did you ever love me?" asked Annabel.

"I thought I did," said Frankie.

"Yes, so did I." Frankie wasn't sure whether Annabel was referring to his feelings for her, or hers for him, but, after all, what did it matter? The waiter arrived with their main course and, when he left, she took a sip of the 1968 Chateau Lafitte Frankie had ordered, and said, "Lovely wine." And then, not pausing for breath, she continued, "I'm getting married, Francis. That's what I wanted to see you about."

Forewarned by the rock on her finger, Frankie felt no surprise, only relief to have his suspicion confirmed. "Congratulations," he said. "When's the happy day?"

"We haven't set a date yet."

His spirits plummeted again. Despite the decree *nisi* tucked away in the safe deposit box in his bank, as long as Annabel didn't belong to someone else she continued to belong to him. On some deep, atavistic level, she remained his responsibility. "Why not?" He could hear the belligerence in his voice.

Instead of answering his question, she said, "Don't you have any curiosity at all about who it is I'm marrying?"

"Certainly," he said. It was not of paramount importance, but yes, now that she mentioned it, he was curious. "Who is it?"

"No one you would know," she said, her voice colored by the faintest whiff of snobbery. Not long ago, a comment like that would have ended in a battle capable of reducing the Edwardian Room to ruins. Now Frankie merely smiled inquisitively. (It was amazing what a little age and self-control could accomplish.) "I meant, know *personally*," continued Annabel. "His name is Richard Gaynor."

"The Australian?"

"Yes," said Annabel. Gaynor was a real estate tycoon, a multinational mover with projects in development in Australia, Canada, England, India, the United States. He was almost, if not so solidly, as rich as Rupert Murdoch, as rich as Annabel needed a husband to be. Frankie remembered reading that he'd recently divorced his wife of thirty years. They had three grown sons, all of whom worked for their father. "I met him with the Burdens. He was one of their guests at Ascot. Flora was after him," continued Annabel. "Hordes of women were. But, well, it was no contest really."

"No," said Frankie. "When you make up your mind, it never is." Lucky Flora. Gaynor had a reputation for being brutal in both his business and personal lives. He deserved someone like Annabel, who could give as good as she got. "I hope you'll both be very happy." And maybe they would be, Annabel with the money, Gaynor with his aristocratic trophy wife.

"Thank you," said Annabel. "So, Flora and I have decided to close the New York store. I really won't have time for it anymore. And I'm selling my share of the London one to her. She needs something to keep her oc-cupied."

"That's very thoughtful of you."

Annabel ignored the sarcasm, and continued, "Which means I won't be spending as much time here as before."

"I guess not," said Frankie, finally beginning to understand why Annabel had wanted to see him.

"Richard's headquarters are in London now. That's where our home will be. And I think, Francis, and I'm sure you'll agree when you give it some thought, that it would be much better for Maud if she was to come live with us."

It took some effort, but Frankie held on to his self control. He poured himself another glass of wine, and said, reasonably, "What would you do about school?"

"That's exactly the point," said Annabel. "There are so many excellent schools in England. I've already had a word with the headmistress of mine, and . . . well, I'm quite certain—given a contribution from Richard—that a place could be found there for Maud."

"Let me see if I've got this right. You want to take Maud away from me, from her family, from her friends, so you can put her in a boarding school in a foreign country?"

"So that she can be near *me*," said Annabel.

"Why? To trot her out on weekends, show her off to your fancy friends, and prove what a devoted mother you are?"

"You're not being fair, Francis. I love Maud."

"I'm sure you do, in your way. It's just not my way. The answer is no. You go where you like. Maud stays in New York." He signaled the waiter.

"You forget, I have joint custody," said Annabel.

The waiter arrived immediately. "The check," said Frankie. "And make it fast, please." He turned to Annabel. "Don't *you* forget, you can't take

Maud out of the country without my permission. According to what I read in the newspapers, Gaynor's got deals pending here. You'll be in New York plenty. If that's not often enough, hop on a plane, come by yourself for a few days."

"I'm her mother, Francis. Girls need their mothers."

Not mothers like you, he thought, but all he said was, "She can spend her vacations with you—when you have the time for her." The waiter brought the check. Frankie looked at it, pulled out a roll of bills, and paid in cash.

"Think about it, Francis, please. Forget your own ego, forget your own selfish desires. Think about what's best for Maud."

Think about what's best for Maud! Frankie started to laugh. "You are some piece of work," he said.

"What, may I ask, is so amusing?"

He stood up. "Let's go, Annabel."

"I want coffee."

"Let's go," he said.

Reluctantly, she stood. He took her arm, and escorted her from the room. They got as far as the lobby without speaking, but then Annabel pulled away from him, and said, "Don't you think we should at least ask Maud what *she* wants?"

"No, I don't. She's a child. She shouldn't be made to choose between us. She shouldn't be put in that position."

"So you'll do the choosing."

"That's right. I'll do it."

"You always were a self-righteous prick," she said.

It occurred to Frankie that Annabel's heart hadn't been in the argument. She'd let him win too easily. Since she didn't need his money any longer, he had no real weapons, other than the court order, which could be fought, especially with Richard Gaynor's wealth at her disposal. Probably all she had hoped to gain was Gaynor's sympathy by playing the Wronged Mother. Well, let her, thought Frankie. He had what he wanted, Maud. He said, "It's been a pleasure, as always, Annabel."

"You never could deal with a real woman."

"A real woman? You mean *you*." There was contempt in his voice. A mistake.

"One with a mind."

"And a mouth?"

"I suppose that little Barbie doll you're going to marry doesn't say a thing but 'Yes, Frankie. Anything you want, Frankie. You're so wonderful, Frankie.' It's pathetic, your constant need to have your ego massaged. *You're* pathetic!"

The anger, on a slow simmer all night, came boiling up. His chest felt like a vast seething cauldron of past grievances, unforgotten hurts, unforgiven wrongs. Involuntarily, his hands lifted. He took a step toward her. She held her ground, and hissed, "You touch me, Francis, and you'll regret it." Her words alone probably wouldn't have stopped him. At that moment, Frankie was beyond rational thought. But a couple walked passed, laughing, and the sound pierced the armor of his rage. He remembered where he was, in the lobby of the Plaza Hotel, and if he hit her, yes, he would regret it. He would be ashamed of himself, embarrassed in front of the world, and, worse, he might lose Maud. Get indicted for assaulting her mother, and any judge would reconsider the question of custody. Frankie's hands dropped to his sides. "I think I'll wait to murder you until we're someplace a little less public," he said.

Annabel gave him a blazing smile. She'd won. She'd made him lose his temper. It wasn't much of a hold to have over someone, but it was better than none. "I suppose, in future, I ought to avoid being alone with you," she said, with a hint of coyness.

"I don't think that's going to be a problem," said Frankie and, good manners be damned, he left her standing there and fled out the door, into a waiting cab.

*O*n the answering machine when he got home, Frankie found a series of messages from Kelly, the gist of which was that he'd forgotten he was to take her to hear some rock star, whose name meant nothing to him, sing at a new club opened by a friend of hers, whose face he could only vaguely recall. Oh, shit, thought Frankie, suddenly remembering the pink slip with Kelly's name on it, lying on his desk when he'd returned from a late afternoon meeting. He'd picked up the phone, started to dial, but an incoming call had interrupted him. That was the last time Kelly had crossed his mind until Annabel mentioned her. A Barbie doll? She was no such thing! She was an intelligent young woman, with a mind very much her own. If she tended to idolize him a bit, well, what was so wrong with thinking the person you loved a paragon? Wasn't that better than believing him to be a fool, a push-over, a patsy?

Feeling genuinely contrite, Frankie poured himself a scotch and then called Kelly, only to get *her* answering machine. He left a suitably abject message, removed his shoes, settled into a chair, and picked up the book he was close to finishing. Maud was staying at Annabel's. The apartment was quiet. It was still early, only nine-thirty, and he found himself savoring the idea of the hours of solitude stretching in front of him. He took another sip of his drink and began to read. It was a thriller, by le Carré. Annabel, Kelly, Maud, everyone slipped from his consciousness as he lost himself in the narrative, as the flow of words carried him into a world where the story made sense and the characters acted from motives he could understand. When the phone rang, irritated by the interruption, he reached for the receiver, and snapped, "Hello?"

"Frankie, where have you been?" It was Kelly.

"I left a message on your machine."

"I'm not home yet."

He searched for a reasonable tone of voice. "I'm sorry, Kelly. Something came up," he said, working his way through his excuses, not very smoothly, aware the whole time that nothing could excuse the one unarguable, unforgivable fact that he'd forgotten her.

"You could have called," she said.

Which of course he would have done—if he hadn't forgotten. "I am sorry," he said again, sick of the sound of his voice apologizing.

"We're still here, at the club. Come and join us. There's another set later. And dancing."

She was giving him a way to redeem himself, and Frankie knew he ought to take it. But he couldn't. He had begun to relax, to feel peaceful. He didn't want to put on his shoes, his jacket, and go off into the night again to brave the lights, the noise. Once, how long ago? months? years? when he was younger and desperate to get laid, he would have done it in a minute, the promise of Kelly's body enough to make him endure the crowds, the babble that passed for conversation, the head-slamming music. Once, he might even have enjoyed it. "I've had a rough night," he said. "I'm going to turn in early."

"You always say that. Lately, you never want to spend time with me."

"Kelly, you know that's not true," said Frankie reassuringly. "I've just had a lot on my plate these past few months." There was a note of self-pity in his voice which he hoped would engage her sympathy. It didn't.

"We hardly ever see each other, or do anything fun anymore. You used to want to make love all the time. And now?"

"Are you in a phone booth?" he asked, imagining the people waiting in line, listening with interest to Kelly hurling accusations at him at the top of her lungs.

"I'm in Clive's office," said Kelly. Clive was the club's owner, Frankie remembered. "He said I could use his phone. He could see how upset I was." She was moving beyond anger toward hysteria.

"I'll make it up to you tomorrow, all right? We'll go somewhere great for dinner, just the two of us. We'll do anything you want." He made a mental note to stop in at Bergdorf's or Tiffany's the next day. It wouldn't hurt to show up at dinner with something pretty. And he'd send flowers, first thing in the morning.

"Tomorrow something else will happen, and you'll forget again. I want you to come tonight. I want you to be with me now!"

"Kelly, try to be reasonable—"

"I'm tired of being reasonable. When I'm reasonable you just ignore me. I want you to pay attention to me, Frankie."

"I'll pay attention to you tomorrow, Kelly. Tonight, I'm tired."

"Frankie, you better come!" It was a shriek.

One scene a day, one angry woman a day, that was enough, he decided. "Hey, I forgot our date. I've apologized. But there are more important things in life than club openings, you know. Like maybe my daughter's future." He was being unfair, but he didn't give a damn. "So cut the melodrama, okay. Stop behaving like a spoiled brat. Go back to your friends and enjoy yourself. I'm going to bed. Good night, Kelly." He hung up and poured himself another scotch. Maybe he hadn't been paying enough attention to her, he thought, but what the hell did she expect? He was busy. He had a million things to deal with. There was a lot of pressure on him. Why the fuck couldn't she understand?

Because she's a spoiled rich kid, came another thought, used to having the whole world revolve around her. She's daddy's little darling.

And you're a self-righteous, egocentric prick. He heard Annabel's voice as clearly as if she were in the room with him.

He sat, sipping his drink. Did he have plans for tomorrow night? He couldn't remember. If he did, he would break them. He would take Kelly away for a weekend again, sometime soon. No, not soon, next weekend. Somewhere romantic. Somewhere they could make love all day, if they wanted to. He stood, picked up his drink and his book, and went into his room. For some reason, the thought of an idyllic weekend alone with Kelly didn't fill him with as much pleasure as it once would have done.

When he got to work the next morning, Frankie asked Carol, his assistant, for the number of a florist, resisted her suggestion that she make the call, and, as a penance, phoned himself to order two dozen long-stemmed roses to be sent to Kelly at work. He decided to wait to talk to her until after lunch, by which time the flowers would have arrived. Let her stew, he thought. Let her wonder if he meant to phone. And, when he did, he would suggest a weekend away. At dinner that night, he would deliver a bracelet, or a pair of earrings, whatever he happened to pick up on the way.

Feeling pleased with himself, Frankie headed for the conference room where he spent the next hour refereeing an argument between the head of his marketing division, his chief designer, and the manager of the factory over the delivery dates of the new sports line, after which he and his lawyer met with Russell Schneider at the gallery to settle the final details of the sale. Afterward, he stopped in at Tiffany's, bought Kelly a pair of two-carat yellow diamond earrings, picked up a turkey sandwich at the deli, and returned to his office feeling that, for the moment at least, he had everything under control.

"This just came for you," said his secretary, handing him a padded envelope. The return address on the mailing label read "Abel Ellis Productions." In the corner was scrawled, in Kelly's handwriting, "By Messenger."

"Thanks," said Frankie. "Is there any coffee around?"

"I just made a fresh pot," she said.

"Would you put this on a dish too, while you're at it?" he said, handing her the bag with the turkey sandwich.

Taking the envelope, he went into his office and sat down. He put the Tiffany box in his bottom drawer, than opened the envelope. Inside was another, a white one, business-size, to which a typed note was pinned with a paper clip. *Frankie,* it said, *it makes me very sad to say this but, after what happened last night, I don't think there's any future left for us. I'm returning your ring. Consider our engagement over. Love always, Kelly.* Stunned, Frankie reread the note, though he had understood it perfectly the first time, then he tore open the white envelope. Inside, wrapped in a tissue, was the six-carat diamond engagement ring he had given Kelly in the spring. Returning it was quite a gesture, he thought. He felt proud of her. He felt relieved, too, but that feeling was quickly subsumed by guilt at not being more upset. He was in love with Kelly, after all. Losing her should be devastating. But it wasn't. It was liberating. And when he realized how precious his freedom suddenly seemed to him, his guilt darkened and deepened, tempting him like the cool depths of a forest lake on a hot day, until finally he plunged headlong into it.

Carol entered with a tray on which sat the turkey sandwich on a ceramic plate, a mug of coffee, and a couple of napkins. Absently he thanked her, then ignored his lunch as he wondered what to do. It occurred to him that he could call Martha and ask her advice, but just as quickly he knew that was a very bad idea, one that should be resisted. Instead, he picked up his phone and called Kelly. He didn't know what he was going to say, but, after hanging on for two or three very long minutes, he got no chance to say anything at all. Kelly wasn't in, or claimed not to be. When he tried her again, several hours later, the receptionist insisted that she was out, possibly for the rest of the day. He left a message for her on her answering machine at home. Sounding more annoyed than conciliatory, he accused her of over-reacting, of seeing only her side of the story and making no attempt to understand his. He insisted that they talk before making any decisions about their future. Forgetting to say he loved her, Frankie replaced the receiver in its cradle, and felt relieved, satisfied, certain that he'd done the right thing, and that now no blame could attach to him for whatever followed.

*L*ate in the afternoon, Martha called to ask if he was planning to stop by to see Hannah that night. (She always said "to see Hannah," never herself.) "I'm meeting Vic for a game of racquetball," he said.

"Come by after that, Frankie. There's something I want to discuss with you."

"What's up?" he said.

"We'll talk about it when you get here. It'll keep till then. See you later," she said, and got off the phone before he could ask any more questions.

First racquetball, then Martha, then Kelly. A full evening. If Kelly continued not answering her phone, he would just go over there and lean on her bell until she let him in. That decided, he took the earrings out of the Tiffany bag, and put them in his inside pocket along with the diamond ring. A perfect time for a mugging, he thought, waiting on the corner outside the building for a taxi to take him downtown to Macklin's.

*H*is mind on other matters, Frankie played badly. "Your body may be here, but the rest of you is somewhere in outer space," said Vic after their second game.

"Kelly broke our engagement. I forgot I promised to take her to some club opening last night and she went ballistic."

"That doesn't sound like Kelly."

"I guess I've been neglecting her lately, since Pop died. I've had a lot to deal with."

"You okay about it?" asked Vic. "I mean about Kelly and the engagement."

"Upset. Confused," said Frankie. "Come on, one more game," he added quickly. He was not in the mood for a heart-to-heart. "I promise to concentrate."

Frankie won that game and called it a night. "I've got to get over to Martha's," he said.

Vic frowned, started to say something, and changed his mind.

"What?" said Frankie.

"Nothing," said Vic. "Give me a call when you want a rematch. I got nothing but time these days." He'd been unemployed for three weeks and, typical of an actor, was beginning to think he would never work again.

"Anytime you want a job with Ferraro Clubs," said Frankie, as he usually did when Vic started looking worried, "just say the word."

Vic laughed. "Thanks. As long as I can start at the top, one of these days, I might just say yes."

"My right-hand man," said Frankie. "Like always."

*L*eaving Vic in the downstairs lockers, Frankie went up to his office, showered and changed, patted his jacket pocket to be sure the earrings and ring were still there, stopped briefly to review some figures with the new manager, then left the club and took a cab back uptown to Martha's. She was putting Hannah to bed when he arrived. Without protest, she allowed Frankie to take her place reading to the child; but Hannah, after a few minutes, began crying for her mother, and Frankie had to cede his place, leaving Martha to soothe her daughter to sleep.

Though he tried not to, Frankie felt hurt by the rejection. Maud had always preferred him to Annabel. But then, Frankie had been the permanent fixture in her life, Annabel the one to come and go. He helped himself to a scotch, which he believed Martha kept strictly for his benefit, turned on the television, and sat watching the news until she joined him. As if she could read his mind, she said, "Children like their bedtime routine."

"I know. I shouldn't let it bother me, but . . ." He shrugged.

Without responding, she continued on into the kitchen, returning a few minutes later with what looked like a glass of seltzer. She sat, took a sip, and said, "Frankie . . ."

"What?" He'd been so preoccupied with Hannah when he arrived that he hadn't noticed how tired she looked. "Are you okay?" he asked. What if she was sick? he thought. Really sick. He thought about Amy Colvington. "You're not sick are you?" He could hear the panic in his voice.

So could Martha. She smiled grimly and shook her head. "No. I'm not sick. I'm just . . . I've been trying to think all day how to tell you . . ." Again she hesitated.

"You're getting married," he said. He didn't seem to like that idea much either.

"No. Mark's just a friend, Frankie. A friend, that's all. There's no one." And then, in what seemed a non sequitur, but wasn't, she added quickly, "I'm pregnant."

It took Frankie a moment to follow that train of thought. "Then how . . ." But before he could complete the thought, he knew the answer. "It's mine," he said.

Martha began to cry. "You can't blame me, Frankie. I never expected you to come that night. I wasn't prepared. It's not my fault."

"I'm not blaming you," he said. He'd never seen Martha like this, so fearful, so out of control. She'd never before allowed him to see this side of her either.

"I had to tell you," she said, sobbing. "I wanted you to know." He went to put his arms around her, but she pushed him away. "I'm keeping it," she said, belligerently, as if in answer to his suggestion. "I don't care what you say, I don't care what you want, I'm keeping it. I'm keeping it," she repeated. "I'm keeping it."

Chapter 34

When he got home, Frankie found three messages on his answering machine. With a sinking stomach, he played them, expecting at least one to be from Kelly. He would have to call her back, and what in the name of God could he say? But there was no message from her. Two were business calls. The third was from Hugo, suggesting that he and Frankie meet. "I don't have to tell you, Frankie, how upset Rose and I are about this little contretemps between you and Kelly," he said. Contretemps. Wait, thought Frankie. Wait until the real shit hits the fan.

Hugo had left a Chicago phone number. It was two hours later there, too late to call, Frankie decided. By morning, with luck, he would have thought of a way to appease Hugo and salvage his relationship with Kelly. After locking the Tiffany box in his desk, he stood staring out the library window, beyond the passing traffic in the lighted street below, into the shadowy recesses of the park. Though he'd had only a couple of drinks at Martha's, he felt a headache coming on. He felt numb, dispirited, boxed into a corner, and too weak to fight his way out. What he needed was for someone to step aside to let him pass.

But that's what they'd done, Kelly and Martha both, stepped aside, moved out of his way. Kelly had broken their engagement. Martha had assumed total responsibility for the new child, just as she had with Hannah. Why then did he feel so trapped?

His sleep was troubled, full of dreams he could remember nothing about in the morning except that his father, looking stern and disapproving, had made guest appearances in several. He awoke feeling tired, no closer to a decision, not even certain he knew what options he had. He showered and shaved and, feeling no better, wandered into the kitchen, frightening his housekeeper, who took one look at his face and fled to the back of the apartment to keep out of his way. Alone again (which seemed to him an ideal way to spend the rest of his life), he poured himself a cup of the coffee the housekeeper had made, called Maud at Annabel's to say good morning, then his mother, who had, she told him, spoken to Rose Helm the night before. "She was very upset," said Dolly. To Frankie's surprise, to his *amazement*, Dolly was not. "Listen, Frankie, you do what you want," she continued in her light, rapid-fire voice. "Kelly's a nice girl, but if you don't love her, don't marry her. You hear me? I don't want you making any more mistakes."

He wished he knew for certain what love was, what it felt like. Was it possible that, for most of his adult life, he hadn't known? Had he been operating under mistaken impressions, confusing it not just with the obvious lust, but with affection, admiration, *acquisitiveness*? "Right now, Ma, I don't know what's going to happen, but whatever does, I don't want you to be upset."

"I won't be upset. Not if you're happy."

That was, he thought, the most honest, the most sensible, the most encouraging conversation he'd ever had with his mother. But the good feeling it engendered lasted only seconds. As soon as he put the receiver down, the phone rang. It was Hugo Helm. "I was just about to call you," said Frankie.

"I expected you would last night." Hugo's voice was as cold as Frankie had ever heard it, making him feel small, insignificant, ashamed. Hugo was a man he longed to please, and Frankie had disappointed him.

"I got in too late." He had never sounded so abject with Sal.

"I didn't sleep. Neither did Rose. Frankie, I'm coming to New York, today."

"I don't think that's really necessary. Kelly and I can work this out."

"I want to talk to you."

"I'm doing what I can, believe me. It's Kelly who won't listen to reason."

"Then we'll have to make her. Plan on having dinner with me. The Four Seasons. Seven o'clock." And the line went dead.

*T*hat day there were enough crises to keep Frankie's mind focused on business, but the temper he'd spent so many years learning to keep kept flying out of his control. The head of the textile plant called to say that he would not, after all, be able to get the new stretch fabric to the factory on time, which would delay the production schedule, meaning the clothes would get shipped to the boutiques well past the delivery date so painstakingly negotiated a few days before. There had been a small fire in the Boston club caused by someone's flicking a cigarette butt into a paper towel bin, causing a great deal of smoke but no serious damage. A Rhinehart painting had been declared a fake by an expert at Sotheby's. Frankie shouted profanities at everyone, including Carol, who cried and said that she quit. It took him half an hour of coaxing to get her to change her mind. "Personal problems. Just keep out of my way. I'll be my usual sunny self tomorrow," he promised. "I don't know what I'd do without you." He smiled at her, and she forgave him everything.

As often as he thought of calling Martha, he decided against it, afraid he might say something he would regret. When Colette phoned, he refused to take the call. She probably wanted to discuss the promotion of the new sportswear line, but it was possible that Martha had confided in her, and he was in no mood to listen to any barbed comments, no matter how oblique. As for Kelly, he might score some points if he kept trying to reach her; but, though he was 99 percent sure that, when the moment of decision came, he'd be ready to kiss and make up, he couldn't make himself dial her number.

Instead he took a call from his sister, who said, "It's none of my business, but you want to tell me what's goin' on?"

"Kelly and I had a fight, that's all. I thought it was a spat. Now it's beginning to look like World War Three. Angela . . ." He hesitated, and then he said, "You love Denny, don't you?"

"Of course I do." She sounded shocked that he could doubt it.

"What does it feel like?"

"Love? I don't know. I mean . . . I don't know how to explain."

"Try," he insisted.

"Love is love, and when you feel it you know it."

"Thanks. That's a lot of help."

"If you're not sure, Frankie, then don't marry her." Why hadn't he noticed before how like their mother Angela was? "Kelly's a real sweetheart, and after Annabel God knows you deserve somebody nice. But she's so young, maybe she doesn't know any better than you did at her age what she wants. Maybe you still don't know. You always had eyes bigger than your stomach," she said.

He wanted to defend himself, to say that ambition was not a crime, that it was the American way; but he didn't need another argument. "Maybe," he said.

"Anyway, I love you," she said. "I want you to be happy. So whatever that takes, it's okay with me."

"I love you too," he said, realizing, as he replaced the receiver, that he meant it. Despite the irritations and resentments, the unkind words and frequent desire to escape their clutches, what he felt for Angela and his mother, for Sal (no doubt about it) was love. And his daughters? Love seemed too mild a word to describe the constriction of his heart just the thought of them could provoke. But Kelly? Settling back in his chair, he considered their first meeting, their first date, the months since. He could isolate moments of affection, admiration, impatience, anger, lust. But love? He wasn't sure. That was the truth. He just wasn't sure.

Every impulse in Frankie suggested that he be early for his meeting with Hugo; but, as he approached the Seagram Building at ten minutes to seven, being early suddenly struck him as too deferential. It seemed to put him in the wrong, to confirm his guilt. So he continued downtown along Park for a few blocks, turned east toward Lexington, and circled back, window-shopping along the way until five minutes past, when he approached the restaurant's entrance, paused under its awning, took a deep breath, and went inside.

Hugo was seated, nursing a martini. He looked thoughtful, somber, and rich, in a navy suit, a paisley tie with a diamond stickpin, a pocket hanky furled in his breast pocket. Still, in gray flannel trousers and a cashmere jacket, Frankie felt he could hold his own. "Sorry I'm late," he said, joining him at the table. "I had a meeting at Sotheby's. It ran a little longer than I expected." There had been a meeting at Sotheby's. That much was true.

Hugo rose slightly and offered his manicured hand to Frankie. "Good to see you, son," he said. His voice was warm, full of affection, not at all what Frankie had expected. "There's been plenty of publicity about the sale. You ought to draw a good crowd."

"Yeah, everything's looking good. It'll be a relief to have it over with." It was set for the following Tuesday. "One less thing to worry about."

A waiter came and took their orders and, when they were alone again, Hugo said, "Now tell me what's going on between you and my little girl."

Feeling much as he had when faced with Father McMann's questions in the confessional, Frankie said, "I've been busier than usual—my father's estate, the auction, problems at work. Kelly feels I've been neglecting her. And I have."

"That's all?" said Hugo. He sounded relieved. "You're sure?"

"What did she say?" asked Frankie.

"She said you don't love her. Do you?"

Frankie looked Hugo Helm in the eye and tried to tell the truth. He tried to say, I don't know. He couldn't. It seemed too terrible a thing to admit to a girl's father. So he said, "Sure I do. Why else would I have asked her to marry me?"

"That's what I told her," said Hugo, beaming. "Rose and I have spoiled Kelly. I know that. But deep down she's a good girl. She deserves the best, which is what we've always tried to give her. And I knew, from the start, that's the way you felt too. I knew I could trust you to take care of her."

"I hope so," said Frankie, wishing he could sound more definite but lacking the stamina for another outright lie.

"I'll get her to see you," said Hugo. "Then the rest is up to you."

"What if she won't change her mind?"

"Son, you're a lot like me. You can charm the birds out of the trees. She'll be like putty in your hands."

"But," said Frankie insistently, "what if she's decided she doesn't love *me*?"

Hugo hesitated a moment, and then said, "I'll be disappointed. But, hell, my little girl's happiness matters to me more than anything in the world."

There was a right thing to do here, thought Frankie. If only he could figure out what it was. "It matters to me, too."

Satisfied, Hugo nodded, and said, "I've always found, in these situations, that a little gift often does the trick. A little oil on troubled waters."

"I picked up a pair of diamond earrings at Tiffany's."

"Nice," said Hugo. "Very nice." He smiled. "I'll have a word with Kelly tonight," he said. "You call her tomorrow. I'm sure she'll speak with you."

*T*he next morning, Frankie flew up to Boston to take a look at the damage and found things in worse shape than he'd expected. The place reeked of smoke. A fine layer of soot covered every surface. Towels had to be washed, the entire place professionally cleaned, and the men's locker room repainted. The manager had closed the club for the day, and it would have to stay closed for at least a week, Frankie estimated, even if all the workmen kept to their optimistic schedules. "You know who did this?" he asked, looking around him in disgust.

"I've got my suspicions."

"An employee?"

"One of the trainers."

"He's out of here," said Frankie. "Find some excuse, and get rid of him. He's a fire hazard."

Even in his office, Frankie could smell the smoke. As he dialed Kelly's number at work, he coughed. He could feel a tightness in his chest. Not anxiety, he assured himself, just bad air. The receptionist put him through without delay when he asked for Kelly, who, sounding subdued and chastened, agreed immediately to his suggestion that they have dinner that night. "You're right," she said firmly, though with a noticeable lack of enthusiasm. "We've got to settle things."

"My place, then. Seven-thirty?" Kelly agreed, and Frankie called his housekeeper to ask her to prepare a casserole. She wasn't as good a cook as Martha, but cuisine was not of paramount importance. What mattered was having a quiet place to talk.

It was a fine mid-September day. The air was crisp, the sun was shining, the leaves were just beginning to turn. Leaving the club, Frankie walked the few blocks to the building that housed the Colvington Mead Publishing Company. Since neither Dan nor he was hungry, they went for a walk along Back Bay, past row after row of tidy Victorian houses, their fronts freshly painted, their stoops swept clean, their window boxes crammed with asters and chrysanthemums.

As they walked, Frankie talked, about Kelly, about Martha, about the new baby. There was a note of irony in his voice, a hint of self-deprecation that kept him from sounding too full of self-pity, without quite hiding how troubled, how confused, he was. "I've really dropped myself in it this time," he said.

"Yes. But the question is, do you go in deeper, or haul yourself out?"

"I think maybe I'll just toss a coin."

Dan didn't reply.

When they reached the Gardner, they went in. "I came here with Miranda," Frankie said. Again, Dan made no comment. They stopped to admire the Sargent in the entry hall, then went upstairs see the Vermeer, the Cranach, the Botticelli. Miranda, Frankie thought, looking at the sweet face of the virgin in *The Madonna of the Eucharist,* the somber face of the angel. Miranda. The pain was there. It always would be, but now it was a bearable dull ache.

On the way out, they came across the Zofany portrait of Isabella Stewart Gardner, looking alive and radiant, exuding a mesmerizing energy, and Frankie said, "She always reminds me a little of Eva. Not in looks . . ."

"No. It's the energy, the will to dominate, the charm . . ."

"How's Craig doing?" asked Frankie.

"Better," said Dan. "He's getting out a little these days."

When they left the museum, they stopped at a coffee shop for a quick sandwich, by which time the conversation had got around to politics and how long Reagan could keep the Democratic Congress buffaloed. They had almost reached Dan's office before he said, hesitantly, as if he found the subject difficult, "I've got some news of my own, Frankie. I'm getting married."

"For chrissake, why'd you let me go on about *me* for so long."

"I didn't know how to tell you. No," he added, stopping Frankie's protest. "Not because of how you're feeling. Because of how *I'm* feeling. Happy, disloyal, guilty."

"Amy would want you to be happy," said Frankie.

"Knowing that doesn't help somehow."

"Who is she?"

"Miss Malvern," said Dan. Then he laughed, and for that moment the only sound in his voice was joy. "She was Lulu's first-grade teacher."

Relieved to have something at last to laugh about, Frankie joined in. "Does she have a first name? Or do we all have to call her Miss Malvern?"

"Minerva. Known as Minnie. Her father was a classics scholar. She's a wonderful woman. Intelligent, warmhearted, open-minded. The children adore her. She has a way of being comfortable, without presuming. You know what I mean?" Frankie thought of Martha and said that he did. "She's made them understand somehow that she doesn't want to take Amy's place. She wants a place all her own, different, maybe not equal, but substantial." She'd been married once, briefly, in her twenties, unhappily enough to believe that she never wanted to try it again. Dan had changed her mind.

"You've known her how long and never said a word?"

"Close to two years." He hesitated a moment, and then added, "Until recently, there was nothing to say." He paused again, then said, "She fills the house with warmth. She makes it feel like a home again. I don't want to be alone anymore, Frankie. And I love her. Maybe not the way I did Amy. But that doesn't make what I feel any less real, any less important. You'll like her," he said finally. "Everybody does. Next time you come, you'll meet her."

On the plane back to New York, an image of the Colvingtons' dining room appeared in Frankie's head, Dan at the head of the table, the children in their usual places, a blur representing Minnie Malvern where Amy used to sit. Frankie too was in his usual place. It was an idealized picture, lacking the bickering of the children, the flashes of temper, the plain food, but the laughter and the general sense of well-being were real. He added Kelly to the scene, and immediately felt the strain. No matter how hard he tried, he couldn't imagine her enjoying herself. She liked Dan and his family, that wasn't the problem. She got along well with Lulu, though she didn't have a clue how to deal with the boys. But when the conversation strayed beyond theatrical productions and pop concerts to politics or books, she stopped listening. Mostly, when she was with the Colvingtons, Kelly's face registered forced concentration, and Frankie fluctuated between guilt at paying her too little attention and irritation at having his own pleasure spoiled.

Banishing the image from his mind, Frankie decided that he wasn't being fair. He reminded himself that Kelly was sweet, and agreeable. She tried, really tried, to enjoy the things he did. It wasn't her fault that she couldn't. Yet. As they spent more time together, their interests would surely begin to intertwine; then they would find a world of things to share. Children, for example.

The thought of children reminded Frankie of Martha. He hadn't spoken to her since she'd told him about the baby. When he'd left her, he'd been upset and angry. And now? Hell, he was still upset and angry, but not with her. With himself, perhaps. With life. With whoever or whatever insisted on retribution for his every thoughtless act. Some people got away with murder. Why not him?

A stack of phone messages awaited him at his office. He returned the most urgent of them and then called Martha. It was close to six. She would be busy with Hannah, but suddenly it seemed important to him not to let any more time pass before speaking to her. Already she would have started to withdraw, like a turtle, pulling back into her shell. When she was in there, he couldn't reach her, couldn't influence her. And he needed to influence her, though to do what, he wasn't sure. Not to have an abortion. As powerless as he felt in the face of Martha's determination to have the child, as furious as it made him that she never even pretended to take his wishes into account, he was again relieved that abortion was not an option. It was one less sin to have on his conscience.

When she answered the phone, Martha sounded strained and tired. "It's all right," she said when he asked if she was busy. "Pina's here. She's feeding Hannah."

"How're you doing?"

"Fine," she said.

"Look, I'm sorry about how I reacted the other night."

"It's all right. I know the news was a shock. It was to me, too."

"It's not all right. I apologize."

"Apology accepted." Her voice had a heavy quality, as if she was on painkillers or tranquilizers.

"We'll work this out," said Frankie. "We've done it before." He laughed, though there was little good humor in the sound. "We're old hands at it."

He could practically hear the effort her mind was making to frame a suitable response. Finally, she said, "I'm moving to Los Angeles."

"You're what?" The question came out as an angry yelp.

"I've been talking with Colette about transferring the office there."

"You can't go."

386 • THE WIVES OF FRANKIE FERRARO

"I have to. I have to get away from you." She was crying. "I thought I could control the situation. I thought we could be friends."

"We can be!"

"We can't! Look at what happens when we try! I need a life. I thought I had one, but I was wrong. All I had were the crumbs of yours."

"What the fuck are you talking about? You have a child, a home, a career. You have no money troubles. You have friends, an interesting social life. You live in the greatest city in the world. What more do you want?"

"You take up too much space, Frankie. You use up too much air. I have to get away."

"Martha, look, I'll be right over. We have to talk."

"Don't come. I don't want to talk. There's nothing to talk about. I've made up my mind."

The line went dead and Frankie felt something close to terror. It would be easier getting a river to change its course than Martha to change her mind. But how could he let her go, take Hannah, and move to Los Angeles? And the new baby? He'd have a child he'd never know, at least not in any way that mattered.

It wouldn't be the end of the world, some part of his mind prompted. Lots of men never saw their kids. They survived. Not only did they survive, but to hear some people tell it, they thrived. They threw out their old lives like rubbish, and moved on to the next one. It kept them young, this constant starting over.

Was that what he was doing with Kelly? he wondered, trying to hold on to his youth by marrying someone more than twenty years his junior? Would the children he was almost certain to have with her blot out the memory of Hannah and the new child? The thought was troubling. He didn't like to think that was the sort of man he was. Not a man at all, according to Sal Ferraro, who considered a real man one with balls enough to accept his responsibilities.

Without stopping to think why, he dialed Colette's number in Boca Raton and when she got on the line, he said, "You can't let Martha go to Los Angeles."

"It's her decision," said Colette calmly.

"I don't want her to go." He knew he was sounding unreasonable, but, hell, that's how he was feeling.

"You want. You don't want. Try for once to think about what Martha wants. What she *needs*."

"How is being in Los Angeles better for her than being here, where I can take care of her and the children?"

"For one thing, maybe with a continent between you, you'll be able to keep your hands off her."

"Twice, Colette. Twice, that's all. And neither time did she say no. Remember that. It's not my fucking fault she's so goddamn fertile."

"All right, your hands off each other. Does that sound fairer to you? Are you satisfied?"

"No. I want her here, in New York. I want to be able to see my kids."

"You're getting married, Frankie," said Colette, sounding like a teacher explaining the way the world worked to a particularly dense student. "You're starting a new life. A new family. Don't you think Martha should have a chance to do the same?"

"She can do that here!"

"Oh, Frankie, *please!*"

"I never tried to stop her," he protested, knowing it was true, yet feeling that he was somehow missing the point.

"How someone as smart as you can be so incredibly stupid!"

"Talk to her Colette, please!"

"Would you grow up!"

Again the line went dead. Angry, he slammed down the receiver. Taking his jacket from the closet, he stormed out of his office, and glared at Carol. "Anybody wants me, leave a message on my machine at home. I'll get back to them as soon as I can."

"You're leaving?" she said. Instantly, she bit her lip, regretting the way she always managed to behave like a cretin when confronted by one of Frankie's moods.

Instead of snapping her head off, he forced a civil response. (One abject apology a month was enough.) "Uh-huh," he said. "Have a nice evening."

Outside, he hailed a cab and was about to give Martha's address when he changed his mind. There was no point trying to reason with her tonight. He would give her a few days to cool off first, and then go to work. Surely, if he tried, if he made a real effort, he could think of some way to get her to stay in New York. He told the cabby to take him home. Which was just as well, he realized, when he entered the apartment and saw the dining room table set for two. Kelly! He'd forgotten all about her. "Shit!" he groaned. He checked his watch. It was close to seven and she was expected at seven-thirty.

In the kitchen, a baguette, fresh from the bakery, lay on the counter next to a note saying that the salad was in the refrigerator, and giving detailed instructions about how to heat the casserole. Frankie turned on the oven, opened a bottle of red wine, and went into his bedroom. Maybe a shower would help clear his mind, he thought, taking off his clothes. Half an hour later, freshly washed and shaved, dressed in sharply creased chinos and a neatly ironed T-shirt, he still had no idea what to say to Kelly when she arrived.

As he put the Tiffany box on the table, next to her plate, he heard the bell ring. Opening the door, he found Kelly on the threshold, looking bedraggled, her plaid suit and navy pumps rain-soaked, her red hair hanging in damp strands. "The skies just opened," she said. He kissed her hello. Then, because she looked so young and fragile, her eyes so dark with trouble, he hugged her. She stood still in his embrace for a moment and then pulled away. "I better tidy myself up," she said.

He let her go, watching as she walked down the corridor, her long legs moving in graceful strides, her neat bottom swaying under the short tight skirt. He felt suddenly, peculiarly, as if he were watching a movie, waiting for the screen to fade to black and the end credits to roll. But the lights stayed up and Kelly turned into the bathroom out of sight.

Going into the kitchen, he sliced the bread, put it into the basket his housekeeper had left on the counter, then took the salad out of the refrigerator and mixed in the dressing. By the time Kelly returned, everything was ready. "First open your present," he said.

She sat at the table, and, with more caution than pleasure, as if expecting to set off a bomb, she untied the white ribbon, took off the blue cover, and lifted the cotton pad. "Oh, Frankie, they're beautiful," she said softly. "You didn't have to. . . ."

"I wanted to. Try them on."

With a sure hand, she removed her earrings, replaced them with the diamond drops, and cocked her head. "How do they look?" she asked.

"Beautiful." Bending, he kissed her, adding, "And so do you. Let's eat," he said, and he served the casserole.

Kelly asked about the trip to Boston and Frankie told her the news about Dan. She tried to amuse him with anecdotes about friends at work, but what seemed to be most on her mind was the latest crisis: Matthew Polansky, the star of one of Abel Ellis's hit musicals, had broken his leg the night before. It would be weeks before he could perform again, and the prevailing opinion was that either a name replacement would have to be found or the show would have to close.

"That's too bad," said Frankie, who remembered meeting Polansky at the opening night party. He'd seemed like a nice kid.

Kelly put down her fork. Her eyes filled with tears. She seemed to struggle for control and then gave up, and said, "It's my fault."

"Your fault? Don't be silly," said Frankie. "How could it be your fault?"

She and Matthew had run into each other occasionally at late-night clubs, explained Kelly, evenings when Frankie was busy with his mother, or whatever it was that was occupying his time these days. Then came lunches, then dinners on days when there were no performances. Unsurprisingly, one thing had led to another. "He thinks he's in love with me," said Kelly. When she told him that her father was coming to New York and that, as a result, she and Frankie were probably going to get back together, "He went a little crazy." They were in the street, and he began kicking out at everything in his path. "I couldn't stop him," she said. Finally, he kicked a garbage can, stumbled, tripped over the curb, and fell.

"How do you feel about him, Kelly? Do you love him?"

She hesitated a moment and then said, "I don't know. I'm not sure. I thought I loved you."

"And I thought I loved *you*. But maybe we've both been wrong."

Instead of the relief he felt, Frankie saw panic in Kelly's eyes. "You don't love me? But Daddy said—"

"Let's keep your father out of this, for a little, anyway. Let's just try to figure out what *we* want, okay?"

Kelly nodded. Her face was solemn. "I'm sorry if I hurt you, Frankie. I didn't mean to."

"I know." Was he hurt? His ego felt a little bruised, that much he knew. He'd been so certain that Kelly was crazy about him. He'd have put money on her being faithful to him.

"It was just . . . well, I was feeling so neglected, so lonely."

Instead of self-righteous, Kelly sounded guilty. She was taking the full weight of what had happened onto herself. For a moment Frankie was tempted to let her go on doing it; but finally he said, "I have a confession to make, too. I haven't been honest with you. I wanted to be, but I was afraid. I didn't know how you'd react, how your parents would react. I didn't want to hurt you, any of you. But now I think it's time to level." Again Kelly nodded. And he told her about Martha, about Hannah, about the new baby.

As he spoke, Kelly's eyes widened in disbelief. Deception on such a grand scale was beyond her ken. "Do you love her?" she asked when Frankie came to a halt.

"I love my daughter," said Frankie. "But Martha? I never thought about it. I like her, that's all. I never meant for any of it to happen."

"You should have told me." She sounded hurt, but not angry. Her own sense of guilt was too great to allow for anger at him. That would come later.

"For a long time, I didn't think it mattered. What happened, happened before I met you."

"Not the new baby," said Kelly.

"No," said Frankie guiltily. "I don't know how to explain that. I was upset about Pop. I didn't plan it, I just wound up there, at Martha's."

"You didn't think of coming to me?"

He remembered the way she'd reacted to his father's death, how distant and self-involved she'd seemed; but what was the point in mentioning it? "I didn't think at all," he said.

Kelly picked up her fork again and began to push her food around on her plate, separating the pieces of chicken from the potatoes, the potatoes from the peppers. Finally, she looked up at Frankie, and said, "I feel as if everything between us has been a lie."

"No," he said. "We cared about each other. We still care. Maybe not enough to spend the rest of our lives married to one another, but we care." She began to cry, and Frankie got up, pulled her from her seat, put his arms around her. "Don't cry. Think how much better it is that we found this out now, before we made an even bigger mistake."

"I don't know what I'm going to say to Daddy," she sobbed.

Neither do I, thought Frankie. Neither do I.

$\mathcal{T}$hey talked until each was assured that neither really wanted to proceed with the wedding. Then, absolved of guilt, they agreed to face Hugo Helm together. Pointing out that her father would be even more upset (and who could blame him?) if he thought Kelly was giving up a successful business man for an unemployed actor, Frankie got Kelly to promise that she wouldn't rush into an engagement with Matthew Polansky. "I'm not a complete fool," she said. "I have no intention of ruining my life. Anyway, I don't think I love him. I was just mad at you."

When they'd talked themselves out, Frankie took Kelly home in a cab and returned immediately. He felt ten years younger and forty pounds lighter. There was a slight tenderness about his ego, but otherwise he was fine, better than fine. He hadn't felt so well in months, since before his father's death. No, even longer ago than that, since before his engagement to Kelly. Relief flooded through his body, followed by a surge of something stronger, less familiar. It took a while for him to realize that it was joy.

That night, Frankie slept soundly and awoke feeling full of energy and determination. While he was asleep, his subconscious had been busy making decisions. He knew what he had to do. Finally, he was going to put his life in order.

It was a Saturday, a good day for that. He called Annabel's, where, fortunately, Mrs. Ashby answered the phone. "Lady Annabel has a hairdresser's appointment, so there will be no problem," she said when Frankie suggested lunch with Maud.

After stopping by the office to catch up with some neglected paperwork, he arrived, with perfect timing, at the apartment just after Annabel had left. However, Richard Gaynor was there. A burly, florid man with sandy hair, a jovial manner, and beady eyes, he had a handshake designed to establish immediate superiority. Frankie tried to give as good as he got, but he came off second in the bone-crushing contest, and took an immediate dislike to the energetic Australian. "Pleased ta meet'ya," said Gaynor.

"Same here," said Frankie.

He refused a drink, and the two men stood around awkwardly, discussing the previous night's Yankee game. "Great sport, baseball," said Gaynor. "Not cricket, but a thinking man's game just the same." Finally Mrs. Ashby arrived with Maud, who looked wary, as if the sudden change in plans boded her no real good. "Nice little girl you've got there," said Gaynor, managing to look fond.

"Thanks," said Frankie. He kissed Maud hello, then took her hand, a defensive maneuver to avoid shaking Gaynor's again. "Let's go, sweetheart."

"See ya," said Gaynor cheerfully.

"Sure thing," said Frankie, fleeing for the door.

At the Carnegie Deli, when the busy combo of busboy and waitress finally allowed them a few minutes peace, Frankie screwed up his courage and, as gently as he could, broke the news to his daughter. "We care about each other a lot," he told her, "and Kelly loves you, you know that, but to get married . . ." He hesitated, and then went on, "Sometimes other things matter more than love." That wasn't exactly what he meant to say, or precisely what he thought, but it was as close as he could get just then.

Maud put down the hot dog she'd been eating carefully, trying to mind her manners the way Mrs. Ashby had taught her. She looked at her father, her eyes welling with tears. "Oh, Daddy," she said, with a wail of distress, "the wedding is all *planned*."

"That's not what matters. What matters is doing the right thing, the best thing, for Kelly and me, and you, too."

"Getting married's best," said Maud stubbornly.

How was he going to make her understand? He pulled out a handkerchief, wiped her eyes and nose. Finally, he said, "You think your cousin Sean is great. You like pretty clothes. Books. Dogs."

"Horses, too." She had not quite abandoned hope that she might get one for her next birthday.

"Could you have a best friend who thought Sean was a jerk, hated to shop, thought books were boring, and was scared of animals?"

"Kelly isn't scared of animals," said Maud. At least she'd stopped crying.

"We're not talking about Kelly. We're talking about a make-believe person. Spending a lot of time with someone who disagreed with you about everything, that wouldn't be a lot of fun, would it?"

Maud thought about it a moment, and then said grudgingly, "I s'pose not."

"I loved your mother when we got married. I thought we were going to be happy. But we were so different. We didn't like the same people, or enjoy the same things. We just grew further and further apart. And ended up hurting each other. And you. I don't want that to happen with Kelly."

"But you like a lot of the same things," said Maud, in one last gasp of protest.

"No, we only pretended to like them to impress each other. When people first fall in love they do that. It's a big mistake. Because, after you're married, all the pretending stops. Only by then, it's too late."

Maud sniffed, then picked up her hot dog and began to eat, silently, thinking things over. Her big dark eyes were troubled. Her heart had been so set on a wedding. Without much appetite, Frankie scooped up a forkful of his scrambled eggs. He'd caused Maud enough pain for one day, he decided. Telling her about Martha and Hannah would have to wait. There was a limit to what a nine-year-old should have to deal with at one time.

After Frankie took Maud home, he picked up his car, and headed for Midford. As he drove through Queens's flat urban wasteland, past the billboards, the factories, the dumps, he rehearsed what he was going to say to his mother, got bored with that, and by the time the increasing density of trees announced suburbia, he was singing along with the radio in an effort to distract himself, "Lean on Me," "What You Get Is What You See," "Wanted Dead or Alive." When he reached his old neighborhood, he stopped. Anxiety was building again. He turned off the radio and drove slowly down his mother's street, on the watch for kids playing ball or riding bikes, past the rows of neat houses, all in prime condition, except for the Cape Cod which, to the scandal of the neighborhood, had missing shingles, peeling paint, and a shutter hanging askew because Mr. Gilligan was too old, too ill, and too poor to keep it up. Angela's car was parked in the driveway. That meant one less explanation, thought Frankie, parking beside it. Instead of using his key, he rang the bell, and Angela came to the door. "Hi," she said. "What's wrong?"

"Nothing," said Frankie. "I just want to talk to you and Ma." He kissed her hello, followed her into the kitchen where his mother was preparing sauce for the next day's pasta, said yes to a cup of coffee, and sat at the kitchen table. It was the same one he'd sat at for breakfast through all of high school, made of imitation wood (or *faux bois* as Annabel might have said), heat and stain resistant.

"What a surprise," said Dolly, smiling to show how pleased she was to see him, moving nimbly around her kitchen, making coffee, getting mugs, sugar, pouring milk into a porcelain pitcher, cutting pieces of pound cake, telling Angela that she didn't need help, to sit down and keep her brother company. There was plenty to talk about. There always was, with a family the size of theirs. And while Angela watched him with some anxiety, Frankie let Dolly tell him about Aunt Millie's latest angina attack and Cousin Joey's new job. "Jimmy and Donna are expecting their first grandchild," she said.

A chill went through Frankie. Jimmy, his peer, his classmate, once his best friend, about to be a grandfather. He was only forty-four. "That's nice," said Frankie.

Finally, Dolly poured the coffee and joined Frankie and Angela at the table. She seemed about to resume her news broadcast when Frankie said, "Ma, there's something I've got to tell you and Angela. Kelly and I had a long talk last night. We decided to call off the wedding."

"If that's what you both want," said Dolly.

"If you think that's best," said Angela.

More than anything, they sounded relieved to have the matter resolved. "That's what we want," said Frankie, who saw no need to go into detail. "There's more, though. Something else. Something I should have told you years ago. There's this woman, a friend, someone I care about. Her name is Martha. She and I . . . well, we have a daughter," said Frankie. "Hannah. She's three years old."

There was a stunned silence, then Dolly gasped, "Oh, my God!"

"Martha, I remember when she worked for you," said Angela. Then, "Didn't she come to Pop's funeral?"

"Yes," said Frankie.

"You sonovabitch!"

"Angela, don't talk to your brother like that!" said Dolly.

Angela stood and glared at Frankie. "You never thought of marrying her, I suppose. Not beautiful enough, or rich enough, I guess."

"I wasn't divorced from Annabel yet," said Frankie. "Anyway, I didn't love her. I didn't think I loved her," he corrected. "And she didn't expect it. She didn't expect anything. Or want anything. It's like trench warfare to get her to take a nickel from me."

"That makes a change," said Angela snidely.

"The thing is," said Frankie, ignoring his sister, "it's happened again. Martha's pregnant."

"Jesus Christ! Frankie!"

"Angela, you watch your mouth!"

"Why are you getting mad at me, Ma? Why aren't you mad at *him*?"

"That's why you broke off your engagement?" asked Dolly.

"Part of the reason." If things had been right between him and Kelly, he would never have gone to Martha. He wouldn't have needed her. "But it wasn't just me, Ma. It was Kelly's decision too. She doesn't love me." That was a hard thing to admit. "At least, not enough," he added.

Dolly's eyes grew bright with tears. "I don't know what your father would've said."

Frankie did. Sal would have hollered about duty, about responsibility. He would have carried on loudly and at length, but, ultimately, he wouldn't have expected Frankie to do any more than he'd already done, to pick up the tab. Boys would be boys, after all. But Dolly, and Angela, too, did expect more. And perhaps it had been to escape their disapproval, and not Sal's, that Frankie had kept Hannah's existence a secret for so long.

"I want you to bring that child here. She's my granddaughter, after all. You have to bring her here. And her mother, too, the poor girl. Promise, Frankie?"

"I promise," he said.

Maybe he'd done it the wrong way around, thought Frankie as he drove back to the city. Maybe he should have talked to Martha first. That might have saved him a lot of explaining. But as he continued to weigh the pros and cons, the more he was certain that he had, instinctively, done the right thing. Martha would have to listen to him now.

It was still early when he got back to the city, about six-thirty. Six-thirty on a Saturday night. Should he risk it? Why not? And, as he had just a few months before, he drove directly to West End Avenue.

"Go away," she said, her voice over the intercom sounding more unhappy than angry.

"Let me in, Martha. We have to talk."

"I told you never to come without calling first."

"Let me in!"

The intercom clicked off. There was silence, and Frankie rang again. And again. Finally, she opened the door.

As he got off the elevator, he saw her, waiting for him, standing in the doorway, looking belligerent. She was wearing jeans and a T-shirt. Her hair was in a ponytail. Without makeup, she looked . . . young. Not a beauty, but good-looking. What she reminded him of, with her regular features and sensible manner, he suddenly realized, was a Jane Austen heroine, a woman made attractive by character. How old was she? He was embarrassed that he didn't know. About thirty-seven, he guessed. "What do you want?" she said, her voice cold.

"I told you, to talk. We have to, if not tonight than some other time. So, it might as well be now."

"Why does everything have to run according to your schedule?"

"I just want to talk," he repeated.

Reluctantly, she stood aside and let him in; and, immediately, he was aware of how at home he felt there, how the chairs begged to be sat on, how the lamps cast a soothing glow, how the curtains and pictures, the knickknacks, the books, Hannah on the floor playing with her toy cars, how comfortable it all was, how inviting. He noticed the drawing he had given her resting on a stand on one of the end tables. "Nice picture," he said.

"Yes," she agreed, refraining from thanking him again.

"Frankie," said Hannah, holding up one of her miniature cars. She opened the doors and said, "Look, it opens."

"Yes," said Frankie, joining her on the floor. It was an old Chevy. "I used to have a car like that," he said.

"Was it blue?

Martha sat on the couch, staring at them glumly, watching as they played. "You wanted to talk?" she said finally.

He looked up from the car he was rolling up the ramp into the toy garage, and said, "I think we should get married." The expression on her face was almost comical—surprised, wary, fearful, as if she'd just discovered a madman loose in her home and wasn't quite sure how to deal with him. "Well," he continued, when she didn't respond. "What do *you* think."

"I think you're out of your mind."

"You love me, don't you?"

"Who said so?" she asked belligerently.

He smiled. "Why else would you have put up with me all these years?"

She blushed. "I don't love you," she said firmly. "Maybe I did once. But I don't."

Maybe she meant it, he thought. Maybe she'd stopped loving him. He felt cold. He almost lost courage. Then, having spent hours deciding what he wanted to say, he decided to say it anyway. After all, he had nothing to lose except his pride, and, after the bashing it had taken in the last twenty-four hours, he was confident it could survive another blow. "Love's not important," he said. "Or at least, it's not as important as other things that matter, like Hannah and the baby."

"I can take care of the children, you know I can. We've been through this before."

"Yes, we have. But I want to take care of them, too. I'm suggesting we get married to do it."

"I'm moving to Los Angeles," she said. "And you're marrying Kelly."

"Kelly and I decided yesterday not to go ahead with the wedding. We agreed it would be a mistake."

There was a sudden flare of hope, of excitement, in Martha's eyes. When she saw Frankie studying her, she turned her face away. "Well, I'm sorry if you're unhappy," she said, "but I don't see how that changes anything."

"I'm not unhappy. I'm relieved." He got up from the floor and, ignoring Hannah's protest, went to sit beside Martha on the couch. He took her hand. "We're friends," he said. "We like each other. When one of us is in trouble, the other wants to help. We enjoy each other's company. And, I bet, if we made a list, we'd find we like a lot of the same things. We're compatible, Martha. And maybe in the long run that's more important than love. Although I think, maybe, I do love you. I'm just not sure what love is anymore."

"Oh, Frankie," she said. "If you loved me, you'd know."

"I know I don't want you to go away. I know I want to be with you. And Hannah. And the baby."

Angry at being ignored, Hannah got up from the floor and came over to join them. "Frankie," she said, "play with me." Before he could pick her up, Martha swept her up into her arms, and stood, holding Hannah in front of her like a shield.

Frankie stood too, and said, "Think about it, Martha. Please." She turned away, but Frankie moved in front of her, putting his hands on her shoulders. Cradled between them, happy now, Hannah took one arm from around Martha's neck and put it around Frankie's, hugging them both. "Hannah loves me," he said.

Martha took a step backward, returned Hannah to the floor, and said slowly, "I don't want you to do anything you'll regret. Or anything I'll regret."

Frankie laughed. She was weakening. "That makes two of us," he said. "I told my mother and sister. They want to meet you."

"You didn't!"

"Maria figured everything out all by herself. The day of Pop's funeral."

"I told you I shouldn't have gone."

"She said Hannah looks just like me."

"She has my mouth," said Martha.

"I haven't told Maud yet. But I will. She'll like having a sister. Marry me," said Frankie. "For better or worse, marry me. You know it's the right thing to do."

Martha was quiet a moment and then, finally, she said, "All right. Yes. I will."

"And try to love me again. It may not be necessary, but I think it would help. I mean, if we want to have a really good life."

"You know I love you," she said. "You've always known."

"I didn't," said Frankie. "I can't believe how dumb I was. But I'm happy you do. I like it."

And, for what seemed to both of them like the first time, they kissed.

Part Four

MARTHA

1997

$$\boxed{Chapter\ 35}$$

*T*he sky was a deep, clear blue, brushed by faint wisps of white cloud. The sun, visible for first time in days, cast a crisp autumn light over the Ferraros' back garden. It was warm, but not humid, a perfect day for a party.

Martha and the girls were in the kitchen with Pina, the housekeeper, preparing the food, which included antipasti of shrimp, cheese, salami, prosciutto, pepperoni, roasted peppers, and olives, to be followed by baked ziti, chicken cacciatore, barbecued flank steak, string beans, fried cauliflower, potato salad made with vinegar, not mayonnaise, sliced tomatoes with olive oil and oregano, a salad of mixed baby greens, and, for dessert, tiramisù, along with assorted Italian pastries—all in all, enough to feed an army.

Though the gardener had done a first-class job the day before, Frankie's assignment was to scrub the gas grill and clean up the patio, chores he enjoyed as long as he was only rarely required to do them. Ten years ago, when Martha had suggested moving to Westchester or Long Island, he'd balked. But with the children, Mrs. Ashby coming and going, and Pina sometimes staying over, they did need more room, and he'd agreed finally to move as far as a brownstone on West Eighty-first Street, off Central Park West. Its small garden was all of suburbia Frankie needed to feel in touch with nature.

Michael was supposed to be helping him, but had gone to his room to write, or so he claimed, a paper he had due on Monday, about wolves, he'd decided after spending hours during the past week poring through books from both the school and the public libraries, reading to his parents (at length and with outrage) heart-rending passages of mistreatment and near extinction. He was first in his class at Blessed Sacrament, an accomplishment that swelled his father's heart with pride. At the same age, thirteen, Frankie had barely been pulling Cs.

When the grill looked clean enough to meet even his mother's demanding criteria, Frankie took the hose and washed a day's collection of city soot and bird droppings from the black wrought-iron garden furniture ("It doesn't show the dirt so much," Dolly had said admiringly the first time she saw it). The patio, laid by a friend of Sal's, with Frankie's tentative assistance, was an intricate pattern of old brick covering the entire yard. A chestnut tree provided shade near the house, while, deeper in the garden stood dogwoods and Japanese maples. There were roses in tubs, borders with flowering shrubs, and, twining up from the stone boundary wall and across the patio overhang, a wisteria from which, in early summer, blossoms dangled in thick, sweet clusters, scenting the air and casting an eerie violet light in the late afternoon sun.

Frankie and the gardener trimmed the shrubs and pruned the roses. Except for cutting an occasional bouquet, Martha confined her activities indoors. When pregnant with Michael, she'd stopped working. Her intention had been to go back when he was three months old, but she'd allowed Frankie to talk her out of it, both then and later when Colette, at last resigned to retirement, had asked her to take over the business. After Martha turned her down, Colette had sold out to a large agency. Her husband had died soon after, but she was still going strong, wreaking havoc, she claimed, among the widowers in Boca Raton.

Getting Martha to stay home had not required much arm twisting. She'd had little emotional commitment to her job. Work to her had been, on one level, simply about money. It was a way to earn a living, to support first herself and then herself and Hannah. On another, deeper, level, Frankie understood, it had been about independence and self-esteem; but she'd agreed—more or less—to surrender the former the day she married. As for self-esteem, she seemed to get all she needed by being a wife and mother, at least he thought she did. But, when Michael started nursery school, Martha had grown restless. By then, however, his business was in trouble. After the crash of October 1987, when the affluent were forced (for a while at least) to start tightening their belts, membership in the Ferraro Clubs dropped and retail sales of the sports line sank into red ink. As Frankie began to cut back and rethink, Martha offered her help, and he took it. What she did was unofficial and without pay, but her advice helped him to cut costs, retain quality, reduce prices, and save the clothing business. It was on her call that he'd ventured into the direct catalogue sales that now accounted for the company's largest profits. Without feeling it necessary to offer her a salary, he was nevertheless grateful to her. And if he couldn't quite think of her as a business partner, if occasionally her stubbornness drove him crazy, if sometimes he felt a hint of resentment at what some demon in him considered her interference, most times he simply admired her.

Martha was smart, tactful; she had enviable management skills. Whatever she did for Ferraro Clubs, Incorporated, she did without neglecting her family. Her children never went without costumes for Halloween, or help with their homework. She organized Frankie to be on time for their plays and dance recitals, for parents' meetings and graduations. A wonderful cook, she entertained family and friends at home, and enjoyed going out with her husband to the theater, to museums, to concerts, to Yankee games. She loved him; and she did what Frankie had known she would, she made a home for him and the children.

After putting the hose away, Frankie dried off the furniture, took the cushions out of the storage benches built especially to hold them, and put them on the seats. He took a final look around, and went inside, entering into a large room with overstuffed chairs and an entertainment unit that contained, among other things, a forty-five inch television set. Pina's room and Martha's little studio were also on this level. Upstairs were the kitchen, dining room, and sitting room. The master bedroom suite was on the floor above that, as well as a guest bedroom and bath. The children's rooms were on the fourth floor, and at the top was another guest suite and the library, with Frankie's books, his desk, a treadmill, and a balcony overlooking the garden. None of the rooms was enormous, but they were sufficient in number to provide everyone a safe haven.

Instead of taking the elevator, which some previous owner had installed (earning Frankie's eternal gratitude), he walked up the steps to the kitchen, where he found every surface covered with food and all his girls, as he called them, busy chopping, stirring, tasting. Pina, her slender body wrapped in an apron, was testing the chicken. Standing side-by-side at the counter, Maud was dicing cucumbers, Hannah stringing beans. Though Hannah was two inches taller, long limbed and willowy, while Maud was graceful and delicate, even a stranger could have seen that they were sisters. They both had Frankie's dark hair (well, his was mostly silver now), his dark eyes, and olive skin; but, while theirs was soft with the sheen of silk, his had roughened with age, though it still, to his relief, had very few wrinkles.

Maud was twenty-two-years old, *already*, thought Frankie. An adult, a woman. Sometimes he could hardly believe it. Still serious and shy, she had high cheekbones, a firm chin, and an aquiline nose, flattened at the bridge, like Sal Ferraro's. She'd wanted to have it fixed when she was sixteen, but Frankie had said no. He loved her nose. And she had come not so much to like *it,* as to approve of the character it added to her face. Last year she'd graduated from Princeton, and now, with a little help from Dan Colvington, was working as an editorial assistant at a publishing house in New York. For peanuts, of course, that being the way of the publishing world. Which annoyed the hell out of Annabel, who thought that, if her daughter had to work, then at least she should be doing something lucrative.

Money, as always, was Annabel's chief concern. Richard Gaynor had lost most of his in the aftermath of the '87 crash and then had suffered a stroke that left him paralyzed. The following year, Annabel had divorced him, receiving what she described as "a pittance" in settlement. Still attractive in that stylized, artificial way that women who have had too many face lifts acquire, she'd quickly found a new protector and was currently living with an aging Central American with vast holdings in sugar. He didn't seem inclined to marry her, perhaps because he already had a wife somewhere, but he would gladly have offered Annabel's daughter a job. Maud, however, wanted nothing to do with sugar. ("Do you know how they exploit people on those plantations?" she'd asked her mother shortly after she'd begun living with Jaime. "They should be grateful to be working," Annabel had replied.) For that matter, Maud wanted nothing to do with health clubs and clothes catalogues. Books were what she loved, the result, thought Frankie proudly, of all those years of his reading her bedtime stories.

Hannah had turned seventeen in April. She had her mother's long legs, clever hands, and her temperament. She was sensible, good-natured, and stubborn. As a young girl, she'd dreamed of being a ballerina, but that had passed, along with her desire to be a race car driver. Now, interested in urban development and low-cost housing (springing from the same source as Martha's desire to make things comfortable for people?), she wanted to study architecture. Unlike her sister, who moved cautiously from one romance to the next, Hannah fell in and out of love regularly and joyfully, bouncing back from each heartbreak to move on to the next conquest. When Frankie complained, Martha would look at him in mock exasperation, and say, "Well, it's not me she takes after."

"Everything under control?" he asked, smiling happily at them from the doorway.

Pina put the lid back on the pot and nodded, her face gleaming with perspiration and confidence. Of course everything was under control. She was in charge.

"Absolutely," said Hannah.

"We're almost done," said Maud.

"Go take your shower," said Martha. "People will be arriving soon." Her hair was streaked blond to conceal the gray, but she was as slender as when they married. No, more so, because then she was pregnant. She looked youthful, happy, pretty. She looked like Martha, the woman he loved more often than not.

"Yes, sir, boss," he said. She laughed. She rarely minded being teased, one of her nicest qualities. Frankie smiled back at her. Their eyes held for a moment, and then he turned back into the hallway, and continued on up the stairs.

Today was their fifteenth wedding anniversary, Martha's and his. Family and friends were gathering to celebrate. Her parents were staying at a nearby hotel, preferring, they said, to have their privacy. What remained of Frankie's aunts and uncles would arrive that afternoon, escorted to the town house by obliging sons and daughters. Having been frustrated in her desire to join her husband at the earliest possible time, Dolly would come with Angela, with whom she'd been living since Denny's death from pancreatic cancer five years before. Frankie had not approved of the arrangement. Their mother was managing fine on her own, he'd told his sister, and, at some point, when she'd finished grieving, Angela might actually want to get on with her own life. He'd not dared to say that she might start dating again, but, understanding very well what he meant, she had burst into tears, and, between sobs, had told him that there would never be another man for her. So far, she'd been right. Though she continued to teach math in the local high school, and occasionally went out to dinner with one of her male colleagues, no romances had developed. But she seemed content. And certainly taking care of Angela had given eighty-year-old Dolly a new lease on life. She looked and acted ten years younger than she was.

Dennis, Angela's oldest son, had married, and would be coming with his wife and baby son. Sean was engaged and would bring his girlfriend. Vic and Maria and their two daughters would arrive late, they'd warned. Their son was in California, a cybercrat at one of the up-and-coming computer software companies. Vic, whose career managed to keep moving at a steady (if unexciting and far from glamorous) pace, was flying in from Vancouver where he was playing a small-time mobster in a Tarantino film. Their older daughter had graduated from the Yale School of Drama and was working as an instructor at Macklin's between small jobs acting. The younger girl was in her last year at Cornell, and had come down for the weekend especially to attend the anniversary party, foregoing a date to a football game. This Maria had told Frankie to counter, with the weight of her singular experience, the common complaint that the younger generation had no family feeling.

Friends were expected, too: Martha's one-time roommate, Jill, and her husband from Del Ray Beach, Colette from Boca Raton. Joan Heller, about to retire as director of a museum in Albuquerque, was bringing her lover. The affection he felt for Joan always surprised Frankie, and not just because she was inevitably a reminder of a painful part of his life. There was also the matter of her sexuality; and, when he considered that, he could never resist congratulating himself for having overcome, so completely it seemed to him, the prejudices of his youth. What would his father, or his Uncle Vic, (who'd died two years after his brother) have made of Joan, and Ginger, the redheaded photographer, who was the love of her life? Dolly, of course, thought they were just good friends. Which was also true.

They were staying for a week at the Stanhope, Joan told Frankie when she phoned to accept the invitation. They had museums and galleries to visit, new restaurants to check out, ethnic cuisine to sample. Albuquerque was great, but it was not, emphatically *not,* New York. And she was eager, as well, to spend some time with Dan. Though there was no blood relationship between the two, they were as close as cousins. Together they'd shared the responsibility for Craig in the last years of his life, caring for him as he dwindled into senility. Both had been with him when he died, comfortably at home, as he'd wished. And it was to them that Craig had left the bulk of his estate (a fortune, resulting from the sale of the Colvington stores to Federated, most of it eaten up with inheritance taxes), allotting token bequests to his other nieces and nephews, and his stepson Philip, Joan's halfbrother, who had threatened to sue. Dan and Joan had placated him with a substantial sum, and the matter had been settled out of court.

Dan and Minnie Colvington were driving down from Boston and would spend the night in the Ferraros' guest bedroom. Ben, studying for a graduate degree in film studies at NYU, was expected to show up at some point during the day, the only one of the Colvington children who would. Lulu, an undergraduate at Stanford, had returned to school at the beginning of the month. Aaron, on the first lap of a trip around the world before settling down to graduate school, was (at least according to his last postcard) in Hong Kong visiting Danny, who'd recently been transferred there by the brokerage house that employed him. William, the youngest, was at home with his nanny.

Though the Ferraros and the Colvingtons usually spent part of each summer together, sometimes at the house on the Cape, sometimes at a rented villa somewhere in Europe, Frankie and Dan saw less of one another during the remainder of the year than they used to. Though both made an effort to stay in touch, with wives, children, and business to deal with, there seemed to be less time now for friendship than when they were younger. Still, in Frankie's opinion, they were better friends than ever. An equity existed between them that hadn't been there at the start, due entirely to the fact that Frankie (to the relief of both) had stopped envying Dan, had stopped considering him the chosen one, the blessed of the gods. That belief, dealt its first blow when Amy died, was vanquished completely when his and Minnie's only child was diagnosed as autistic.

For a while it had seemed as if the Colvington marriage wouldn't survive the diagnosis. Minnie had focused all her attention on William. Dan had withdrawn into himself. It was as if Amy's death had used up all his emotional resources, leaving no reserves to deal with this new trial. He wouldn't talk about it. When he and Frankie saw each other, they discussed sports or politics, the latest films, the latest books, anything but their personal lives. Ultimately, however, Dan wasn't able to leave Minnie out there alone to fend for herself and the boy. His sense of duty wouldn't allow it, and the crack that duty made in his defenses allowed love to come flooding back in, love for his son, love for his wife. Now their marriage was a joint venture committed to ensuring that William led as normal a life as possible.

No, though he knew his own life had fallen far short of his once grand ambitions, Frankie no longer envied Dan, but he respected him, admired him, and was grateful, not only for Dan's introducing him all those years ago to new and interesting worlds, but for teaching him one last, all-important lesson: nobody's life is golden. Life is simply life, and the lucky ones are those who rise to meet its trials with courage, who accept its gifts with gratitude and joy.

As always, thinking about William made Frankie anxious about his own son. Needing to make sure that disaster hadn't struck while he'd been otherwise preoccupied, he continued up the stairs to Michael's room, knocked on the door, heard a gruff "Come in," and entered to find him, in shorts and a T-shirt with a skull-and-crossbones motif, right where he was supposed to be, at his desk, in front of his computer.

"How's it going?"

"Not bad," he said. Long and lanky, with a voice given to changing pitch, and arms and legs that often seemed to act of their own volition, he had his mother's coloring and his father's temper. Girls were already clamoring for his attention, writing him letters, phoning the house to speak to him. To his father's relief, he wasn't interested. Yet. "I'm almost done," he added, looking up from the screen. "Do you want to read it?"

"When you're finished," said Frankie. He walked across the room to him anyway, just to touch him. Putting his hands on Michael's shoulders, he leaned over him to look at the screen. " 'Assurance' is spelled with an 'a,' not an 'e,' " he said. Michael's spelling was abysmal. So was Hannah's. Which Frankie attributed to newfangled and completely worthless teaching methods. Thanks to Mrs. Ashby, now retired and living near her son, somewhere in the vicinity of Castle Melton, Maud was an excellent speller.

"I haven't spell checked it yet," said Michael, not in the least concerned. Nevertheless, to please his father, he made the correction.

He had almost not been born. Shortly after the hurried marriage, fifteen years ago today, Martha had miscarried, in Paris, where she and Frankie were honeymooning. As they were leaving the Jeu de Paume, she'd complained of stomach cramps. By the time their taxi stopped in front of the Raphael, where they were staying, both had known it was serious and he had asked the driver to wait while he ran in to ask the concierge the best place to take her. Frankie could still remember the terror, seeing Martha so pale and in pain, not knowing a doctor, or the reputation of any hospital, his few words of French so inadequate to the situation. Not that language had ultimately mattered. The doctor at the clinic spoke excellent English. He knew his job. It was just one of those things, he said. It was no one's fault. Some babies were not destined to be born.

Martha couldn't stop crying. Frankie felt dazed and unable to comfort her. Neither was thinking clearly. The loss of the baby who had rushed them into marriage now made that exercise seem futile. Waiting for Martha to recover enough to fly, they spent their last few days in Paris in silence, each wrapped in separate misery. Then, just before their plane touched down in New York, numb with depression, overwhelmed by guilt, Martha suggested a divorce. Relief swept through Frankie when he heard the word, followed immediately by resentment. As always when Martha offered him the escape route he'd been looking for, he found himself reluctant to take it. "Let's not decide anything now. We're too shell-shocked. Let's give ourselves a little time." Then, like a revelation, the face of a little girl materialized in his mind. "There's Hannah," he said. "We have to think about what's best for her, too."

For a few weeks, it was touch and go. Martha's pride and his temper combined to make life hell. Sometimes it seemed to Frankie that only embarrassment kept him from agreeing to a divorce. Having announced Martha and Hannah's existence to the world, having lost Kelly and the Helms, devastated Maud, shocked his family, how could he now admit that it had all been for nothing? How could he admit that his marrying Martha had been a mistake? How could he face a third failed marriage when that, above all else, had been what he most wanted to avoid?

They lived separately, Martha in her apartment, Frankie in his. If those who knew thought it strange, they refrained from saying so. Dutifully, Frankie continued to visit Martha and Hannah, often taking Maud with him. Though Martha balked (after one duty visit to Dolly) at visiting his family, she agreed to go with him and the children to the zoo, the Botanical Gardens, the Natural History Museum. Frankie was determined that, whatever happened between Martha and him, the girls would grow up as sisters.

The children tipped the scales. As they grew increasingly more attached to each other, and even Maud began to look to Martha for mothering, she rallied. She stopped insisting that the marriage was a farce, by which time Frankie had already decided that a divorce was the last thing he wanted. He'd remembered by then that he loved her, maybe not with the overwhelming, all-consuming passion of his love for Miranda, or the madness to possess that he'd felt for Annabel, maybe not even completely without those veils of illusion that Kalima considered so destructive, but what he felt for Martha was love all the same, deep and steady, built on a foundation of admiration and respect.

One night, about six weeks after their return from Paris, Frankie went alone to Martha's to discuss their future. He poured himself a scotch, and, while she read Hannah to sleep, sat drinking it, rehearsing what he meant to say. "There's something we've got to get straight," he said when she came back into the room. "When you agreed to marry me, you said it was because you loved me. Well, did you or didn't you?"

Biting her lip, Martha dropped into an armchair opposite, and, sitting awkwardly on its edge, leaning toward him, she said sadly, "I feel as if I trapped you."

"And I said I loved *you*," he continued, ignoring her remark. "Losing the baby hasn't changed that for me. I admit for a while I was confused. I was feeling a lot of pain and I wasn't sure of the cause. But now I know I hurt for the same reason you do. Because I lost a child. I don't want to compound that hurt by losing you, too." Martha began to cry, and this time, Frankie was able to do more than watch. He pulled her out of the chair and into his arms. "I love you," he had repeated. "I do. I really do." Given the prompt arrival of Michael nine months later, it was possible he was conceived that night.

Resisting the urge to kiss his son, who these days hated overt signs of affection, Frankie ruffled his dark hair, and said, "You're a good kid."

Looking up again from the computer screen, Michael flashed him a smile, and said, "Remember that when I ask you to buy me a new bike."

"I'll take it into account," promised Frankie. He turned and headed back to the door, saying, as he went, "Change before you come down, okay? Nothing too fancy, just a T-shirt that won't give your grandmother heart failure?"

"Mom already warned me," said Michael, rolling his eyes. "Don't worry."

*R*etracing his steps, Frankie went back downstairs and entered the master bedroom. It had a king-sized bed, two huge chests of drawers, an oversized armchair, and two walk-in closets. The walls, the curtains, the bedcover, were in varied fabrics of an eggshell color, making the room feel both spacious and tranquil, qualities that Martha had managed to incorporate into the decor of the entire house, which seemed elegant yet informal, a comfortable place to live, a home. The Matisse drawing he had given her rested on a stand on one of the chests.

Stripping off his clothes, he threw them in the hamper and turned on the shower. Fifteen years, he thought, stepping under the spray of hot water. Not so long really.

There had been another bad patch in the marriage. With the benefit of hindsight, Frankie could now see that it had arrived with embarrassing predictability just before his fiftieth birthday. Feeling suddenly restless, he'd begun to wonder if life didn't have a little more to offer than he was currently getting. On the one hand, everything was great: he had a good wife, three terrific kids, his business had started to recover from a series of setbacks. On the other, he was bored. That's all. Nothing more serious than that. He was bored. And not even the terror of AIDS (which by then had claimed his friend, Tom Murray), prevented his picking up a girl in the Macklin's bar. It seemed as if, instead of 1989, it was 1978 all over again, only this time it was Martha he was lying to and not Annabel, and without even the excuse of detesting his wife. On the contrary, he loved her. Whatever else he was feeling, at bottom that remained, his love for Martha and his children. Within weeks of initiating the affair, Frankie ended it. He went to his doctor, got a clean bill of health, and swore to himself that he'd never do anything that crazy again.

Martha, thank God, had never found out. She might have forgiven him for betraying her trust, but he couldn't be sure. It wasn't something he wished ever to put to the test. So, though the boredom came and went, though sometimes he felt frustrated by the predictability of his sex life or tempted by the desire to conquer new territories, he'd been a faithful husband ever since, and a reasonably contented one, as contented as anyone had a right to be, as contented as life ever allowed.

$\mathcal{H}$earing the bedroom door open, Frankie turned and saw Martha come into the room. He was naked, his hair still wet from the shower, his face freshly shaven. He turned away again, opened the dresser drawer, and pulled out a clean pair of shorts. "Everything under control?"

"Uh-huh," she said, coming up behind him, wrapping her arms around his waist, resting her cheek against his bare back. "You smell good," she said. "I'm all hot and sweaty from cooking."

"You should have come up a few minutes sooner," he said, turning in her arms. "We could have showered together." He leered at her and she laughed.

"No time for fooling around now," she said. "Your mother and sister just got here."

If Frankie sometimes felt like Prufrock, if he regretted the fading of his early dreams, his failure to accomplish the great things he'd hoped for, if he could hear too clearly and too often, that eternal footman's snicker, yet he had the good sense to cherish what he did have, to value what (mostly by luck, by accident, without planning) he had done. He kissed Martha lightly, then said, "I've been thinking all day how glad I am I married you."

"All things considered," she said happily, "it didn't turn out so bad."

"All things considered, I'd say it turned out damn good." He kissed her again.

When he stopped, she twisted out of his arms, and said, "To be continued later?"

"You bet," he promised. "Absolutely."